O HENRY
100 Selected Stories

O HENRY
100 Selected Stories

―――――――◆―――――――

Chosen by Sapper

WORDSWORTH CLASSICS

The paper in this book is produced from pure wood
pulp, without the use of chlorine or any other substance
harmful to the environment. The energy used in its
production consists almost entirely of hydroelectricity
and heat generated from waste materials, thereby
conserving fossil fuels and contributing little to the
greenhouse effect.

This edition published 1995 by
Wordsworth Editions Limited
Cumberland House, Crib Street, Ware,
Hertfordshire SG12 9ET

ISBN 1 85326 241 2

© Wordsworth Editions Limited 1995

Printed and bound in Denmark by Nørhaven
Typeset in the UK by R & B Creative Services Ltd

INTRODUCTION

THE STORIES OF O HENRY are in the great tradition of American short story writing that stretches from Irving and Poe through to Damon Runyon and even P J O'Rourke. In all, Henry wrote two hundred and seventy stories, and they consist of a rich mixture of semi-realism, sentiment and surprise endings. Though he is frequently thought of as a 'funny' writer, O Henry was, like Runyon, capable of addressing the darker side of life – *A Municipal Report* and *The Furnished Room* are two such stories. At the same time, his genius for comic invention flows through the pages of this book, exemplified by the epicurean exchange in *Hostages to Momus* between the narrator and Caligula Polk.

The extraordinary life and experiences of O Henry inform all his stories. He is as at home describing life south of the Rio Grande as he is with 'the four million' – the ordinary inhabitants of teeming, turn-of-the-century New York. Although he has been criticised for relying too much on coincidence and contrived circumstance, O Henry had a genuine sympathy for the downtrodden and oppressed which was unusual in writers of his era. And it is an era that he depicts with remarkable clarity; though some of the reportage and some of the conversations may grate on those whose consciousness is attuned to political attitudes of the late twentieth century rather than the realities of the early twentieth century, the stories are valuable examples of how life was lived at a time when slavery and the Indian Wars were only a generation or so in the past.

This selection of one hundred of O Henry's stories does not include any from his first collection, *Of Cabbages and Kings* (1904). Those were all set in South America and have a common thread running through them. This book seeks rather to represent in the widest way the sheer variety and scope of O Henry's writing and to bring it to the wide audience that his talent deserves, and to restore him to his rightful place in the mainstream of American short story writing.

O Henry (1862-1910) was born William Sydney Porter in North Carolina. His schooling was rudimentary, and after working in a drug store, he went to Texas in 1882; he became a rancher for a time, then a bank teller and journalist, founding a comic weekly magazine, The Rolling Stone (1894-5) before being employed by the Houston Post *to write a humorous daily column.*

In 1896 he was indicted for alleged embezzlement by the bank for which he had worked, and fled to Honduras. He returned three years later to be with his dying wife, was arrested and spent three years in the federal penitentiary in Columbus, Ohio. Here Porter started to write short stories under the pseudonym of O Henry, thought to be adopted from a French . pharmacist mentioned in The US Dispensary, *a reference book which Porter came across in his work in the prison pharmacy. His collections of stories were immediately popular, and include* The Four Million (1906), Heart of the West (1907), The Trimmed Lamp (1907), The Gentle Grafter (1908), The Voice of the City (1908), Options (1909), Roads of Destiny (1909), Whirligigs (1910) *and* Strictly Business (1910). *Other collections were published after Porter's death of a wasting disease in 1910. O Henry Memorial Awards were established to be given annually for the best magazine stories.*

Further reading:
Biographies of O Henry by G Longford (1967) and Richard O'Connor (1970), together with a study by J Gallegly (1970) and a bibliography by P S Clarkson (1938).

CONTENTS

O HENRY
100 Selected Stories

The Gift of the Magi

ONE DOLLAR AND EIGHTY-SEVEN CENTS. That was all. And sixty cents of it was in pennies. Pennies saved one and two at a time by bulldozing the grocer and the vegetable man and the butcher until one's cheek burned with the silent imputation of parsimony that such close dealing implied. Three times Della counted it. One dollar and eighty-seven cents. And the next day would be Christmas.

There was clearly nothing left to do but flop down on the shabby little couch and howl. So Della did it. Which instigates the moral reflection that life is made up of sobs, sniffles, and smiles, with sniffles predominating.

While the mistress of the home is gradually subsiding from the first stage to the second, take a look at the home. A furnished flat at $8 per week. It did not exactly beggar description, but it certainly had that word on the look-out for the mendicancy squad.

In the vestibule below was a letter-box into which no letter would go, and an electric button from which no mortal finger could coax a ring. Also appertaining thereunto was a card bearing the name 'Mr. James Dillingham Young.'

The 'Dillingham' had been flung to the breeze during a former period of prosperity when its possessor was being paid $30 per week. Now, when the income was shrunk to $20, the letters of 'Dillingham' looked blurred, as though they were thinking seriously of contracting to a modest and unassuming D. But whenever Mr. James Dillingham Young came home and reached his flat above he was called 'Jim' and greatly hugged by Mrs. James Dillingham Young, already introduced to you as Della. Which is all very good.

Della finished her cry and attended to her cheeks with the powder rag. She stood by the window and looked out dully at a grey cat walking a grey fence in a grey backyard. To-morrow would be Christmas Day, and she had only $1.87 with which to buy Jim a present. She had been saving every penny she could for months, with this result. Twenty dollars a week doesn't go far. Expenses had been greater than she had calculated. They always are. Only $1.87 to buy a present for Jim. Her Jim. Many a happy hour she had spent planning for something nice for him. Something fine and rare and sterling – something just a little bit near to being worthy of the honour of being owned by Jim.

There was a pier-glass between the windows of the room. Perhaps you have seen a pier-glass in an $8 flat. A very thin and very agile person may, by observing his reflection in a rapid sequence of longitudinal strips, obtain a fairly accurate conception of his looks. Della, being slender, had mastered the art.

Suddenly she whirled from the window and stood before the glass. Her eyes were shining brilliantly, but her face had lost its colour within twenty seconds. Rapidly she pulled down her hair and let it fall to its full length.

Now, there were two possessions of the James Dillingham Youngs in which they both took a mighty pride. One was Jim's gold watch that had been his father's and his grandfather's. The other was Della's hair. Had the Queen of Sheba lived in the flat across the airshaft, Della would have let her hair hang out the window some day to dry just to depreciate Her Majesty's jewels and gifts. Had King Solomon been the janitor, with all his treasures piled up in the basement, Jim would have pulled out his watch every time he passed, just to see him pluck at his beard from envy.

So now Della's beautiful hair fell about her, rippling and shining like a cascade of brown waters. It reached below her knee and made itself almost a garment for her. And then she did it up again nervously and quickly. Once she faltered for a minute and stood still while a tear or two splashed on the worn red carpet.

On went her old brown jacket; on went her old brown hat. With a whirl of skirts and with the brilliant sparkle still in her eyes, she fluttered out of the door and down the stairs to the street.

Where she stopped the sign read: 'Mme. Sofronie. Hair Goods of All Kinds.' One flight up Della ran, and collected herself, panting. Madame, large, too white, chilly, hardly looked the 'Sofronie.'

'Will you buy my hair?' asked Della.

'I buy hair,' said Madame. 'Take yer hat off and let's have a sight at the looks of it.'

Down rippled the brown cascade.

'Twenty dollars,' said Madame, lifting the mass with a practised hand.

'Give it to me quick,' said Della.

Oh, and the next two hours tripped by on rosy wings. Forget the hashed metaphor. She was ransacking the stores for Jim's present.

She found it at last. It surely had been made for Jim and no one else. There was no other like it in any of the stores, and she had turned all of them inside out. It was a platinum fob chain simple and chaste in design, properly proclaiming its value by substance alone and not by meretricious ornamentation – as all good things should do. It was even worthy of The Watch. As soon as she saw it she knew that it must be Jim's. It was like him. Quietness and value – the description applied to both. Twenty-one dollars they took from her for it, and she hurried home with the 87 cents. With that chain on his watch Jim might be properly anxious about the time in any company. Grand as the watch was, he sometimes looked at it on the sly on account of the old leather strap that he used in place of a chain.

When Della reached home her intoxication gave way a little to prudence and reason. She got out her curling irons and lighted the gas and went to work repairing the ravages made by generosity added to love. Which is always a tremendous task, dear friends – a mammoth task.

Within forty minutes her head was covered with tiny, close-lying curls that made her look wonderfully like a truant schoolboy. She looked at her reflection in the mirror long, carefully, and critically.

'If Jim doesn't kill me,' she said to herself, 'before he takes a second look at me, he'll say I look like a Coney Island chorus girl. But what could I do – oh! what could I do with a dollar and eighty-seven cents?'

At seven o'clock the coffee was made and the frying-pan was on the back of the stove, hot and ready to cook the chops.

Jim was never late. Della doubled the fob chain in her hand and sat on the corner of the table near the door that he always entered. Then she heard his step on the stair away down on the first flight, and she turned white for just a moment. She had a habit of saying little silent prayers about the simplest everyday things, and now she whispered: 'Please God, make him think I am still pretty.'

The door opened and Jim stepped in and closed it. He looked thin and very serious. Poor fellow, he was only twenty-two – and to be burdened with a family! He needed a new overcoat and he was without gloves.

Jim stepped inside the door, as immovable as a setter at the scent of quail. His eyes were fixed upon Della, and there was an expression in them that she could not read, and it terrified her. It was not anger, nor surprise, nor disapproval, nor horror, nor any of the sentiments that she had been prepared for. He simply stared at her fixedly with that peculiar expression on his face.

Della wriggled off the table and went for him.

'Jim, darling,' she cried, 'don't look at me that way. I had my hair cut off and sold it because I couldn't have lived through Christmas without giving you a present. It'll grow out again – you won't mind, will you? I just had to do it. My hair grows awfully fast. Say "Merry Christmas!" Jim, and let's be happy. You don't know what a nice – what a beautiful, nice gift I've got for you.'

'You've cut off your hair?' asked Jim, laboriously, as if he had not arrived at that patent fact yet even after the hardest mental labour.

'Cut it off and sold it,' said Della. 'Don't you like me just as well, anyhow? I'm me without my hair, ain't I?'

Jim looked about the room curiously.

'You say your hair is gone?' he said with an air almost of idiocy.

'You needn't look for it,' said Della. 'It's sold, I tell you – sold and gone, too. It's Christmas Eve, boy. Be good to me, for it went for you. Maybe the hairs of my head were numbered,' she went on with a sudden serious sweetness, 'but nobody could ever count my love for you. Shall I put the chops on, Jim?'

Out of his trance Jim seemed quickly to wake. He enfolded his Della. For ten seconds let us regard with discreet scrutiny some inconsequential object in the other direction. Eight dollars a week or a million a year – what is the difference? A mathematician or a wit would give you the wrong answer. The magi brought valuable gifts, but that was not among them. This dark assertion will be illuminated later on.

Jim drew a package from his overcoat pocket and threw it upon the table.

'Don't make any mistake, Dell,' he said, 'about me. I don't think there's anything in the way of a haircut or a shave or a shampoo that could make me like my girl any less. But if you'll unwrap that package you may see why you had me going awhile at first.'

White fingers and nimble tore at the string and paper. And then an ecstatic scream of joy; and then, alas! a quick feminine change to hysterical tears and wails, necessitating the immediate employment of all the comforting powers of the lord of the flat.

For there lay The Combs – the set of combs, side and back, that Della had worshipped for long in a Broadway window. Beautiful combs, pure tortoiseshell, with jewelled rims – just the shade to wear in the beautiful vanished hair. They were expensive combs, she knew, and her heart had simply craved and yearned over them without the least hope of possession. And now they were hers, but the tresses that should have adorned the coveted adornments were gone.

But she hugged them to her bosom, and at length she was able to look up with dim eyes and a smile and say: 'My hair grows so fast, Jim!'

And then Della leaped up like a little singed cat and cried, 'Oh, oh!'

Jim had not yet seen his beautiful present. She held it out to him eagerly upon her open palm. The dull precious metal seemed to flash with a reflection of her bright and ardent spirit.

'Isn't it a dandy, Jim? I hunted all over town to find it. You'll have to look at the time a hundred times a day now. Give me your watch. I want to see how it looks on it.'

Instead of obeying, Jim tumbled down on the couch and put his hands under the back of his head and smiled.

'Dell,' said he, 'let's put our Christmas presents away and keep 'em awhile. They're too nice to use just at present. I sold the watch to get the money to buy your combs. And now suppose you put the chops on.'

The magi, as you know, were wise men – wonderfully wise men – who brought gifts to the Babe in the manger. They invented the art of giving Christmas presents. Being wise, their gifts were no doubt wise ones, possibly bearing the privilege of exchange in case of duplication. And here I have lamely related to you the uneventful chronicle of two foolish children in a flat who most unwisely sacrificed for each other the greatest treasures of their house. But in a last word to the wise of these days, let it be said that of all who give gifts these two were the wisest. Of all who give and receive gifts, such as they are wisest. Everywhere they are wisest. They are the magi.

II

A Cosmopolite in a Café

AT MIDNIGHT THE CAFÉ was crowded. By some chance the little table at which I sat had escaped the eye of incomers, and two vacant chairs at it extended their arms with venal hospitality to the influx of patrons.

And then a cosmopolite sat in one of them, and I was glad, for I held a theory that since Adam no true citizen of the world has existed. We hear of them, and we see foreign labels on much luggage, but we find travellers instead of cosmopolites.

I invoke your consideration of the scene – the marble-topped tables, the range of leather-upholstered wall seats, the gay company, the ladies dressed in demi-state toilets, speaking in an exquisite visible chorus of taste, economy, opulence or art, the sedulous and largess-loving *garçons*, the music wisely catering to all with its raids upon the composers; the *mélange* of talk and laughter – and, if you will, the Würzburger in the tall glass cones that bend to your lips as a ripe cherry sways on its branch to the beak of a robber jay. I was told by a sculptor from Mauch Chunk that the scene was truly Parisian.

My cosmopolite was named E. Rushmore Coglan, and he will be heard from next summer at Coney Island. He is to establish a new 'attraction' there, he informed me, offering kingly diversion. And then his conversation rang along parallels of latitude and longitude. He took the great, round world in his hand, so to speak, familiarly, contemptuously, and it seemed no larger than the seed of a Maraschino cherry in a table-d'hôte grape fruit. He spoke disrespectfully of the equator, he skipped from continent to continent, he derided the zones, he mopped up the high seas with his napkin. With a wave of his hand he would speak of a certain bazaar in Hyderabad. Whiff! He would have you on skis in Lapland. Zip! Now you rode the breakers with the Kanakas at Kealaikahiki. Presto! He dragged you through an Arkansas post-oak swamp, let you dry for a moment on the alkali plains of his Idaho ranch, then whirled you into the society of Viennese archdukes. Anon he would be telling you of a cold he acquired in a Chicago lake breeze and how old Escamila cured it in Buenos Ayres with a hot infusion of the *chuchula* weed. You would have addressed the letter to 'E. Rushmore Coglan, Esq., the Earth, Solar System, the Universe,' and have mailed it, feeling confident that it would be delivered to him.

I was sure that I had at last found the one true cosmopolite since Adam, and I listened to his world-wide discourse fearful lest I should discover in it the local note of the mere globe-trotter. But his opinions never fluttered or drooped; he was as impartial to cities, countries and continents as the winds or gravitation.

And as E. Rushmore Coglan prattled of this little planet I thought with glee of a great almost-cosmopolite who wrote for the whole world and dedicated himself to Bombay. In a poem he has to say that there is pride and rivalry between the cities of the earth, and that 'the men that breed from them, they traffic up and down, but cling to their cities' hem as a child to the mother's gown.' And whenever they walk 'by roaring streets unknown' they remember their native city 'most faithful, foolish, fond; making her mere-breathed name their bond upon their bond.' And my glee was roused because I had caught Mr. Kipling napping. Here I had found a man not made from dust; one who had no narrow boasts of birthplace or country, one who, if he bragged at all, would brag of his whole round globe against the Martians and the inhabitants of the Moon.

Expression on these subjects was precipitated from E. Rushmore Coglan by the third corner to our table. While Coglan was describing to me the topography along the Siberian Railway the orchestra glided into a medley. The concluding air was 'Dixie,' and as the exhilarating notes tumbled forth they were almost overpowered by a great clapping of hands from almost every table.

It is worth a paragraph to say that this remarkable scene can be witnessed every evening in numerous cafés in the City of New York. Tons of brew have been consumed over theories to account for it. Some have conjectured hastily that all Southerners in town hie themselves to cafés at nightfall. This applause of the 'rebel' air in a Northern city does puzzle a little; but it is not insolvable. The war with Spain, many years' generous mint and water-melon crops, a few long-shot winners at the New Orleans race-track, and the brilliant banquets given by the Indiana and Kansas citizens who compose the North Carolina Society, have made the South rather a 'fad' in Manhattan. Your manicure will lisp softly that your left forefinger reminds her so much of a gentleman's in Richmond, Va. Oh, certainly; but many a lady has to work now – the war, you know.

When 'Dixie' was being played a dark-haired young man sprang up from somewhere with a Mosby guerrilla yell and waved frantically his soft-brimmed hat. Then he strayed through the smoke, dropped into the vacant chair at our table and pulled out cigarettes.

The evening was at the period when reserve is thawed. One of us mentioned three Würzburgers to the waiter; the dark-haired young man acknowledged his inclusion in the order by a smile and a nod. I hastened to ask him a question because I wanted to try out a theory I had.

'Would you mind telling me,' I began, 'whether you are from –'

The fist of E. Rushmore Coglan banged the table and I was jarred into silence.

'Excuse me,' said he, 'but that's a question I never like to hear asked. What does it matter where a man is from? Is it fair to judge a man by his post-office address? Why, I've seen Kentuckians who hated whisky, Virginians who weren't descended from Pocahontas, Indianians who hadn't written a novel, Mexicans who didn't wear velvet trousers with silver dollars sewed along the seams, funny Englishmen, spendthrift Yankees, cold-blooded Southerners, narrow-minded Westerners, and New Yorkers who were too busy to stop for an hour on the street to watch a one-armed grocer's clerk do up cranberries in paper bags. Let a man be a man and don't handicap him with the label of any section.'

'Pardon me,' I said, 'but my curiosity was not altogether an idle one. I know the South, and when the band plays "Dixie" I like to observe. I have formed the belief that the man who applauds that air with special violence and ostensible sectional loyalty is invariably a native of either Secaucus, N.J., or the district between Murray Hill Lyceum and the Harlem River, this city. I was about to put my opinion to the test by inquiring of this gentleman when you interrupted with your own – larger theory, I must confess.'

And now the dark-haired young man spoke to me, and it became evident that his mind also moved along its own set of grooves.

'I should like to be a periwinkle,' said he, mysteriously, 'on the top of a valley, and sing too-ralloo-ralloo.'

This was clearly too obscure, so I turned again to Coglan.

'I've been around the world twelve times,' said he. 'I know an Esquimau in Upernavik who sends to Cincinati for his neckties, and I saw a goat-herder in Uruguay who won a prize in a Battle Creek breakfast-food puzzle competition. I pay rent on a room in

Cairo, Egypt, and another in Yokohama all the year round. I've got slippers waiting for me in a tea-house in Shanghai, and I don't have to tell 'em how to cook my eggs in Rio de Janeiro or Seattle. It's a mighty little old world. What's the use of bragging about being from the North, or the South, or the old manor-house in the dale, or Euclid Avenue, Cleveland, or Pike's Peak, or Fairfax County, Va., or Hooligan's Flats or any place? It'll be a better world when we quit being fools about some mildewed town or ten acres of swampland just because we happened to be born there.'

'You seem to be a genuine cosmopolite,' I said admiringly. 'But it also seems that you would decry patriotism.'

'A relic of the stone age,' declared Coglan warmly. 'We are all brothers – Chinamen, Englishmen, Zulus, Patagonians, and the people in the bend of the Kaw River. Some day all this petty pride in one's city or state or section or country will be wiped out, and we'll all be citizens of the world, as we ought to be.'

'But while you are wandering in foreign lands,' I persisted, 'do not your thoughts revert to some spot – some dear and –'

'Nary a spot,' interrupted E. R. Coglan flippantly. 'The terrestrial, globular, planetary hunk of matter, slightly flattened at the poles, and known as the Earth, is my abode. I've met a good many object-bound citizens of this country abroad. I've seen men from Chicago sit in a gondola in Venice on a moonlight night and brag about their drainage canal. I've seen a Southerner on being introduced to the King of England hand that monarch, without batting his eyes, the information that his grandaunt on his mother's side was related by marriage to the Perkinses, of Charleston. I knew a New Yorker who was kidnapped for ransom by some Afghanistan bandits. His people sent over the money and he came back to Kabul with the agent. "Afghanistan?" the natives said to him through an interpreter. "Well, not so slow, do you think?" "Oh, I don't know," says he, and he begins to tell them about a cab-driver at Sixth Avenue and Broadway. Those ideas don't suit me. I'm not tied down to anything that isn't 8,000 miles in diameter. Just put me down as E. Rushmore Coglan, citizen of the terrestrial sphere.'

My cosmopolite made a large adieu and left me, for he thought that he saw someone through the chatter and smoke whom he knew. So I was left with the would-be periwinkle, who was reduced to Würzburger without further ability to voice his aspirations to perch, melodious, upon the summit of a valley.

I sat reflecting upon my evident cosmopolite and wondering how the poet had managed to miss him. He was my discovery and

I believed in him. How was it? 'The men that breed from them they traffic up and down, but cling to their cities' hem as a child to the mother's gown.'

Not so E. Rushmore Coglan. With the whole world for his –

My meditations were interrupted by a tremendous noise and conflict in another part of the café. I saw above the heads of the seated patrons E. Rushmore Coglan and a stranger to me engaged in terrific battle. They fought between the tables like Titans, and glasses crashed, and men caught their hats up and were knocked down, and a brunette screamed, and a blonde began to sing 'Teasing.'

My cosmopolite was sustaining the pride and reputation of the Earth when the waiters closed in on both combatants with their famous flying wedge formation and bore them outside, still resisting.

I called McCarthy, one of the French garçons, and asked him the cause of the conflict.

'The man with the red tie' (that was my cosmopolite), said he, 'got hot on account of things said about the bum sidewalks and water supply of the place he come from by the other guy.'

'Why,' said I, bewildered, 'that man is a citizen of the world – a cosmopolite. He –'

'Originally from Mattawamkeag, Maine, he said,' continued McCarthy, 'and he wouldn't stand for no knockin' the place.'

III

Between Rounds

THE MAY MOON SHONE BRIGHT upon the private boarding-house of Mrs. Murphy. By reference to the almanac a large amount of territory will be discovered upon which its rays also fell. Spring was in its heyday, with hay fever soon to follow. The parks were green with new leaves and buyers for the Western and Southern trade. Flowers and summer-resort agents were blowing; the air and answers to Lawson were growing milder; hand-organs, fountains and pinochle were playing everywhere.

The windows of Mrs. Murphy's boarding-house were open. A group of boarders were seated on the high stoop upon round, flat mats like German pancakes.

In one of the second-floor front windows Mrs. McCaskey

awaited her husband. Supper was cooling on the table. Its heat went into Mrs. McCaskey.

At nine Mr. McCaskey came. He carried his coat on his arm and his pipe in his teeth; and he apologized for disturbing the boarders on the steps as he selected spots of stone between them on which to set his size 9, width Ds.

As he opened the door of his room he received a surprise. Instead of the usual stove-lid or potato-masher for him to dodge, came only words.

Mr. McCaskey reckoned that the benign May moon had softened the breast of his spouse.

'I heard ye,' came the oral substitutes for kitchenware. 'Ye can apollygize to riff-raff of the streets for settin' yer unhandy feet on the tails of their frocks, but ye'd walk on the neck of yer wife the length of a clothes-line without so much as a "Kiss me fut," and I'm sure it's that long from rubberin' out the windy for ye and the victuals cold such as there's money to buy after drinkin' up yer wages at Gallegher's every Saturday evenin', and the gas man here twice to-day for his.'

'Woman!' said Mr. McCaskey, dashing his coat and hat upon a chair, 'the noise of ye is an insult to me appetite. When ye run down politeness ye take the mortar from between the bricks of the foundations of society. 'Tis no more than exercisin' the acrimony of a gentleman when ye ask the dissent of ladies blockin' the way for steppin' between them. Will ye bring the pig's face of ye out of the windy and see to the food?'

Mrs. McCaskey arose heavily and went to the stove. There was something in her manner that warned Mr. McCaskey. When the corners of her mouth went down suddenly like a barometer it usually foretold a fall of crockery and tinware.

'Pig's face, is it?' said Mrs. McCaskey, and hurled a stewpan full of bacon and turnips at her lord.

Mr. McCaskey was no novice at repartee. He knew what should follow the entree. On the table was a roast sirloin of pork, garnished with shamrocks. He retorted with this, and drew the appropriate return of a bread pudding in an earthen dish. A hunk of Swiss cheese accurately thrown by her husband struck Mrs. McCaskey below one eye. When she replied with a well-aimed coffee-pot full of a hot, black, semi-fragrant liquid the battle, according to courses, should have ended.

But Mr. McCaskey was no 50 cent table d'hôter. Let cheap Bohemians consider coffee the end, if they would. Let them make that *faux pas*. He was foxier still. Finger-bowls were not beyond the compass of his experience. They were not to be had in the Pension Murphy; but their equivalent was at hand. Triumphantly he sent the granite-ware wash-basin at the head of his matrimonial adversary. Mrs. McCaskey dodged in time. She reached for a flat-iron, with which, as a sort of cordial, she hoped to bring the gastronomical duel to a close. But a loud, wailing scream downstairs caused both her and Mr. McCaskey to pause in a sort of involuntary armistice.

On the sidewalk at the corner of the house Policeman Cleary was standing with one ear upturned, listening to the crash of household utensils.

' 'Tis Jawn McCaskey and his missus at it again,' meditated the policeman. 'I wonder shall I go up and stop the row. I will not. Married folks they are; and few pleasures they have. 'Twill not last long. Sure, they'll have to borrow more dishes to keep it up with.'

And just then came the loud scream below-stairs, betokening fear or dire extremity. ' 'Tis probably the cat,' said Policeman Cleary, and walked hastily in the other direction.

The boarders on the steps were fluttered. Mr. Toomey, an insurance solicitor by birth and an investigator by profession, went inside to analyse the scream. He returned with the news that Mrs. Murphy's little boy Mike was lost. Following the messenger, out bounced Mrs. Murphy – two hundred pounds in tears and hysterics, clutching the air and howling to the sky for the loss of thirty pounds of freckles and mischief. Bathos, truly; but Mr. Toomey sat down at the side of Miss Purdy, milliner, and their hands came together in sympathy. The two old maids, Misses Walsh, who complained every day about the noise in the halls, inquired immediately if anybody had looked behind the clock.

Major Grigg, who sat by his fat wife on the top step, arose and buttoned his coat. 'The little one lost?' he exclaimed. 'I will scour the city.' His wife never allowed him out after dark. But now she said: 'Go, Ludovic!' in a baritone voice. 'Whoever can look upon that mother's grief without springing to her relief has a heart of stone.' 'Give me some thirty or – sixty cents, my love,' said the Major. 'Lost children sometimes stray far. I may need car-fares.'

Old man Denny, hall-room, fourth floor back, who sat on the lowest step, trying to read a paper by the street lamp, turned over a page to follow up the article about the carpenters' strike. Mrs. Murphy shrieked to the moon: 'Oh, ar-r-Mike, fr Gawd's sake, where is me little bit av a boy?'

'When'd ye see him last?' asked old man Denny, with one eye on the report of the Building Trades League.

'Oh,' wailed Mrs. Murphy, ' 'twas yisterday, or maybe four hours ago! I dunno. But it's lost he is, me little boy Mike. He was playin' on the sidewalk only this mornin' – or was it Wednesday? I'm that busy with work 'tis hard to keep up with dates. But I've looked the house over from top to cellar, and it's gone he is. Oh, for the love av Hiven –'

Silent, grim, colossal, the big city has ever stood against its revilers. They call it hard as iron; they say that no pulse of pity beats in its bosom; they compare its streets with lonely forests and deserts of lava. But beneath the hard crust of the lobster is found a delectable and luscious food. Perhaps a different simile would have been wiser. Still, nobody should take offence. We would call no one a lobster without good and sufficient claws.

No calamity so touches the common heart of humanity as does the straying of a little child. Their feet are so uncertain and feeble; the ways are so steep and strange.

Major Griggs hurried down to the corner, and up the avenue into Billy's place. 'Gimme a rye-high,' he said to the servitor. 'Haven't seen a bow-legged, dirty-faced little devil of a six-year-old lost kid around here anywhere, have you?'

Mr. Toomey retained Miss Purdy's hand on the steps. 'Think of that dear little babe,' said Miss Purdy, 'lost from his mother's side – perhaps already fallen beneath the iron hoofs of galloping steeds – oh, isn't it dreadful?'

'Ain't that right?' agreed Mr. Toomey, squeezing her hand. 'Say I start out and help look for um!'

'Perhaps,' said Miss Purdy, 'you should. But oh, Mr. Toomey, you are so dashing – so reckless – suppose in your enthusiasm some accident should befall you, then what –'

Old man Denny read on about the arbitration agreement, with one finger on the lines.

In the second floor front Mr. and Mrs. McCaskey came to the window to recover their second wind. Mr. McCaskey was scooping turnips out of his vest with a crooked forefinger, and his lady was wiping an eye that the salt of the roast pork had not benefited. They heard the outcry below, and thrust their heads out of the window.

' 'Tis little Mike is lost,' said Mrs. McCaskey in a hushed voice, 'the beautiful, little, trouble-making angel of a gossoon!'

'The bit of a boy mislaid?' said Mr. McCaskey leaning out of the window. 'Why, now, that's bad enough, entirely. The childer, they be different. If 'twas a woman I'd be willin', for they leave peace behind 'em when they go.'

Disregarding the thrust, Mrs. McCaskey caught her husband's arm.

'Jawn,' she said sentimentally, 'Missis Murphy's little bye is lost. 'Tis a great city for losing little boys. Six years old he was. Jawn, 'tis the same age our little bye would have been if we had had one six years ago.'

'We never did,' said Mr. McCaskey, lingering with the fact.

'But if we had, Jawn, think what sorrow would be in our hearts this night, with our little Phelan run away and stolen in the city nowheres at all.'

'Ye talk foolishness,' said Mr. McCaskey. ' 'Tis Pat he would be named, after me old father in Cantrim.'

'Ye lie!' said Mrs. McCaskey, without anger. 'Me brother was worth tin dozen bog-trotting McCaskeys. After him would the bye be named.' She leaned over the window-sill and looked down at the hurrying and bustle below.

'Jawn,' said Mrs. McCaskey softly, 'I'm sorry I was hasty wid ye.'

' 'Twas hasty puddin', as ye say,' said her husband, 'and hurry-up turnips and get-a-move-on-ye coffee. 'Twas what ye could call a quick lunch, all right, and tell no lie.'

Mrs. McCaskey slipped her arm inside her husband's and took his rough hand in hers.

'Listen at the cryin' of poor Mrs. Murphy,' she said. ' 'Tis an awful thing for a bit of a bye to be lost in this great big city. If 'twas our little Phelan, Jawn, I'd be breakin' me heart.'

Awkwardly Mr. McCaskey withdrew his hand. But he laid it around the nearing shoulders of his wife.

' 'Tis foolishness, of course,' said he, roughly, 'but I'd be cut up some meself, if our little – Pat was kidnapped or anything. But there never was any childer for us. Sometimes I've been ugly and hard with ye, Judy. Forget it.'

They leaned together, and looked down at the heart-drama being acted below.

Long they sat thus. People surged along the sidewalk, crowding, questioning, filling the air with rumours and inconsequent surmises. Mrs. Murphy ploughed back and forth in their midst, like a soft mountain down which plunged an audible cataract of tears. Couriers came and went.

Loud voices and a renewed uproar were raised in front of the boarding-house.

'What's up now, Judy?' asked Mr. McCaskey.

' 'Tis Missis Murphy's voice,' said Mrs. McCaskey, harking. 'She says she's after finding little Mike asleep behind the roll of old linoleum under the bed in her room.'

Mr. McCaskey laughed loudly.

'That's yer Phelan,' he shouted sardonically 'Divil a bit would a Pat have done that trick If the bye we never had is strayed and stole, by the powers, call him Phelan, and see him hide out under the bed like a mangy pup.'

Mrs. McCaskey arose heavily, and went toward the dish closet, with the corners of her mouth drawn down.

Policeman Cleary came back around the corner as the crowd dispersed. Surprised, he upturned an ear toward the McCaskey apartment where the crash of irons and chinaware and the ring of hurled kitchen utensils seemed as loud as before. Policeman Cleary took out his timepiece.

'By the deported snakes!' he exclaimed, 'Jawn McCaskey and his lady have been fightin' for an hour and a quarter by the watch. The missis could give him forty pounds weight. Strength to his arm.'

Policeman Cleary strolled back around the corner.

Old man Denny folded his paper and hurried up the steps just as Mrs. Murphy was about to lock the door for the night.

IV

The Skylight Room

FIRST MRS. PARKER would show you the double parlours. You would not dare to interrupt her description of their advantages and of the merits of the gentleman who had occupied them for eight years. Then you would manage to stammer forth the confession that you were neither a doctor nor a dentist. Mrs. Parker's manner of receiving the admission was such that you could never afterward entertain the same feeling toward your parents, who had neglected to train you up in one of the professions that fitted Mrs. Parker's parlours.

Next you ascended one flight of stairs and looked at the second floor back at $8. Convinced by her second-floor manner that it

was worth the $12 that Mr. Toosenberry always paid for it until
he left to take charge of his brother's orange plantation in Florida
near Palm Beach, where Mrs. McIntyre always spent the winters
that had the double front room with private bath, you managed to
babble that you wanted something still cheaper.

If you survived Mrs. Parker's scorn, you were taken to look at
Mr. Skidder's large hall-room on the third floor. Mr. Skidder's
room was not vacant. He wrote plays and smoked cigarettes in it
all day long. But every room-hunter was made to visit his room to
admire the lambrequins. After each visit, Mr. Skidder, from the
fright caused by possible eviction, would pay something on his
rent.

Then – oh, then – if you still stood on one foot with your hot
hand clutching the three moist dollars in your pocket, and
hoarsely proclaimed your hideous and culpable poverty, never-
more would Mrs. Parker be cicerone of yours. She would honk
loudly the word 'Clara,' she would show you her back, and march
downstairs. Then Clara, the coloured maid, would escort you up
the carpeted ladder that served for the fourth flight, and show you
the Skylight Room. It occupied 7 by 8 feet of floorspace at the
middle of the hall. On each side of it was a dark lumber closet or
store-room.

In it was an iron cot, a washstand and a chair A shelf was the
dresser. Its four bare walls seemed to close in upon you like the
sides of a coin. Your hand crept to your throat, you gasped, you
looked up as from a well – and breathed once more. Through the
glass of the little skylight you saw a square of blue infinity.

'Two dollars, suh,' Clara would say in her half-contemptuous,
half-Tuskegeenial tones.

One day Miss Leeson came hunting for a room. She carried a
typewriter made to be lugged around by a much larger lady. She
was a very little girl, with eyes and hair that kept on growing after
she had stopped and that always looked as if they were saying:
'Goodness me. Why didn't you keep up with us?'

Mrs. Parker showed her the double parlours. 'In this closet,' she
said, 'one could keep a skeleton or anæsthetic or coal –'

'But I am neither a doctor nor a dentist,' said Miss Leeson with
a shiver.

Mrs. Parker gave her the incredulous, pitying, sneering, icy
stare that she kept for those who failed to qualify as doctors or
dentists, and led the way to the second floor back.

'Eight dollars?' said Miss Leeson. 'Dear me! I'm not Hetty if I do look green. I'm just a poor little working girl. Show me something higher and lower.'

Mr. Skidder jumped and strewed the floor with cigarette stubs at the rap on his door.

'Excuse me, Mr. Skidder,' said Mrs. Parker, with her demon's smile at his pale looks. 'I didn't know you were in. I asked the lady to have a look at your lambrequins.'

'They're too lovely for anything,' said Miss Leeson, smiling in exactly the way the angels do.

After they had gone Mr. Skidder got very busy erasing the tall, black-haired heroine from his latest (unproduced) play and inserting a small, roguish one with heavy, bright hair and vivacious features.

'Anna Held'll jump at it,' said Mr. Skidder to himself, putting his feet up against the lambrequins and disappearing in a cloud of smoke like an aerial cuttlefish.

Presently the tocsin call of 'Clara!' sounded to the world the state of Miss Leeson's purse. A dark goblin seized her, mounted a Stygian stairway, thrust her into a vault with a glimmer of light in its top and muttered the menacing and cabalistic words 'Two dollars!'

'I'll take it!' sighed Miss Leeson, sinking down upon the squeaky iron bed.

Every day Miss Leeson went out to work. At night she brought home papers with handwriting on them and made copies with her typewriter. Sometimes she had no work at night, and then she would sit on the steps of the high stoop with the other roomers. Miss Leeson was not intended for a skylight room when the plans were drawn for her creation. She was gay-hearted and full of tender, whimsical fancies. Once she let Mr. Skidder read to her three acts of his great (unpublished) comedy, 'It's No Kid; or, The Heir of the Subway.'

There was rejoicing among the gentlemen roomers whenever Miss Leeson had time to sit on the steps for an hour or two. But Miss Longnecker, the tall blonde who taught in a public school and said 'Well, really!' to everything you said, sat on the top step and sniffed. And Miss Dorn, who shot at the moving ducks at Coney every Sunday and worked in a department store, sat on the bottom step and sniffed. Miss Leeson sat on the middle step, and the men would quickly group around her.

Especially Mr. Skidder, who had cast her in his mind for the star part in a private, romantic (unspoken) drama in real life. And

especially Mr. Hoover, who was forty-five, fat, flushed and foolish.
And especially very young Mr. Evans, who set up a hollow cough
to induce her to ask him to leave off cigarettes. The men voted her
'the funniest and jolliest ever,' but the sniffs on the top step and
the lower step were implacable.

●　　●　　●　　●　　●

I pray you let the drama halt while Chorus stalks to the footlights and drops an epicedian tear upon the fatness of Mr. Hoover.
Tune the pipes to the tragedy of tallow, the bane of bulk, the
calamity of corpulence. Tried out, Falstaff might have rendered
more romance to the ton than would have Romeo's rickety ribs to
the ounce. A lover may sigh, but he must not puff. To the train of
Momus are the fat men remanded. In vain beats the faithfullest
heart above a 52-inch belt. Avaunt, Hoover! Hoover, forty-five,
flush and foolish, might carry off Helen herself; Hoover, forty-
five, flush, foolish and fat, is meat for perdition. There was never a
chance for you, Hoover.

As Mrs. Parker's roomers sat thus one summer's evening, Miss
Leeson looked up into the firmament and cried with her little gay
laugh:

'Why, there's Billy Jackson! I can see him from down here, too.'

All looked up – some at the windows of skyscrapers, some casting about for an airship, Jackson-guided.

'It's that star,' explained Miss Leeson, pointing with a tiny
finger. 'Not the big one that twinkles – the steady blue one near it.
I can see it every night through my skylight. I named it Billy Jackson.'

'Well, really!' said Miss Longnecker. 'I didn't know you were an
astronomer, Miss Leeson.'

'Oh, yes,' said the small star-gazer, 'I know as much as any of
them about the style of sleeves they're going to wear next fall in
Mars.'

'Well, really!' said Miss Longnecker. 'The star you refer to is
Gamma, of the constellation Cassiopeia. It is nearly of the second
magnitude, and its meridian passage is –'

'Oh,' said the very young Mr. Evans, 'I think Billy Jackson is a
much better name for it.'

'Same here,' said Mr. Hoover, loudly breathing defiance to Miss
Longnecker. 'I think Miss Leeson has just as much right to name
stars as any of those old astrologers had.'

'Well, really!' said Miss Longnecker.

'I wonder whether it's a shooting star,' remarked Miss Dorn. 'I hit nine ducks and a rabbit out of ten in the gallery at Coney Sunday.'

'He doesn't show up very well from down here,' said Miss Leeson. 'You ought to see him from my room. You know you can see stars even in the daytime from the bottom of a well. At night my room is like the shaft of a coal-mine, and it makes Billy Jackson look like the big diamond pin that Night fastens her kimono with.'

There came a time after that when Miss Leeson brought no formidable papers home to copy. And when she went in the morning, instead of working, she went from office to office and let her heart melt away in the drip of cold refusals transmitted through insolent office boys. This went on.

There came an evening when she wearily climbed Mrs. Parker's stoop at the hour when she always returned from her dinner at the restaurant. But she had had no dinner.

As she stepped into the hall Mr. Hoover met her and seized his chance. He asked her to marry him, and his fatness hovered above her like an avalanche. She dodged, and caught the balustrade. He tried for her hand, and she raised it and smote him weakly in the face. Step by step she went up, dragging herself by the railing. She passed Mr. Skidder's door as he was red-inking a stage direction for Myrtle Delorme (Miss Leeson) in his (unaccepted) comedy, to 'pirouette across stage from L to the side of the Count.' Up the carpeted ladder she crawled at last and opened the door of the skylight room.

She was too weak to light the lamp or to undress. She fell upon the iron cot, her fragile body scarcely hollowing the worn springs. And in that Erebus of a room she slowly raised her heavy eyelids, and smiled.

For Billy Jackson was shining down on her, calm and bright and constant through the skylight. There was no world about her. She was sunk in a pit of blackness, with but that small square of pallid light framing the star that she had so whimsically, and oh, so ineffectually, named. Miss Longnecker must be right; it was Gamma, of the constellation Cassiopeia, and not Billy Jackson. And yet she could not let it be Gamma.

As she lay on her back she tried twice to raise her arm. The third time she got two thin fingers to her lips and blew a kiss out of the black pit to Billy Jackson. Her arm fell back limply.

'Good-bye, Billy,' she murmured faintly. 'You're millions of miles away and you won't even twinkle once. But you kept where I could see you most of the time up there when there wasn't anything else but darkness to look at, didn't you? . . . Millions of miles. . . . Good-bye, Billy Jackson.'

Clara, the coloured maid, found the door locked at ten the next day, and they forced it open. Vinegar, and the slapping of wrists and even burnt feathers, proving of no avail, someone ran to 'phone for an ambulance.

In due time it backed up to the door with much gong-clanging, and the capable young medico, in his white linen coat, ready, active, confident, with his smooth face half debonair, half grim, danced up the steps.

'Ambulance call to 49,' he said briefly. 'What's the trouble?'

'Oh yes, doctor,' sniffed Mrs. Parker, as though her trouble that there should be trouble in the house was the greater. 'I can't think what can be the matter with her. Nothing we could do would bring her to. It's a young woman, a Miss Elsie − yes, a Miss Elsie Leeson. Never before in my house −'

'What room?' cried the doctor in a terrible voice, to which Mrs. Parker was a stranger.

'The skylight room. It −'

Evidently the ambulance doctor was familiar with the location of skylight rooms. He was gone up the stairs, four at a time. Mrs. Parker followed slowly, as her dignity demanded.

On the first landing she met him coming back bearing the astronomer in his arms. He stopped and let loose the practised scalpel of his tongue, not loudly. Gradually Mrs. Parker crumpled as a stiff garment that slips down from a nail. Ever afterwards there remained crumples in her mind and body. Sometimes her curious roomers would ask her what the doctor said to her.

'Let that be,' she would answer. 'If I can get forgiveness for having heard it I will be satisfied.'

The ambulance physician strode with his burden through the pack of hounds that follow the curiosity chase, and even they fell back along the sidewalk abashed, for his face was that of one who bears his own dead.

They noticed that he did not lay down upon the bed prepared for it in the ambulance the form that he carried, and all that he said was: 'Drive like h − 1, Wilson,' to the driver.

That is all. Is it a story? In the next morning's paper I saw a little news item, and the last sentence of it may help you (as it helped me) to weld the incidents together.

It recounted the reception into Bellevue Hospital of a young woman who had been removed from No. 49 East - Street, suffering from debility induced by starvation. It concluded with these words:

'Dr. William Jackson, the ambulance physician who attended the case, says the patient will recover.'

V

A Service of Love

WHEN ONE LOVES ONES ART no service seems too hard.

That is our premise. This story shall draw a conclusion from it, and show at the same time that the premise is incorrect. That will be a new thing in logic, and a feat in story-telling somewhat older than the Great Wall of China.

Joe Larrabee came out of the post-oak flats of the Middle West pulsing with a genius for pictorial art. At six he drew a picture of the town pump with a prominent citizen passing it hastily. This effort was framed and hung in the drug store window by the side of the ear of corn with an uneven number of rows. At twenty he left for New York with a flowing necktie and a capital tied up somewhat closer.

Delia Caruthers did things in six octaves so promisingly in a pine-tree village in the South that her relatives chipped in enough in her chip hat for her to go 'North' and 'finish.' They could not see her f -, but that is our story

Joe and Delia met in an atelier where a number of art and music students had gathered to discuss chiaroscuro, Wagner, music, Rembrandt's works pictures, Waldteufel, wall-paper, Chopin, and Oolong.

Joe and Delia became enamoured one of the other or each of the other, as you please, and in a short time were married - for (see above), when one loves one's Art no service seem too hard.

Mr. and Mrs. Larrabee began housekeeping in a flat. It was a lonesome flat - something like the A sharp way down at the left-hand end of the keyboard. And they were happy; for they had their Art and they had each other. And my advice to the rich young man would be - sell all thou hast, and give it to the poor - janitor for the privilege of living in a flat with your Art and your Delia.

Flat-dwellers shall endorse my dictum that theirs is the only true happiness. If a home is happy it cannot fit too close – let the dresser collapse and become a billiard table; let the mantel turn to a rowing machine, the escritoire to a spare bedchamber, the wash-stand to an upright piano; let the four walls come together, if they will, so you and your Delia are between. But if home be the other kind, let it be wide and long – enter you at the Golden Gate, hang your hat on Hatteras, your cape on Cape Horn, and go out by Labrador.

Joe was painting in the class of the great Magister – you know his fame. His fees are high; his lessons are light – his high-lights have brought him renown. Delia was studying under Rosenstock – you know his repute as a disturber of the piano keys.

They were mighty happy as long as their money lasted. So is every – but I will not be cynical. Their aims were very clear and defined. Joe was to become capable very soon of turning out pictures that old gentlemen with thin side-whiskers and thick pocket-books would sandbag one another in his studio for the privilege of buying. Delia was to become familiar and then contemptuous with Music, so that when she saw the orchestra seats and boxes unsold she could have sore throat and lobster in a private dining-room and refuse to go on the stage.

But the best, in my opinion, was the home life in the little flat – the ardent, voluble chats after the day's study; the cosy dinners and fresh, light breakfasts; the interchange of ambitions – ambitions interwoven each with the other's or else inconsiderable – the mutual help and inspiration; and – overlook my artlessness – stuffed olives and cheese sandwiches at 11p.m.

But after awhile Art flagged. It sometimes does, even if some switchman doesn't flag it. Everything going out and nothing coming in, as the vulgarians say. Money was lacking to pay Mr. Magister and Herr Rosenstock their prices. When one loves one's Art no service seems too hard. So, Delia said she must give music lessons to keep the chafing dish bubbling.

For two or three days she went out canvassing for pupils. One evening she came home elated.

'Joe, dear,' she said gleefully, 'I've a pupil. And, oh, the loveliest people! General – General A. B. Pinkney's daughter – on Seventy-first Street. Such a splendid house, Joe – you ought to see the front door! Byzantine I think you would call it. And inside! Oh, Joe, I never saw anything like it before.

'My pupil is his daughter Clementina. I dearly love her already. She's a delicate thing – dresses always in white; and the sweetest, simplest manners! Only eighteen years old. I'm to give three lessons a week; and, just think, Joe! $5 a lesson. I don't mind it a bit; for when I get two or three more pupils I can resume my lessons with Herr Rosenstock. Now, smooth out that wrinkle between your brows, dear, and let's have a nice supper.'

'That's all right for you, Dele,' said Joe, attacking a can of peas with a carving knife and a hatchet, 'but how about me? Do you think I'm going to let you hustle for wages while I philander in the regions of high art? Not by the bones of Benvenuto Cellini! I guess I can sell papers or lay cobblestones, and bring in a dollar or two.'

Delia came and hung about his neck.

'Joe, dear, you are silly. You must keep on at your studies. It is not as if I had quit my music and gone to work at something else. While I teach I learn. I am always with my music. And we can live as happily as millionaires on $15 a week. You mustn't think of leaving Mr. Magister.'

'All right,' said Joe, reaching for the blue scalloped vegetable dish. 'But I hate for you to be giving lessons. It isn't Art. But you're a trump and a dear to do it.'

'When one loves one's Art no service seems too hard,' said Delia.

'Magister praised the sky in that sketch I made in the park,' said Joe. 'And Tinkle gave me permission to hang two of them in his window. I may sell one if the right kind of a moneyed idiot sees them.'

'I'm sure you will,' said Delia sweetly. 'And now let's be thankful for General Pinkney and this veal roast.'

During all of the next week the Larrabees had an early breakfast. Joe was enthusiastic about some morning-effect sketches he was doing in Central Park, and Delia packed him off breakfasted, coddled, praised, and kissed at seven o'clock. Art is an engaging mistress. It was most times seven o'clock when he returned in the evening.

At the end of the week Delia, sweetly proud but languid, triumphantly tossed three five-dollar bills on the 8 by 10 (inches) centre table of the 8 by 10 (feet) flat parlour.

'Sometimes,' she said, a little wearily, 'Clementina tries me. I'm afraid she doesn't practise enough, and I have to tell her the same things so often. And then she always dresses entirely in white, and that does get monotonous. But General Pinkney is the dearest old man! I wish you could know him, Joe. He comes in sometimes when I am with Clementina at the piano — he is a widower, you know — and stands there pulling his white goatee. "And how are the semiquavers and the demi-semiquavers progressing?" he always asks.

'I wish you could see the wainscoting in that drawing-room, Joe! And those Astrakhan rug *portières*. And Clementina has such a funny little cough. I hope she is stronger than she looks. Oh, I really am getting attached to her, she is so gentle and high bred. General Pinkney's brother was once Minister to Bolivia.'

And then Joe, with the air of a Monte Cristo, drew forth a ten, a five, a two and a one — all legal tender notes — and laid them beside Delia's earnings.

'Sold that water-colour of the obelisk to a man from Peoria,' he announced overwhelmingly

'Don't joke with me,' said Delia — 'not from Peoria!'

'All the way. I wish you could see him, Dele. Fat man with a woollen muffler and a quill toothpick. He saw the sketch in Tinkle's window and thought it was a windmill at first. He was game, though, and bought it anyhow. He ordered another — an oil sketch of the Lackawanna freight depot — to take back with him. Music lessons! Oh, I guess Art is still in it.'

'I'm so glad you've kept on,' said Delia heartily. 'You're bound to win, dear. Thirty-three dollars! We never had so much to spend before. We'll have oysters to-night.'

'And filet mignon with champignons,' said Joe. 'Where is the olive fork?'

On the next Saturday evening Joe reached home first. He spread his $18 on the parlour table and washed what seemed to be a great deal of dark paint from his hands.

Half an hour later Delia arrived, her right hand tied up in a shapeless bundle of wraps and bandages.

'How is this?' asked Joe after the usual greetings

Delia laughed, but not very joyously

'Clementina,' she explained, 'insisted upon a Welsh rabbit after her lesson. She is such a queer girl. Welsh rabbits at five in the afternoon. The General was there. You should have seen him run for the chafing dish, Joe, just as if there wasn't a servant in the house. I know Clementina isn't in good health; she is so nervous. In serving the rabbit she spilled a great lot of it, boiling hot, over my hand and wrist. It hurt awfully, Joe. And the dear girl was so sorry! But General Pinkney! — Joe, that old man nearly went distracted. He rushed downstairs and sent somebody — they said the

furnace man or somebody in the basement – out to a drug store
for some oil and things to bind it up with. It doesn't hurt so much
now.'

'What's this?' asked Joe, taking the hand tenderly and pulling at
some white strands beneath the bandages.

'It's something soft,' said Delia, 'that had oil on it. Oh, Joe, did
you sell another sketch?' She had seen the money on the table.

'Did I?' said Joe. 'Just ask the man from Peoria. He got his
depot to-day, and he isn't sure but he thinks he wants another
parkscape and a view on the Hudson. What time this afternoon
did you burn your hand, Dele?'

'Five o'clock, I think,' said Dele plaintively. 'The iron – I mean
the rabbit came off the fire about that time. You ought to have
seen General Pinkney, Joe, when –'

'Sit down here a moment, Dele,' said Joe. He drew her to the
couch, sat down beside her and put his arm across her shoulders.

'What have you been doing for the last two weeks, Dele?' he
asked.

She braved it for a moment or two with an eye full of love and
stubbornness, and murmured a phrase or two vaguely of General
Pinkney; but at length down went her head and out came the truth
and tears.

'I couldn't get any pupils,' she confessed. 'And I couldn't bear to
have you give up your lessons; and I got a place ironing shirts in
that big Twenty-fourth Street laundry. And I think I did very well
to make up both General Pinkney and Clementina, don't you,
Joe? And when a girl in the laundry set down a hot iron on my
hand this afternoon I was all the way home making up that story
about the Welsh rabbit. You're not angry are you, Joe? And if I
hadn't got the work you mightn't have sold your sketches to that
man from Peoria.'

'He wasn't from Peoria,' said Joe slowly

'Well, it doesn't matter where he was from. How clever you are,
Joe – and – kiss me, Joe – and what made you ever suspect that I
wasn't giving music lessons to Clementina?'

'I didn't,' said Joe, 'until to-night. And I wouldn't have then,
only I sent up this cotton waste and oil from the engine-room this
afternoon for a girl upstairs who had her hand burned with a
smoothing-iron. I've been firing the engine in that laundry for the
last two weeks.'

'And then you didn't –'

'My purchaser from Peoria,' said Joe, 'and General Pinkney are both creations of the same art – but you wouldn't call it either painting or music.

And then they both laughed, and Joe began:

'When one loves one's Art no service seems –'

But Delia stopped him with her hand on his lips. 'No,' she said – 'just "When one loves." '

VI

The Coming-out of Maggie

EVERY SATURDAY NIGHT the Clover Leaf Social Club gave a hop in the hall of the Give and Take Athletic Association on the East Side. In order to attend one of these dances you must be a member of the Give and Take – or, if you belong to the division that starts off with the right foot in waltzing, you must work in Rhinegold's paper-box factory. Still, any Clover Leaf was privileged to escort or be escorted by an outsider to a single dance. But mostly each Give and Take brought the paper-box girl that he affected; and few strangers could boast of having shaken a foot at the regular hops.

Maggie Toole, on account of her dull eyes, broad mouth and left-handed style of footwork in the two-step, went to the dances with Anna McCarty and her 'fellow.' Anna and Maggie worked side by side in the factory, and were the greatest chums ever. So Anna always made Jimmy Burns take her by Maggie's house every Saturday night so that her friend could go to the dance with them.

The Give and Take Athletic Association lived up to its name. The hall of the association in Orchard Street was fitted out with muscle-making inventions. With the fibres thus builded up the members were wont to engage the police and rival social and athletic organizations in joyous combat. Between these more serious occupations the Saturday night hops with the paper-box factory girls came as a refining influence and as an efficient screen. For sometimes the tip went 'round, and if you were among the elect that tiptoed up the dark back stairway you might see as neat and satisfying a little welter-weight affair to a finish as ever happened inside the ropes.

On Saturdays Rhinegold's paper-box factory closed at 3 p.m. On one such afternoon Anna and Maggie walked homeward together. At Maggie's door Anna said, as usual: 'Be ready at seven, sharp, Mag; and Jimmy and me'll come by for you.'

But what was this? Instead of the customary humble and grateful thanks from the non-escorted one there was to be perceived a high-poised head, a prideful dimpling at the corners of a broad mouth, and almost a sparkle in a dull brown eye.

'Thanks, Anna,' said Maggie; 'but you and Jimmy needn't bother to-night. I've a gentleman friend that's coming 'round to escort me to the hop.'

The comely Anna pounced upon her friend, shook her, chided and beseeched her. Maggie Toole catch a fellow! Plain, dear, loyal, unattractive Maggie, so sweet as a chum, so unsought for a two-step or a moonlit bench in the little park. How was it? When did it happen? Who was it?

'You'll see to-night,' said Maggie, flushed with the wine of the first grapes she had gathered in Cupid's vineyard. 'He's swell all right. He's two inches taller than Jimmy, and an up-to-date dresser. I'll introduce him, Anna, just as soon as we get to the hall.'

Anna and Jimmy were among the first Clover Leafs to arrive that evening. Anna's eyes were brightly fixed upon the door of the hall to catch the first glimpse of her friend's 'catch.'

At 8.30 Miss Toole swept into the hall with her escort. Quickly her triumphant eye discovered her chum under the wing of her faithful Jimmy.

'Oh, gee!' cried Anna, 'Mag ain't made a hit – oh, no! Swell fellow? Well, I guess! Style? Look at 'um.'

'Go as far as you like,' said Jimmy, with sandpaper in his voice. 'Cop him out if you want him. These new guys always win out with the push. Don't mind me. He don't squeeze all the limes, I guess. Huh!'

'Shut up, Jimmy. You know what I mean. I'm glad for Mag. First fellow she ever had. Oh, here they come.'

Across the floor Maggie sailed like a coquettish yacht convoyed by a stately cruiser. And truly, her companion justified the encomiums of the faithful chum. He stood two inches taller than the average Give and Take athlete; his dark hair curled; his eyes and his teeth flashed whenever he bestowed his frequent smiles. The young men of the Clover Leaf Club pinned not their faith to the graces of person as much as they did to its prowess, its achievements in hand-to-hand conflicts, and its preservation from the legal duress that constantly menaced it. The member of the association who would bind a paper-box maiden to his conquering chariot scorned to employ Beau Brummel airs. They were not considered honourable methods of warfare. The swelling biceps,

the coat straining at its buttons over the chest, the air of conscious
conviction of the super-eminence of the male in the cosmogony of
creation, even a calm display of bow legs as subduing and enchant-
ing agents in the gentle tourneys of Cupid – these were the
approved arms and ammunition of the Clover Leaf gallants. They
viewed, then, the genuflexions and alluring poses of this visitor
with their chins at a new angle.

'A friend of mine, Mr. Terry O'Sullivan,' was Maggie's formula
of introduction. She led him around the room, presenting him to
each new-arriving Clover Leaf. Almost was she pretty now, with
the unique luminosity in her eyes that comes to a girl with her
first suitor and a kitten with its first mouse.

'Maggie Toole's got a fellow at last,' was the word that went
round among the paper-box girls. 'Pipe Mag's floor-walker' – thus
the Give and Takes expressed their indifferent contempt.

Usually at the weekly hops Maggie kept a spot on the wall warm
with her back. She felt and showed so much gratitude whenever a
self-sacrificing partner invited her to dance that his pleasure was
cheapened and diminished. She had even grown used to noticing
Anna joggle the reluctant Jimmy with her elbow as a signal for
him to invite her chum to walk over his feet through a two-step.

But to-night the pumpkin had turned to a coach and six. Terry
O'Sullivan was a victorious Prince Charming, and Maggie Toole
winged her first butterfly flight. And though our tropes of fairyland be mixed with those of entomology they shall not spill one
drop of ambrosia from the rose-crowned melody of Maggie's one
perfect night.

The girls besieged her for introductions to her 'fellow.' The
Clover Leaf young men, after two years of blindness, suddenly
perceived charms in Miss Toole. They flexed their compelling
muscles before her and bespoke her for the dance.

Thus she scored; but to Terry O'Sullivan the honours of the
evening fell thick and fast. He shook his curls; he smiled and went
easily through the seven motions for acquiring grace in your own
room before an open window ten minutes each day. He danced like
a faun; he introduced manner and style and atmosphere; his words
came trippingly upon his tongue, and – he waltzed twice in succession with the paper-box girl that Dempsey Donovan brought.

Dempsey was the leader of the association. He wore a dress suit,
and could chin the bar twice with one hand. He was one of 'Big
Mike' O'Sullivan's lieutenants, and was never troubled by trouble.
No cop dared to arrest him. Whenever he broke a push-cart man's

head or shot a member of the Heinrick B. Sweeney Outing and
Literary Association in the kneecap, an officer would drop around
and say:

'The Cap'n'd like to see ye a few minutes round to the office
whin ye have time, Dempsey, me boy.'

But there would be sundry gentlemen there with large gold fob
chains and black cigars; and somebody would tell a funny story,
and then Dempsey would go back and work half an hour with the
six-pound dumb-bells. So, doing a tight-rope act on a wire
stretched across Niagara was a safe terpsichorean performance
compared with waltzing twice with Dempsey Donovan's paper-
box girl. At ten o'clock the jolly round face of 'Big Mike' O'Sullivan shone at the door for five minutes upon the scene. He always
looked in for five minutes, smiled at the girls and handed out real
perfectos to the delighted boys.

Dempsey Donovan was at his elbow instantly, talking rapidly.
'Big Mike' looked carefully at the dancers, smiled, shook his head
and departed.

The music stopped. The dancers scattered to the chairs along
the walls. Terry O'Sullivan, with his entrancing bow, relinquished
a pretty girl in blue to her partner and started back to find
Maggie. Dempsey intercepted him in the middle of the floor.

Some fine instinct that Rome must have bequeathed to us
caused nearly every one to turn and look at them — there was a
subtle feeling that two gladiators had met in the arena. Two or
three Give and Takes with tight coat-sleeves drew nearer.

'One moment, Mr. O'Sullivan,' said Dempsey. 'I hope you're
enjoying yourself. Where did you say you lived?

The two gladiators were well matched. Dempsey had, perhaps,
ten pounds of weight to give away. The O'Sullivan had breadth
with quickness Dempsey had a glacial eye, a dominating slit of a
mouth, an indestructible jaw, a complexion like a belle's and the
coolness of a champion. The visitor showed more fire in his contempt and less control over his conspicuous sneer. They were enemies by the law written when the rocks were molten. They were
each too splendid, too mighty, too incomparable to divide pre-
eminence. One only must survive.

'I live on Grand,' said O'Sullivan insolently; 'and no trouble to
find me at home. Where do you live?'

Dempsey ignored the question.

'You say your name's O'Sullivan,' he went on. 'Well, "Big
Mike" says he never saw you before.'

'Lots of things he never saw,' said the favourite of the hop.

'As a rule,' went on Dempsey, huskily sweet, 'O'Sullivans in this district know one another. You escorted one of our lady members here, and we want a chance to make good. If you've got a family tree let's see a few historical O'Sullivan buds come out on it. Or do you want us to dig it out of you by the roots?'

'Suppose you mind your own business, suggested O'Sullivan blandly.

Dempsey's eyes brightened. He held up an inspired forefinger as though a brilliant idea had struck him.

'I've got it now,' he said cordially. 'It was just a little mistake. You ain't no O'Sullivan. You are a ring-tailed monkey. Excuse us for not recognizing you at first.'

O'Sullivan's eye flashed. He made a quick movement, but Andy Geoghan was ready and caught his arm.

Dempsey nodded at Andy and William McMahan, the secretary of the club, and walked rapidly toward a door at the rear of the hall. Two other members of the Give and Take Association swiftly joined the little group. Terry O'Sullivan was now in the hands of the Board of Rules and Social Referees. They spoke to him briefly and softly, and conducted him out through the same door at the rear.

This movement on the part of the Clover Leaf members requires a word of elucidation. Back of the association hall was a smaller room rented by the club. In this room personal difficulties that arose on the ballroom floor were settled, man to man, with the weapons of nature, under the supervision of the Board. No lady could say that she had witnessed a fight at a Clover Leaf hop in several years. Its gentlemen members guaranteed that.

So easily and smoothly had Dempsey and the Board done their preliminary work that many in the hall had not noticed the checking of the fascinating O'Sullivan's social triumph. Among these was Maggie. She looked about for her escort.

'Smoke up!' said Rose Cassidy. 'Wasn't you on? Demps Donovan picked a scrap with your Lizzie-boy, and they've waltzed out to the slaughter-room with him. How's my hair look done up this way, Mag?'

Maggie laid a hand on the bosom of her cheesecloth waist.

'Gone to fight with Dempsey!' she said breathlessly. 'They've got to be stopped. Dempsey Donovan can't fight him. Why, he'll – he'll kill him!'

'Ah, what do you care?' said Rosa. 'Don't some of 'em fight every hop?'

But Maggie was off, darting her zigzag way through the maze of dancers. She burst through the rear door into the dark hall and then threw her solid shoulder against the door of the room of single combat. It gave way, and in the instant that she entered her eye caught the scene — the Board standing about with open watches; Dempsey Donovan in his shirt-sleeves dancing, light-footed, with the wary grace of the modern pugilist, within easy reach of his adversary; Terry O'Sullivan standing with arm folded and a murderous look in his dark eyes. And without slacking the speed of her entrance she leaped forward with a scream — leaped in time to catch and hang upon the arm of O'Sullivan that was suddenly uplifted, and to whisk from it the long, bright stiletto that he had drawn from his bosom.

The knife fell and rang upon the floor. Cold steel drawn in the rooms of the Give and Take Association! Such a thing had never happened before. Every one stood motionless for a minute. Andy Geoghan kicked the stiletto with the toe of his shoe curiously, like an antiquarian who has come upon some ancient weapon unknown to his learning.

And then O'Sullivan hissed something unintelligible between his teeth. Dempsey and the Board exchanged looks. And then Dempsey looked at O'Sullivan without anger as one looks at a stray dog, and nodded his head in the direction of the door.

'The back stairs, Giuseppi,' he said briefly. 'Somebody'll pitch your hat down after you.'

Maggie walked up to Dempsey Donovan. There was a brilliant spot of red in her cheeks, down which slow tears were running. But she looked him bravely in the eye.

'I knew it, Dempsey,' she said, as her eyes grew dull even in their tears. 'I knew he was a Guinea. His name's Tony Spinelli. I hurried in when they told me you and him was scrappin'. Them Guineas always carries knives. But you don't understand, Dempsey. I never had a fellow in my life. I got tired of comin' with Anna and Jimmy every night, so I fixed it with him to call himself O'Sullivan, and brought him along. I knew there'd be nothin' doin' for him if he came as a Dago. I guess I'll resign from the club now.'

Dempsey turned to Andy Geoghan.

'Chuck that cheese slicer out of the window,' he said, 'and tell 'em inside that Mr. O'Sullivan has had a telephone message to go down to Tammany Hall.'

And then he turned back to Maggie.

'Say, Mag,' he said, 'I'll see you home. And how about next Saturday night? Will you come to the hop with me if I call around for you?'

It was remarkable how quickly Maggie's eyes could change from dull to a shining brown.

'With you, Dempsey?' she stammered. 'Say – will a duck swim?'

VII

The Cop and the Anthem

ON HIS BENCH IN MADISON SQUARE Soapy moved uneasily. When wild goose honk high of nights, and when women without sealskin coats grow kind to their husbands, and when Soapy moves uneasily on his bench in the park, you may know that winter is near at hand.

A dead leaf fell in Soapy's lap. That was Jack Frost s card. Jack is kind to the regular denizens of Madison Square, and gives fair warning of his annual call. At the corners of four streets he hands his pasteboard to the North Wind, footman of the mansion of All Outdoors, so that the inhabitants thereof may make ready.

Soapy's mind became cognizant of the fact that the time had come for him to resolve himself into a singular Committee of Ways and Means to provide against the coming rigour. And therefore he moved uneasily on his bench.

The hibernatorial ambitions of Soapy were not of the highest. In them were no considerations of Mediterranean cruises, of soporific Southern skies or drifting in the Vesuvian Bay. Three months on the Island was what his soul craved. Three months of assured board and bed and congenial company, safe from Boreas and bluecoats, seemed to Soapy the essence of things desirable.

For years the hospitable Blackwell's had been his winter quarters. Just as his more fortunate fellow New Yorkers had bought their tickets to Palm Beach and the Riviera each winter, so Soapy had made his humble arrangements for his annual hegira to the Island. And now the time was come. On the previous night three Sabbath newspapers, distributed beneath his coat, about his ankles and over his lap, had failed to repulse the cold as he slept on his bench near the spurting fountain in the ancient square. So the Island loomed large and timely in Soapy's mind. He scorned the provisions made in the name of charity for the city's dependents.

In Soapy's opinion the Law was more benign than Philanthropy. There was an endless round of institutions, municipal and eleemosynary, on which he might set out and receive lodging and food accordant with the simple life. But to one of Soapy's proud spirit the gifts of charity are encumbered. If not in coin you must pay in humiliation of spirit for every benefit received at the hands of philanthropy. As Cæsar had his Brutus, every bed of charity must have its toll of a bath, every loaf of bread its compensation of a private and personal inquisition. Wherefore it is better to be a guest of the law, which, though conducted by rules, does not meddle unduly with a gentleman's private affairs

Soapy, having decided to go to the Island, at once set about accomplishing his desire. There were many easy ways of doing this. The pleasantest was to dine luxuriously at some expensive restaurant; and then, after declaring insolvency, be handed over quietly and without uproar to a policeman. An accommodating magistrate would do the rest.

Soapy left his bench and strolled out of the square and across the level sea of asphalt, where Broadway and Fifth Avenue flow together. Up Broadway he turned, and halted at a glittering café, where are gathered together nightly the choicest products of the grape, the silkworm and the protoplasm.

Soapy had confidence in himself from the lowest button of his vest upward. He was shaven, and his coat was decent and his neat black, ready-tied four-in-hand had been presented to him by a lady missionary on Thanksgiving Day. If he could reach a table in the restaurant unsuspected success would be his. The portion of him that would show above the table would raise no doubt in the waiter's mind. A roasted mallard duck, thought Soapy, would be about the thing − with a bottle of Chablis, and then Camembert, a demi-tasse and a cigar. One dollar for the cigar would be enough. The total would not be so high as to call forth any supreme manifestation of revenge from the café management; and yet the meat would leave him filled and happy for the journey to his winter refuge.

But as Soapy set foot inside the restaurant door the head waiter's eye fell upon his frayed trousers and decadent shoes. Strong and ready hands turned him about and conveyed him in silence and haste to the sidewalk and averted the ignoble fate of the menaced mallard.

Soapy turned off Broadway. It seemed that his route to the coveted Island was not to be an epicurean one. Some other way of entering limbo must be thought of.

At a corner of Sixth Avenue electric lights and cunningly displayed wares behind plate-glass made a shop window conspicuous. Soapy took a cobblestone and dashed it through the glass. People came running round the corner, a policeman in the lead. Soapy stood still, with his hands in his pockets, and smiled at the sight of brass buttons.

'Where's the man that done that?' inquired the officer excitedly.

'Don't you figure out that I might have had something to do with it?' said Soapy, not without sarcasm, but friendly, as one greets good fortune.

The policeman's mind refused to accept Soapy even as a clue. Men who smash windows do not remain to parley with the law's minions. They take to their heels. The policeman saw a man halfway down the block running to catch a car. With drawn club he joined in the pursuit. Soapy, with disgust in his heart, loafed along, twice unsuccessful.

On the opposite side of the street was a restaurant of no great pretensions. It catered to large appetites and modest purses. Its crockery and atmosphere were thick; its soup and napery thin. Into this place Soapy took his accusive shoes and tell-tale trousers without challenge. At a table he sat and consumed beefsteak, flapjacks, doughnuts and pie. And then to the waiter he betrayed the fact that the minutest coin and himself were strangers.

'Now, get busy and call a cop,' said Soapy. 'And don't keep a gentleman waiting.'

'No cop for youse,' said the waiter, with a voice like butter cakes and an eye like the cherry in a Manhattan cocktail. 'Hey, Con!'

Neatly upon his left ear on the callous pavement two waiters pitched Soapy. He arose, joint by joint, as a carpenter's rule opens, and beat the dust from his clothes. Arrest seemed but a rosy dream. The Island seemed very far away. A policeman who stood before a drug store two doors away laughed and walked down the street.

Five blocks Soapy travelled before his courage permitted him to woo capture again. This time the opportunity presented what he fatuously termed to himself a 'cinch.' A young woman of a modest and pleasing guise was standing before a show window gazing with sprightly interest at its display of shaving mugs and inkstands, and two yards from the window a large policeman of severe demeanour leaned against a water-plug.

It was Soapy's design to assume the role of the despicable and execrated 'masher.' The refined and elegant appearance of his victim and the contiguity of the conscientious cop encouraged him to believe that he would soon feel the pleasant official clutch upon his arm that would ensure his winter quarters on the right little, tight little isle.

Soapy straightened the lady missionary's ready-made tie, dragged his shrinking cuffs into the open, set his hat at a killing cant and sidled toward the young woman. He made eyes at her, was taken with sudden coughs and 'hems,' smiled, smirked and went brazenly through the impudent and contemptible litany of the 'masher.' With half an eye Soapy saw that the policeman was watching him fixedly. The young woman moved away a few steps, and again bestowed her absorbed attention upon the shaving mugs. Soapy followed, boldly stepping to her side, raised his hat and said:

'Ah there, Bedelia! Don't you want to come and play in my yard?'

The policeman was still looking. The persecuted young woman had but to beckon a finger and Soapy would be practically *en route* for his insular haven. Already he imagined he could feel the cosy warmth of the station-house. The young woman faced him and, stretching out a hand, caught Soapy's coat-sleeve.

'Sure, Mike,' she said joyfully, 'if you'll blow me to a pail of suds. I'd have spoke to you sooner, but the cop was watching.'

With the young woman playing the clinging ivy to his oak Soapy walked past the policeman, overcome with gloom. He seemed doomed to liberty.

At the next corner he shook off his companion and ran. He halted in the district where by night are found the lightest streets, hearts, vows and librettos. Women in furs and men in greatcoats moved gaily in the wintry air. A sudden fear seized Soapy that some dreadful enchantment had rendered him immune to arrest. The thought brought a little of panic upon it, and when he came upon another policeman lounging grandly in front of a transplendent theatre he caught at the immediate straw of 'disorderly conduct.'

On the sidewalk Soapy began to yell drunken gibberish at the top of his harsh voice. He danced, howled, raved and otherwise disturbed the welkin.

The policeman twirled his club, turned his back to Soapy and remarked to a citizen:

' 'Tis one of them Yale lads celebratin' the goose egg they give to the Hartford College. Noisy; but no harm. We've instructions to lave them be.'

Disconsolate, Soapy ceased his unavailing racket. Would never a policeman lay hands on him? In his fancy the Island seemed an unattainable Arcadia. He buttoned his thin coat against the chilling wind.

In a cigar store he saw a well-dressed man lighting a cigar at a swinging light. His silk umbrella he had set by the door on entering. Soapy stepped inside, secured the umbrella and sauntered off with it slowly. The man at the cigar light followed hastily.

'My umbrella,' he said sternly.

'Oh, is it?' sneered Soapy, adding insult to petit larceny. 'Well, why don't you call a policeman? I took it. Your umbrella! Why don't you call a cop? There stands one at the corner.'

The umbrella owner slowed his steps. Soapy did likewise, with a presentiment that luck would again run against him. The policeman looked at the two curiously.

'Of course,' said the umbrella man – 'that is – well, you know how these mistakes occur – I – if it's your umbrella I hope you'll excuse me – I picked it up this morning in a restaurant – If you recognize it as yours, why – I hope you'll –'

'Of course it's mine,' said Soapy viciously.

The ex-umbrella man retreated. The policeman hurried to assist a tall blonde in an opera cloak across the street in front of a street car that was approaching two blocks away.

Soapy walked eastward through a street damaged by improvements. He hurled the umbrella wrathfully into an excavation. He muttered against the men who wear helmets and carry clubs. Because he wanted to fall into their clutches, they seemed to regard him as a king who could do no wrong.

At length Soapy reached one of the avenues to the east where the glitter and turmoil was but faint. He set his face down this toward Madison Square, for the homing instinct survives even when the home is a park bench.

But on an unusually quiet corner Soapy came to a standstill. Here was an old church, quaint and rambling and gabled. Through one violet-stained window a soft light glowed, where, no doubt, the organist loitered over the keys, making sure of his mastery of the coming Sabbath anthem. For there drifted out to Soapy's ears sweet music that caught and held him transfixed against the convolutions of the iron fence.

The moon was above, lustrous and serene; vehicles and pedestrians were few; sparrows twittered sleepily in the eaves – for a little while the scene might have been a country churchyard. And the anthem that the organist played cemented Soapy to the iron fence, for he had known it well in the days when his life contained such things as mothers and roses and ambitions and friends and immaculate thoughts and collars.

The conjunction of Soapy's receptive state of mind and the influences about the old church wrought a sudden and wonderful change in his soul. He viewed with swift horror the pit into which he had tumbled, the degraded days, unworthy desires, dead hopes, wrecked faculties and base motives that made up his existence.

And also in a moment his heart responded thrillingly to this novel mood. An instantaneous and strong impulse moved him to battle with his desperate fate. He would pull himself out of the mire; he would make a man of himself again; he would conquer the evil that had taken possession of him. There was time; he was comparatively young yet; he would resurrect his old eager ambitions and pursue them without faltering. Those solemn but sweet organ notes had set up a revolution in him. To-morrow he would go into the roaring down-town district and find work. A fur importer had once offered him a place as driver. He would find him to-morrow and ask for the position. He would be somebody in the world. He would –

Soapy felt a hand laid on his arm. He looked quickly around into the broad face of a policeman.

'What are you doin' here?' asked the officer.

'Nothin',' said Soapy.

'Then come along,' said the policeman.

'Three months on the Island,' said the Magistrate in the Police Court the next morning.

VIII

Memoirs of a Yellow Dog

I DON'T SUPPOSE it will knock any of you people off your perch to read a contribution from an animal. Mr. Kipling and a good many others have demonstrated the fact that animals can express themselves in remunerative English, and no magazine goes to press nowadays without an animal story in it, except the old-style monthlies that are still running pictures of Bryan and the Mont Pelée horror.

But you needn't look for any stuck-up literature in my piece, such as Bearoo, the bear, and Snakoo, the snake, and Tammanoo, the tiger, talk in the jungle books. A yellow dog that's spent most of his life in a cheap New York flat, sleeping in a corner on an old sateen underskirt (the one she spilled port wine on at the Lady Longshoremen's banquet), mustn't be expected to perform any tricks with the art of speech.

I was born a yellow pup; date, locality, pedigree and weight unknown. The first thing I can recollect, an old woman had me in a basket at Broadway and Twenty-third trying to sell me to a fat lady. Old Mother Hubbard was boosting me to beat the band as a genuine Pomeranian-Hambletonian-Red-Irish-Cochin-China-Stoke-Pogis fox terrier. The fat lady chased a V around among the samples of gros grain flannelette in her shopping-bag till she cornered it, and gave up. From that moment I was a pet – a mamma's own wootsey squidlums. Say, gentle reader, did you ever have a 200-pound woman breathing a flavour of Camembert cheese and Peau d'Espagne pick you up and wallop her nose all over you, remarking all the time in an Emma Eames tone of voice: 'Oh, oo's um oodlum, doodlum, woodlum, toodlum, bitsy-witsy skoodlums?'

From a pedigreed yellow pup I grew up to be an anonymous yellow cur looking like a cross between an Angora cat and a box of lemons. But my mistress never tumbled. She thought that the two primeval pups that Noah chased into the ark were but a collateral branch of my ancestors. It took two policemen to keep her from entering me at the Madison Square Garden for the Siberian bloodhound prize.

I'll tell you about that flat. The house was the ordinary thing in New York, paved with Parian marble in the entrance hall and cobblestones above the first floor. Our flat was three fl – well, not flights – climbs up. My mistress rented it unfurnished, and put in the regular things – 1903 antique upholstered parlour set, oil chromo of geishas in a Harlem tea-house, rubber plant and husband.

By Sirius! there was a biped I felt sorry for. He was a little man with sandy hair and whiskers a good deal like mine. Hen-pecked? – well, toucans and flamingoes and pelicans all had their bills in him. He wiped the dishes and listened to my mistress tell about the cheap, ragged things the lady with the squirrel-skin coat on the second floor hung out on her line to dry. And every evening while she was getting supper she made him take me out on the end of a string for a walk.

If men knew how women pass the time when they are alone they'd never marry. Laura Lean Jibbey, peanut brittle, a little almond cream on the neck muscles, dishes unwashed, half an hour's talk with the iceman, reading a package of old letters, a couple of pickles and two bottles of malt extract, one hour peeking through a hole in the window shade into the flat across the air-shaft – that's about all there is to it. Twenty minutes before time for him to come home from work she straightens up the house, fixes her rat so it won't show, and gets out a lot of sewing for a ten-minute bluff.

I led a dog's life in that flat. 'Most all day I lay there in my corner watching the fat woman kill time. I slept sometimes and had pipe dreams about being out chasing cats into basements and growling at old ladies with black mittens, as a dog was intended to do. Then she would pounce upon me with a lot of that drivelling poodle palaver and kiss me on the nose – but what could I do? A dog can't chew cloves.

I began to feel sorry for Hubby, dog my cats if I didn't. We looked so much alike that people noticed it when we went out; so we shook the streets that Morgan's cab drives down, and took to climbing the piles of last December's snow on the streets where cheap people live.

One evening when we were thus promenading, and I was trying to look like a prize St. Bernard, and the old man was trying to look like he wouldn't have murdered the first organ-grinder he heard play Mendelssohn's wedding-march, I looked up at him and said, in my way:

'What are you looking so sour about, you oakum trimmed lobster? She don't kiss you. You don't have to sit on her lap and listen to talk that would make the book of a musical comedy sound like the maxims of Epictetus. You ought to be thankful you're not a dog. Brace up, Benedick, and bid the blues begone.'

The matrimonial mishap looked down at me with almost canine intelligence in his face.

'Why, doggie,' says he, 'good doggie. You almost look like you could speak. What is it, doggie – Cats?'

Cats! Could speak!

But, of course, he couldn't understand. Humans were denied the speech of animals. The only common ground of communication upon which dogs and men can get together is in fiction.

In the flat across the hall from us lived a lady with a black-and-tan terrier. Her husband strung it and took it out every evening, but he always came home cheerful and whistling. One day I touched noses with the black-and-tan in the hall, and I struck him for an elucidation.

'See, here, Wiggle-and-Skip,' I says, 'you know that it ain't the nature of a real man to play dry-nurse to a dog in public. I never saw one leashed to a bow-wow yet that didn't look like he'd like to lick every other man that looked at him. But your boss comes in every day as perky and set up as an amateur prestidigitator doing the egg trick. How does he do it? Don't tell me he likes it.'

'Him?' says the black-and-tan. 'Why, he uses Nature's Own Remedy. He gets spifflicated. At first when we go out he's as shy as the man on the steamer who would rather play pedro when they make 'em all jackpots. By the time we've been in eight saloons he don't care whether the thing on the end of his line is a dog or a catfish. I've lost two inches of my tail trying to sidestep those swinging doors.'

The pointer I got from that terrier – vaudeville please copy – set me to thinking.

One evening about six o'clock my mistress ordered him to get busy and do the ozone act for Lovey. I have concealed it until now, but that is what she called me. The black-and-tan was called 'Tweetness.' I consider that I have the bulge on him as far as you could chase a rabbit. Still 'Lovey' is something of a nomenclatural tin-can on the tail of one's self-respect.

At a quiet place on a safe street I tightened the line of my custodian in front of an attractive, refined saloon. I made a dead-ahead scramble for the doors, whining like a dog in the press despatches that lets the family know that little Alice is bogged while gathering lilies in the brook.

'Why, darn my eyes,' says the old man, with a grin; 'darn my eyes if the saffron-coloured son of a seltzer lemonade ain't asking me in to take a drink. Lemme see – how long's it been since I saved shoe leather by keeping one foot on the footrest? I believe I'll –'

I knew I had him. Hot Scotches he took, sitting at a table. For an hour he kept the Campbells coming. I sat by his side rapping for the waiter with my tail, and eating free lunch such as mamma in her flat never equalled with her homemade truck bought at a delicatessen store eight minutes before papa comes home.

When the products of Scotland were all exhausted except the rye bread the old man unwound me from the table leg and played me outside like a fisherman plays a salmon. Out there he took off my collar and threw it into the street.

'Poor doggie,' says he; 'good doggie. She shan't kiss you any more. 'S a darned shame. Good doggie, go away and get run over by a street car and be happy.'

I refused to leave. I leaped and frisked around the old man's legs happy as a pug on a rug.

'You old flea-headed woodchuck-chaser,' I said to him – 'you moon-baying, rabbit-pointing, egg-stealing old beagle, can't you see that I don't want to leave you? Can't you see that we're both Pups in the Wood and the missis is the cruel uncle after you with the dish towel and me with the flea liniment and a pink bow to tie on my tail. Why not cut that all out and be pards for evermore?'

Maybe you'll say he didn't understand – maybe he didn't. But he kind of got a grip on the Hot Scotches, and stood still for a minute, thinking.

'Doggie,' says he finally, 'we don't live more than a dozen lives on this earth, and very few of us live to be more than 300. If I ever see that flat any more I'm a flat, and if you do you're flatter; and that's no flattery. I'm offering 60 to 1 that Westward Ho wins out by the length of a dachshund.'

There was no string, but I frolicked along with my master to the Twenty-third Street ferry. And the cats on the route saw reason to give thanks that prehensile claws had been given them.

On the Jersey side my master said to a stranger who stood eating a currant bun:

'Me and my doggie, we are bound for the Rocky Mountains.'

But what pleased me most was when my old man pulled both of my ears until I howled, and said:

'You common, monkey-headed, rat-tailed, sulphur-coloured son of a door-mat, do you know what I'm going to call you?'

I thought of 'Lovey,' and I whined dolefully.

'I'm going to call you "Pete," ' says my master; and if I'd had five tails I couldn't have done enough wagging to do justice to the occasion.

IX

The Love-philtre of Ikey Shoenstein

THE BLUE LIGHT DRUG STORE is down-town, between the Bowery and First Avenue, where the distance between the two streets is the shortest. The Blue Light does not consider that pharmacy is a thing of bric-a-brac, scent and ice-cream soda. If you ask it for a pain-killer it will not give you a bonbon.

The Blue Light scorns the labour-saving arts of modern pharmacy. It macerates its opium and percolates its own laudanum and paregoric. To this day pills are made behind its tall prescription desk – pills rolled out on its own pill-tile, divided with a spatula, rolled with the finger and thumb, dusted with calcined magnesia and delivered in little round, pasteboard pill-boxes. The store is on a corner about which coveys of ragged-plumed, hilarious children play and become candidates for the cough-drops and soothing syrups that wait for them inside.

Ikey Schoenstein was the night clerk of the Blue Light and the friend of his customers. Thus it is on the East Side, where the heart of pharmacy is not *glacé*. There, as it should be, the druggist is a counsellor, a confessor, an adviser, an able and willing missionary and mentor whose learning is respected, whose occult wisdom is venerated and whose medicine is often poured, untasted, into the gutter. Therefore Ikey's corniform, bespectacled nose and narrow, knowledge-bowed figure was well known in the vicinity of the Blue Light, and his advice and notice were much desired.

Ikey roomed and breakfasted at Mrs. Riddle's, two squares away. Mrs. Riddle had a daughter named Rosy. The circumlocution has been in vain – you must have guessed it – Ikey adored Rosy. She tinctured all his thoughts; she was the compound extract of all that was chemically pure and officinal – the dispensatory contained nothing equal to her. But Ikey was timid, and his hopes remained insoluble in the menstruum of his backwardness and fears. Behind his counter he was a superior being, calmly conscious of special knowledge and worth; outside, he was a weak-kneed, purblind, motorman-cursed rambler, with ill-fitting clothes stained with chemicals and smelling of socotrine aloes and valerianate of ammonia.

The fly in Ikey's ointment (thrice welcome, pat trope!) was Chunk McGowan.

Mr. McGowan was also striving to catch the bright smiles tossed about by Rosy. But he was no out-fielder as Ikey was; he picked them off the bat. At the same time he was Ikey's friend and customer, and often dropped in at the Blue Light Drug Store to have a bruise painted with iodine or get a cut rubber-plastered after a pleasant evening spent along the Bowery.

One afternoon McGowan drifted in in his silent, easy way, and sat, comely, smoothed-faced, hard, indomitable, good-natured, upon a stool.

'Ikey,' said he, when his friend had fetched his mortar and sat opposite, grinding gum benzoin to a powder, 'get busy with your ear. It's drugs for me if you've got the line I need.'

Ikey scanned the countenance of Mr. McGowan for the usual evidences of conflict, but found none.

'Take your coat off,' he ordered. 'I guess already that you have been stuck in the ribs with a knife. I have many times told you those Dagoes would do you up.'

Mr. McGowan smiled. 'Not them,' he said. 'Not any Dagoes. But you've located the diagnosis all right enough – it's under my coat, near the ribs. Say! Ikey – Rosy and me are goin' to run away and get married to-night.'

Ikey's left forefinger was doubled over the edge of the mortar, holding it steady. He gave it a wild rap with the pestle, but felt it not. Meanwhile Mr. McGowan's smile faded to a look of perplexed gloom.

'That is,' he continued, 'if she keeps in the notion until the time comes. We've been layin' pipes for the gateway for two weeks. One day she says she will; the same evenin' she says nixy. We've agreed on to-night, and Rosy's stuck to the affirmative this time for two whole days. But it's five hours yet till the time, and I'm afraid she'll stand me up when it comes to the scratch.'

'You said you wanted drugs,' remarked Ikey.

Mr. McGowan looked ill at ease and harassed – a condition opposed to his usual line of demeanour. He made a patent-medicine almanac into a roll and fitted it with unprofitable carefulness about his finger.

'I wouldn't have this double handicap make a false start to-night for a million,' he said. 'I've got a little flat up in Harlem all ready, with chrysanthemums on the table and a kettle ready to boil. And I've engaged a pulpit pounder to be ready at his house for us at 9.30. It's got to come off. And if Rosy don't change her mind again!' – Mr. McGowan ceased, a prey to his doubts.

'I don't see then yet,' said Ikey shortly, 'what makes it that you talk of drugs, or what I can be doing about it.'

'Old man Riddle don't like me a little bit,' went on the uneasy suitor, bent upon marshalling his arguments. 'For a week he hasn't let Rosy step outside the door with me. If it wasn't for losin' a boarder they'd have bounced me long ago. I'm makin' $20 a week and she'll never regret flyin' the coop with Chunk McGowan.'

'You will excuse me, Chunk,' said Ikey. 'I must make a prescription that is to be called for soon.'

'Say,' said McGowan, looking up suddenly, 'say, Ikey, ain't there a drug of some kind – some kind of powders that'll make a girl like you better if you give 'em to her?'

Ikey's lip beneath his nose curled with the scorn of superior enlightenment; but before he could answer, McGowan continued:

'Tim Lacy told me once that he got some from a croaker up-town and fed 'em to his girl in soda water. From the very first dose he was ace-high and everybody else looked like thirty cents to her. They was married in less than two weeks.'

Strong and simple was Chunk McGowan. A better reader of men than Ikey was could have seen that his tough frame was strung upon fine wires. Like a good general who was about to invade the enemy's territory he was seeking to guard every point against possible failure.

'I thought,' went on Chunk hopefully, 'that if I had one of them powders to give Rosy when I see her at supper to-night it might brace her up and keep her from reneging on the proposition to skip. I guess she don't need a mule team to drag her away, but women are better at coaching than they are at running bases. If the stuff'll work just for a couple of hours it'll do the trick.'

'When is this foolishness of running away to be happening?' asked Ikey.

'Nine o'clock,' said Mr. McGowan. 'Supper's at seven. At eight Rosy goes to bed with a headache. At nine old Parvenzano lets me through to his backyard, where there's a board off Riddle's fence, next door. I go under her window and help her down the fire-escape. We've got to make it early on the preacher's account. It's all dead easy if Rosy don't balk when the flag drops. Can you fix me one of them powders, Ikey?'

Ikey Schoenstein rubbed his nose slowly.

'Chunk,' said he, 'it is of drugs of that nature that pharma-ceutists must have much carefulness. To you alone of my acquaintance would I entrust a powder like that. But for you I shall make it, and you shall see how it makes Rosy to think of you.'

Ikey went behind the prescription desk. There he crushed to a powder two soluble tablets, each containing a quarter of a grain of morphia. To them he added a little sugar of milk to increase the bulk, and folded the mixture neatly in a white paper. Taken by an adult this powder would ensure several hours of heavy slumber without danger to the sleeper. This he handed to Chunk

McGowan, telling him to administer it in a liquid, if possible, and received the hearty thanks of the backyard Lochinvar.

The subtlety of Ikey's action becomes apparent upon recital of his subsequent move. He sent a messenger for Mr. Riddle and disclosed the plans of McGowan for eloping with Rosy. Mr. Riddle was a stout man, brick-dusty of complexion and sudden in action.

'Much obliged,' he said briefly to Ikey. 'The lazy Irish loafer! My own room's just above Rosy's. I'll just go up there myself after supper and load the shot-gun and wait. If he comes in my backyard he'll go away in an ambulance instead of a bridal chaise.'

With Rosy held in the clutches of Morpheus for a many-hours' deep slumber, and the bloodthirsty parent waiting, armed and forewarned, Ikey felt that his rival was close, indeed, upon discomfiture.

All night in the Blue Light Store he waited at his duties for chance news of the tragedy, but none came.

At eight o'clock in the morning the day clerk arrived and Ikey started hurriedly for Mrs. Riddle's to learn the outcome. And, lo! as he stepped out of the store who but Chunk McGowan sprang from a passing street-car and grasped his hand – Chunk McGowan with a victor's smile and flushed with joy.

'Pulled it off,' said Chunk with Elysium in his grin. 'Rosy hit the fire-escape on time to a second and we was under the wire at the Reverend's at 9.30 ¼. She's up at the flat – she cooked eggs this mornin' in a blue kimono – Lord I how lucky I am! You must pace up some day, Ikey, and feed with us. I've got a job down near the bridge, and that's where I'm heading for now.'

'The – the powder?' stammered Ikey.

'Oh, that stuff you gave me!' said Chunk broadening his grin; 'well, it was this way. I sat down at the supper table last night at Riddle's, and I looked at Rosy, and I says to myself, "Chunk, if you get the girl get her on the square – don't try any hocus-pocus with a thoroughbred like her." And I keeps the paper you give me in my pocket. And then my lamps falls on another party present, who, I says to myself, is failin' in a proper affection toward his comin' son-in-law, so I watches my chance and dumps that powder in old man Riddle's coffee – see?'

X

Mammon and the Archer

OLD ANTHONY ROCKWALL, retired manufacturer and proprietor of Rockwall's Eureka Soap, looked out the library window of his Fifth Avenue mansion and grinned. His neighbour to the right – the aristocratic clubman, G. Van Schuylight Suffolk-Jones – came out to his waiting motor-car, wrinkling a contumelious nostril, as usual, at the Italian renaissance sculpture of the soap palace's front elevation.

'Stuck-up old statuette of nothing doing!' commented the ex-Soap King. 'The Eden Musee'll get that old frozen Nesselrode yet if he don't watch out. I'll have this house painted red, white, and blue next summer and see if that'll make his Dutch nose turn up any higher.'

And then Anthony Rockwall, who never cared for bells, went to the door of his library and shouted 'Mike!' in the same voice that had once chipped off pieces of the welkin on the Kansas prairies.

'Tell my son,' said Anthony to the answering menial, 'to come in here before he leaves the house.'

When young Rockwall entered the library the old man laid aside his newspaper, looked at him with a kindly grimness on his big, smooth, ruddy countenance, rumpled his mop of white hair with one hand and rattled the keys in his pocket with the other.

'Richard,' said Anthony Rockwall, 'what do you pay for the soap that you use?'

Richard, only six months home from college, was startled a little. He had not yet taken the measure of this sire of his, who was as full of unexpectednesses as a girl at her first party.

'Six dollars a dozen, I think, dad.'

'And your clothes?'

'I suppose about sixty dollars, as a rule.'

'You're a gentleman,' said Anthony decidedly. 'I've heard of these young bloods spending $24 a dozen for soap, and going over the hundred mark for clothes. You've got as much money to waste as any of 'em, and yet you stick to what's decent and moderate. Now I use the old Eureka – not only for sentiment, but it's the purest soap made. Whenever you pay more than ten cents a cake for soap you buy bad perfumes and labels. But fifty cents is doing very well for a young man in your generation, position and condition. As I said, you're a gentleman. They say it takes three generations to make one. They're off. Money'll do it as slick as soap grease. It's made you one. By hokey! it's almost made one of me. I'm nearly as impolite and disagreeable and ill-mannered as these two old Knickerbocker gents on each side of me that can't sleep of nights because I bought in between 'em.'

'There are some things that money can't accomplish,' remarked young Rockwall rather gloomily.

'Now, don't say that,' said old Anthony, shocked. 'I bet my money on money every time. I've been through the encyclopædia down to Y looking for something you can't buy with it; and I expect to have to take up the appendix next week. I'm for money against the field. Tell me something money won't buy.'

'For one thing,' answered Richard, rankling a little, 'it won't buy one into the exclusive circles of society.'

'Oho I won't it?' thundered the champion of the root of evil. 'You tell me where your exclusive circles would be if the first Astor hadn't had the money to pay for his steerage passage over?'

Richard sighed.

'And that's what I was coming to,' said the old man less boister- ously. 'That's why I asked you to come in. There's something going wrong with you, boy. I've been noticing it for two weeks. Out with it. I guess I could lay my hands on eleven millions within twenty-four hours, besides the real estate. If it's your liver, there's the *Rambler* down in the bay, coaled, and ready to steam down to the Bahamas in two days.'

'Not a bad guess, dad; you haven't missed it far.'

'Ah,' said Anthony keenly; 'what's her name?'

Richard began to walk up and down the library floor. There was enough comradeship and sympathy in this crude old father of his to draw his confidence.

'Why don't you ask her?' demanded old Anthony. 'She'll jump at you. You've got the money and the looks, and you're a decent boy. Your hands are clean. You've got no Eureka soap on 'em. You've been to college, but she'll overlook that.'

'I haven't had a chance,' said Richard.

'Make one,' said Anthony. 'Take her for a walk in the park, or a straw ride, or walk home with her from church. Chancel Pshaw!'

'You don't know the social mill, dad. She's part of the stream that turns it. Every hour and minute of her time is arranged for days in advance. I must have that girl, dad, or this town is a blackjack swamp for evermore. And I can't write it — I can't do that.'

'Tut!' said the old man. 'Do you mean to tell me that with all the money I've got you can't get an hour or two of a girl's time for yourself?'

'I've put it off too late. She's going to sail for Europe at noon day after to-morrow for a two years' stay. I'm to see her alone to-morrow evening for a few minutes. She's at Larchmont now at her aunt's. I can't go there. But I'm allowed to meet her with a cab at the Grand Central Station to-morrow evening at the 8.30 train. We drive down Broadway to Wallack's at a gallop, where her mother and a box party will be waiting for us in the lobby. Do you think she would listen to a declaration from me during those six or eight minutes under those circumstances? No. And what chance would I have in the theatre or afterward? None. No, dad, this is one tangle that your money can't unravel. We can't buy one minute of time with cash; if we could, rich people would live longer. There's no hope of getting a talk with Miss Lantry before she sails.'

'All right, Richard, my boy,' said old Anthony cheerfully. 'You may run along down to your club now. I'm glad it ain't your liver. But don't forget to burn a few punk sticks in the joss-house to the great god Mazuma from time to time. You say money won't buy time? Well, of course, you can't order eternity wrapped up and delivered at your residence for a price, but I've seen Father Time get pretty bad stone bruises on his heels when he walked through the gold diggings.'

That night came Aunt Ellen, gentle, sentimental, wrinkled, sighing, oppressed by wealth, in to Brother Anthony at his evening paper, and began discourse on the subject of lovers' woes.

'He told me all about it,' said brother Anthony yawning. 'I told him my bank account was at his service. And then he began to knock money. Said money couldn't help. Said the rules of society couldn't be buckled for a yard by a team of ten-millionaires.'

'Oh, Anthony,' sighed Aunt Ellen, 'I wish you would not think so much of money. Wealth is nothing where a true affection is concerned. Love is all-powerful. If he only had spoken earlier! She could not have refused our Richard. But now I fear it is too late. He will have no opportunity to address her. All your gold cannot bring happiness to your son.'

At eight o'clock the next evening Aunt Ellen took a quaint old gold ring from a moth-eaten case and gave it to Richard.

'Wear it to-night, nephew,' she begged. 'Your mother gave it to me. Good luck in love, she said it brought. She asked me to give it to you when you had found the one you loved.'

Young Rockwall took the ring reverently and tried it on his smallest finger. It slipped as far as the second joint and stopped. He took it off and stuffed it into his vest pocket, after the manner of man. And then he 'phoned for his cab.

At the station he captured Miss Lantry out of the gadding mob at 8.32.

'We mustn't keep mamma and the others waiting,' said she.

'To Wallack's Theatre as fast as you can drive!' said Richard loyally.

They whirled up Forty-second to Broadway, and then down the white-starred lane that leads from the soft meadows of sunset to the rocky hills of morning.

At Thirty-fourth Street young Richard quickly thrust up the trap and ordered the cabman to stop.

'I've dropped a ring,' he apologized, as he climbed out. 'It was my mother's, and I'd hate to lose it. I won't detain you a minute – I saw where it fell.'

In less than a minute he was back in the cab with the ring.

But within that minute a cross-town car had stopped directly in front of the cab. The cabman tried to pass to the left, but a heavy express wagon cut him off. He tried the right, and had to back away from a furniture van that had no business to be there. He tried to back out, but dropped his reins and swore dutifully. He was blockaded in a tangled mess of vehicles and horses.

One of those street blockades had occurred that sometimes tie up commerce and movement quite suddenly in the big city.

'Why don't you drive on?' said Miss Lantry impatiently. 'We'll be late.'

Richard stood up in the cab and looked around. He saw a congested flood of wagons, trucks, cabs, vans and street-cars filling the vast space where Broadway, Sixth Avenue and Thirty-fourth Street cross one another as a twenty-six-inch maiden fills her twenty-two-inch girdle. And still from all the cross-streets they were hurrying and rattling toward the converging point at full speed, and hurling themselves into the struggling mass, locking wheels and adding their drivers imprecations to the clamour. The entire traffic of Manhattan seemed to have jammed itself around them. The oldest New Yorker among the thousands of spectators that lined the sidewalks had not witnessed a street blockade of the proportions of this one.

'I'm very sorry,' said Richard, as he resumed his seat, 'but it looks as if we are stuck. They won't get this jumble loosened up in an hour. It was my fault. If I hadn't dropped the ring we –'

'Let me see the ring,' said Miss Lantry. 'Now that it can't be helped, I don't care. I think theatres are stupid, anyway.'

At eleven o'clock that night somebody tapped lightly on Anthony Rockwall's door.

'Come in,' shouted Anthony, who was in a red dressing-gown, reading a book of piratical adventures.

Somebody was Aunt Ellen, looking like a grey-haired angel that had been left on earth by mistake.

'They're engaged, Anthony,' she said softly. 'She has promised to marry our Richard. On their way to the theatre there was a street blockade, and it was two hours before their cab could get out of it.

'And oh, brother Anthony, don't ever boast of the power of money again. A little emblem of true love – a little ring that symbolized unending and unmercenary affection – was the cause of our Richard finding his happiness. He dropped it in the street, and got out to recover it. And before they could continue the blockade occurred. He spoke to his love and won her there while the cab was hemmed in. Money is dross compared with true love, Anthony.'

'All right,' said old Anthony. 'I'm glad the boy has got what he wanted. I told him I wouldn't spare any expense in the matter if –'

'But, brother Anthony, what good could your money have done?'

'Sister,' said Anthony Rockwall, 'I've got my pirate in a devil of a scrape. His ship has just been scuttled, and he's too good a judge of the value of money to let drown. I wish you would let me go on with this chapter.'

The story should end here. I wish it would as heartily as you who read it wish it did. But we must go to the bottom of the well for truth.

The next day a person with red hands and a blue polka-dot necktie, who called himself Kelly, called at Anthony Rockwall's house, and was at once received in the library.

'Well,' said Anthony, reaching for his chequebook, 'it was a good bilin' of soap. Let's see – you had $5,000 in cash.'

'I paid out $300 more of my own,' said Kelly. 'I had to go a little above the estimate. I got the express wagons and cabs mostly for $5; but the trucks and two-horse teams mostly raised me to $10. The motor-men wanted $10, and some of the loaded teams $20. The cops struck me hardest – $50 I paid two, and the rest $20 and $25. But didn't it work beautiful, Mr. Rockwall? I'm glad William

A. Brady wasn't on to that little outdoor vehicle mob scene. I wouldn't want William to break his heart with jealousy. And never a rehearsal, either! The boys was on time to the fraction of a second. It was two hours before a snake could get below Greeley's statue.'

'Thirteen hundred – there you are, Kelly,' said Anthony, tearing off a cheque. 'Your thousand, and the $300 you were out. You don't despise money, do you, Kelly?'

'Me?' said Kelly. 'I can lick the man that invented poverty.'

Anthony called Kelly when he was at the door.

'You didn't notice,' said he, 'anywhere in the tie-up, a kind of a fat boy without any clothes on shooting arrows around with a bow, did you?'

'Why, no,' said Kelly, mystified. 'I didn't. If he was like you say, maybe the cops pinched him before I got there.'

'I thought the little rascal wouldn't be on hand,' chuckled Anthony. 'Good-bye, Kelly.'

XI

Springtime à la Carte

IT WAS A DAY IN MARCH.

Never, never begin a story this way when you write one. No opening could possibly be worse. It is unimaginative, flat, dry and likely to consist of mere wind. But in this instance it is allowable. For the following paragraph, which should have inaugurated the narrative, is too wildly extravagant and preposterous to be flaunted in the face of the reader without preparation.

Sarah was crying over her bill of fare.

Think of a New York girl shedding tears on the menu card!

To account for this you will be allowed to guess that the lobsters were all out, or that she had sworn ice-cream off during Lent, or that she had ordered onions, or that she had just come from a Hackett matinée. And then, all these theories being wrong, you will please let the story proceed.

The gentleman who announced that the world was an oyster which he with his sword would open made a larger hit than he deserved. It is not difficult to open an oyster with a sword. But did you ever notice anyone try to open the terrestrial bivalve with a typewriter? Like to wait for a dozen raw opened that way?

Sarah had managed to pry apart the shells with her unhandy weapon far enough to nibble a wee bit at the cold and clammy world within. She knew no more shorthand than if she had been a graduate in stenography just let slip upon the world by a business college. So, not being able to stenog, she could not enter that bright galaxy of office talent. She was a free-lance typewriter and canvassed for odd jobs of copying.

The most brilliant and crowning feat of Sarah's battle with the world was the deal she made with Schulenberg's Home Restaurant. The restaurant was next door to the old red brick in which she hall-roomed. One evening after dining at Schulenberg's 40-cent five-course table d'hôte (served as fast as you throw the five baseballs at the coloured gentleman's head) Sarah took away with her the bill of fare. It was written in an almost unreadable script neither English nor German, and so arranged that if you were not careful you began with a toothpick and rice pudding and ended with soup and the day of the week.

The next day Sarah showed Schulenberg a neat card on which the menu was beautifully typewritten with the viands temptingly marshalled under their right and proper heads from 'hors d'œuvre' to 'not responsible for overcoats and umbrellas.'

Schulenberg became a naturalized citizen on the spot. Before Sarah left him she had him willingly committed to an agreement. She was to furnish typewritten bills of fare for the twenty-one tables in the restaurant – a new bill for each day's dinner, and new ones for breakfast and lunch as often as changes occurred in the food or as neatness required.

In return for this Schulenberg was to send three meals per diem to Sarah's hall-room by a waiter – an obsequious one if possible – and furnish her each afternoon with a pencil draft of what Fate had in store for Schulenberg's customers on the morrow.

Mutual satisfaction resulted from the agreement. Schulenberg's patrons now knew what the food they ate was called even if its nature sometimes puzzled them. And Sarah had food during a cold, dull winter, which was the main thing with her.

And then the almanac lied, and said that spring had come. Spring comes when it comes. The frozen snows of January still lay like adamant in the cross-town streets. The hand-organs still played 'In the Good Old Summertime,' with their December vivacity and expression. Men began to make thirty-day notes to buy Easter dresses. Janitors shut off steam. And when these things happen one may know that the city is still in the clutches of winter.

One afternoon Sarah shivered in her elegant hall-bedroom; 'house heated; scrupulously clean; conveniences; seen to be appreciated.' She had no work to do except Schulenberg's menu cards. Sarah sat in her squeaky willow rocker, and looked out the window. The calendar on the wall kept crying to her: 'Springtime is here, Sarah – springtime is here, I tell you. Look at me, Sarah, my figures show it. You've got a neat figure yourself, Sarah – a – nice, springtime figure – why do you look out the window so sadly?'

Sarah's room was at the back of the house. Looking out the window she could see the windowless rear brick wall of the box factory on the next street. But the wall was clearest crystal; and Sarah was looking down a grassy lane shaded with cherry trees and elms and bordered with raspberry bushes and Cherokee roses.

Spring's real harbingers are too subtle for the eye and ear. Some must have the flowering crocus, the wood-starring dogwood, the voice of bluebird – even so gross a reminder as the farewell handshake of the retiring buckwheat and oyster before they can welcome the Lady in Green to their dull bosoms. But to old earth's choicest kin there come straight, sweet messages from his newest bride, telling them they shall be no stepchildren unless they choose to be.

On the previous summer Sarah had gone into the country and loved a farmer.

(In writing your story never hark back thus. It is bad art, and cripples interest. Let it march, march.)

Sarah stayed two weeks at Sunnybrook Farm. There she learned to love old Farmer Franklin's son, Walter. Farmers have been loved and wedded and turned out to grass in less time. But young Walter Franklin was a modern agriculturist. He had a telephone in his cow-house, and he could figure up exactly what effect next year's Canada wheat crop would have on potatoes planted in the dark of the moon.

It was in this shaded and raspberried lane that Walter had wooed and won her. And together they had sat and woven a crown of dandelions for her hair. He had immoderately praised the effect of the yellow blossoms against her brown tresses; and she had left the chaplet there, and walked back to the house swinging her straw sailor in her hands.

They were to marry in the spring – at the very first signs of spring, Walter said. And Sarah came back to the city to pound her typewriter.

A knock at the door dispelled Sarah's visions of that happy day. A waiter had brought the rough pencil draft of the Home Restaurant's next day fare in old Schulenberg's angular hand.

Sarah sat down at her typewriter and slipped a card between the rollers. She was a nimble worker. Generally in an hour and a half the twenty-one menu cards were written and ready.

To-day there were more changes on the bill of fare than usual. The soups were lighter; pork was eliminated from the entrees, figuring only with Russian turnips among the roasts. The gracious spirit of spring pervaded the entire menu. Lamb, that lately capered on the greening hill-sides, was becoming exploited with the sauce that commemorated its gambols. The song of the oyster, though not silenced, was *diminuendo con amore*. The frying-pan seemed to be held, inactive, behind the beneficent bars of the broiler. The pie list swelled; the richer puddings had vanished; the sausage, with his drapery wrapped about him, barely lingered in a pleasant thanatopsis with the buckwheats and the sweet but doomed maple.

Sarah's fingers danced like midgets above a summer stream. Down through the courses she worked, giving each item its position according to its length with an accurate eye.

Just above the desserts came the list of vegetables. Carrots and peas, asparagus on toast, the perennial tomatoes and corn and succotash, lima beans, cabbage – and then –

Sarah was crying over her bill of fare. Tears from the depths of some divine despair rose in her heart and gathered to her eyes. Down went her head on the little typewriter stand; and the keyboard rattled a dry accompaniment to her moist sobs.

For she had received no letter from Walter in two weeks, and the next item on the bill of fare was dandelions – dandelions with some kind of egg – but bother the egg! – dandelions, with whose golden blooms Walter had crowned her his queen of love and future bride – dandelions, the harbingers of spring, her sorrow's crown of sorrow – reminder of her happiest days.

Madam, I dare you to smile until you suffer this test: Let the Maréchal Niel roses that Percy brought you on the night you gave him your heart be served as a salad with French dressing before your eyes at a Schulenberg table d'hôte. Had Juliet so seen her love tokens dishonoured the sooner would she have sought the lethean herbs of the good apothecary.

But what a witch is Spring! Into the great cold city of stone and iron a message had to be sent. There was none to convey it but the little hardy courier of the fields with his rough, green coat and modest air. He is a true soldier of fortune, this *dent-de-lion* - this lion's tooth, as the French chefs call him. Flowered, he will assist at love-making, wreathed in my lady's nut-brown hair; young and callow and unblossomed, he goes into the boiling pot and delivers the word of his sovereign mistress.

By and by Sarah forced back her tears. The cards must be written. But, still in a faint, golden glow from her dandeleonine dream, she fingered the typewriter keys absently for a little while, with her mind and heart in the meadow lane with her young farmer. But soon she came swiftly back to the rock-bound lanes of Manhattan, and the typewriter began to rattle and jump like a strike-breaker's motor-car.

At six o'clock the waiter brought her dinner and carried away the typewritten bill of fare. When Sarah ate she set aside, with a sigh, the dish of dandelions with its crowning ovarious accompaniment. As this dark mass had been transformed from a bright and love-endorsed flower to be an ignominious vegetable, so had her summer hopes wilted and perished. Love may, as Shakespeare said, feed on itself: but Sarah could not bring herself to eat the dandelions that had graced, as ornaments, the first spiritual banquet of her heart's true affection.

At 7.30 the couple in the next room began to quarrel; the man in the room above sought for A on his flute; the gas went a little lower; three coal wagons started to unload - the only sound of which the phonograph is jealous; cats on the back fences slowly retreated toward Mukden. By these signs Sarah knew that it was time for her to read. She got out *The Cloister and the Hearth*, the best non-selling book of the month, settled her feet on her trunk, and began to wander with Gerard.

The front-door bell rang. The landlady answered it. Sarah left Gerard and Denys treed by a bear and listened. Oh, yes; you would, just as she did!

And then a strong voice was heard in the hall below, and Sarah jumped for her door, leaving the book on the floor and the first round easily the bear's.

You have guessed it. She reached the top of the stairs just as her farmer came up, three at a jump, and reaped and garnered her, with nothing left for the gleaners.

'Why haven't you written - oh, why?' cried Sarah.

'New York is a pretty large town,' said Walter Fanklin. I came in a week ago to your old address. I found that you went away on a

Thursday. That consoled some; it eliminated the possible Friday bad luck. But it didn't prevent my hunting for you with police and otherwise ever since!'

'I wrote!' said Sarah vehemently

'Never got it!'

'Then how did you find me?'

The young farmer smiled a springtime smile.

'I dropped into that Home Restaurant next door this evening,' said he. 'I don't care who knows it; I like a dish of some kind of greens at this time of the year. I ran my eye down that nice, type-written bill of fare looking for something in that line. When I got below cabbage I turned my chair over and hollered for the proprietor. He told me where you lived.'

'I remember,' sighed Sarah happily. 'That was dandelions below cabbage.'

'I'd know that cranky capital W 'way above the line that your typewriter makes anywhere in the world,' said Franklin.

'Why, there's no W in dandelions,' said Sarah, in surprise.

The young man drew the bill of fare from his pocket, and pointed to a line.

Sarah recognized the first card she had typewritten that afternoon. There was still the rayed splotch in the upper right-hand corner where a tear had fallen. But over the spot where one should have read the name of the meadow plant, the clinging memory of their golden blossoms had allowed her fingers to strike strange keys.

Between the red cabbage and the stuffed green peppers was the item:

'DEAREST WALTER, WITH HARD-BOILED EGG.'

XII

From the Cabby's Seat

THE CABBY HAS HIS POINT OF VIEW. It is more single-minded, perhaps, than that of a follower of any other calling. From the high, swaying seat of his hansom he looks upon his fellowmen as nomadic particles, of no account except when possessed of migratory desires. He is Jehu, and you are goods in transit. Be you President or vagabond, to cabby you are only a fare. He takes you up, cracks his whip, joggles your vertebræ and sets you down.

When time for payment arrives, if you exhibit a familiarity with legal rates, you come to know what contempt is; if you find that you have left your pocket-book behind you, you are made to realize the mildness of Dante's imagination.

It is not an extravagant theory that the cabby's singleness of purpose and concentrated view of life are the results of the hansom's peculiar construction. The cock-of-the-roost sits aloft like Jupiter on an unsharable seat, holding your fate between two thongs of inconstant leather. Helpless, ridiculous, confined, bobbing like a toy mandarin, you sit like a rat in a trap – you, before whom butlers cringe on solid land – and must squeak upward through a slit in your peripatetic sarcophagus to make your feeble wishes known.

Then, in a cab, you are not even an occupant; you are contents. You are a cargo at sea, and the 'cherub that sits up aloft' has Davy Jones's street and number by heart.

One night there were sounds of revelry in the big brick tenement-house next door but one to McGary's Family Café. The sounds seemed to emanate from the apartments of the Walsh family. The sidewalk was obstructed by an assortment of interested neighbours, who opened a lane from time to time for a hurrying messenger bearing from McGary's goods pertinent to festivity and diversion. The sidewalk contingent was engaged in comment and discussion from which it made no effort to eliminate the news that Norah Walsh was being married.

In the fullness of time there was an eruption of the merrymakers to the sidewalk. The uninvited guests enveloped and permeated them, and upon the night air rose joyous cries, congratulations laughter and unclassified noises born of McGary's oblations to the hymeneal scene.

Close to the kerb stood Jerry O'Donovan's cab. Night-hawk was Jerry called; but no more lustrous or cleaner hansom than his ever closed its doors upon point lace and November violets. And Jerry's horse! I am within bounds when I tell you that he was stuffed with oats until one of those old ladies who leave their dishes unwashed at home and go about having expressmen arrested, would have smiled – yes, smiled – to have seen him.

Among the shifting, sonorous, pulsing crowd glimpses could be had of Jerry's high hat, battered by the winds and rains of many years; of his nose like a carrot, battered by the frolicsome, athletic progeny of millionaires and by contumacious fares; of his brass-buttoned green coat, admired in the vicinity of McGary's. It was

plain that Jerry had usurped the functions of his cab, and was carrying a 'load.' Indeed, the figure may be extended and he be
likened to a bread-wagon if we admit the testimony of a youthful
spectator, who was heard to remark 'Jerry has got a bun.'

From somewhere among the throng in the street or else out of
the thin stream of pedestrians a young woman tripped and stood by
the cab. The professional hawk's eye of Jerry caught the movement. He made a lurch for the cab, overturning three or four
onlookers and himself – no! he caught the cap of a water-plug and
kept his feet. Like a sailor shinning up the ratlins during a squall,
Jerry mounted to his professional seat. Once he was there
McGary's liquids were baffled. He seesawed on the mizzen-mast
of his craft as safe as a steeplejack rigged to the flagpole of a
skyscraper.

'Step in, lady,' said Jerry, gathering his lines.

The young woman stepped into the cab; the doors shut with a
bang; Jerry's whip cracked in the air; the crowd in the gutter
scattered, and the fine hansom dashed away 'cross-town.

When the oat-spry horse had hedged a little his first spurt of
speed Jerry broke the lid of his cab and called down through the
aperture in the voice of a cracked megaphone trying to please:

'Where, now, will ye be drivin' to?'

'Anywhere you please,' came up the answer, musical and contented.

' 'Tis drivin' for pleasure she is,' thought Jerry. And then he
suggested as a matter of course:

'Take a thrip around in the park, lady. 'Twill be ilegant cool and
fine.'

'Just as you like,' answered the fare pleasantly.

The cab headed for Fifth Avenue and sped up that perfect
street. Jerry bounced and swayed in his seat. The potent fluids of
McGary were disquieted and they sent new fumes to his head. He
sang an ancient song of Killisnook and brandished his whip like a
baton.

Inside the cab the fare sat up straight on the cushions, looking
to right and left at the lights and houses. Even in the shadowed
hansom her eyes shone like stars at twilight.

When they reached Fifty-ninth Street Jerry's head was bobbing
and his reins were slack. But his horse turned in through the park
gate and began the old familiar, nocturnal round. And then the fare
leaned back entranced, and breathed deep the clean, wholesome
odours of grass and leaf and bloom. And the wise beast in the

shafts, knowing his ground, struck into his by-the-hour gait and kept to the right of the road.

Habit also struggled successfully against Jerry's increasing torpor. He raised the hatch of his storm-tossed vessel and made the inquiry that cabbies do make in the park.

'Like shtop at the Cas-sino, lady? Gezzer r'freshm's, 'n lish'n the music. Ev'body shtops.'

'I think that would be nice,' said the fare.

They reined up with a plunge at the Casino entrance. The cab doors flew open. The fare stepped directly upon the floor. At once she was caught in a web of ravishing music and dazzled by a panorama of lights and colours. Someone slipped a little square card into her hand on which was printed a number - 34. She looked around and saw her cab twenty yards away already lining up in its place among the waiting mass of carriages, cabs and motor-cars. And then a man who seemed to be all shirt-front danced backward before her; and next she was seated at a little table by a railing over which climbed a Jessamine vine.

There seemed to be a wordless invitation to purchase; she consulted a collection of small coins in a thin purse, and received from them licence to order a glass of beer. There she sat, inhaling and absorbing it all - the new-coloured, new-shaped life in a fairy palace in an enchanted wood.

At fifty tables sat princes and queens clad in all the silks and gems of the world. And now and then one of them would look curiously at Jerry's fare. They saw a plain figure dressed in a pink silk of the kind that is tempered by the word 'foulard,' and a plain face that wore a look of love of life that the queens envied.

Twice the long hands of the clocks went round. Royalties thinned from their *alfresco* thrones, and buzzed or clattered away in their vehicles of state. The music retired into cases of wood and bags of leather and baize. Waiters removed cloths pointedly near the plain figure sitting almost alone.

Jerry's fare rose, and held out her numbered card simply:

'Is there anything coming on the ticket?' she asked.

A waiter told her it was her cab check, and that she should give it to the man at the entrance. This man took it, and called the number. Only three hansoms stood in line. The driver of one of them went and routed out Jerry, asleep in his cab. He swore deeply, climbed to the captain's bridge and steered his craft to the pier. His fare entered, and the cab whirled into the cool fastnesses of the park along the shortest homeward cuts.

At the gate a glimmer of reason in the form of sudden suspicion seized upon Jerry's beclouded mind. One or two things occurred to him. He stopped his horse, raised the trap and dropped his phonographic voice, like a lead plummet, through the aperture:

'I want to see four dollars before goin' any further on th' thrip. Have ye got th' dough?'

'Four dollars!' laughed the fare softly, 'dear me, no. I've only got a few pennies and a dime or two.'

Jerry shut down the trap and slashed his oatfed horse. The clatter of hoofs strangled but could not drown the sound of his profanity. He shouted choking and gurgling curses at the starry heavens; he cut viciously with his whip at passing vehicles; he scattered fierce and ever-changing oaths and imprecations along the streets, so that a late truck driver, crawling homeward, heard and was abashed. But he knew his recourse, and made for it at a gallop.

At the house with the green lights beside the steps he pulled up. He flung wide the cab doors and tumbled heavily to the ground.

'Come on, you,' he said roughly.

His fare came forth with the Casino dreamy smile still on her plain face. Jerry took her by the arm and led her into the police station. A grey-moustached sergeant looked keenly across the desk. He and the cabby were no strangers.

'Sargeant,' began Jerry in his old raucous, martyred, thunderous tones of complaint. 'I've got a fare here that –'

Jerry paused. He drew a knotted, red hand across his brow. The fog set up by McGary was beginning to clear away.

'A fare, sargeant,' he continued, with a grin, 'that I want to inthroduce to ye. It's me wife that I married at ould man Walsh's this avening. And a divil of a time we had, 'tis thrue. Shake hands wid th' sargeant, Norah, and we'll be off to home.'

Before stepping into the cab Norah sighed profoundly.

'I've had such a nice time, Jerry,' said she.

XIII

An Unfinished Story

WE NO LONGER GROAN and heap ashes upon our heads when the flames of Tophet are mentioned. For, even the preachers have begun to tell us that God is radium, or ether or some scientific compound, and that the worst we wicked ones may expect is a chemical reaction. This is a pleasing hypothesis; but there lingers yet some of the old, goodly terror of orthodoxy.

There are but two subjects upon which one may discourse with a free imagination, and without the possibility of being controverted. You may talk of your dreams; and you may tell what you heard a parrot say. Both Morpheus and the bird are incompetent witnesses; and your listener dare not attack your recital. The baseless fabric of a vision, then, shall furnish my theme – chosen with apologies and regrets instead of the more limited field of Pretty Polly's small talk.

I had a dream that was so far removed from the higher criticism that it had to do with the ancient, respectable, and lamented bar-of-judgment theory.

Gabriel had played his trump; and those of us who could not follow suit were arraigned for examination. I noticed at one side a gathering of professional bondsmen in solemn black and collars that buttoned behind; but it seemed there was some trouble about their real estate titles; and they did not appear to be getting any of us out.

A fly cop – an angel policeman – flew over to me and took me by the left wing. Near at hand was a group of very prosperous-looking spirits arraigned for Judgment.

'Do you belong with that bunch?' the policeman asked.

'Who are they?' was my answer.

'Why,' said he, 'they are –'

But this irrelevant stuff is taking up space that the story should occupy.

Dulcie worked in a department store. She sold Hamburg edging, or stuffed peppers, or automobiles, or other little trinkets such as they keep in department stores. Of what she earned, Dulcie received six dollars per week. The remainder was credited to her and debited to somebody else's account in the ledger kept by G – Oh, primal energy, you say, Reverend Doctor – Well then, in the Ledger of Primal Energy.

During her first year in the store, Dulcie was paid five dollars per week. It would be instructive to know how she lived on that amount. Don't care? Very well; probably you are interested in larger amounts. Six dollars is a larger amount. I will tell you how she lived on six dollars per week.

One afternoon at six, when Dulcie was sticking her hat-pin within an eighth of an inch of her *medulla oblongata*, she said to her chum, Sadie – the girl that waits on you with her left side:

'Say, Sade, I made a date for dinner this evening with Piggy.'

'You never did!' exclaimed Sadie admiringly. 'Well, ain't you the lucky one? Piggy's an awful swell; and he always takes a girl to swell places. He took Blanche up to the Hoffman House one evening, where they have swell music, and you see a lot of swells. You'll have a swell time, Dulcie.'

Dulcie hurried off homeward. Her eyes were shining, and her cheeks showed the delicate pink of life's – real life's – approaching dawn. It was Friday; and she had fifty cents left of her last week's wages.

The streets were filled with the rush-hour floods of people. The electric lights of Broadway were glowing – calling moths from miles, from leagues, from hundreds of leagues out of darkness around to come in and attend the singeing school. Men in accurate clothes, with faces like those carved on cherry-stones by the old salts in sailors' homes, turned and stared at Dulcie as she sped, unheeding, past them. Manhattan, the night-blooming cereus, was beginning to unfold its dead-white, heavy-odoured petals.

Dulcie stopped in a store where goods were cheap and bought an imitation lace collar with her fifty cents. That money was to have been spent otherwise – fifteen cents for supper, ten cents for breakfast, ten cents for lunch. Another dime was to be added to her small store of savings; and five cents was to be squandered for liquorice drops – the kind that made your cheek look like the toothache, and last as long. The liquorice was an extravagance – almost a carouse – but what is life without pleasures?

Dulcie lived in a furnished room. There is this difference between a furnished room and a boarding-house. In a furnished room, other people do not know it when you go hungry.

Dulcie went up to her room – the third floor back in a West Side brownstone-front. She lit the gas. Scientists tell us that the diamond is the hardest substance known. Their mistake. Land-ladies know of a compound beside which the diamond is as putty. They pack it in the tips of gas-burners; and one may stand on a chair and dig at it in vain until one's fingers are pink and bruised. A hairpin will not remove it; therefore let us call it immovable.

So Dulcie lit the gas. In its one-fourth-candlepower glow we will observe the room.

Couch-bed, dresser, table, washstand, chair – of this much the landlady was guilty. The rest was Dulcie's. On the dresser were her treasures – a gilt china vase presented to her by Sadie, a calendar issued by a pickle works, a book on the divination of dreams, some rice powder in a glass dish, and a cluster of artificial cherries tied with a pink ribbon.

Against the wrinkly mirror stood pictures of General Kitchener, William Muldoon, the Duchess of Marlborough, and Benvenuto Cellini. Against one wall was a plaster of Paris plaque of an O'Callahan in a Roman helmet. Near it was a violent oleograph of a lemon-coloured child assaulting an inflammatory butterfly. This was Dulcie's final judgment in art; but it had never been upset. Her rest had never been disturbed by whispers of stolen copes; no critic had elevated his eyebrows at her infantile entomologist.

Piggy was to call for her at seven. While she swiftly makes ready, let us discreetly face the other way and gossip.

For the room, Dulcie paid two dollars per week. On weekdays her breakfast cost ten cents; she made coffee and cooked an egg over the gaslight while she was dressing. On Sunday mornings she feasted royally on veal chops and pineapple fritters at 'Billy's' restaurant, at a cost of twenty-five cents – and tipped the waitress ten cents. New York presents so many temptations for one to run into extravagance. She had her lunches in the department-store restaurant at a cost of sixty cents for the week; dinners were $1.05. The evening papers – show me a New Yorker going without his daily paper! – came to six cents; and two Sunday papers – one for the personal column and the other to read – were ten cents. The total amounts to $4.76. Now, one has to buy clothes, and –

I give it up. I hear of wonderful bargains in fabrics, and of miracles performed with needle and thread; but I am in doubt. I hold my pen poised in vain when I would add to Dulcie's life some of those joys that belong to woman by virtue of all the unwritten, sacred, natural, inactive ordinances of the equity of heaven. Twice she had been to Coney Island and had ridden the hobby-horses. 'Tis a weary thing to count your pleasures by summers instead of by hours.

Piggy needs but a word. When the girls named him, an undeserving stigma was cast upon the noble family of swine. The words-of-three-letters lesson in the old blue spelling-book begins with Piggy's biography. He was fat; he had the soul of a rat, the habits of a bat, and the magnanimity of a cat. . . . He wore expensive clothes; and was a connoisseur in starvation. He could look at a show-girl and tell you to an hour how long it had been since she had eaten anything more nourishing than marsh-mallows and tea. He hung about the shopping districts, and prowled around in department stores with his invitations to dinner. Men who escort dogs upon the streets at the end of a string look down upon him. He is a type; I can dwell upon him no longer; my pen is not the kind intended for him; I am no carpenter.

At ten minutes to seven Dulcie was ready. She looked at herself in the wrinkly mirror. The reflection was satisfactory. The dark blue dress, fitting without a wrinkle, the hat with its jaunty black feather, the but-slightly-soiled gloves – all representing self-denial, even of food itself – were vastly becoming.

Dulcie forgot everything else for a moment except that she was beautiful, and that life was about to lift a corner of its mysterious veil for her to observe its wonders. No gentleman had ever asked her out before. Now she was going for a brief moment into the glitter and exalted show.

The girls said that Piggy was a 'spender.' There would be a grand dinner, and music, and splendidly dressed ladies to look at, and things to eat that strangely twisted the girls' jaws when they tried to tell about them. No doubt she would be asked out again.

There was a blue pongee suit in a window that she knew – by saving twenty cents a week instead of ten, in – let's see – Oh, it would run into years! But there was a second-hand store in Seventh Avenue where –

Somebody knocked at the door. Dulcie opened it. The landlady stood there with a spurious smile, sniffing for cooking by stolen gas. 'A gentleman's downstairs to see you,' she said. 'Name is Mr. Wiggins.'

By such epithet was Piggy known to unfortunate ones who had to take him seriously.

Dulcie turned to the dresser to get her handkerchief; then she stopped still, and bit her underlip hard. While looking in her mirror she had seen fairyland and herself, a princess, just awakening from a long slumber. She had forgotten one that was watching her with sad, beautiful, stern eyes – the only one there was to approve or condemn what she did. Straight and slender and tall, with a look of sorrowful reproach on his handsome, melancholy face, General Kitchener fixed his wonderful eyes on her out of his gilt photograph frame on the dresser.

Dulcie turned like an automatic doll to the landlady.

'Tell him I can't go,' she said dully. 'Tell him I'm sick, or something. Tell him I'm not going out.'

After the door was closed and locked, Dulcie fell upon her bed, crushing her black tip, and cried for ten minutes. General Kitchener was her only friend. He was Dulcie's ideal of a gallant knight.

He looked as if he might have a secret sorrow, and his wonderful moustache was a dream, and she was a little afraid of that stern yet tender look in his eyes. She used to have little fancies that he would call at the house some time, and ask for her, with his sword clanking against his high boots. Once, when a boy was rattling a piece of chain against a lamp-post she had opened the window and looked out. But there was no use. She knew that General Kitchener was away over in Japan leading his army against the savage Turks; and he would never step out of his gilt frame for her. Yet one look from him had vanquished Piggy that night. Yes, for that night.

When her cry was over Dulcie got up and took off her best dress, and put on her old blue kimono. She wanted no dinner. She sang two verses of 'Sammy.' Then she became intensely interested in a little red speck on the side of her nose. And after that was attended to, she drew up a chair to the rickety table, and told her fortune with an old deck of cards.

'The horrid, impudent thing!' she said aloud 'And I never gave him a word or a look to make him think it!'

At nine o'clock Dulcie took a tin box of crackers and a little pot of raspberry jam out of her trunk and had a feast. She offered General Kitchener some jam on a cracker; but he only looked at her as the Sphinx would have looked at a butterfly – if there are butterflies in the desert.

'Don't eat if you don't want to,' said Dulcie 'And don't put on so many airs and scold so with your eyes. I wonder if you'd be so superior and snippy if you had to live on six dollars a week.'

It was not a good sign for Dulcie to be rude to General Kitchener. And then she turned Benvenuto Cellini face downward with a severe gesture. But that was not inexcusable; for she had always thought he was Henry VIII, and she did not approve of him.

At half-past nine Dulcie took a last look at the pictures on the dresser, turned out the light, and skipped into bed. It's an awful thing to go to bed with a good-night look at General Kitchener, William Muldoon, the Duchess of Marlborough, and Benvenuto Cellini.

This story really doesn't get anywhere at all. The rest of it comes later – some time when Piggy asks Dulcie again to dine with him, and she is feeling lonelier than usual, and General Kitchener happens to be looking the other way; and then –

As I said before, I dreamed that I was standing near a crowd of prosperous-looking angels, and a policeman took me by the wing and asked if I belonged with them.

'Who are they?' I asked.

'Why,' said he, 'they are the men who hired working-girls, and paid 'em five or six dollars a week to live on. Are you one of the bunch?'

'Not on your immortality,' said I. 'I'm only the fellow that set fire to an orphan asylum, and murdered a blind man for his pennies.'

XIV

Sisters of the Golden Circle

THE RUBBERNECK AUTO was about ready to start. The merry top-riders had been assigned to their seats by the gentlemanly conductor. The sidewalk was blockaded with sightseers who had gathered to stare at sightseers, justifying the natural law that every creature on earth is preyed upon by some other creature.

The megaphone man raised his instrument of torture; the inside of the great automobile began to thump and throb like the heart of a coffee drinker. The top-riders nervously clung to the seats; the old lady from Valparaiso, Indiana, shrieked to be put ashore. But, before a wheel turns, listen to a brief preamble through the cardiaphone, which shall point out to you an object of interest on life s sight-seeing tour.

Swift and comprehensive is the recognition of white man for white man in African wilds; instant and sure is the spiritual greeting between mother and babe; unhesitatingly do master and dog commune across the slight gulf between animal and man; immeasurably quick and sapient are the brief messages between one and one's beloved. But all these instances set forth only slow and groping interchange of sympathy and thought beside one other instance which the Rubberneck coach shall disclose. You shall learn (if you have not learned already) what two beings of all earth's living inhabitants most quickly look into each other's hearts and souls when they meet face to face.

The gong whirred, and the Glaring-at-Gotham car moved majestically upon its instructive tour.

On the highest, rear seat was James Williams, of Cloverdale, Missouri, and his Bride.

Capitalize it, friend typo – that last word – word of words in the epiphany of life and love. The scent of the flowers, the booty of the bee, the primal dip of spring waters, the overture of the lark, the twist of lemon peel on the cocktail of creation – such is the bride. Holy is the wife; revered the mother; galliptious is the summer girl – but the bride is the certified cheque among the wedding presents that the gods send in when man is married to mortality.

The car glided up the Golden Way. On the bridge of the great cruiser the captain stood, trumpeting the sights of the big city to his passengers. Wide-mouthed and open-eared, they heard the sights of the metropolis thundered forth to their eyes. Confused, delirious with excitement and provincial longings, they tried to make ocular responses to the megaphonic ritual. In the solemn spires of spreading cathedrals they saw the home of the Vanderbilts; in the busy bulk of the Grand Central depot they viewed, wonderingly, the frugal cot of Russell Sage. Bidden to observe the highlands of the Hudson, they gaped, unsuspecting, at the upturned mountains of a new-laid sewer. To many the elevated railroad was the Rialto, on the stations of which uniformed men sat and made chop suey of your tickets. And to this day in the outlying districts many have it that Chuck Connors, with his hand on his heart, leads reform; and that but for the noble municipal efforts of one Parkhurst, a district attorney, the notorious 'Bishop' Potter gang would have destroyed law and order from the Bowery to the Harlem River.

But I beg you to observe Mrs. James Williams – Hattie Chalmers that was – once the belle of Cloverdale. Pale-blue is the bride's, if she will; and this colour she had honoured. Willingly had the moss rosebud loaned to her cheeks of its pink – and as for the violet! – her eyes will do very well as they are, thank you. A useless strip of white chaf – oh, no, he was guiding the auto-car – of white chiffon – or perhaps it was grenadine or tulle – was tied beneath her chin, pretending to hold her bonnet in place. But you know as well as I do that the hatpins did the work.

And on Mrs. James Williams's face was recorded a little library of the world's best thoughts in three volumes. Volume No. I contained the belief that James Williams was about the right sort of thing. Volume No. 2 was an essay on the world, declaring it to be a very excellent place. Volume No. 3 disclosed the belief that in occupying the highest seat in a Rubberneck auto they were travelling the pace that passes all understanding.

James Williams, you would have guessed, was about twenty-four. It will gratify you to know that your estimate was so accurate. He was exactly twenty-three years, eleven months and twenty-nine days old. He was well-built, active, strong-jawed, good-natured and rising. He was on his wedding-trip.

Dear kind fairy, please cut out those orders for money and 40 h.p. touring cars and fame and a new growth of hair and the presidency of the boat club. Instead of any of them turn backward – oh, turn backward and give just a teeny-weeny bit of our wedding-trip over again. Just an hour, dear fairy, so we can remember how the grass and poplar trees looked, and the bow of those bonnet strings tied beneath her chin – even if it was the hatpins that did the work. Can't do it? Very well; hurry up with that touring car and the oil stock, then.

Just in front of Mrs. James Williams sat a girl in a loose tan jacket and a straw hat adorned with grapes and roses. Only in dreams and milliners' shops do we, alas! gather grapes and roses at one swipe. This girl gazed with large blue eyes, credulous, when the megaphone man roared his doctrine that millionaires were things about which we should be concerned. Between blasts she resorted to Epictetian philosophy in the form of pepsin chewing gum.

At this girl's right hand sat a young man about twenty-four. He was well-built, active, strong-jawed and good-natured. But if his description seems to follow that of James Williams, divest it of anything Cloverdalian. This man belonged to hard streets and sharp corners. He looked keenly about him, seeming to begrudge the asphalt under the feet of those upon whom he looked down from his perch.

While the megaphone barks at a famous hostelry, let me whisper you through the low-tuned cardiaphone to sit tight; for now things are about to happen, and the great city will close over them again as over a scrap of ticker tape floating down from the den of a Broad Street bear.

The girl in the tan jacket twisted around to view the pilgrims on the last seat. The other passengers she had absorbed; the seat behind her was her Bluebeard's chambers.

Her eyes met those of Mrs. James Williams. Between two ticks of a watch they exchanged their life's-experiences, histories, hopes and fancies. And all, mind you, with the eye, before two men could have decided whether to draw steel or borrow a match.

The bride leaned forward low. She and the girl spoke rapidly together, their tongues moving quickly like those of two serpents – a comparison that is not meant to go further. Two smiles and a dozen nods closed the conference.

And now in the broad, quiet avenue in front of the Rubberneck car a man in dark clothes stood with uplifted hand. From the sidewalk another hurried to join him.

The girl in the fruitful hat quickly seized her companion by the arm and whispered in his ear. That young man exhibited proof of ability to act promptly. Crouching low, he slid over the edge of the car, hung lightly for an instant, and then disappeared. Half a dozen of the top-riders observed his feat, wonderingly, but made no comment, deeming it prudent not to express surprise at what might be the conventional manner of alighting in this bewildering city. The truant passenger dodged a hansom and then floated past, like a leaf on a stream between a furniture van and a florist's delivery wagon.

The girl in the tan jacket turned again, and looked in the eyes of Mrs. James Williams. Then she faced about and sat still while the Rubberneck auto stopped at the flash of the badger under the coat of the plain-clothes man.

'What's eatin' you?' demanded the megaphonist, abandoning his professional discourse for pure English.

'Keep her at anchor for a minute,' ordered the officer. 'There's a man on board we want – a Philadelphia burglar called "Pinky" McGuire. There he is on the back seat. Look out for the side, Donovan.'

Donovan went to the hind wheel and looked up at James Williams.

'Come down, old sport,' he said pleasantly. 'We've got you. Back to Sleepytown for yours. It ain't a bad idea, hidin' on a Rubberneck, though. I'll remember that.'

Softly through the megaphone came the advice of the conductor:

'Better step off, sir, and explain. The car must proceed on its tour.'

James Williams belonged among the level heads. With necessary slowness he picked his way through the passengers down to the steps at the front of the car. His wife followed, but she first turned her eyes and saw the escaped tourist glide from behind the furniture van and slip behind a tree on the edge of the little park, not fifty feet away.

Descended to the ground, James Williams faced his captors with a smile. He was thinking what a good story he would have to tell in Cloverdale about having been mistaken for a burglar. The Rubberneck coach lingered, out of respect for its patrons What could be a more interesting sight than this?

'My name is James Williams, of Cloverdale, Missouri,' he said
kindly, so that they would not be too greatly mortified. 'I have letters here that will show —'

'You'll come with us, please,' announced the plain-clothes man.
' "Pinky" McGuire's description fits you like a flannel washed in
hot suds. A detective saw you on the Rubberneck up at Central
Park and 'phoned down to take you in. Do your explaining at the
station-house.'

James Williams's wife — his bride of two weeks — looked him in
the face with a strange, soft radiance in her eyes and a flush on her
cheeks, looked him in the face and said:

'Go with 'em quietly, "Pinky," and maybe it'll be in your favour.'

And then as the Glaring-at-Gotham car rolled away she turned
and threw a kiss — his wife threw a kiss — at someone high up on
the seats of the Rubberneck.

'Your girl gives you good advice, McGuire,' said Donovan.
'Come on, now.'

And then madness descended upon and occupied James
Williams. He pushed his hat far upon the back of his head.

'My wife seems to think I am a burglar,' he said recklessly. 'I never
heard of her being crazy, therefore I must be. And if I'm crazy, they
can't do anything to me for killing you two fools in my madness.'

Whereupon he resisted arrest so cheerfully and industriously
that cops had to be whistled for, and afterwards the reserves, to
disperse a few thousand delighted spectators.

At the station-house the desk sergeant asked for his name.

'McDoodle, the Pink, or Pinky the Brute, I forget which,' was
James Williams's answer. 'But you can bet I'm a burglar; don't
leave that out. And you might add that it took five of 'em to pluck
the Pink. I'd especially like to have that in the records.'

In an hour came Mrs. James Williams, with Uncle Thomas, of
Madison Avenue, in a respect-compelling motor-car and proofs of
the hero's innocence — for all the world like the third act of a
drama backed by an automobile mfg. co.

After the police had sternly reprimanded James Williams for
imitating a copyrighted burglar and given him as honourable a
discharge as the department was capable of, Mrs. Williams re-
arrested him and swept him into an angle of the stationhouse.
James Williams regarded her with one eye. He always said that
Donovan closed the other while somebody was holding his good
right hand. Never before had he given her a word of reproach or
of reproof.

'If you can explain,' he began rather stiffly, 'why you –'

'Dear,' she interrupted, 'listen. It was an hour's pain and trial to you. I did it for her – I mean the girl who spoke to me on the coach. I was so happy, Jim – so happy with you that I didn't dare to refuse that happiness to another. Jim, they were married only this morning – those two; and I wanted him to get away. While they were struggling with you I saw him slip from behind his tree and hurry across the park. That's all of it, dear – I had to do it.'

Thus does one sister of the plain gold band know another who stands in the enchanted light that shines but once and briefly for each one. By rice and satin bows does mere man become aware of weddings. But bride knoweth bride at the glance of an eye. And between them swiftly passes comfort and meaning in a language that man and widows wot not of.

XV

The Romance of a Busy Broker

PITCHER, CONFIDENTIAL CLERK in the office of Harvey Maxwell, broker, allowed a look of mild interest and surprise to visit his usually expressionless countenance when his employer briskly entered at half past nine in company with his young lady stenographer. With a snappy 'Good morning, Pitcher,' Maxwell dashed at his desk as though he were intending to leap over it, and then plunged into the great heap of letters and telegrams waiting there for him.

The young lady had been Maxwell's stenographer for a year. She was beautiful in a way that was decidedly unstenographic. She forwent the pomp of the alluring pompadour. She wore no chains, bracelets or lockets. She had not the air of being about to accept an invitation to luncheon. Her dress was grey and plain, but it fitted her figure with fidelity and discretion. In her neat black turban hat was the gold-green wing of a macaw. On this morning she was softly and shyly radiant. Her eyes were dreamily bright, her cheeks genuine peachblow, her expression a happy one, tinged with reminiscence.

Pitcher, still mildly curious, noticed a difference in her ways this morning. Instead of going straight into the adjoining room, where her desk was, she lingered, slightly irresolute, in the outer office. Once she moved over by Maxwell's desk, near enough for him to be aware of her presence.

The machine sitting at that desk was no longer a man; it was a busy New York broker, moved by buzzing wheels and uncoiling springs.

'Well – what is it? Anything?' asked Maxwell sharply. His opened mail lay like a bank of stage snow on his crowded desk. His keen grey eye, impersonal and brusque, flashed upon her half impatiently.

'Nothing,' answered the stenographer, moving away with a little smile.

'Mr. Pitcher,' she said to the confidential clerk, 'did Mr. Maxwell say anything yesterday about engaging another stenographer?'

'He did,' answered Pitcher. 'He told me to get another one. I notified the agency yesterday afternoon to send over a few samples this morning. It's 9.45 o'clock, and not a single picture hat or piece of pineapple chewing gum has showed up yet.'

'I will do the work as usual, then,' said the young lady, 'until someone comes to fill the place.' And she went to her desk at once and hung the black turban hat with the gold-green macaw wing in its accustomed place.

He who has been denied the spectacle of a busy Manhattan broker during a rush of business is handicapped for the profession of anthropology. The poet sings of the 'crowded hour of glorious life.' The broker's hour is not only crowded, but the minutes and seconds are hanging to all the straps and packing both front and rear platforms.

And this day was Harvey Maxwell's busy day. The ticker began to reel out jerkily its fitful coils of tape, the desk telephone had a chronic attack of buzzing. Men began to throng into the office and call at him over the railing, jovially, sharply, viciously, excitedly. Messenger boys ran in and out with messages and telegrams. The clerks in the office jumped about like sailors during a storm. Even Pitcher's face relaxed into something resembling animation.

On the Exchange there were hurricanes and landslides and snowstorms and glaciers and volcanoes, and those elemental disturbances were reproduced in miniature in the broker's offices. Maxwell shoved his chair against the wall and transacted business after the manner of a toe-dancer. He jumped from ticker to 'phone, from desk to door with the trained agility of a harlequin.

In the midst of this growing and important stress the broker became suddenly aware of a high-rolled fringe of golden hair under a nodding canopy of velvet and ostrich tips, an imitation sealskin sacque and a string of beads as large as hickory nuts, ending near the floor with a silver heart. There was a self-possessed young lady connected with these accessories; and Pitcher was there to construe her.

'Lady from the Stenographer's Agency to see about the position,' said Pitcher.

Maxwell turned half around, with his hands full of papers and ticker tape.

'What position?' he asked, with a frown.

'Position of stenographer,' said Pitcher. 'You told me yesterday to call them up and have one sent over this morning.

'You are losing your mind, Pitcher,' said Maxwell. 'Why should I have given you any such instructions? Miss Leslie has given perfect satisfaction during the year she has been here. The place is hers as long as she chooses to retain it. There's no place open here, madam. Countermand that order with the agency, Pitcher, and don't bring any more of 'em in here.'

The silver heart left the office, swinging and banging itself independently against the office furniture as it indignantly departed. Pitcher seized a moment to remark to the bookkeeper that the 'old man' seemed to get more absent-minded and forgetful every day of the world.

The rush and pace of business grew fiercer and faster. On the floor they were pounding half a dozen stocks in which Maxwell's customers were heavy investors. Orders to buy and sell were coming and going as swift as the flight of swallows. Some of his own holdings were imperilled, and the man was working like some high-geared, delicate, strong machine – strung to full tension, going at full speed, accurate, never hesitating, with the proper word and decision and act ready and prompt as clockwork. Stocks and bonds, loans and mortgages, margins and securities – here was a world of finance, and there was no room in it for the human world or the world of nature.

When the luncheon hour drew near there came a slight lull in the uproar.

Maxwell stood by his desk with his hands full of telegrams and memoranda, with a fountain pen over his right ear and his hair hanging in disorderly strings over his forehead. His window was open, for the beloved janitress Spring had turned on a little warmth through the waking registers of the earth.

And through the window came a wandering – perhaps a lost – odour – a delicate, sweet odour of lilac that fixed the broker for a moment immovable. For this odour belonged to Miss Leslie; it was her own, and hers only.

The odour brought her vividly, almost tangibly before him. The world of finance dwindled suddenly to a speck. And she was in the next room – twenty steps away.

'By George, I'll do it now,' said Maxwell, half aloud. 'I'll ask her now. I wonder I didn't do it long ago.'

He dashed into the inner office with the haste of a short trying to cover. He charged upon the desk of the stenographer.

She looked up at him with a smile. A soft pink crept over her cheek, and her eyes were kind and frank. Maxwell leaned one elbow on her desk. He still clutched fluttering papers with both hands and the pen was above his ear.

'Miss Leslie,' he began hurriedly, 'I have but a moment to spare. I want to say something in that moment. Will you be my wife? I haven't had time to make love to you in the ordinary way, but I really do love you. Talk quick, please – those fellows are clubbing the stuffing out of Union Pacific.'

'Oh, what are you talking about?' exclaimed the young lady. She rose to her feet and gazed upon him, round-eyed.

'Don't you understand?' said Maxwell restively. 'I want you to marry me. I love you, Miss Leslie. I wanted to tell you, and I snatched a minute when things had slackened up a bit. They're calling me for the 'phone now. Tell 'em to wait a minute, Pitcher. Won't you, Miss Leslie?'

The stenographer acted very queerly. At first she seemed over-come with amazement; then tears flowed from her wondering eyes; and then she smiled sunnily through them, and one of her arms slid tenderly about the broker's neck.

'I know now,' she said softly. 'It's this old business that has driven everything else out of your head for the time. I was fright-ened at first. Don't you remember, Harvey? We were married last evening at eight o'clock in the Little Church Around the Corner.'

XVI

The Furnished Room

RESTLESS, SHIFTING, FUGACIOUS as time itself, is a certain vast bulk of the population of the redbrick district of the lower West Side.

Homeless, they have a hundred homes. They flit from furnished room to furnished room, transients for ever – transients in abode, transients in heart and mind. They sing 'Home Sweet Home' in ragtime; they carry their *lares et penates* in a bandbox; their vine is entwined about a picture hat; a rubber plant is their fig tree.

Hence the houses of this district, having had a thousand dwellers, should have a thousand tales to tell, mostly dull ones, no doubt; but it would be strange if there could not be found a ghost or two in the wake of all these vagrant ghosts.

One evening after dark a young man prowled among these crumbling red mansions, ringing their bells. At the twelfth he rested his lean hand-baggage upon the step and wiped the dust from his hat-band and forehead. The bell sounded faint and far away in some remote, hollow depths.

To the door of this, the twelfth house whose bell he had rung, came a housekeeper who made him think of an unwholesome, sur-feited worm that had eaten its nut to a hollow shell and now sought to fill the vacancy with edible lodgers.

He asked if there was a room to let.

'Come in,' said the housekeeper. Her voice came from her throat; her throat seemed lined with fur. 'I have the third floor back, vacant since a week back. Should you wish to look at it?'

The young man followed her up the stairs. A faint light from no particular source mitigated the shadows of the halls. They trod noiselessly upon a stair carpet that its own loom would have for-sworn. It seemed to have become vegetable; to have degenerated in that rank, sunless air to lush lichen or spreading moss that grew in patches to the staircase and was viscid under the foot like organic matter. At each turn of the stairs were vacant niches in the wall. Perhaps plants had once been set within them. If so they had died in that foul and tainted air. It may be that statues of the saints had stood there, but it was not difficult to conceive that imps and devils had dragged them forth in the darkness and down to the unholy depths of some furnished pit below.

'This is the room,' said the housekeeper, from her furry throat. 'It's a nice room. It ain't often vacant. I had some most elegant people in it last summer – no trouble at all, and paid in advance to the minute. The water's at the end of the hall. Sprowls and Mooney-kept it three months. They done a vaudeville sketch. Miss B'retta Sprowls – you may have heard of her – Oh, that was just the stage names – right there over the dresser is where the marriage certificate hung, framed. The gas is here, and you see there is plenty of closet room. It's a room everybody likes. It never stays idle long.'

'Do you have many theatrical people rooming here?' asked the young man.

'They comes and goes. A good proportion of my lodgers is connected with the theatres. Yes, sir, this is the theatrical district. Actor people never stays long anywhere. I get my share. Yes, they comes and they goes.'

He engaged the room, paying for a week in advance. He was tired, he said, and would take possession at once. He counted out the money. The room had been made ready, she said, even to towels and water. As the housekeeper moved away he put, for the thousandth time, the question that he carried at the end of his tongue.

'A young girl – Miss Vashner – Miss Eloise Vashner – do you remember such a one among your lodgers? She would be singing on the stage, most likely. A fair girl, of medium height and slender, with reddish gold hair and a dark mole near her left eyebrow.'

'No, I don't remember the name. Them stage people has names they change as often as their rooms. They comes and they goes. No, I don't call that one to mind.'

No. Always no. Five months of ceaseless interrogation and the inevitable negative. So much time spent by day in questioning managers, agents, schools and choruses; by night among the audiences of theatres from all-star casts down to music-halls so low that he dreaded to find what he most hoped for. He who had loved her best had tried to find her. He was sure that since her disappearance from home this great water-girt city held her somewhere, but it was like a monstrous quicksand, shifting its particles constantly, with no foundation, its upper granules of to-day buried to-morrow in ooze and slime.

The furnished room received its latest guest with a first glow of pseudo-hospitality, a hectic, haggard, perfunctory welcome like the specious smile of a demirep. The sophistical comfort came in reflected gleams from the decayed furniture, the ragged brocade upholstery of a couch and two chairs, a footwide cheap pier glass between the two windows, from one or two gilt picture frames and a brass bedstead in a corner.

The guest reclined, inert, upon a chair, while the room, confused in speech as though it were an apartment in Babel, tried to discourse to him of its divers tenantry.

A polychromatic rug like some brilliant-flowered, rectangular, tropical islet lay surrounded by a billowy sea of soiled matting. Upon the gay-papered wall were those pictures that pursue the homeless one from house to house – The Huguenot Lovers, The First Quarrel, The Wedding Breakfast, Psyche at the Fountain. The mantel's chastely severe outline was ingloriously veiled behind some pert drapery drawn rakishly askew like the sashes of the Amazonian ballet. Upon it was some desolate flotsam cast aside by the room's marooned when a lucky sail had borne them to a fresh port – a trifling vase or two, pictures of actresses, a medicine bottle, some stray cards out of a deck.

One by one, as the characters of a cryptograph become explicit, the little signs left by the furnished room's procession of guests developed a significance. The threadbare space in the rug in front of the dresser told that lovely woman had marched in the throng. Tiny finger-prints on the wall spoke of little prisoners trying to feel their way to sun and air. A splattered stain, raying like the shadow of a bursting bomb, witnessed where a hurled glass or bottle had splintered with its contents against the wall. Across the pier glass had been scrawled with a diamond in staggering letters the name 'Marie.' It seemed that the succession of dwellers in the furnished room had turned in fury – perhaps tempted beyond forbearance by its garish coldness – and wreaked upon it their passions. The furniture was chipped and bruised; the couch, distorted by bursting springs, seemed a horrible monster that had been slain during the stress of some grotesque convulsion. Some more potent upheaval had cloven a great slice from the marble mantel. Each plank in the floor owned its particular cant and shriek as from a separate and individual agony. It seemed incredible that all this malice and injury had been wrought upon the room by those who had called it for a time their home; and yet it may have been the cheated home instinct surviving blindly, the resentful rage at false household gods that had kindled their wrath. A hut that is our own we can sweep and adorn and cherish.

The young tenant in the chair allowed these thoughts to file, soft-shod, through his mind, while there drifted into the room furnished sounds and furnished scents. He heard in one room a tittering and incontinent, slack laughter; in others the monologue of a scold, the rattling of dice, a lullaby, and one crying dully; above him a banjo tinkled with spirit. Doors banged somewhere; the elevated trains roared intermittently; a cat yowled miserably upon a back fence. And he breathed the breath of the house – a dank savour rather than a smell – a cold, musty effluvium as from underground vaults mingled with the reeking exhalations of linoleum and mildewed and rotten woodwork.

Then, suddenly, as he rested there, the room was filled with the strong, sweet odour of mignonette. It came as upon a single buffet of wind with such sureness and fragrance and emphasis that it almost seemed a living visitant. And the man cried aloud, 'What, dear?' as if he had been called, and sprang up and faced about. The rich odour clung to him and wrapped him about. He reached out his arms for it, all his senses for the time confused and commingled. How could one be peremptorily called by an odour? Surely it must have been a sound. But, was it not the sound that had touched, that had caressed him?

'She has been in this room,' he cried, and he sprang to wrest from it a token, for he knew he would recognize the smallest thing that had belonged to her or that she had touched. This enveloping scent of mignonette, the odour that she had loved and made her own – whence came it?

The room had been but carelessly set in order. Scattered upon the flimsy dresser scarf were half a dozen hairpins – those discreet, indistinguishable friends of womankind, feminine of gender, infinite of mood and uncommunicative of tense. These he ignored, conscious of their triumphant lack of identity. Ransacking the drawers of the dresser he came upon a discarded, tiny, ragged handkerchief. He pressed it to his face. It was racy and insolent with heliotrope; he hurled it to the floor. In another drawer he found odd buttons, a theatre programme, a pawnbroker's card, two lost marshmallows, a book on the divination of dreams. In the last was a woman's black satin hair-bow, which halted him, poised between ice and fire. But the black satin hair-bow also is femininity's demure, impersonal, common ornament, and tells no tales.

And then he traversed the room like a hound on the scent, skimming the walls, considering the corners of the bulging matting on his hands and knees, rummaging mantel and tables, the curtains and hangings, the drunken cabinet in the corner, for a visible sign unable to perceive that she was there beside, around, against, within, above him, clinging to him, wooing him, calling him so poignantly through the finer senses that even his grosser ones became cognizant of the call. Once again he answered loudly, 'Yes, dear!' and turned, wild-eyed, to gaze on vacancy, for he could not yet discern form and colour and love and outstretched arms in the odour of mignonette. Oh, God! whence that odour, and since when have odours had a voice to call? Thus he groped.

He burrowed in crevices and corners, and found corks and cigarettes. These he passed in passive contempt. But once he found in
a fold of the matting a half-smoked cigar, and this he ground
beneath his heel with a green and trenchant oath. He sifted the
room from end to end. He found dreary and ignoble small records
of many a peripatetic tenant; but of her whom he sought, and who
may have lodged there, and whose spirit seemed to hover there, he
found no trace.

And then he thought of the housekeeper.

He ran from the haunted room downstairs and to a door that
showed a crack of light. She came out to his knock. He smothered
his excitement as best he could.

'Will you tell me, madam,' he besought her, 'who occupied the
room I have before I came?'

'Yes, sir. I can tell you again. 'Twas Sprowls and Mooney, as I
said. Miss B'retta Sprowls it was in the theatres, but Missis
Mooney she was. My house is well known for respectability. The
marriage certificate hung, framed, on a nail over –'

'What kind of a lady was Miss Sprowls – in looks, I mean?'

'Why, black-haired, sir, short and stout, with a comical face.
They left a week ago Tuesday.'

'And before they occupied it?'

'Why, there was a single gentleman connected with the draying
business. He left owing me a week. Before him was Missis Crowder
and her two children, that stayed four months; and back of them
was old Mr. Doyle, whose sons paid for him. He kept the room six
months. That goes back a year, sir, and further I do not remember.'

He thanked her and crept back to his room. The room was
dead. The essence that had vivified it was gone. The perfume of
mignonette had departed. In its place was the old, stale odour of
mouldy house furniture, of atmosphere in storage.

The ebbing of his hope drained his faith. He sat staring at the
yellow, singing gaslight. Soon he walked to the bed and began to
tear the sheets into strips. With the blade of his knife he drove
them tightly into every crevice around windows and door. When
all was snug and taut he turned out the light turned the gas full on
again and laid himself gratefully upon the bed.

●　　●　　●　　●　　●

It was Mrs. McCool's night to go with the can for beer. So she
fetched it and sat with Mrs. Purdy in one of those subterranean

retreats where housekeepers foregather and the worm dieth seldom.

'I rented out my third floor back, this evening,' said Mrs. Purdy, across a fine circle of foam. 'A young man took it. He went up to bed two hours ago.

'Now, did ye, Mrs. Purdy, ma'am?' said Mrs. McCool, with intense admiration. 'You do be a wonder for rentin' rooms of that kind. And did ye tell him, then?' she concluded in a husky whisper, laden with mystery.

'Rooms,' said Mrs. Purdy, in her furriest tones, 'are furnished for to rent. I did not tell him, Mrs. McCool.'

' 'Tis right ye are, ma'am; 'tis by renting rooms we kape alive. Ye have the rale sense for business, ma'am. There be many people will rayjict the rentin' of a room if they be tould a suicide has been after dyin' in the bed of it.'

'As you say, we has our living to be making,' remarked Mrs. Purdy.

'Yis, ma'am; 'tis true. 'Tis just one wake ago this day I helped ye lay out the third floor back. A pretty slip of a colleen she was to be killin' herself wid the gas a swate little face she had, Mrs. Purdy, ma'am.'

'She'd a-been called handsome, as you say,' said Mrs. Purdy, assenting but critical, 'but for that mole she had a-growin' by her left eyebrow. Do fill up your glass again, Mrs. McCool.'

XVII

The Brief Debut of Tildy

IF YOU DO NOT KNOW Bogle's Chop House and Family Restaurant it is your loss. For if you are one of the fortunate ones who dine expensively you should be interested to know how the other half consumes provisions. And if you belong to the half to whom waiters' checks are things of moment, you should know Bogle's, for there you get your money's worth – in quantity, at least.

Bogle's is situated in that highway of *bourgeoisie*, that boulevard of Brown-Jones-and-Robinson, Eighth Avenue. There are two rows of tables in the room, six in each row. On each table is a castor-stand, containing cruets of condiments and seasons. From the pepper cruet you may shake a cloud of something tasteless and melancholy, like volcanic dust. From the salt cruet you may expect nothing. Though a man should extract a sanguinary stream from the pallid turnip, yet will his prowess be balked when he comes to wrest salt from Bogle's cruets. Also upon each table stands the counterfeit of that benign sauce made 'from the recipe of a nobleman in India.'

At the cashier's desk sits Bogle, cold, sordid, slow, smouldering, and takes your money. Behind a mountain of toothpicks he makes your change, files your check, and ejects at you, like a toad, a word about the weather. Beyond a corroboration of his meteorological statement you would better not venture. You are not Bogle's friend; you are a fed, transient customer, and you and he may not meet again until the blowing of Gabriel's dinner horn. So take your change and go – to the devil if you like. There you have Bogle's sentiments.

The needs of Bogle's customers were supplied by two waitresses and a Voice. One of the waitresses was named Aileen. She was tall, beautiful, lively, gracious and learned in persiflage. Her other name? There was no more necessity for another name at Bogle's than there was for finger-bowls.

The name of the other waitress was Tildy. Why do you suggest Matilda? Please listen this time – Tildy – Tildy. Tildy was dumpy, plain-faced, and too anxious to please to please. Repeat the last clause to yourself once or twice, and make the acquaintance of the duplicate infinite.

The Voice at Bogle's was invisible. It came from the kitchen, and did not shine in the way of originality. It was a heathen Voice, and contented itself with vain repetitions of exclamations emitted by the waitresses concerning food.

Will it tire you to be told again that Aileen was beautiful? Had she donned a few hundred dollars' worth of clothes and joined the Easter parade, and had you seen her, you would have hastened to say so yourself.

The customers at Bogle's were her slaves. Six tables full she could wait upon at once. They who were in a hurry restrained their impatience for the joy of merely gazing upon her swiftly moving, graceful figure. They who had finished eating ate more that they might continue in the light of her smiles. Every man there – and they were mostly men – tried to make his impression upon her.

Aileen could successfully exchange repartee against a dozen at once. And every smile that she sent forth lodged, like pellets from a scatter-gun, in as many hearts. And all this while she would be performing astounding feats with orders of pork and beans, pot roasts, ham-and, sausage-and-the-wheats, and any quantity of things on the iron and in the pan and straight up and on the side. With all this feasting and flirting and merry exchange of wit Bogle's came mighty near being a salon, with Aileen for its Madame Récamier.

If the transients were entranced by the fascinating Aileen, the regulars were her adorers. There was much rivalry among many of the steady customers. Aileen could have had an engagement every evening. At least twice a week someone took her to a theatre or to a dance. One stout gentleman whom she and Tildy had privately christened 'The Hog' presented her with a turquoise ring. Another one known as 'Freshy,' who rode on the Traction Company's repair wagon, was going to give her a poodle as soon as his brother got the hauling contract in the Ninth. And the man who always ate spareribs and spinach and said he was a stockbroker asked her to go to 'Parsifal' with him.

'I don't know where this place is,' said Aileen while talking it over with Tildy, 'but the wedding-ring's got to be on before I put a stitch into a travelling dress – ain't that right? Well, I guess!'

But, Tildy!

In steaming, chattering, cabbage-scented Bogle's there was almost a heart tragedy. Tildy with the blunt nose, the hay-coloured hair, the freckled skin the bag-o'-meal figure. had never had an admirer. Not a man followed her with his eyes when she went to and fro in the restaurant save now and then when they glared with the beast-hunger for food. None of them bantered her gaily to coquettish interchanges of wit. None of them loudly 'jollied' her of mornings as they did Aileen, accusing her, when the eggs were slow in coming, of late hours in the company of envied swains. No one had ever given her a turquoise ring or invited her upon a voyage to mysterious distant 'Parsifal.'

Tildy was a good waitress, and the men tolerated her. They who sat at her tables spoke to her briefly with quotations from the bill of fare; and then raised their voices in honeyed and otherwise-flavoured accents, eloquently addressed to the fair Aileen. They writhed in their chairs to gaze around and over the impending form of Tildy, that Aileen's pulchritude might season and make ambrosia of their bacon and eggs.

And Tildy was content to be the unwooed drudge if Aileen could receive the flattery and the homage. The blunt nose was loyal to the short Grecian. She was Aileen's friend; and she was

glad to see her rule hearts and wean the attention of men from
smoking pot-pie and lemon meringue. But deep below our freckles and hay-coloured hair the unhandsomest of us dream of a
prince or a princess, not vicarious, but coming to us alone.

There was a morning when Aileen tripped in to work with a
slightly bruised eye; and Tildy's solicitude was almost enough to
heal any optic.

'Fresh guy,' explained Aileen, 'last night as I was going home at
Twenty-third and Sixth. Sashayed up, so he did, and made a break.
I turned him down, cold, and he made a sneak; but followed me
down to Eighteenth, and tried his hot air again. Gee! but I slapped
him a good one, side of the face. Then he give me that eye. Does
it look real awful, Til? I should hate that Mr. Nicholson should
see it when he comes in for his tea and toast at ten.'

Tildy listened to the adventure with breathless admiration. No
man had ever tried to follow her. She was safe abroad at any hour
of the twenty-four. What bliss it must have been to have had a
man follow one and black one's eye for love!

Among the customers at Bogle's was a young man named Seeders, who worked in a laundry office. Mr. Seeders was thin and had
light hair, and appeared to have been recently rough-dried and
starched. He was too diffident to aspire to Aileen's notice; so he
usually sat at one of Tildy's tables, where he devoted himself to
silence and boiled weakfish.

One day when Mr. Seeders came in to dinner he had been
drinking beer. There were only two or three customers in the
restaurant. When Mr. Seeders had finished his weakfish he got up,
put his arm around Tildy s waist, kissed her loudly and impudently, walked out upon the street, snapped his fingers in the
direction of the laundry, and hied himself to play pennies in the
slot machines at the Amusement Arcade.

For a few moments Tildy stood petrified. Then she was aware
of Aileen shaking at her an arch forefinger, and saying:

'Why, Til, you naughty girl! Ain't you getting to be awful, Miss
Slyboots! First thing I know you'll be stealing some of my fellows.
I must keep an eye on you, my lady.'

Another thing dawned upon Tildy's recovering wits. In a
moment she had advanced from a hopeless, lowly admirer to be an
Eve-sister of the potent Aileen. She herself was now a man-
charmer, a mark for Cupid, a Sabine who must be coy when the
Romans were at their banquet boards. Man had found her waist
achievable and her lips desirable. The sudden and amatory Seeders

had, as it were, performed for her a miraculous piece of one-day laundry-work. He had taken the sackcloth of her uncomeliness, had washed, dried, starched and ironed it, and returned it to her sheer embroidered lawn – the robe of Venus herself.

The freckles on Tildy's cheeks merged into a rosy flush. Now both Circe and Psyche peeped from her brightened eyes. Not even Aileen herself had been publicly embraced and kissed in the restaurant.

Tildy could not keep the delightful secret. When trade was slack she went and stood at Bogle's desk. Her eyes were shining; she tried not to let her words sound proud and boastful.

'A gentleman insulted me to-day,' she said. 'He hugged me around the waist and kissed me.'

'That so?' said Bogle, cracking open his business armour. 'After this week you get a dollar a week more.'

At the next regular meal when Tildy set food before customers with whom she had acquaintance she said to each of them modestly, as one whose merit needed no bolstering:

'A gentleman insulted me to-day in the restaurant. He put his arm around my waist and kissed me.'

The diners accepted the revelation in various ways – some incredulously, some with congratulations; others turned upon her the stream of badinage that had hitherto been directed at Aileen alone. And Tildy's heart swelled in her bosom, for she saw at last the towers of Romance rise above the horizon of the grey plain in which she had for so long travelled.

For two days Mr. Seeders came not again. During that time Tildy established herself firmly as a woman to be wooed. She bought ribbons, and arranged her hair like Aileen's, and tightened her waist two inches. She had a thrilling but delightful fear that Mr. Seeders would rush in suddenly and shoot her with a pistol. He must have loved her desperately; and impulsive lovers are always blindly jealous.

Even Aileen had not been shot at with a pistol. And then Tildy rather hoped that he would not shoot at her, for she was always loyal to Aileen; and she did not want to overshadow her friend.

At four o'clock on the afternoon of the third day Mr. Seeders came in. There were no customers at the tables. At the back end of the restaurant Tildy was refilling the mustard pots and Aileen was quartering pies Mr. Seeders walked back to where they stood.

Tildy looked up and saw him, gasped, and pressed the mustard spoon upon her heart. A red hair-bow was in her hair; she wore

Venus's Eighth Avenue badge, the blue bead necklace with the swinging silver symbolic heart.

Mr. Seeders was flushed and embarrassed. He plunged one hand into his hip pocket and the other into a fresh pumpkin pie.

'Miss Tildy,' said he, 'I want to apologize for what I done the other evenin'. Tell you the truth, I was pretty well tanked up or I wouldn't of done it. I wouldn't do no lady that a-way when I was sober. So I hope, Miss Tildy, you'll accept my "pology, and believe that I wouldn't of done it if I'd known what I was doin' and hadn't of been drunk.'

With this handsome plea Mr. Seeders backed away, and departed, feeling that reparation had been made.

But behind the convenient screen Tildy had thrown herself flat upon a table among the butter chips and the coffee cups, and was sobbing her heart out – out and back again to the grey plain wherein travel they with blunt noses and hay-coloured hair. From her knot she had torn the red hair-bow and cast it upon the floor. Seeders she despised utterly; she had but taken his kiss as that of a pioneer and prophetic prince who might have set the clocks going and the pages to running in fairyland. But the kiss had been maudlin and unmeant; the court had not stirred at the false alarm; she must for evermore remain the Sleeping Beauty.

Yet not all was lost. Aileen's arm was around her; and Tildy's red hand groped among the butter chips till it found the warm grasp of her friend's.

'Don't you fret, Til,' said Aileen, who did not understand entirely. 'That turnip-faced little clothes-pin of a Seeders ain't worth it. He ain't anything of a gentleman or he wouldn't ever of apologized.'

XVIII

Hearts and Crosses

BALDY WOODS REACHED for the bottle, and got it. Whenever Baldy went for anything he usually – but this is not Baldy's story. He poured out a third drink that was larger by a finger than the first and second. Baldy was in consultation; and the consultee is worthy of his hire.

'I'd be king if I was you,' said Baldy, so positively that his holster creaked and his spurs rattled.

Webb Yeager pushed back his flat-brimmed Stetson, and made further disorder in his straw-coloured hair. The tonsorial recourse being without avail, he followed the liquid example of the more resourceful Baldy.

'If a man marries a queen, it oughtn't to make him a two-spot,' declared Webb, epitomizing his grievances.

'Sure not,' said Baldy, sympathetic, still thirsty, and genuinely solicitous concerning the relative value of the cards. 'By rights you're a king. If I was you, I'd call for a new deal. The cards have been stacked on you. I'll tell you what you are, Webb Yeager.'

'What?' asked Webb, with a hopeful look in his pale blue eyes.

'You're a prince consort.'

'Go easy,' said Webb, 'I never blackguarded you none.'

'It's a title,' explained Baldy, 'up among the picture cards; but it don't take no tricks I'll tell you, Webb. It's a brand they've got for certain animals in Europe. Say that you or me or one of them Dutch dukes marries in a royal family. Well, by and by our wife gets to be queen. Are we king? Not in a million years. At the coronation ceremonies we march between little casino and the Ninth Grand Custodian of the Royal Hall Bedchamber. The only use we are is to appear in photographs, and accept the responsibility for the heir-apparent That ain't any square deal. Yes, sir, Webb, you're a prince consort; and if I was you, I'd start a interregnum or a habeas corpus or somethin'; and I'd be king *if I* had to turn from the bottom of the deck.'

Baldy emptied his glass to the ratification of his Warwick pose.

'Baldy,' said Webb solemnly, 'me and you punched cows in the same outfit for years. We been runnin' on the same range, and ridin' the same trails since we was boys. I wouldn't talk about my family affairs to nobody but you. You was line-rider on the Nopalito Ranch when I married Santa McAllister. I was foreman then; but what am I now? I don't amount to a knot in a stake rope.'

'When old McAllister was the cattle king of West Texas,' continued Baldy with Satanic sweetness, 'you was some tallow. You had as much to say on the ranch as he did.'

'I did,' admitted Webb, 'up to the time he found out I was tryin' to get my rope over Santa's head. Then he kept me out on the range as far from the ranch-house as he could. When the old man died they commenced to call Santa the "cattle queen." I'm boss of the cattle – that's all. She 'tends to all the business; she handles all the money; I can't sell even a beef-steer to a party of campers, myself. Santa's the "queen"; and I'm Mr. Nobody.'

'I'd be king if I was you,' repeated Baldy Woods, the royalist. 'When a man marries a queen he ought to grade up with her – on the hoof – dressed – dried – corned – any old way from the chaparral to the packing-house. Lots of folks thinks it's funny, Webb, that you don't have the say so on the Nopalito. I ain't reflectin' none on Miz Yeager – she's the finest little lady between the Rio Grande and next Christmas – but a man ought to be boss of his own camp.'

The smooth, brown face of Yeager lengthened to a mask of wounded melancholy. With that expression, and his rumpled yellow hair and guileless blue eyes, he might have been likened to a schoolboy whose leadership had been usurped by a youngster of superior strength. But his active and sinewy seventy-two inches, and his girded revolvers forbade the comparison.

'What was that you called me, Baldy?' he asked. 'What kind of a concert was it?'

'A "consort," ' corrected Baldy – 'a "prince consort." It's a kind of short-card pseudonym. You come in sort of between Jack-high and a four-card flush.'

Webb Yeager sighed, and gathered the strap of his Winchester scabbard from the floor.

'I'm ridin' back to the ranch to-day,' he said half-heartedly. 'I've got to start a bunch of beeves for San Antone in the morning.'

'I'm your company as far as Dry Lake,' announced Baldy. 'I've got a round-up camp on the San Marcos cuttin' out two-year-olds.'

The two *compañeros* mounted their ponies and trotted away from the little railroad settlement, where they had foregathered in the thirsty morning.

At Dry Lake, where their routes diverged, they reined up for a parting cigarette. For miles they had ridden in silence save for the soft drum of the ponies' hoofs on the matted mesquite grass, and the rattle of the chaparral against their wooden stirrups. But in Texas discourse is seldom continuous. You may fill in a mile, a meal, and a murder between your paragraphs without detriment to your thesis. So, without apology, Webb offered an addendum to the conversation that had begun ten miles away.

'You remember, yourself, Baldy, that there was a time when Santa wasn't quite so independent. You remember the days when old McAllister was keepin' us apart, and how she used to send me the sign that she wanted to see me? Old man Mac promised to make me look like a colander if I ever come in gunshot of the ranch. You remember the sign she used to send, Baldy – the heart with a cross inside of it?'

'Me?' cried Baldy, with intoxicated archness. 'You old sugar-stealing coyote! Don't I remember. Why, you dad-blamed old long-horned turtle-dove, the boys in camp was all cognoscious about them hiroglyphs. The "gizzard and crossbones" we used to call it. We used to see 'em on truck that was sent out from the ranch. They was marked in charcoal on the sacks of flour and in lead pencil on the newspapers. I see one of 'em once chalked on the back of a new cook that old man McAllister sent out from the ranch – danged if I didn't.'

'Santa's father,' explained Webb gently, 'got her to promise that she wouldn't write to me or send me any word. That heart-and-cross sign was her scheme. Whenever she wanted to see me in particular she managed to put that mark on somethin' at the ranch that she knew I'd see. And I never laid eyes on it but what I burnt the wind for the ranch the same night. I used to see her in that coma mott back of the little horse corral.'

'We knowed it,' chanted Baldy; 'but we never let on. We was all for you. We knowed why you always kept that fast paint in camp. And when we see that gizzard and crossbones figured out on the truck from the ranch we knowed old Pinto was going to eat up miles that night instead of grass. You remember Scurry – that educated horse-wrangler we had – the college fellow that tangle-foot drove to the range? Whenever Scurry saw that come-meet-your-honey brand on anything from the ranch, he'd wave his hand like that, and say, "Our friend Lee Andrews will again swim the Hell's point to-night." '

'The last time Santa sent me the sign,' said Webb, 'was once when she was sick. I noticed it as soon as I hit camp, and I galloped Pinto forty mile that night. She wasn't at the coma mott. I went to the house; and old McAllister met me at the door. "Did you come here to get killed?" says he; "I'll disoblige you for once. I just started a Mexican to bring you. Santa wants you. Go in that room and see her. And then come out here and see me."

'Santa was lyin' in bed pretty sick. But she gives out a kind of a smile, and her hand and mine lock horns, and I sets down by the bed – mud and spurs and chaps and all. "I've heard you ridin' across the grass for hours, Webb," she says. "I was sure you'd come. You saw the sign?" she whispers. "The minute I hit camp," says I. " 'Twas marked on the bag of potatoes and onions." "They're always together," says she, soft like – "always together in life." "They go well together," I says, "in a stew." "I mean hearts and crosses," says Santa. "Our sign – to love and to suffer – that's what they mean."

'And there was old Doc Musgrove amusin' himself with whisky and a palm-leaf fan. And by and by Santa goes to sleep; and Doc feels her forehead; and he says to me: "You're not such a bad febrifuge But you'd better slide out now; for the diagnosis don't call for you in regular doses. The little lady'll be all right when she wakes up."

'I seen old McAllister outside. "She's asleep," says I. "And now you can start in with your colander work. Take your time; for I left my gun on my saddle-horn."

'Old Mac laughs, and he says to me: "Pumpin' lead into the best ranch-boss in West Texas don't seem to me good business policy. I don't know where I could get as good a one. It's the son-in-law idea, Webb, that makes me admire for to use you as a target. You ain't my idea for a member of the family. But I can use you on the Nopalito if you'll keep outside of a radius with the ranchhouse in the middle of it. You go upstairs and lay down on a cot, and when you get some sleep we'll talk it over." '

Baldy Woods pulled down his hat, and uncurled his leg from his saddle-horn. Webb shortened his rein, and his pony danced, anxious to be off. The two men shook hands with Western ceremony.

'Adios, Baldy,' said Webb, 'I'm glad I seen you and had this talk.'

With a pounding rush that sounded like the rise of a covey of quail, the riders sped away toward different points of the compass. A hundred yards on his route Baldy reined in on the top of a bare knoll, and emitted a yell. He swayed on his horse; had he been on foot, the earth would have risen and conquered him; but in the saddle he was a master of equilibrium, and laughed at whisky, and despised the centre of gravity.

Webb turned in his saddle at the signal.

'If I was you,' came Baldy's strident and perverting tones, 'I'd be king!'

At eight o'clock on the following morning Bud Turner rolled from his saddle in front of the Nopalito ranch-house, and stumbled with whizzing rowels towards the gallery. Bud was in charge of the bunch of beef-cattle that was to strike the trail that morning for San Antonio. Mrs. Yeager was on the gallery watering a cluster of hyacinths growing in a red earthenware jar.

'King' McAllister had bequeathed to his daughter many of his strong characteristics – his resolution, his gay courage, his contumacious self-reliance, his pride as a reigning monarch of hoofs and horns. Allegro and fortissimo had been McAllister's tempo and tone.

In Santa they survived, transposed to the feminine key. Substantially, she preserved the image of the mother who had been summoned to wander in other and less finite green pastures long before the waxing herds of kine had conferred royalty upon the house. She had her mother's slim, strong figure and grave, soft prettiness that relieved in her the severity of the imperious McAllister eve and the McAllister air of royal independence.

Webb stood on one end of the gallery giving orders to two or three sub-bosses of various camps and outfits who had ridden in for instructions.

' 'Morning,' said Bud briefly. 'Where do you want them beeves to go in town – to Barber's, as usual?'

Now, to answer that had been the prerogative of the queen. All the reins of business – buying, selling, and banking – had been held by her capable fingers. The handling of the cattle had been entrusted fully to her husband. In the days of 'King' McAllister, Santa had been his secretary and helper; and she had continued her work with wisdom and profit. But before she could reply, the prince consort spake up with calm decision –

'You drive that bunch to Zimmerman and Nesbit's pens; I spoke to Zimmerman about it some time ago.'

Bud turned on his high boot-heels.

'Wait!' called Santa quickly. She looked at her husband with surprise in her steady grey eyes.

'Why, what do you mean, Webb?' she asked, with a small wrinkle gathering between her brows. 'I never deal with Zimmerman and Nesbit. Barber has handled every head of stock from this ranch in that market for five years. I'm not going to take the business out of his hands.' She faced Bud Turner. 'Deliver those cattle to Barber,' she concluded positively.

Bud gazed impartially at the water-jar hanging on the gallery, stood on his other leg, and chewed a mesquite leaf.

'I want this bunch of beeves to go to Zimmerman and Nesbit,' said Webb, with a frosty light in his blue eyes.

'Nonsense,' said Santa impatiently. 'You'd better start on, Bud, so as to noon at the Little Elm water-hole. Tell Barber we'll have another lot of culls ready in about a month.'

Bud allowed a hesitating eye to steal upward and meet Webb's. Webb saw apology in his look, and fancied he saw commiseration.

'You deliver them cattle,' he said grimly, 'to –'

'Barber,' finished Santa sharply. 'Let that settle it. Is there anything else you are waiting for, Bud?'

'No, m'm,' said Bud. But before going he lingered while a cow's tail could have switched thrice; for man is man's ally; and even the Philistines must have blushed when they took Samson in the way they did.

'You hear your boss!' cried Webb sardonically. He took off his hat, and bowed until it touched the floor before his wife.

'Webb,' said Santa rebukingly, 'you're acting mighty foolish to-day.'

'Court fool, your Majesty,' said Webb, in his slow tones, which had changed their quality. 'What else can you expect? Let me tell you. I was a man before I married a cattle queen. What am I now? The laughing-stock of the camps. I'll be a man again.'

Santa looked at him closely.

'Don't be unreasonable, Webb,' she said calmly. 'You haven't been slighted in any way. Do I ever interfere in your management of the cattle? I know the business side of the ranch much better than you do. I learned it from Dad. Be sensible.'

'Kingdoms and queendoms,' said Webb, 'don't suit me unless I am in the pictures, too. I punch the cattle and you wear the crown. All right. I'd rather be High Lord Chancellor of a cow-camp than the eight-spot in a queen-high flush. It's your ranch; and Barber gets the beeves.'

Webb's horse was tied to the rack. He walked into the house and brought out his roll of blankets that he never took with him except on long rides, and his 'slicker,' and his longest stake rope of plaited raw-hide. These he began to tie deliberately upon his saddle. Santa, a little pale, followed him.

Webb swung up into the saddle. His serious, smooth face was without expression, except for a stubborn light that smouldered in his eyes.

'There's a herd of cows and calves,' said he, 'near the Hondo Water-hole on the Frio that ought to be moved away from timber. Lobos have killed three of the calves. I forgot to leave orders. You'd better tell Simms to attend to it.'

Santa laid a hand on the horse's bridle, and looked her husband in the eye.

'Are you going to leave me, Webb?' she asked quietly.

'I am going to be a man again,' he answered.

'I wish you success in a praiseworthy attempt,' she said, with a sudden coldness. She turned and walked directly into the house.

Webb Yeager rode to the south-east as straight as the topography of West Texas permitted. And when he reached the horizon he might have ridden on into blue space as far as knowledge of him on the Nopalito went. And the days, with Sundays at their head, formed into hebdomadal squads; and the weeks, captained by the full moon, closed ranks into menstrual companies carrying 'Tempus fugit' on their banners; and the months marched on toward the vast camp-ground of the years; but Webb Yeager came no more to the dominions of his queen.

One day a being named Bartholomew, a sheepman – and therefore of little account – from the lower Rio Grande country, rode in sight of the Nopalito ranch-house and felt hunger assail him. *Ex consuetudine* he was soon seated at the midday dining-table of that hospitable kingdom. Talk like water gushed from him: he might have been smitten with Aaron's rod – that is your gentle shepherd when an audience is vouchsafed him whose ears are not overgrown with wool.

'Missis Yeager,' he babbled, 'I see a man the other day on the Rancho Seco down in Hidalgo County by your name – Webb Yeager was his. He'd just been engaged as manager. He was a tall, light-haired man, not saying much. Maybe he was some kin of yours, do you think?'

'A husband.' said Santa cordially. 'The Seco has done well. Mr. Yeager is one of the best stockmen in the West.'

The dropping out of a prince consort rarely disorganizes a monarchy. Queen Santa had appointed as *mayordomo* of the ranch a trusty subject, named Ramsay, who had been one of her father's faithful vassals. And there was scarcely a ripple on the Nopalito ranch save when the gulf breeze created undulations in the grass of its wide acres.

For several years the Nopalito had been making experiments with an English breed of cattle that looked down with aristocratic contempt upon the Texas long-horns. The experiments were found satisfactory; and a pasture had been set apart for the blue-bloods. The fame of them had gone forth into the chaparral and pear as far as men ride in saddles. Other ranches woke up, rubbed their eyes, and looked with new dissatisfaction upon the long-horns.

As a consequence, one day a sunburned, capable, silk-kerchiefed, nonchalant youth, garnished with revolvers, and attended by three Mexican *vaqueros*, alighted at the Nopalito ranch and presented the following business-like epistle to the queen thereof –

'Mrs. Yeager – The Nopalito Ranch –

DEAR MADAM –

'I am instructed by the owners of the Rancho Seco to purchase 100 head of two and three-year-old cows of the Sussex breed owned by you. If you can fill the order please deliver the cattle to the bearer; and a cheque will be forwarded to you at once.

'Respectfully,

WEBSTER YEAGER,

'Manager the Rancho Seco.'

Business is business, even – very scantily did it escape being written 'especially' – in a kingdom.

That night the 100 head of cattle were driven up from the pasture and penned in a corral near the ranch-house for delivery in the morning.

When night closed down and the house was still, did Santa Yeager throw herself down, clasping that formal note to her bosom, weeping, and calling out a name that pride (either in one or the other) had kept from her lips many a day? Or did she file the letter in her business way, retaining her royal balance and strength?

Wonder, if you will; but royalty is sacred; and there is a veil. But this much you shall learn –

At midnight Santa slipped softly out of the ranchhouse, clothed in something dark and plain. She paused for a moment under the live-oak tree. The prairies were somewhat dim, and the moonlight was pale orange, diluted with particles of an impalpable flying mist. But the mock-bird whistled on every bough of vantage; leagues of flowers scented the air; and a kindergarten of little shadowy rabbits leaped and played in an open space near by. Santa turned her face to the south-east and threw three kisses thitherward; for there was none to see.

Then she sped silently to the blacksmith-shop, fifty yards away; and what she did there can only be surmised. But the forge glowed red; and there was a faint hammering such as Cupid might make when he sharpens his arrow-points.

Later she came forth with a queer-shaped, handled thing in one hand, and a portable furnace, such as are seen in branding-camps, in the other. To the corral where the Sussex cattle were penned she sped with these things swiftly in the moonlight.

She opened the gate and slipped inside the corral. The Sussex cattle were mostly a dark red. But among this bunch was one that was milky white – notable among the others.

And now Santa shook from her shoulder something that we had not seen before – a rope lasso. She freed the loop of it, coiling the length in her left hand, and plunged into the thick of the cattle.

The white cow was her object. She swung the lasso, which caught one horn and slipped off. The next throw encircled the forefeet and the animal fell heavily. Santa made for it like a panther; but it scrambled up and dashed against her, knocking her over like a blade of grass.

Again she made the cast, while the aroused cattle milled around the four sides of the corral in a plunging mass. This throw was fair; the white cow came to earth again; and before it could rise Santa had made the lasso fast around a post of the corral with a swift and simple knot, and had leaped upon the cow again with the raw-hide hobbles.

In one minute the feet of the animal were tied (no record-breaking deed) and Santa leaned against the corral for the same space of time, panting and lax.

And then she ran swiftly to her furnace at the gate and brought the branding-iron, queerly-shaped and white-hot.

The bellow of the outraged white cow, as the iron was applied, should have stirred the slumbering auricular nerves and consciences of the near-by subjects of the Nopalito, but it did not. And it was amid the deepest nocturnal silence that Santa ran like a lapwing back to the ranch-house and there fell upon a cot and sobbed – sobbed as though queens had hearts as simple ranch-men's wives have, and as though she would gladly make kings of prince consorts, should they ride back again from over the hills and far away.

In the morning the capable revolvered youth and his *vaqueros* set forth, driving the bunch of Sussex cattle across the prairies to the Rancho Seco. Ninety miles it was; a six days' journey, grazing and watering the animals on the way.

The beasts arrived at Rancho Seco one evening at dusk; and were received and counted by the foreman of the ranch.

The next morning at eight o'clock a horseman loped out of the brush to the Nopalito ranch-house. He dismounted stiffly, and strode, with whizzing spurs, to the house. His horse gave a great sigh and swayed foam-streaked, with down-drooping head and closed eyes.

But waste not your pity upon Belshazzar, the flea-bitten sorrel. To-day, in Nopalito horse pasture he survives, pampered, beloved, unridden, cherished record-holder of long-distance rides.

The horseman stumbled into the house. Two arms fell around his neck, and someone cried out in the voice of woman and queen alike: 'Webb – oh, Webb!'

'I was a skunk,' said Webb Yeager.

'Hush,' said Santa, 'did you see it?'

'I saw it,' said Webb.

What they meant God knows; and you shall know, if you rightly read the primer of events.

'Be the cattle-queen,' said Webb; 'and overlook it if you can. I was a mangy, sheep-stealing coyote.'

'Hush!' said Santa again, laying her fingers upon his mouth. 'There's no queen here. Do you know who I am? I am Santa Yeager, First Lady of the Bedchamber. Come here.'

She dragged him from the gallery into the room to the right. There stood a cradle with an infant in it – a red, ribald, unintelligible, babbling, beautiful infant, sputtering at life in an unseemly manner.

'There's no queen on this ranch,' said Santa again. 'Look at the king. He's got your eyes, Webb. Down on your knees and look at His Highness.'

But jingling rowels sounded on the gallery, and Bud Turner stumbled there again with the same query that he had brought, lacking a few days, a year ago.

' 'Morning. Them beeves is just turned out on the trail. Shall I drive 'em to Barber's, or –'

He saw Webb and stopped, open-mouthed.

'Ba-ba-ba-ba-ba-ba!' shrieked the king in his cradle, beating the air with his fists.

'You hear your boss, Bud,' said Webb Yeager, with a broad grin – just as he had said a year ago.

And that is all, except that when old man Quinn, owner of the Rancho Seco, went out to look over the herd of Sussex cattle that he had bought from the Nopalito ranch, he asked his new manager –

'What's the Nopalito ranch brand, Wilson?'

'X Bar Y,' said Wilson.

'I thought so,' said Quinn. 'But look at that white heifer there; she's got another brand – a heart with a cross inside of it. What brand is that?'

XIX

Telemachus, Friend

RETURNING FROM A HUNTING TRIP, I waited at the little town of
Los Piños, in New Mexico, for the south-bound train, which was
one hour late. I sat on the porch of the Summit House and discussed the functions of life with Telemachus Hicks, the hotel
proprietor.

Perceiving that personalities were not out of order, I asked him
what species of beast had long ago twisted and mutilated his left
ear. Being a hunter, I was concerned in the evils that may befall
one in the pursuit of game.

'That ear,' said Hicks, 'is the relic of true friendship.'

'An accident?' I persisted.

'No friendship is an accident,' said Telemachus; and I was
silent.

'The only perfect case of true friendship I ever knew,' went on
my host, 'was a cordial intent between a Connecticut man and a
monkey. The monkey climbed palms in Barranquilla and threw
down coco-nuts to the man. The man sawed them in two and made
dippers, which he sold for two *reales* each and bought rum. The
monkey drank the milk of the nuts. Through each being satisfied
with his own share of the graft, they lived like brothers.

'But in the case of human beings, friendship is a transitory art,
subject to discontinuance without further notice.

'I had a friend once, of the entitlement of Paisley Fish, that I
imagined was sealed to me for an endless space of time. Side by
side for seven years we had mined, ranched, sold patent churns,
herded sheep, took photographs and other things, built wire fences,
and picked prunes. Thinks I, neither homicide nor flattery nor
riches nor sophistry nor drink can make trouble between me and
Paisley Fish. We was friends an amount you could hardly guess at.
We was friends in business, and we let our amicable qualities lap
over and season our hours of recreation and folly. We certainly had
days of Damon and nights of Pythias.

'One summer me and Paisley gallops down into these San
Andrés mountains for the purpose of a month's surcease and
levity, dressed in the natural store habiliments of man. We hit this
town of Los Piños, which certainly was a roof-garden spot of the

world, and flowing with condensed milk and honey. It had a street
or two, and air, and hens, and a eating-house; and that was enough
for us.

'We strikes the town after supper-time, and we concludes to
sample whatever efficacy there is in this eating-house down by the
railroad tracks. By the time we had set down and pried up our
plates with a knife from the red oil-cloth, along intrudes Widow
Jessup with the hot biscuit and the fried liver.

'Now, there was a woman that would have tempted an anchovy
to forget his vows. She was not so small as she was large; and a kind
of welcome air seemed to mitigate her vicinity. The pink of her
face was the *in hoc signo if* a culinary temper and a warm disposition,
and her smile would have brought out the dogwood blossoms in
December.

'Widow Jessup talks to us a lot of garrulousness about the climate and history and Tennyson and prunes and the scarcity of
mutton, and finally wants to know where we came from.

' "Spring Valley," says I.

' "Big Spring Valley," chips in Paisley, out of a lot of potatoes
and knuckle-bone of ham in his mouth.

'That was the first sign I noticed that the old *fidus Diogenes* business between me and Paisley Fish was ended for ever. He knew
how I hated a talkative person, and yet he stampedes into the conversation with his amendments and addendums of syntax. On the
map it was Big Spring Valley; but I had heard Paisley himself call
it Spring Valley a thousand times.

'Without saying any more, we went out after supper and set on
the railroad track. We had been pardners too long not to know
what was going on in each other's mind.

' "I reckon you understand," says Paisley, "that I've made up
my mind to accrue that widow woman as part and parcel in and to
my hereditaments for ever, both domestic, sociable, legal, and
otherwise, until death us do part."

' "Why, yes," says I. "I read it between the lines, though you
only spoke one. And I suppose you are aware," says I, "that I have
a movement on foot that leads up to the widow's changing her
name to Hicks, and leaves you writing to the society column *to*
inquire whether the best man wears a japonica or seamless socks at
the wedding!"

' "There'll be some hiatuses in your programme," says Paisley,
chewing up a piece of a railroad tie. "I'd give in to you," says he,
"in 'most any respect if it was secular affairs, but this is not so. The

smiles of woman," goes on Paisley, "is the whirlpool of Squills and Chalybeates, into which vortex the good ship Friendship is often drawn and dismembered. I'd assault a bear that was annoying you," says Paisley, or I'd endorse your note, or rub the place between your shoulder-blades with opodeldoc the same as ever; but there my sense of etiquette ceases. In this fracas with Mrs. Jessup we play it alone. I've notified you fair."

'And then I collaborates with myself, and offers the following resolutions and bye-laws –

' "Friendship between man and man," says I, "is an ancient historical virtue enacted in the days when men had to protect each other against lizards with eighty-foot tails and flying turtles. And they've kept up the habit to this day, and stand by each other till the bellboy comes up and tells them the animals are not really there. I've often heard," I says, "about ladies stepping in and breaking up a friendship between men. Why should that be? I'll tell you, Paisley, the first sight and hot biscuit of Mrs. Jessup appears to have inserted a oscillation into each of our bosoms. Let the best man of us have her. I'll play you a square game, and won't do any underhanded work. I'll do all of my courting of her in your presence, so you will have an equal opportunity. With that arrangement I don't see why our steamboat of friendship should fall overboard in the medicinal whirlpools you speak of, whichever of us wins out."

' "Good old hoss!" says Paisley, shaking my hand. "And I'll do the same," says he. "We'll court the lady synonymously, and without any of the prudery and bloodshed usual to such occasions. And we'll be friends still, win or lose."

'At one side of Mrs. Jessup's eating-house was a bench under some trees where she used to sit in the breeze after the southbound had been fed and gone. And there me and Paisley used to congregate after supper and make partial payments on our respects to the lady of our choice. And we was so honourable and circuitous in our calls that if one of us got there first we waited for the other before beginning any gallivantery.

'The first evening that Mrs. Jessup knew about our arrangement I got to the bench before Paisley did. Supper was just over, and Mrs. Jessup was out there with a fresh pink dress on, and almost cool enough to handle.

'I sat down by her and made a few specifications about the moral surface of nature as set forth by the landscape and the contiguous perspective. That evening was surely a case in point. The

moon was attending to business in the section of sky where it
belonged, and the trees was making shadows on the ground
according to science and nature, and there was a kind of conspicuous hullabaloo going on in the bushes between the bullbats and
the orioles and the jack rabbits and other feathered insects of the
forest. And the wind out of the mountains was singing like a jew's
harp in the pile of old tomato cans by the railroad track.

'I felt a kind of sensation in my left side – something like dough
rising in a crock by the fire. Mrs. Jessup had moved up closer.

' "Oh, Mr. Hicks," says she, "when one is alone in the world,
don't they feel it more aggravated on a beautiful night like this?"

'I rose up off of the bench at once.

' "Excuse me, ma'am," says I, "but I'll have to wait till Paisley
comes before I can give a audible hearing to leading questions like
that."

'And then I explained to her how we was friends cinctured by
years of embarrassment and travel and complicity, and how we
had agreed to take no advantage of each other in any of the more
mushy walks of life, such as might be fomented by sentiment and
proximity. Mrs. Jessup appears to think serious about the matter
for a minute, and then she breaks into a species of laughter that
makes the wild wood resound.

'In a few minutes Paisley drops around, with oil of bergamot on
his hair, and sits on the other side of Mrs. Jessup, and inaugurates
a sad tale of adventure in which him and Pieface Lumley has a
skinning match of dead cows in '95 for a silver-mounted saddle in
the Santa Rita valley during the nine months drought.

'Now, from the start of that courtship I had Paisley Fish hobbled and tied to, a post. Each one of us had a different system of
reaching out for the easy places in the female heart. Paisley's
scheme was to petrify 'em with wonderful relations of events that
he had either come across personally or in large print. I think he
must have got his idea of subjugation from one of Shakespeare's
shows I see once called *Othello*. There is a coloured man in it who
acquires a duke's daughter by disbursing to her a mixture of the
talk turned out by Rider Haggard Lew Dockstader, and Dr.
Parkhurst. But that style of courting don't work well off the stage.

'Now, I give you my own recipe for inveigling a woman into that
state of affairs when she can be referred to as *"née* Jones." Learn
how to pick up her hand and hold it, and she's yours. It ain't so easy.
Some men grab at it so much like they was going to set a dislocation
of the shoulder that you can smell the arnica and hear 'em tearing

off bandages. Some take it up like a hot horseshoe, and hold it off at arm's length like a druggist pouring tincture of asafœtida in a bottle. And most of 'em catch hold of it and drag it right out before the lady's eyes like a boy finding a baseball in the grass, without giving her a chance to forget that the hand is growing on the end of her arm. Them ways are all wrong.

'I'll tell you the right way. Did you ever see a man sneak out in the back yard and pick up a rock to throw at a tom-cat that was sitting on a fence looking at him? He pretends he hasn't got a thing in his hand, and that the cat don't see him, and that he don't see the cat. That's the idea. Never drag her hand out where she'll have to take notice of it. Don't let her know that you think she knows you have the least idea she is aware you are holding her hand. That was my rule of tactics; and as far as Paisley's serenade about hostilities and misadventure went, he might as well have been reading to her a time-table of the Sunday trains that stop at Ocean Grove, New Jersey.

'One night when I beat Paisley to the bench by one pipeful, my friendship gets subsidized for a minute, and I asks Mrs. Jessup if she didn't think a "H" was easier to write than a "J." In a second her head was mashing the oleander flower in my buttonhole, and I leaned over and – but I didn't.

' "If you don't mind," says I, standing up, "we'll wait for Paisley to come before finishing this. I've never done anything dishonourable yet to our friendship, and this won't be quite fair."

' "Mr. Hicks," says Mrs. Jessup, looking at me peculiar in the dark, "if it wasn't for but one thing, I'd ask you to hike yourself down the gulch and never disresume your visits to my house."

' "And what is that, ma'am?" I asks.

' "You are too good a friend not to make a good husband," says she.

'In five minutes Paisley was on his side of Mrs. Jessup.

' "In Silver City, in the summer of '98," he begins, "I see Jim Bartholomew chew off a Chinaman's ear in the *Blue Light Saloon* on account of a cross-barred muslin shirt that – what was that noise?"

'I had resumed matters again with Mrs. Jessup right where we had left off.

' "Mrs. Jessup," says I, "has promised to make it Hicks. And this is another of the same sort."

'Paisley winds his feet around a leg of the bench and kind of groans."

' "Lem," says he, "we been friends for seven years. Would you mind not kissing Mrs. Jessup quite so loud? I'd do the same for you."

' "All right," says I. "The other kind will do as well."

' "This Chinaman," goes on Paisley, "was the one that shot a man named Mullins in the spring of '97, and that was –"

'Paisley interrupted himself again.

' "Lem," says he, "if you was a true friend you wouldn't hug Mrs. Jessup quite so hard. I felt the bench shake all over just then. You know you told me you would give me an even chance as long as there was any."

' "Mr. Man," says Mrs. Jessup, turning around to Paisley, "if you was to drop in to the celebration of mine and Mr. Hicks's silver wedding, twenty-five years from now, do you think you could get it into that Hubbard squash you call your head that you are *nix cum rous* in this business? I've put up with you a long time because you was Mr. Hicks's friend; but it seems to me it's time for you to wear the willow and trot off down the hill."

' "Mrs. Jessup," says I, without losing my grasp on the situation as fiancé, "Mr. Paisley is my friend, and I offered him a square deal and a equal opportunity as long as there was a chance."

' "A chance!" says she. "Well, he may think he has a chance; but I hope he won't think he's got a cinch, after what he's been next to all the evening."

'Well, a month afterward me and Mrs. Jessup was married in the Los Piños Methodist Church; and the whole town closed up to see the performance.

'When we lined up in front, and the preacher was beginning to sing out his rituals and observances, I looks around and misses Paisley. I calls time on the preacher. "Paisley ain't here," says I. "We've got to wait for Paisley. A friend once, a friend always – that's Telemachus Hicks," says I. Mrs. Jessup's eyes snapped some; but the preacher holds up the incantations according to instructions.

'In a few minutes Paisley gallops up the aisle, putting on a cuff as he comes. He explains that the only dry-goods store in town was closed for the wedding, and he couldn't get the kind of a boiled shirt that his taste called for until he had broke open the back window of the store and helped himself. Then he ranges up on the other side of the bride, and the wedding goes on. I always imagined that Paisley calculated as a last chance that the preacher might marry him to the widow by mistake.

'After the proceedings was over we had tea and jerked antelope and canned apricots, and then the populace hiked itself away. Last of all Paisley shook me by the hand and told me I'd acted square and on the level with him, and he was proud to call me a friend.

'The preacher had a small house on the side of the street that he'd fixed up to rent; and he allowed me and Mrs. Hicks to occupy it till the ten-forty train the next morning, when we was going on a bridal tour to El Paso. His wife had decorated it all up with hollyhocks and poison ivy, and it looked real festal and bowery.

'About ten o'clock that night I sets down in the front door and pulls off my boots a while in the cool breeze, while Mrs. Hicks was fixing around in the room. Right soon the light went out inside; and I sat there a while reverberating over old times and scenes. And then I heard Mrs. Hicks call out "Ain't you coming in soon, Lem?"

' "Well, well!" says I, kind of rousing up. "Durn me if I wasn't waiting for old Paisley to –"

'But when I got that far,' concluded Telemachus Hicks, 'I thought somebody had shot this left ear of mine off with a forty-five. But it turned out to be only a lick from a broom-handle in the hands of Mrs. Hicks.'

XX

The Handbook of Hymen

'TIS THE OPINION OF MYSELF, Sanderson Pratt, who sets this down, that the educational system of the United States should be in the hands of the weather bureau. I can give you good reasons for it; and you can't tell me why our college professors shouldn't be transferred to the meteorological department. They have been learned to read; and they could very easily glance at the morning papers and then wire in to the main office what kind of weather to expect. But there's the other side of the proposition. I am going on to tell you how the weather furnished me and Idaho Green with a elegant education.

We was up in the Bitter Root Mountains over the Montana line prospecting for gold. A chin-whiskered man in Walla-Walla, carrying a line of hope as excess baggage, had grubstaked us; and there we was in the foothills pecking away, with enough grub on hand to last an army through a peace conference.

Along one day comes a mail-rider over the mountains from Carlos, and stops to eat three cans of greengages, and leave us a newspaper of modern date. This paper prints a system of premonitions of the weather, and the card it dealt Bitter Root Mountains from the bottom of the deck was 'warmer and fair, with light westerly breezes.'

That evening it began to snow, with the wind strong in the east. Me and Idaho moved camp into an old empty cabin higher up the mountain, thinking it was only a November flurry. But after falling three foot on a level it went to work in earnest; and we knew we was snowed in. We got in plenty of firewood before it got deep, and we had grub enough for two months, so we let the elements rage and cut up all they thought proper.

If you want to instigate the art of manslaughter just shut two men up in a eighteen by twenty-foot cabin for a month. Human nature won't stand it.

When the first snowflakes fell me and Idaho Green laughed at each other's jokes and praised the stuff we turned out of a skillet and called bread. At the end of three weeks Idaho makes this kind of a edict to me. Says he –

'I never exactly heard sour milk dropping out of a balloon on the bottom of a tin pan, but I have an idea it would be music of the spears compared to this attenuated stream of asphyxiated thought that emanates out of your organs of conversation. The kind of half-masticated noises that you emit every day puts me in mind of a cow's cud, only she s lady enough to keep hers to herself, and you ain't.'

'Mr. Green,' says I, 'you having been a friend of mine once, I have some hesitations in confessing to you that if I had my choice for society between you and a common yellow, three-legged cur pup, one of the inmates of this here cabin would be wagging a tail just at present.'

This way we goes on for two or three days, and then we quits speaking to one another. We divides up the cooking implements, and Idaho cooks his grub on one side of the fireplace and me on the other. The snow is up to the windows, and we have to keep a fire all day.

You see me and Idaho never had any education beyond reading and doing 'if John had three apples and James five' on a slate. We never felt any special need for a university degree, though we had acquired a species of intrinsic intelligence in knocking around the world that we could use in emergencies. But, snow-bound in that

cabin in the Bitter Roots, we felt for the first time that if we had
studied Homer or Greek and fractions and the higher branches of
information, we'd have had some resources in the line of medita-
tion and private thought. I've seen them Eastern college fellows
working in camps all through the West, and I never noticed but
what education was less of a drawback to 'em than you would
think. Why, once over on Snake River, when Andrew
McWilliam's saddle-horse got the botts, he sent a buckboard ten
miles for one of these strangers that claimed to be a botanist. But
that horse died.

One morning Idaho was poking around with a stick on top of a
little shelf that was too high to reach. Two books fell down to the
floor. I started toward 'em, but caught Idaho's eye. He speaks for
the first time in a week.

'Don't burn your fingers,' says he. 'In spite of the fact that
you're only fit to be the companion of a sleeping mud-turtle, I'll
give you a square deal. And that's more than your parents did
when they turned you loose in the world with the sociability of a
rattlesnake and the bedside manner of a frozen turnip. I'll play you
a game of seven-up, the winner to pick up his choice of the books,
the loser to take the other.'

We played; and Idaho won. He picked up his book, and I took
mine. Then each of us got on his side of the house and went to
reading.

I never was as glad to see a ten-ounce nugget as I was that book.
And Idaho looked at his like a kid looks at a stick of candy.

Mine was a little book about five by six inches called *Herkimer's
Handbook of Indispensable Information*. I may be wrong, but I think
that was the greatest book that ever was written. I've got it to-day;
and I can stump you or any man fifty times in five minutes with
the information in it. Talk about Solomon or the New York *Tri-
bune!* Herkimer had cases on both of 'em. That man must have put
in fifty years and travelled a million miles to find out all that stuff.
There was the population of all cities in it, and the way to tell a
girl's age, and the number of teeth a camel has. It told you the
longest tunnel in the world, the number of the stars, how long it
takes for chicken-pox to break out, what a lady's neck ought to
measure, the veto powers of Governors, the dates of the Roman
aqueducts, how many pounds of rice going without three beers a
day would buy, the average annual temperature of Augusta,
Maine, the quantity of seed required to plant an acre of carrots in
drills, antidotes for poisons, the number of hairs on a blonde lady's

head, how to preserve eggs, the height of all the mountains in the world, and the dates of all wars and battles, and how to restore drowned persons, and sunstroke, and the number of tacks in a pound, and how to make dynamite and flowers and beds, and what to do before the doctor comes – and a hundred times as many things besides. If there was anything Herkimer didn't know I didn't miss it out of the book.

I sat and read that book for four hours. All the wonders of education was compressed in it. I forgot the snow, and I forgot that me and old Idaho was on the outs. He was sitting still on a stool reading away with a kind of partly soft and partly mysterious look shining through his tan-bark whiskers.

'Idaho,' says I, 'what kind of a book is yours?'

Idaho must have forgot, too, for he answered moderate, without any slander or malignity.

'Why,' says he, 'this here seems to be a volume by Homer K. M.'

'Homer K. M. what?' I asks.

'Why, just Homer K. M.,' says he.

'You're a liar,' says I, a little riled that Idaho should try to put me up a tree. 'No man is going 'round signing books with his initials. If it's Homer K. M. Spoopendyke, or Homer K. M. McSweeney, or Homer K. M. Jones, why don't you say so like a man instead of biting off the end of it like a calf chewing off the tail of a shirt on a clothes-line?'

'I put it to you straight, Sandy,' says Idaho, quiet. 'It's a poem book,' says he, 'by Homer K. M. I couldn't get colour out of it at first, but there's a vein if you follow it up. I wouldn't have missed this book for a pair of red blankets.'

'You're welcome to it,' says I. 'What I want is a disinterested statement of facts for the mind to work on, and that's what I seem to find in the book I've drawn.'

'What you've got,' says Idaho, 'is statistics, the lowest grade of information that exists. They'll poison your mind. Give me old K. M.'s system of surmises. He seems to be a kind of a wine agent. His regular toast is "nothing doing," and he seems to have a grouch, but he keeps it so well lubricated with booze that his worst kicks sound like an invitation to split a quart. But it's poetry,' says Idaho, 'and I have sensations of scorn for that truck of yours that tries to convey sense in feet and inches. When it comes to explaining the instinct of philosophy through the art of nature, old K. M. has got your man beat by drills, rows, paragraphs, chest measurement, and average annual rainfall.'

So that's the way me and Idaho had it. Day and night all the excitement we got was studying our books. That snowstorm sure fixed us with a fine lot of attainments apiece. By the time the snow melted, if you had stepped up to me suddenly and said: 'Sanderson Pratt, what would it cost per square foot to lay a roof with twenty by twenty-eight tin at nine dollars and fifty cents per box?' I'd have told you as quick as light could travel the length of a spade-handle at the rate of one hundred and ninety-two thousand miles per second. How many can do it? You wake up 'most any man you know in the middle of the night, and ask him quick to tell you the number of bones in the human skeleton exclusive of the teeth, or what percentage of the vote of the Nebraska Legislature overrules a veto. Will he tell you? Try him and see.

About what benefit Idaho got out of his poetry book I didn't exactly know. Idaho boosted the wine agent every time he opened his mouth; but I wasn't so sure.

This Homer K. M., from what leaked out of his libretto through Idaho, seemed to me to be a kind of a dog who looked at life like it was a tin can tied to his tail. After running himself half to death, he sits down, hangs his tongue out, and looks at the can and says —

'Oh, well, since we can't shake the growler, let's get it filled at the corner, and all have a drink on me.'

Besides that, it seems he was a Persian; and I never hear of Persia producing anything worth mentioning unless it was Turk-ish rugs and Maltese cats.

That spring me and Idaho struck pay ore. It was a habit of ours to sell out quick and keep moving. We unloaded on our grub-staker for eight thousand dollars apiece; and then we drifted down to this little town of Rosa, on the Salmon River, to rest up, and get some human grub, and have our whiskers harvested.

Rosa was no mining camp. It laid in the valley, and was as free of uproar and pestilence as one of them rural towns in the coun-try. There was a three-mile trolley line champing its bit in the environs; and me and Idaho spent a week riding on one of the cars, dropping off of nights at the *Sunset View Hotel*. Being now well read as well as travelled, we was soon *pro re nata* with the best society in Rosa, and was invited out to the most dressed-up and high-toned entertainments. It was at a piano recital and quail-eating contest in the city hall, for the benefit of the fire company, that me and Idaho first met Mrs. De Ormond Sampson, the queen of Rosa society.

Mrs. Sampson was a widow, and owned the only two-story house in town. It was painted yellow, and whichever way you looked from you could see it as plain as egg on the chin of an O'Grady on a Friday. Twenty-two men in Rosa besides me and Idaho was trying to stake a claim on that yellow house.

There was a dance after the song-books and quail bones had been raked out of the hall. Twenty-three of the bunch galloped over to Mrs. Sampson and asked for a dance. I side-stepped the two-step, and asked permission to escort her home. That's where I made a hit.

On the way home says she –

'Ain't the stars lovely and bright to-night, Mr Pratt?'

'For the chance they've got,' says I, 'they're humping themselves in a mighty creditable way. That big one you see is sixty-six billions of miles distant. It took thirty-six years for its light to reach us. With an eighteen-foot telescope you can see forty-three millions of 'em, including them of the thirteenth magnitude, which, if one was to go out now, you would keep on seeing it for twenty-seven hundred years.'

'My!' says Mrs. Sampson. 'I never knew that before. How warm it is! I'm as damp as I can be from dancing so much.'

'That's easy to account for,' says I, 'when you happen to know that you've got two million sweat-glands working all at once. If every one of your perspiratory ducts, which are a quarter of an inch long, was placed end to end, they would reach a distance of seven miles.'

'Lawsy!' says Mrs. Sampson. 'It sounds like an irrigation ditch you was describing, Mr. Pratt. How do you get all this knowledge of information?'

'From observation, Mrs. Sampson,' I tells her. 'I keep my eyes open when I go about the world.'

'Mr. Pratt,' says she, 'I always did admire a man of education. There are so few scholars among the sap-headed plug-uglies of this town that it is a real pleasure to converse with a gentleman of culture. I'd be gratified to have you call at my house whenever you feel so inclined.'

And that was the way I got the goodwill of the lady in the yellow house. Every Tuesday and Friday evenings I used to go there and tell her about the wonders of the universe as discovered, tabulated, and compiled from nature by Herkimer. Idaho and the other gay Lutherans of the town got every minute of the rest of the week that they could.

I never imagined that Idaho was trying to work on Mrs. Sampson with old K. M.'s rules of courtship till one afternoon when I was on my way over to take her a basket of wild hog-plums. I met the lady coming down the lane that led to her house. Her eyes was snapping, and her hat made a dangerous dip over one eye.

'Mr. Pratt,' she opens up, 'this Mr. Green is a friend of yours, I believe.'

'For nine years,' say I.

'Cut him out,' says she. 'He's no gentleman!'

'Why, ma'am,' says I, 'he's a plain incumbent of the mountains, with asperities and the usual failings of a spendthrift and a liar, but I never on the most momentous occasion had the heart to deny that he was a gentleman. It may be that in haberdashery and the sense of arrogance and display Idaho offends the eye, but inside, ma'am, I've found him impervious to the lower grades of crime and obesity. After nine years of Idaho's society, Mrs. Sampson,' I winds up, 'I should hate to impute him, and I should hate to see him imputed.'

'It's right plausible of you, Mr. Pratt,' says Mrs. Sampson, 'to take up the curmudgeons in your friend's behalf; but it don't alter the fact that he has made proposals to me sufficiently obnoxious to ruffle the ignominy of any lady.'

'Why, now, now, now!' says I. 'Old Idaho do that! I could believe it of myself sooner. I never knew but one thing to deride in him; and a blizzard was responsible for that. Once while we was snowbound in the mountains he became a prey to a kind of spurious and uneven poetry, which may have corrupted his demeanour.'

'It has,' says Mrs. Sampson. 'Ever since I knew him he has been reciting to me a lot of irreligious rhymes by some person he calls Ruby Ott, and who is no better than she should be, if you judge by her poetry.'

'Then Idaho has struck a new book,' says I, 'for the one he had was by a man who writes under the *nom de plume* of K. M.'

'He'd better have stuck to it,' says Mrs. Sampson, 'whatever it was. And to-day he caps the vortex. I get a bunch of flowers from him, and on 'em is pinned a note. Now, Mr. Pratt, you know a lady when you see her; and you know how I stand in Rosa society. Do you think for a moment that I'd skip out to the woods with a man along with a jug of wine and a loaf of bread, and go singing and cavorting up and down under the trees with him? I take a little claret with my meals, but I'm not in the habit of packing a jug of it into the brush and raising Cain in any such style as that. And of course he'd bring his book of verses along too. He said so. Let him go on his scandalous picnics alone! Or let him take his Ruby Ott with him. I reckon she wouldn't kick unless it was on account of there being too much bread along. And what do you think of your gentleman friend now, Mr. Pratt?'

'Well, 'm,' says I, 'it may be that Idaho's invitation was a kind of poetry, and meant no harm. Maybe it belonged to the class of rhymes they call figurative. They offend law and order, but they get sent through the mails on the ground that they mean something that they don't say. I'd be glad on Idaho's account if you'd overlook it,' says I, 'and let us extricate our minds from the low regions of poetry to the higher planes of fact and fancy. On a beautiful afternoon like this, Mrs. Sampson,' I goes on, 'we should let our thoughts dwell accordingly. Though it is warm here, we should remember that at the equator the line of perpetual frost is at an altitude of fifteen thousand feet. Between the latitudes of forty degrees and forty-nine degrees it is from four thousand to nine thousand feet.'

'Oh, Mr. Pratt,' says Mrs. Sampson, 'it's such a comfort to hear you say them beautiful facts after getting such a jar from that minx of a Ruby's poetry!'

'Let us sit on this log at the roadside,' says I, 'and forget the inhumanity and ribaldry of the poets It is in the glorious columns of ascertained facts and legalized measures that beauty is to be found. In this very log we sit upon, Mrs. Sampson,' says I, 'is statistics more wonderful than any poem. The rings show it was sixty years old. At the depth of two thousand feet it would become coal in three thousand years. The deepest coal mine in the world is at Killingworth, near Newcastle. A box four feet long, three feet wide, and two feet eight inches deep will hold one ton of coal. If an artery is cut, compress it above the wound. A man's leg contains thirty bones. The Tower of London was burned in 1841.'

'Go on, Mr. Pratt,' says Mrs. Sampson. 'Them ideas is so original and soothing. I think statistics are just as lovely as they can be.'

But it wasn't till two weeks later that I got all that was coming to me out of Herkimer.

One night I was waked up by folks hollering 'Fire!' all around. I jumped up and dressed and went out of the hotel to enjoy the scene. When I seen it was Mrs. Sampson's house, I gave forth a kind of yell, and I was there in two minutes.

The whole lower story of the yellow house was in flames, and every masculine, feminine, and canine in Rosa was there, screeching and barking and getting in the way of the firemen. I saw Idaho trying to get away from six firemen who were holding him. They was telling him the whole place was on fire downstairs, and no man could go in it and come out alive.

'Where's Mrs. Sampson?' I asks.

'She hasn't been seen,' says one of the firemen. 'She sleeps upstairs. We've tried to get in, but we can't, and our company hasn't got any ladders yet.

I runs around to the light of the big blaze, and pulls the Handbook out of my inside pocket. I kind of laughed when I felt it in my hands – I reckon I was some daffy with the sensation of excitement.

'Herky, old boy,' I says to it, as I flipped over the pages, 'you ain't ever lied to me yet, and you ain't ever throwed me down at a scratch yet. Tell me what, old boy, tell me what!' says I.

I turned to 'What to do in Case of Accidents,' on page 117. I run my finger down the page, and struck it. Good old Herkimer, he never overlooked anything! It said –

'SUFFOCATION FROM INHALING SMOKE OR GAS. – There is nothing better than flax-seed. Place a few seed in the outer corner of the eye.'

I shoved the Handbook back in my pocket, and grabbed a boy that was running by.

'Here,' says I, giving him some money, 'run to the drug store and bring a dollar's worth of flaxseed. Hurry, and you'll get another one for yourself. Now,' I sings out to the crowd, 'we'll have Mrs. Sampson!' And I throws away my coat and hat.

Four of the firemen and citizens grabs hold of me. It's sure death, they say, to go in the house, for the floors was beginning to fall through

'How in blazes,' I sings out, kind of laughing yet, but not feeling like it, 'do you expect me to put flax-seed in a eye without the eye?'

I jabbed each elbow in a fireman's face, kicked the bark off of one citizen's shin, and tripped the other one with a side hold. And then I busted into the house. If I die first I'll write you a letter and tell you if it's any worse down there than the inside of that yellow house was; but don't believe it yet. I was a heap more cooked than the hurry-up orders of broiled chicken that you get in restaurants. The fire and smoke had me down on the floor twice, and was about to shame Herkimer, but the firemen helped me with their little stream of water, and I got to Mrs. Sampson's room. She'd lost conscientiousness from the smoke, so I wrapped her in the bed-clothes and got her on my shoulder. Well, the floors wasn't as bad as they said, or I never could have done it – not by no means.

I carried her out fifty yards from the house and laid her on the grass. Then, of course, every one of them other twenty-two plaintiffs to the lady's hand crowded around with tin dippers of water ready to save her. And up runs the boy with the flax-seed.

I unwrapped the covers from Mrs. Sampson's head. She opened her eyes and says –

'Is that you, Mr. Pratt?'

'S-s-sh,' says I. 'Don't talk till you've had the remedy.'

I runs my arm around her neck and raises her head, gentle, and breaks the bag of flax-seed with the other hand; and as easy as I could I bends over and slips three or four of the seeds in the outer corner of her eye.

Up gallops the village doc. by this time, and snorts around, and grabs at Mrs. Sampson's pulse, and wants to know what I mean by such sandblasted nonsense.

'Well, old Jalap and Jerusalem oak-seed,' says I, 'I'm no regular practitioner, but I'll show you my authority, anyway.'

They fetch my coat, and I gets out the Handbook.

'Look on page 117,' says I, 'at the remedy for suffocation by smoke or gas. Flax-seed in the outer corner of the eye, it says, I don't know whether it works as a smoke consumer or whether it hikes the compound gastro-hippopotamus nerve into action, but Herkimer says it, and he was called to the case first. If you want to make it a consultation there's no objection.'

Old doc. takes the book and looks at it by means of his specs. and a fireman's lantern.

'Well, Mr. Pratt,' says he, 'you evidently got on the wrong line in reading your diagnosis. The recipe for suffocation says: 'Get the patient into fresh air as quickly as possible, and place in a reclining position.' The flax-seed remedy is for 'Dust and Cinders in the Eye,' on the line above. But, after all –'

'See here,' interrupts Mrs. Sampson, 'I reckon I've got something to say in this consultation. That flax-seed done me more good than anything I ever tried.' And then she raises up her head and lays it back on my arm again, and says: 'Put some in the other eye, Sandy dear.'

And so if you was to stop off at Rosa to-morrow, or any other day, you'd see a fine new yellow house, with Mrs. Pratt, that was

Mrs. Sampson, embellishing and adorning it. And if you was to step inside you'd see on the marble-top centre table in the parlour *Herkimer's Handbook of Indispensable Information,* all re-bound in red morocco, and ready to be consulted on any subject pertaining to human happiness and wisdom.

XXI

The Trimmed Lamp

OF COURSE THERE ARE TWO SIDES to the question. Let us look at the other. We often hear 'shop-girls' spoken of. No such persons exist. There are girls who work in shops. They make their living that way. But why turn their occupation into an adjective? Let us be fair. We do not refer to the girls who live on Fifth Avenue as 'marriage-girls.'

Lou and Nancy were chums. They came to the big city to find work because there was not enough to eat at their homes to go around. Nancy was nineteen; Lou was twenty. Both were pretty, active, country girls who had no ambition to go on the stage.

The little cherub that sits up aloft guided them to a cheap and respectable boarding-house. Both found positions and became wage-earners. They remained chums. It is at the end of six months that I would beg you to step forward and be introduced to them. Meddlesome Reader: My Lady friends, Miss Nancy and Miss Lou. While you are shaking hands please take notice – cautiously – of their attire. Yes, cautiously; for they are as quick to resent a stare as a lady in a box at the horse show is.

Lou is a piece-work ironer in a hand laundry. She is clothed in a badly-fitting purple dress, and her hat plume is four inches too long; but her ermine muff and scarf cost $25, and its fellow beasts will be ticketed in the windows at $7.98 before the season is over. Her cheeks are pink, and her light blue eyes bright. Contentment radiates from her.

Nancy you would call a shop-girl – because you have the habit. There is no type; but a perverse generation is always seeking a type; so this is what the type should be. She has the high-ratted pompadour, and the exaggerated straight-front. Her skirt is shoddy, but has the correct flare. No furs protect her against the bitter spring air, but she wears her short broadcloth jacket as jauntily as though it were Persian lamb! On her face and in her eyes, remorseless type-seeker, is the typical shop-girl expression. It is a look of silent but contemptuous revolt against cheated woman-hood; of sad prophecy of the vengeance to come. When she laughs her loudest the look is still there. The same look can be seen in the eyes of Russian peasants; and those of us left will see it some day on Gabriel's face when he comes to blow us up. It is a look that should wither and abash man; but he has been known to smirk at it and offer flowers – with a string tied to them.

Now lift your hat and come away, while you receive Lou's cheery 'See you again,' and the sardonic, sweet smile of Nancy that seems, somehow, to miss you and go fluttering like a white moth up over the house-tops to the stars.

The two waited on the corner for Dan. Dan was Lou's steady company. Faithful? Well, he was on hand when Mary would have had to hire a dozen subpœna servers to find her lamb.

'Ain't you cold, Nance?' said Lou. 'Say, what a chump you are for working in that old store for $8 a week! I made $18.50 last week. Of course ironing ain't as swell work as selling lace behind a counter, but it pays. None of us ironers make less than $10. And I don't know that it's any less respecrful work, either.'

'You can have it,' said Nancy, with uplifted nose. 'I'll take my eight a week and hall-bedroom. I like to be among nice things and swell people. And look what a chance I've got! Why, one of our glove girls married a Pittsburg – steel maker, or blacksmith or something – the other day worth a million dollars. I'll catch a swell myself some time. I ain't bragging on my looks or anything; but I'll take my chances where there's big prizes offered. What show would a girl have in a laundry?'

'Why, that's where I met Dan,' said Lou triumphantly. 'He came in for his Sunday shirt and collars and saw me at the first board ironing. We all try to get to work at the first board. Ella Maginnis was sick that day, and I had her place. He said he noticed my arms first, how round and white they was. I had my sleeves rolled up. Some nice fellows come into laundries. You can tell 'em by their bringing their clothes in suit-cases, and turning in the door sharp and sudden.'

'How can you wear a waist like that, Lou?' said Nancy, gazing down at the offending article with sweet scorn in her heavy-lidded eyes. 'It shows fierce taste.'

'This waist?' cried Lou, with wide-eyed indignation. 'Why, I paid $16 for this waist. It's worth twenty-five. A woman left it to be laundered, and never called for it. The boss sold it to me. It's got yards and yards of hand embroidery on it. Better talk about that ugly, plain thing you've got on.'

'This ugly, plain thing,' said Nancy calmly, 'was copied from one that Mrs. Van Alstyne Fisher was wearing. The girls say her bill in the store last year was $12,000. I made mine myself. It cost me $1.50. Ten feet away you couldn't tell it from hers.'

'Oh, well,' said Lou good-naturedly, 'if you want to starve and put on airs, go ahead. But I'll take my job and good wages; and after hours give me something as fancy and attractive to wear as I am able to buy.'

But just then Dan came – a serious young man with a ready-made necktie, who had escaped the city's brand of frivolity – an electrician earning $30 per week who looked upon Lou with the sad eyes of Romeo, and thought her embroidered waist a web in which any fly should delight to be caught.

'My friend, Mr. Owens – shake hands with Miss Danforth,' said Lou.

'I'm mighty glad to know you, Miss Danforth,' said Dan, with outstretched hand. 'I've heard Lou speak of you so often.'

'Thanks,' said Nancy, touching his fingers with the tips of her cool ones, 'I've heard her mention you – a few times.'

Lou giggled.

'Did you get that handshake from Mrs. Van Alstyne Fisher, Nance?' she asked.

'If I did, you can feel safe in copying it,' said Nancy.

'Oh, I couldn't use it at all. It's too stylish for me. It's intended to set off diamond rings, that high shake is. Wait till I get a few and then I'll try it.'

'Learn it first,' said Nancy wisely, 'and you'll be more likely to get the rings.'

'Now, to settle this argument,' said Dan with his ready, cheerful smile, 'let me make a proposition. As I can't take both of you up to Tiffany's and do the right thing, what do you say to a little vaude-ville? I've got the tickets. How about looking at stage diamonds since we can't shake hands with the real sparklers?'

The faithful squire took his place close to the kerb; Lou next, a little peacocky in her bright and pretty clothes; Nancy on the inside, slender, and soberly clothed as the sparrow, but with the true Van Alstyne Fisher walk – thus they set out for their evening's moderate diversion.

I do not suppose that many look upon a great department store as an educational institution. But the one in which Nancy worked

was something like that to her. She was surrounded by beautiful
things that breathed of taste and refinement. If you live in an
atmosphere of luxury, luxury is yours whether your money pays
for it, or another's.

The people she served were mostly women whose dress, manners, and position in the social world were quoted as criterions.
From them Nancy began to take toll − the best from each according
to her view.

From one she would copy and practise a gesture, from another
an eloquent lifting of an eyebrow, from others, a manner of walking, of carrying a purse, of smiling, of greeting a friend, of
addressing 'inferiors in station.' From her best beloved model,
Mrs. Van Alstyne Fisher, she made requisition for that excellent
thing, a soft, low voice as clear as silver and as perfect in articula-
tion as the notes of a thrush. Suffused in the aura of this high
social refinement and good breeding, it was impossible for her to
escape a deeper effect of it. As good habits are said to be better
than good principles, so, perhaps, good manners are better than
good habits. The teachings of your parents may not keep alive
your New England conscience; but if you sit on a straight-back
chair and repeat the words 'prisms and pilgrims' forty times the
devil will flee from you. And when Nancy spoke in the Van
Alstyne Fisher tones she felt the thrill of *noblesse oblige* to her very
bones.

There was another source of learning in the great departmental
school. Whenever you see three or four shop-girls gather in a
bunch and jingle their wire bracelets as an accompaniment to
apparently frivolous conversation, do not think that they are there
for the purpose of criticizing the way Ethel does her back hair.
The meeting may lack the dignity of the deliberative bodies of
man; but it has all the importance of the occasion on which Eve
and her first daughter first put their heads together to make Adam
understand his proper place in the household. It is a Woman's
Conference for Common Defence and Exchange of Strategical
Theories of Attack and Repulse upon and against the World,
which is a Stage, and Man, its Audience who Persists in Throwing
Bouquets Thereupon. Woman, the most helpless of the young of
any animal − with the fawn's grace but without its fleetness; with
the bird's beauty but without its power of flight; with the honey-
bee's burden of sweetness but without its − Oh, let's drop that
simile − some of us may have been stung.

During this council of war they pass weapons one to another, and exchange stratagems that each has devised and formulated out of the tactics of life.

'I says to 'im,' says Sadie, 'ain't you the fresh thing! Who do you suppose I am, to be addressing such a remark to me? And what do you think he says back to me?'

The heads, brown, black, flaxen, red, and yellow bob together; the answer is given; and the parry to the thrust is decided upon, to be used by each thereafter in passages-at-arms with the common enemy, man.

Thus Nancy learned the art of defence; and to women successful defence means victory.

The curriculum of a department store is a wide one. Perhaps no other college could have fitted her as well for her life's ambition – the drawing of a matrimonial prize.

Her station in the store was a favoured one. The music-room was near enough for her to hear and become familiar with the works of the best composers – at least to acquire the familiarity that passed for appreciation in the social world in which she was vaguely trying to set a tentative and aspiring foot. She absorbed the educating influence of artwares, of costly and dainty fabrics, of adornments that are almost culture to women.

The other girls soon became aware of Nancy's ambition. 'Here comes your millionaire, Nance,' they would call to her whenever any man who looked the role approached her counter. It got to be a habit of men, who were hanging about while their women folk were shopping, to stroll over to the handkerchief counter and dawdle over the cambric squares. Nancy's imitation high-bred air and genuine dainty beauty was what attracted. Many men thus came to display their graces before her. Some of them may have been millionaires; others were certainly not more than their sedulous apes. Nancy learned to discriminate. There was a window at the end of the handkerchief counter; and she could see the rows of vehicles waiting for the shoppers in the street below. She looked, and perceived that automobiles differ as well as do their owners.

Once a fascinating gentleman bought four dozen handkerchiefs, and wooed her across the counter with a King Cophetua air. When he had gone one of the girls said:

'What's wrong, Nance, that you didn't warm up to that fellow? He looks the swell article, all right, to me.'

'Him?' said Nancy, with her coolest, sweetest, most impersonal, Van Alstyne Fisher smile; 'not for mine. I saw him drive up outside. A 12 H.P. machine and an Irish chauffeur! And you saw what kind of handkerchiefs he bought – silk! And he's got dactylis on him. Give me the real thing or nothing, if you please.'

Two of the most 'refined' women in the store – a forelady and a cashier – had a few 'swell gentlemen friends' with whom they now and then dined. Once they included Nancy in an invitation. The dinner took place in a spectacular café whose tables are engaged for New Year's Eve a year in advance. There were two 'gentlemen friends' – one without any hair on his head – high living ungrew it; and we can prove it – the other a young man whose worth and sophistication he impressed upon you in two convincing ways – he swore that all the wine was corked; and he wore diamond cuff buttons. This young man perceived irresistible excellences in Nancy. His taste ran to show-girls; and here was one that added the voice and manner of his high social world to the franker charms of her own caste. So, on the following day, he appeared in the store and made her a serious proposal of marriage over a box of hem-stitched, grass-bleached Irish linens. Nancy declined. A brown pompadour ten feet away had been using her eyes and ears. When the rejected suitor had gone she heaped carboys of upbraidings and horror upon Nancy's head.

'What a terrible little fool you are! That fellow's a millionaire – he's a nephew of old Van Skittles himself. And he was talking on the level, too. Have you gone crazy, Nance?'

'Have I?' said Nancy. 'I didn't take him, did I? He isn't a millionaire so hard that you could notice it, anyhow. His family only allows him $20,000 a year to spend. The bald-headed fellow was guying him about it the other night at supper.'

The brown pompadour came nearer and narrowed her eyes.

'Say, what do you want?' she inquired, in a voice hoarse for lack of chewing-gum. 'Ain't that enough for you? Do you want to be a Mormon, and marry Rockefeller and Gladstone Dowie and the King of Spain and the whole bunch? Ain't $20,000 a year good enough for you?'

Nancy flushed a little under the level gaze of the black, shallow eyes.

'It wasn't altogether the money, Carrie,' she explained. 'His friend caught him in a rank lie the other night at dinner. It was about some girl he said he hadn't been to the theatre with. Well, I can't stand a liar. Put everything together – I don't like him; and that settles it. When I sell out it's not going to be on any bargain day. I've got to have something that sits up in a chair like a man, anyhow. Yes, I'm looking out for a catch; but it's got to be able to do something more than make a noise like a toy bank.'

'The physiopathic ward for yours!' said the brown pompadour, walking away.

The high ideas, if not ideals – Nancy continued to cultivate on $8 per week. She bivouacked on the trail of the great unknown 'catch,' eating her dry bread and tightening her belt day by day. On her face was the faint, soldierly, sweet, grim smile of the pre-ordained man-hunter. The store was her forest; and many times she raised her rifle at game that seemed broad-antlered and big; but always some deep, unerring instinct – perhaps of the huntress, perhaps of the woman – made her hold her fire and take up the trail again.

Lou flourished in the laundry. Out of her $18.50 per week she paid $6 for her room and board. The rest went mainly for clothes. Her opportunities for bettering her taste and manners were few compared with Nancy's. In the steaming laundry there was nothing but work, work and her thoughts of the evening pleasures to come. Many costly and showy fabrics passed under her iron; and it may be that her growing fondness for dress was thus transmitted to her through the conducting metal.

When the day's work was over Dan awaited her outside, her faithful shadow in whatever light she stood.

Sometimes he cast an honest and troubled glance at Lou's clothes that increased in conspicuity rather than in style; but this was no disloyalty; he deprecated the attention they called to her in the streets.

And Lou was no less faithful to her chum. There was a law that Nancy should go with them on whatsoever outings they might take. Dan bore the extra burden heartily and in good cheer. It might be said that Lou furnished the colour, Nancy the tone, and Dan the weight of the distraction-seeking trio. The escort, in his neat but obviously ready-made suit, his ready-made tie and unfailing, genial, ready-made wit never startled or clashed. He was of that good kind that you are likely to forget while they are present, but remember distinctly after they are gone.

To Nancy's superior taste the flavour of these ready-made pleasures was sometimes a little bitter: but she was young! and youth is a gourmand, when it cannot be a gourmet.

'Dan is always wanting me to marry him right away,' Lou told her once. 'But why should I? I'm independent. I can do as I please with the money I earn; and he never would agree for me to keep on working afterward. And say, Nance, what do you want to stick to that old store for, and half dress yourself? I could get you a place in the laundry right now if you'd come. It seems to me that you could afford to be a little less stuck-up if you could make a good deal more money.'

'I don't think I'm stuck-up, Lou,' said Nancy, 'but I'd rather live on half rations and stay where I am. I suppose I've got the habit. It's the chance that I want. I don't expect to be always behind a counter. I'm learning something new every day. I'm right up against refined and rich people all the time – even if I do only wait on them; and I'm not missing any pointers that I see passing around.'

'Caught your millionaire yet?' asked Lou, with her teasing laugh.

'I haven't selected one yet,' answered Nancy. 'I've been looking them over.'

'Goodness! the idea of picking over 'em! Don't you ever let one get by you, Nance – even if he's a few dollars shy. But of course you're joking – millionaires don't think about working girls like us.'

'It might be better for them if they did,' said Nancy, with cool wisdom. 'Some of us could teach them how to take care of their money.'

'If one was to speak to me,' laughed Lou, 'I know I'd have a duck-fit.'

'That's because you don't know any. The only difference between swells and other people is you have to watch 'em closer. Don't you think that red silk lining is just a little bit too bright for that coat, Lou?'

Lou looked at the plain, dull olive jacket of her friend.

'Well, no I don't – but it may seem so beside that faded-looking thing you've got on.'

'This jacket,' said Nancy complacently, 'has exactly the cut and fit of one that Mrs. Van Alstyne Fisher was wearing the other day. The material cost me $3.98. I suppose hers cost about $100 more.'

'Oh, well,' said Lou lightly, 'it don't strike me as millionaire bait. Shouldn't wonder if I catch one before you do, anyway.'

Truly it would have taken a philosopher to decide upon the values of the theories held by the two friends. Lou, lacking that certain pride and fastidiousness that keeps stores and desks filled with girls working for the barest living, thumped away gaily with her iron in the noisy and stifling laundry. Her wages supported her even beyond the point of comfort; so that her dress profited until sometimes she cast a sidelong glance of impatience at the neat but inelegant apparel of Dan — Dan the constant, the immutable, the undeviating.

As for Nancy, her case was one of tens of thousands. Silk and jewels and laces and ornaments and the perfume and music of the fine world of good-breeding and taste — these were made for woman; they are her equitable portion. Let her keep near them if they are a part of life to her, and if she will. She is no traitor to herself, as Esau was; for she keeps her birthright, and the pottage she earns is often very scant.

In this atmosphere Nancy belonged, and she throve in it and ate her frugal meals and schemed over her cheap dresses with a determined and contented mind. She already knew woman; and she was studying man, the animal, both as to his habits and eligibility. Some day she would bring down the game that she wanted; but she promised herself it would be what seemed to her the biggest and the best, and nothing smaller.

Thus she kept her lamp trimmed and burning to receive the bridegroom when he should come.

But, another lesson she learned, perhaps unconsciously. Her standard of values began to shift and change. Sometimes the dollar-mark grew blurred in her mind's eye, and shaped itself into letters that spelled such words as 'truth' and 'honour' and now and then just 'kindness.' Let us make a likeness of one who hunts the moose or elk in some mighty wood. He sees a little dell, mossy and embowered, where a rill trickles, babbling to him of rest and comfort. At these times the spear of Nimrod himself grows blunt.

So Nancy wondered sometimes if Persian lamb was always quoted at its market value by the hearts that it covered.

One Thursday evening Nancy left the store and turned across Sixth Avenue, westward to the laundry. She was expected to go with Lou and Dan to a musical comedy.

Dan was just coming out of the laundry when she arrived. There was a queer, strained look on his face.

'I thought I would drop around to see if they had heard from her,' he said.

'Heard from who?' asked Nancy. 'Isn't Lou there?'

'I thought you knew,' said Dan. 'She hasn't been there or at the house where she lived since Monday. She moved all her things there. She told one of the girls in the laundry she might be going to Europe.'

'Hasn't anybody seen her anywhere?' asked Nancy.

Dan looked at her with his jaws set grimly and a steely gleam in his steady grey eyes.

'They told me in the laundry,' he said harshly, 'that they saw her pass yesterday – in an automobile. With one of the millionaires, I suppose, that you and Lou were for ever busying your brains about.'

For the first time Nancy quailed before a man. She laid her hand, that trembled slightly, on Dan's sleeve.

'You've no right to say such a thing to me, Dan – as if I had anything to do with it!'

'I didn't mean it that way,' said Dan, softening. He fumbled in his vest pocket.

'I've got the tickets for the show to-night,' he said, with a gallant show of lightness. 'If you –'

Nancy admired pluck whenever she saw it.

'I'll go with you, Dan,' she said.

Three months went by before Nancy saw Lou again.

At the twilight one evening the shop-girl was hurrying home along the border of a little quiet park. She heard her name called, and wheeled about in time to catch Lou rushing into her arms.

After the first embrace they drew their heads back as serpents do, ready to attack or to charm, with a thousand questions trembling on their swift tongues. And then Nancy noticed that prosperity had descended upon Lou, manifesting itself in costly furs, flashing gems, and creations of the tailor's art.

'You little fool!' cried Lou, loudly and affectionately. 'I see you are still working in that store, and as shabby as ever. And how about that big catch you were going to make – nothing doing yet, I suppose?

And then Lou looked, and saw that something better than prosperity had descended upon Nancy – something that shone brighter than gems in her eyes and redder than a rose in her cheeks, and that danced like electricity anxious to be loosed from the tip of her tongue.

'Yes, I'm still in the store,' said Nancy, 'but I'm going to leave it next week. I've made my catch – the biggest catch in the world. You won't mind now, Lou, will you? – I'm going to be married to Dan – to Dan! – he's my Dan now – why, Lou!'

Around the corner of the park strolled one of those new-crop, smooth-faced young policemen that are making the force more endurable – at least to the eye. He saw a woman with an expensive fur coat and diamond-ringed hands crouching down against the iron fence of the park, sobbing turbulently, while a slender, plainly dressed working girl leaned close, trying to console her. But the Gibsonian cop, being of the new order, passed on, pretending not to notice, for he was wise enough to know that these matters are beyond help, so far as the power he represents is concerned, though he rap the pavement with his night-stick till the sound goes up to the farthermost stars.

XXII

The Pendulum

'EIGHTY-FIRST STREET — let 'em out, please,' yelled the shepherd in blue.

A flock of citizen sheep scrambled out and another flock scrambled aboard. Ding-ding! The cattle cars of the Manhattan Elevated rattled away, and John Perkins drifted down the stairway of the station with the released flock.

John walked slowly toward his flat. Slowly, because in the lexicon of his daily life there was no such word as 'perhaps.' There are no surprises awaiting a man who has been married two years and lives in a flat. As he walked John Perkins prophesied to himself with gloomy and downtrodden cynicism the foregone conclusions of the monotonous day.

Katy would meet him at the door with a kiss flavoured with cold cream and butterscotch. He would remove his coat, sit upon a macadamized lounge and read, in the evening paper, of Russians and Japs slaughtered by the deadly linotype. For dinner there would be pot roast; a salad flavoured with a dressing warranted not to crack or injure the leather, stewed rhubarb and the bottle of strawberry marmalade blushing at the certificate of chemical purity on its label. After dinner Katy would show him the new patch in her crazy quilt that the iceman had cut for her off the end of his four-in-hand. At half-past seven they would spread newspapers over the furniture to catch the pieces of plastering that fell when the fat man in the flat overhead began to take his physical culture exercises. Exactly at eight Hickey & Mooney, of the vaudeville team (unbooked) in the flat across the hall would yield to the gentle influence of delirium tremens and begin to overturn chairs under the delusion that Hammerstein was pursuing them with a five-hundred-dollar-a-week contract. Then the gent at the window across the air-shaft would get out his flute; the nightly gas leak would steal forth to frolic in the high-ways; the dumb-waiter would slip off its trolley; the janitor would drive Mrs. Zanowitski's five children once more across the Yalu, the lady with the champagne shoes and the Skye terrier would trip downstairs and paste her Thursday name over her bell and letter-box – and the evening routine of the Frogmore flats would be under way.

John Perkins knew these things would happen. And he knew that at a quarter-past eight he would summon his nerve and reach for his hat, and that his wife would deliver this speech in a querulous tone:

'Now, where are you going, I'd like to know, John Perkins?

'Thought I'd drop up to McCloskey's,' he would answer, 'and play a game or two of pool with the fellows.'

Of late such had been John Perkins' habit. At ten or eleven he would return. Sometimes Katy would be asleep; sometimes wait-ing up; ready to melt in the crucible of her ire a little more gold plating from the wrought-steel chains of matrimony. For these things Cupid will have to answer when he stands at the bar of justice with his victims from the Frogmore flats.

To-night John Perkins encountered a tremendous upheaval of the commonplace when he reached his door. No Katy was there with her affectionate, confectionate kiss. The three rooms seemed in portentous disorder. All about lay her things in confusion. Shoes in the middle of the floor, curling tongs, hair bows, kimonos, powder-box, jumbled together on dresser and chairs – this was not Katy's way. With a sinking heart John saw the comb with a curling cloud of her brown hair among its teeth. Some unusual hurry and perturbation must have possessed her, for she always carefully placed these combings in the little blue base on the mantel, to be some day formed into the coveted feminine 'rat.'

Hanging conspicuously to the gas jet by a string was a folded paper. John seized it. It was a note from his wife running thus:

DEAR JOHN, –

'I just had a telegram saying mother is very sick. I am going to take the 4.30 train. Brother Sam is going to meet me at the depot there. There is cold mutton in the ice-box. I hope it isn't her quinsy again. Pay the milkman 60 cents. She had it bad last spring. Don't forget to write to the company about the gas meter, and your good socks are in the top drawer. I will write to-morrow.

'Hastily,

'KATY.'

Never during their two years of matrimony had he and Katy been separated for a night. John read the note over and over in a dumbfounded way. Here was a break in a routine that had never varied, and it left him dazed.

There on the back of a chair hung, pathetically empty and formless, the red wrapper with black dots that she always wore while getting the meals. Her week-day clothes had been tossed here and there in her haste. A little paper bag of her favourite butter-scotch lay with its string yet unwound. A daily paper sprawled on the floor, gaping rectangularly where a railroad time-table had been clipped from it. Everything in the room spoke of a loss, of an essence gone, of its soul and life departed. John Perkins stood among the dead remains with a queer feeling of desolation in his heart.

He began to set the rooms tidy as well as he could. When he touched her clothes a thrill of something like terror went through him. He had never thought what existence would be without Katy. She had become so thoroughly annealed into his life that she was like the air he breathed – necessary but scarcely noticed. Now, without warning, she was gone, vanished, as completely absent as if she had never existed. Of course it would be only for a few days, or at most a week or two, but it seemed to him as if the very hand of death had pointed a finger at his secure and uneventful home.

John dragged the cold mutton from the ice-box, made coffee and sat down to a lonely meal face to face with the strawberry marmalade's shameless certificate of purity. Bright among withdrawn blessings now appeared to him the ghosts of pot roast and the salad with tan polish dressing. His home was dismantled. A quinsied mother-in-law had knocked his lares and penates sky-high. After his solitary meal John sat at a front window.

He did not care to smoke. Outside the city roared to him to come join in its dance of folly and pleasure. The night was his. He might go forth unquestioned and thrum the strings of jollity as free as any gay bachelor there. He might carouse and wander and have his fling until dawn if he liked; and there would be no wrathful Katy waiting for him, bearing the chalice that held the dregs of his joy. He might play pool at McCloskey's with his roistering friends until Aurora dimmed the electric bulbs if he chose. The hymeneal strings that had curbed him always when the Frogmore flats had palled upon him were loosened. Katy was gone.

John Perkins was not accustomed to analysing his emotions. But as he sat in his Katy-bereft 10 x 12 parlour he hit unerringly upon the keynote of his discomfort. He knew now that Katy was necessary to his happiness. His feeling for her, lulled into unconsciousness by the dull round of domesticity, had been sharply stirred by the loss of her presence. Has it not been dinned into us by proverb and sermon and fable that we never prize the music till the sweet voiced bird has flown – or in other no less florid and true utterances?

'I'm a double-dyed dub,' mused John Perkins, 'the way I've been treating Katy. Off every night playing pool and bumming with the boys instead of staying home with her. The poor girl here all alone with nothing to amuse her, and me acting that way! John Perkins, you're the worst kind of a shine. I'm going to make it up for the little girl. I'll take her out and let her see some amusement. And I'll cut out the McCloskey gang right from this minute.'

Yes, there was the city roaring outside for John Perkins to come dance in the train of Momus. And at McCloskey's the boys were knocking the balls idly into the pockets against the hour for the nightly game. But no primrose way nor clicking cue could woo the remorseful soul of Perkins, the bereft. The thing that was his, lightly held and half scorned, had been taken away from him, and he wanted it. Backward to a certain man named Adam, whom the cherubim bounced from the orchard, could Perkins, the remorseful, trace his descent.

Near the right hand of John Perkins stood a chair. On the back of it stood Katy's blue shirtwaist. It still retained something of her contour. Midway of the sleeves were fine, individual wrinkles made by the movements of her arms in working for his comfort and pleasure. A delicate but impelling odour of bluebells came from it. John took it and looked long and soberly at the unresponsive grenadine. Katy had never been unresponsive. Tears – yes, tears – came into John Perkins' eyes. When she came back things would be different. He would make up for all his neglect. What was life without her?

The door opened. Katy walked in carrying a little hand satchel. John stared at her stupidly.

'My! I'm glad to get back,' said Katy. 'Ma wasn't sick to amount to anything. Sam was at the depot, and said she just had a little spell, and got all right soon after they telegraphed. So I took the next train back. I'm just dying for a cup of coffee."

Nobody heard the click and the rattle of the cogwheels as the third-floor front of the Frogmore flats buzzed its machinery back into the Order of Things. A band slipped, a spring was touched, the gear was adjusted and the wheels revolved in their old orbits.

John Perkins looked at the clock. It was 8.15. He reached for his hat and walked to the door.

'Now, where are you going, I'd like to know, John Perkins?' asked Katy, in a querulous tone.

'Thought I'd drop up to McCloskey's,' said John, 'and play a game or two of pool with the fellows.'

XXIII

The Assessor of Success

HASTINGS BEAUCHAMP MORLEY sauntered across Union Square with a pitying look at the hundreds that lolled upon the park benches. They were a motley lot, he thought; the men with stolid, animal, unshaven faces; the women wriggling and self-conscious, twining and untwining their feet that hung four inches above the gravelled walks.

Were I Mr. Carnegie or Mr. Rockefeller I would put a few millions in my inside pocket and make an appointment with all the Park Commissioners (around the corner, if necessary), and arrange for benches in all the parks of the world low enough for women to sit upon, and rest their feet upon the ground. After that I might furnish libraries to towns that would pay for 'em, or build sanatoriums for crank professors, and call 'em colleges, if I wanted to.

Women's rights societies have been labouring for many years after equality with man. With what result? When they sit on a bench they must twist their ankles together and uncomfortably swing their highest French heels clear of earthly support. Begin at the bottom, ladies. Get your feet on the ground, and then rise to theories of mental equality.

Hastings Beauchamp Morley was carefully and neatly dressed. That was the result of an instinct due to his birth and breeding. It is denied us to look farther into a man's bosom than the starch on his shirt front; so it is left to us only to recount his walks and conversation.

Morley had not a cent in his pockets; but he smiled pityingly at a hundred grimy, unfortunate ones who had no more, and who would have no more when the sun's first rays yellowed the tall paper-cutter building on the west side of the square. But Morley would have enough by then. Sundown had seen his pockets empty before; but sunrise had always seen them lined.

First he went to the house of a clergyman off Madison Avenue and presented a forged letter of introduction that holily purported to issue from a pastorate in Indiana. This netted him $5 when backed up by a realistic romance of a delayed remittance.

On the sidewalk, twenty steps from the clergyman's door, a pale-faced, fat man huskily enveloped him with a raised, red fist, and the voice of a bell buoy, demanding payment of an old score.

'Why, Bergman, man,' sang Morley dulcetly, 'is this you? I was just on my way up to your place to settle up. That remittance from my aunt arrived only this morning. Wrong address was the trouble. Come up to the corner and I'll square up. Glad to see you. Saves me a walk.'

Four drinks placated the emotional Bergman. There was an air about Morley when he was backed by money in hand that would have stayed off a call loan at Rothschilds'. When he was penniless his bluff was pitched half a tone lower, but few are competent to detect the difference in the notes.

'You gum to mine blace und bay me to-morrow, Mr. Morley,' said Bergman. 'Oxcuse me dat I dun you on der street. But I haf not seen you in dree mont'. Pros't!'

Morley walked away with a crooked smile on his pale, smooth face. The credulous, drink-softened German amused him. He would have to avoid Twenty-ninth Street in the future. He had not been aware that Bergman ever went home by that route.

At the door of a darkened house two squares to the north Morley knocked with a peculiar sequence of raps. The door opened to the length of a six-inch chain, and the pompous, important black face of an African guardian imposed itself in the opening. Morley was admitted.

In a third-story room, in an atmosphere opaque with smoke, he hung for ten minutes above a roulette wheel. Then downstairs he crept, and was out-sped by the important negro, jingling in his pocket the forty cents in silver that remained to him of his five dollar capital. At the corner he lingered, undecided.

Across the street was a drug store well lighted; sending forth gleams from the German silver and crystal of its soda fountain and glasses. Along came a youngster of five, headed for the dispensary, stepping high with the consequence of a big errand, possibly one to which his advancing age had earned him promotion. In his hand he clutched something tightly, publicly, proudly, conspicuously.

Morley stopped him with his winning smile and soft speech.

'Me?' said the youngster. 'I'm doin' to the drug 'tore for mamma. She dave me a dollar to buy a bottle of med'cin.'

'Now, now, now!' said Morley. 'Such a big man you are to be doing errands for mamma. I must go along with my little man to see that the cars don't run over him. And on the way we'll have some chocolates. Or would he rather have lemon drops?'

Morley entered the drug store leading the child by the hand. He presented the prescription that had been wrapped around the money.

On his face was a smile, predatory, parental, politic, profound.

'Aqua pura, one pint,' said he to the druggist. 'Sodium chloride, ten grains. Fiat solution. And don't try to skin me, because I know all about the number of gallons of H_2O in the Croton reservoir, and I always use the other ingredient on my potatoes.'

'Fifteen cents,' said the druggist, with a wink, after he had compounded the order. 'I see you understand pharmacy. A dollar is the regular price.

'To gulls,' said Morley smilingly.

He settled the wrapped bottle carefully in the child's arms and escorted him to the corner. In his own pocket he dropped the eighty-five cents accruing to him by virtue of his chemical knowledge.

'Look out for the cars, sonny,' he said cheerfully, to his small victim.

Two street-cars suddenly swooped in opposite directions upon the youngster. Morley dashed between them and pinned the infantile messenger by the neck, holding him in safety. Then, from the corner of his street he sent him on his way, swindled, happy, and sticky with vile, cheap candy from the Italian's fruit stand.

Morley went to a restaurant and ordered a sirloin and a pint of inexpensive Chateau Breuille. He laughed noiselessly, but so genuinely that the waiter ventured to premise that good news had come his way.

'Why, no,' said Morley, who seldom held conversation with anyone. 'It is not that. It is something else that amuses me. Do you know what three divisions of people are easiest to overreach in transactions of all kinds?'

'Sure,' said the waiter, calculating the size of the tip promised by the careful knot of Morley's tie; 'there's the buyers from the dry goods stores in the South during August, and honeymooners from Staten Island, and —'

'Wrong!' said Morley, chuckling happily. 'The answer is just – men, women and children. The world – well, say New York and as far as summer boarders can swim out from Long Island – it is full of greenhorns. Two minutes longer on the broiler would have made this steak fit to be eaten by a gentleman, François.'

'If yez t'inks it's on de bum,' said the waiter, 'Oi'll –'

Morley lifted his hand in protest – slightly martyred protest.

'It will do,' he said magnanimously. 'And now, green Chartreuse, frappe and a demitasse.'

Morley went out leisurely and stood on a corner where two tradeful arteries of the city cross. With a solitary dime in his pocket he stood on the kerb watching with confident, cynical, smiling eyes the tides of people that flowed past him. Into that stream he must cast his net and draw fish for his further sustenance and need. Good Izaak Walton had not the half of his self-reliance and bait-lore.

A joyful party of four – two women and two men – fell upon him with cries of delight. There was a dinner party on – where had he been for a fortnight past? – what luck to thus run upon him! They surrounded and engulfed him – he must join them – tra la la – and the rest.

One, with a white hat-plume curving to the shoulder, touched his sleeve, and cast at the others a triumphant look that said: 'See what I can do with him!' and added her queen's command to the invitations.

'I leave you to imagine,' said Morley, pathetically, 'how it desolates me to forgo the pleasure. But my friend Carruthers, of the New York Yacht Club, is to pick me up here in his motor-car at eight.'

The white plume tossed, and the quartette danced like midgets around an arc light down the frolicsome way.

Morley stood, turning over and over the dime in his pocket and laughing gleefully to himself.

' "Front," ' he chanted under his breath; ' "front" does it. It is trumps in the game. How they take it in! Men, women and children – forgeries, water-and-salt lies – how they all take it in!'

An old man with an ill-fitting suit, a straggling, grey beard and a corpulent umbrella hopped from the conglomeration of cabs and street-cars to the sidewalk at Morley's side.

'Stranger,' said he, 'excuse me for troubling you, but do you know anybody in this here town named Solomon Smothers? He's my son, and I've come down from Ellenville to visit him. Be darned if I know what I done with his street and number.'

'I do not, sir,' said Morley, half closing his eyes to veil the joy in them. 'You had better apply to the police.'

'The police!' said the old man. 'I ain't done nothin' to call in the police about. I just come down to see Ben. He lives in a five-story house, he writes me. If you know anybody by that name and could –'

'I told you I did not,' said Morley coldly. 'I know no one by the name of Smithers, and I advise you to –'

'Smothers, not Smithers,' interrupted the old man hopefully. 'A heavy-sot man, sandy complected, about twenty-nine, two front teeth out, about five foot –'

'Oh, "Smothers"!' exclaimed Morley. 'Sol Smothers? Why, he lives in the next house to me. I thought you said "Smithers." '

Morley looked at his watch. You must have a watch. You can do it for a dollar. Better go hungry than forgo a gunmetal or the ninety-eight-cent one that the railroads – according to these watchmakers – are run by.

'The Bishop of Long Island,' said Morley, 'was to meet me here at eight to dine with me at the Kingfishers' Club. But I can't leave the father of my friend Sol Smothers alone on the street. By St. Swithin, Mr. Smothers, we Wall Street men have to work! Tired is no name for it! I was about to step across to the other corner and have a glass of ginger ale with a dash of sherry when you approached me. You must let me take you to Sol's house, Mr. Smothers. But before we take the car I hope you will join me in –'

An hour later Morley seated himself on the end of a quiet bench in Madison Square, with a twenty-five-cent cigar between his lips and $140 in deeply creased bills in his inside pocket. Content, light-hearted, ironical, keenly philosophic, he watched the moon drifting in and out amidst a maze of flying clouds. An old, ragged man with a low-bowed head sat at the other end of the bench.

Presently the old man stirred and looked at his bench compan-ion. In Morley's appearance he seemed to recognize something superior to the usual nightly occupants of the benches.

'Kind sir,' he whined, 'if you could spare a dime or even a few pennies to one who –'

Morley cut short his stereotyped appeal by throwing him a dollar.

'God bless you!' said the old man. 'I've been trying to find work for –'

'Work!' echoed Morley with his ringing laugh. 'You are a fool, my friend. The world is a rock to you, no doubt; but you must be an Aaron and smite it with your rod. Then things better than water will gush out of it for you. That is what the world is for. It gives to me whatever I want from it.'

'God has blessed you,' said the old man. 'It is only work that I have known. And now I can get no more.'

'I must go home,' said Morley, rising and buttoning his coat. 'I stopped here only for a smoke. I hope you may find work.'

'May your kindness be rewarded this night,' said the old man.

'Oh,' said Morley, 'you have your wish already. I am satisfied. I think good luck follows me like a dog. I am for yonder bright hotel across the square for the night. And what a moon that is lighting up the city to-night. I think no one enjoys the moonlight and such little things as I do. Well, a good night to you.'

Morley walked to the corner where he would cross to his hotel. He blew slow streamers of smoke from his cigar heavenward. A policeman, passing, saluted to his benign nod. What a fine moon it was.

The clock struck nine as a girl just entering womanhood stopped on the corner waiting for the approaching car. She was hurrying as if homeward from employment or delay. Her eyes were clear and pure, she was dressed in simple white, she looked eagerly for the car and neither to the right nor the left.

Morley knew her. Eight years before he had sat on the same bench with her at school. There had been no sentiment between them – nothing but the friendship of innocent days.

But he turned down the side-street to a quiet spot and laid his suddenly burning face against the cool iron of a lamp-post, and said dully:

'God! I wish I could die.'

XXIV

The Buyer from Cactus City

IT IS WELL THAT HAY FEVER and colds do not obtain in the health-ful vicinity of Cactus City, Texas, for the dry goods emporium of Navarro & Platt, situated there, is not to be sneezed at.

Twenty thousand people in Cactus City scatter their silver coin with liberal hands for the things that their hearts desire. The bulk of this semiprecious metal goes to Navarro & Platt. Their huge brick building covers enough ground to graze a dozen head of sheep. You can buy of them a rattlesnake-skin necktie, an automobile, or an eighty-five-dollar, latest style, ladies' tan coat in twenty different shades. Navarro & Platt first introduced pennies west of the Colorado River. They had been ranchmen with business heads, who saw that the world did not necessarily have to cease its revolutions after free grass went out.

Every spring, Navarro, senior partner, fifty-five, half Spanish, cosmopolitan, able, polished, had 'gone on' to New York to buy goods. This year he shied at taking up the long trail. He was undoubtedly growing older; and he looked at his watch several times a day before the hour came for his siesta.

'John,' he said, to his junior partner, 'you shall go on this year to buy the goods.'

Platt looked tired.

'I'm told,' said he, 'that New York is a plumb dead town; but I'll go. I can take a whirl in San Antone for a few days on my way and have some fun.

Two weeks later a man in a Texas full dresssuit – black frock-coat, broad-brimmed, soft, white hat, and lay-down collar 3-4 inch high, with black, wrought-iron necktie – entered the wholesale cloak and suit establishment of Zizzbaum & Son, on Lower Broadway.

Old Zizzbaum had the eye of an osprey, the memory of an elephant and a mind that unfolded from him in three movements like the puzzle of the carpenter's rule. He rolled to the front like a brunette polar bear, and shook Platt's hand.

'And how is the good Mr. Navarro in Texas?' he said. 'The trip was too long for him this year, so? We welcome Mr. Platt instead.'

'A bull's eye,' said Platt, 'and I'd give forty acres of unirrigated Pecos County land to know how you did it.'

'I knew,' grinned Zizzbaum, 'just as I know that the rainfall in El Paso for the year was 28.5 inches, or an increase of 15 inches, and that therefore Navarro & Platt will buy a $15,000 stock of suits this spring instead of $10,000, as in a dry year. But that will be to-morrow. There is first a cigar in my private office that will remove from your mouth the taste of the ones you smuggle across the Rio Grande and like – because they are smuggled.'

It was late in the afternoon and business for the day had ended, Zizzbaum left Platt with a half-smoked cigar and came out of the private office to Son, who was arranging his diamond scarfpin before a mirror, ready to leave.

'Abey,' he said, 'you will have to take Mr. Platt around to-night

and show him things. They are customers for ten years. Mr.
Navarro and I we played chess every moment of spare time when
he came. That is good, but Mr. Platt is a young man and this is his
first visit to New York. He should amuse easily.'

'All right,' said Abey, screwing the guard tightly on his pin. 'I'll
take him on. After he's seen the Flatiron and the head waiter at
the Hotel Astor and heard the phonograph play "Under the old
Apple Tree" it'll be half-past ten, and Mr. Texas will be ready to
roll up in his blanket. I've got a supper engagement at 11.30, but
he'll be all to the Mrs. Winslow before then.'

The next morning at ten Platt walked into the store ready to do
business. He had a bunch of hyacinths pinned on his lapel.
Zizzbaum himself waited on him. Navarro & Platt were good customers, and never failed to take their discount for cash.

'And what did you think of our little town?' asked Zizzbaum,
with the fatuous smile of the Manhattanite.

'I shouldn't care to live in it,' said the Texan. 'Your son and I
knocked around quite a little last night. You've got good water,
but Cactus City is better lit up.'

'We've got a few lights on Broadway, don't you think, Mr.
Platt?'

'And a good many shadows,' said Platt. 'I think I like your
horses best. I haven't seen a crowbait since I've been in town.'

Zizzbaum led him upstairs to show the samples of suits

'Ask Miss Asher to come,' he said to a clerk.

Miss Asher came, and Platt, of Navarro & Platt, felt for the first
time the wonderful bright light of romance and glory descend
upon him. He stood still as a granite cliff above the canon of the
Colorado, with his wide-open eyes fixed upon her. She noticed his
look and flushed a little, which was contrary to her custom.

Miss Asher was the crack model of Zizzbaum & Son. She was of
the blonde type known as 'medium,' and her measurements even
went the required 38-25-42 standard a little better. She had been
at Zizzbaum's two years, and knew her business. Her eye was
bright, but cool; and had she chosen to match her gaze against the
optic of the famed basilisk, that fabulous monster's gaze would
have wavered and softened first. Incidentally, she knew buyers.

'Now, Mr. Platt,' said Zizzbaum, 'I want you to see these
princesse gowns in the light shades. They will be the thing in your
climate. This first, if you please, Miss Asher.'

Swiftly in and out of the dressing-room the prize model flew,
each time wearing a new costume and looking more stunning with

every change. She posed with absolute self-possession before the stricken buyer, who stood, tongue-tied and motionless, while Zizzbaum orated oilily of the styles. On the model's face was her faint, impersonal professional smile that seemed to cover something like weariness or contempt.

When the display was over Platt seemed to hesitate. Zizzbaum was a little anxious, thinking that his customer might be inclined to try elsewhere. But Platt was only looking over in his mind the best building sites in Cactus City, trying to select one on which to build a house for his wife-to-be — who was just then in the dressing-room taking off an evening gown of lavender and tulle.

'Take your time, Mr. Platt,' said Zizzbaum. 'Think it over to-night. You won't find anybody else meet our prices on goods like these. I'm afraid you're having a dull time in New York, Mr. Platt. A young man like you — of course, you miss the society of the ladies. Wouldn't you like a nice young lady to take out to dinner this evening? Miss Asher, now, is a very nice young lady; she will make it agreeable for you.'

'Why, she doesn't know me,' said Platt wonderingly. 'She doesn't know anything about me. Would she go? I'm not acquainted with her.'

'Would she go?' repeated Zizzbaum, with uplifted eyebrows. 'Sure, she would go. I will introduce you, Sure, she would go.'

He called Miss Asher loudly.

She came, calm and slightly contemptuous, in her white shirt waist and plain black shirt.

'Mr. Platt would like the pleasure of your company to dinner this evening,' said Zizzbaum, walking away.

'Sure,' said Miss Asher, looking at the ceiling. 'I'd be much pleased. Nine-eleven West Twentieth Street. What time?'

'Say seven o'clock.'

'All right, but please don't come ahead of time. I room with a school-teacher, and she doesn't allow any gentlemen to call in the room. There isn't any parlour, so you'll have to wait in the hall. I'll be ready.'

At half-past seven Platt and Miss Asher sat at a table in a Broadway restaurant. She was dressed in a plain filmy black. Platt didn't know that it was all a part of her day's work.

With the unobtrusive aid of a good waiter he managed to order a respectable dinner, minus the usual Broadway preliminaries.

Miss Asher flashed upon him a dazzling smile.

'Mayn't I have something to drink?' she asked.

'Why, certainly,' said Platt. 'Anything you want.'

'A dry Martini,' she said to the waiter.

When it was brought and set before her Platt reached over and took it away.

'What is this?' he asked.

'A cocktail, of course.'

'I thought it was some kind of tea you ordered. This is liquor. You can't drink this. What is your first name?'

'To my intimate friends,' said Miss Asher freezingly, 'it is "Helen."'

'Listen, Helen,' said Platt, leaning over the table. 'For many years every time the spring flowers blossomed out on the prairies I got to thinking of somebody that I'd never seen or heard of. I knew it was you the minute I saw you yesterday. I'm going back home to-morrow and you're going with me. I know it, for I saw it in your eyes when you first looked at me. You needn't kick, for you've got to fall into line. Here's a little trick I picked out for you on my way over.'

He flicked a two-carat diamond solitaire ring across the table. Miss Asher flipped it back to him with her fork.

'Don't get fresh,' she said severely.

'I'm worth a hundred thousand dollars,' said Platt. 'I'll build you the finest house in West Texas.'

'You can't buy me, Mr. Buyer,' said Miss Asher, 'if you had a hundred million. I didn't think I'd have to call you down. You didn't look like the others to me at first, but I see you're all alike.'

'All who?' asked Platt.

'All you buyers. You think because we girls have to go out to dinner with you or lose our jobs that you're privileged to say what you please. Well, forget it. I thought you were different from the others, but I see I was mistaken.'

Platt struck his fingers on the table with a gesture of sudden, illuminating satisfaction.

'I've got it!' he exclaimed, almost hilariously – 'the Nicholson place, over on the north side. There's a big grove of live oaks and a natural lake. The old house can be pulled down and the new one set farther back.'

'Put out your pipe,' said Miss Asher. 'I'm sorry to wake you up, but you fellows might as well get wise, once for all, to where you stand. I'm supposed to go to dinner with you and help jolly you along so you'll trade with old Zizzy, but don't expect to find me in any of the suits you buy.'

'Do you mean to tell me,' said Platt, 'that you go out this way with customers, and they all – they all talk to you like I have?'

'They all make plays,' said Miss Asher. 'But I must say that you've got 'em beat in one respect. They generally talk diamonds while you've actually dug one up.'

'How long have you been working, Helen?'

'Got my name pat, haven't you? I've been supporting myself for eight years. I was a cash girl, and a wrapper, and then a shop-girl until I was grown, and then I got to be a suit model. Mr. Texas Man, don't you think a little wine would make this dinner a little less dry?'

'You're not going to drink wine any more, dear. It's awful to think how – I'll come to the store to-morrow and get you. I want you to pick out an automobile before we leave. That's all we need to buy here.'

'Oh, cut that out. If you knew how sick I am of hearing such talk.'

After the dinner they walked down Broadway and came upon Diana's little wooded park. The trees caught Platt's eye at once, and he must turn along under the winding walk beneath them. The lights shone upon two bright tears in the model's eyes.

'I don't like that,' said Platt. 'What's the matter?'

'Don't you mind,' said Miss Asher. 'Well, it's because – well, I didn't think you were that kind when I first saw you. But you are all alike. And now will you take me home, or will I have to call a cop?'

Platt took her to the door of her boarding-house. They stood for a minute in the vestibule. She looked at him with such scorn in her eyes that even his heart of oak began to waver. His arm was half-way around her waist, when she struck him a stinging blow on the face with her open hand.

As he stepped back a ring fell from somewhere and bounded on the tiled floor. Platt groped for it and found it.

'Now, take your useless diamond and go, Mr. Buyer,' she said.

'This was the other one – the wedding ring,' said the Texan, holding the smooth, gold band on the palm of his hand.

Miss Asher's eyes blazed upon him in the half darkness.

'Was that what you meant? – did you –'

Somebody opened the door from inside the house.

'Good night,' said Platt. 'I'll see you at the store to-morrow.'

Miss Asher ran up to her room and shook the school-teacher until she sat up in bed ready to scream 'Fire!'

'Where is it?' she cried.

'That's what I want to know,' said the model. 'You've studied geography, Emma, and you ought to know. Where is a town called Cac – Cac – Carac – Caracas City, I think they called it?'

'How dare you wake me up for that?' said the school-teacher. 'Caracas is in Venezuela, of course.'

'What's it like?'

'Why, it's principally earthquakes and negroes and monkeys and malarial fever and volcanoes.'

'I don't care,' said Miss Asher blithely; 'I'm going there to-morrow.'

XXV

The Badge of Policeman O'Roon

IT CANNOT BE DENIED that men and women have looked upon one another for the first time and become instantly enamoured. It is a risky process, this love at first sight, before she has seen him in Bradstreet or he has seen her in curl papers. But these things do happen; and one instance must form a theme for this story – though not, thank Heaven, to the over-shadowing of more vital and important subjects, such as drink, policemen, horses, and earldoms.

During a certain war a troop calling itself the Gentle Riders rode into history and one or two ambuscades. The Gentle Riders were recruited from the aristocracy of the wild men of the West, and the wild men of the aristocracy of the East. In khaki there is little telling them one from another, so they became good friends and comrades all around.

Ellsworth Remsen, whose old Knickerbocker descent atoned for his modest rating at only ten millions, ate his canned beef gaily by the camp-fires of the Gentle Riders. The war was a great lark to him, so that he scarcely regretted polo and planked shad.

One of the troopers was a well-set-up, affable, cool young man, who called himself O'Roon. To this young man Remsen took an especial liking. The two rode side by side during the famous mooted up-hill charge that was disputed so hotly at the time by the Spaniards and afterwards by the Democrats.

After the war Remsen came back to his polo and shad. One day a well-set-up, affable, cool young man disturbed him at his club, and he and O'Roon were soon pounding each other and exchanging opprobious epithets after the manner of long-lost friends. O'Roon looked seedy and out of luck and perfectly contented. But it seemed that his content was only apparent.

'Get me a job, Remsen,' he said. 'I've just handed a barber my last shilling.'

'No trouble at all,' said Remsen. 'I know a lot of men who have banks and stores and things down-town. Any particular line you fancy?'

'Yes,' said O'Roon, with a look of interest. 'I took a walk in your Central Park this morning. I'd like to be one of those bobbies on horseback. That would be about the ticket. Besides, it's the only thing I could do. I can ride a little and the fresh air suits me. Think you could land that for me?'

Remsen was sure that he could. And in a very short time he did. And they who were not above looking at mounted policemen might have seen a well-set-up, affable, cool young man on a prancing chestnut steed attending to his duties along the driveways of the park.

And now at the extreme risk of wearying old gentlemen who carry leather fob chains, and elder ladies who – but no! grandmother herself yet thrills at foolish, immortal Romeo – there must be a hint of love at first sight.

It came just as Remsen was strolling into Fifth Avenue from his club a few doors away.

A motor-car was creeping along foot by foot impeded by a freshet of vehicles that filled the street. In the car was a chauffeur and an old gentleman with snowy side-whiskers and a Scotch plaid cap which could not be worn while automobiling except by a personage. Not even a wine agent would dare to do it. But these two were of no consequence – except, perhaps, for the guiding of the machine and the paying for it. At the old gentleman's side sat a young lady more beautiful than pomegranate blossoms, more exquisite than the first quarter moon viewed at twilight through the tops of oleanders. Remsen saw her and knew his fate. He could have flung himself under the very wheels that conveyed her, but he knew that would be the last means of attracting the attention of those who ride in motor-cars. Slowly the auto passed, and, if we place the poets above the autoists, carried the heart of Remsen with it. Here was a large city of millions and many women who at a certain distance appear to resemble pomegranate blossoms. Yet he hoped to see her again; for each one fancies that his romance has its own tutelary guardian and divinity.

Luckily for Remsen's peace of mind there came a diversion in the guise of a reunion of the Gentle Riders of the city. There were not many of them – perhaps a score – and there was wassail, and things to eat, and speeches and the Spaniard was bearded again in recapitulation. And when daylight threatened them the survivors prepared to depart. But some remained upon the battlefield. One of these was Trooper O'Roon, who was not seasoned to potent liquids. His legs declined to fulfil the obligations they had sworn to the police department.

'I'm stewed, Remsen,' said O'Roon to his friend. 'Why do they build hotels that go round and round like catherine wheels? They'll take away my shield and break me. I can think and talk con-con-consec-sec-secutively, but I s-s-s-stammer with my feet. I've got to go on duty in three hours. The jig is up, Remsen. The jig is up, I tell you.'

'Look at me,' said Remsen, who was his smiling self, pointing to his own face; 'whom do you see here?'

'Goo' fellow,' said O'Roon dizzily. 'Goo' old Remsen.'

'Not so,' said Remsen. 'You see Mounted Policeman O'Roon. Look at your face – no; you can't do that without a glass – but look at mine, and think of yours. How much alike are we? As two French table d'hôte dinners. With your badge, on your horse, in your uniform, will I charm nursemaids and prevent the grass from growing under people's feet in the Park this day. I will save your badge and your honour, besides having the jolliest lark I've been blessed with since we licked Spain.'

Promptly on time the counterfeit presentment of Mounted Policeman O'Roon single-footed into the Park on his chestnut steed. In a uniform two men who are unlike will look like; two who somewhat resemble each other in feature and figure will appear as twin brothers. So Remsen trotted down the bridle-paths, enjoying himself hugely, so few real pleasures do ten-millionaires have.

Along the driveway in the early morning spun a victoria drawn by a pair of fiery bays. There was something foreign about the affair, for the Park is rarely used in the morning except by unimportant people who love to be healthy, poor and wise. In the vehicle sat an old gentleman with snowy side-whiskers and Scotch plaid cap which could not be worth while driving except by a personage. At his side sat the lady of Remsen's heart – the lady who looked like pomegranate blossoms and the gibbous moon.

Remsen met them coming. At the instant of their passing her

eyes looked into his, and but for the ever-coward heart of a true lover he could have sworn that she flushed a faint pink. He trotted on for twenty yards, and then wheeled his horse at the sound of runaway hoofs. The bays had bolted.

Remsen sent his chestnut after the victoria like a shot. There was work cut out for the impersonator of Policeman O'Roon. The chestnut ranged alongside the off bay thirty seconds after the chase began, rolled his eye back at Remsen, and said in the only manner open to policemen's horses:

'Well, you duffer, are you going to do your share? You're not O'Roon, but it seems to me if you'd lean to the right you could reach the reins of the foolish, slow-running bay – ah! you're all right; O'Roon couldn't have done it more neatly!'

The runaway team was tugged to an inglorious halt by Remsen's tough muscles. The driver released his hands from the wrapped reins, jumped from his seat and stood at the heads of the team. The chestnut, approving his new rider, danced and pranced, reviling equinely the subdued bays. Remsen, lingering, was dimly conscious of a vague, impossible, unnecessary old gentleman in a Scotch cap who talked incessantly about something. And he was acutely conscious of a pair of violet eyes that would have drawn Saint Pyrites from his iron pillar – or whatever the illusion is – and of the lady's smile and look – a little frightened, but a look that, with the ever-coward heart of a true lover, he could not yet construe. They were asking his name and bestowing upon him well-bred thanks for his heroic deed, and the Scotch cap was especially babbling and insistent. But the eloquent appeal was in the eyes of the lady.

A little thrill of satisfaction ran through Remsen because he had a name to give which, without undue pride, was worthy of being spoken in high places, and a small fortune which, with due pride, he could leave at his end without disgrace.

He opened his lips to speak, and closed them again.

Who was he? Mounted Policeman O'Roon. The badge and the honour of his comrade were in his hands. If Ellesworth Remsen, ten-millionaire and Knickerbocker, had just rescued pomegranate blossoms and Scotch cap from possible death, where was Policeman O'Roon? Off his beat, exposed, disgraced, discharged. Love had come, but before that there had been something that demanded precedence – the fellowship of men on battlefields fighting an alien foe.

Remsen touched his cap, looked between the chestnut's ears, and took refuge in vernacularity.

'Don't mention it,' he said stolidly. 'We policemen are paid to do these things. It's our duty.'

And he rode away – rode away cursing *noblesse oblige*, but knowing he could never have done anything else.

At the end of the day Remsen sent the chestnut to his stable and went to O'Roon's room. The policeman was again a well-set-up, affable, cool young man who sat by the window smoking cigars.

'I wish you and the rest of the police force and all badges, horses, brass buttons and men who can't drink two glass of *brut* without getting upset were at the devil,' said Remsen feelingly.

O'Roon smiled with evident satisfaction.

'Good old Remsen,' he said affably, 'I know all about it. They trailed me down and cornered me here two hours ago. There was a little row at home, you know, and I cut sticks just to show them. I don't believe I told you that my governor was the Earl of Ardsley. Funny you should bob against them in the Park. If you damaged that horse of mine I'll never forgive you. I'm going to buy him and take him back with me. Oh yes, and I think my sister – Lady Angela, you know – wants particularly for you to come up to the hotel with me this evening. Didn't lose my badge, did you, Remsen? I've got to turn that in at Headquarters when I resign.'

XXVI

Brickdust Row

BLINKER WAS DISPLEASED. A man of less culture and poise and wealth would have sworn. But Blinker always remembered that he was a gentleman – a thing that no gentleman should do. So he merely looked bored and sardonic while he rode in a hansom to the centre of disturbance, which was the Broadway office of Lawyer Oldport, who was agent for the Blinker estate.

'I don't see,' said Blinker, 'why I should be always signing confounded papers. I am packed, and was to have left for the North Woods this morning. Now I must wait until to-morrow morning. I hate night trains. My best razors are, of course, at the bottom of some unidentifiable trunk. It is a plot to drive me to bay rum and a monologueing, thumb-handed barber. Give me a pen that doesn't scratch. I hate pens that scratch.'

'Sit down,' said double-chinned, grey Lawyer Oldport. 'The worst has not been told you. Oh, the hardships of the rich! The papers are not yet ready to sign. They will be laid before you tomorrow at eleven. You will miss another day. Twice shall the barber tweak the helpless nose of a Blinker. Be thankful that your sorrows do not embrace a hair-cut.'

'If,' said Blinker, rising, 'the act did not involve more signing of papers I would take my business out of your hands at once. Give me a cigar, please.'

If, said Lawyer Oldport, 'I had cared to see an old friend's son gulped down at one mouthful by sharks I would have ordered you to take it away long ago. Now, let's quit fooling, Alexander. Besides the grinding task of signing your name some thirty times to-morrow, I must impose upon you the consideration of a matter of business — of business, and I may say humanity or right. I spoke to you about this five years ago, but you would not listen — you were in a hurry for a coaching trip, I think. The subject has come up again. The property —'

'Oh, property!' interrupted Blinker. 'Dear Mr. Oldport, I think you mentioned to-morrow. Let's have it all at one dose to-morrow — signatures and property and snappy rubber bands and that smelly sealing-wax and all. Have luncheon with me? Well, I'll try to remember to drop in at eleven to-morrow. Morning.'

The Blinker wealth was in lands, tenements and hereditaments, as the legal phrase goes. Lawyer Oldport had once taken Alexander in his little pulmonary gasoline runabout to see the many buildings and rows of buildings that he owned in the city. For Alexander was sole heir. They had amused Blinker very much. The houses looked so incapable of producing the big sums of money that Lawyer Oldport kept piling up in banks for him to spend.

In the evening Blinker went to one of his clubs, intending to dine. Nobody was there except some old fogies playing whist who spoke to him with grave politeness and glared at him with savage contempt. Everybody was out of town. But here he was kept in like a schoolboy to write his name over and over on pieces of paper. His wounds were deep.

Blinker turned his back on the fogies, and said to the club steward who had come forward with some nonsense about cold fresh salmon roe:

'Symons, I'm going to Coney Island.' He said it as one might say: 'All's off; I'm going to jump into the river.'

The joke pleased Symons. He laughed within a sixteenth of a note of the audibility permitted by the laws governing employees.

'Certainly, sir,' he tittered. 'Of course, sir, I think I can see you at Coney, Mr. Blinker.'

Blinker got a paper and looked up the movements of Sunday steamboats. Then he found a cab at the first corner and drove to a North River pier. He stood in line, as democratic as you or I, and bought a ticket, and was trampled upon and shoved forward until, at last, he found himself on the upper deck of the boat staring brazenly at a girl who sat alone upon a camp stool. But Blinker did not intend to be brazen; the girl was so wonderfully good looking that he forgot for one minute that he was the prince incog, and behaved just as he did in society.

She was looking at him, too, and not severely. A puff of wind threatened Blinker's straw hat. He caught it warily and settled it again. The movement gave the effect of a bow. The girl nodded and smiled, and in another instant he was seated at her side. She was dressed all in white, she was paler than Blinker imagined milk-maids and girls of humble stations to be, but she was as tidy as a cherry blossom, and her steady, supremely frank grey eyes looked out from the intrepid depths of an unshadowed and untroubled soul.

'How dare you raise your hat to me?' she asked, with a smile-redeemed severity.

'I didn't,' Blinker said, but he quickly covered the mistake by extending it to 'I didn't know how to keep from it after I saw you.'

'I do not allow gentlemen to sit by me to whom I have not been introduced,' she said, with a sudden haughtiness that deceived him. He rose reluctantly, but her clear, teasing laugh brought him down to his chair again.

'I guess you weren't going far,' she declared, with beauty's magnificent self-confidence.

'Are you going to Coney Island?' asked Blinker.

'Me?' She turned upon him wide-open eyes full of bantering surprise. 'Why, what a question! Can't you see that I'm riding a bicycle in the park?' Her drollery took the form of impertinence.

'And I am laying brick on a tall factory chimney,' said Blinker. 'Mayn't we see Coney together? I'm all alone and I've never been there before.'

'It depends,' said the girl, 'on how nicely you behave. I'll consider your application until we get there.'

Blinker took pains to provide against the rejection of his application. He strove to please. To adopt the metaphor of his nonsensical phrase, he laid brick upon brick on the tall chimney of his devoirs until, at length, the structure was stable and complete. The manners of the best society come around finally to simplicity; and as the girl's way was that naturally, they were on a mutual plane of communication from the beginning.

He learned that she was twenty, and her name was Florence; that she trimmed hats in a millinery shop; that she lived in a furnished room with her best chum, Ella, who was cashier in a shoe store; and that a glass of milk from the bottle on the window-sill and an egg that boils itself while you twist up your hair makes a breakfast good enough for anyone. Florence laughed when she heard 'Blinker.'

'Well,' she said. 'It certainly shows that you have imagination. It gives the "Smiths" a chance for a little rest, anyhow.'

They landed at Coney, and were dashed on the crest of a great human wave of mad pleasure-seekers into the walks and avenues of Fairyland gone into vaudeville.

With a curious eye, a critical mind and a fairly withheld judgment, Blinker considered the temples, pagodas and kiosks of popularized delights. Hoi polloi trampled, hustled and crowded him. Basket parties bumped him; sticky children tumbled, howling, under his feet, candying his clothes. Insolent youths strolling among the booths with hard-won canes under one arm and easily won girls on the other, blew defiant smoke from cheap cigars into his face. The publicity gentlemen with megaphones, each before his own stupendous attraction, roared like Niagara in his ears. Music of all kinds that could be tortured from brass, reed, hide or string, fought in the air to gain space for its vibrations against its competitors. But what held Blinker in awful fascination was the mob, the multitude, the proletariat, shrieking, struggling, hurrying, panting, hurling itself in incontinent frenzy, with unabashed abandon, into the ridiculous sham palaces of trumpery and tinsel pleasures. The vulgarity of it, its brutal overriding of all the tenets of repression and taste that were held by his caste, repelled him strongly.

In the midst of his disgust he turned and looked down at Florence by his side. She was ready with her quick smile and upturned, happy eyes, as bright and clear as the water in trout pools. The eyes were saying that they had the right to be shining and happy, for was their owner not with her (for the present) Man, her Gentleman Friend and holder of the keys to the enchanted city of fun?

Blinker did not read her look accurately, but by some miracle he suddenly saw Coney aright.

He no longer saw a mass of vulgarians seeking gross joys. He now looked clearly upon a hundred thousand true idealists. Their offences were wiped out. Counterfeit and false though the garish joys of these spangled temples were, he perceived that deep under the gilt surface they offered saving and apposite balm and satisfaction to the restless human heart. Here, at least, was the husk of Romance, the empty but shining casque of Chivalry, the breath-catching though safe-guarded dip and flight of Adventure, the magic carpet that transports you to the realms of fairyland, though its journey be through but a few poor yards of space. He no longer saw a rabble, but his brothers seeking the ideal. There was no magic of poesy here or of art; but the glamour of their imagination turned yellow calico into cloth of gold and the megaphones into the silver trumpets of joy's heralds.

Almost humbled, Blinker rolled up the shirt sleeves of his mind and joined the idealists.

'You are the lady doctor,' he said to Florence. 'How shall we go about doing this jolly conglomeration of fairy tales, incorporated?'

'We will begin there,' said the Princess, pointing to a fun pagoda on the edge of the sea, 'and we will take them all in, one by one.'

They caught the eight o'clock returning boat and sat, filled with pleasant fatigue against the rail in the bow, listening to the Italians' fiddle and harp. Blinker had thrown off all care. The North Woods seemed to him an uninhabitable wilderness. What a fuss he had made over signing his name – pooh! he could sign it a hundred times. And her name was as pretty as she was – 'Florence,' he said it to himself a great many times.

As the boat was nearing its pier in the North River a two-funnelled, drab, foreign-looking, seagoing steamer was dropping down toward the bay. The boat turned its nose in toward its slip. The steamer veered as if to seek mid-stream, and then yawed, seemed to increase its speed and struck the Coney boat on the side near the stern, cutting into it with a terrifying shock and crash.

While the six hundred passengers on the boat were mostly tumbling about the decks in a shrieking panic the captain was shouting at the steamer that it should not back off and leave the rent exposed for the water to enter. But the steamer tore its way out like a savage sawfish and cleaved its heartless way, full speed ahead.

The boat began to sink at its stern, but moved slowly toward the slip. The passengers were a frantic mob, unpleasant to behold.

Blinker held Florence tightly until the boat had righted itself. She made no sound or sign of fear. He stood on a camp stool, ripped off the slats above his head and pulled down a number of the life preservers. He began to buckle one around Florence. The rotten canvas split and the fraudulent granulated cork came pouring out in a stream. Florence caught a handful of it and laughed gleefully.

'It looks like breakfast food,' she said. 'Take it off. They're no good.'

She unbuckled it and threw it on the deck. She made Blinker sit down, and sat by his side and put her hand in his. 'What'll you bet we don't reach the pier all right?' she said, and began to hum a song.

And now the captain moved among the passengers and compelled order. The boat would undoubtedly make her slip, he said, and ordered the women and children to the bow, where they could land first. The boat, very low in the water at the stern, tried gallantly to make his promise good.

'Florence,' said Blinker, as she held him close by an arm and hand, 'I love you.'

'That's what they all say,' she replied lightly.

'I am not one of "they all," ' he persisted. 'I never knew anyone I could love before. I could pass my life with you and be happy every day. I am rich. I can make things all right for you.'

'That's what they all say,' said the girl again, weaving the words into her little, reckless song.

'Don't say that again,' said Blinker in a tone that made her look at him in frank surprise.

'Why shouldn't I say it?' she asked calmly. 'They all do.'

'Who are "they"?' he asked, jealous for the first time in his existence.

'Why, the fellows I know.'

'Do you know so many?'

'Oh, well, I'm not a wallflower,' she answered with modest complacency.

'Where do you see these – these men? At your home?'

'Of course not. I meet them just as I did you. Sometimes on the boat, sometimes in the park, sometimes on the street. I'm a pretty good judge of a man. I can tell in a minute if a fellow is one who is likely to get fresh.'

'What do you mean by "fresh"?'

'Why, try to kiss you – me, I mean.'

'Do any of them try that?" asked Blinker, clenching his teeth.

'Sure. All men do. You know that.'

'Do you allow them?'

'Some. Not many. They won't take you out anywhere unless you do.'

She turned her head and looked searchingly at Blinker. Her eyes were as innocent as a child's. There was a puzzled look in them, as though she did not understand him.

'What's wrong about my meeting fellows?' she asked, wonderingly.

'Everything,' he answered, almost savagely. 'Why don't you entertain your company in the house where you live? Is it necessary to pick up Tom, Dick and Harry on the streets?'

She kept her absolutely ingenuous eyes upon his.

'If you could see the place where I live you wouldn't ask that. I live in Brickdust Row. They call it that because there's red dust from the bricks crumbling over everything. I've lived there for more than four years. There's no place to receive company. You can't have anybody come to your room. What else is there to do? A girl has got to meet the men, hasn't she?'

'Yes,' he said hoarsely. 'A girl has got to meet a – has got to meet the men.'

'The first time one spoke to me on the street,' she continued, 'I ran home and cried all night. But you get used to it. I meet a good many nice fellows at church. I go on rainy days and stand in the vestibule until one comes up with an umbrella. I wish there was a parlour, so I could ask you to call, Mr. Blinker – are you really sure it isn't "Smith," now?'

The boat landed safely. Blinker had a confused impression of walking with the girl through quiet cross-town streets until she stopped at a corner and held out her hand.

'I live just one more block over,' she said. 'Thank you for a very pleasant afternoon.'

Blinker muttered something and plunged northward till he found a cab. A big, grey church loomed slowly at his right. Blinker shook his fist at it through the window.

'I gave you a thousand dollars last week,' he cried under his breath, 'and she meets them in your very doors. There is something wrong; there is something wrong.'

At eleven the next day Blinker signed his name thirty times with a new pen provided by Lawyer Oldport.

'Now let me go to the woods,' he said surlily.

'You are not looking well,' said Lawyer Oldport. 'The trip will do you good. But listen, if you will, to that little matter of business of which I spoke to you yesterday, and also five years ago. There are some buildings, fifteen in number, of which there are new five-year leases to be signed. Your father contemplated a change in the lease provisions, but never made it. He intended that the parlours of these houses should not be sub-let, but that the tenants should be allowed to use them for reception rooms. These houses are in the shopping district, and are mainly tenanted by young working girls. As it is they are forced to seek companionship outside. This row of red brick –'

Blinker interrupted him with a loud, discordant laugh.

'Brickdust Row for an even hundred,' he cried. 'And I own it. Have I guessed right?'

'The tenants have some such name for it,' said Lawyer Oldport.

Blinker arose and jammed his hat down to his eyes.

'Do what you please with it,' he said harshly. 'Remodel it, burn it, raze it to the ground. But, man, it's too late, I tell you. It's too late. It's too late. It's too late.'

XXVII

The Making of a New Yorker

BESIDES MANY OTHER THINGS, Raggles was a poet. He was called a tramp; but that was only an elliptical way of saying that he was a philosopher, an artist, a traveller, a naturalist and a discoverer. But most of all he was a poet. In all his life he never wrote a line of verse; he lived his poetry. His Odyssey would have been a Limerick, had it been written. But, to linger with the primary proposition, Raggles was a poet.

Raggles's speciality, had he been driven to ink and paper, would have been sonnets to the cities. He studied cities as women study their reflections in mirrors; as children study the glue and sawdust of a dislocated doll; as the men who write about wild animals study the cages in the Zoo. A city to Raggles was not merely a pile of bricks and mortar, peopled by a certain number of inhabitants; it was a thing with a soul characteristic and distinct; an individual conglomeration of life, with its own peculiar essence, flavour and feeling. Two thousand miles to the north and south, east and west, Raggles wandered in poetic fervour, taking the cities to his breast. He footed it on dusty roads, or sped magnificently in freight cars, counting time as of no account. And when he had found the heart of a' city and listened to its secret confession, he strayed on, restless, to another. Fickle Raggles! – but perhaps he had not met the civic corporation that could engage and hold his critical fancy.

Through the ancient poets we have learned that the cities are feminine. So they were to poet Raggles; and his mind carried a concrete and clear conception of the figure that symbolized and typified each one that he had wooed.

Chicago seemed to swoop down upon him with a breezy suggestion of Mrs. Partington, plumes and patchouli, and to disturb his rest with a soaring and beautiful song of future promise. But Raggles would awake to a sense of shivering cold and a haunting impression of ideals lost in a depressing aura of potato salad and fish.

Thus Chicago affected him. Perhaps there is a vagueness and inaccuracy in the description; but that is Raggles's fault. He should have recorded his sensations in magazine poems.

Pittsburg impressed him as the play of *Othello* performed in the Russian language in a railroad station by Dockstader's minstrels. A royal and generous lady this Pittsburg, though – homely, hearty, with flushed face, washing the dishes in a silk dress and white kid slippers, and bidding Raggles sit before the roaring fireplace and drink champagne with his pigs' feet and fried potatoes.

New Orleans had simply gazed down upon him from a balcony. He could see her pensive, starry eyes and catch the flutter of her fan, and that was all. Only once he came face to face with her. It was at dawn, when she was flushing the red bricks of the banquette with a pail of water. She laughed and hummed a chansonette and filled Raggles's shoes with ice-cold water. Allons!

Boston construed herself to the poetic Raggles in an erratic and singular way. It seemed to him that he had drunk cold tea and that the city was a white, cold cloth that had been bound tightly around his brow to spur him to some unknown but tremendous mental effort. And, after all, he came to shovel snow for a livelihood; and the cloth, becoming wet, tightened its knots and could not be removed.

Indefinite and unintelligible ideas, you will say, but your disapprobation should be tempered with gratitude, for these are poets' fancies – and suppose you had come upon them in verse!

One day Raggles came and laid siege to the heart of the great city of Manhattan. She was the greatest of all; and he wanted to learn her note in the scale; to taste and appraise and classify and solve and label her and arrange her with the other cities that had given him up the secret of their individuality. And here we cease to be Raggles's translator and become his chronicler.

Raggles landed from a ferry-boat one morning and walked into the core of the town with the blasé air of a cosmopolite. He was dressed with care to play the role of an 'unidentified man.' No country, race, class, clique, union, party, clan or bowling association could have claimed him. His clothing, which had been donated to him piece-meal by citizens of different height, but same number of inches around the heart, was not yet as uncomfortable to his figure as those specimens of raiment, self-measured, that are railroaded to you by transcontinental tailors with a suit-case, suspenders, silk handkerchief and pearl studs as a bonus. Without money – as a poet should be – but with the ardour of an astronomer discovering a new star in the chorus of the Milky Way, or a man who has seen ink suddenly flow from his fountain pen, Raggles wandered into the great city.

Late in the afternoon he drew out of the roar and commotion with a look of dumb terror on his countenance. He was defeated, puzzled, discomfited, frightened. Other cities had been to him as long primer to read; as country maidens quickly to fathom; as send-price-of-subscription-with-answer rebuses to solve; as oyster cocktails to swallow; but here was one as cold, glittering, serene, impossible as a four-carat diamond in a window to a lover outside fingering damply in his pocket his ribbon-counter salary.

The greetings of the other cities he had known – their home-spun kindliness, their human gamut of rough charity, friendly curses, garrulous curiosity and easily estimated credulity or indifference. This city of Manhattan gave him no clue; it was walled against him. Like a river of adamant it flowed past him in the streets. Never an eye was turned upon him; no voice spoke to him. His heart yearned for the clap of Pittsburg's sooty hand on his shoulder; for Chicago's menacing but social yawp in his ear; for the pale and eleemosynary stare through the Bostonian eyeglass – even for the precipitate but unmalicious boot-toe of Louisville or St. Louis.

On Broadway, Raggles, successful suitor of many cities, stood, bashful, like any country swain. For the first time he experienced the poignant humiliation of being ignored. And when he tried to reduce this brilliant, swiftly changing, ice-cold city to a formula he failed utterly. Poet though he was, it offered him no colour, no similes, no points of comparison, no flaw in its polished facets, no handle by which he could hold it up and view its shape and structure, as he familiarly and often contemptuously had done with other towns. The houses were interminable ramparts loopholed for defence; the people were bright but bloodless spectres passing in sinister and selfish array.

The thing that weighed heaviest on Raggles's soul and clogged his poet's fancy was the spirit of absolute egotism that seemed to saturate the people as toys are saturated with paint. Each one that he considered appeared a monster of abominable and insolent conceit. Humanity was gone from them; they were toddling idols of stone and varnish, worshipping themselves and greedy for, though oblivious of, worship from their fellow graven images. Frozen, cruel, implacable, impervious, cut to an identical pattern, they hurried on their ways like statues brought by some miracles to motion, while soul and feeling lay unaroused in the reluctant marble.

Gradually Raggles became conscious of certain types. One was an elderly gentleman with a snow-white short beard, pink unwrinkled face and stony sharp blue eyes, attired in the fashion of a gilded youth, who seemed to personify the city's wealth, ripeness and frigid unconcern. Another type was a woman, tall, beautiful, clear as a steel engraving, goddess-like, calm, clothed like the princesses of old, with eyes as coldly blue as the reflection of sunlight on a glacier. And another was a by-product of this town of marionettes — a broad, swaggering, grim, threateningly sedate fellow, with a jowl as large as a harvested wheatfield, the complexion of a baptized infant and the knuckles of a prize-fighter. This type leaned against cigar signs and viewed the world with frapped contumely.

A poet is a sensitive creature, and Raggles soon shrivelled in the bleak embrace of the undecipherable. The chill, sphinx-like, ironical, illegible, unnatural, ruthless expression of the city left him downcast and bewildered. Had it no heart? Better the woodpile, the scolding of vinegar-faced housewives at back doors, the kindly spleen of bartenders behind provincial free-lunch counters, the amiable truculence of rural constables, the kicks, arrests and happy go lucky chances of the other vulgar, loud, crude cities than this freezing heartlessness.

Raggles summoned his courage and sought alms from the populace. Unheeding, regardless, they passed on without the wink of an eyelash to testify that they were conscious of his existence. And then he said to himself that this fair but pitiless city of Manhattan was without a soul; that its inhabitants were manikins moved by wires and springs, and that he was alone in a great wilderness.

Raggles started to cross the street. There was a blast, a roar, a hissing and a crash as something struck him and hurled him over and over six yards from where he had been. As he was coming down like the stick of a rocket the earth and all the cities thereof turned to a fractured dream.

Raggles opened his eyes. First an odour made itself known to him – an odour of the earliest spring flowers of Paradise. And then a hand soft as a falling petal touched his brow. Bending over him was the woman clothed like the princess of old, with blue eyes, now soft and humid with human sympathy. Under his head on the pavement were silks and furs. With Raggles's hat in his hand and with his face pinker than ever from a vehement burst of oratory against reckless driving, stood the elderly gentleman who personified the city's wealth and ripeness. From a near-by café hurried the by-product with the vast jowl and baby complexion, bearing a glass full of a crimson fluid that suggested delightful possibilities.

'Drink dis, sport,' said the by-product, holding the glass to Raggles's lips.

Hundreds of people huddled around in a moment, their faces wearing the deepest concern. Two flattering and gorgeous policemen got into the circle and pressed back the overplus of Samaritans. An old lady in a black shawl spoke loudly of camphor a newsboy slipped one of his papers beneath Raggles's elbow, where it lay on the muddy pavement. A brisk young man with a notebook was asking for names.

A bell clanged importantly, and the ambulance cleared a lane through the crowd. A cool surgeon slipped into the midst of affairs.

'How do you feel, old man?' asked the surgeon stooping easily to his task. The princess of silks and satins wiped a red drop or two from Raggles's brow with a fragrant cobweb.

'Me?' said Raggles, with a seraphic smile. 'I feel fine.'

He had found the heart of his new city.

In three days they let him leave his cot for the convalescent ward in the hospital. He had been in there an hour when the attendants heard sounds of conflict. Upon investigation they found that Raggles had assaulted and damaged a brother convalescent – a glowering transient whom a freight train collision had sent in to be patched up.

'What's all this about?' inquired the head nurse.

'He was runnin' down me town,' said Raggles

'What town?' asked the nurse.

'Noo York,' said Raggles.

XXVIII

Vanity and some Sables

WHEN 'KID' BRADY was sent to the ropes by Molly McKeever's blue-black eyes he withdrew from the Stovepipe Gang. So much for the power of a colleen's blanderin' tongue and stubborn true-heartedness. If you are a man who read this, may such an influence be sent you before two o'clock to-morrow; if you are a woman, may your Pomeranian greet you this morning with a cold nose – a sign of dog-health and your happiness.

The Stovepipe Gang borrowed its name from a subdistrict of the city called the 'Stovepipe,' which is a narrow and natural extension of the familiar district known as 'Hell's Kitchen.' The 'Stovepipe' strip of town runs along Eleventh and Twelfth avenues on the river, and bends a hard and sooty elbow around little, lost, homeless DeWitt Clinton park. Consider that a stovepipe is an important factor in any kitchen and the situation is analysed. The chefs in 'Hell's Kitchen' are many, and the Stovepipe Gang wears the cordon blue.

The members of this unchartered but widely known brotherhood appeared to pass their time on street corners arrayed like the lilies of the conservatory and busy with nail files and pen-knives. Thus displayed as a guarantee of good faith, they carried on an innocuous conversation in a 200-word vocabulary, to the casual observer as innocent and immaterial as that heard in the clubs seven blocks to the east.

But off exhibition the 'Stovepipes' were not mere street-corner ornaments addicted to posing and manicuring. Their serious occupation was the separating of citizens from their coin and valuables. Preferably this was done by weird and singular tricks without noise or bloodshed; but whenever the citizen honoured by their attentions refused to impoverish himself gracefully his objections came to be spread finally upon some police-station blotter or hospital register.

The police held the Stovepipe Gang in perpetual suspicion and respect. As the nightingale's liquid note is heard in the deepest shadows, so along the 'Stovepipe's' dark and narrow confines the whistle for reserves punctures the dull ear of night. Whenever there was smoke in the 'Stovepipe' the tasselled men in blue knew there was fire in 'Hell's Kitchen.'

'Kid' Brady promised Molly to be good. 'Kid' was the vainest, the strongest, the wariest and the most successful plotter in the gang. Therefore the boys were sorry to give him up.

But they witnessed his fall to a virtuous life without protest. For, in the Kitchen it is considered neither unmanly nor improper for a guy to do as his girl advises.

Black her eye for love's sake, if you will; but it is all-to-the-good business to do a thing when she wants you to do it.

'Turn off the hydrant,' said the Kid, one night when Molly, tearful, besought him to amend his ways. 'I'm going to cut out the gang. You for mine, and the simple life on the side. I'll tell you, Moll – I'll get work; and in a year we'll get married. I'll do it for you. We'll get a flat and a flute, and a sewing machine, and a rubber plant, and live as honest as we can.'

'Oh, Kid,' sighed Molly, wiping the powder off his shoulder with her handkerchief, 'I'd rather hear you say that than to own all of New York. And we can be happy on so little!'

The Kid looked down at his speckless cuffs and shining patent leathers with a suspicion of melancholy.

'It'll hurt hardest in the rags department,' said he. 'I've kind of always liked to rig out swell when I could. You know how I hate cheap things, Moll. This suit set me back sixty-five. Anything in the wearing apparel line has got to be just so, or it's to the misfit parlours for it, for mine. If I work I won't have so much coin to hand over to the little man with the big shears.'

'Never mind, Kid. I'll like you just as much in a blue jumper as I would in a red automobile.'

Before the Kid had grown large enough to knock out his father he had been compelled to learn the plumber's art. So now back to this honourable and useful profession he returned. But it was as an assistant that he engaged himself; and it is the master plumber and not the assistant, who wears diamonds as large as hailstones and looks contemptuously upon the marble colonnades of Senator Clark's mansion.

Eight months went by as smoothly and surely as though they had 'elapsed' on a theatre programme. The Kid worked away at his pipes and solder with no symptoms of backsliding. The

Stovepipe Gang continued its piracy on the high avenues, cracked policemen's heads, held up late travellers, invented new methods of peaceful plundering, copied Fifth Avenue's cut of clothes and neckwear fancies and comported itself according to its lawless by-laws. But the Kid stood firm and faithful to his Molly, even though the polish was gone from his finger-nails and it took him fifteen minutes to tie his purple silk ascot so that the worn places would not show.

One evening he brought a mysterious bundle with him to Molly's house.

'Open that, Moll!' he said in his large, quiet way. 'It's for you.'

Molly's eager fingers tore off the wrappings. She shrieked aloud, and in rushed a sprinkling of little McKeevers, and Ma McKeever, dishwashy, but an undeniable relative of the late Mrs. Eve.

Again Molly shrieked, and something dark and long and sinuous flew and enveloped her neck like an anaconda.

'Russian sables,' said the Kid pridefully, enjoying the sight of Molly's round cheek against the clinging fur. 'The real thing. They don't grow anything in Russia too good for you, Moll.'

Molly plunged her hands into the muff, overturned a row of the family infants and flew to the mirror. Hint for the beauty column. To make bright eyes, rosy cheeks and a bewitching smile: Recipe – one set Russian sables. Apply.

When they were alone Molly became aware of a small cake of the ice of common sense floating down the full tide of her happiness.

'You're a bird, all right, Kid,' she admitted gratefully. 'I never had any furs on before in my life. But ain't Russian sables awful expensive? Seems to me I've heard they were.'

'Have I ever chucked any bargain-sale stuff at you, Moll?' asked the Kid, with calm dignity. 'Did you ever notice me leaning on the remnant counter or peering in the window of the five-and-ten? Call that scarf $250 and the muff $175 and you won't make any mistake about the price of Russian sables. The swell goods for me. Say, they look fine on you, Moll.'

Molly hugged the sables to her bosom in rapture. And then her smile went away little by little, and she looked the Kid straight in the eye sadly and steadily.

He knew what every look of hers meant; and he laughed with a faint flush upon his face.

'Cut it out,' he said, with affectionate roughness. 'I told you I was done with that. I bought 'em and paid for 'em all right, with my own money.'

'Out of the money you worked for, Kid? Out of $75 a month?'

'Sure. I been saving up.'

'Let's see – saved $425 in eight months, Kid?'

'Ah, let up,' said the Kid, with some heat. 'I had some money when I went to work. Do you think I've been holding 'em up again? I told you I'd quit. They're paid for on the square. Put 'em on and come out for a walk.'

Molly calmed her doubts. Sables are soothing. Proud as a queen she went forth in the streets at the Kid's side. In all that region of low-lying streets Russian sables had never been seen before. The word sped, and doors and windows blossomed with heads eager to see the swell furs Kid Brady had given his girl. All down the street there were 'Oh's' and 'Ah's,' and the reported fabulous sum paid for the sables was passed from lip to lip, increasing as it went. At her right elbow sauntered the Kid with the air of princes. Work had not diminished his love of pomp and show, and his passion for the costly and genuine. On a corner they saw a group of the Stovepipe Gang loafing, immaculate. They raised their hats to the Kid's girl and went on with their calm, unaccented palaver.

Three blocks behind the admired couple strolled Detective Ransom, of the Central Office. Ransom was the only detective on the force who could walk abroad with safety in the Stovepipe district. He was fair dealing and unafraid, and went there with the hypothesis that the inhabitants were human. Many liked him, and now and then one would tip off to him something that he was looking for.

'What's the excitement down the street?' asked Ransom of a pale youth in a red sweater.

'Dey're out rubberin' at a set of buffalo robes Kid Brady staked his girl to,' answered the youth. 'Some say he paid $900 for de skins. Dey're swell all right enough.'

'I hear Brady has been working at his old trade for nearly a year,' said the detective. 'He doesn't travel with the gang any more, does he?'

'He's workin', all right,' said the red sweater, 'but – say, sport, are you trailin' anything in the fur line? A job in a plumbin' shop don't match wid dem skins de Kid's girl's got on.'

Ransom overtook the strolling couple on an empty street near the river bank. He touched the Kid's arm from behind.

'Let me see you a moment, Brady,' he said, quietly. His eye rested for a second on the long fur scarf thrown stylishly back over Molly's left shoulder. The Kid, with his old-time police-hating frown on his face, stepped a yard or two aside with the detective.

'Did you go to Mrs. Hethcote's on West 7th Street yesterday to fix a leaky waterpipe?' asked Ransom.

'I did,' said the Kid. 'What of it?'

'The lady's $1,000 set of Russian sables went out of the house about the same time you did. The description fits the ones this lady has on.'

'To h – Harlem with you,' cried the Kid angrily. 'You know I've cut out that sort of thing, Ransom. I bought them sables yesterday at –'

The Kid stopped short.

'I know you've been working straight lately,' said Ransom. 'I'll give you every chance. I'll go with you where you bought the furs and investigate. The lady can wear 'em along with us and nobody'll be on. That's fair, Brady.'

'Come on,' agreed the Kid hotly. And then he stopped suddenly in his tracks and looked with an odd smile at Molly's distressed and anxious face.

'No use,' he said grimly. 'They're the Hethcote sables, all right. You'll have to turn 'em over, Moll, but they ain't too good for you if they cost a million.'

Molly, with anguish in her face, hung upon the Kid's arm.

'Oh, Kiddy, you've broke my heart,' she said. 'I was so proud of you – and now they'll do you – and where's our happiness gone?'

'Go home,' said the Kid wildly. 'Come on, Ransom – take the furs. Let's get away from here. Wait a minute – I've a good mind to – no, I'll be d – if I can do it – run along, Moll – I'm ready, Ransom.'

Around the corner of a lumber-yard came Policeman Kohen on his way to his beat along the river. The detective signed to him for assistance. Kohen joined the group. Ransom explained.

'Sure,' said Kohen. 'I hear about those saples dat vas stole. You say you have dem here?'

Policeman Kohen took the end of Molly's late scarf in his hands and looked at it closely.

'Once,' he said, 'I sold furs in Sixth Avenue. Yes, dese are saples. Dey come from Alaska. Dis scarf is vort $12 and dis muff –'

'Biff!' came the palm of the Kid's powerful hand upon the policeman's mouth. Kohen staggered and rallied. Molly screamed.

The detective threw himself upon Brady and with Kohen's aid got the nippers on his wrist.

'The scarf is vort $12 and the muff is vort $9,' persisted the policeman. 'Vot is dis talk about $1,000 saples?'

The Kid sat upon a pile of lumber and his face turned dark red.

'Correct, Solomonski!' he declared viciously. 'I paid $21.50 for the set. I'd rather have got six months and not have told it. Me, the swell guy that wouldn't look at anything cheap! I'm a plain bluffer. Moll – my salary couldn't spell sables in Russian.'

Molly cast herself upon his neck.

'What do I care for all the sables and money in the world,' she cried. 'It's my Kiddy I want. Oh, you dear, stuck-up, crazy blockhead!'

'You can take dose nippers off,' said Kohen to the detective. 'Before I leaf de station de report come in dat de lady vind her saples – hanging in her wardrobe. Young man, I excuse you dat punch in my face – dis von time.'

Ransom handed Molly her furs. Her eyes were smiling upon the Kid. She wound the scarf and threw the end over her left shoulder with a duchess's grace.

'A gouple of young vools,' said Policeman Kohen to Ransom: 'come on away.'

XXIX

The Social Triangle

AT THE STROKE OF SIX Ikey Snigglefritz laid down his goose. Ikey was a tailor's apprentice. Are there tailor's apprentices nowadays?

At any rate, Ikey toiled and snipped and basted and pressed and patched and sponged all day in the steamy fetor of a tailor-shop. But when work was done Ikey hitched his wagon to such stars as his firmament let shine.

It was Saturday night, and the boss laid twelve begrimed and begrudged dollars in his hand. Ikey dabbled discreetly in water, donned coat, hat and collar with its frazzled tie and chalcedony pin, and set forth in pursuit of his ideals.

For each of us, when our day's work is done, must seek our ideal, whether it be love or pinochle or lobster à la Newburg, or the sweet silence of the musty bookshelves.

Behold Ikey as he ambles up the street beneath the roaring 'El' between the rows of reeking sweatshops. Pallid, stooping, insignificant, squalid, doomed to exist for ever in penury of body and mind, yet, as he swings his cheap cane and projects the noisome inhalations from his cigarette, you perceive that he nurtures in his narrow bosom the bacillus of society.

Ikey's legs carried him to and into that famous place of entertainment known as the Café Maginnis — famous because it was the rendezvous of Billy McMahan, the greatest man, the most wonderful man, Ikey thought, that the world had ever produced.

Billy McMahan was the district leader. Upon him the Tiger purred, and his hand held manna to scatter. Now, as Ikey entered, McMahan stood, flushed and triumphant and mighty, the centre of a huzzaing concourse of his lieutenants and constituents. It seems there had been an election; a signal victory had been won; the city had been swept back into line by a resistless besom of ballots.

Ikey slunk along the bar and gazed, breath-quickened, at his idol.

How magnificent was Billy McMahan, with his great, smooth, laughing face; his grey eye, shrewd as a chicken hawks; his diamond ring, his voice like a bugle call, his prince's air, his plump and active roll of money, his clarion call to friend and comrade — oh, what a king of men he was! How he obscured his lieutenants, though they themselves loomed large and serious, blue of chin and important of mien, with hands buried deep in the pockets of their short overcoats! But Billy — oh, what small avail are words to paint for you his glory as seen by Ikey Snigglefritz!

The Café Maginnis rang to the note of victory. The white-coated bartenders threw themselves featfully upon bottle, cork and glass. From a score of clear Havanas the air received its paradox of clouds. The leal and the hopeful shook Billy McMahan's hand. And there was born suddenly in the worshipful soul of Ikey Snigglefritz an audacious, thrilling impulse.

He stepped forward into the little cleared space in which majesty moved, and held out his hand.

Billy McMahan grasped it unhesitatingly, shook it and smiled.

Made mad now by the gods who were about to destroy him, Ikey threw away his scabbard and charged upon Olympus.

'Have a drink with me, Billy,' he said familiarly, 'you and your friends?'

'Don't mind if I do, old man,' said the great leader, 'just to keep the ball rolling.'

The last spark of Ikey's reason fled.

'Wine,' he called to the bartender, waving a trembling hand.

The corks of three bottles were drawn; the champagne bubbled in the long row of glasses set upon the bar. Billy McMahan took his and nodded, with his beaming smile, at Ikey. The lieutenants and satellites took theirs and growled 'Here's to you.' Ikey took his nectar in delirium. All drank.

Ikey threw his week's wages in a crumpled roll upon the bar.

'C'rect,' said the bartender, smoothing the twelve one-dollar notes. The crowd surged around Billy McMahan again. Someone was telling how Brannigan fixed 'em over in the Eleventh. Ikey leaned against the bar a while and then went out.

He went down Hester Street and up Chrystie, and down Delancey to where he lived. And there his womenfolk, a bibulous mother and three dingy sisters, pounced upon him for his wages. And at his confession they shrieked and objurgated him in the pithy rhetoric of the locality.

But even as they plucked at him and struck him, Ikey remained in his ecstatic trance of joy. His head was in the clouds; the star was drawing his wagon. Compared with what he had achieved the loss of wages and the bray of women's tongues were slight affairs.

He had shaken the hand of Billy McMahan.

•   •   •   •   •

Billy McMahan had a wife, and upon her visiting cards was engraved the name 'Mrs. William Darragh McMahan.' And there was a certain vexation attendant upon these cards; for, small as they were, there were houses in which they could not be inserted. Billy McMahan was a dictator in politics, a four-walled tower in business, a mogul: dreaded, loved and obeyed among his own people. He was growing rich; the daily papers had a dozen men on his trail to chronicle his every word of wisdom; he had been honoured in caricature holding the Tiger cringing in leash.

But the heart of Billy was sometimes sore within him. There was a race of men from which he stood apart but that he viewed with the eye of Moses looking over into the Promised Land. He, too, had ideals, even as had Ikey Snigglefritz; and sometimes, hopeless of attaining them, his own solid success was as dust and ashes in his mouth. And Mrs. William Darragh McMahan wore a look of discontent upon her plump but pretty face, and the very rustle of her silks seemed a sigh.

There was a brave and conspicuous assemblage in the dining-saloon of a noted hostelry where Fashion loves to display her charms. At one table sat Billy McMahan and his wife. Mostly silent they were, but the accessories they enjoyed little needed the endorsement of speech. Mrs. McMahan's diamonds were out-shone by few in the room. The waiter bore the costliest brands of wine to their table. In evening dress, with an expression of gloom upon his smooth and massive countenance, you would look in vain for a more striking figure than Billy's.

Four tables away sat alone a tall, slender man, about thirty, with thoughtful, melancholy eyes, a Van Dyke beard and pecu-liarly white, thin hands. He was dining on filet mignon, dry toast and apollinaris. That man was Cortlandt Van Duyckink, a man worth eighty millions, who inherited and held a sacred seat in the exclusive inner circle of society.

Billy McMahan spoke to no one around him, because he knew no one. Van Duyckink kept his eyes on his plate because he knew that every eye present was hungry to catch his. He could bestow knighthood and prestige by a nod, and he was chary of creating a too-extensive nobility.

And then Billy McMahan conceived and accomplished the most startling and audacious act of his life. He rose deliberately and walked over to Cortlandt Van Duyckink's table and held out his hand.

'Say, Mr. Van Duyckink,' he said. 'I've heard you was talking about starting some reforms among the poor people down in my district. I'm McMahan, you know. Say, now, if that's straight I'll do all I can to help you. And what I says goes in that neck of the woods, don't it? Oh, say, I rather guess it does.'

Van Duyckink's rather sombre eyes lighted up. He rose to his lank height and grasped Billy McMahan's hand.

'Thank you, Mr. McMahan,' he said in his deep, serious tones. 'I have been thinking of doing some work of that sort. I shall be glad of your assistance. It pleases me to have become acquainted with you.'

Billy walked back to his seat. His shoulder was tingling from the accolade bestowed by royalty. A hundred eyes were now turned upon him in envy and new admiration. Mrs. William Darragh McMahan trembled with ecstasy, so that her diamonds smote the eye almost with pain. And now it was apparent that at many tables there were those who suddenly remembered that they enjoyed Mr McMahan's acquaintance. He saw smiles and bows about him. He became enveloped in the aura of dizzy greatness. His campaign coolness deserted him.

'Wine for that gang!' he commanded the waiter, pointing with his finger. 'Wine over there. Wine to those three gents by that green bush. Tell 'em it's on me. D – n it! Wine for everybody!'

The waiter ventured to whisper that it was perhaps inexpedient to carry out the order, in consideration of the dignity of the house and its custom.

'All right,' said Billy, 'if it's against the rules. I wonder if 'twould do to send my friend Van Duyckink a bottle. No? Well, it'll flow all right at the caffy to-night, just the same. It'll be rubber boots for anybody who comes in there any time up to 2 a.m.'

Billy McMahan was happy.

He had shaken the hand of Cortlandt Van Duyckink.

•   •   •   •   •   •

The big pale-grey auto with its shining metal work looked out of place moving slowly among the push-carts and trash-heaps on the lower East Side. So did Cortlandt Van Duyckink, with his aristocratic face and white, thin hands, as he steered carefully between the groups of ragged, scurrying youngsters in the streets. And so did Miss Constance Schuyler, with her dim, ascetic beauty, seated at his side.

'Oh, Cortlandt,' she breathed, 'isn't it sad that human beings have to live in such wretchedness and poverty? And you – how noble it is of you to think of them, to give your time and money to improve their condition!'

Van Duyckink turned his solemn eyes upon her.

'It is little,' he said sadly, 'that I can do. The question is a large one, and belongs to society. But even individual effort is not thrown away. Look, Constance! On this street I have arranged to build soup kitchens, where no one who is hungry will be turned away. And down this other street are the old buildings that I shall cause to be torn down, and there erect others in place of those death-traps of fire and disease.'

Down Delancey slowly crept the pale-grey auto. Away from it toddled coveys of wondering, tangle-haired, barefooted, unwashed children. It stopped before a crazy brick structure, foul and awry.

Van Duyckink alighted to examine at a better perspective one of the leaning walls. Down the steps of the building came a young man who seemed to epitomize its degradation, squalor and infelicity – a narrow-chested, pale, unsavoury young man, puffing at a cigarette.

Obeying a sudden impulse, Van Duyckink stepped out and warmly grasped the hand of what seemed to him a living rebuke.

'I want to know you people,' he said sincerely. 'I am going to help you as much as I can. We shall be friends.

As the auto crept carefully away Cortlandt Van Duyckink felt an unaccustomed glow about his heart. He was near to being a happy man

He had shaken the hand of Ikey Snigglefritz.

XXX

The Lost Blend

SINCE THE BAR HAS BEEN blessed by the clergy, and cocktails open the dinners of the elect one may speak of the saloon. Teetotalers need not listen, if they choose; there is always the slot restaurant, where a dime dropped into the cold bouillon aperture will bring forth a dry Martini.

Con Lantry worked on the sober side of the bar in Kenealy's café. You and I stood, one-legged like geese, on the other side and went into voluntary liquidation with our week's wages. Opposite danced Con, clean, temperate, clearheaded, polite, white-jacketed, punctual, trustworthy, young, responsible, and took our money.

The saloon (whether blessed or cursed) stood in one of those little 'places' which are parallelograms instead of streets, and inhabited by laundries, decayed Knickerbocker families and Bohemians who have nothing to do with either

Over the café lived Kenealy and his family. His daughter Katherine had eyes of dark Irish – but why should you be told? Be content with your Geraldine or your Eliza Ann. For Con dreamed of her; and when she called softly at the foot of the back stairs for the pitcher of beer for dinner, his heart went up and down like a milk punch in the shaker. Orderly and fit are the rules of Romance; and if you hurl the last shilling of your fortune upon the bar for whisky, the bartender shall take it, and marry his boss's daughter, and good will grow out of it.

But not so Con. For in the presence of woman he was tongue-tied and scarlet. He who would quell with his eye the sonorous youth whom the claret punch made loquacious, or smash with lemon squeezer the obstreperous, or hurl gutterward the cantankerous without a wrinkle coming to his white lawn tie, when he stood before woman he was voiceless, incoherent, stuttering, buried beneath a hot avalanche of bashfulness and misery. What, then, was he before Katherine? A trembler, with no word to say for himself, a stone without blarney, the dumbest lover that ever babbled of the weather in the presence of his divinity.

There came to Kenealy's two sunburned men, Riley and McQuirk. They had conference with Kenealy; and then they took possession of a back room which they filled with bottles and siphons and jugs and druggist's measuring glasses. All the appurtenances and liquids of a saloon were there, but they dispensed no drinks. All day long the two sweltered in there, pouring and mixing unknown brews and decoctions from the liquors in their store. Riley had the education, and he figured on reams of paper, reducing gallons to ounces and quarts to fluid drams. McQuirk, a morose man with a red eye, dashed each unsuccessful completed mixture into the waste pipes with curses gentle, husky and deep. They laboured heavily and untiringly to achieve some mysterious solution, like two alchemists striving to resolve gold from the elements.

Into this back room one evening when his watch was done sauntered Con. His professional curiosity had been stirred by these occult bartenders at whose bar none drank, and who daily drew upon Kenealy's store of liquors to follow their consuming and fruitless experiments.

Down the back stairs came Katherine with her smile like sunrise on Gweebarra Bay.

'Good evening, Mr. Lantry,' says she. 'And what is the news to-day, if you please?'

It looks like r-rain,' stammered the shy one, backing to the wall.

'It couldn't do better,' said Katherine. 'I'm thinking there's nothing the worse off for a little water.'

In the back room Riley and McQuirk toiled like bearded witches over their strange compounds. From fifty bottles they drew liquids carefully measured after Riley's figures, and shook the whole together in a great glass vessel. Then McQuirk would dash it out, with gloomy profanity, and they would begin again.

'Sit down,' said Riley to Con, 'and I'll tell you.

'Last summer me and Tim concludes that an American bar in this nation of Nicaragua would pay. There was a town on the coast where there's nothing to eat but quinine and nothing to drink but rum. The natives and foreigners lay down with chills and get up with fevers; and a good mixed drink is nature's remedy for all such tropical inconveniences.

'So we lays in a fine stock of wet goods in New York, and bar fixtures and glassware, and we sails for that Santa Palma town on a line steamer. On the way me and Tim sees flying fish and plays seven-up with the captain and steward, and already begins to feel like the high-ball kings of the tropic of Capricorn.

'When we gets in five hours of the country that we was going to introduce to long drinks and short change the captain calls us over to the starboard binnacle and recollects a few things.

' "I forgot to tell you, boys," says he, "that Nicaragua slapped an import duty of 48 per cent. *ad valorem* on all bottled goods last month. The President took a bottle of Cincinnati hair tonic by mistake for tabasco sauce, and he's getting even. Barrelled goods is free."

' "Sorry you didn't mention it sooner," says we. And we bought two forty-two gallon casks from the captain, and opened every bottle we had and dumped the stuff all together in the casks. That 48 per cent. would have ruined us; so we took the chances on making that $1,200 cocktail rather than throw the stuff away.

'Well, when we landed we tapped one of the barrels. The mixture was something heartrending. It was the colour of a plate of Bowery pea-soup, and it tasted like one of those coffee substitutes your aunt makes you take for the heart trouble you get by picking losers. We gave a nigger four fingers of it to try it, and he lay under a coco-nut tree three days beating the sand with his heels and refused to sign a testimonial.

'But the other barrel! Say, bartender, did you ever put on a straw hat with a yellow band around it and go up in a balloon with a pretty girl with $8,000,000 in your pocket all at the same time? That's what thirty drops of it would make you feel like. With two fingers of it inside you you would bury your face in your hands and cry because there wasn't anything more worth while around for you to lick than little Jim Jeffries. Yes, sir, the stuff in that second barrel was distilled elixir of battle money and high life. It was the colour of gold and as clear as glass, and it shone after dark like the sunshine was still in it. A thousand years from now you'll get a drink like that across the bar

'Well, we started up business with that one line of drinks, and it was enough. The piebald gentry of that country stuck to it like a hive of bees. If that barrel had lasted that country would have become the greatest on earth. When we opened up of mornings we had a line of Generals and Colonels and ex-Presidents and revolutionists a block long waiting to be served. We started in at fifty cents silver a drink. The last ten gallons went easy at $5 a gulp. It was wonderful stuff. It gave a man courage and ambition and nerve to do anything; at the same time he didn't care whether his money was tainted or fresh from the Ice Trust. When that barrel was half gone Nicaragua had repudiated the National Debt, removed the duty on cigarettes and was about to declare war on the United States and England.

' 'Twas by accident we discovered this king of drinks, and 'twill be by good luck if we strike it again. For ten months we've been trying. Small lots at a time, we've mixed barrels of all the harmful ingredients known to the profession of drinking. Ye could have stocked ten bars with the whiskies, brandies, cordials, bitters, gins and wines me and Tim have wasted. A glorious drink like that to be denied to the world! 'tis a sorrow and a loss of money. The United States as a nation would welcome a drink of the sort, and pay for it.'

All the while McQuirk had been carefully measuring and pouring together small quantities of various spirits, as Riley called them, from his latest pencilled prescription. The completed mixture was of a vile, mottled chocolate colour. McQuirk tasted it, and hurled it, with appropriate epithets, into the waste sink.

' 'Tis a strange story, even if true,' said Con. I'll be going now along to my supper.'

'Take a drink,' said Riley. 'We've all kinds except the lost blend.'

'I never drink,' said Con, 'anything stronger than water. I am just after meeting Miss Katherine by the stairs. She said a true word. "There's not anything," says she, "but is better off for a little water." '

When Con had left them Riley almost felled McQuirk by a blow on the back.

'Did ye hear that?' he shouted. 'Two fools are we. The six dozen bottles of 'pollinaris we had on the ship – ye opened them yourself – which barrel did ye pour them in – which barrel, ye mud-head?'

'I mind,' said McQuirk, slowly, ' 'twas in the second barrel we opened. I mind the blue piece of paper pasted on the side of it.'

'We've got it now,' cried Riley. ' 'Twas that we lacked. 'Tis the water that does the trick. Everything else we had right. Hurry, man, and get two bottles of 'pollinaris from the bar, while I figure out the proportionments with me pencil.'

An hour later Con strolled down the sidewalk toward Kenealy's café. Thus faithful employees haunt, during their recreation hours, the vicinity where they labour, drawn by some mysterious attraction.

A police patrol wagon stood at the side door. Three able cops were half carrying, half hustling Riley and McQuirk up its rear steps. The eyes and faces of each bore the bruises and cuts of sanguinary and assiduous conflict. Yet they whooped with strange joy, and directed upon the police the feeble remnants of their pugnacious madness.

'Began fighting each other in the back room,' explained Kenealy to Con. 'And singing! That was worse. Smashed everything pretty much up. But they're good men. They'll pay for everything. Trying to invent some new kind of cocktail, they was. I'll see they come out all right in the morning.'

Con sauntered into the back room to view the battlefield. As he went through the hall Katherine was just coming down the stairs.

'Good evening again, Mr. Lantry,' said she. 'And is there no news from the weather yet?'

'Still threatens r-rain,' said Con, slipping past with red in his smooth, pale cheek.

Riley and McQuirk had indeed waged a great and friendly battle. Broken bottles and glasses were everywhere. The room was full of alcohol fumes; the floor was variegated with spirituous puddles.

On the table stood a 32-ounce glass graduated measure. In the bottom of it were two tablespoonfuls of liquid — a bright golden liquid that seemed to hold the sunshine a prisoner in its auriferous depths.

Con smelled it. He tasted it. He drank it.

As he returned through the hall Katherine was just going up the stairs.

'No news yet, Mr. Lantry?' she asked, with her teasing laugh.

Con lifted her clear from the floor and held her there.

'The news is,' he said, 'that we're to be married.'

'Put me down, sir!' she cried indignantly, 'or I will – Oh, Con, where, oh, wherever did you get the nerve to say it?'

XXXI

A Harlem Tragedy

HARLEM.

Mrs. Fink has dropped into Mrs. Cassidy's flat one flight below.

'Ain't it a beaut?' said Mrs. Cassidy.

She turned her face proudly for her friend Mrs. Fink to see.

One eye was nearly closed, with a great, greenish-purple bruise around it. Her lip was cut and bleeding a little and there were red finger-marks on each side of her neck.

'My husband wouldn't ever think of doing that to me,' said Mrs. Fink, concealing her envy.

'I wouldn't have a man,' declared Mrs. Cassidy, 'that didn't beat me up at least once a week. Shows he thinks something of you. Say! but that last dose Jack gave me wasn't no homœpathic one. I can see stars yet. But he'll be the sweetest man in town for the rest of the week to make up for it. This eye is good for theatre tickets and a silk shirt waist at the very least.'

'I should hope,' said Mrs. Fink, assuming complacency, 'that Mr. Fink is too much of a gentleman ever to raise his hand against me.'

'Oh, go on, Maggie!' said Mrs. Cassidy, laughing and applying wych-hazel, 'you're only jealous. Your old man is too frapped and slow to ever give you a punch. He just sits down and practises physical culture with a newspaper when he comes home – now ain't that the truth?'

'Mr. Fink certainly peruses of the papers when he comes home,' acknowledged Mrs. Fink, with a toss of her head; 'but he certainly don't ever make no Steve O'Donnell out of me just to amuse himself – that's a sure thing.'

Mrs. Cassidy laughed the contented laugh of the guarded and happy matron. With the air of Cornelia exhibiting her jewels, she drew down the collar of her kimono and revealed another treasured bruise, maroon-coloured, edged with olive and orange – a bruise now nearly well, but still to memory dear.

Mrs. Fink capitulated. The formal light in her eye softened to envious admiration. She and Mrs. Cassidy had been chums in the down-town paper-box factory before they had married, one year before. Now she and her man occupied the flat above Mame and her man. Therefore she could not put on airs with Mame.

'Don't it hurt when he soaks you?' asked Mrs. Fink curiously.

'Hurt!' – Mrs. Cassidy gave a soprano scream of delight. 'Well, say did you ever have a brick house fall on you? – well, that's just the way it feels – just like when they're digging you out of the ruins. Jack's got a left that spells two matinees and a new pair of Oxfords – and his right! – well, it takes a trip to Coney and six pairs of openwork, silk lisle threads to make that good.'

'But what does he beat you for?' inquired Mrs. Fink, with wide-open eyes.

'Silly!' said Mrs. Cassidy, indulgently. 'Why, because he's full. It's generally on Saturday nights.'

'But what cause do you give him?' persisted the seeker after knowledge.

'Why, didn't I marry him? Jack comes in tanked up; and I'm here, ain't I? Who else has he got a right to beat? I'd just like to catch him once beating anybody else! Sometimes it's because supper ain't ready; and sometimes it's because it is. Jack ain't particular about causes. He just lushes till he remembers he's married, and then he makes for home and does me up. Saturday nights I just move the furniture with sharp corners out of the way, so I won't cut my head when he gets his work in. He's got a left swing that jars you! Sometimes I take the count in the first round; but when I feel like having a good time during the week, or want some new rags, I come up again for more punishment. That's what I done last night. Jack knows I've been wanting a black silk waist for a month, and I didn't think just one black eye would bring it. Tell you what, Mag, I'll bet you the ice cream he brings it to-night.'

Mrs. Fink was thinking deeply.

'My Mart,' she said, 'never hit me a lick in his life. It's just like you said, Mame; he comes in grouchy and ain't got a word to say. He never takes me out anywhere. He's a chairwarmer at home for fair. He buys me things, but he looks so glum about it that I never appreciate 'em.'

Mrs. Cassidy slipped an arm around her chum.

'You poor thing!' she said. 'But everybody can't have a husband like Jack. Marriage wouldn't be no failure if they was all like him. These discontented wives you hear about – what they need is a man to come home and kick their slats in once a week, and then make it up in kisses and chocolate creams. That'd give 'em some interest in life. What I want is a masterful man that slugs you when he's jagged and hugs you when he ain't jagged. Preserve me from the man that ain't got the sand to do neither!'

Mrs. Fink sighed.

The hallways were suddenly filled with sound. The door flew open at the kick of Mr. Cassidy. His arms were occupied with bundles. Mame flew and hung about his neck. Her sound eye sparkled with the love-light that shines in the eye of the Maori maid when she recovers consciousness in the hut of the wooer who has stunned and dragged her there.

'Hello, old girl!' shouted Mr. Cassidy. He shed his bundles and lifted her off her feet in a mighty hug. 'I got tickets for Barnum &

Bailey's, and if you'll bust the string of one of them bundles I guess you'll find that silk waist – why, good evening, Mrs. Fink, I didn't see you at first. How's old Mart coming along?'

'He's very well, Mr. Cassidy – thanks,' said Mrs. Fink. 'I must be going along up now. Mart 'll be home for supper soon. I'll bring you down that pattern you wanted to-morrow, Mame.'

Mrs. Fink went up to her flat and had a little cry. It was a meaningless cry, the kind of cry that only a woman knows about, a cry from no particular cause, altogether an absurd cry; the most transient and the most hopeless cry in the repertory of grief. Why had Martin never thrashed her? He was as big and strong as Jack Cassidy. Did he not care for her at all? He never quarrelled; he came home and lounged about, silent, glum, idle. He was a fairly good provider, but he ignored the spices of life.

Mrs. Fink's ship of dreams was becalmed. Her captain ranged between plum-duff and his hammock. If only he would shiver his timbers or stamp his foot on the quarter-deck now and then! And she had thought to sail so merrily, touching at ports in the Delectable Isles! But now, to vary the figure, she was ready to throw up the sponge, tired out, with a scratch to show for all those tame rounds with her sparring partner. For one moment she almost hated Mame – Mame, with her cuts and bruises, her salve of presents and kisses, her stormy voyage with her fighting, brutal, loving mate.

Mr. Fink came home at seven. He was permeated with the curse of domesticity. Beyond the portal of his cosy home he cared not to roam. He was the man who had caught the street-car, the anaconda that had swallowed its prey, the tree that lay as it had fallen.

'Like the supper, Mart?' asked Mrs. Fink, who had striven over it.

'M-m-m-yep,' grunted Mr. Fink.

After supper he gathered his newspapers to read. He sat in his stockinged feet.

Arise, some new Dante, and sing me the befitting corner of perdition for the man who sitteth in the house in his stockinged feet! Sisters of Patience who by reason of ties or duty have endured it in silk, yarn, cotton, lisle thread or woollen – does not the new canto belong?

The next day was Labour Day. The occupations of Mr. Cassidy and Mr. Fink ceased for one passage of the sun. Labour, triumphant, would parade and otherwise disport itself.

Mrs. Fink took Mrs. Cassidy's pattern down early. Mame had

on her new silk waist. Even her damaged eye managed to emit a
holiday gleam. Jack was fruitfully penitent, and there was an hilarious scheme for the day afoot, with parks and picnics and Pilsener
in it.

A rising, indignant jealousy seized Mrs. Fink as she returned to
her flat above. Oh, happy Mame, with her bruises and her quick-
following balm! But was Mame to have a monopoly of happiness?
Surely Martin Fink was as good a man as Jack Cassidy. Was his
wife to go always unbelaboured and uncaressed? A sudden, brilliant, breathless idea came to Mrs. Fink. She would show Mame
that there were husbands as able to use their fists and perhaps to
be as tender afterward as any Jack.

The holiday promised to be a nominal one with the Finks. Mrs.
Fink had the stationary wash-tubs in the kitchen filled with a two
weeks' wash that had been soaking overnight. Mr. Fink sat in his
stockinged feet reading a newspaper. Thus Labour Day presaged
to speed.

Jealousy surged high in Mrs. Fink's heart, and higher still
surged an audacious resolve. If her man would not strike her – if
he would not so far prove his manhood, his prerogative and his
interest in conjugal affairs, he must be prompted to his duty.

Mr. Fink lit his pipe and peacefully rubbed an ankle with a
stockinged toe. He reposed in the state of matrimony like a limp
of unblended suet in a pudding. This was his level Elysium – to sit
at ease vicariously girdling the world in print amid the wifely
splashing of suds and the agreeable smells of breakfast dishes
departed and dinner ones to come. Many ideas were far from his
mind; but the furthest one was the thought of beating his wife.

Mrs. Fink turned on the hot water and set the washboards in the
suds. Up from the flat below came the gay laugh of Mrs. Cassidy.
It sounded like a taunt, a flaunting of her own happiness in the
face of the unslugged bride above. Now was Mrs. Fink's time.

Suddenly she turned like a fury upon the man reading.

'You lazy loafer!' she cried, 'must I work my arms off washing
and toiling for the ugly likes of you? Are you a man or are you a
kitchen hound?'

Mr. Fink dropped his paper, motionless from surprise. She
feared that he would not strike – that the provocation had been
insufficient. She leaped at him and struck him fiercely in the face
with her clenched hand. In that instant she felt a thrill of love for
him such as she had not felt for many a day. Rise up, Martin Fink,
and come into your kingdom! Oh, she must feel the weight of his

hand now – just to show that he cared – just to show that he cared!

Mr. Fink sprang to his feet – Maggie caught him again on the jaw with a wide swing of her other hand. She closed her eyes in that fearful, blissful moment before his blow should come – she whispered his name to herself – she leaned to the expected shock, hungry for it.

In the flat below, Mr. Cassidy, with a shamed and contrite face, was powdering Mame's eye in preparation for their junket. From the flat above came the sound of a woman's voice, high-raised, a bumping, a stumbling and a shuffling, a chair overturned – unmistakable sounds of domestic conflict.

'Mart and Mag scrapping?' postulated Mr. Cassidy. 'Didn't know they ever indulged. Shall I trot up and see if they need a sponge-holder?'

One of Mrs. Cassidy's eyes sparkled like a diamond. The other twinkled at least like paste.

'Oh, oh,' she said softly and without apparent meaning, in the feminine ejaculatory manner. 'I wonder if – I wonder if! Wait, Jack, till I go up and see.'

Up the stairs she sped. As her foot struck the hallway above, out from the kitchen door of her flat wildly flounced Mrs. Fink.

'Oh, Maggie,' cried Mrs. Cassidy, in a delighted whisper; 'did he? Oh, did he?'

Mrs. Fink ran and laid her face upon her chum's shoulder and sobbed hopelessly.

Mrs. Cassidy took Maggie's face between her hands and lifted it gently. Tear-stained it was, flushing and paling, but its velvety, pink-and-white, becomingly freckled surface was unscratched, unbruised, unmarred by the recreant fist of Mr. Fink.

'Tell me, Maggie,' pleaded Mame, 'or I'll go in there and find out. What was it? Did he hurt you – what did he do?'

Mrs. Fink's face went down again despairingly on the bosom of her friend.

'For Gawd's sake don't open that door, Mame,' she sobbed. 'And don't ever tell nobody – keep it under your hat. He – he never touched me, and – he's – oh, Gawd – he's washin' the clothes – he's washin' the clothes!'

XXXII

'The Guilty Party'

A RED-HAIRED, UNSHAVEN, untidy man sat in a rocking-chair by a window. He had just lighted a pipe, and was puffing blue clouds with great satisfaction. He had removed his shoes and donned a pair of blue, faded carpet-slippers. With the morbid thirst of the confirmed daily news drinker, he awkwardly folded back the pages of an evening paper, eagerly gulping down the strong, black headlines, to be followed as a chaser by the milder details of the smaller type.

In an adjoining room a woman was cooking supper. Odours from strong bacon and boiling coffee contended against the cut-plug fumes from the vespertine pipe.

Outside was one of those crowded streets of the East Side, in which, as twilight falls, Satan sets up his recruiting office. A mighty host of children danced and ran and played in the street. Some in rags, some in clean white and beribboned, some wild and restless as young hawks, some gentlefaced and shrinking, some shrieking rude and sinful words, some listening, awed, but soon, grown familiar, to embrace – here were the children playing in the corridors of the House of Sin. Above the playground for ever hovered a great bird. The bird was known to humorists as the stork. But the people of Chrystie Street were better ornithologists. They called it a vulture.

A little girl of twelve came up timidly to the man reading and resting by the window, and said:

'Papa, won't you play a game of checkers with me if you aren't too tired?'

The red-haired, unshaven, untidy man sitting shoeless by the window answered, with a frown:

'Checkers! No, I won't. Can't a man who works hard all day have a little rest when he comes home? Why don't you go out and play with the other kids on the sidewalk?'

The woman who was cooking came to the door.

'John,' she said, 'I don't like for Lizzie to play in the street. They learn too much there that ain't good for 'em. She's been in the house all day long. It seems that you might give up a little of your time to amuse her when you come home.'

'Let her go out and play like the rest of 'em if she wants to be

amused,' said the red-haired, unshaven, untidy man, 'and don't
bother me.'

•   •   •   •   •

'You're on,' said Kid Mullaly. 'Fifty dollars to $25 I take Annie
to the dance. Put up.'

The Kid's black eyes were snapping with the fire of the baited and
challenged. He drew out his 'roll' and slapped five tens upon the bar.
The three or four young fellows who were thus 'taken' more slowly
produced their stake. The bartender, ex-officio stakeholder, took the
money, laboriously wrapped it, recorded the bet with an inch-long
pencil and stuffed the whole into a corner of the cash register.

'And, oh, what'll be done to you'll be a plenty,' said a better,
with anticipatory glee.

'That's my look-out,' said the Kid sternly. 'Fill 'em up all
around, Mike.'

After the round Burke, the Kid's sponge, spongeholder, pal,
mentor and Grand Vizier, drew him out to the bootblack stand at
the saloon corner, where all the official and important matters of
the Small Hours Social Club were settled. As Tony polished the
light tan shoes of the club's President and Secretary for the fifth
time that day, Burke spake words of wisdom to his chief.

'Cut that blonde out, Kid,' was his advice, 'or there'll be trouble. What do you want to throw down that girl of yours for?
You'll never find one that'll freeze to you like Liz has. She's worth
a hallfull of Annies.'

'I'm no Annie admirer!' said the Kid, dropping a cigarette ash
on his polished toe, and wiping it off on Tony's shoulder. 'But I
want to teach Liz a lesson. She thinks I belong to her. She's been
bragging that I daren't speak to another girl. Liz is all right — in
some ways. She's drinking a little too much lately. And she uses
language that a lady oughtn't.'

'You're engaged, ain't you?' asked Burke.

'Sure. We'll get married next year, maybe.'

'I saw you make her drink her first glass of beer,' said Burke.
'That was two years ago, when she used to come down to the
corner of Chrystie, bareheaded, to meet you after supper. She was
a quiet sort of a kid then, and couldn't speak without blushing.'

'She's a little spitfire, sometimes, now,' said the Kid. 'I hate jealousy. That's why I'm going to the dance with Annie. It'll teach her
some sense.'

'Well, you better look a little out,' were Burke's last words. 'If Liz was my girl and I was to sneak out to a dance coupled up with an Annie, I'd want a suit of chain armour on under my gladsome rags, all right.'

Through the land of the stork vulture wandered Liz. Her black eyes searched the passing crowds fierily but vaguely. Now and then she hummed bars of foolish little songs. Between times she set her small, white teeth together, and spake crisp words that the East Side has added to language.

Liz's skirt was green silk. Her waist was a large brown-and-pink plaid, well-fitting and not without style. She wore a cluster ring of huge imitation rubies, and a locket that banged her knees at the bottom of a silver chain. Her shoes were run down over twisted high heels, and were strangers to polish. Her hat would scarcely have passed into a flour barrel.

The 'Family Entrance' of the Blue Jay Café received her. At a table she sat, and punched the button with the air of milady ringing for her carriage. The waiter came with his large-chinned, low-voiced manner of respectful familiarity. Liz smoothed her silken skirt with a satisfied wriggle. She made the most of it. Here she could order and be waited upon. It was all that her world offered her of the prerogative of woman.

'Whisky, Tommy,' she said as her sisters further uptown murmur, 'Champagne, James.'

'Sure, Miss Lizzie. What'll the chaser be?'

'Seltzer. And say, Tommy, has the Kid been around to-day?'

'Why, no, Miss Lizzie, I haven't saw him today.'

Fluently came the 'Miss Lizzie,' for the Kid was known to be one who required rigid upholdment of the dignity of his fiancée.

'I'm lookin' for 'm,' said Liz, after the chaser had sputtered under her nose. 'It's got to me that he says he'll take Annie Karlson to the dance. Let him. The pink-eyed white rat! I'm lookin' for 'm. You know me, Tommy. Two years me and the Kid 've been engaged. Look at that ring. Five hundred, he said it cost. Let him take her to the dance. What'll I do? I'll cut his heart out. Another whisky, Tommy.'

'I wouldn't listen to no such reports, Miss Lizzie,' said the waiter smoothly, from the narrow opening above his chin. 'Kid Mullaly's not the guy to throw a lady like you down. Seltzer on the side?'

'Two years,' repeated Liz, softening a little to sentiment under the magic of the distiller's art. 'I always used to play out on the street of evenin's 'cause there was nothin' doin' for me at home. For a long time I just sat on doorsteps and looked at the lights and the people goin' by. And then the Kid came along one evenin' and sized me up, and I was mashed on the spot for fair. The first drink he made me take I cried all night at home, and got a lickin' for makin' a noise. And now – say, Tommy, you ever see this Annie Karlson? If it wasn't for peroxide the chloroform limit would have put her out long ago. Oh, I'm lookin' for 'm. You tell the Kid if he comes in. Me? I'll cut his heart out. Leave it to me. Another whisky, Tommy.'

A little unsteadily, but with watchful and brilliant eyes, Liz walked up the avenue. On the doorstep of a brick tenement a curly-haired child sat, puzzling over the convolutions of a tangled string. Liz flopped down beside her, with a crooked, shifting smile on her flushed face. But her eyes had grown clear and artless of a sudden.

'Let me show you how to make a cats-cradle, kid,' she said, tucking her green silk skirt under her rusty shoes.

And while they sat there the lights were being turned on for the dance in the hall of the Small Hours Social Club. It was the bi-monthly dance, a dress affair in which the members took great pride and bestirred themselves huskily to further and adorn.

At nine o'clock the President, Kid Mullaly, paced upon the floor with a lady on his arm. As the Loreley's was her hair golden. Her 'yes' was softened to a 'yah,' but its quality of assent was patent to the most Milesian ears. She stepped upon her own train and blushed, and – she smiled into the eyes of Kid Mullaly.

And then, as the two stood in the middle of the waxed floor, the thing happened to prevent which many lamps are burning nightly in many studies and libraries.

Out from the circle of spectators in the hall leaped Fate in a green silk skirt, under the *nom de guerre* of 'Liz.' Her eyes were hard and blacker than jet. She did not scream or waver. Most unwomanly, she cried out one oath – the Kid's own favourite oath – and in his own deep voice; and then while the Small Hours Social Club went frantically to pieces, she made good her boast to Tommy, the waiter – made good as far as the length of her knife blade and the strength of her arm permitted.

And next came the primal instinct of self-preservation – or was it self-annihilation, the instinct that society has grafted on the natural branch?

Liz ran out and down the street swift and true as a woodcock flying through a grove of saplings at dusk.

And then followed the big city's biggest shame, its most ancient and rotten surviving canker, its pollution and disgrace, its blight and perversion, its forever infamy and guilt, fostered, unreproved and cherished, handed down from a long-ago century of the basest barbarity – the Hue and Cry. Nowhere but in the big cities does it survive, and here most of all, where the ultimate perfection of culture, citizenship and alleged superiority joins, bawling, in the chase.

They pursued – a shrieking mob of fathers, mothers, lovers and maidens – howling, yelling, calling, whistling, crying for blood. Well may the wolf in the big city stand outside the door. Well may his heart, the gentler, falter at the siege.

Knowing her way, and hungry for her surcease, she darted down the familiar ways until at last her feet struck the dull solidity of the rotting pier. And then it was but a few more panting steps – and good mother East River took Liz to her bosom, soothed her muddily but quickly, and settled in five minutes the problem that keeps lights burning o' nights in thousands of pastorates and colleges.

•　　•　　•　　•　　•

It's mighty funny what kind of dreams one has sometimes. Poets call them visions, but a vision is only a dream in blank verse. I dreamed the rest of this story.

I thought I was in the next world. I don't know how I got there, I suppose I had been riding on the Ninth Avenue elevated or taking patent medicine, or trying to pull Jim Jeffries's nose, or doing some such little injudicious stunt. But, anyhow, there I was, and there was a great crowd of us outside the court-room where the judgments were going on. And every now and then a very beautiful and imposing court-officer angel would come outside the door and call another case.

While I was considering my own wordly sins and wondering whether there would be any use of my trying to prove an alibi by claiming that I lived in New Jersey, the bailiff angel came to the door and rang out:

'Case No. 99,852,743.'

Up stepped a plain-clothes man – there were lots of 'em there, dressed exactly like preachers, and hustling us spirits around just like cops do on earth – and by the arm he dragged – whom do you think? Why, Liz!

The court officer took her inside and closed the door. I went up to Mr. Fly-cop and inquired about the case.

'A very sad one,' says he, laying the points of his manicured fingers together. 'An utterly incorrigible girl. I am Special Terrestrial Officer the Reverend Jones. The case was assigned to me. The girl murdered her fiancé and committed suicide. She had no defence. My report to the court relates the facts in detail, all of which are substantiated by reliable witnesses. The wages of sin is death. Praise the Lord.'

The court officer opened the door and stepped out.

'Poor girl,' said Special Terrestrial Officer the Reverend Jones, with a tear in his eye. 'It was one of the saddest cases that I ever met with. Of course she was –'

'Discharged,' said the court officer. 'Come here, Jonesy. First thing you know you'll be switched to the pot-pie squad. How would you like to be on the missionary force in the South Sea Islands – hey? Now, you quit making these false arrests, or you'll be transferred – see? The guilty party you've got to look for in this case is a red-haired, unshaven, untidy man, sitting by the window reading, in his stocking feet, while his children play in the streets. Get a move on you.'

Now, wasn't that a silly dream?

XXXIII

The Last Leaf

IN A LITTLE DISTRICT west of Washington Square the streets have run crazy and broken themselves into small strips called 'places.' These 'places' make strange angles and curves. One street crosses itself a time or two. An artist once discovered a valuable possibility in this street. Suppose a collector with a bill for paints, paper and canvas should, in traversing this route, suddenly meet himself coming back, without a cent having been paid on account!

So, to quaint old Greenwich Village the art people soon came prowling, hunting for north windows and eighteenth-century gables and Dutch attics and low rents. Then they imported some pewter mugs and a chafing dish or two from Sixth Avenue, and became a 'colony.'

At the top of a squatty, three-story brick Sue and Johnsy had their studio. 'Johnsy' was familiar for Joanna. One was from Maine, the other from California. They had met at the table d'hôte of an Eighth Street 'Delmonico's,' and found their tastes in art, chicory salad and bishop sleeves so congenial that the joint studio resulted.

That was in May. In November a cold, unseen stranger, whom the doctors called Pneumonia, stalked about the colony, touching one here and there with his icy finger. Over on the East Side this ravager strode boldly, smiting his victims by scores, but his feet trod slowly through the maze of the narrow and moss-grown 'places.'

Mr. Pneumonia was not what you would call a chivalric old gentleman. A mite of a little woman with blood thinned by Californian zephyrs was hardly fair game for the red-fisted, short-breathed old duffer. But Johnsy he smote; and she lay, scarcely moving, on her painted iron bedstead, looking through the small Dutch window-panes at the blank side of the next brick house.

One morning the busy doctor invited Sue into the hallway with a shaggy, grey eyebrow.

'She has one chance in – let us say, ten,' he said, as he shook down the mercury in his clinical thermometer. 'And that chance is for her to want to live. This way people have of lining-up on the side of the undertaker makes the entire pharmacopœia look silly. Your little lady has made up her mind that she's not going to get well. Has she anything on her mind?'

'She – she wanted to paint the Bay of Naples some day,' said Sue.

'Paint? – bosh! Has she anything on her mind worth thinking about twice – a man, for instance?'

'A man?' said Sue, with a jews'-harp twang in her voice. 'Is a man worth – but, no, doctor; there is nothing of the kind.'

'Well, it is the weakness, then,' said the doctor. 'I will do all that science, so far as it may filter through my efforts, can accomplish. But whenever my patient begins to count the carriages in her funeral procession I subtract 50 per cent from the curative power of medicines. If you will get her to ask one question about the new winter styles in cloak sleeves I will promise you a one-in five chance for her, instead of one in ten.'

After the doctor had gone, Sue went into the workroom and cried a Japanese napkin to a pulp. Then she swaggered into Johnsy's room with her drawing-board, whistling ragtime.

Johnsy lay, scarcely making a ripple under the bedclothes, with her face toward the window. Sue stopped whistling, thinking she was asleep.

She arranged her board and began a pen-and-ink drawing to

illustrate a magazine story. Young artists must pave their way to Art by drawing pictures for magazine stories that young authors write to pave their way to Literature.

As Sue was sketching a pair of elegant horseshow riding trousers and a monocle on the figure of the hero, an Idaho cowboy, she heard a low sound, several times repeated. She went quickly to the bedside.

Johnsy's eyes were open wide. She was looking out the window and counting – counting backward.

'Twelve,' she said, and a little later, 'eleven'; and then 'ten,' and 'nine'; and then 'eight' and 'seven,' almost together.

Sue looked solicitously out the window. What was there to count? There was only a bare, dreary yard to be seen, and the blank side of the brick house twenty feet away. An old, old ivy vine, gnarled and decayed at the roots, climbed half-way up the brick wall. The cold breath of autumn had stricken its leaves from the vine until its skeleton branches clung, almost bare, to the crumbling bricks.

'What is it, dear?' asked Sue.

'Six,' said Johnsy, in almost a whisper. 'They're falling faster now. Three days ago there were almost a hundred. It made my head ache to count them. But now it's easy. There goes another one. There are only five left now.'

'Five what, dear? Tell your Sudie.'

'Leaves. On the ivy vine. When the last one falls I must go too. I've known that for three days. Didn't the doctor tell you?'

'Oh, I never heard of such nonsense,' complained Sue, with magnificent scorn. 'What have old ivy leaves to do with your getting well? And you used to love that vine so, you naughty girl. Don't be a goosey. Why, the doctor told me this morning that your chances for getting well real soon were – let's see exactly what he said – he said the chances were ten to one! Why, that's almost as good a chance as we have in New York when we ride on the street-cars or walk past a new building. Try to take some broth now, and let Sudie go back to her drawing, so she can sell the editor man with it, and buy port wine for her sick child, and pork chops for her greedy self.'

'You needn't get any more wine,' said Johnsy, keeping her eyes fixed out the window.

'There goes another. No, I don't want any broth. That leaves just four. I want to see the last one fall before it gets dark. Then I'll go too.'

'Johnsy, dear,' said Sue, bending over her, 'will you promise me to keep your eyes closed, and not look out of the window until I am done working? I must hand those drawings in by to-morrow. I need the light or I would draw the shade down.'

'Couldn't you draw in the other room?' asked Johnsy coldly.

'I'd rather be here by you,' said Sue. 'Besides, I don't want you to keep looking at those silly ivy leaves.'

'Tell me as soon as you have finished,' said Johnsy, closing her eyes, and lying white and still as a fallen statue, 'because I want to see the last one fall. I'm tired of waiting. I'm tired of thinking. I want to turn loose my hold on everything, and go sailing down, down, just like one of those poor, tired leaves.'

'Try to sleep,' said Sue. 'I must call Behrman up to be my model for the old hermit miner. I'll not be gone a minute. Don't try to move till I come back.'

Old Behrman was a painter who lived on the ground floor beneath them. He was past sixty and had a Michael Angelo's Moses beard curling down from the head of a satyr along the body of an imp. Behrman was a failure in art. Forty years he had wielded the brush without getting near enough to touch the hem of his Mistress's robe. He had been always about to paint a masterpiece, but had never yet begun it. For several years he had painted nothing except now and then a daub in the line of commerce or advertising. He earned a little by serving as a model to those young artists in the colony who could not pay the price of a professional. He drank gin to excess, and still talked of his coming masterpiece. For the rest he was a fierce little old man, who scoffed terribly at softness in anyone, and who regarded himself as especial mastiff-in-waiting to protect the two young artists in the studio above.

Sue found Behrman smelling strongly of juniper berries in his dimly-lighted den below. In one corner was a blank canvas on an easel that had been waiting there for twenty-five years to receive the first line of the masterpiece. She told him of Johnsy's fancy, and how she feared she would, indeed, light and fragile as a leaf herself, float away when her slight hold upon the world grew weaker.

Old Behrman, with his red eyes plainly streaming, shouted his contempt and derision for such idiotic imaginings.

'Vass!' he cried. 'Is dere people in de world mit der foolishness to die because leafs dey drop off from a confounded vine? I haf not heard of such a thing. No, I vill not bose as a model for your fool hermit-dunderhead. Vy do you allow dot silly pusiness to come in der prain of her? Ach, dot poor little Miss Yohnsy.'

'She is very ill and weak,' said Sue, 'and the fever has left her mind morbid and full of strange fancies. Very well, Mr. Behrman, if you do not care to pose for me, you needn't. But I think you are a horrid old – old flibberti-gibbet.'

'You are just like a woman!' yelled Behrman. 'Who said I vill not bose? Go on. I come mit you. For half an hour I haf peen trying to say dot I am ready to bose. Gott! dis is not any blace in which one so goot as Miss Yohnsy shall lie sick. Some day I vill baint a masterpiece, and ve shall all go avay. Gott! yes.'

Johnsy was sleeping when they went upstairs. Sue pulled the shade down to the window-sill and motioned Behrman into the other room. In there they peered out the window fearfully at the ivy vine. Then they looked at each other for a moment without speaking. A persistent, cold rain was falling, mingled with snow. Behrman, in his old blue shirt, took his seat as the hermit-miner on an upturned kettle for a rock.

When Sue awoke from an hour's sleep the next morning she found Johnsy with dull, wide-open eyes staring at the drawn green shade.

'Pull it up! I want to see,' she ordered, in a whisper.

Wearily Sue obeyed.

But, lo! after the beating rain and fierce gusts of wind that had endured through the livelong night, there yet stood out against the brick wall one ivy leaf. It was the last on the vine. Still dark green near its stem, but with its serrated edges tinted with the yellow of dissolution and decay, it hung bravely from a branch some twenty feet above the ground.

'It is the last one,' said Johnsy. 'I thought it would surely fall during the night. I heard the wind. It will fall to-day, and I shall die at the same time.'

'Dear, dear!' said Sue, leaning her worn face down to the pillow; 'think of me, if you won't think of yourself. What would I do?'

But Johnsy did not answer. The lonesomest thing in all the world is a soul when it is making ready to go on its mysterious, far journey. The fancy seemed to possess her more strongly as one by one the ties that bound her to friendship and to earth were loosed.

The day wore away, and even through the twilight they could see the lone ivy leaf clinging to its stem against the wall. And then, with the coming of the night the north wind was again loosed, while the rain still beat against the windows and pattered down from the low Dutch eaves.

When it was light enough Johnsy, the merciless, commanded that the shade be raised.

The ivy leaf was still there.

Johnsy lay for a long time looking at it. And then she called to Sue, who was stirring her chicken broth over the gas stove.

'I've been a bad girl, Sudie,' said Johnsy. 'Something has made that last leaf stay there to show me how wicked I was. It is a sin to want to die. You may bring me a little broth now, and some milk with a little port in it, and – no; bring me a hand-mirror first; and then pack some pillows about me, and I will sit up and watch you cook.'

An hour later she said –

'Sudie, some day I hope to paint the Bay of Naples.'

The doctor came in the afternoon, and Sue had an excuse to go into the hallway as he left.

'Even chances,' said the doctor, talking Sue's thin, shaking hand in his. 'With good nursing you'll win. And now I must see another case I have downstairs. Behrman, his name is – some kind of an artist, I believe. Pneumonia, too. He is an old, weak man, and the attack is acute. There is no hope for him; but he goes to the hospital to-day to be made more comfortable.'

The next day the doctor said to Sue: 'She's out of danger. You've won. Nutrition and care now – that's all.'

And that afternoon Sue came to the bed where Johnsy lay, contentedly knitting a very blue and very useless woollen shoulder scarf, and put one arm around her, pillows and all.

'I have something to tell you, white mouse,' she said. 'Mr. Behrman died of pneumonia today in hospital. He was ill only two days. The janitor found him on the morning of the first day in his room downstairs helpless with pain. His shoes and clothing were wet through and icy cold. They couldn't imagine where he had been on such a dreadful night. And then they found a lantern, still lighted, and a ladder that had been dragged from its place, and some scattered brushes, and a palette with green and yellow colours mixed on it, and – look out the window, dear, at the last ivy leaf on the wall. Didn't you wonder why it never fluttered or moved when the wind blew? Ah, darling, it's Behrman's masterpiece – he painted it there the night that the last leaf fell.'

XXXIV

The Count and the Wedding Guest

ONE EVENING WHEN Andy Donovan went to dinner at his Second Avenue boarding-house, Mrs. Scott introduced him to a new boarder, a young lady, Miss Conway. Miss Conway was small and unobtrusive. She wore a plain, snuffy-brown dress, and bestowed her interest, which seemed languid, upon her plate. She lifted her diffident eyelids and shot one perspicuous, judicial glance at Mr. Donovan, politely murmured his name, and returned to her mutton. Mr. Donovan bowed with the grace and beaming smile that was rapidly winning for him social, business and political advancement, and erased the snuffy-brown one from the tablets of his consideration.

Two weeks later Andy was sitting on the front steps enjoying his cigar. There was a soft rustle behind and above him, and Andy turned his head − and had his head turned.

Just coming out of the door was Miss Conway. She wore a night-black dress of *crêpe de* − *crêpe de* − oh, this thin black goods. Her hat was black, and from it drooped and fluttered an ebon veil, filmy as a spider's web. She stood on the top step and drew on black silk gloves. Not a speck of white or a spot of colour about her dress anywhere. Her rich golden hair was drawn, with scarcely a ripple, into a shining, smooth knot low on her neck. Her face was plain rather than pretty, but it was now illuminated and made almost beautiful by her large grey eyes that gazed above the houses across the street into the sky with an expression of the most appealing sadness and melancholy.

Gather the idea, girls − all black, you know, with the preference for *crêpe de* − oh, *crêpe de chine* − that's it. All black, and that sad, far-away look, and the hair shining under the black veil (you have to be a blonde, of course), and try to look as if, although your young life had been blighted just as it was about to give a hop-skip-and-a-jump over the threshold of life, a walk in the park might do you good, and be sure to happen out the door at the right moment, and − oh, it'll fetch 'em every time. But it's fierce, now, how cynical I am, ain't it? − to talk about mourning costumes this way.

Mr. Donovan suddenly reinscribed Miss Conway upon the tables of his consideration. He threw away the remaining inch-and-a-quarter of his cigar, that would have been good for eight minutes yet, and quickly shifted his centre of gravity to his low-cut patent leathers.

'It's a fine, clear evening, Miss Conway,' he said; and if the Weather Bureau could have heard the confident emphasis of his tones it would have hoisted the square white signal and nailed it to the mast.

'To them that has the heart to enjoy it, it is, Mr. Donovan,' said Miss Conway, with a sigh.

Mr. Donovan, in his heart, cursed fair weather. Heartless weather! It should hail and blow and snow to be consonant with the mood of Miss Conway.

'I hope none of your relatives – I hope you haven't sustained a loss?' ventured Mr. Donovan.

'Death has claimed,' said Miss Conway, hesitating – 'not a relative, but one who – but I will not intrude my grief upon you, Mr. Donovan.'

'Intrude?' protested Mr. Donovan. 'Why, say, Miss Conway, I'd be delighted, that is, I'd be sorry – I mean I'm sure nobody could sympathize with you truer than I would.'

Miss Conway smiled a little smile. And oh, it was sadder than her expression in repose.

' "Laugh, and the world laughs with you; weep, and they give you the laugh," ' she quoted. 'I have learned that, Mr. Donovan. I have no friends or acquaintances in this city. But you have been kind to me. I appreciate it highly.'

He had passed her the pepper twice at the table.

'It's tough to be alone in New York – that's a cinch,' said Mr. Donovan. 'But, say – whenever this little old town does loosen up and get friendly it goes the limit. Say you took a little stroll in the park, Miss Conway – don't you think it might chase away some of your mullygrubs? And if you'd allow me –'

'Thanks, Mr. Donovan. I'd be pleased to accept of your escort if you think the company of one whose heart is filled with gloom could be anyways agreeable to you.'

Through the open gates of the iron-railed, old, down-town park, where the elect once took the air, they strolled, and found a quiet bench.

There is this difference between the grief of youth and that of old age; youth's burden is lightened by as much of it as another shares; old age may give and give, but the sorrow remains the same.

'He was my fiancé,' confided Miss Conway, at the end of an hour. 'We were going to be married next spring. I don't want you to think that I am stringing you, Mr. Donovan, but he was a real Count. He had an estate and a castle in Italy. Count Fernando Mazzini was his name. I never saw the beat of him for elegance. Papa objected, of course, and once we eloped, but papa overtook us, and took us back. I thought sure papa and Fernando would fight a duel. Papa has a livery business – in P'kipsee, you know.

'Finally, papa came round, all right, and said we might be married next spring. Fernando showed him proofs of his title and wealth, and then went over to Italy to get the castle fixed up for us. Papa's very proud, and when Fernando wanted to give me several thousand dollars for my trousseau he called him down something awful. He wouldn't even let me take a ring or any presents from him. And when Fernando sailed I came to the city and got a position as cashier in a candy store.

'Three days ago I got a letter from Italy, forwarded from P'kipsee, saying that Fernando had been killed in a gondola accident.

'That is why I am in mourning. My heart, Mr. Donovan, will remain for ever in his grave. I guess I am poor company, Mr. Donovan, but I cannot take any interest in no one. I should not care to keep you from gaiety and your friends who can smile and entertain you. Perhaps you would prefer to walk back to the house?'

Now, girls, if you want to observe a young man hustle out after a pick and shovel, just tell him that your heart is in some other fellow's grave. Young men are grave-robbers by nature. Ask any widow. Something must be done to restore that missing organ to weeping angels in *crêpe de chine*. Dead men certainly got the worst of it from all sides.

'I'm awfully sorry,' said Mr. Donovan gently. 'No, we won't walk back to the house just yet. And don't say you haven't no friends in this city, Miss Conway. I'm awful sorry, and I want you to believe I'm your friend, and that I'm awful sorry.'

'I've got his picture here in my locket,' said Miss Conway, after wiping her eyes with her handkerchief. 'I never showed it to anybody; but I will to you, Mr. Donovan, because I believe you to be a true friend.'

Mr. Donovan gazed long and with much interest at the photograph in the locket that Miss Conway opened for him. The face of Count Mazzini was one to command interest. It was a smooth, intelligent, bright, almost a handsome face – the face of a strong, cheerful man who might well be a leader among his fellows.

'I have a larger one, framed, in my room,' said Miss Conway. 'When we return I will show you that. They are all I have to remind me of Fernando. But he ever will be present in my heart, that's a sure thing.'

A subtle task confronted Mr. Donovan – that of supplanting the unfortunate Count in the heart of Miss Conway. This his admiration for her determined him to do. But the magnitude of the undertaking did not seem to weigh upon his spirits. The sympathetic but cheerful friend was the role he essayed; and he played it so successfully that the next half-hour found them conversing pensively across two plates of ice-cream, though yet there was no diminution of the sadness in Miss Conway's large grey eyes.

Before they parted in the hall that evening she ran upstairs and brought down the framed photograph wrapped lovingly in a white silk scarf. Mr. Donovan surveyed it with inscrutable eyes.

'He gave me this the night he left for Italy,' said Miss Conway. 'I had the one for the locket made from this.'

'A fine-looking man,' said Mr. Donovan heartily. 'How would it suit you, Miss Conway, to give me pleasure of your company to Coney next Sunday afternoon?'

A month later they announced their engagement to Mrs. Scott and the other boarders. Miss Conway continued to wear black.

A week after the announcement the two sat on the same bench in the down-town park, while the fluttering leaves of the trees made a dim kinetoscopic picture of them in the moonlight. But Donovan had worn a look of abstracted gloom all day. He was so silent to-night that love's lips could not keep back any longer the questions that love's heart propounded.

'What's the matter, Andy, you are so solemn and grouchy to-night?'

'Nothing, Maggie.'

'I know better. Can't I tell? You never acted this way before. What is it?'

'It's nothing much, Maggie.'

'Yes, it is; and I want to know. I'll bet it's some other girl you are thinking about. All right. Why don't you go get her if you want her. Take your arm away, if you please.'

'I'll tell you, then,' said Andy wisely, 'but I guess you won't understand it exactly. You've heard of Mike Sullivan, haven't you? "Big Mike" Sullivan, everybody calls him.'

'No, I haven't,' said Maggie. 'And I don't want to, if he makes you act like this. Who is he?'

'He's the biggest man in New York,' said Andy, almost reverently. 'He can about do anything he wants to with Tammany or any other old thing in the political line. He's a mile high and as broad as East River. You say anything against Big Mike, and you'll have a million men on your collarbone in about two seconds. Why, he made a visit over to the old country awhile back, and the kings took to their holes like rabbits.

'Well, Big Mike's a friend of mine. I ain't more than deuce-high in the district as far as influence goes, but Mike's as good a friend to a little man, or a poor man, as he is to a big one. I met him to-day on the Bowery, and what do you think he does? Comes up and shakes hands. "Andy," says he. "I've been keeping cases on you. You've been putting in some good licks over on your side of the street, and I'm proud of you. What'll you take to drink?" He takes a cigar, and I take a highball. I told him I was going to get married in two weeks. "Andy," says he, "send me an invitation, so I'll keep in mind of it, and I'll come to the wedding." That's what Big Mike says to me; and he always does what he says.

'You don't understand it, Maggie, but I'd have one of my hands cut off to have Big Mike Sullivan at our wedding. It would be the proudest day of my life. When he goes to a man's wedding, there's a guy being married that's made for life. Now, that's why I'm maybe looking sore to-night.'

'Why don't you invite him, then, if he's so much to the mustard?' said Maggie lightly.

'There's a reason why I can't,' said Andy sadly. 'There's a reason why he mustn't be there. Don't ask me what it is, for I can't tell you.'

'Oh, I don't care,' said Maggie. 'It's something about politics, of course. But it's no reason why you can't smile at me.'

'Maggie,' said Andy presently, 'do you think as much of me as you did of your – as you did of the Count Mazzini?'

He waited a long time, but Maggie did not reply. And then, suddenly she leaned against his shoulder and began to cry – to cry and shake with sobs, holding his arm tightly, and wetting the *crêpe de chine* with tears.

'There, there, there!' soothed Andy, putting aside his own trouble. 'And what is it, now?'

'Andy,' sobbed Maggie, 'I've lied to you, and you'll never marry me, or love me any more. But I feel that I've got to tell. Andy, there never was so much as the little finger of a count. I never had a beau in my life. But all the other girls had; and they talked about 'em; and that seemed to make the fellows like 'em more. And, Andy, I look swell in black – you know I do. So I went out to a photograph store and bought that picture, and had a little one made for my locket, and made up all that story about the Count, and about his being killed, so I could wear black. And nobody can love a liar, and you'll shake me, Andy, and I'll die for shame. Oh, there never was anybody I liked but you – and that's all.'

But instead of being pushed away, she found Andy's arm folding her closer. She looked up and saw his face cleared and smiling.

'Could you – could you forgive me, Andy?'

'Sure,' said Andy. 'It's all right about that. Back to the cemetery for the Count. You've straightened everything out, Maggie. I was in hopes you would before the wedding-day. Bully girl!'

'Andy,' said Maggie, with a somewhat shy smile, after she had been thoroughly assured of forgiveness, 'did you believe all that story about the Count?'

'Well, not to any large extent,' said Andy, reaching for his cigar case; 'because it's Big Mike Sullivan's picture you've got in that locket of yours.'

XXXV

The Tale of a Tainted Tenner

MONEY TALKS. But you may think that the conversation of a little old ten-dollar bill in New York would be nothing more than a whisper. Oh, very well! Pass up this *sotto voce* autobiography of an X if you like. If you are one of the kind that prefers to listen to John D.'s chequebook roar at you through a megaphone as it passes by, all right. But don't forget that small change can say a word to the point now and then. The next time you tip your grocer's clerk a silver quarter to give you extra weight of his boss's goods read the four words above the lady's head. How are they for repartee?

I am a ten-dollar Treasury note, series of 1901. You may have seen one in a friend's hand. On my face, in the centre, is a picture of the bison Americanus, miscalled a buffalo by fifty or sixty millions of Americans. The heads of Capt. Lewis and Capt. Clark adorn the ends. On my back is the graceful figure of Liberty, or

Ceres, or Maxine Elliott standing in the centre of the stage on a conservatory plant. My references is – or are – Section 3,588, Revised Statutes. Ten cold, hard dollars – I don't say whether silver, gold, lead or iron – Uncle Sam will hand you over his counter if you want to cash me in.

I beg you will excuse any conversational breaks that I make thanks, I knew you would – got that sneaking little respect and agreeable feeling toward even an X, haven't you? You see, a tainted bill doesn't have much chance to acquire a correct form of expression. I never knew a really cultured and educated person that could afford to hold a ten-spot any longer than it would take to do an Arthur Duffy to the nearest That's All! sign or delicatessen store.

For a six-year-old, I've had a lively and gorgeous circulation. I guess I've paid as many debts as the man who dies. I've been owned by a good many kinds of people. But a little old ragged, damp, dingy five-dollar silver certificate gave me a jar one day. I was next to it in the fat and bad-smelling purse of a butcher.

'Hey, you Sitting Bull,' says I, 'don't scrouge so. Anyhow, don't you think it's about time you went in on a customs payment and got reissued? For a series of 1899 you're a sight.'

'Oh, don't get crackly just because you're a Buffalo bill,' says the fiver. 'You'd be limp, too, if you'd been stuffed down in a thick cotton-and-lisle-thread under an elastic all day, and the thermometer not a degree under 85 in the store.'

'I never heard of a pocket-book like that,' says I. 'Who carried you?'

'A shop-girl,' says the five-spot.

'What's that?' I had to ask.

'You'll never know till their millennium comes,' says the fiver.

Just then a two-dollar bill behind me with a George Washington head, spoke up to the fiver:

'Aw, cut out yer kicks. Ain't lisle thread good enough for yer? If you was under all cotton like I've been to-day, and choked up with factory dust till the lady with the cornucopia on me sneezed half a dozen times, you'd have some reason to complain.'

That was the next day after I arrived in New York. I came in a $500 package of tens to a Brooklyn bank from one of its Pennsylvania correspondents – and I haven't made the acquaintance of any of the five and two spots' friends' pocketbooks yet. Silk for mine, every time.

I was lucky money. I kept on the move. Sometimes I changed hands twenty times a day. I saw the inside of every business; I fought for my owner's every pleasure. It seemed that on Saturday nights I never missed being slapped down on a bar. Tens were always slapped down, while ones and twos were slid over to the bartenders folded. I got in the habit of looking for mine, and I managed to soak in a little straight or some spilled Martini or Manhattan whenever I could. Once I got tied up in a great greasy roll of bills in a pushcart pedlar's jeans. I thought I never would get in circulation again, for the future department store owner lived on eight cents' worth of dog-meat and onions a day. But this pedlar got into trouble one day on account of having his cart too near a crossing, and I was rescued. I always will feel grateful to the cop that got me. He changed me at a cigar store near the Bowery that was running a crap game in the back room. So it was the Captain of the precinct, after all, that did me the best turn, when he got his. He blew me for wine the next evening in a Broadway restaurant; and I really felt as glad to get back again as an Astor does when he sees the lights of Charing Cross.

A tainted ten certainly does get action on Broadway. I was alimony once, and got folded in a little dogskin purse among a lot of dimes. They were bragging about the busy times there were in Ossining whenever three girls got hold of one of them during the ice-cream season. But it's Slow Moving Vehicles Keep to the Right for the little Bok tips when you think of the way we bison plasters refuse to stick to anything during the rush lobster hour.

The first I ever heard of tainted money was one night when a good thing with a Van to his name threw me over with some other bills to buy a stack of blues.

About midnight a big, easy-going man with a fat face like a monk's and the eye of a janitor with his wages raised took me and a lot of other notes and rolled us into what is termed a 'wad' among the money tainters.

'Ticket me for five hundred,' said he to the banker, 'and look out for everything, Charlie. I'm going out for a stroll in the glen before the moonlight fades from the brow of the cliff. If anybody finds the roof in their way there's $60,000 wrapped in a comic supplement in the upper left-hand corner of the safe. Be bold; everywhere be bold, but be not bowled over. 'Night.'

I found myself between two $20 gold certificates. One of 'em says to me:

'Well, old shorthorn, you're in luck to-night. You'll see something of life. Old Jack's going to make the Tenderloin look like a Hamburg steak.'

'Explain,' says I. 'I'm used to joints, but I don't care for filet mignon with the kind of sauce you serve.'

' 'Xcuse me,' said the twenty. 'Old Jack is the proprietor of this gambling house. He's going on a whiz to-night because he offered $50,000 to a church and it refused to accept it because they said his money was tainted.'

'What is a church?' I asked.

'Oh, I forgot,' says the twenty, 'that I was talking to a tenner. Of course you don't know. You're too much to put into the contribution basket, and not enough to buy anything at a bazzar. A church is – a large building in which penwipers and tidies are sold at $20 each.'

I don't care much about chinning with gold certificates. There's a streak of yellow in 'em. All is not gold that's quitters.

Old Jack certainly was a gilt-edged sport. When it came his time to loosen up he never referred the waiter to an actuary.

By and by it got around that he was smiting the rock in the wilderness; and all along Broadway things with cold noses and hot gullets fell in on our trail. The third Jungle Book was there waiting for somebody to put covers on it. Old Jack's money may have had a taint to it, but all the same he had orders for his Camembert piling up on him every minute. First his friends rallied round him; and then the fellows that his friends knew by sight; and then a few of his enemies buried the hatchet; and finally he was buying souvenirs for so many Neapolitan fisher-maidens and butterfly octettes that the head waiters were 'phoning all over town for Julian Mitchell to please come around and get them into some kind of order.

At last we floated into an up-town café that I knew by heart. When the hod-carriers' union in jackets and aprons saw us coming the chief goal-kicker called out: 'Six – eleven – forty-two – nineteen – twelve' to his men, and they put on nose guards till it was clear whether we meant Port Arthur or Portsmouth. But Old Jack wasn't working for the furniture and glass factories that night. He sat down quiet and sang 'Ramble' in a half-hearted way. His feelings had been hurt, so the twenty told me, because his offer to the church had been refused.

But the wassail went on; and Brady himself couldn't have hammered the thirst mob into a better imitation of the real penchant for the stuff that you screw out of a bottle with a napkin.

Old Jack paid the twenty above me for a round, leaving me on the outside of his roll. He laid the roll on the table and sent for the proprietor.

'Mike,' says he, 'here's money that the good people have refused. Will it buy of your wares in the name of the devil? They say it's tainted.'

'It will,' says Mike, 'and I'll put it in the drawer next to the bills that was paid to the parson's daughter for kisses at the church fair to build a new parsonage for the parson's daughter to live in.'

At one o'clock when the hod-carriers were making ready to close up the front and keep the inside open, a woman slips in the door of the restaurant and comes up to Old Jack's table. You've seen the kind – black shawl, creepy hair, ragged skirt, white face, eyes a cross between Gabriel's and a sick kitten's – the kind of woman that's always on the look-out for an automobile or the mendicancy squad – and she stands there without a word and looks at the money.

Old Jack gets up, peels me off the roll and hands me to her with a bow.

'Madam,' says he, just like actors I've heard, 'here is a tainted bill. I am a gambler. This bill came to me to-night from a gentleman's son. Where he got it I do not know. If you will do me the favour to accept it, it is yours.'

The woman took me with a trembling hand.

'Sir,' said she, 'I counted thousands of this issue of bills into packages when they were virgin from the presses. I was a clerk in the Treasury Department. There was an official to whom I owed my position. You say they are tainted now. If you only knew – but I won't say any more. Thank you with all my heart, sir – thank you – thank you.'

Where do you suppose that woman carried me almost at a run? To a bakery. Away from Old Jack and a sizzling good time to a bakery. And I get changed, and she does a Sheridan-twenty-miles-away with a dozen rolls and a section of jelly cake as big as a turbine water-wheel. Of course I lost sight of her then, for I was snowed up in the bakery, wondering whether I'd get changed at the drug store the next day in an alum deal or paid over to the cement works.

A week afterward I butted up against one of the one-dollar bills the baker had given the woman for change.

'Hallo, E35039669,' says I, 'weren't you in the change for me in a bakery last Saturday night?'

'Yep,' says the solitaire in his free and easy style.

'How did the deal turn out?' I asked.

'She blew E17051431 for milk and round steak,' says the one-spot. 'She kept me till the rent man came. It was a bum room with a sick kid in it. But you ought to have seen him go for the bread and tincture of formaldehyde. Half starved, I guess. Then she prayed some. Don't get stuck up, tenner. We one-spots hear ten prayers where you hear one. She said something about "who giveth to the poor." Oh, let's cut out the slum talk. I'm certainly tired of the company that keeps me. I wish I was big enough to move in society with you tainted bills.'

'Shut up,' says I; 'there's no such thing. I know the rest of it. There's a "lendeth to the Lord" somewhere in it. Now look on my back and read what you see there.'

'This note is a legal tender at its face value for all debts public and private.'

'This talk about tainted money makes me tired,' says I.

XXXVI

Jeff Peters as a Personal Magnet

JEFF PETERS HAS BEEN ENGAGED in as many schemes for making money as there are recipes for cooking rice in Charleston, S.C.

Best of all I like to hear him tell of his earlier days when he sold liniments and cough cures on street corners, living hand to mouth, heart to heart, with the people? throwing heads or tails with fortune for his last coin.

'I struck Fisher Hill, Arkansaw,' said he, 'in a buckskin suit, moccasins, long hair and a thirty-carat diamond ring that I got from an actor in Texarkana. I don't know what he ever did with the pocket-knife I swapped him for it.

'I was Dr. Waugh-hoo, the celebrated Indian medicine man. I carried only one best bet just then, and that was Resurrection Bitters. It was made of life-giving plants and herbs accidentally discovered by Ta-qua-la, the beautiful wife of the chief of the Choctaw Nation, while gathering truck to garnish a platter of boiled dog for the annual corn dance.

'Business hadn't been good at the last town, so I only had five dollars. I went to the Fisher Hill druggist and he credited me for half a gross of eight-ounce bottles and corks. I had the labels and ingredients in my valise, left over from the last town. Life began to look rosy again after I got in my hotel room with the water running from the tap, and the Resurrection Bitters lining up on the table by the dozen.

'Fake? No, sir. There was two dollars' worth of fluid extract of cinchona and a dime's worth of aniline in that half-gross of bitters. I've gone through towns years afterwards and had folks ask for 'em again.

'I hired a wagon that night and commenced selling the bitters on Main Street. Fisher Hill was a low, malarial town; and a compound hypothetical pneumocardiac anti-scorbutic tonic was just what I diagnosed the crowd as needing. The bitters started off like sweetbreads-on-toast at a vegetarian dinner. I had sold two dozen at fifty cents apiece when I felt somebody pull my coat tail. I knew what that meant; so I climbed down and sneaked a five-dollar bill into the hand of a man with a German silver star on his lapel.

' "Constable," says I, "it's a fine night."

' "Have you got a city licence," he asks, "to sell this illegitimate essence of spooju that you flatter by the name of medicine?"

' "I have not," says I. "I didn't know you had a city. If I can find it to-morrow I'll take one out if it's necessary."

' "I'll have to close you up till you do," says the constable.

'I quit selling and went back to the hotel. I was talking to the landlord about it.

' "Oh, you won't stand no show in Fisher Hill," says he. "Dr. Hoskins, the only doctor here, is a brother-in-law of the Mayor, and they won't allow no fake doctor to practise in town."

' "I don't practise medicine," says I, "I've got a State pedlar's licence, and I take out a city one wherever they demand it."

'I went to the Mayor's office the next morning and they told me he hadn't showed up yet. They didn't know when he'd be down. So Doc Waughhoo hunches down again in a hotel chair and lights a jimpson-weed regalia, and waits.

'By and by a young man in a blue neck-tie slips into the chair next to me and asks the time.

' "Half-past ten," says I, "and you are Andy Tucker. I've seen you work. Wasn't it you that put up the Great Cupid Combination package on the Southern States? Let's see, it was a Chilian diamond engagement ring, a wedding-ring, a potato masher, a bottle of soothing syrup and Dorothy Vernon – all for fifty cents."

'Andy was pleased to hear that I remembered him. He was a good street man; and he was more than that – he respected his profession, and he was satisfied with 300 per cent. profit. He had plenty of offers to go into the illegitimate drug and garden seed business; but he was never to be tempted off of the straight path.

'I wanted a partner; so Andy and me agreed to go out together. I told him about the situation in Fisher Hill and how finances was low on account of the local mixture of politics and jalap. Andy had just got in on the train that morning. He was pretty low himself, and was going to canvass the town for a few dollars to build a new battleship by popular subscription at Eureka Springs. So we went out and sat on the porch and talked it over.

'The next morning at eleven o'clock, when I was sitting there alone, an Uncle Tom shuffles into the hotel and asked for the doctor to come and see Judge Banks, who, it seems, was the mayor and a mighty sick man.

' "I'm no doctor," says I. "Why don't you go and get the doctor?"

' "Boss," says he, "Doc Hoskins am done gone twenty miles in de country to see some sick persons. He's de only doctor in de town, and Massa Banks am powerful bad off. He sent me to ax you to please, suh, come."

' "As man to man," says I, "I'll go and look him over." So I put a bottle of Resurrection Bitters in my pocket and goes up on the hill to the Mayor's mansion, the finest house in town, with a mansard roof and two cast-iron dogs on the lawn.

'This Mayor Banks was in bed all but his whiskers and feet. He was making internal noises that would have had everybody in San Francisco hiking for the parks. A young man was standing by the bed holding a cup of water.

' "Doc," says the Mayor, "I'm awful sick. I'm about to die. Can't you do nothing for me?"

' "Mr. Mayor," says I, "I'm not a regular preordained disciple of S. Q. Lapius. I never took a course in a medical college," says I, "I've just come as a fellow-man to see if I could be of assistance."

' "I'm deeply obliged," says he. "Doc Waughhoo, this is my nephew, Mr. Biddle. He has tried to alleviate my distress, but without success. Oh, Lordy! Ow-ow-ow!!" he sings out.

'I nods at Mr. Biddle and sets down by the bed and feels the Mayor's pulse. "Let me see your liver – your tongue, I mean," says I. Then I turns up the lids of his eyes and looks close at the pupils of 'em.

' "How long have you been sick?" I asked.

'I was taken down – ow-ouch – last night," says the Mayor. "Gimme something for it, doc, won't you?"

' "Mr. Fiddle," says I, "raise the window shade a bit, will you?"

' "Biddle," says the young man. "Do you feel like you could eat some ham and eggs, Uncle James?"

' "Mr. Mayor," says I, after laying my ear to his right shoulder-blade and listening, "you've got a bad attack of super-inflammation of the right clavicle of the harpsichord!"

' "Good Lord!" says he, with a groan. "Can't you rub something on it, or set it or anything?"

'I picks up my hat and starts for the door.

' "You ain't going, doc?" says the Mayor with a howl. "You ain't going away and leave me to die with this – superfluity of the clapboards, are you?"

' "Common humanity, Dr. Whoa-ha," says Mr. Biddle, "ought to prevent your deserting a fellow-human in distress." '

' "Dr. Waugh-hoo, when you get through ploughing," says I. And then I walks back to the bed and throws back my long hair.

' "Mr. Mayor," says I, "there is only one hope for you. Drugs will do you no good. But there is another power higher yet, although drugs are high enough," says I.

' "And what is that?" says he.

' "Scientific demonstrations," says I. "The triumph of mind over sarsaparilla. The belief that there is no pain and sickness except what is produced when we ain't feeling well. Declare yourself in arrears. Demonstrate."

' "What is this paraphernalia you speak of, doc?" says the Mayor. "You ain't a Socialist, are you?"

' "I am speaking," says I, "of the great doctrine of psychic financiering of the enlightened school of long-distance, subcon-scientious treatment of fallacies and meningitis – of that wonderful indoor sport known as personal magnetism."

' "Can you work it, doc?" asks the Mayor

' "I'm one of the Sole Sanhedrims and Ostensible Hooplas of the Inner Pulpit," says I. "The lame talk and the blind rubber whenever I make a pass at 'em. I am a medium, a coloratura hyp-notist and a spirituous control. It was only through me at the recent seances at Ann Arbour that the late president of the Vine-gar Bitters Company could revisit the earth to communicate with his sister Jane. You see me peddling medicine on the streets," says I, "to the poor. I don't practise personal magnetism on them. I do not drag it in the dust," says I, "because they haven't got the dust."

' "Will you treat my case?" asks the Mayor.

' "Listen," says I. "I've had a good deal of trouble with medical societies everywhere I've been. I don't practise medicine. But, to save your life, I'll give you the psychic treatment if you'll agree as mayor not to push the licence question."

' "Of course I will," says he. "And now get to work, doc, for them pains are coming on again."

' "My fee will be $250.00, cure guaranteed in two treatments, says I.

' "All right," says the Mayor. "I'll pay it. I guess my life's worth that much."

'I sat down by the bed and looked him straight in the eye.

' "Now," says I, "get your mind off the disease. You ain't sick. You haven't got a heart or a clavicle or a funny-bone or brains or anything. You haven't got any pain. Declare error. Now you feel the pain that you didn't have leaving, don't you?"

' "I do feel some little better, doc," says the Mayor, "darned if I don't. Now state a few lies about my not having this swelling in my left side, and I think I could be propped up and have some sausage and buckwheat cakes."

'I made a few passes with my hands.

' "Now," says I, "the inflammation's gone. The right lobe of the perihelion has subsided. You're getting sleepy. You can't hold your eyes open any longer. For the present the disease is checked. Now, you are asleep."

'The Mayor shut his eyes slowly and began to snore.

' "You observe, Mr. Tiddle," says I, "the wonders of modern science."

' "Biddle," says he. "When will you give uncle the rest of the treatment, Dr. Pooh-pooh?"

' "Waugh-hoo," says I. "I'll come back at eleven to-morrow. When he wakes up give him eight drops of turpentine and three pounds of steak. Good morning."

'The next morning I went back on time. "Well, Mr. Riddle," says I, when he opened the bedroom door, "and how is uncle this morning?"

' "He seems much better," says the young man.

'The Mayor's colour and pulse was fine. I gave him another treatment, and he said the last of the pain left him.

' "Now," says I, "you'd better stay in bed for a day or two, and you'll be all right. It's a good thing I happened to be in Fisher Hill, Mr. Mayor," says I, "for all the remedies in the cornucopia that the regular schools of medicine use couldn't have saved you. And now that error has flew and pain proved a perjurer, let's allude to a cheerfuller subject – say the fee of $250. No cheques, please; I hate to write my name on the back of a cheque almost as bad as I do on the front."

' "I've got the cash here," says the Mayor, pulling a pocket-book from under his pillow.

'He counts out five fifty-dollar notes and holds 'em in his hand.

' "Bring the receipt," he says to Biddle.

'I signed the receipt and the Mayor handed me the money. I put it in my inside pocket careful.

' "Now do your duty, officer," says the Mayor, grinning much unlike a sick man.

'Mr. Biddle lays his hand on my arm.

' "You're under arrest, Dr. Waugh-hoo, alias Peters," says he, "for practising medicine without authority under the State law."

' "Who are you?" I asks.

' "I'll tell you who he is," says Mr. Mayor, sitting up in bed. "He's a detective employed by the State Medical Society. He's been following you over five counties. He came to me yesterday and we fixed up this scheme to catch you. I guess you won't do any more doctoring around these parts, Mr. Faker. What was it you said I had? doc?" the Mayor laughs, "compound — well it wasn't softening of the brain, I guess, anyway."

' "A detective," says I.

' "Correct," says Biddle. "I'll have to turn you over to the sheriff."

' "Let's see you do it," says I, and I grabs Biddle by the throat and half throws him out of the window, but he pulls a gun and sticks it under my chin, and I stand still. Then he puts handcuffs on me, and takes the money out of my pocket.

' "I witness," says he, "that they're the same bills that you and I marked, Judge Banks. I'll turn them over to the sheriff when we get to his office, and he'll send you a receipt. They'll have to be used as evidence in the case."

' "All right, Mr. Biddle," says the Mayor. "And now, Doc Waugh-hoo," he goes on, "why don't you demonstrate? Can't you pull the cork out of your magnetism with your teeth and hocus-pocus them handcuffs off?'

' "Come on, officer," says I, dignified. "I may as well make the best of it." And then I turns to old Banks and rattles my chains.

' "Mr. Mayor," says I, "the time will come soon when you'll believe that personal magnetism is a success. And you'll be sure that it succeeded in this case, too."

'And I guess it did.

'When we got nearly to the gate, I says: "We might meet somebody now, Andy. I reckon you better take 'em off, and —" Hey?

Why, of course it was Andy Tucker. That was his scheme; and that's how we got the capital to go into business together.'

XXXVII

The Hand that Riles the World

'MANY OF OUR GREAT MEN,' said I (apropos of many things), have declared that they owe their success to the aid and encouragement of some brilliant woman.'

'I know,' said Jeff Peters. 'I've read in history and mythology about Joan of Arc and Mme. Yale and Mrs. Caudle and Eve and other noted females of the past. But, in my opinion, the woman of to-day is of little use in politics or business, What's she best in, anyway? – men make the best cooks, milliners, nurses, housekeepers, stenographers, clerks, hairdressers and launderers. About the only job left that a woman can beat a man in is female impersonator in vaudeville.'

'I would have thought,' said I, 'that occasionally, anyhow, you would have found the wit and intuition of woman invaluable to you in your lines of – er – business.'

'Now, wouldn't you,' said Jeff, with an emphatic nod – 'wouldn't you have imagined that? But a woman is an absolutely unreliable partner in any straight swindle. She's liable to turn honest on you when you are depending upon her the most. I tried 'em once.

'Bill Humble, an old friend of mine in the Territories, conceived the illusion that he wanted to be appointed United States Marshal. At that time me and Andy was doing a square, legitimate business of selling walking-canes. If you unscrewed the head of one and turned it up to your mouth a half-pint of good rye whisky would go trickling down your throat to reward you for your act of intelligence. The deputies was annoying me and Andy some, and when Bill spoke to me about his officious aspirations, I saw how the appointment as Marshal might help along the firm of Peters & Tucker.

' "Jeff," says Bill to me, "you are a man of learning and education, besides having knowledge and information concerning not only rudiments but facts and attainments."

' "I do so," says I, "and I have never regretted it. I am not one," says I, "who would cheapen education by making it free. Tell me," says I, "which is of the most value to mankind, literature or horse-racing?"

' "Why – er – playing the po – I mean, of course, the poets and the great writers have got the call, of course," says Bill.

' "Exactly," says I. "Then why do the master minds of finance and philanthropy," says I, "charge us $2 to get into a race-track and let us into a library free? Is that distilling into the masses," says I, "a correct estimate of the relative value of the two means of self-culture and disorder?"

' "You are arguing outside of my faculties of sense and rhetoric," says Bill. "What I wanted you to do is to go to Washington and dig out this appointment for me. I haven't no ideas of cultivation and intrigue. I'm a plain citizen and I need the job. I've killed seven men," says Bill; "I've got nine children; I've been a good Republican ever since the first of May; I can't read nor write, and I see no reason why I ain't illegible for the office. And I think your partner, Mr. Tucker," goes on Bill, "is also a man of sufficient ingratiation and connected system of mental delinquency to assist you in securing the appointment. I will give you preliminary," says Bill, "$1,000 for drinks, bribes and car-fare in Washington. If you land the job I will pay you $1,000 more, cash down, and guarantee you impunity in boot-legging whisky for twelve months. Are you patriotic to the West enough to help me put this thing through the Whitewashed Wigwam of the Great Father of the most eastern flag station of the Pennsylvania Railroad?" says Bill.

'Well, I talked to Andy about it, and he liked the idea immense. Andy was a man of an involved nature. He was never content to plod along, as I was, selling to the peasantry some little tool like a combination steak beater, shoe horn, marcel waver, monkey wrench, nail file, potato masher and Multum in Parvo tuning-fork. Andy had the artistic temper, which is not to be judged as a preacher's or a moral man's is by purely commercial deflections. So we accepted Bill's offer, and strikes out for Washington.

'Says I to Andy, when we got located at a hotel on South Dakota Avenue, G. S. S. W., "now, Andy, for the first time in our lives we've got to do a real dishonest act. Lobbying is something we've never been used to; but we've got to scandalize ourselves for Bill Humble's sake. In a straight and legitimate business," says I, "we could afford to introduce a little foul play and chicanery, but in a disorderly and heinous piece of malpractice like this it seems to me that the straightforward and aboveboard way is the best. I propose," says I, "that we hand over $500 of this money to the chairman of the national campaign committee, get a receipt, lay the receipt on the President's desk and tell him about Bill. The President is a man who would appreciate a candidate who went about getting office that way instead of pulling wires."

'Andy agreed with me, but after we talked the scheme over with the hotel clerk we give that plan up. He told us that there was only one way to get an appointment in Washington, and that was through a lady lobbyist. He gave us the address of one he recommended, a Mrs. Avery, who, he said, was high up in sociable and diplomatic rings and circles.

'The next morning at ten o'clock me and Andy called at her hotel, and was shown up to her reception room.

'This Mrs. Avery was a solace and a balm to the eyesight. She had hair the colour of the back of a twenty-dollar gold certificate, blue eyes and a system of beauty that would make the girl on the cover of a July magazine look like a cook on a Monongahela coal barge.

'She had on a low-necked dress covered with silver spangles, and diamond rings and ear-bobs. Her arms was bare; and she was using a desk telephone with one hand, and drinking tea with the other.

' "Well, boys," says she after a bit, "what is it?"

'I told her in as few words as possible what we wanted for Bill, and the price we could pay.

' "Those western appointments," says she, "are easy. Le'me see, now," says she, "who could put that through for us? No use fooling with Territorial delegates. I guess," says she, "that Senator Sniper would be about the man. He's from somewhere in the West. Let's see how he stands on my private menu card." She takes some papers out of a pigeon-hole with the letter "S" over it.

' "Yes," says she, "he's marked with a star; that means 'ready to serve.' Now, let's see. 'Age 55; married twice; Presbyterian, likes blondes Tolstoi, poker and stewed terrapin; sentimental at third bottle of wine.' Yes," she goes on, "I am sure I can have your friend, Mr. Bummer, appointed Minister to Brazil."

' "Humble," says I. "And United States Marshal was the berth."

' "Oh, yes," says Mrs. Avery. "I have so many deals of this sort I sometimes get them confused. Give me all the memoranda you have of the case, Mr. Peters, and come back in four days. I think it can be arranged by then."

'So me and Andy goes back to our hotel and waits. Andy walks up and down and chews the left end of his moustache.

' "A woman of high intellect and perfect beauty is a rare thing, Jeff," says he.

' "As rare," says I, "as an omelet made from the eggs of the fabulous bird known as the epidermis," says I.

' "A woman like that," says Andy, "ought to lead a man to the
highest positions of opulence and fame."

' "I misdoubt," says I, "if any woman ever helped a man to
secure a job any more than to have his meals ready promptly and
spread a report that the other candidate's wife had once been a
shoplifter. They are no more adapted for business and politics,"
says I, "than Algernon Charles Swinburne is to be floor manager
at one of Chuck Connor's annual balls. I know," says I to Andy,
"that sometimes a woman seems to step out into the kalsomine
light as the charge d'affaires of her man's political job. But how
does it come out? Say, they have a neat little berth somewhere as
foreign consul of record to Afghanistan or lock-keeper on the
Delaware and Raritan Canal. One day this man finds his wife
putting on her overshoes and three months' supply of bird-seed
into the canary's cage. 'Sioux Falls?' he asks with a kind of hopeful
light in his eye. 'No, Arthur,' says she, 'Washington. We're wasted
here,' says she. 'You ought to be Toady Extraordinary to the
Court of St. Bridget or Head Porter of the Island of Porto Rico.
I'm going to see about it.' "

' "Then this lady," I says to Andy, "moves against the authorities at Washington with her baggage and munitions, consisting of
five dozen indiscriminating letters written to her by a member of
the Cabinet when she was 15; a letter of introduction from King
Leopold to the Smithsonian Institution, and a pink silk costume
with canary-coloured spats.

' "Well, and then what?" I goes on. "She has the letters printed
in the evening papers that match her costume, she lectures at an
informal tea given in the palm room of the B. & O. depot and
then calls on the President. The ninth Assistant Secretary of Commerce and Labour, the first aide-de-camp of the Blue Room and
an unidentified coloured man are waiting there to grasp her by the
hands – and feet. They carry her out to S. W. B. street and leave
her on a cellar door. That ends it. The next time we hear of her
she is writing postal cards to the Chinese Minister asking him to
get Arthur a job in a tea store."

' "Then," says Andy, "you don't think Mrs. Avery will land the
Marshalship for Bill?"

' "I do not," says I. "I do not wish to be a sceptic, but I doubt if
she can do as well as you and me could have done."

' "I don't agree with you," says Andy; "I'll bet you she does. I'm proud of having a higher opinion of the talent and the powers of negotiation of ladies."

'We was back at Mrs. Avery's hotel at the time she appointed. She was looking pretty and fine enough, as far as that went, to make any man let her name every officer in the country. But I hadn't much faith in looks, so I was certainly surprised when she pulls out a document with the great seal of the United States on it, and "William Henry Humble" in a fine, big hand on the back

' "You might have had it the next day, boys,; says Mrs. Avery, smiling. "I hadn't the slightest trouble in getting it," says she. "I just asked for it, that's all. Now, I'd like to talk to you a while," she goes on, "but I'm awfully busy, and I know you'll excuse me. I've got an Ambassadorship, two Consulates and a dozen other minor applications to look after. I can hardly find time to sleep at all. You'll give my compliments to Mr. Humble when you get home, of course."

'Well, I handed her the $500, which she pitched into her desk drawer without counting. I put Bill's appointment in my pocket and me and Andy made our adieux.

'We started back for the Territory the same day. We wired Bill: "Job landed; get the tall glasses ready," and we felt pretty good.

'Andy joshed me all the way about how little I knew about women.

' "All right," says I. "I'll admit that she surprised me. But it's the first time I ever knew one of 'em to manipulate a piece of business on time without getting it bungled up in some way," says I.

'Down about the edge of Arkansas I got out Bill's appointment and looked it over, and then I handed it to Andy to read. Andy read it, but didn't add any remarks to my silence.

'The paper was for Bill, all right, and a genuine document, but it appointed him postmaster of Dade City, Fla.

'Me and Andy got off the train at Little Rock and sent Bill's appointment to him by mail. Then we struck north-east towards Lake Superior.

'I never saw Bill Humble after that.'

XXXVIII

The Exact Science of Matrimony

'AS I HAVE TOLD YOU BEFORE,' said Jeff Peters, 'I never had much confidence in the perfidiousness of woman. As partners or coeducators in the most innocent line of graft they are not trustworthy.'

'They deserve the compliment,' said I. 'I think they are entitled to be called the honest sex.'

'Why shouldn't they be?' said Jeff. 'They've got the other sex either grafting or working overtime for 'em. They're all right in business until they get their emotions or their hair touched up too much. Then you want to have a flat-footed, heavy-breathing man with sandy whiskers, five kids and a building and loan mortgage ready as an understudy to take her desk. Now there was that widow lady that me and Andy Tucker engaged to help us in a little matrimonial agency scheme we floated out in Cairo.

'When you've got enough advertising capital – say a roll as big as the little end of a wagon tongue – there's money in matrimonial agencies. We had about $6,000 and we expected to double it in two months, which is about as long as a scheme like ours can be carried on without taking out a New Jersey charter.

'We fixed up an advertisement that read about like this:

'Charming widow, beautiful, home loving, 32 years, possessing $3,000 cash and owning valuable country property, would remarry. Would prefer a poor man with affectionate disposition to one with means, as she realizes that the solid virtues are oftenest to be found in the humble walks of life. No objection to elderly man or one of homely appearance if faithful and true and competent to manage property and invest money with judgment. Address, with particulars,

LONELY,

Care of Peters & Tucker, agents, Cairo, Ill.

' "So far, so pernicious," says I, when we had finished the literary concoction. "And now," says I, "where is the lady?"

'Andy gives me one of his looks of calm irritation.

' "Jeff," says he, "I thought you had lost them ideas of realism in your art. Why should there be a lady? When they sell a lot of watered stock on Wall Street would you expect to find a mermaid in it? What has a matrimonial ad got to do with a lady?"

' "Now listen," says I. "You know my rule, Andy, that in all my illegitimate inroads against the legal letter of the law the article sold must be existent, visible, producible. In that way and by a careful study of city ordinances and train schedules I have kept out of all trouble with the police that a five-dollar bill and a cigar could not square. Now, to work this scheme we've got to be able to produce bodily a charming widow or its equivalent with or without the beauty, hereditaments and appurtenances set forth in the catalogue and writ of errors, or hereafter be held by a justice of the peace."

' "Well," says Andy, reconstructing his mind, "maybe it would be safer in case the post office or the peace commission should try to investigate our agency. But where," he says, "could you hope to find a widow who would waste time on a matrimonial scheme that had no matrimony in it?"

'I told Andy that I thought I knew of the exact party. An old friend of mine, Zeke Trotter, who used to draw soda-water and teeth in a tent show, had made his wife a widow a year before by drinking some dyspepsia cure of the old doctor's instead of the liniment that he always got boozed up on. I used to stop at their house often, and I thought we could get her to work with us.

' 'Twas only sixty miles to the little town where she lived, so I jumped out on the I. C. and finds her in the same cottage with the same sunflowers and roosters standing on the wash-tub. Mrs. Trotter fitted our ad first-rate except, maybe, for beauty and age and property valuation. But she looked feasible and praiseworthy to the eye, and it was a kindness to Zeke's memory to give her the Job.

' "Is this an honest deal you are putting on, Mr. Peters?" she asks me when I tell her what we want.

' "Mrs. Trotter," says I, "Andy Tucker and me have computed the calculation that 3,000 men in this broad and unfair country will endeavour to secure your fair hand and ostensible money and property through our advertisement. Out of that number something like thirty hundred will expect to give you in exchange, if they should win you, the carcass of a lazy and mercenary loafer, a failure in life, a swindler and contemptible fortune-seeker.

' "Me and Andy," says I, "propose to teach these preyers upon society a lesson. It was with difficulty," says I, "that me and Andy could refrain from forming a corporation under the title of the Great Moral and Millennial Malevolent Matrimonial Agency. Does that satisfy you?"

' "It does, Mr. Peters," says she. "I might have known you wouldn't have gone into anything that wasn't opprobrious. But what will my duties be? Do I have to reject personally these 3,000 ramscallions you speak of, or can I throw them out in bunches?"

' "Your job, Mrs. Trotter," says I, "will be practically a cynosure. You will live at a quiet hotel and will have no work to do. Andy and I will attend to all the correspondence and business end of it.

' "Of course," says I, "some of the more ardent and impetuous suitors who can raise the railroad fare may come to Cairo to personally press their suit or whatever fraction of a suit they may be wearing. In that case you will be probably put to the inconvenience of kicking them out face to face. We will pay you $25 per week and hotel expenses."

' "Give me five minutes," says Mrs. Trotter, "to get my powder rag and leave the front door key with a neighbour and you can let my salary begin."

'So I conveys Mrs. Trotter to Cairo and establishes her in a family hotel far enough away from mine and Andy's quarters to be unsuspicious and available, and I tell Andy.

' "Great," says Andy. "And now that your conscience is appeased as to the tangibility and proximity of the bait, and leaving mutton aside, suppose we revenoo a noo fish."

'So, we began to insert our advertisement in newspapers covering the country far and wide. One ad was all we used. We couldn't have used more without hiring so many clerks and marcelled paraphernalia that the sound of the gum-chewing would have disturbed the Postmaster-General.

'We placed $2,000 in a bank to Mrs. Trotter's credit and gave her the book to show in case anybody might question the honesty and good faith of the agency. I knew Mrs. Trotter was square and reliable and it was safe to leave it in her name.

'With that one ad Andy and me put in twelve hours a day answering letters.

'About one hundred a day was what came in. I never knew there was so many large-hearted but indigent men in the country who were willing to acquire a charming widow and assume the burden of investing her money.

'Most of them admitted that they ran principally to whiskers and lost jobs and were misunderstood by the world, but all of 'em were sure that they were so chock-full of affection and manly qualities that the widow would be making the bargain of her life to get em.

'Every applicant got a reply from Peters & Tucker informing them that the widow had been deeply impressed by his straightforward and interesting letter and requesting them to write again; stating more particulars; and enclosing photograph if convenient. Peters & Tucker also informed the applicant that their fee for handing over the second letter to their fair client would be $2, enclosed therewith.

'There you see the simple beauty of the scheme. About 90 per cent. of them domestic foreign noblemen raised the price somehow and sent it in. That was all there was to it. Except that me and

Andy complained an amount about being put to the trouble of slicing open them envelopes, and taking the money out.

'Some few clients called in person. We sent 'em to Mrs. Trotter and she did the rest; except for three or four who came back to strike us for car-fare. After the letters began to get in from the r.f.d. districts Andy and me were taking in about $200 a day.

'One afternoon when we were busiest and I was stuffing the two and ones into cigar boxes and Andy was whistling "No Wedding Bells for Her," a small, slick man drops in and runs his eye over the walls like he was on the trail of a lost Gainsborough painting or two. As soon as I saw him I felt a glow of pride, because we were running our business on the level.

' "I see you have quite a large mail to-day," says the man.

'I reached and got my hat.

' "Come on," says I. "We've been expecting you. I'll show you the goods. How was Teddy when you left Washington?"

'I took him down to the Riverview Hotel and had him shake hands with Mrs. Trotter. Then I showed him her bank book with the $2,000 to her credit.

' "It seems to be all right," says the Secret Service.

' "It is," says I. "And if you're not a married man I'll leave you to talk a while with the lady. We won't mention the two dollars."

' "Thanks," says he. "If I wasn't, I might. Good day, Mrs. Peters."

'Toward the end of three months we had taken in something over $5,000, and we saw it was time to quit. We had a good many complaints made to us; and Mrs. Trotter seemed to be tired of the job. A good many suitors had been calling to see her, and she didn't seem to like that.

'So we decides to pull out, and I goes down to Mrs. Trotter's hotel to pay her last week's salary and say farewell and get her cheque for the $2,000.

'When I got there I found her crying like a kid that don't want to go to school.

' "Now, now," says I, "what's it all about? Somebody sassed you or you getting home-sick?"

' "No, Mr. Peters," says she. "I'll tell you. You was always a friend of Zeke's, and I don't mind. Mr. Peters, I'm in love. I just love a man so hard I can't bear not to get him. He's just the ideal I've always had in mind."

' "Then take him," says I. "That is, if it's a mutual case. Does he return the sentiment according to the specilications and painfulness you have described?

' "He does," says she. "But he's one of the gentlemen that's been coming to see me about the advertisement and he won't marry me unless I give him the $2,000. His name is William Wilkinson." And then she goes off again in the agitations and hysterics of romance.

' "Mrs. Trotter," says I, "there's no man more sympathizing with a woman's affections than I am. Besides, you was once the life partner of one of my best friends. If it was left to me I'd say take this $2,000 and the man of your choice and be happy.

' "We could afford to do that, because we have cleaned up over $5,000 from these suckers that wanted to marry you. But," says I, "Andy Tucker is to be consulted.

' "He is a good man, but keen in business. He is my equal partner financially. I will talk to Andy," says I, "and see what can be done."

'I goes back to our hotel and lays the case before Andy.

' "I was expecting something like this all the time," says Andy. "You can't trust a woman to stick by you in any scheme that involves her emotions and preferences."

' "It's a sad thing, Andy," says I, "to think that we've been the cause of the breaking of a woman's heart."

' "It is," says Andy, "and I tell you what I'm willing to do, Jeff. You've always been a man of a soft and generous heart and disposition. Perhaps I've been too hard and worldly and suspicious, for once I'll meet you half-way. Go to Mrs. Trotter and tell her to draw the $2,000 from the bank and give it to this man she's infatuated with and be happy."

'I jumps up and shakes Andy's hand for five minutes, and then I goes back to Mrs. Trotter and tells her, and she cries as hard for joy as she did for sorrow.

'Two days afterward me and Andy packed up to go.

' "Wouldn't you like to go down and meet Mrs. Trotter once before we leave?" I asks him. "She'd like mightily to know you and express her encomiums and gratitude."

' "Why, I guess not," says Andy. "I guess we'd better hurry and catch that train."

'I was strapping our capital around me in a memory belt like we always carried it, when Andy pulls a roll of large bills out of his pocket and asks me to put 'em with the rest.

' "What's this?" says I.

' "It's Mrs. Trotter's two thousand," says Andy.

' "How do you come to have it?" I asks.

' "She gave it to me," says Andy. "I've been calling on her three
evenings a week for more than a month."

' "Then are you William Wilkinson?" says I.

' "I was," says Andy.

XXXIX

Conscience in Art

'I NEVER COULD HOLD MY PARTNER, Andy Tucker, down to
legitimate ethics of pure swindling,' said Jeff Peters to me one
day.

'Andy had too much imagination to be honest. He used to
devise schemes of money-getting so fraudulent and high-financial
that they wouldn't have been allowed in the by-laws of a railroad
rebate system.

'Myself, I never believed in taking any man's dollars unless I
gave him something for it – something in the way of rolled gold
jewellery, garden seeds, lumbago lotion, stock certificates, stove
polish or a crack on the head to show for his money. I guess I must
have had New England ancestors away back and inherited some of
their staunch and rugged fear of the police.

'But Andy's family tree was in different kind. I don't think he
could have traced his descent any further back than a corporation.

'One summer while he was in the Middle West, working down
the Ohio valley with a line of family albums, headache powders
and roach destroyer Andy takes one of his notions of high and
actionable financiering.

' "Jeff," says he, "I've been thinking that we oughe to drop these
rutabaga fanciers and give our attention to something more nourishing and prolific. If we keep on snapshooting these hinds for
their egg money we'll be classed as nature fakers. How about
plunging into the fastnesses of the sky-scraper country and biting
some big bull caribous in the chest?"

' "Well," says I, "you know my idiosyncrasies. I prefer a square,
non-illegal style of business such as we are carrying on now.
When I take money I want to leave some tangible object in the
other fellow's hands for him to gaze at and to distract his attention
from my spoor, even if it's only a Komical Kuss Trick Finger Ring
for Squirting Perfume in a Friend's Eye. But if you've got a fresh
idea, Andy," says I, "let's have a look at it. I'm not so wedded to

petty graft that I would refuse something better in the way of a subsidy."

' "I was thinking," says Andy, "of a little hunt without horn, hound or camera among the great herd of the Midas Americanus, commonly known as the Pittsburg millionaires."

' "In New York?" I asks.

' "No, sir," says Andy, "in Pittsburg. That's their habitat. They don't like New York. They go there now and then just because it's expected of 'em."

' "A Pittsburg millionaire in New York is like a fly in a cup of hot coffee — he attracts attention and comment, but he don't enjoy it. New York ridicules him for 'blowing' so much money in that town of sneaks and snobs, and sneers. The truth is, he don't spend anything while he is there. I saw a memorandum of expenses for a ten-days' trip to Bunkum Town made by a Pittsburg man worth $15,000,000 once. Here's the way he set it down:

R. R. fare to and from	$21	00
Cab fare to and from hotel	2	00
Hotel bill @ $5 per day	50	00
Tips	5,750	00
Total	$5,823 00	

' "That's the voice of New York," goes on Andy. "The town's nothing but a head waiter. If you tip it too much it'll go and stand by the door and make fun of you to the hat check boy. When a Pittsburger wants to spend money and have a good time he stays at home. That's where we'll go to catch him."

'Well, to make a dense story more condensed, me and Andy cached our Paris green and anti-pyrine powders and albums in a friend's cellar, and took the trail to Pittsburg. Andy didn't have any especial prospectus of chicanery and violence drawn up, but he always had plenty of confidence that his immoral nature would rise to any occasion that presented itself.

'As a concession to my ideas of self-preservation and rectitude he promised that if I should take an active and incriminating part in any little business venture that we might work up there should be something actual and cognizant to the senses of touch, sight, taste or smell to transfer to the victim for the money so my conscience might rest easy. After that I felt better and entered more cheerfully into the foul play.

' "Andy," says I, as we strayed through the smoke along the cinderpath they call Smithfield Street, "had you figured out how we are going to get acquainted with these coke kings and pig-iron squeezers? Not that I would decry my own worth or system of drawing-room deportment, and work with the olive fork and pie knife," says I, "but isn't the entree nous into the salons of the stogie smokers going to be harder than you imagined?"

' "If there's any handicap at all," says Andy, "it's our own refinement and inherent culture. Pittsburg millionaires are a fine body of plain, whole-hearted, unassuming, democratic men.

' "They are rough but uncivil in their manners, and though their ways are boisterous and unpolished, under it all they have a great deal of impoliteness and discourtesy. Nearly every one of 'em rose from obscurity," says Andy, "and they'll live in it till the town gets to using smoke consumers. If we act simple and unaffected and don't go too far from the saloons and keep making a noise like an import duty on steel rails we won't have any trouble in meeting some of 'em socially."

'Well, Andy and me drifted about town three or four days getting our bearings. We got to knowing several millionaires by sight.

'One used to stop his automobile in front of our hotel and have a quart of champagne brought out to him. When the waiter opened it he'd turn it up to his mouth and drink it out of the bottle. That showed he used to be a glass-blower before he made his money.

'One evening Andy failed to come to the hotel for dinner. About eleven o'clock he came into my room.

' "Landed one, Jeff," says he. "Twelve millions. Oil, rolling mills, real estate and natural gas. He's a fine man; no airs about him. Made all his money in the last five years. He's got professors posting him up now in education — art and literature and haberdashery and such things.

' "When I saw him he'd just won a bet of $10,000 with a Steel Corporation man that there'd be four suicides in the Allegheny rolling mills to-day. So everybody in sight had to walk up and have drinks on him. He took a fancy to me and asked me to dinner with him. We went to a restaurant in Diamond Alley and sat on stools and had sparkling Moselle and clam powder and apple fritters.

' "Then he wanted to show me his bachelor apartment on Liberty Street. He's got ten rooms over a fish market with privilege of the bath on the next floor above. He told me it cost him $18,000 to furnish his apartment, and I believe it.

' "He's got $40,000 worth of pictures in one room, and $20,000 worth of curios and antiques in another. His name's Scudder, and he's 45, and taking lessons on the piano and 15,000 barrels of oil a day out of his wells."

' "All right," says I. "Preliminary canter satisfactory. But, kay vooly, voo? What good is the art junk to us? And the oil?"

' "Now, that man," says Andy, sitting thoughtfully on the bed, "ain't what you would call an ordinary scutt. When he was showing me his cabinet of art curios his face lighted up like the door of a coke oven. He says that if some of his big deals go through he'll make J. P. Morgan's collection of sweetshop tapestry and Augusta, Me., beadwork look like the contents of an ostrich's craw thrown on a screen by a magic lantern.

' "And then he showed me a little carving," went on Andy, "that anybody could see was a wonderful thing. It was something like 2,000 years old, he said. It was a lotus flower with a woman's face in it carved out of a solid piece of ivory.

' "Scudder looks it up in a catalogue and describes it. An Egyptian carver named Khafra made two of 'em for King Rameses II about the year B.C. The other one can't be found. The junkshops and antique bugs have rubbered all Europe for it, but it seems to be out of stock. Scudder paid $2,000 for the one he has."

' "Oh, well," says I, "this sounds like the purling of a rill to me. I thought we came here to teach the millionaires business, instead of learning art from 'em?"

' "Be patient," says Andy kindly. "Maybe we will see a rift in the smoke ere long."

'All the next morning Andy was out. I didn't see him until about noon. He came to the hotel and called me into his room across the hall. He pulled a roundish bundle about as big as a goose egg out of his pocket and unwrapped it. It was an ivory carving just as he had described the millionaire's to me.

' "I went in an old second-hand store and pawnshop a while ago," says Andy, "and I see this half hidden under a lot of old daggers and truck. The pawnbroker said he'd had it several years and thinks it was soaked by some Arabs or Turks or some foreign dubs that used to live down by the river.

' "I offered him $2 for it, and I must have looked like I wanted it, for he said it would be taking the pumpernickel out of his children's mouths to hold any conversation that did not lead up to a price of $35. I finally got it for $25.

' "Jeff," goes on Andy, "this is the exact counterpart of Scudder's carving. It's absolutely a dead ringer for it. He'll pay $2,000 for it as quick as he'd tuck a napkin under his chin. And why shouldn't it be the genuine other one, anyhow, that the old gipsy whittled out?"

' "Why not, indeed?" says I. "And how shall we go about compelling him to make a voluntary purchase of it?"

'Andy had his plan all ready, and I'll tell you how we carried it out.

'I got a pair of blue spectacles, put on my black frock-coat, rumpled my hair up and became Prof. Pickleman. I went to another hotel, registered, and sent a telegram to Scudder to come to see me at once on important art business. The elevator dumped him on me in less than an hour. He was a foggy man with a clarion voice, smelling of Connecticut wrappers and naphtha.

' "Hello, Profess!" he shouts. "How's your conduct?"

'I rumpled my hair some more and gave him a blue-glass stare.

' "Sir," says I. "Are you Cornelius T. Scudder? Of Pittsburg, Pennsylvania?"

' "I am," says he. "Come out and have a drink."

' "I have neither the time nor the desire," says I, "for such harmful and deleterious amusements. I have come from New York," says I, "on a matter of busi – on a matter of art.

' "I learned there that you are the owner of an Egyptian ivory carving of the time of Rameses II, representing the head of Queen Isis in a lotus flower. There were only two of such carvings made. One has been lost for many years. I recently discovered and purchased the other in a pawn – in an obscure museum in Vienna. I wish to purchase yours. Name your price."

' "Well, the great ice jams, Profess!" says Scudder. "Have you found the other one? Me sell? No. I don't guess Cornelius Scudder needs to sell anything that he wants to keep. Have you got the carving with you, Profess?"

'I shows it to Scudder. He examines it careful all over.

' "It's the article," says he. "It's a duplicate of mine, every line and curve of it. Tell you what I'll do," he says. "I won't sell, but I'll buy. Give you $2,500 for yours."

' "Since you won't sell, I will," says I. "Large bills, please. I'm a man of few words. I must return to New York to-night. I lecture to-morrow at the aquarium."

'Scudder sends a cheque down and the hotel cashes it. He goes off with his piece of antiquity and I hurry back to Andy's hotel, according to arrangement.

'Andy is walking up and down the room looking at his watch.

' "Well?" he says.

' "Twenty-five hundred," says I. "Cash."

' "We've got just eleven minutes," says Andy, "to catch the B. & O. west-bound. Grab your baggage."

' "What's the hurry?" says I. "It was a square deal. And even if it was only an imitation of the original carving it'll take him some time to find it out. He seemed to be sure it was the genuine article."

' "It was," says Andy. "It was his own. When I was looking at his curios yesterday he stepped out of the room for a moment and I pocketed it. Now, will you pick up your suit-case and hurry?"

' "Then," says I, "why was that story about finding another one in the pawn –'

' "Oh," says Andy, "out of respect for that conscience of yours. Come on." '

XL

The Man Higher Up

ACROSS OUR TWO DISHES of spaghetti, in a corner of Provenzano's restaurant, Jeff Peters was explaining to me the three kinds of graft.

Every winter Jeff comes to New York to eat spaghetti, to watch the shipping in East River from the depths of his chinchilla overcoat, and to lay in a supply of Chicago-made clothing at one of the Fulton Street stores. During the other three seasons he may be found further west – his range is from Spokane to Tampa. In his profession he takes a pride which he supports and defends with a serious and unique philosophy of ethics. His profession is no new one. He is an incorporated, uncapitalized, unlimited asylum for the reception of the restless and unwise dollars of his fellow-men.

In the wilderness of stone in which Jeff seeks his annual lonely holiday he is glad to palaver of his many adventures, as a boy will whistle after sundown in a wood. Wherefore, I mark on my calendar the time of his coming, and open a question of privilege at Provenzano's concerning the little wine-stained table in the corner between the rakish rubber plant and the framed palazzio della something on the wall.

'There are two kinds of grafts,' said Jeff, 'that ought to be wiped out by law. I mean Wall Street speculation, and burglary.'

'Nearly everybody will agree with you as to one of them,' said I, with a laugh.

'Well, burglary ought to be wiped out too,' said Jeff; and I wondered whether the laugh had been redundant.

'About three months ago,' said Jeff, 'it was my privilege to become familiar with a sample of each of the aforesaid branches of illegitimate art. I was *sine qua grata* with a member of the house-breakers' union and one of the John D. Napoleons of finance at the same time.'

'Interesting combination,' said I, with a yawn. 'Did I tell you I bagged a duck and a ground-squirrel at one shot last week over in the Ramapos?' I knew well how to draw Jeff's stories.

'Let me tell you first about these barnacles that clog the wheels of society by poisoning the springs of rectitude with their upas-like eye,' said Jeff, with the pure gleam of the muck-raker in his own.

'As I said, three months ago I got into bad company. There are two times in a man's life when he does this – when he's dead broke, and when he's rich.

'Now and then the most legitimate business runs out of luck. It was out in Arkansas I made the wrong turn at a cross-road, and drives into this town of Peavine by mistake. It seems I had already assaulted and disfigured Peavine the spring of the year before. I had sold $600 worth of young fruit trees there – plums, cherries, peaches and pears. The Peaviners were keeping an eye on the country road and hoping I might pass that way again. I drove down Main Street as far as the Crystal Palace drug-store before I realized I had committed ambush upon myself and my white horse Bill.

'The Peaviners took me by surprise and Bill by the bridle and began a conversation that wasn't entirely dissociated with the subject of fruit trees. A committee of 'em ran some trace-chains through the armholes of my vest, and escorted me through their gardens and orchards.

'Their fruit trees hadn't lived up to their labels. Most of 'em had turned out to be persimmons and dogwoods, with a grove or two of blackjacks and poplars. The only one that showed any signs of bearing anything was a fine young cottonwood that had put forth a hornet's nest and half of an old corset-cover.

'The Peaviners protracted our fruitless stroll to the edge of town. They took my watch and money on account; and they kept Bill and the wagon as hostages. They said the first time one of them dogwood trees put forth an Amsden's June peach I might come back and get my things. Then they took off the trace-chains and jerked their thumbs in the direction of the Rocky Mountains; and I struck a Lewis and Clark lope for the swollen rivers and impenetrable forests.

'When I regained intellectualness I found myself walking into an unidentified town on the A., T. & S. F. railroad. The Peaviners hadn't left anything in my pockets except a plug of chewing – they wasn't after my life – and that saved it. I bit off a chunk and sits down on a pile of ties by the track to recogitate my sensations of thought and perspicacity.

'And then along comes a fast freight which slows up a little at the town; and off of it drops a black bundle that rolls for twenty yards in a cloud of dust and then gets up and begins to spit soft coal and interjections. I see it is a young man broad across the face, dressed more for Pullmans than freights, and with a cheerful kind of smile in spite of it all that made Phœbe Snow's job look like a chimney-sweep's.

' "Fall off?" says I.

' "Nunk," says he. "Got off. Arrived at my destination. What town is this?"

' "Haven't looked it up on the map yet," says I. "I got in about five minutes before you did. How does it strike you?"

' "Hard," says he, twisting one of his arms around. "I believe that shoulder – no, it's all right."

'He stoops over to brush the dust off his clothes, when out of his pocket drops a fine, nine-inch burglar's steel jimmy. He picks it up and looks at me sharp, and then grins and holds out his hand.

' "Brother," says he, "greetings. Didn't I see you in Southern Missouri last summer selling coloured sand at half a dollar a tea-spoonful to put into lamps to keep the oil from exploding?"

' "Oil," says I, "never explodes. It's the gas that forms that explodes." But I shake hands with him, anyway.

' "My name's Bill Bassett," says he to me, "and if you'll call it professional pride instead of conceit, I'll inform you that you have the pleasure of meeting the best burglar that ever set a gum-shoe on ground drained by the Mississippi River."

'Well, me and this Bill Bassett sits on the ties and exchanges brags as artists in kindred lines will do. It seems he didn't have a cent, either, and we went into close caucus. He explained why an able burglar sometimes had to travel on freights by telling me that a servant girl had played him false in Little Rock, and he was making a quick get-away.

' "It's part of my business," says Bill Bassett, "to play up the ruffles when I want to make a riffle as Raffles. 'Tis loves that makes the hit go 'round. Show me a house with the swag in it and a pretty parlour-maid, and you might as well call the silver melted down and sold, and me spilling truffles and that Chateau stuff on the napkin under my chin, while the police are calling it an inside job just because the old lady's nephew teaches a Bible class. I first make an impression on the girl," says Bill, "and when she lets me inside I make an impression on the locks. But this one in Little Rock done me," says he. "She saw me taking a trolley ride with another girl, and when I came round on the night she was to leave the door open for me it was fast. And I had keys made for the doors upstairs. But, no, sir. She had sure cut off my locks. She was a Delilah," says Bill Bassett.

'It seems that Bill tried to break in anyhow with his jimmy, but the girl emitted a succession of bravura noises like the top-riders of a tally-ho, and Bill had to take all the hurdles between there and the depot. As he had no baggage they tried hard to check his departure, but he made a train that was just pulling out.

' "Well," says Bill Bassett, when we had exchanged memoirs of our dead lives, "I could eat. This town don't look like it was kept under a Yale lock. Suppose we commit some mild atrocity that will bring in temporary expense money. I don't suppose you've brought along any hair tonic or rolled-gold watch-chains, or similar law-defying swindles that you could sell on the plaza to the pikers of the paretic populace, have you?"

' "No," says I, "I left an elegant line of Patagonian diamond ear-rings and rainy-day sunbursts in my valise at Peavine. But they're to stay there till some of them black-gum trees begin to glut the market with yellow clings and Japanese plums. I reckon we can't count on them unless we take Luther Burbank in for a partner."

' "Very well," says Bassett, "we'll do the best we can. Maybe after dark I'll borrow a hairpin from some lady, and open the Farmers' and Drovers' Marine Bank with it."

'While we were talking, up pulls a passenger train to the depot near by. A person in a high hat gets off on the wrong side of the train and comes tripping down the track towards us. He was a little, fat man with a big nose and rat's eyes, but dressed expensive, and carrying a hand-satchel careful, as if it had eggs or railroad bonds in it. He passes by us and keeps on down the track, not appearing to notice the town.

' "Come on," says Bill Bassett to me, starting after him.

' "Where?" I asks.

' "Lordy!" says Bill, "had you forgot you was in the desert? Didn't you see Colonel Manna drop down right before your eyes? Don't you hear the rustling of General Raven's wings? I'm surprised at you, Elijah."

'We overtook the stranger in the edge of some woods, and, as it was after sundown and in a quiet place, nobody saw us stop him. Bill takes the silk hat off the man's head and brushes it with his sleeve and puts it back.

' "What does this mean, sir?" says the man.

' "When I wore one of these," says Bill, "and felt embarrassed, I always done that. Not having one now, I had to use yours. I hardly know how to begin, sir, in explaining our business with you, but I guess we'll try your pockets first."

'Bill Bassett felt in all of them, and looked disgusted.

' "Not even a watch," he says. "Ain't you ashamed of yourself, you whited sculpture? Going about dressed like a head-waiter, and financed like a Count! You haven't even got car-fare. What did you do with your transfer?"

'The man speaks up and says he has no assets or valuables of any sort. But Bassett takes his hand-satchel and opens it. Out comes some collars and socks and a half a page of a newspaper clipped out. Bill reads the clipping careful, and holds out his hand to the held-up party.

' "Brother," says he, "greetings! Accept the apologies of friends. I am Bill Bassett, the burglar. Mr. Peters, you must make the acquaintance of Mr. Alfred E. Ricks. Shake hands. Mr. Peters," says Bill, "stands about half-way between me and you, Mr. Ricks, in the line of havoc and corruption. He always gives something for the money he gets. I'm glad to meet you, Mr. Ricks – you and Mr. Peters. This is the first time I ever attended a full gathering of the National Synod of Sharks – housebreaking, swindling, and financiering all represented. Please examine Mr. Ricks's credentials, Mr. Peters."

'The piece of newspaper that Bill Bassett handed me had a good picture of this Ricks on it. It was a Chicago paper, and it had obloquies of Ricks in every paragraph. By reading it over I harvested the intelligence that said alleged Ricks had laid off all that portion of the State of Florida that lies under water into town lots and sold 'em to alleged innocent investors from his magnificently furnished offices in Chicago. After he had taken in a hundred thousand or so dollars one of these fussy purchasers that are always making trouble – (I've had 'em actually try gold watches I've sold 'em with acid) – took a cheap excursion down to the land where it is always just before supper to look at his lot and see if it didn't need a new paling or two on the fence, and market a few lemons in time for the Christmas present trade. He hires a surveyor to find his lot for him. They run the line out and find the flourishing town of Paradise Hollow, so advertised, to be about 40 rods and 16 poles S., 27° E., of the middle of Lake Okeechobee. This man's lot was under thirty-six feet of water, and, besides, had been pre-empted so long by the alligators and gars that his title looked fishy.

'Naturally, the man goes back to Chicago and makes it as hot for Alfred E. Ricks as the morning after a prediction of snow by the weather bureau. Ricks defied the allegation, but he couldn't deny the alligators. One morning the papers came out with a column about it, and Ricks come out by the fire-escape. It seems the alleged authorities had beat him to the safe-deposit box where he kept his winnings, and Ricks has to westward ho! with only feet-wear and a dozen 15½ English pokes in his shopping bag. He happened to have some mileage left in his book, and that took him as far as the town in the wilderness where he was spilled out on me and Bill Bassett as Elijah III with not a raven in sight for any of us.

'Then this Alfred E. Ricks lets out a squeak that he is hungry, too, and denies the hypothesis that he is good for the value, let alone the price, of a meal. And so, there was the three of us, representing, if we had a mind to draw syllogisms and parabolas, labour and trade and capital. Now, when trade has no capital there isn't a dicker to be made. And when capital has no money there's a stagnation in steak and onions. That put it up to the man with the jimmy.

' "Brother bushrangers," says Bill Bassett, "never yet, in trouble, did I desert a pal. Hard by, in yon wood, I seem to see unfurnished lodgings. Let us go there and wait till dark."

'There was an old, deserted cabin in the grove, and we three took possession of it. After dark Bill Bassett tells us to wait, and goes out for half an hour. He comes back with a armful of bread and spareribs and pies.

' "Panhandled 'em at a farm-house on Washita Avenue," says he. "Eat, drink and be leary."

'The full moon was coming up bright, so we sat on the floor of the cabin and ate in the light of it. And this Bill Bassett begins to brag.

' "Sometimes," says he, with his mouth full of country produce, "I lose all patience with you people that think you are higher up in the profession than I am. Now, what could either of you have done in the present emergency to set us on our feet again? Could you do it, Ricksy?"

' "I must confess, Mr. Bassett," says Ricks, speaking nearly inaudible out of a slice of pie, "that at this immediate juncture I could not, perhaps, promote an enterprise to relieve the situation. Large operations, such as I direct, naturally require careful preparation in advance. I –'

' "I know, Ricksy," breaks in Bill Bassett. "You needn't finish. You need $500 to make the first payment on a blonde typewriter, and four roomsful of quartered oak furniture. And you need $500 more for advertising contracts. And you need two weeks' time for the fish to begin to bite. Your line of relief would be about as useful in an emergency as advocating municipal ownership to cure a man suffocated by eighty-cent gas. And your graft ain't much swifter, Brother Peters," he winds up.

' "Oh," says I, "I haven't seen you turn anything into gold with your wand yet, Mr. Good Fairy. Most anybody could rub the magic ring for a little left-over victuals."

' "That was only getting the pumpkin ready," says Bassett, braggy and cheerful. "The coach and six'll drive up to the door before you know it, Miss Cinderella. Maybe you've got some scheme under your sleeve-holders that will give us a start."

' "Son," says I, "I'm fifteen years older than you are, and young enough yet to take out an endowment policy. I've been broke before. We can see the lights of that town not half a smile away. I learned under Montague Silver, the greatest street man that ever spoke from a wagon. There are hundreds of men walking those streets this moment with grease-spots on their clothes. Give me a gasoline lamp, a dry-goods box, and a two-dollar bar of white castile soap, cut into little –"

' "Where's your two dollars?" snickered Bill Bassett into my discourse. There was no use arguing with that burglar.

' "No," he goes on; "you're both babes-in-the-wood. Finance has closed the mahogany desk, and trade has put the shutters up. Both of you look to labour to start the wheels going. All right. You admit it. To-night I'll show you what Bill Bassett can do."

'Bassett tells me and Ricks not to leave the cabin till he comes back, even if it's daylight, and then he starts off toward town, whistling gay.

'This Alfred E. Ricks pulls off his shoes and his coat, lays a silk handkerchief over his hat, and lays down on the floor.

' "I think I will endeavour to secure a little slumber," he squeaks. "The day has been fatiguing. Good night, my dear Mr. Peters."

' "My regards to Morpheus," says I. "I think I'll sit up a while."

'About two o'clock, as near as I could guess by my watch in Peavine, home comes our labouring man and kicks up Ricks, and calls us to the streak of bright moonlight shining in the cabin door. Then he spreads out five packages of one thousand dollars each on the floor, and begins to cackle over the nest-egg like a hen.

' "I'll tell you a few things about that town,' says he. "It's named Rocky Springs, and they're building a Masonic temple, and it looks like the Democratic candidate for mayor is going to get soaked by a Pop, and Judge Tucker's wife, who has been down with pleurisy, is some better. I had a talk on these lilliputian thesises before I could get a siphon in the fountain of knowledge that I was after. And there's a bank there called the Lumberman's Fidelity and Ploughman's Savings Institution. It closed for business yesterday with $23,000 cash on hand. It will open this morning with $18,000 – all silver – that's the reason didn't bring more. There you are, trade and capital. Now, will you be bad?"

' "My young friend," says Alfred E. Ricks, holding up his hands, "have you robbed this bank? Dear me, dear me!"

' "You couldn't call it that," says Bassett. "'Robbing' sounds harsh. All I had to do was to find out what street it was on. That town is so quiet that I could stand on the corner and hear the tumblers clicking in that safe lock – 'right to 45; left twice to 80; right once to 60; left to 15' – as plain as the Yale captain giving orders in the football dialect. Now, boys," says Bassett, "this is an early rising town. They tell me the citizens are all up and stirring before daylight. I asked what for, and they said because breakfast was ready at that time. And what of merry Robin Hood? It must be Yoicks! and away with the tinkers' chorus. I'll stake you. How much do you want? Speak up, Capital."

' "My dear young friend," says this ground squirrel of a Ricks, standing on his hind legs and juggling nuts in his paws, "I have friends in Denver who would assist me. If I had a hundred dollars I –"

'Bassett unpins a package of the currency and throws five twenties to Ricks.

' "Trade, how much?" he says to me.

' "Put your money up, Labour," says I. "I never yet drew upon

honest toil for its hard-earned pittance. The dollars I get are surplus ones that are burning the pockets of damfools and greenhorns. When I stand on a street corner and sell a solid gold
diamond ring to a yap for $3.00, I make just $2.60. And I know
he's going to give it to a girl in return for all the benefits accruing
from a $125.00 ring. His profits are $122.00. Which of us is the
biggest faker?"

' "And when you sell a poor woman a pinch of sand for fifty
cents to keep her lamp from exploding," says Bassett, "what do
you figure her gross earnings to be, with sand at forty cents a
ton?"

' "Listen," says I. "I instruct her to keep her lamp clean and well
filled. If she does that it can't burst. And with the sand in it she
knows it can't, and she don't worry. It's a kind of Industrial Christian Science. She pays fifty cents, and gets both Rockefeller and
Mrs. Eddy on the job. It ain't everybody that can let the gold-dust
twins do their work."

'Alfred E. Ricks all but licks the dust off of Bill Bassett's shoes.

' "My dear young friend," says he, "I will never forget your generosity. Heaven will reward you. But let me implore you to turn
from your ways of violence and crime."

' "Mousie," says Bill, "the hole in the wainscoting for yours.
Your dogmas and inculcations sound to me like the last words of a
bicycle pump. What has your high moral, elevator-service system
of pillage brought you to? Penuriousness and want. Even Brother
Peters, who insists upon contaminating the art of robbery with
theories of commerce and trade, admitted he was on the lift. Both
of you live by the gilded rule. Brother Peters," says Bill, "you'd
better choose a slice of this embalmed currency. You're welcome."

'I told Bill Bassett once more to put his money in his pocket. I
had never had the respect for burglary that some people have. I
always gave something for the money I took, even if it was only
some little trifle for a souvenir to remind 'em not to get caught
again.

'And then Alfred E. Ricks grovels at Bill's feet again, and bids us
adieu. He says he will have a team at a farm-house, and drive to
the station below, and take the train for Denver. It salubrified the
atmosphere when that lamentable boll-worm took his departure.
He was a disgrace to every non-industrial profession in the country. With all his big schemes and fine offices he had wound up
unable even to get an honest meal except by the kindness of a
strange and maybe unscrupulous burglar. I was glad to see him go,

though I felt a little sorry for him, now that he was ruined for
ever. What could such a man do without a big capital to work
with? Why, Alfred E. Ricks, as we left him, was as helpless as a
turtle on its back. He couldn't have worked a scheme to beat a
little girl out of a penny slate-pencil.

'When me and Bill Bassett was left alone I did a little sleight-of-
mind turn in my head with a trade secret at the end of it. Thinks I,
I'll show this Mr. Burglar Man the difference between business
and labour. He had hurt some of my professional self-adulation by
casting his Persians upon commerce and trade.

' "I won't take any of your money as a gift, Mr. Bassett," says I
to him, "but if you'll pay my expenses as a travelling companion
until we get out of the danger zone of the immoral deficit you
have caused in this town's finances to-night, I'll be obliged."

'Bill Bassett agreed to that, and we hiked westward as soon as we
could catch a safe train.

'When we got to a town in Arizona called Los Perros I suggested that we once more try our luck on terra-cotta. That was the
home of Montague Silver, my old instructor, now retired from
business. I knew Monty would stake me to web money if I could
show him a fly buzzing 'round in the locality. Bill Bassett said all
towns looked alike to him as he worked mainly in the dark. So we
got off the train in Los Perros, a fine little town in the silver
region.

'I had an elegant little sure thing in the way of a commercial
slungshot that I intended to hit Bassett behind the ear with. I
wasn't going to take his money while he was asleep, but I was
going to leave him with a lottery ticket that would represent in
experience to him $4,755 – I think that was the amount he had
when we got off the train. But the first time I hinted to him about
an investment, he turns on me and disencumbers himself of the
following terms and expressions.

' "Brother Peters," says he, "it ain't a bad idea to go into an
enterprise of some kind, as you suggest. I think I will. But if I do
it will be such a cold proposition that nobody but Robert E.
Peary and Charlie Fairbanks will be able to sit on the board of
directors."

' "I thought you might want to turn your money over," says I.

' "I do," says he, "frequently. I can't sleep on one side all
night. I'll tell you, Brother Peters," says he, I'm going to start a
poker room. I don't seem to care for the humdrum in swindling,
such as peddling egg-beaters and working off breakfast food on

Barnum and Bailey for sawdust to strew in their circus rings. But the gambling business," says he, "from the profitable side of the table is a good compromise between swiping silver spoons and selling penwipers at a Waldorf-Astoria charity bazaar."

' "Then," says I, "Mr. Bassett, you don't care to talk over my little business proposition?"

' "Why," says he, "do you know, you can't get a Pasteur institute to start up within fifty miles of where I live. I bite so seldom."

'So, Bassett rents a room over a saloon and looks around for some furniture and chromos. The same night I went to Monty Silver's house, and he let me have $200 on my prospects. Then I went to the only store in Los Perros that sold playing cards and bought every deck in the house. The next morning when the store opened I was there bringing all the cards back with me. I said that my partner that was going to back me in the game had changed his mind; and I wanted to sell the cards back again. The storekeeper took 'em at half price.

'Yes, I was seventy-five dollars loser up to that time. But while I had the cards that night I marked every one in every deck. That was labour. And then trade and commerce had their innings, and the bread I had cast upon the waters began to come back in the form of cottage pudding with wine sauce.

'Of course I was among the first to buy chips at Bill Bassett's game. He had bought the only cards there was to be had in town, and I knew the back of every one of them better than I know the back of my head when the barber shows me my haircut in the two mirrors.

'When the game closed I had the five thousand and a few odd dollars, and all Bill Bassett had was the wanderlust and a black cat he had bought for a mascot. Bill shook hands with me when I left.

' "Brother Peters," says he, "I have no business being in business. I was preordained to labour. When a No. 1 burglar tries to make a James out of his jimmy he perpetrates an improfundity. You have a well-oiled and efficacious system of luck at cards," says he. "Peace go with you." And I never afterward sees Bill Bassett again.'

'Well, Jeff,' said I, when the Autolycan adventurer seemed to have divulged the gist of his tale, 'I hope you took care of the money. That would be a respecta – that is a considerable working capital if you should choose some day to settle down to some sort of regular business.'

'Me?' said Jeff virtuously. 'You can bet I've taken care of that five thousand.'

He tapped his coat over the region of his chest exultantly.

'Gold mining stock,' he explained, 'every cent of it. Shares par value one dollar. Bound to go up 500 per cent. within a year. Non-assessable. The Blue Gopher Mine. Just discovered a month ago. Better get in yourself if you've any spare dollars on hand.'

'Sometimes,' said I, 'these mines are not –'

'Oh, this one's solid as an old goose,' said Jeff. 'Fifty thousand dollars' worth of ore in sight, and 10 per cent. monthly earnings guaranteed.'

He drew a long envelope from his pocket and cast it on the table.

'Always carry it with me,' said he. 'So the burglar can't corrupt or the capitalist break in and water it.'

'I looked at the beautifully engraved certificate of stock.

'In Colorado, I see,' said I. 'And, by the way, Jeff, what was the name of the little man who went to Denver – the one you and Bill met at the station?'

'Alfred E. Ricks,' said Jeff, 'was the toad's designation.'

'I see,' said I, 'the president of this mining company signs himself A. L. Fredericks. I was wondering –'

'Let me see that stock,' said Jeff quickly, almost snatching it from me.

To mitigate, even though slightly, the embarrassment I summoned the waiter and ordered another bottle of the Barbera. I thought it was the least I could do.

XLI

A Tempered Wind

THE FIRST TIME my optical nerves was disturbed by the sight of Buckingham Skinner was in Kansas City. I was standing on a corner when I see Buck stick his straw-coloured head out of a third-story window of a business block and holler, 'Whoa, there! Whoa!' like you would in endeavouring to assuage a team of runaway mules.

I looked around; but all the animals I see in sight is a policeman, having his shoes shined, and a couple of delivery wagons hitched to posts. Then in a minute downstairs tumbles this Buckingham

Skinner, and runs to the corner, and stands and gazes down the other street at the imaginary dust kicked up by the fabulous hoofs of the fictitious team of chimerical quadrupeds. And then B. Skinner goes back up to the third-story room again and I see that the lettering on the window is 'The Farmers' Friend Loan Company.'

By and by Straw-top comes down again, and I crossed the street to meet him, for I had my ideas. Yes, sir, when I got close I could see where he overdone it. He was Reub all right as far as his blue jeans and cowhide boots went, but he had a matinée actor's hands, and the rye straw stuck over his ear looked like it belonged to the property man of the Old Homestead Co. Curiosity to know what his graft was got the best of me.

'Was that your team broke away and run just now?' I asks him, polite. 'I tried to stop 'em,' says I, 'but I couldn't. I guess they're half-way back to the farm by now.'

'Gosh blame them darned mules,' says Strawtop, in a voice so good that I nearly apologized; 'they're a'lus bustin' loose.' And then he looks at me close, and then he takes off his hayseed hat, and says, in a different voice: 'I'd like to shake hands with Parleyvoo Pickens, the greatest street man in the West, barring only Montague Silver, which you can no more than allow.'

I let him shake hands with me.

'I learned under Silver,' I said; 'I don't begrudge him the lead. But what's your graft, son? I admit that the phantom flight of the non-existing animals at which you remarked "Whoa!" has puzzled me somewhat. How do you win out on the trick?'

Buckingham Skinner blushed.

'Pocket money,' says he; 'that's all. I am temporarily unfinanced. This little coup de rye straw is good for forty dollars in a town of this size. How do I work it? Why, I involve myself, as you perceive, in the loathsome apparel of the rural dub. Thus embalmed I am Jonas Stubblefield – a name impossible to improve upon. I repair noisily to the office of some loan company conveniently located in the third floor front. There I lay my hat and yarn gloves on the floor and ask to mortgage my farm for $2,000 to pay for my sister's musical education in Europe. Loans like that always suit the loan companies. It's ten to one that when the note falls due the foreclosure will be leading the semiquavers by a couple of lengths.

'Well, sir, I reach in my pocket for the abstract of title; but I suddenly hear my team running away. I run to the window and emit the word – or exclamation, whichever it may be – viz.

"Whoa!" Then I rush downstairs and down the street, returning in a few minutes. "Dang them mules," I says; "they done run away and busted the doubletree and two traces. Now I got to hoof it home, for I never brought no money along. Reckon we'll talk about that loan some other time, gen'lemen."

'Then I spreads out my tarpaulin, like the Israelites, and waits for the manna to drop.

' "Why, no, Mr. Stubblefield," says the lobster-coloured party in the specs and dotted piqué vest; "oblige us by accepting this ten-dollar bill until to-morrow. Get your harness repaired and call in at ten. We'll be pleased to accommodate you in the matter of this loan."

'It's a slight thing,' says Buckingham Skinner, modest, 'but, as I said, only for temporary loose change.

'It's nothing to be ashamed of,' says I, in respect for his mortification; 'in case of an emergency. Of course, it's small compared to organizing a trust or bridge whist, but even the Chicago University had to be started in a small way.'

'What's your graft these days?' Buckingham Skinner asks me.

'The legitimate,' says I. 'I'm handling rhinestones and Dr. Oleum Sinapi's Electric Headache Battery and the Swiss Warbler's Bird Call, a small lot of the new queer ones and twos, and the Bonanza Budget, consisting of a rolled-gold wedding and engagement ring, six Egyptian lily bulbs, a combination pickle fork and nail-clipper, and fifty engraved visiting cards – no two names alike – all for the sum of thirty-eight cents.'

'Two months ago,' says Buckingham Skinner, 'I was doing well down in Texas with a patent instantaneous fire kindler, made of compressed wood ashes and benzine. I sold loads of 'em in towns where they like to burn niggers quick, without having to ask somebody for a light. And just when I was doing the best they strikes oil down there and puts me out of business. "Your machine's too slow, now, pardner," they tells me. "We can have a coon in hell with this here petroleum before your old flint-and-tinder truck can get him warm enough to perfess religion." And so I gives up the kindler and drifts up here to K.C. This little curtain-raiser you seen me doing, Mr. Pickens, with the simulated farm and the hypothetical team, ain't in my line at all, and I'm ashamed you found me working it.'

'No man,' says I, kindly, 'need to be ashamed of putting the ski-bunk on a loan corporation for even so small a sum as ten dollars, when he is financially abashed. Still, it wasn't quite the proper thing. It's too much like borrowing money without paying it back.'

I liked Buckingham Skinner from the start, for as good a man as ever stood over the axles and breathed gasoline smoke. And pretty soon we gets thick, and I let him in on a scheme I'd had in mind for some time, and offers to go partners.

'Anything,' says Buck, 'that is not actually dishonest will find me willing and ready. Let us perforate into the inwardness of your proposition. I feel degraded when I am forced to wear property straw in my hair and assume a bucolic air for the small sum of ten dollars. Actually, Mr. Pickens, it makes me feel like the Ophelia of the Great Occidental All-Star One-Night Consolidated Theatrical Aggregation.'

This scheme of mine was one that suited my proclivities. By nature I am some sentimental, and have always felt gentle toward the mollifying elements of existence. I am disposed to be lenient with the arts and sciences, and I find time to instigate a cordiality for the more human works of nature, such as romance and the atmosphere and grass and poetry and the Seasons. I never skin a sucker without admiring the prismatic beauty of his scales. I never sell a little auriferous trifle to the man with the hoe without noticing the beautiful harmony there is between gold and green. And that's why I liked this scheme; it was so full of outdoor air and landscapes and easy money.

We had to have a young lady assistant to help us work this graft; and I asked Buck if he knew of one to fill the bill.

'One,' says I, 'that is cool and wise and strictly business from her pompadour to her Oxfords. No ex-toe-dancers or gum-chewers or crayon portrait canvassers for this.'

Buck claimed he knew a suitable feminine and he takes me around to see Miss Sarah Malloy. The minute I see her I am pleased. She looked to be the goods as ordered. No sign of the three p's about her – no peroxide, patchouli, nor peau de soie; about twenty-two, brown hair, pleasant ways – the kind of a lady for the place.

'A description of the sandbag, if you please,' she begins.

'Why, ma'am,' says I, 'this graft of ours is so nice and refined and romantic, it would make the balcony scene in "Romeo and Juliet" look like second-story work.'

We talked it over, and Miss Malloy agreed to come in as a business partner. She said she was glad to get a chance to give up her place as stenographer and secretary to a suburban lot company, and go into something respectable.

This is the way we worked our scheme. First, I figured it out by a kind of a proverb. The best grafts in the world are built up on copy-book maxims and psalms and proverbs and Esau's fables. l hey seem to kind of hit off human nature. Our peaceful little swindle was constructed on the old saying: 'The whole push loves a lover.'

One evening Buck and Miss Malloy drives up like blazes in a buggy to a farmer's door. She is pale but affectionate, clinging to his arm – always clinging to his arm. And one can see that she is a peach and of the cling variety. They claim they are eloping for to be married on account of cruel parents. They ask where they can find a preacher. Farmer says, 'B'gum there ain't any preacher nigher than Reverend Abels, four miles over on Caney Creek.' Farmeress wipes her hand on her apron and rubbers through her specs.

Then, lo and look ye! Up the road from the other way jogs Parleyvoo Pickens in a gig, dressed in black, white necktie, long face, sniffing his nose, emitting a spurious kind of noise resembling the long metre doxology.

'B'jinks!' says farmer, 'if thar ain't a preacher now!'

It transpires that I am Rev. Abijah Green, travelling over to Little Bethel school-house for to preach next Sunday.

The young folks will have it they must be married, for pa is pursuing them with the plough mules and the buckboard. So the Reverend Green, after hesitation, marries 'em in farmer's parlour. And farmer grins, and has in cider, and says, 'B'gum!' and farmeress sniffles a bit and pats the bride on the shoulder. And Parleyvoo Pickens, the wrong reverend, writes out a marriage certificate, and farmer and farmeress sign it as witnesses. And the parties of the first, second, and third part gets in their vehicles and rides away. Oh, that was an idyllic graft! True love and the lowing kine and the sun shining on the red barns – it certainly had all other impostures I know about beat to a batter.

I suppose I happened along in time to marry Buck and Miss Malloy at about twenty farmhouses. I hated to think how the romance was going to fade later on when all them marriage certificates turned up in banks where we'd discounted 'em, and the farmers had to pay them notes of hand they'd signed, running from $300 to $500.

On the 15th day of May us three divided about $6,000. Miss Malloy nearly cried with joy. You don't often see a tender-hearted girl or one that was so bent on doing right.

'Boys,' says she, dabbing her eyes with a little handkerchief, 'this stake comes in handier than a powder rag at a fat man's ball. It gives me a chance to reform. I was trying to get out of the real estate business when you fellows came along. But if you hadn't taken me in on this neat little proposition for removing the cuticle of the rutabaga propagators I'm afraid I'd have got into something worse. I was about to accept a place in one of these Women's Auxiliary Bazaars, where they build a parsonage by selling a spoonful of chicken salad and a cream-puff for seventy-five cents and calling it a Business Men's Lunch.

'Now I can go into a square, honest business, and give all them queer jobs the shake. I'm going to Cincinnati and start a palm reading and clairvoyant joint. As Madame Saramaloi, the Egyptian Sorceress, I shall give everybody a dollar's worth of good honest prognostication. Good bye, boys. Take my advice and go into some decent fake. Get friendly with the police and newspapers and you'll be all right.'

So then we all shook hands, and Miss Malloy left us. Me and Buck also rose up and sauntered off a few hundred miles; for we didn't care to be around when them marriage certificates fell due.

With about $4,000 between us we hit that bumptious little town off the New Jersey coast they call New York.

If there ever was an aviary overstocked with jays it is that Yaptown-on-the-Hudson. Cosmopolitan they call it. You bet. So's a piece of fly-paper. You listen close when they're buzzing and trying to pull their feet out of the sticky stuff. 'Little old New York's good enough for us' – that's what they sing.

There's enough Reubs walk down Broadway in one hour to buy up a week's output of the factory in Augusta, Maine, that makes Knaughty Knovelties and the little Phine Phun oroide gold finger ring that sticks a needle in your friend's hand.

You'd think New York people was all wise; but no. They don't get a chance to learn. Everything's too compressed. Even the hayseeds are baled hayseeds. But what else can you expect from a town that's shut off from the world by the ocean on one side and New Jersey on the other?

It's no place for an honest grafter with a small capital. There's too big a protective tariff on bunco. Even when Giovanni sells a quart of warm worms and chestnut hulls he has to hand out a pint to an insectivorous cop. And the hotel man charges double for everything in the bill that he sends by the patrol wagon to the altar where the duke is about to marry the heiress.

But old Badville near-Coney is the ideal hurg for a refined piece of piracy if you can pay the bunco duty. Imported grafts come pretty high. The custom-house officers that look after it carry clubs, and it's hard to smuggle in even a bib-and-tucker swindle to work Brooklyn with unless you can pay the toll. But now, me and Buck, having capital, descends upon New York to try and trade the metropolitan backwoodsmen a few glass beads for real estate just as the Vans did a hundred or two years ago.

At an East Side hotel we gets acquainted with Romulus G. Atterbury, a man with the finest head for financial operations I ever saw. It was all bald and glossy except for grey side whiskers. Seeing that head behind an office railing, you'd deposit a million with it without a receipt. This Atterbury was well dressed, though he ate seldom; and the synopsis of his talk would make the conversation of a siren sound like a cab-driver's kick. He said he used to be a member of the Stock Exchange, but some of the big capitalists got jealous and formed a ring that forced him to sell his seat.

Atterbury got to liking me and Buck and he begun to throw on the canvas for us some of the schemes that had caused his hair to evacuate. He had one scheme for starting a National Bank on $45 that made the Mississippi Bubble look as solid as a glass marble. He talked this to us for three days, and when his throat was good and sore we told him about the roll we had. Atterbury borrowed a quarter from us and went out and got a box of throat lozenges and started all over again. This time he talked bigger things, and we got to see 'em as he did. The scheme he laid out looked like a sure winner, and he talked me and Buck into putting our capital against his burnished dome of thought. It looked all right for a kid-gloved graft. It seemed to be just about an inch and a half outside of the reach of the police, and as moneymaking as a mint. It was just what me and Buck wanted – a regular business at a permanent stand, with no open-air spieling with tonsillitis on the street corners every evening.

So, in six weeks you see a handsome furnished set of offices down in the Wall Street neighbourhood, with 'The Golconda Gold Bond and Investment Company' in gilt letters on the door. And you see in his private room, with the door open, the secretary and treasurer, Mr. Buckingham Skinner, costumed like the lilies of the conservatory, with his high silk hat close to his hand. Nobody yet ever saw Buck outside of an instantaneous reach for his hat.

And you might perceive the president and general manager, Mr. R. G. Atterbury, with his priceless polished poll, busy in the main office room dictating letters to a shorthand contess, who has got pomp and a pompadour that is no less than a guarantee to investors.

There is a book-keeper and an assistant, and a general atmosphere of varnish and culpability.

At another desk the eye is relieved by the sight of an ordinary man, attired with unscrupulous plainness, sitting with his feet up, eating apples, with his obnoxious hat on the back of his head. That man is no other than Colonel Tecumseh (once 'Parleyvoo') Pickens, the vice-president of the company.

'No recherché rags for me,' I says to Atterbury, when we was organizing the stage properties of the robbery. 'I'm a plain man,' says I, 'and I do not use pajamas, French, or military hair-brushes. Cast me for the role of the rhinestone-in-the-rough or I don't go on exhibition. If you can use me in my natural, though displeasing form, do so.'

'Dress you up?' says Atterbury. 'I should say not! Just as you are you're worth more to the business than a whole roomful of the things they pin chrysanthemums on. You're to play the part of the solid but dishevelled capitalist from the Far West. You despise the conventions. You've got so many stocks you can afford to shake socks. Conservative, homely, rough, shrewd, saving – that's your pose. It's a winner in New York. Keep your feet on the desk and eat apples. Whenever anybody comes in eat an apple. Let 'em see you stuff the peelings in a drawer of your desk. Look as economical and rich and rugged as you can.

I followed out Atterbury's instructions. I played the Rocky Mountain capitalist without ruching or frills. The way I deposited apple peelings to my credit in a drawer when any customers came in made Hetty Green look like a spendthrift. I could hear Atterbury saying to victims, as he smiled at me, indulgent and venerating, 'That's our vice-president, Colonel Pickens . . . fortune in Western investments . . . delightfully plain manners, but . . . could sign his cheque for half a million . . . simple as a child . . . wonderful head . . . conservative and careful almost to a fault '

Atterbury managed the business. Me and Buck never quite understood all of it, though he explained it to us in full. It seems the company was a kind of co-operative one, and everybody that bought stock shared in the profits. First, we officers bought up a controlling interest – we had to have that – of the shares at fifty cents a hundred – just what the printer charged us – and the rest went to the public at a dollar each. The company guaranteed the stockholders a profit of ten per cent. each month, payable on the last day thereof.

When any stockholder had paid in as much as $100, the company issued him a Gold Bond and he became a bond-holder. I asked Atterbury one day what benefits and appurtenances these Gold Bonds was to an investor more so than the immunities and privileges enjoyed by the common sucker who only owned stock. Atterbury picked up one of them Gold Bonds, all gilt and lettered up with flourishes and a big red seal tied with a blue ribbon in a bow-knot, and he looked at me like his feelings was hurt.

'My dear Colonel Pickens,' says he, 'you have no soul for Art. Think of a thousand homes made happy by possessing one of these beautiful gems of the lithographer's skill! Think of the joy in the household where one of these Gold Bonds hangs by a pink cord to the whatnot, or is chewed by the baby, carolling gleefully upon the floor! Ah, I see your eye growing moist, Colonel – I have touched you, have I not?'

'You have not,' says I, 'for I've been watching you. The moisture you see is apple juice. You can't expect one man to act as a human cider-press and an art connoisseur too.'

Atterbury attended to the details of the concern. As I understand it, they was simple. The investors in stock paid in their money, and – well, I guess that's all they had to do. The company received it, and – I don't call to mind anything else. Me and Buck knew more about selling corn salve than we did about Wall Street, but even we could see how the Golconda Gold Bond Investment Company was making money. You take in money and pay back ten per cent. of it; it's plain enough that you make a clean, legitimate profit of 90 per cent., less expenses, as long as the fish bite.

Atterbury wanted to be president and treasurer too, but Buck winks an eye at him and says: 'You was to furnish the brains. Do you call it good brain-work when you propose to take in money at the door too? Think again. I hereby nominate myself treasurer *ad valorem, sine die*, and by acclamation. I chip in that much brain-work free. Me and Pickens, we furnished the capital, and we'll handle the unearned increment as it incremates.'

It cost us $500 for office rent and first payment on furniture; $1,500 more went for printing and advertising. Atterbury knew his business. 'Three months to a minute we'll last,' says he. 'A day longer than that and we'll have to either go under or go under an alias. By that time we ought to clean up $60,000. And then a

money belt and a lower berth for me, and the yellow journals and
the furniture men can pick the bones.'

Our ads. done the work. 'Country weeklies and Washington
hand-press dailies, of course,' says I when we was ready to make
contracts.

'Man,' says Atterbury, 'as its advertising manager you would
cause a Limburger cheese factory to remain undiscovered during a
hot summer. The game we're after is right here in New York and
Brooklyn and the Harlem reading-rooms. They're the people that
the street-car fenders and the Answers to Correspondents columns
and the pickpocket notices are made for. We want our ads. in the
biggest city dailies, top of column, next to editorials on radium
and pictures of the girl doing health exercises.'

Pretty soon the money begins to roll in. Buck didn't have to
pretend to be busy; his desk was piled high up with money orders
and cheques and green-backs. People began to drop in the office
and buy stock every day.

Most of the shares went in small amounts – $10 and $25 and
$50, and a good many $2 and $3 lots. And the bald and inviolate
cranium of President Atterbury shines with enthusiasm and
demerit, while Colonel Tecumseh Pickens, the rude but reputable
Crœsus of the West, consumes so many apples that the peelings
hang to the floor from the mahogany garbage chest that he calls
his desk.

Just as Atterbury said, we ran along about three months without
being troubled. Buck cashed the paper as fast as it came in and
kept the money in a safe deposit vault a block or so away. Buck
never thought much of banks for such purposes. We paid the
interest regular on the stock we'd sold, so there was nothing for
anybody to squeal about. We had nearly $50,000 on hand and all
three of us had been living as high as prize-fighters out of training.

One morning, as me and Buck sauntered into the office, fat and
flippant, from our noon grub, we met an easy-looking fellow, with
a bright eye and a pipe in his mouth, coming out. We found Atterbury looking like he'd been caught a mile from home in a wet
shower.

'Know that man?' he asked us.

We said we didn't.

'I don't either,' says Atterbury, wiping off his head; 'but I'll bet
enough Gold Bonds to paper a cell in the Tombs that he's a newspaper reporter.'

'What did he want?' asks Buck.

'Information,' says our president. 'He said he was thinking of buying some stock and asked me about nine hundred questions, and every one of 'em hit some sore place in the business. I know he's on a paper. You can't fool me. You see a man about half shabby, with an eye like a gimlet, smoking cut plug, with dandruff on his coat collar, and knowing more than J. P. Morgan and Shakespeare put together – if that ain't a reporter I never saw one. I was afraid of this. I don't mind detectives and post-office inspectors – I talk to 'em eight minutes and then sell 'em stock – but them reporters take the starch out of my collar. Boys, I recommend that we declare a dividend and fade away. The signs point that way.'

Me and Buck talked to Atterbury and got him to stop sweating and stand still. That fellow didn't look like a reporter to us. Reporters always pull out a pencil and tablet on you, and tell you a story you've heard, and strike you for the drinks. But Atterbury was shaky and nervous all day.

The next day me and Buck comes down from the hotel about ten-thirty. On the way we buys the papers, and the first thing we see is a column on the front page about our little imposition. It was a shame the way that reporter intimated that we were no blood relatives of the late George W. Childs. He tells all about the scheme as he sees it, in a rich, racy kind of a guying style that might amuse most anybody except a stockholder. Atterbury was right; it behooveth the gaily clad treasurer and the pearly pated president and the rugged vice-president of the Golconda Gold Bond and Investment Company to go away real sudden and quick that their days might be longer upon the land.

Me and Buck hurries down to the office. We finds on the stairs and in the hall a crowd of people trying to squeeze into our office, which is already jammed full inside to the railing. They've nearly all got Golconda stock and Gold Bonds in their hands. Me and Buck judged they'd been reading the papers, too.

We stopped and looked at our stockholders, some surprised. It wasn't quite the kind of a gang we supposed had been investing. They all looked like poor people; there was plenty of old women and lots of young girls that you'd say worked in factories and mills. Some was old men that looked like war veterans, and some was crippled, and a good many was just kids – bootblacks and newsboys and messengers. Some was workingmen in overalls, with their sleeves rolled up. Not one of the gang looked like a stockholder in anything unless it was a peanut stand. But they all had Golconda stock and looked as sick as you please.

I saw a queer kind of a pale look come on Buck's face when he sized up the crowd. He stepped up to a sickly looking woman and says: 'Madam, do you own any of this stock?'

'I put in a hundred dollars,' says the woman, faint like. 'It was all I had saved in a year. One of my children is dying at home now and I haven't a cent in the house. I came to see if I could draw out some. The circulars said you could draw it at any time. But they say now I will lose it all.'

There was a smart kind of a kid in the gang — I guess he was a newsboy. 'I got in twenty-fi', mister,' he says, looking hopeful at Buck's silk hat and clothes. 'Dey paid me two-fifty a mont' on it. Say, a man tells me dey can't do dat and be on de square. Is dat straight? Do you guess I can get out my twent-fi'?'

Some of the old women was crying. The factory girls was plumb distracted. They'd lost all their savings and they'd be docked for the time they lost coming to see about it.

There was one girl — a pretty one in a red shawl, crying in a corner like her heart would dissolve. Buck goes over and asks her about it.

'It ain't so much losing the money, mister,' says she, shaking all over, 'though I've been two years saving it up; but Jakey won't marry me now. He'll take Rosa Steinfeld. I know J — J — Jakey. She's got $400 in the savings bank. Ai, ai, ai —' she sings out.

Buck looks all around with that same funny look on his face. And then we see leaning against the wall, puffing at his pipe, with his eye shining at us, this newspaper reporter. Buck and me walks over to him.

'You're a real interesting writer,' says Buck. 'How far do you mean to carry it? Anything more up your sleeve?

'Oh, I'm just waiting around,' says the reporter, smoking away, 'in case any news turns up. It's up to your stockholders now. Some of them might complain, you know. Isn't that the patrol wagon now?' he says, listening to a sound outside. 'No,' he goes on, 'that's Doc. Whittleford's old cadaver coupe from the Roosevelt. I ought to know that gong. Yes, I suppose I've written some interesting stuff at times.'

'You wait,' says Buck; 'I'm going to throw an item of news in your way.'

Buck reaches in his pocket and hands me a key. I knew what he meant before he spoke. Confounded old buccaneer — I knew what he meant. They don't make them any better than Buck.

'Pick,' says he, looking at me hard, 'ain't this graft a little out of our line? Do we want Jakey to marry Rosa Steinfeld?'

'You've got my vote,' says I. 'I'll have it here in ten minutes.' And I starts for the safe deposit vaults.

I comes back with the money done up in a big bundle, and then Buck and me takes the journalist reporter around to another door and we let ourselves into one of the office rooms.

'Now, my literary friend,' says Buck, 'take a chair, and keep still, and I'll give you an interview. You see before you two grafters from Graftersville, Grafter County, Arkansas. Me and Pick have sold brass jewellery, hair tonic, song books, marked cards, patent medicines, Connecticut Smyrna rugs, furniture polish, and albums in every town from Old Point Comfort to the Golden Gate. We've grafted a dollar whenever we saw one that had a surplus look to it. But we never went after the simoleon in the toe of the sock under the loose brick in the corner of the kitchen hearth. There's an old saying you may have heard – "fussily decency averni" – which means it's an easy slide from the street-faker's dry-goods box to a desk in Wall Street. We've took that slide, but we didn't know exactly what was at the bottom of it. Now, you ought to be wise, but you ain't. You've got New York wiseness, which means that you judge a man by the outside of his clothes. That ain't right. You ought to look at the lining and seams and the button-holes. While we are waiting for the patrol wagon you might get out your little stub pencil and take notes for another funny piece in the paper.'

And then Buck turns to me and says: 'I don't care what Atterbury thinks. He only put in brains, and if he gets his capital out he's lucky But what do you say, Pick?'

'Me?' said I. 'You ought to know me, Buck. I didn't know who was buying the stock.'

'All right,' says Buck. And then he goes through the inside door into the main office and looks at the gang trying to squeeze through the railing. Atterbury and his hat was gone. And Buck makes 'em a short speech.

'All you lambs get in line. You're going to get your wool back. Don't shove so. Get in a line – a *line* – not in a pile. Lady, will you please stop bleating? Your money's waiting for you Here, sonny, don't climb over that railing; your dimes are safe. Don't cry, sis; you ain't out a cent. Get in *line*, I say. Here, Pick, come and straighten 'em out and let 'em through and out by the other door.'

Buck takes off his coat, pushes his silk hat on the back of his head, and lights up a reina victoria. He sets at the table with the boodle before him, all done up in neat packages. I gets the stockholders strung out and marches 'em, single file, through from the main room; and the reporter man passes 'em out of the side door into the hall again. As they go by, Buck takes up the stock and the Gold Bonds, paying 'em cash, dollar for dollar, the same as they paid in.

The shareholders of the Golconda Gold Bond and Investment Company can't hardly believe it. They almost grabs the money out of Buck's hands. Some of the women keep on crying, for it's a custom of the sex to cry when they have sorrow, to weep when they have joy, and to shed tears whenever they find themselves without either.

The old women's fingers shake when they stuff the skads in the bosom of their rusty dresses. The factory girls just stoop over and flap their dry goods a second, and you hear the elastic go 'pop' as the currency goes down in the ladies' department of the 'Old Domestic Lisle-Thread Bank.'

Some of the stockholders that had been doing the Jeremiah act the loudest outside had spasms of restored confidence and wanted to leave the money invested. 'Salt away that chicken feed in your duds, and skip along,' says Buck. 'What business have you got investing in bonds? The tea-pot or the crack in the wall behind the clock for your hoard of pennies.'

When the pretty girl in the red shawl cashes in Buck hands her an extra twenty.

'A wedding present,' says our treasurer, 'from the Golconda Company. And say — if Jakey ever follows his nose, even at a respectful distance, around the corner where Rosa Steinfeld lives, you are hereby authorized to knock a couple of inches of it off.'

When they was all paid off and gone, Buck calls the newspaper reporter and shoves the rest of the money over to him.

'You begun this,' says Buck; 'now finish it. Over there are the books, showing every share and bond issued. Here's the money to cover, except what we've spent to live on. You'll have to act as receiver. I guess you'll do the square thing on account of your paper. This is the best way we know how to settle it. Me and our substantial but apple-weary vice-president are going to follow the example of our revered president, and skip. Now, have you got enough news for to-day, or do you want to interview us on etiquette and the best way to make over an old taffeta skirt?'

'News!' says the newspaper man, taking his pipe out; 'do you think I could use this? I don't want to lose my job. Suppose I go around to the office and tell 'em this happened. What'll the managing editor say? He'll just hand me a pass to Bellevue and tell me to come back when I get cured. I might turn in a story about a sea serpent wiggling up Broadway, but I haven't got the nerve to try 'em with a pipe like this. A get-rich-quick – excuse me – gang giving back the boodle! Oh, no. I'm not on the comic supplement.'

'You can't understand it, of course,' says Buck, with his hand on the door-knob. 'Me and Pick ain't Wall Streeters like you know 'em. We never allowed to swindle sick old women and working girls and take nickels off of kids. In the lines of graft we've worked we took money from the people the Lord made to be buncoed – sports and rounders and smart Alecks and street crowds, that always have a few dollars to throw away, and farmers that wouldn't ever be happy if the grafters didn't come around and play with 'em when they sold their crops. We never cared to fish for the kid of suckers that bite here. No, sir. We got too much respect for the profession and for ourselves. Good-bye to you, Mr. Receiver.'

'Here!' says the journalist reporter; 'wait a minute. There's a broker I know on the next floor. Wait till I put this truck in his safe. I want you fellows to take a drink on me before you go.'

'On you?' says Buck, winking solemn. 'Don't you go and try to make 'em believe at the office you said that. Thanks. We can't spare the time, I reckon. So long.'

And me and Buck slides out the door; and that's the way the Golconda Company went into involuntary liquefaction.

If you had seen me and Buck the next night you'd have had to go to a little bum hotel over near the West Side ferry landings. We was in a little back room, and I was filling up a gross of six-ounce bottles with hydrant water coloured red with aniline and flavoured with cinnamon. Buck was smoking, contented, and he wore a decent brown derby in place of his silk hat.

'It's a good thing, Pick,' says he, as he drove in the corks, 'that we got Brady to loan us his horse and wagon for a week. We'll rustle up a stake by then. This hair tonic'll sell right along over in Jersey. Bald heads ain't popular over there on account of the mosquitoes.'

Directly I dragged out my valise and went down in it for labels.

'Hair tonic labels are out,' says I. 'Only about a dozen on hand.'

'Buy some more,' says Buck.

We investigated our pockets and found we had just enough money to settle our hotel bill in the morning and pay our passage over the ferry.

'Plenty of the "Shake-the-Shakes Chill Cure" labels,' says I, after looking.

'What more do you want?' says Buck. 'Slap 'em on. The chill season is just opening up in the Hackensack low grounds. What's hair, anyway, if you have to shake it off?'

We posted on the Chill Cure labels about half an hour and Buck says:

'Making an honest livin's better than that Wall Street, anyhow; ain't it, Pick?'

'You bet,' says I.

XLII

Hostages to Momus

I

I NEVER GOT INSIDE of the legitimate line of graft but once. But, one time, as I say, I reversed the decision of the revised statutes and undertook a thing that I'd have to apologize for even under the New Jersey trust laws.

Me and Caligula Polk, of Muskogee in the Creek Nation, was down in the Mexican State of Tamaulipas running a peripatetic lottery and monte game. Now, selling lottery tickets is a government graft in Mexico, just like selling forty-eight cents' worth of postage-stamps for forty-nine cents is over here. So Uncle Porfirio he instructs the *rurales* to attend to our case.

Rurales? They're a sort of country police; but don't draw any mental crayon portraits of the worthy constable with a tin star and a grey goatee. The *rurales* – well, if we'd mount our Supreme Court on broncos, arm 'em with Winchesters, and start 'em out after John Doe *et al.*, we'd have about the same thing.

When the *rurales* started for us we started for the States. They chased us as far as Matamoras. We hid in a brickyard; and that night we swum the Rio Grande, Caligula with a brick in each hand, absent-minded, which he drops upon the soil of Texas, forgetting he had 'em.

From there we emigrated to San Antone, and then over to New Orleans, where we took a rest. And in that town of cotton bales and other adjuncts to female beauty we made the acquaintance of drinks invented by the Creoles during the period of Louey Cans, in which they are still served at the side doors. The most I can remember of this town is that me and Caligula and a Frenchman named McCarty – wait a minute; Adolph McCarty – was trying to make the French Quarter pay up the back trading-stamps due on the Louisiana Purchase, when somebody hollers that the john-darms are coming. I have an insufficient recollection of buying two yellow tickets through a window; and I seemed to see a man swing a lantern and say 'All aboard!' I remembered no more, except that the train butcher was covering me and Caligula up with Augusta J. Evans' works and figs.

When we become revised, we find that we have collided up against the State of Georgia at a spot hitherto unaccounted for in time-tables except by an asterisk, which means that trains stop every other Thursday on signal by tearing up a rail. We was waked up in a yellow pine hotel by the noise of flowers and the smell of birds. Yes, sir, for the wind was banging sunflowers as big as buggy wheels against the weather-boarding and the chicken-coop was right under the window. Me and Caligula dressed and went downstairs. The landlord was shelling peas on the front porch. He was six feet of chills and fever, and Hong-Kong in complexion, though in other respects he seemed amenable in the exercise of his sentiments and features.

Caligula, who is a spokesman by birth, and a small man, though red-haired and impatient of painfulness of any kind, speaks up.

'Pardner,' says he, 'good morning, and be darned to you. Would you mind telling us why we are at? We know the reason we are where, but can't exactly figure out on account of at what place.'

'Well, gentlemen,' says the landlord, 'I reckoned you-all would be inquiring this morning. You-all dropped off at the nine-thirty train here last night; and you was right tight. Yes, you was right smart in liquor. I can inform you that you are now in the town of Mountain Valley, in the State of Georgia.'

'On top of that,' says Caligula, 'don't say that we can't have anything to eat.'

'Sit down, gentlemen,' says the landlord, 'and in twenty minutes I'll call you to the best breakfast you can get anywhere in town.'

That breakfast turned out to be composed of fried bacon and a yellowish edifice that proved up something between pound cake and flexible sandstone. The landlord calls it corn pone; and then he sets out a dish of the exaggerated breakfast food known as hominy; and so me and Caligula makes the acquaintance of the celebrated food that enabled every Johnny Reb to lick one and two-thirds Yankees for nearly four years at a stretch.

'The wonder to me is,' says Caligula, 'that Uncle Robert Lee's boys didn't chase the Grant and Sherman outfit clear up into Hudson's Bay. It would have made me that mad to eat this truck they call mahogany!'

'Hog and hominy,' I explains, 'is the staple food of this section.'

'Then,' says Caligula, 'they ought to keep it where it belongs. I thought this was a hotel and not a stable. Now, if we was in Muskogee at the St. Lucifer House, I'd show you some breakfast grub. Antelope steaks and fried liver to begin on, and venison cutlets with *chili con carne* and pineapple fritters, and then some sardines and mixed pickles; and top it off with a can of yellow clings and a bottle of beer. You won't find a layout like that on the bill of affairs of any of your Eastern restauraws.'

'Too lavish,' say I. 'I've travelled, and I'm unprejudiced. There'll never be a perfect breakfast eaten until some man grows arms long enough to stretch down to New Orleans for his coffee and over to Norfolk for his rolls, and reaches up to Vermont and digs a slice of butter out of a spring-house, and then turns over a beehive close to a white clover patch out in Indiana for the rest. Then he'd come pretty close to making a meal on the amber that the gods eat on Mount Olympia.'

'Too ephemeral,' says Caligula. 'I'd want ham and eggs, or rabbit stew, anyhow, for a chaser. What do you consider the most edifying and casual in the way of a dinner?'

'I've been infatuated from time to time,' I answers, 'with fancy ramifications of grub such as terrapins, lobsters, reed birds, jambolaya, and canvas-covered ducks; but, after all, there's nothing less displeasing to me than a beefsteak smothered in mushrooms on a balcony in sound of the Broadway street-cars, with a hand organ playing down below, and the boys hollering extras about the latest suicide. For the wine, give me a reasonable Ponty Cany. And that's all, except a *demi-tasse*.'

'Well,' says Caligula, 'I reckon in New York you get to be a conniseer; and when you go around with the *demi-tasse you* are naturally bound to buy 'em stylish grub.'

'It's a great town for epicures,' says I. 'You'd soon fall into their ways if you was there.'

'I've heard it was,' says Caligula. 'But I reckon I wouldn't. I can polish my finger-nails all they need myself.'

II

After breakfast we went out on the front porch, lighted up two of the landlord's *flor de upas* perfectos, and took a look at Georgia.

The instalment of scenery visible to the eye looked mighty poor. As far as we could see was red hills all washed down with gullies and scattered over with patches of piny woods. Blackberry bushes was all that kept the rail fences from falling down. About fifteen miles over to the north was a little range of well-timbered mountains.

That town of Mountain Valley wasn't going. About a dozen people permeated along the sidewalks; but what you saw mostly was rain-barrels and roosters, and boys poking around with sticks in piles of ashes made by burning the scenery of Uncle Tom shows.

And just then there passes down on the other side of the street a high man in a long black coat and a beaver hat. All the people in sight bowed, and some crossed the street to shake hands with him; folks came out of stores and houses to holler at him; women leaned out of windows and smiled; and all the kids stopped playing to look at him. Our landlord stepped out on the porch and bent himself double like a carpenter's rule, and sung out, 'Good morning, Colonel,' when he was a dozen yards gone by.

'And is that Alexander, pa?' says Caligula to the landlord; 'and why is he called great?'

'That, gentlemen,' says the landlord, 'is no less than Colonel Jackson T. Rockingham, the president of the Sunrise & Edenville Tap Railroad, mayor of Mountain Valley, and chairman of the Perry County board of immigration and public improvements.'

'Been away a good many years, hasn't he?' I asked.

'No, sir; Colonel Rockingham is going down to the post office for his mail. His fellow-citizens take pleasure in greeting him thus every morning. The colonel is our most prominent citizen. Besides the height of the stock of the Sunrise & Edenville Tap Railroad, he owns a thousand acres of that land across the creek. Mountain Valley delights, sir, to honour a citizen of such worth and public spirit.'

For an hour that afternoon Caligula sat on the back of his neck on the porch and studied a newspaper, which was unusual in a man who despised print. When he was through he took me to the end of the porch among the sunlight and drying dish-towels. I knew that Caligula had invented a new graft. For he chewed the ends of his moustache and ran the left catch of his suspenders up and down, which was his way.

'What is it now?' I asks. 'Just so it ain't floating mining stocks or raising Pennsylvania pinks, we'll talk it over.'

Pennsylvania pinks? Oh, that refers to a coin-raising scheme of the Keystoners. They burn the soles of old women s feet to make them tell where their money's hid.

Caligula's words in business was always few and bitter.

'You see them mountains,' said he, pointing. 'And you seen that colonel man that owns railroads and cuts more ice when he goes to the post office than Roosevelt does when he cleans 'em out. What w-e're going to do is to kidnap the latter into the former, and inflict a ransom of ten thousand dollars.'

'Illegality,' says I, shaking my head.

'I knew you'd say that,' says Caligula. 'At first sight it does seem to jar peace and dignity. But it don't. I got the idea out of that newspaper. Would you commit aspersions on a equitable graft that the United States itself has condoned and indorsed and ratified?'

'Kidnapping,' says I, 'is an immoral function in the derogatory list of the statutes. If the United States upholds it, it must be a recent enactment of ethics, along with race suicide and rural delivery.'

'Listen,' says Caligula, 'and I'll explain the case set down in the papers. Here was a Greek citizen named Burdick Harris,' says he, 'captured for a graft by Africans; and the United States sends two gunboats to the State of Tangiers and makes the King of Morocco give up seventy thousand dollars to Raisuli.'

'Go slow,' says I 'That sounds too international to take in all at once. It's like "thimble, thimble, who's got the naturalization papers?" '

' 'Twas Press despatches from Constantinople,' says Caligula. 'You'll see, six months from now. They'll be confirmed by the monthly magazines; and then it won't be long till you'll notice 'em alongside of photos of the Mount Pelée eruption photos in the while-you-get-your-hair-cut weeklies. It's all right, Pick. This African man Raisuli hides Burdick Harris up in the mountains, and advertises his price to the governments of different nations. Now, you wouldn't think for a minute,' goes on Caligula, 'that John Hay would have chipped in and helped this graft along if it wasn't a square game, would you?'

'Why, no,' says I. 'I've always stood right in with Bryan's policies, and I couldn't consciously say a word against the Republican administration just now. But if Harris was a Greek, on what system of international protocols did Hay interfere?'

'It ain't exactly set forth in the papers,' says Caligula. 'I suppose it's a matter of sentiment. You know he wrote this poem, "Little

Breeches"; and them Greeks wear little or none. But anyhow, John Hay sends the *Brooklyn* and the *Olympia* over, and they cover Africa with thirty-inch guns. And then Hay cables after the health of the *persona grata*. "And how are they this morning?" he wires. "Is Burdick Harris alive yet, or Mr. Raisuli dead?" And the King of Morocco sends up the seventy thousand dollars, and they turn Burdick Harris loose. And there's not half the hard feelings among the nations about this little kidnapping matter as there was about the peace congress. And Burdick Harris says to the reporters, in the Greek language, that he's often heard about the United States, and he admires Roosevelt next to Raisuli, who is one of the whitest and most gentlemanly kidnappers that he ever worked alongside of. So you see, Pick,' winds up Caligula, 'we've got the law of nations on our side. We'll cut this colonel man out of the herd, and corral him in them little mountains, and stick up his heirs and assigns for ten thousand dollars.'

'Well, you seldom little red-headed territorial terror,' I answers, 'you can't bluff your uncle Tecumseh Pickens! I'll be your company in this graft. But I misdoubt if you've absorbed the inwardness of this Burdick Harris case, Calig; and if on any morning we get a telegram from the Secretary of State asking about the health of the scheme, I propose to acquire the most propinquitous and celeritous mule in this section and gallop diplomatically over into the neighbouring and peaceful nation of Alabama.'

III

Me and Caligula spent the next three days investigating the bunch of mountains into which we proposed to kidnap Colonel Jackson T. Rockingham. We finally selected an upright slice of topography covered with bushes and trees that you could only reach by a secret path that we cut out up the side of it. And the only way to reach the mountain was to follow up the bend of a brand that wound among the elevations.

Then I took in hand an important sub-division of the proceedings. I went up to Atlanta on the train and laid in a two-hundred-and-fifty-dollar supply of the most gratifying and efficient lines of grub that money could buy. I always was an admirer of viands in their more palliative and revised stages. Hog and hominy are not only inartistic to my stomach, but they give indigestion to my moral sentiments. And I thought of Colonel Jackson T. Rockingham, president of the Sunrise & Edenville Tap Railroad, and how he would miss the luxury of his home fare as is so famous among wealthy Southerners. So I sunk half of mine and Caligula's capital in as elegant a layout of fresh and canned provisions as Burdick Harris or any other professional kidnappee ever saw in a camp.

I put another hundred in a couple of cases of Bordeaux, two quarts of cognac, two hundred Havana regalias with gold bands, and a camp-stove and stools and folding cots. I wanted Colonel Rockingham to be comfortable; and I hoped after he gave up the ten thousand dollars he would give me and Caligula as good a name for gentlemen and entertainers as the Greek man did the friend of his that made the United States his bill collector against Africa.

When the goods came down from Atlanta, we hired a wagon, moved them up on the little mountain, and established camp. And then we laid for the colonel.

We caught him one morning about two miles out from Mountain Valley, on his way to look after some of his burnt umber farm land. He was an elegant old gentleman, as thin and tall as a trout rod, with frazzled shirt-cuffs and specs on a black string. We explained to him, brief and easy, what we wanted; and Caligula showed him, careless, the handle of his forty-five under his coat.

'What?' says Colonel Rockingham. 'Bandits in Perry County, Georgia! I shall see that the board of immigration and public improvements hears of this!'

'Be so unfoolhardy as to climb into that buggy,' says Caligula, 'by order of the board of perforation and public depravity. This is a business meeting, and we're anxious to adjourn *sine qua non*.'

We drove Colonel Rockingham over the mountain and up the side of it as far as the buggy could go. Then we tied the horse, and took our prisoner on foot up to the camp.

'Now, colonel,' I says to him, 'we're after the ransom, me and my partner; and no harm will come to you if the King of Mor – if your friends send up the dust. In the meantime we are gentlemen the same as you. And if you give us your word not to try to escape, the freedom of the camp is yours.'

'I give you my word,' says the colonel.

'All right,' says I; 'and now it's eleven o'clock, and me and Mr. Polk will proceed to inoculate the occasion with a few well-timed trivialities in the line of grub.'

'Thank you,' says the colonel; 'I believe I could relish a slice of bacon and a plate of hominy.'

'But you won't,' says I emphatic. 'Not in this camp. We soar in higher regions than them occupied by your celebrated but repulsive dish.'

While the colonel read his paper, me and Caligula took off our coats and went in for a little luncheon *de luxe* just to show him. Caligula was a fine cook of the Western brand. He could toast a buffalo or fricassee a couple of steers as easy as a woman could make a cup of tea. He was gifted in the way of knocking together edibles when haste and muscle and quantity was to be considered. He held the record west of the Arkansas River for frying pancakes with his left hand, broiling venison cutlets with his right, and skinning a rabbit with his teeth at the same time. But I could do things *en casserole* and *à la creole*, and handle the oil and tobasco as gently and nicely as a French *chef*.

So at twelve o'clock we had a hot lunch ready that looked like a banquet on a Mississippi River steamboat. We spread it on the tops of two or three big boxes, opened two quarts of the red wine, set the olives and a canned oyster cocktail and a ready-made Martini by the colonel's plate, and called him to grub.

Colonel Rockingham drew up his camp-stool, wiped off his specs, and looked at the things on the table. Then I thought he was swearing; and I felt mean because I hadn't taken more pains with the victuals. But he wasn't; he was asking a blessing; and me and Caligula hung our heads, and I saw a tear drop from the colonel's eye into his cocktail.

I never saw a man eat with so much earnestness and application – not hastily, like a grammarian, or one of the canal, but slow and appreciative, like a anaconda, or a real vive *bonjour*.

In an hour and a half the colonel leaned back I brought him a pony of brandy and his black coffee, and set the box of Havana regalias on the table.

'Gentlemen,' says he, blowing out the smoke and trying to breathe it back again, 'when we view the eternal hills and the smiling and beneficent landscape, and reflect upon the goodness of the Creator who –'

'Excuse me, colonel,' says I, 'but there's some business to attend to now'; and I brought out paper and pen and ink and laid 'em before him. 'Who do you want to send to for the money?' I asks.

'I reckon,' says he, after thinking a bit, 'to the vice-president of our railroad, at the general offices of the Company in Edenville.'

'How far is it to Edenville from here?' I asked.

'About ten miles,' says he.

Then I dictated these lines, and Colonel Rockingham wrote them out:

'I am kidnapped and held a prisoner by two desperate outlaws in a place which is useless to attempt to find. They demand ten thousand dollars at once for my release. The amount must be raised immediately, and these directions followed. Come alone with the money to Stony Creek, which runs out of Blacktop Mountains. Follow the bed of the creek till you come to a big flat rock on the left bank, on which is marked a cross in red chalk. Stand on the rock and wave a white flag. A guide will come to you and conduct you to where I am held. Lose no time.'

After the colonel had finished this, he asked permission to tack on a postscript about how white he was being treated, so the railroad wouldn't feel uneasy in its bosom about him. We agreed to that. He wrote down that he had just had lunch with the two desperate ruffians; and then he set down the whole bill of fare, from cocktails to coffee. He wound up with the remark that dinner would be ready about six, and would probably be a more licentious and intemperate affair than lunch.

Me and Caligula read it, and decided to let it go; for we, being cooks, were amenable to praise, though it sounded out of place on a sight draft for ten thousand dollars.

I took the letter over to the Mountain Valley road and watched for a messenger. By and by a coloured equestrian came along on horseback, riding toward Edenville. I gave him a dollar to take the letter to the railroad offices; and then I went back to camp.

IV

About four o'clock in the afternoon, Caligula, who was acting as look-out, calls to me:

'I have to report a white shirt signalling on the starboard bow, sir.'

I went down the mountain and brought back a fat, red man in an alpaca coat and no collar.

'Gentlemen,' says Colonel Rockingham, 'allow me to introduce my brother, Captain Duval C. Rockingham, vice-president of the Sunrise & Edenville Tap Railroad.'

'Otherwise the King of Morocco,' says I. 'I reckon you don't mind my counting the ransom, just as a business formality.'

'Well, no, not exactly,' says the fat man, 'not when it comes. I turned that matter over to our second vice-president. I was anxious after Brother Jackson's safetiness. I reckon he'll be along right soon. What does that lobster salad you mentioned taste like, Brother Jackson?'

'Mr. Vice-President,' says I, 'you'll oblige us by remaining here till the second V.-P. arrives. This is a private rehearsal, and we don't want any roadside speculators selling tickets.'

In half an hour Caligula sings out again:

Sail ho! Looks like an apron on a broomstick.'

I perambulated down the cliff again, and escorted up a man six foot three, with a sandy beard and no other dimensions that you could notice. Thinks I to myself, if he's got ten thousand dollars on his person it's in one bill and folded lengthwise.

'Mr. Patterson G. Coble, our second vice-president,' announces the colonel.

'Glad to know you, gentlemen,' says this Coble 'I came up to disseminate the tidings that Major Tallahassee Tucker, our general passenger agent, is now negotiating a peach-crate full of our railroad bonds with the Perry County Bank for a loan. My dear Colonel Rockingham, was that chicken gumbo or cracked goobers on the bill of fare in your note? Me and the conductor of fifty-six was having a dispute about it.'

'Another white wings on the rocks!' hollers Caligula. 'If I see any more I'll fire on 'em and swear they was torpedo-boats!'

The guide goes down again, and convoys into the lair a person in blue overalls carrying an amount of inebriety and a lantern. I am so sure that this is Major Tucker that I don't even ask him until we are up above; and then I discover that it is Uncle Timothy, the yard switchman at Edenville, who is sent ahead to flag our understandings with the gossip that Judge Pendergast, the railroad's attorney, is in the process of mortgaging Colonel Rockingham's farming lands to make up the ransom.

While he is talking, two men crawl from under the bushes into camp, and Caligula, with no white flag to disinter him from his plain duty, draws his gun. But again Colonel Rockingham intervenes and introduces Mr. Jones and Mr. Batts, engineer and fireman of train number forty-two.

'Excuse us,' says Batts, 'but me and Jim have hunted squirrels all over this mounting, and we don't need no white flag. Was that straight, colonel, about the plum pudding and pineapples and real store cigars?'

'Towel on a fishing-pole in the offing!' howls Caligula. 'Suppose it's the firing-line of the freight conductors and brake-men.'

'My last trip down,' says I, wiping off my face. 'If the S. & E. T. wants to run an excursion up here just because we kidnapped their president, let 'em. We'll put out our sign. "The Kidnapper's Café and Trainmen's Home."'

This time I caught Major Tallahassee Tucker by his own confession, and I felt easier. I asked him into the creek, so I could
drown him if he happened to be a track-walker or caboose porter.
All the way up the mountain he drivelled to me about asparagus
on toast, a thing that his intelligence in life had skipped.

Up above I got his mind segregated from food and asked if he
had raised the ransom.

'My dear sir,' says he, 'I succeeded in negotiating a loan on
thirty thousand dollars' worth of the bonds of our railroad, and –'

'Never mind just now, major,' says I. 'It's all right, then. Wait
till after dinner, and we'll settle the business. All of you gentlemen,' I continues to the crowd, 'are invited to stay to dinner. We
have mutually trusted one another, and the white flag is supposed
to wave over the proceedings.'

'The correct idea,' says Caligula, who was standing by me. 'Two
baggage-masters and a ticket-agent dropped out of a tree while
you was below the last time. Did the major man bring the money?'

'He says,' I answered, 'that he succeeded in negotiating the
loan.'

If any cooks ever earned ten thousand dollars in twelve hours,
me and Caligula did that day. At six o'clock we spread the top of
the mountain with as fine a dinner as the personnel of any railroad
ever engulfed. We opened all the wine, and we concocted entrees
and *pièces de resistance*, and stirred up little savoury *chef de cuisines*
and organized a mass of grub such as has been seldom instigated
out of canned and bottled goods. The railroad gathered around it,
and the wassail and diversions was intense.

After the feast, me and Caligula, in the line of business, takes
Major Tucker to one side and talks ransom. The major pulls out
an agglomeration of currency about the size of the price of a town
lot in the suburbs of Rabbitville, Arizona, and makes this outcry:

'Gentlemen,' says he, 'the stock of the Sunrise & Edenville Railroad has depreciated some. The best I could do with thirty thousand dollars' worth of the bonds was to secure a loan of
eighty-seven dollars and fifty cents. On the farming lands of
Colonel Rockingham, Judge Pendergast was able to obtain, on a
ninth mortgage, the sum of fifty dollars. You will find the amount,
one hundred and thirty-seven fifty, correct.'

'A railroad president,' said I, looking this Tucker in the eye,
'and the owner of a thousand acres of land; and yet –'

'Gentlemen,' says Tucker, 'the railroad is ten miles long. There
don't any train run on it except when the crew goes out in the

pines and gathers enough light-wood knots to get up steam. A long time ago, when times was good, the net earnings used to run as high as eighteen dollars a week. Colonel Rockingham's land has been sold for taxes thirteen times. There hasn't been a peach crop in this part of Georgia for two years. The wet spring killed the water-melons. Nobody around here has money enough to buy fertilizer; and land is so poor the corn crop failed, and there wasn't enough grass to support the rabbits. All the people have had to eat in this section for over a year is hog and hominy, and –'

'Pick,' interrupts Caligula, mussing up his red hair, 'what are you going to do with that chicken-feed?'

I hands the money back to Major Tucker; and then I goes over to Colonel Rockingham and slaps him on the back.

'Colonel,' says I, 'I hope you've enjoyed our little joke. We don't want to carry it too far. Kidnappers! Well, wouldn't it tickle your uncle? My name's Rhinegelder, and I'm a nephew of Chaucey Depew. My friend's a second cousin of the editor of *Puck*. So you can see. We are down South enjoying ourselves in our humorous way. Now, there's two quarts of cognac to open yet, and then the joke's over.'

What's the use to go into details? One or two will be enough. I remember Major Tallahassee Tucker playing on a jews' harp, and Caligula waltzing with his head on the watch-pocket of a tall baggage-master. I hesitate to refer to the cakewalk done by me and Mr. Patterson G. Coble with Colonel Jackson T. Rockingham between us.

And even on the next morning, when you wouldn't think it possible, there was a consolation for me and Caligula. We knew that Raisuli himself never made half the hit with Burdick Harris that we did with the Sunrise & Edenville Tap Railroad.

XLIII

The Ethics of Pig

ON AN EAST-BOUND TRAIN I went into the smoker and found Jefferson Peters, the only man with a brain west of the Wabash River who can use his cerebrum cerebellum and medulla oblongata at the same time.

Jeff is in the line of unillegal graft. He is not to be dreaded by widows and orphans; he is a reducer of surplusage. His favourite disguise is that of the target-bird at which the spendthrift or the reckless investor may shy a few inconsequential dollars. He is readily vocalized by tobacco; so, with the aid of two thick and easy-burning brevas, I got the story of his latest Autolycan adventure.

'In my line of business,' said Jeff, 'the hardest thing is to find an upright, trustworthy, strictly honourable partner to graft with. Some of the best men I ever worked with in a swindle would resort to trickery at times.

'So, last summer, I thinks I will go over into this section of country where I hear the serpent has not yet entered, and see if I can find a partner naturally gifted with a talent for crime, but not yet contaminated by success.

'I found a village that seemed to show the right kind of a layout. The inhabitants hadn't found out that Adam had been dispossessed, and were going right along naming the animals and killing snakes just as if they were in the Garden of Eden. They call this town Mount Nebo, and it's up near the spot where Kentucky and West Virginia and North Carolina corner together. Them States don't meet? Well, it was in that neighbourhood, anyway.

'After putting in a week proving I wasn't a revenue officer, I went over to the store where the rude fourflushers of the hamlet lied, to see if I could get a line on the kind of man I wanted.

' "Gentlemen," says I, after we had rubbed noses and gathered around the dried-apple barrel. "I don't suppose there's another community in the whole world into which sin and chicanery has less extensively permeated than this. Life here, where all the women are brave and propitious and all the men honest and expedient, must, indeed, be an idol. It reminds me," says I, "of Goldstein's beautiful ballad entitled 'The Deserted Village,' which says:

> "Ill fares the land, to hastening ills a prey;
> What art can drive its charms away?
> The judge rode slowly down the lane, mother,
> For I'm to be Queen of the May."

' "Why, yes, Mr. Peters," says the storekeeper. "I reckon we air about as moral and torpid a community as there be on the mounting, according to censuses of opinion; but I reckon you ain't ever met Rufe Tatum."

' "Why, no," says the town constable, "he can't hardly have ever. That air Rufe is shore the monstrousest scalawag that has escaped hangin' on the galluses. And that puts me in mind that I ought to have turned Rufe out of the lock-up day before yesterday. The thirty days he got for killin' Yance Goodloe was up then. A day or two more won't hurt Rufe any, though."

' "Shucks, now," says I, in the mountain idiom, "don't tell me there's a man in Mount Nebo as bad as that."

' "Worse," says the storekeeper. "He steals hogs."

'I think I will look up this Mr. Tatum; so a day or two after the constable turned him out I got acquainted with him and invited him out on the edge of town to sit on a log and talk business.

'What I wanted was a partner with a natural rural make-up to play a part in some little one-act outrages that I was going to book with the Pitfall & Gin circuit in some of the Western towns; and this R. Tatum was born for the role as sure as nature cast Fairbanks for the stuff that kept *Eliza* from sinking into the river.

'He was about the size of a first base-man; and he had ambiguous blue eyes like the china dog on the mantelpiece that Aunt Harriet used to play with when she was a child. His hair waved a little bit like the statue of the dinkus-thrower in the Vacation at Rome, but the colour of it reminded you of the "Sunset in the Grand Canon, by an American Artist," that they hang over the stovepipe holes in the salongs. He was the Reub, without needing a touch. You'd have known him for one, even if you'd seen him on the vaudeville stage with one cotton suspender and a straw over his ear.

'I told him what I wanted, and found him ready to jump at the job.

' "Overlooking such a trivial little peccadillo as the habit of manslaughter," says I, "what have you accomplished in the way of indirect brigandage or non-actionable thriftiness that you could point to, with or without pride, as an evidence of your qualifications for the position?"

' "Why," says he, in his kind of Southern system of procrastinated accents, "hain't you heard tell? There ain't any man, black or white, in the Blue Ridge that can tote off a shoat as easy as I can without bein' heard, seen, or cotched. I can lift a shoat," he goes on, "out of a pen, from under a porch, at the trough, in the woods, day or night, anywhere or anyhow, and I guarantee nobody won't hear a squeal. It's all in the way you grab hold of 'em and carry 'em afterwards. Some day," goes on this gentle despoiler of pig-pens, "I hope to become reckernized as the champion shoat-stealer of the world."

' "It's proper to be ambitious," says I; "and hog-stealing will do very well for Mount Nebo; but in the outside world, Mr. Tatum, it would be considered as crude a piece of business as a bear raid on Bay State Gas. However, it will do as a guarantee of good faith. We'll go into partnership. I've got a thousand dollars cash capital; and with that homeward-plods atmosphere of yours we ought to be able to win out a few shares of Soon Parted, preferred, in the money market."

'So I attaches Rufe, and we go away from Mount Nebo down into the lowlands. And all the way I coach him for his part in the grafts I had in mind. I had idled away two months on the Florida coast, and was feeling all to the Ponce de Leon, besides having so many new schemes up my sleeve that I had to wear kimonos to hold 'em.

'I intended to assume a funnel shape and mow a path nine miles wide through the farming belt of the Middle West; so we headed in that direction. But when we got as far as Lexington we found Binkley Brothers' circus there, and the blue-grass peasantry romping into town and pounding the Belgian blocks with their hand-pegged sabots as artless and arbitrary as an extra session of a Datto Bryan duma. I never pass a circus without pulling the valve-cord and coming down for a little Key West money; so I engaged a couple of rooms and board for Rufe and me at a house near the circus grounds run by a widow lady named Peevy. Then I took Rufe to a clothing store and gent's-outfitted him. He showed up strong, as I knew he would, after he was rigged up in the ready-made rutabaga regalia. Me and old Misfitzky stuffed him into a bright blue suit with a Nile green visible plaid effect, and riveted on a fancy vest of a light Tuskegee Normal tan colour, a red neck-tie, and the yellowest pair of shoes in town.

'They were the first clothes Rufe had ever worn except the gingham layette and the butternut top-dressing of his native kraal, and he looked as selfconscious as an Igorrote with a new nose-ring.

'That night I went down to the circus tents and opened a small shell game. Rufe was to be the capper. I gave him a roll of phony currency to bet with and kept a bunch of it in a special pocket to pay his winnings out of. No; I didn't mistrust him; but I simply can't manipulate the ball to lose when I see real money bet. My fingers go on a strike every time I try it.

'I set up my little table and began to show them how easy it was to guess which shell the little pea was under. The unlettered hinds gathered in a thick semicircle and began to nudge elbows and banter one another to bet. Then was when Rufe ought to have single-footed up and called the turn on the little joker for a few tens and fives to get them started. But, no Rufe. I'd seen him two or three times walking about and looking at the sideshow pictures with his mouth full of peanut candy; but he never came nigh.

'The crowd piked a little; but trying to work the shells without a capper is like fishing without bait. I closed the game with only forty-two dollars of the unearned increment, while I had been counting on yanking the yeomen for two hundred at least. I went home at eleven and went to bed. I supposed that the circus had proved too alluring for Rufe, and that he had succumbed to it, concert and all; but I meant to give him a lecture on general business principles in the morning.

'Just after Morpheus had got both my shoulders to the shuck mattress I hears a houseful of unbecoming and ribald noises like a youngster screeching with green-apple colic. I opens my door and calls out in the hall for the widow lady, and when she sticks her head out, I says: "Mrs. Peevy, ma'am, would you mind choking off that kid of yours so that honest people can get their rest?"

' "Sir," says she, "it's no child of mine. It's the pig squealing that your friend Mr. Tatum brought home to his room a couple of hours ago. And if you are uncle or second cousin or brother to it, I'd appreciate your stopping its mouth, sir, yourself, if you please."

'I put on some of the polite outside habiliments of external society and went into Rufe's room. He had gotten up and lit his lamp, and was pouring some milk into a tin pan on the floor for a dingy-white, half-grown, squealing pig.

' "How is this, Rufe?" says I. "You flimflammed in your part of the work to-night and put the game on crutches. And how do you explain the pig? It looks like backsliding to me."

' "Now, don't be too hard on me, Jeff," says he. "You know how long I've been used to stealing shoats. It's got to be a habit with me. And to-night, when I see such a fine chance, I couldn't help takin' it."

' "Well," says I, "maybe you've really got kleptopigia. And maybe when we get out of the pig belt you'll turn your mind to higher and more remunerative misconduct. Why you should want to stain your soul with such a distasteful, feebleminded, perverted, roaring beast as that I can't understand."

' "Why, Jeff," says he, "you ain't in sympathy with shoats. You don't understand 'em like I do. This here seems to me to be an animal of more than common powers of ration and intelligence. He walked half across the room on his hind legs a while ago.

' "Well, I'm going back to bed," says I. "See if you can impress it upon your friend's ideas of intelligence that he's not to make so much noise."

' "He was hungry," says Rufe. "He'll go to sleep and keep quiet now."

'I always get up before breakfast and read the morning paper whenever I happen to be within the radius of a Hoe cylinder or a Washington hand-press. The next morning I got up early and found a Lexington daily on the front porch where the carrier had thrown it. The first thing I saw in it was a double-column ad. on the front page that read like this:

FIVE THOUSAND DOLLARS REWARD

The above amount will be paid, and no questions asked, for the return, alive and uninjured, of Beppo, the famous European educated pig, that strayed or was stolen from the side-show tents of Binkley Bros.' circus last night.

GEO. B. TAPLEY, Business Manager.

At the Circus Grounds.

'I folded up the paper flat, put it into my inside pocket, and went to Rufe's room. He was nearly dressed, and was feeding the pig with the rest of the milk and some apple-peelings.

' "Well, well, well, good morning all," I says, hearty and amiable. "So we are up? And piggy is having his breakfast. What had you intended doing with that pig, Rufe?"

' "I'm going to crate him up," says Rufe, "and express him to ma in Mount Nebo. He'll be company for her while I am away."

' "He's a mighty fine pig," says I, scratching him on the back.

' "You called him a lot of names last night," says Rufe.

' "Oh, well," says I, "he looks better to me this morning. I was raised on a farm, and I'm very fond of pigs. I used to go to bed at sundown, so I never saw one by lamplight before. Tell you what I'll do, Rufe," I says. "I'll give you ten dollars for that pig."

' "I reckon I wouldn't sell this shoat," says he. "If it was any other one I might."

' "Why not this one?" I asked, fearful that he might know something.

' "Why, because," says he, "it was the grandest achievement of my life. There ain't airy other man that could have done it. If I ever have a fireside and children, I'll sit beside it and tell 'em how their daddy toted off a shoat from a whole circus full of people. And maybe my grandchildren, too. They'll certainly be proud a whole passel. Why," says he, "there was two tents, one openin' into the other. This shoat was on a platform, tied with a little chain. I seen a giant and a lady with a fine chance of bushy white hair in the other tent. I got the shoat and crawled out from under the canvas again without him squeakin' as loud as a mouse. I put him under my coat, and I must have passed a hundred folks before I got out where the streets was dark. I reckon I wouldn't sell that shoat, Jeff. I'd want ma to keep it, so there'd be a witness to what I done."

' "The pig won't live long enough," I says, "to use as an exhibit in your senile fireside mendacity. Your grandchildren will have to take your word for it. I'll give you one hundred dollars for the animal."

'Rufe looked at me astonished.

' "The shoat can't be worth anything like that to you," he says. "What do you want him for?"

' "Viewing me casuistically," says I, with a rare smile, "you wouldn't think that I've got an artistic side to my temper. But I have. I'm a collector of pigs. I've scoured the world for unusual pigs. Over in the Wabash Valley I've got a hog ranch with most every specimen on it, from a Merino to a Poland China. This looks like a blooded pig to me, Rufe," says I. "I believe it's a genuine Berkshire. That's why I'd like to have it."

' "I'd shore like to accommodate you," says he, "but I've got the artistic tenement, too. I don't see why it ain't art when you can steal a shoat better than anybody else can. Shoats is a kind of inspiration and genius with me. Specially this one. I wouldn't take two hundred and fifty for that animal."

' "Now, listen," says I, wiping off my forehead. "It's not so much a matter of business with me as it is art; and not so much art as it is philosophy. Being a connoisseur and disseminator of pigs, I wouldn't feel like I'd done my duty to the world unless I added that Berkshire to my collection. Not intrinsically, but according to the ethics of pigs as friends and coadjutors of mankind, I offer you five hundred dollars for the animal."

' "Jeff," says this pork esthete, "it ain't money; it's sentiment with me."

' "Seven hundred," says I.

' "Make it eight hundred," says Rufe, "and I'll crush the sentiment out of my heart."

'I went under my clothes for my money-belt, and counted him out forty twenty-dollar gold certificates.

' "I'll just take him into my own room," says I, "and lock him up till after breakfast."

'I took the pig by the hind leg. He turned on a squeal like the steam calliope at the circus.

' "Let me tote him in for you," says Rufe; and he picks up the beast under one arm, holding his snout with the other hand, and packs him into my room like a sleeping baby.

'After breakfast Rufe, who had a chronic case of haberdashery ever since I got his trousseau, says he believes he will amble down to Misfitzky's and look over some royal-purple socks. And then I got as busy as a one-armed man with the nettle-rash pasting on wallpaper. I found an old negro man with an express wagon to hire; and we tied the pig in a sack and drove down to the circus grounds.

'I found George B. Tapley in a little tent with a window flap open. He was a fattish man with an immediate eye, in a black skull-cap, with a four-ounce diamond screwed into the bosom of his red sweater.

' "Are you George B. Tapley?" I asks.

' "I swear it," says he.

' "Well, I've got it," says I.

' "Designate," says he. "Are you the guinea pigs for the Asiatic python or the alfalfa for the sacred buffalo?"

' "Neither," says I. "I've got Beppo, the educated hog, in a sack in that wagon. I found him rooting up the flowers in my front yard this morning. I'll take the five thousand dollars in large bills, if it's handy."

'George B. hustles out of his tent, and asks me to follow. We went into one of the side-shows. In there was a jet-black pig with a pink ribbon around his neck lying on some hay and eating carrots that a man was feeding to him.

' "Hey, Mac," calls G. B. "Nothing wrong with the world-wide this morning, is there?"

' "Him? No," says the man. "He's got an appetite like a chorus girl at 1 a.m."

' "How'd you get this pipe?" says Tapley to me. "Eating too many pork chops last night?"

'I pulls out the paper and shows him the ad.

' "Fake," says he. "Don't know anything about it. You've beheld with your own eyes the marvellous, world-wide porcine wonder of the four-footed kingdom eating with preternatural sagacity his matutinal meal, unstrayed and unstole. Good morning."

'I was beginning to see. I got in the wagon and told Uncle Ned to drive to the most adjacent orifice of the nearest alley. There I took out my pig, got the range carefully for the other opening, set his sights, and gave him such a kick that he went out the other end of the alley twenty feet ahead of his squeal.

'Then I paid Uncle Ned his fifty cents, and walked down to the newspaper office. I wanted to hear it in cold syllables. I got the advertising man to his window.

' "To decide a bet," says I, "wasn't the man who had this ad. put in last night short and fat, with long, black whiskers and a club-foot?"

' "He was not," says the man. "He would measure about six feet by four and a half inches, with corn-silk hair, and dressed like the pansies of the conservatory."

'At dinner-time I went back to Mrs. Peevy's.

' "Shall I keep some soup hot for Mr. Tatum till he comes back?" she asks.

' "If you do, ma'am," says I, "you'll more than exhaust for firewood all the coal in the bosom of the earth and all the forests on the outside of it."

'So there, you see,' said Jefferson Peters, in conclusion, 'how hard it is ever to find a fairminded and honest business-partner.'

'But,' I began, with the freedom of long acquaintance, 'the rule should work both ways. If you had offered to divide the reward you would not have lost –'

Jeff's look of dignified reproach stopped me

'That don't involve the same principles at all,' said he. 'Mine was a legitimate and moral attempt at speculation. Buy low and sell high – don't Wall Street endorse it? Bulls and bears and pigs – what's the difference? Why not bristles as well as horns and fur?'

XLIV

Strictly Business

I SUPPOSE YOU KNOW all about the stage and stage people. You've been touched with and by actors, and you read the newspaper criticisms and the jokes in the weeklies about the Rialto and the chorus girls and the long-haired tragedians. And I suppose that a condensed list of your ideas about the mysterious stageland would boil down to something like this:

Leading ladies have five husbands, paste diamonds, and figures no better than your own (madam) if they weren't padded. Chorus girls are inseparable from peroxide, Panhards and Pittsburg. All shows walk back to New York on tan oxford and railroad ties. Irreproachable actresses reserve the comic-landlady part for their mothers on Broadway and their step-aunts on the road. Kyrle Bellew's real name is Boyle O'Kelley. The ravings of John McCullough in the phonograph were stolen from the first sale of the Ellen Terry memoirs. Joe Weber is funnier than E. H. Sothern; but Henry Miller is getting older than he was.

All theatrical people on leaving the theatre at night drink champagne and eat lobsters until noon the next day. After all, the moving pictures have got the whole bunch pounded to a pulp.

Now, few of us know the real life of the stage people. If we did, the profession might be more overcrowded than it is. We look askance at the players with an eye full of patronizing superiority – and we go home and practise all sorts of elocution and gestures in front of our looking-glasses.

Latterly there has been much talk of the actor people in a new light. It seems to have been divulged that instead of being motoring bacchanalians and diamond-hungry *loreleis* they are businesslike folk, students and ascetics with childer and homes and libraries, owning real estate, and conducting their private affairs in as orderly and unsensational a manner as any of us good citizens who are bound to the chariot wheels of the gas, rent, coal, ice, and ward men.

Whether the old or the new report of the sock-and-buskiners be the true one is a surmise that has no place here. I offer you merely this little story of two strollers; and for proof of its truth I can show you only the dark patch above the cast-iron handle of the stage-entrance door of Keetor's old vaudeville theatre made there by the petulant push of gloved hands too impatient to finger the clumsy thumb-latch – and where I last saw Cherry whisking through like a swallow into her nest, on time to the minute, as usual, to dress for her act.

The vaudeville team of Hart & Cherry was an inspiration. Bob Hart had been roaming through the Eastern and Western circuits for four years with a mixed-up act comprising a monologue, three lightning changes, with songs, a couple of imitations of celebrated imitators, and a buck-and-wing dance that had drawn a glance of approval from the bassviol player in more than one house – than which no performer ever received more satisfactory evidence of good work.

The greatest treat an actor can have is to witness the pitiful performance with which all other actors desecrate the stage. In order to give himself this pleasure he will often forsake the sunniest Broadway corner between Thirty-fourth and Forty-fourth to attend a matinee offering by his less gifted brothers. Once during the lifetime of a minstrel joke one comes to scoff and remains to go through with that most difficult exercise of Thespian muscles – the audible contact of the palm of one hand against the palm of the other.

One afternoon Bob Hart presented his solvent, serious, well-known vaudevillian face at the box-office window of a rival attraction and got his d.h. coupon for an orchestra seat.

A, B, C, and D glowed successively on the announcement spaces and passed into oblivion, each plunging Mr. Hart deeper into gloom. Others of the audience shrieked, squirmed, whistled and applauded; but Bob Hart, 'All the Mustard and a Whole Show in Himself,' sat with his face as long and his hands as far apart as a boy holding a hank of yarn for his grandmother to wind into a ball.

But when H came on, 'The Mustard' suddenly sat up straight. H was the happy alphabetical prognosticator of Winona Cherry in Character Songs and Impersonations. There were scarcely more than two bites to Cherry; but she delivered the merchandise tied with a pink cord and charged to the old man's account. She first showed you a deliciously dewy and ginghamy country girl with a basket of property daisies who informed you ingenuously that there were other things to be learned at the old log schoolhouse besides cipherin' and nouns, especially 'When the Teach-er kept Me in.' Vanishing, with a quick flirt of gingham apronstrings, she reappeared in considerably less than a 'trice' as a fluffy 'Parisienne' – so near does Art bring the old red mill to the Moulin Rouge. And then –

But you know the rest. And so did Bob Hart; but he saw somebody else. He thought he saw that Cherry was the only professional on the short order stage that he had seen who seemed exactly to fit the part of 'Helen Grimes' in the sketch he had written and kept tucked away in the tray of his trunk. Of course Bob Hart, as well as every other normal actor, grocer, newspaper man, professor, kerb broker, and farmer, has a play tucked away somewhere. They tuck 'em in trays of trunks, trunks of trees, desks, haymows, pigeon-holes, inside pockets, safe-deposit vaults, handboxes, and coal cellars, waiting for Mr. Frohman to call. They belong among the fifty-seven different kinds.

But Bob Hart's sketch was not destined to end in a pickle jar. He called it 'Mice Will Play.' He had kept it quiet and hidden away ever since he wrote it, waiting to find a partner who fitted his conception of 'Helen Grimes.' And here was 'Helen' herself, with all the innocent abandon, the youth, the sprightliness, and the flawless stage art that his critical taste demanded.

After the act was over Hart found the manager in the box office, and got Cherry's address. At five the next afternoon he called at the musty old house in the West Forties and sent up his professional card.

By daylight, in a secular shirt waist and plain *voile* skirt, with her hair curbed and her Sister of Charity eyes, Winona Cherry might have been playing the part of Prudence Wise, the deacon's daughter, in the great (unwritten) New England drama not yet entitled anything.

'I know your act, Mr. Hart,' she said after she had looked over his card carefully. 'What did you wish to see me about?'

'I saw you work last night,' said Hart 'I've written a sketch that I've been saving up. It's for two; and I think you can do the other part. I thought I'd see you about it.'

'Come in the parlour,' said Miss Cherry. 'I've been wishing for something of the sort. I think I'd like to act instead of doing turns.'

Bob Hart drew his cherished 'Mice Will Play' from his pocket, and read it to her.

'Read it again, please,' said Miss Cherry.

And then she pointed out to him clearly how it could be improved by introducing a messenger instead of a telephone call, and cutting the dialogue just before the climax while they were struggling for the pistol, and by completely changing the lines and business of Helen Grimes at the point where her jealousy overcomes her. Hart yielded to all her strictures without argument. She had at once put her finger on the sketch's weaker points. That was her woman's intuition that he had lacked. At the end of their talk Hart was willing to stake the judgment, experience, and savings of his four years of vaudeville that 'Mice Will Play' would blossom into a perennial flower in the garden of the circuits. Miss Cherry was slower to decide. After many puckerings of her

smooth young brow and tappings on her small, white teeth with
the end of a lead pencil she gave out her dictum.

'Mr. Hart,' said she, 'I believe your sketch is going to win out.
That Grimes part fits me like a shrinkable flannel after its first trip
to a handless hand laundry. I can make it stand out like the colonel
of the Forty-fourth Regiment at a Little Mothers' Bazaar. And
I've seen you work. I know what you can do with the other part.
But business is business. How much do you get a week for the
stunt you do now?'

'Two hundred,' answered Hart.

'I get one hundred for mine,' said Cherry. 'That's about the natural discount for a woman. But I live on it and put a few simoleons
every week under the loose brick in the old kitchen hearth. The
stage is all right. I love it; but there's something else I love better –
that's a little country home, some day, with Plymouth Rock chickens
and six ducks wandering around the yard.

'Now, let me tell you, Mr. Hart, I am STRICTLY BUSINESS. If you
want me to play the opposite part in your sketch, I'll do it. And I
believe we can make it go. And there's something else I want to
say: There's no nonsense in my make-up; I'm *on the level*, and I'm
on the stage for what it pays me, just as other girls work in stores
and offices. I'm going to save my money to keep me when I'm past
doing my stunts. No Old Ladies' Home or Retreat for Imprudent
Actresses for me.

'If you want to make this a business partnership, Mr. Hart, with
all nonsense cut out of it, I'm in on it. I know something about
vaudeville teams in general; but this would have to be one in particular. I want you to know that I'm on the stage for what I can
cart away from it every pay-day in a little manila envelope with
nicotine stains on it, where the cashier has licked the flap. It's kind
of a hobby of mine to want to cravenette myself for plenty of rainy
days in the future. I want you to know just how I am. I don't know
what an all-night restaurant looks like; I drink only weak tea; I
never spoke to a man at a stage entrance in my life, and I've got
money in five savings banks.'

'Miss Cherry,' said Bob Hart in his smooth, serious tones,
'you're in on your own terms. I've got "strictly business" pasted in
my hat and stencilled on my make-up box. When I dream of
nights I always see a five-room bungalow on the north shore of
Long Island, with a Jap cooking clam broth and duckling in the
kitchen, and me with the title deeds to the place in my pongee
coat pocket, swinging in a hammock on the side-porch, reading

Stanley's *Explorations into Africa*. And nobody else around. You never was interested in Africa, was you, Miss Cherry?'

'Not any,' said Cherry. 'What I'm going to do with my money is to bank it. You can get four per cent. on deposits. Even at the salary I've been earning, I've figured out that in ten years I'd have an income of about $50 a month just from the interest alone. Well, I might invest some of the principal in a little business – say, trimming hats or a beauty parlour, and make more.'

'Well,' said Hart, 'you've got the proper idea all right, anyhow. There are mighty few actors that amount to anything at all who couldn't fix themselves for the wet days to come if they'd save their money instead of blowing it. I'm glad you've got the correct business idea of it, Miss Cherry. I think the same way; and I believe this sketch will more than double what both of us earn now when we get it shaped up.'

The subsequent history of 'Mice Will Play' is the history of all successful writings for the stage. Hart & Cherry cut it, pieced it, remodelled it, performed surgical operations on the dialogue and business, changed the lines, restored 'em, added more, cut 'em out, renamed it, gave it back the old name, rewrote it, substituted a dagger for the pistol, restored the pistol – put the sketch through all the known processes of condensation and improvement.

They rehearsed it by the old-fashioned boarding-house clock in the rarely used parlour until its warning click at five minutes to the hour would occur every time exactly half a second before the click of the unloaded revolver that Helen Grimes used in rehearsing the thrilling climax of the sketch.

Yes, that was a thriller and a piece of excellent work. In the act a real 32-calibre revolver was used loaded with a real cartridge. Helen Grimes, who is a Western girl of decidedly Buffalo Billish skill and daring, is tempestuously in love with Frank Desmond, the private secretary and confidential prospective son-in-law of her father, 'Arapahoe' Grimes, quarter-million-dollar cattle king, owing a ranch that, judging by the scenery, is in either the Bad Lands or Amagansett, L.I. Desmond (in private life Mr. Bob Hart) wears puttees and Meadow Brook Hunt riding trousers, and gives his address as New York, leaving you to wonder why he comes to the Bad Lands or Amagansett (as the case may be) and at the same time to conjecture mildly why a cattleman should want puttees about his ranch with a secretary in 'em.

Well, anyhow, you know as well as I do that we all like that kind of play, whether we admit it or not – something along in between 'Bluebeard, Jr.,' and 'Cymbeline' played in the Russian.

There were only two parts and a half in 'Mice Will Play.' Hart and Cherry were the two, of course; and the half was a minor part always played by a stage hand, who merely came in once in a Tuxedo coat and a panic to announce that the house was surrounded by Indians, and to turn down the gas-fire in the grate by the manager's orders.

There was another girl in the sketch – a Fifth Avenue society swelless – who was visiting the ranch and who had sirened Jack Valentine when he was a wealthy clubman on lower Third Avenue before he lost his money. This girl appeared on the stage only in the photographic state – Jack had her Sarony stuck up on the mantel of the Amagan – of the Bad Lands droring-room. Helen was jealous, of course.

And now for the thriller. Old 'Arapahoe' Grimes dies of angina pectoris one night – so Helen informs us in a stage-ferryboat whisper over the footlights – while only his secretary was present. And that same day he was known to have had $647,000 in cash in his (ranch) library just received for the sale of a drove of beeves in the East (that accounts for the prices we pay for steak!). The cash disappears at the same time. Jack Valentine was the only person with the ranchman when he made his (alleged) croak.

'Gawd knows I love him; but if he has done this deed –' you sabe, don't you? And then there are some mean things said about the Fifth Avenue girl – who doesn't come on the stage – and can we blame her, with the vaudeville trust holding down prices until one actually must be buttoned in the back by a call-boy, maids cost so much?

But, wait. Here's the climax. Helen Grimes, chaparralish as she can be, is goaded beyond imprudence. She convinces herself that Jack Valentine is not only a falsetto, but a financier. To lose at one fell swoop $647,000 and a lover in riding trousers with angles in the sides like the variations on the chart of a typhoid-fever patient is enough to make any perfect lady mad. So, then!

They stand in the (ranch) library, which is furnished with mounted elk heads (didn't the Elks have a fish fry in Amagansett once?), and the denouement begins. I know of no more interesting time in the run of a play unless it be when the prologue ends.

Helen thinks Jack has taken the money. Who else was there to take it? The box-office manager was at the front on his job; the orchestra hadn't left their seats; and no man could get past 'Old Jimmy,' the stage doorman, unless he could show a Syke terrier or an automobile as a guarantee of eligibility.

Goaded beyond imprudence (as before said), Helen says to Jack Valentine: 'Robber and thief – and worse yet, stealer of trusting hearts, this should be your fate!'

With that out she whips, of course, the trusty 32-calibre.

'But I will be merciful,' goes on Helen. 'You shall live – that will be your punishment. I will show you how easily I could have sent you to the death that you deserve. There is *her* picture on the mantel. I will send through her more beautiful face the bullet that should have pierced your craven heart.'

And she does it. And there's no fake blank cartridges or assistants pulling strings. Helen fires. The bullet – the actual bullet – goes through the face of the photograph – and then strikes the hidden spring of the sliding panel in the wall – and lo! the panel slides, and there is the missing $647,000 in convincing stacks of currency and bags of gold. It's great. You know how it is. Cherry practised for two months at a target on the roof of her boarding-house. It took good shooting. In the sketch she had to hit a brass disk only three inches in diameter, covered by wall-paper in the panel; and she had to stand in exactly the same spot every night, and the photo had to be in exactly the same spot, and she had to shoot steady and true every time.

Of course old 'Arapahoe' had tucked the funds away there in the secret place; and, of course, Jack hadn't taken anything except his salary (which really might have come under the head of 'obtaining money under'; but that is neither here nor there); and, of course, the New York girl was really engaged to a concrete house contractor in the Bronx; and, necessarily, Jack and Helen ended in a half-Nelson – and there you are.

After Hart and Cherry had gotten 'Mice Will Play' flawless, they had a try-out at a vaudeville house that accommodates. The sketch was a house wrecker. It was one of those rare strokes of talent that inundates a theatre from the roof down. The gallery wept; and the orchestra seats, being dressed for it, swam in tears.

After the show the booking agents signed blank cheques and pressed fountain pens upon Hart and Cherry. Five hundred dollars a week was what it panned out.

That night at 11.30 Bob Hart took off his hat and bade Cherry good night at her boarding-house door.

'Mr. Hart,' said she thoughtfully, 'come inside just a few minutes. We've got our chance now to make good and to make money. What we want to do is to cut expenses every cent we can, and save all we can.'

'Right,' said Bob. 'It's business with me. You've got your scheme for banking yours; and I dream every night of that bungalow with the Jap cook and nobody around to raise trouble. Anything to enlarge the net receipts will engage my attention.'

'Come inside just a few minutes,' repeated Cherry, deeply thoughtful. 'I've got a proposition to make to you that will reduce our expenses a lot and help you work out your own future and help me work out mine – and all on business principles.'

'Mice Will Play' had a tremendously successful run in New York for ten weeks – rather neat for a vaudeville sketch – and then it started on the circuits. Without following it, it may be said that it was a solid drawing card for two years without a sign of abated popularity.

Sam Packard, manager of one of Keetor's New York houses, said of Hart & Cherry:

'As square and high-toned a little team as ever came over the circuit. It's a pleasure to read their names on the booking list. Quiet, hard workers, no Johnny and Mabel nonsense, on the job to the minute, straight home after their act, and each of 'em as gentlemanlike as a lady. I don't expect to handle any attractions that give me less trouble or more respect for the profession.'

And now, after so much cracking of a nutshell, here is the kernel of the story:

At the end of its second season 'Mice Will Play' came back to New York for another run at the roof gardens and summer theatres. There was never any trouble in booking it at the top-notch price. Bob Hart had his bungalow nearly paid for, and Cherry had so many savings-deposit bank books that she had begun to buy sectional bookcases on the instalment plan to hold them.

I tell you these things to assure you, even if you can't believe it, that many, very many of the stage people are workers with abiding ambitions – just the same as the man who wants to be president, or the grocery clerk who wants a home in Flatbush, or a lady who is anxious to flop out of the Count-pan into the Prince-fire. And I hope I may be allowed to say, without chipping into the contribution basket, that they often move in a mysterious way their wonders to perform.

But, listen.

At the first performance of 'Mice Will Play' in New York at the new Westphalia (no hams alluded to) Theatre, Winona Cherry was nervous. When she fired at the photograph of the Eastern beauty on the mantel, the bullet, instead of penetrating the photo and then striking the disk, went into the lower left side of Bob Hart's neck. Not expecting to get it there, Hart collapsed neatly, while Cherry fainted in a most artistic manner.

The audience, surmising that they viewed a comedy instead of a tragedy in which the principals were married or reconciled, applauded with great enjoyment. The Cool Head, who always graces such occasions, rang the curtain down, and two platoons of scene shifters respectively and more or less respectfully removed Hart & Cherry from the stage. The next turn went on, and all went as merry as an alimony bell.

The stage hands found a young doctor at the stage entrance who was waiting for a patient with a decoction of Am. B'ty roses. The doctor examined Hart carefully and laughed heartily.

'No headlines for you, Old Sport,' was his diagnosis. 'If it had been two inches to the left it would have undermined the carotid artery as far as the Red Front Drug Store in Flatbush and Back Again. As it is, you just get the property man to bind it up with a flounce torn from any one of the girls' Valenciennes and go home and get it dressed by the parlour-floor practitioner on your block, and you'll be all right. Excuse me; I've got a serious case outside to look after.'

After that Bob Hart looked up and felt better. And then to where he lay came Vincente, the Tramp Juggler, great in his line. Vincente, a solemn man from Brattleboro, Vt., named Sam Griggs at home, sent toys and maple sugar home to two small daughters from every town he played. Vincente had moved on the same circuits with Hart & Cherry, and was their peripatetic friend.

'Bob,' said Vincente in his serious way, 'I'm glad it's no worse. The little lady is wild about you.'

'Who?' asked Hart.

'Cherry,' said the juggler. 'We didn't know how bad you were hurt; and we kept her away. It's taking the manager and three girls to hold her.'

'It was an accident, of course,' said Hart. 'Cherry's all right. She wasn't feeling in good trim or she couldn't have done it. There's no hard feelings. She's strictly business. The doctor says I'll be on the job again in three days. Don't let her worry.'

'Man,' said Sam Griggs severely, puckering his old smooth, lined face, 'are you a chess automaton or a human pincushion? Cherry's crying her heart out for you – calling "Bob, Bob," every second, with them holding her hands and keeping her from coming to you.

'What's the matter with her;' asked Hart, with wide-open eyes. 'The sketch'll go on again in three days. I'm not hurt bad, the doctor says. She won't lose out half a week's salary. I know it was an accident. What's the matter with her?'

'You seem to be blind, or a sort of a fool,' said Vincente. 'The girl loves you and is almost mad about your hurt. What's the matter with you? Is she nothing to you? I wish you could hear her call you.'

'Loves me?' asked Bob Hart, rising from the stack of scenery on which he lay. 'Cherry loves me? Why, it's impossible.'

'I wish you could see her and hear her,' said Griggs.

'But man,' said Bob Hart, sitting up, 'it's impossible. It's impossible, I tell you. I never dreamed of such a thing.'

'No human being,' said the Tramp Juggler, 'could mistake it. She's wild for love of you. How have you been so blind?'

'But, my God,' said Bob Hart, rising to his feet, *it's too late*. It's too late, I tell you, Sam; *it's too late*. It can't be. You must be wrong. It's *impossible*. There's some mistake.'

'She's crying for you,' said the Tramp Juggle. 'For love of you she's fighting three, and calling your name so loud they don't dare to raise the curtain. Wake up, man.'

'For love of me?' said Bob Hart with staring eyes. 'Don't I tell you it's too late? It's too late, man. *Why, Cherry and I have been married two years!*'

XLV

The Day Resurgent

I CAN SEE THE ARTIST bite the end of his pencil and frown when it comes to drawing his Easter picture; for his legitimate pictorial conceptions of figures pertinent to the festival are but four in number.

First comes Easter, pagan goddess of spring. Here his fancy may have free play. A beautiful maiden with decorative hair and the proper number of toes will fill the bill. Miss Clarice St. Vavasour, the well-known model, will pose for it in the 'Lethergogallagher,' or whatever it was that Trilby called it.

Second – the melancholy lady with upturned eyes in a framework of lilies. This is magazine-covery, but reliable.

Third – Miss Manhattan in the Fifth Avenue Easter Sunday parade.

Fourth – Maggie Murphy with a new red feather in her old straw hat, happy and self-conscious, in the Grand Street turnout.

Of course, the rabbits do not count. Nor the Easter eggs, since the higher criticism has hard-boiled them.

The limited field of its pictorial possibilities proves that Easter, of all our festival days, is the most vague and shifting in our conception. It belongs to all religions, although the pagans invented it. Going back still further to the first spring, we can see Eve choosing with pride a new green leaf from the tree *ficus carica*.

Now, the object of this critical and learned preamble is to set forth the theorem that Easter is neither a date, a season, a festival, a holiday nor an occasion. What it is you shall find out if you follow in the footsteps of Danny McCree.

Easter Sunday dawned as it should, bright and early in its place on the calendar between Saturday and Monday. At 5.24 the sun rose, and at 10.30 Danny followed its example. He went into the kitchen and washed his face at the sink. His mother was frying bacon. She looked at his hard, smooth, knowing countenance as he juggled with the round cake of soap, and thought of his father when she first saw him stopping a hot grounder between second and third twenty-two years before on a vacant lot in Harlem, where the La Paloma apartment-house now stands. In the front room of the flat Danny's father sat by an open window smoking his pipe, with his dishevelled grey hair tossed about by the breeze. He still clung to his pipe, although his sight had been taken from him two years before by a precocious blast of giant powder that went off without permission. Very few blind men care for smoking, for the reason that they cannot see the smoke. Now, could you enjoy having the news read to you from an evening newspaper unless you could see the colours of the headlines?

' 'Tis Easter Day,' said Mrs. McCree.

'Scramble mine,' said Danny.

After breakfast he dressed himself in the Sabbath morning costume of the Canal Street importing house dray chauffeur – frockcoat, striped trousers, patent leathers, gilded trace chain across front of vest, and wing collar, rolled-brim derby and butterfly bow from Schonstein's (between Fourteenth Street and Tony's fruit stand) Saturday night sale.

'You'll be goin' out this day, of course, Danny,' said old man McCree, a little wistfully. ' 'Tis a kind of holiday, they say. Well, it's fine spring weather. I can feel it in the air.'

'Why should I not be going out?' demanded Danny in his

grumpiest chest tones. 'Should I stay in? Am I as good as a horse? One day of rest my team has a week. Who earns the money for the rent and the breakfast you've just eat, I'd like to know? Answer me that!'

'All right, lad,' said the old man. 'I'm not complainin'. While me two eyes was good there was nothin' better to my mind than a Sunday out. There's a smell of turf and burnin' brush comin' in the windy. I have me tobaccy. A good fine day and rist to ye, lad. Times I wish your mother had larned to read, so I might hear the rest about the hippopotamus – but let that be.'

'Now, what is this foolishness he talks of hippopotamuses?' asked Danny of his mother, as he passed through the kitchen. 'Have you been taking him to the Zoo? And for what?'

'I have not,' said Mrs. McCree. 'He sets by the windy all day. 'Tis little recreation a blind man among the poor gets at all. I'm thinkin' they wander in their minds at times. One day he talks of grease without stoppin' for the most of an hour. I looks to see if there's lard burnin' in the fryin' pan. There is not. He says I do not understand. 'Tis weary days, Sundays, and holidays, and all, for a blind man, Danny. There was no better nor stronger than him when he had his two eyes. 'Tis a fine day, son. Injoy yeself ag'inst the morning. There will be cold supper at six.'

'Have you heard any talk of a hippopotamus?' asked Danny of Mike, the janitor, as he went out the door downstairs.

'I have not,' said Mike, pulling his shirt sleeves higher. 'But 'tis the only subject in the animal, natural and illegal lists of outrages that I've not been complained to about these two days. See the landlord. Or else move out if ye like. Have ye hippopotamuses in the lease? No, then?'

'It was the old man who spoke of it,' said Danny. 'Likely there's nothing in it.'

Danny walked up the street to the Avenue and then struck northward into the heart of the district where Easter – modern Easter, in new, bright raiment – leads the pascal march. Out of towering, brown churches came the blithe music of anthems from the choirs. The broad sidewalks were moving parterres of living flowers – so it seemed when your eye looked upon the Easter girl.

Gentlemen, frock-coated, silk-hatted, gardeniaed, sustained the background of the tradition. Children carried lilies in their hands. The windows of the brown-stone mansions were packed with the most opulent creations of Flora, the sister of the Lady of the Lilies.

Around a corner, white-gloved, pink-gilled and tightly buttoned, walked Corrigan, the cop, shield to the kerb. Danny knew him.

'Why, Corrigan,' he asked, 'is Easter? I know it comes the first time you're full after the moon rises on the seventeenth of March – but why? Is it a proper and religious ceremony, or does the Governor appoint it out of politics?'

' 'Tis an annual celebration,' said Corrigan, with the judicial air of the Third Deputy Police Commissioner, 'peculiar to New York. It extends up to Harlem. Sometimes they has the reserves out at One Hundred and Twenty-fifth Street. In my opinion 'tis not political.'

'Thanks,' said Danny. 'And say – did you ever hear a man complain of hippopotamuses? When not specially in drink, I mean.'

'Nothing larger than sea turtles,' said Corrigan, reflecting, 'and there was wood alcohol in that.'

Danny wondered. The double, heavy incumbency of enjoying simultaneously a Sunday and a festival day was his.

The sorrows of the hand-toiler fit him easily. They are worn so often that they hang with the picturesque lines of the best tailor-made garments. That is why well-fed artists of pencil and pen find in the griefs of the common people their most striking models. But when the Philistine would disport himself, the grimness of Melpomene, herself, attends upon his capers. Therefore, Danny set his jaw hard at Easter, and took his pleasure sadly.

The family entrance of Dugan's café was feasible; so Danny yielded to the vernal season as far as a glass of bock. Seated in a dark, linoleumed, humid back room, his heart and mind still groped after the mysterious meaning of the springtime jubilee.

'Say, Tim,' he said to the waiter, 'why do they have Easter?'

'Skiddoo!' said Tim, closing a sophisticated eye. 'Is that a new one? All right. Tony Pastor's for you last night, I guess. I give it up. What's the answer – two apples or a yard and a half?'

From Dugan's Danny turned back eastward. The April sun seemed to stir in him a vague feeling that he could not construe. He made a wrong diagnosis and decided that it was Katy Conlon.

A block from her house on Avenue A he met her going to church. They pumped hands on the corner.

'Gee! but you look dumpish and dressed up,' said Katy. 'What's wrong? Come away with me to church and be cheerful.'

'What's doing at church?' asked Danny.

'Why, it's Easter Sunday. Silly! I waited till after eleven expectin' you might come around to go.'

'What does this Easter stand for, Katy?' asked Danny gloomily. 'Nobody seems to know.'

'Nobody as blind as you,' said Katy with spirit. 'You haven't even looked at my new hat. And skirt. Why, it's when all the girls put on new spring clothes. Silly! Are you coming to church with me?'

'I will,' said Danny. 'If this Easter is pulled off there, they ought to be able to give some excuse for it. Not that the hat ain't a beauty. The green roses are great.'

At church the preacher did some expounding with no pounding. He spoke rapidly, for he was in a hurry to get home to his early Sabbath dinner; but he knew his business. There was one word that controlled his theme – resurrection. Not a new creation; but a new life arising out of the old. The congregation had heard it often before. But there was a wonderful hat, a combination of sweet-peas and lavender, in the sixth pew from the pulpit. It attracted much attention.

After church Danny lingered on a corner while Katy waited, with pique in her sky-blue eyes.

'Are you coming along to the house?' she asked. 'But don't mind me. I'll get there all right. You seem to be studyin' a lot about something. All right. Will I see you at any time specially, Mr. McCree?'

'I'll be around Wednesday night as usual,' said Danny, turning and crossing the street.

Katy walked away with the green roses dangling indignantly. Danny stopped two blocks away. He stood still with his hands in his pockets, at the kerb on the corner. His face was that of a graven image. Deep in his soul something stirred so small, so fine, so keen and leavening that his hard fibres did not recognize it. It was something more tender than the April day, more subtle than the call of the senses, purer and deeper-rooted than the love of woman – for had he not turned away from green roses and eyes that had kept him chained for a year? And Danny did not know what it was. The preacher, who was in a hurry to go to his dinner, had told him, but Danny had had no libretto with which to follow the drowsy intonation. But the preacher spoke the truth.

Suddenly Danny slapped his leg and gave forth a hoarse yell of delight.

'Hippopotamus!' he shouted to an elevated road pillar. 'Well, how is that for a bum guess? Why, blast my skylights! I know what he was driving at now.

'Hippopotamus! Wouldn't that send you to the Bronx? It's been a year since he heard it; and he didn't miss it so very far. We quit at 469 B.C., and this comes next. Well, a wooden man wouldn't have guessed what he was trying to get out of him.'

Danny caught a crosstown car and went up to the rear flat that his labour supported.

Old man McCree was still sitting by the window. His extinct pipe lay on the sill.

'Will that be you, lad?' he asked.

Danny flared into the rage of a strong man who is surprised at the outset of committing a good deed.

'Who pays the rent and buys the food that is eaten in this house?' he snapped viciously. 'Have I no right to come in?'

'Ye're a faithful lad,' said old man McCree, with a sigh. 'Is it evening yet?'

Danny reached up on a shelf and took down a thick book labelled in gilt letters, 'The History of Greece.' Dust was on it half an inch thick. He laid it on the table and found a place in it marked by a strip of paper. And then he gave a short roar at the top of his voice, and said:

'Was it the hippopotamus you wanted to be read to about then?'

'Did I hear ye open the book?' said old man McCree. 'Many and weary be the months since my lad has read it to me. I dinno; but I took a great likings to them Greeks. Ye left off at a place. 'Tis a fine day outside, lad. Be out and take rest from your work. I have gotten used to me chair by the windy and me pipe.'

'Pel-Peloponnesus was the place where we left off, and not hippopotamus,' said Danny. 'The war began there. It kept something doing for thirty years. The headlines says that a guy named Philip of Macedon, in 338 b.c., got to be boss of Greece by getting the decision at the battle of Cher-Cheronæa. I'll read it.'

With his hand to his ear, rapt in the Peioponnesian War, old man McCree sat for an hour, listening.

Then he got up and felt his way to the door of the kitchen. Mrs. McCree was slicing cold meat. She looked up. Tears were running from old man McCree's eyes.

'Do ye hear our lad readin' to me?' he said. 'There is none finer in the land. My two eyes have come back to me again.'

After supper he said to Danny: ' 'tis a happy day, this Easter. And now ye will be off to see Katy in the evening. Well enough.'

'Who pays the rent and buys the food that is eaten in this house?' said Danny angrily. 'Have I no right to stay in it? After supper there is yet to come the reading of the battle of Corinth, 146 B.C., when the kingdom, as they say, became an inintegral portion of the Roman Empire. Am I nothing in this house?'

XLVI

The Fifth Wheel

THE RANKS OF THE BED LINE moved closer together; for it was cold, cold. They were alluvial deposit of the stream of life lodged in the delta of Fifth Avenue and Broadway. The Bed Liners stamped their freezing feet, looked at the empty benches in Madison Square whence Jack Frost had evicted them, and muttered to one another in a confusion of tongues. The Flatiron Building, with its impious, cloud-piercing architecture looming mistily above them on the opposite delta, might well have stood for the tower of Babel, whence these polyglot idlers had been called by the winged walking delegate of the Lord.

Standing on a pine box a head higher than his flock of goats, the Preacher exhorted whatever transient and shifting audience the north wind doled out to him. It was a slave market. Fifteen cents bought you a man. You deeded him to Morpheus; and the recording angel gave you credit.

The Preacher was incredibly earnest and unwearied. He had looked over the list of things one may do for one's fellow-man, and had assumed for himself the task of putting to bed all who might apply at his soap-box on the nights of Wednesday and Sunday. That left but *five* nights for other philanthropists to handle; and had they done their part as well, this wicked city might have become a vast Arcadian dormitory, where all might snooze and snore the happy hours away, letting problem plays and the rent man and business go to the deuce.

The hour of eight was but a little while past; sightseers in a small, dark mass of pay ore were gathered in the shadow of General Worth's monument. Now and then, shyly, ostentatiously, carelessly, or with conscientious exactness, one would step forward and bestow upon the Preacher small bills or silver. Then a lieutenant of Scandinavian colouring and enthusiasm would march away to a lodging-house with a squad of the redeemed. All the while the Preacher exhorted the crowd in terms beautifully devoid of eloquence — splendid with the deadly, accusive monotony of truth. Before the picture of the Bed Liners fades you must hear one phrase of the Preacher's – the one that formed his theme that night. It is worthy of being stencilled on all the white ribbons in the world.

'*No man ever learned to be a drunkard on five-cent whisky.*'

Think of it, tippler. It covers the ground from the sprouting rye to the Potter's Field.

A clean-profiled, erect young man in the rear rank of the bedless emulated the terrapin, drawing his head far down into the shell of his coat collar. It was a well-cut tweed coat; and the trousers still showed signs of having flattened themselves beneath the compelling goose. But, conscientiously, I must warn the milliner's apprentice who reads this, expecting a Reginald Montressor in straits, to peruse no further. The young man was no other than Thomas McQuade, ex-coachman, discharged for drunkenness one month before, and now reduced to the grimy ranks of the one-night bed seekers.

If you live in smaller New York you must know the Van Smuythe family carriage, drawn by the two 1,500-pound, 100-to-1-shot bays. The carriage is shaped like a bath-tub. In each end of it reclines an old lady Van Smuythe holding a black sunshade the size of a New Year's Eve feather tickler. Before his downfall Thomas McQuade drove the Van Smuythe bays and was himself driven by Annie, the Van Smuythe lady's maid. But it is one of the saddest things about romance that a tight shoe or an empty commissary or an aching tooth will make a temporary heretic of any Cupid-worshipper. And Thomas's physical troubles were not few. Therefore, his soul was less vexed with thoughts of his lost lady's maid than it was by the fancied presence of certain non-existent things that his racked nerves almost convinced him were flying, dancing, crawling, and wriggling on the asphalt and in the air above and around the dismal campus of the Bed Line army. Nearly four weeks of straight whisky and a diet limited to crackers, bologna, and pickles often guarantees a psycho-zoological sequel. Thus desperate, freezing, angry, beset by phantoms as he was, he felt the need of human sympathy and intercourse.

The Bed Liner standing at his right was a young man of about his own age, shabby but neat.

'What's the diagnosis of your case, Freddy?' asked Thomas, with the freemasonic familiarity of the damned – 'Booze? That's mine. You don't look like a panhandler. Neither am I. A month ago I was pushing the lines over the backs of the finest team of

Percheron buffaloes that ever made their way down Fifth Avenue in 2-85. And look at me now! Say; how do you come to be at this bed bargain-counter rummage sale?'

The other young man seemed to welcome the advances of the airy ex-coachman.

'No,' said he, 'mine isn't exactly a case of drink. Unless we allow that Cupid is a bartender. I married unwisely, according to the opinion of my unforgiving relatives. I've been out of work for a year because I don't know how to work; and I've been sick in Bellevue and other hospitals four months. My wife and kid had to go back to her mother. I was turned out of the hospital yesterday. And I haven't a cent. That's my tale of woe.'

'Tough luck,' said Thomas. 'A man alone can pull through all right. But I hate to see the women and kids get the worst of it.'

Just then there hummed up Fifth Avenue a motorcar so splendid, so red, so smoothly running, so craftily demolishing the speed regulations, that it drew the attention even of the listless Bed Liners. Suspended and pinioned on its left side was an extra tyre.

When opposite the unfortunate company the fastenings of this tyre became loosed. It fell to the asphalt, bounded and rolled rapidly in the wake of the flying car.

Thomas McQuade, scenting an opportunity, darted from his place among the Preacher's goats. In thirty seconds he had caught the rolling tyre, swung it over his shoulder, and was trotting smartly after the car. On both sides of the avenue people were shouting, whistling, and waving canes at the red car, pointing to the enterprising Thomas coming up with the lost tyre.

One dollar, Thomas had estimated, was the smallest guerdon that so grand an automobilist could offer for the service he had rendered, and save his pride.

Two blocks away the car had stopped. There was a little, brown, muffled chauffeur driving, and an imposing gentleman wearing a magnificent sealskin coat and a silk hat on a rear seat.

Thomas proffered the captured tyre with his best ex-coachman manner and a look in the brighter of his reddened eyes that was meant to be suggestive to the extent of a silver coin or two and receptive up to higher denominations.

But the look was not so construed. The seal-skinned gentleman received the tyre, placed it inside the car, gazed intently at the ex-coachman, and muttered to himself inscrutable words

'Strange – strange!' said he. 'Once or twice even I, myself, have fancied that the Chaldean Chiroscope has availed. Could it be possible?'

Then he addressed less mysterious words to the waiting and hopeful Thomas.

'Sir, I thank you for your kind rescue of my tyre. And I would ask you, if I may, a question. Do you know the family of Van Smuythes living in Washington Square North?'

'Oughtn't I to?' replied Thomas. 'I lived there. Wish I did yet.'

The seal-skinned gentleman opened a door of the car.

'Step in, please,' he said. 'You have been expected.'

Thomas McQuade obeyed with surprise but without hesitation. A seat in a motor-car seemed better than standing room in the Bed Line. But after the lap-robe had been tucked about him and the auto had sped on its course, the peculiarity of the invitation lingered in his mind.

'Maybe the guy hasn't got any change,' was his diagnosis. 'Lots of these swell rounders don't lug about any ready money. Guess he'll dump me out when he gets to some joint where he can get cash on his mug. Anyhow, it's a cinch that I've got that open-air bed convention beat to a finish.'

Submerged in his greatcoat, the mysterious automobilist seemed, himself, to marvel at the surprises of life. 'Wonderful! amazing! strange!' he repeated to himself constantly.

When the car had well entered the crosstown Seventies it swung easily a half block and stopped before a row of high-stooped, brown-stone-front houses.

'Be kind enough to enter my house with me,' said the seal-skinned gentleman when they had alighted.

'He's going to dig up, sure,' reflected Thomas, following him inside.

There was a dim light in the hall. His host conducted him through a door to the left, closing it after him and leaving them in absolute darkness. Suddenly a luminous globe, strangely decorated, shone faintly in the centre of an immense room that seemed to Thomas more splendidly appointed than any he had ever seen on the stage or read of in fairy stories.

The walls were hidden by gorgeous red hangings embroidered with fantastic gold figures. At the rear end of the room were draped portieres of dull gold spangled with silver crescents and stars. The furniture was of the costliest and rarest styles. The ex-coachman's feet sank into rugs as fleecy and deep as snowdrifts. There were three or four oddly shaped stands or tables covered with black velvet drapery.

Thomas McQuade took in the splendours of this palatial

apartment with one eye. With the other he looked for his imposing conductor – to find that he had disappeared.

'B'gee!' muttered Thomas, 'this listens like a spook shop. Shouldn't
wonder if it ain't one of these Moravian Nights' adventures that you
read about. Wonder what became of the furry guy.'

Suddenly a stuffed owl that stood on an ebony perch near the
illuminated globe slowly raised his wings and emitted from his
eyes a brilliant electric glow.

With a fright-born imprecation, Thomas seized a bronze statuette of Hebe from a cabinet near by and hurled it with all his
might at the terrifying and impossible fowl. The owl and his perch
went over with a crash. With the sound there was a click, and the
room was flooded with light from a dozen frosted globes along the
walls and ceiling. The gold portieres parted and closed, and the
mysterious automobilist entered the room. He was tall and wore
evening dress of perfect cut and accurate taste. A Vandyke beard
of glossy, golden brown, rather long and wavy hair, smoothly
parted, and large, magnetic, orientally occult eyes, gave him a
most impressive and striking appearance. If you can conceive a
Russian Grand Duke in a Rajah's throne-room advancing to greet
a visiting Emperor, you will gather something of the majesty of his
manner. But Thomas McQuade was too near his *d t's* to be mind-
ful of his *p's* and *q's*. When he viewed this silken, polished, and
somewhat terrifying host he thought vaguely of dentists.

'Say, doc,' said he resentfully, 'that's a hot bird you keep on tap.
I hope I didn't break anything. But I've nearly got the williwalloos,
and when he threw them 32-candle-power lamps of his on me, I
took a snap-shot at him with that little brass Flatiron Girl that
stood on the sideboard.'

'That is merely a mechanical toy,' said the gentleman with a
wave of his hand. 'May I ask you to be seated while I explain why I
brought you to my house. Perhaps you would not understand nor
be in sympathy with the psychological prompting that caused me
to do so. So I will come to the point at once by venturing to refer
to your admission that you know the Van Smuythe family, of
Washington Square North.'

'Any silver missing?' asked Thomas tartly. 'Any joolry dis-
placed? Of course I know 'em. Any of the old ladies' sunshades
disappeared? Well, I know 'em. And then what?'

The Grand Duke rubbed his white hands together softly.

'Wonderful!' he murmured. 'Wonderful! Shall I come to
believe in the Chaldean Chiroscope myself? Let me assure you,'

he continued, 'that there is nothing for you to fear. Instead, I think I can promise you that very good fortune awaits you. We will see.'

'Do they want me back?' asked Thomas, with something of his old professional pride in his voice. 'I'll promise to cut out the booze and do the right thing if they'll try me again. But how did you get wise, doc? B'gee, it's the swellest employment agency I was ever in, with its flashlight owls and so fourth.'

With an indulgent smile the gracious host begged to be excused for two minutes. He went out to the sidewalk and gave an order to the chauffeur, who still waited with the car. Returning to the mysterious apartment, he sat by his guest and began to entertain him so well by his witty and genial converse that the poor Bed Liner almost forgot the cold streets from which he had been so recently and so singularly rescued. A servant brought some tender cold fowl and tea biscuits and a glass of miraculous wine; and Thomas felt the glamour of Arabia envelop him. Thus half an hour sped quickly; and then the honk of the returned motor-car at the door suddenly drew the Grand Duke to his feet, with another soft petition for a brief absence.

Two women, well muffled against the cold, were admitted at the front door and suavely conducted by the master of the house down the hall through another door to the left and into a smaller room, which was screened and segregated from the larger front room by heavy double portieres. Here the furnishings were even more elegant and exquisitely tasteful than in the other. On a gold-inlaid rosewood table were scattered sheets of white paper and a queer, triangular instrument or toy, apparently of gold, standing on little wheels.

The taller woman threw back her black veil and loosened her cloak. She was fifty, with a wrinkled and sad face. The other, young and plump, took a chair a little distance away to the rear as a servant or an attendant might have done.

'You sent for me, Professor Cherubusco,' said the elder woman wearily. 'I hope you have something more definite than usual to say. I've about lost the little faith I had in your art. I would not have responded to your call this evening if my sister had not insisted upon it.'

'Madam,' said the professor, with his princeliest smile, 'the true Art cannot fail. To find the true psychic and potential branch sometimes requires time. We have not succeeded, I admit, with the cards, the crystal, the stars, the magic formulæ of Zarazin, nor the Oracle of Po. But we have at last discovered the true psychic route. The Chaldean Chiroscope has been successful in our search.'

The professor's voice had a ring that seemed to proclaim his belief in his own words. The elderly lady looked at him with a little more interest.

'Why, there was no sense in those words that it wrote with my hands on it,' she said. 'What do you mean?'

'The words were these,' said Professor Cherubusco, rising to his full magnificent height:

' "*By the fifth wheel of the chariot he shall come.*" '

'I haven't seen many chariots,' said the lady, 'but I never saw one with five wheels.'

'Progress,' said the professor – 'progress in science and mechanics has accomplished it – though, to be exact, we may only speak of it as an extra tyre. Progress in occult art has advanced in proportion. Madam, I repeat that the Chaldean Chiroscope has succeeded. I can not only answer the question that you have propounded, but I can produce before your eyes the proof thereof.'

And now the lady was disturbed both in her disbelief and in her poise.

'Oh, professor!' she cried anxiously – 'When? – where? Has he been found? Do not keep me in suspense.'

'I beg you will excuse me for a very few minutes,' said Professor Cherubusco, 'and I think I can demonstrate to you the efficacy of the true Art.'

Thomas was contentedly munching the last crumbs of the bread and fowl when the enchanter appeared suddenly at his side.

'Are you willing to return to your old home if you are assured of a welcome and restoration to favour?' he asked, with his courteous, royal smile.

'Do I look bughouse?' answered Thomas. 'Enough of the footback life for me. But will they have me again? The old lady is as fixed in her ways as a nut on a new axle.'

'My dear young man,' said the other, 'she has been searching for you everywhere.'

'Great!' said Thomas. 'I'm on the job. That team of dropsical dromedaries they call horses is a handicap for a first-class coachman like myself; but I'll take the job back, sure, doc. They're good people to be with.'

And now a change came o'er the suave countenance of the

Caliph of Bagdad. He looked keenly and suspiciously at the ex-coachman.

'May I ask what your name is?' he said shortly.

'You've been looking for me,' said Thomas, 'and don't know my name? You're a funny kind of sleuth. You must be one of the Central Office gumshoers. I'm Thomas McQuade, of course; and I've been chauffeur of the Van Smuythe elephant team for a year. They fired me a month ago for – well, doc, you saw what I did to your old owl. I went broke on booze, and when I saw the tyre drop off your whiz wagon I was standing in that squad of hoboes at the Worth monument waiting for a free bed. Now, what's the prize for the best answer to all this?'

To his intense surprise Thomas felt himself lifted by the collar and dragged, without a word of explanation, to the front door. This was opened, and he was kicked forcibly down the steps with one heavy, disillusionizing, humiliating impact of the stupendous Arabian's shoe.

As soon as the ex-coachman had recovered his feet and his wits he hastened as fast as he could eastward toward Broadway.

'Crazy guy,' was his estimate of the mysterious automobilist. 'Just wanted to have some fun kiddin', I guess. He might have dug up a dollar, anyhow. Now I've got to hurry up and get back to that gang of bum bed hunters before they all get preached to sleep.'

When Thomas reached the end of his two-mile walk he found the ranks of the homeless reduced to a squad of perhaps eight or ten. He took the proper place of a new-comer at the left end of the rear rank. In the file in front of him was the young man who had spoken to him of hospitals and something of a wife and child.

'Sorry to see you back again,' said the young man, turning to speak to him. 'I hoped you had struck something better than this.'

'Me?' said Thomas. 'Oh, I just took a run around the block to keep warm! I see the public ain't lending to the Lord very fast to-night.'

'In this kind of weather,' said the young man, 'charity avails itself of the proverb, and both begins and ends at home.'

And now the Preacher and his vehement lieutenant struck up a last hymn of petition to Providence and man. Those of the Bed Liners whose windpipes still registered above 32 degrees hopelessly and tunelessly joined in.

In the middle of the second verse Thomas saw a sturdy girl with wind-tossed drapery battling against the breeze and coming straight toward him from the opposite sidewalk. 'Annie!' he yelled, and ran toward her.

'You fool, you fool!' she cried, weeping and laughing, and hanging upon his neck. 'Why did you do it?'

'The Stuff,' explained Thomas briefly. 'You know. But subsequently nit. Not a drop.' He led her to the kerb. 'How did you happen to see me?'

'I came to find you,' said Annie, holding tight to his sleeve. 'Oh, you big fool! Professor Cherubusco told us that we might find you here.'

'Professor Ch – Don't know the guy. What saloon does he work in?'

'He's a clearvoyant, Thomas; the greatest in the world. He found you with the Chaldean telescope, he said.'

'He's a liar,' said Thomas. 'I never had it. He never saw me have anybody's telescope.'

'And he said you came in a chariot with five wheels or something.'

'Annie,' said Thomas solicitously, 'you're giving me the wheels now. If I had a chariot I'd have gone to bed in it long ago. And without any singing and preaching for a nightcap, either.'

'Listen, you big fool. The Missis says she'll take you back. I begged her to. But you must behave. And you can go up to the house to-night; and your old room over the stable is ready.'

'Great!' said Thomas earnestly. 'You are It, Annie. But when did these stunts happen?'

'To-night at Professor Cherubusco's. He sent his automobile for the Missis, and she took me along. I've been there with her before.'

'What's the professor's line?'

'He's a clearvoyant and a witch. The Missis consults him. He knows everything. But he hasn't done the Missis any good yet, though she's paid him hundreds of dollars. But he told us that the stars told him we could find you here.'

'What's the old lady want this cherry-buster to do?'

'That's a family secret,' said Annie. 'And now you've asked enough questions. Come on home, you big fool.'

They had moved but a little way up the street when Thomas stopped.

'Got any dough with you, Annie?' he asked.

Annie looked at him sharply.

'Oh, I know what that look means,-' said Thomas. 'You're wrong. Not another drop. But there's a guy that was standing next to me in the Bed Line over there that's in a bad shape. He's the right kind, and he's got wives or kids or something, and he's on the sick-list. No booze. If you could dig up half a dollar for him so he could get a decent bed I'd like it.'

Annie's fingers began to wiggle in her purse.

'Sure, I've got money,' said she. 'Lots of it. Twelve dollars.' And then she added, with woman's ineradicable suspicion of vicarious benevolence: 'Bring him here and let me see him first.'

Thomas went on his mission. The wan Bed Liner came readily enough. As the two drew near, Annie looked up from her purse and screamed:

'Mr. Walter – oh – Mr. Walter!'

'Is that you, Annie?' said the young man weakly.

'Oh, Mr. Walter! – and the Missis hunting high and low for you!'

'Does mother want to see me?' he asked, with a flush coming out on his pale cheek.

'She's been hunting for you high and low. Sure, she wants to see you. She wants you to come home. She's tried police and morgues and lawyers and advertising and detectives and rewards and everything. And then she took up clearvoyants. You'll go right home, won't you, Mr. Walter?'

'Gladly, if she wants me,' said the young man, 'Three years is a long time. I suppose I'll have to walk up, though, unless the street-cars are giving free rides. I used to walk and beat that old plug team of bays we used to drive to the carriage. Have they got them yet?'

'They have,' said Thomas feelingly. 'And they'll have 'em ten years from now. The life of the royal elephantibus truckhorseibus is one hundred and forty-nine years. I'm the coachman. Just got my reappointment five minutes ago. Let's all ride up in a surface car – that is – er – if Annie will pay the fares.'

On the Broadway car Annie handed each one of the prodigals a nickel to pay the conductor.

'Seems to me you are mighty reckless the way you throw large sums of money around,' said Thomas sarcastically.

'In that purse,' said Annie decidedly, 'is exactly $11.85. I shall take every cent of it to-morrow and give it to Professor Cherubusco, the greatest man in the world.'

'Well,' said Thomas, 'I guess he must be a pretty fly guy to pipe off things the way he does. I'm glad his spooks told him where you could find me. If you'll give me his address, some day I'll go up there myself, and shake his hand.'

Presently Thomas moved tentatively in his seat, and thoughtfully felt an abrasion or two on his knees and elbows.

'Say, Annie,' said he confidentially, 'maybe it's one of the last dreams of the booze, but I've a kind of a recollection of riding in an automobile with a swell guy that took me to a house full of eagles and arc lights. He fed me on biscuits and hot air, and then kicked me down the front steps. If it was the *d t's*, why am I so sore?'

'Shut up, you fool,' said Annie.

'If I could find that funny guy's house,' said Thomas, in conclusion, 'I'd go up there some day and punch his nose for him.'

XLVII

The Poet and the Peasant

THE OTHER DAY a poet friend of mine, who has lived in close communication with nature all his life, wrote a poem and took it to an editor.

It was a living pastoral, full of the genuine breath of the fields, the song of birds, and the pleasant chatter of trickling streams.

When the poet called again to see about it, with hopes of a beefsteak dinner in his heart, it was handed back to him with the comment:

'Too artificial.'

Several of us met over spaghetti and Dutchess County chianti, and swallowed indignation with the slippery forkfuls.

And there we dug a pit for the editor. With us was Conant, a well-arrived writer of fiction − a man who had trod on asphalt all his life, and who had never looked upon bucolic scenes except with sensations of disgust from the windows of express trains.

Conant wrote a poem and called it 'The Doe and the Brook.' It was a fine specimen of the kind of work you would expect from a poet who had strayed with Amaryllis only as far as the florist's windows, and whose sole ornithological discussion had been carried on with a waiter. Conant signed this poem, and we sent it to the same editor.

But this has very little to do with the story.

Just as the editor was reading the first line of the poem, on the next morning, a being stumbled off the West Shore ferryboat, and loped slowly up Forty-second Street.

The invader was a young man with light blue eyes, a hanging

lip, and hair the exact colour of the little orphan's (afterward discovered to be the earl's daughter) in one of Mr. Blaney's plays. His
trousers were corduroy, his coat short-sleeved, with buttons in the
middle of his back. One bootleg was outside the corduroys. You
looked expectantly, though in vain, at his straw hat for ear-holes,
its shape inaugurating the suspicion that it had been ravaged from
a former equine possessor. In his hand was a valise – description of
it is an impossible task; a Boston man would not have carried his
lunch and law books to his office in it. And above one ear, in his
hair, was a wisp of hay – the rustic's letter of credit, his badge of
innocence, the last clinging touch of the Garden of Eden lingering
to shame the goldbrick men.

Knowingly, smilingly, the city crowds passed him by. They saw
the raw stranger stand in the gutter and stretch his neck at the tall
buildings. At this they ceased to smile, and even to look at him. It
had been done so often. A few glanced at the antique valise to see
what Coney 'attraction' or brand of chewing-gum he might be
thus dinning into his memory. But for the most part he was
ignored. Even the newsboys looked bored when he scampered like
a circus clown out of the way of cabs and street-cars.

At Eighth Avenue stood 'Bunco Harry,' with his dyed moustache and shiny, good-natured eyes. Harry was too good an artist
not to be pained at the sight of an actor overdoing his part. He
edged up to the countryman, who had stopped to open his mouth
at a jewellery store window, and shook his head.

'Too thick, pal,' he said critically – 'too thick by a couple of
inches I don't know what your lay is; but you've got the properties
on too thick. That hay, now – why, they don't even allow that on
Proctor's circuit any more.'

'I don't understand you, mister,' said the green one. 'I'm not
lookin' for any circus. I've just run down from Ulster County to
look at the town, bein' that the hayin's over with. Gosh! but it's a
whopper. I thought Poughkeepsie was some punkins; but this here
town is five times as big.'

'Oh, well,' said 'Bunco Harry,' raising his eyebrows, 'I didn't
mean to butt in. You don't have to tell. I thought you ought to
tone down a little, so I tried to put you wise. Wish you success at
your graft, whatever it is. Come and have a drink, anyhow.'

'I wouldn't mind having a glass of lager beer,' acknowledged the
other.

They went to a café frequented by men with smooth faces and
shifty eyes, and sat at their drinks.

'I'm glad I come across you, mister,' said Haylocks. 'How'd you like to play a game or two of seven-up? I've got the keerds.'

He fished them out of Noah's valise – a rare, inimitable deck, greasy with bacon suppers and grimy with the soil of cornfields.

'Bunco Harry' laughed loud and briefly.

'Not for me, sport,' he said firmly. 'I don't go against that make-up of yours for a cent. But I still say you've overdone it. The Reubs haven't dressed like that since '79. I doubt if you could work Brooklyn for a key-winding watch with that lay-out.'

'Oh, you needn't think I ain't got the money,' boasted Haylocks. He drew forth a tightly rolled mass or bills as large as a teacup, and laid it on the table.

'Got that for my share of grandmother's farm,' he announced. 'There's $950 in that roll. Thought I'd come into the city and look around for a likely business to go into.'

'Bunco Harry' took up the roll of money and looked at it with almost respect in his smiling eyes.

'I've seen worse,' he said critically. 'But you'll never do it in them clothes. You want to get light tan shoes and a black suit and a straw hat with a coloured band, and talk a good deal about Pittsburg and freight differentials, and drink sherry for breakfast in order to work off phony stuff like that.'

'What's his line?' asked two or three shifty-eyed men of 'Bunco Harry' after Haylocks had gathered up his impugned money and departed.

'The queer, I guess,' said Harry. 'Or else he's one of Jerome's men. Or some guy with a new graft. He's too much hayseed. Maybe that his – I wonder now – oh no, it couldn't have been real money.'

Haylocks wandered on. Thirst probably assailed him again, for he dived into a dark groggery on a side-street and bought beer. Several sinister fellows hung upon one end of the bar. At first sight of him their eyes brightened; but when his insistent and exaggerated rusticity became apparent their expressions changed to wary suspicion.

Haylocks swung his valise across the bar.

'Keep that awhile for me, mister,' he said, chewing at the end of a virulent claybank cigar. 'I'll be back after I knock around a spell. And keep your eye on it, for there's $950 inside of it, though maybe you wouldn't think so to look at me.'

Somewhere outside a phonograph struck up a band piece, and Haylocks was off for it, his coat-tail buttons flopping in the middle of his back.

'Divvy? Mike,' said the men hanging upon the bar, winking openly at one another.

'Honest, now,' said the bartender, kicking the valise to one side. 'You don't think I'd fall to that, do you? Anybody can see he ain't no jay. One of McAdoo's come-on squad, I guess. He's a shine if he made himself up. There ain't no parts of the country now where they dress like that since they run rural free delivery to Providence, Rhode Island. If he's got nine-fifty in that valise it's a ninety-eight-cent Waterbury that's stopped at ten minutes to ten.'

When Haylocks had exhausted the resources of Mr. Edison to amuse he returned for his valise. And then down Broadway he gallivanted, culling the sights with his eager blue eyes. But still and evermore Broadway rejected him with curt glances and sardonic smiles. He was the oldest of the 'gags' that the city must endure. He was so flagrantly impossible, so ultra-rustic, so exaggerated beyond the most freakish products of the barnyard, the hayfield and the vaudeville stage, that he excited only weariness and suspicion. And the wisp of hay in his hair was so genuine, so fresh and redolent of the meadows, so clamorously rural, that even a shell-game man would have put up his peas and folded his table at the sight of it.

Haylocks seated himself upon a flight of stone steps and once more exhumed his roll of yellow-backs from the valise. The outer one, a twenty, he shucked off and beckoned to a newsboy.

'Son,' said he, 'run somewhere and get this changed for me. I'm mighty nigh out of chicken feed; I guess you'll get a nickel if you'll hurry up.'

A hurt look appeared through the dirt on the newsy's face.

'Aw, watchert'ink! G'wan and get yer funny bill changed yerself. Dey ain't no farm clothes yer got on. G'wan wit yer stage money.'

On a corner lounged a keen-eyed steerer for a gambling-house. He saw Haylocks, and his expression suddenly grew cold and virtuous.

'Mister,' said the rural one. 'I've heard of places in this here town where a fellow could have a good game of old sledge or peg a card at keno. I got $950 in this valise, and I come down from old Ulster to see the sights. Know where a fellow could get action on about $9 or $10? I'm goin' to have some sport, and then maybe I'll buy out a business of some kind.'

The steerer looked pained, and investigated a white speck on his left forefinger nail.

'Cheese it, old man,' he murmured reproachfully. 'The Central

Office must be bughouse to send you out looking like such a gillie. You couldn't get within two blocks of a sidewalk crap game in them Tony Pastor props. The recent Mr. Scotty from Death Valley has got you beat a crosstown block in the way of Elizabethan scenery and mechanical accessories. Let it be skiddoo for yours. Nay, I know of no gilded halls where one may bet a patrol wagon on the ace.'

Rebuffed again by the great city that is so swift to detect artificialities, Haylocks sat upon the kerb and presented his thoughts to hold a conference.

'It's my clothes,' said he; 'durned if it ain't. They think I'm a hayseed and won't have nothin' to do with me. Nobody never made fun of this hat in Ulster County. I guess if you want folks to notice you in New York you must dress up like they do.'

So Haylocks went shopping in the bazaars where men spake through their noses and rubbed their hands and ran the tape line ecstatically over the bulge in his inside pocket where reposed a red nubbin of corn with an even number of rows. And messengers bearing parcels and boxes streamed to his hotel on Broadway within the lights of Long Acre.

At nine o'clock in the evening one descended to the sidewalk whom Ulster County would have forsworn. Bright tan were his shoes; his hat the latest block. His light grey trousers were deeply creased; a gay blue silk handkerchief flapped from the breast pocket of his elegant English walking-coat. His collar might have graced a laundry window; his blond hair was trimmed close; the wisp of hay was gone.

For an instant he stood, resplendent, with the leisurely air of a boulevardier concocting in his mind the route for his evening pleasures. And then he turned down the gay, bright street with the easy and graceful tread of a millionaire.

But in the instant that he had paused the wisest and keenest eyes in the city had enveloped him in their field of vision. A stout man with grey eyes picked two of his friends with a lift of his eyebrows from the row of loungers in front of the hotel.

'The juiciest jay I've seen in six months,' said the man with grey eyes. 'Come along.'

It was half-past eleven when a man galloped into the West Forty-seventh Street police-station with the story of his wrongs.

'Nine hundred and fifty dollars,' he gasped, 'all my share of grandmother's farm.'

The desk sergeant wrung from him the name Jabez Bulltongue,

of Locust Valley Farm, Ulster County, and then began to take descriptions of the strong-arm gentlemen.

When Conant went to see the editor about the fate of his poem, he was received over the head of the office boy into the inner office that is decorated with the statuettes by Rodin and J. G. Brown.

'When I read the first line of "The Doe and the Brook," ' said the editor, 'I knew it to be the work of one whose life has been heart to heart with nature. The finished art of the line did not blind me to that fact. To use a somewhat homely comparison, it was as if a wild, free child of the woods and fields were to don the garb of fashion and walk down Broadway. Beneath the apparel the man would show.'

'Thanks,' said Conant. 'I suppose the cheque will be round on Thursday, as usual.'

The morals of this story have somehow gotten mixed. You can take your choice of 'Stay on the Farm' or 'Don't write Poetry.'

XLVIII

The Thing's the Play

BEING ACQUAINTED WITH a newspaper reporter who had a couple of free passes, I got to see the performance a few nights ago at one of the popular vaudeville houses.

One of the numbers was a violin solo by a striking-looking man not much past forty, but with very grey, thick hair. Not being afflicted with a taste for music, I let the system of noises drift past my ears while I regarded the man.

'There was a story about that chap a month or two ago,' said the reporter. 'They gave me the assignment. It was to run a column and was to be on the extremely light and joking order. The old man seems to like the funny touch I give to local happenings. Oh yes, I'm working on a farce comedy now. Well, I went down to the house and got all the details; but I certainly fell down on that job. I went back and turned in a comic write-up of an east side funeral instead. Why? Oh, I couldn't seem to get hold of it with my funny hooks, somehow. Maybe you could make a one-act tragedy out of it for a curtain-raiser. I'll give you the details.'

After the performance my friend, the reporter, recited to me the facts over the Würzburger.

'I see no reason,' said I, when he had concluded, 'why that shouldn't make a rattling good funny story. Those three people couldn't have acted in a more absurd and preposterous manner if they had been real actors in a real theatre. I'm really afraid that all the stage is a world, anyhow, and all the players merely men and women. "The thing's the play," is the way I quote Mr. Shakespeare.'

'Try it,' said the reporter.

'I will,' said I; and I did, to show him how he could have made a humorous column of it for his paper.

There stands a house near Abingdon Square. On the ground floor there has been for twenty-five years a little store where toys and notions and stationery are sold.

One night, twenty years ago, there was a wedding in the rooms above the store. The Widow Mayo owned the house and store. Her daughter, Helen, was married to Frank Barry. John Delaney was best man. Helen was eighteen, and her picture had been printed in a morning paper next to the headlines of a 'Wholesale Female Murderess' story from Butte, Mont. But after your eye and intelligence had rejected the connection, you seized your magnifying glass and read beneath the portrait her description as one of a series of Prominent Beauties and Belles of the lower west side.

Frank Barry and John Delaney were 'prominent' young beaux of the same side, and bosom friends, whom you expected to turn upon each other every time the curtain went up. One who pays his money for orchestra seats and fiction expects this. That is the first funny idea that has turned up in the story yet. Both had made a great race for Helen's hand. When Frank won, John shook his hand and congratulated him – honestly, he did.

After the ceremony Helen ran upstairs to put on her hat. She was getting married in a travelling-dress. She and Frank were going to Old Point Comfort for a week. Downstairs the usual horde of gibbering cave-dwellers were waiting with their hands full of old Congress gaiters and paper bags of hominy.

Then there was a rattle of the fire-escape, and into her room jumps the mad and infatuated John Delaney, with a damp curl drooping upon his forehead, and made violent and reprehensible love to his lost one, entreating her to flee or fly with him to the Riviera, or the Bronx, or any old place where there are Italian skies and *dolce far niente*.

It would have carried Blaney off his feet to see Helen repulse him. With blazing and scornful eyes she fairly withered him by

demanding whatever he meant by speaking to respectable people
that way.

In a few moments she had him going. The manliness that had
possessed him departed. He bowed low, and said something about
'irresistible impulse' and 'for ever carry in his heart the memory
of' – and she suggested that he catch the first fire-escape going
down.

'I will away,' said John Delaney, 'to the furthermost parts of the
earth. I cannot remain near you and know that you are another's. I
will to Africa, and there amid other scenes strive to for –'

'For goodness' sake, get out,' said Helen. 'Somebody might
come in.'

He knelt upon one knee, and she extended him one white hand
that he might give it a farewell kiss.

Girls, was this choice boon of the great little god Cupid ever
vouchsafed you – to have the fellow you want hard and fast, and
have the one you don't want come with a damp curl on his forehead, and kneel to you and babble of Africa and love which, in
spite of everything, shall for ever bloom, an amaranth, in his
heart? To know your power, and to feel the sweet security of your
own happy state; to send the unlucky one, broken-hearted, to foreign climes, while you congratulate yourself, as he presses his last
kiss upon your knuckles, that your nails are well manicured – say,
girls, it's galluptious – don't ever let it get by you.

And then, of course – how did you guess it? – the door opened
and in stalked the bridegroom, jealous of slow-tying bonnet-
strings.

The farewell kiss was imprinted upon Helen's hand, and out of
the window and down the fire-escape sprang John Delaney,
Africa-bound.

A little slow music, if you please – faint violin just a breath in
the clarinet and a touch of the 'cello. Imagine the scene. Frank,
white-hot, with the cry of a man wounded to death bursting from
him. Helen, rushing and clinging to him, trying to explain. He
catches her wrists and tears them from his shoulders – once, twice,
thrice he sways her this way and that – the stage manager will
show you how – and throws her from him to the floor a huddled
crushed, moaning thing. Never, he cries, will he look upon her
face again, and rushes from the house through the staring groups
of astonished guests.

And, now, because it is the Thing instead of the Play, the audience must stroll out into the real lobby of the world and marry,

die, grow grey, rich, poor, happy or sad during the intermission of twenty years which must precede the rising of the curtain again.

Mrs. Barry inherited the shop and the house. At thirty-eight she could have bested many an eighteen-year-old at a beauty show on points and general results. Only a few people remembered her wedding comedy, but she made of it no secret. She did not pack it in lavender or moth-balls, nor did she sell it to a magazine.

One day a middle-aged, money-making lawyer who bought his legal cap and ink of her, asked her across the counter to marry him.

'I'm really much obliged to you,' said Helen cheerfully, 'but I married another man twenty years ago. He was more a goose than a man, but I think I love him yet. I have never seen him since about half an hour after the ceremony. Was it copying ink that you wanted or just writing fluid?'

The lawyer bowed over the counter with old-time grace and left a respectful kiss on the back of her hand. Helen sighed. Parting salutes, however romantic, may be overdone. Here she was at thirty-eight, beautiful and admired; and all that she seemed to have got from her lovers were reproaches and adieus. Worse still, in the last one she had lost a customer, too.

Business languished, and she hung out a Room to Let card. Two large rooms on the third floor were prepared for desirable tenants. Roomers came, and went regretfully, for the house of Mrs. Barry was the abode of neatness, comfort and taste

One day came Ramonti, the violinist, and engaged the front room above. The discord and clatter uptown offended his nice ear; so a friend had sent him to this oasis in the desert of noise.

Ramonti, with his still youthful face, his dark eyebrows, his short, pointed, foreign, brown beard, his distinguished head of grey hair, and his artist's temperament – revealed in his light, gay and sympathetic manner – was a welcome tenant in the old house near Abingdon Square.

Helen lived on the floor above the store. The architecture of it was singular and quaint. The hall was large and almost square. Up one side of it, and then across the end of it ascended an open stairway to the floor above. This hall space she had furnished as a sitting-room and office combined. There she kept her desk and wrote her business letters; and there she sat of evenings by a warm fire and a bright red light and sewed or read. Ramonti found the atmosphere so agreeable that he spent much time there, describing to Mrs. Barry the wonders of Paris, where he had studied with a particularly notorious and noisy fiddler.

Next comes lodger No. 2, a handsome, melancholy man in the early 40's, with a brown, mysterious beard, and strangely pleading, haunting eyes. He, too, found the society of Helen a desirable thing. With the eyes of Romeo and Othello's tongue, he charmed her with tales of distant climes and wooed her by respectful innuendo.

From the first Helen felt a marvellous and compelling thrill in the presence of this man. His voice somehow took her swiftly back to the days of her youth's romance. This feeling grew, and she gave way to it, and it led her to an instinctive belief that he had been a factor in that romance. And then with a woman's reasoning (oh yes, they do, sometimes) she leaped over common syllogisms and theory, and logic, and was sure that her husband had come back to her. For she saw in his eyes love, which no woman can mistake, and a thousand tons of regret and remorse, which aroused pity, which is perilously near to love requited, which is the *sine qua non* in the house that Jack built.

But she made no sign. A husband who steps around the corner for twenty years and then drops in again should not expect to find his slippers laid out too conveniently near nor a match ready lighted for his cigar. There must be expiation, explanation, and possibly execration. A little purgatory, and then, maybe, if he were properly humble, he might be trusted with a harp and crown. And so she made no sign that she knew or suspected.

And my friend, the reporter, could see nothing funny in this! Sent out on an assignment to write up a roaring, hilarious, brilliant joshing story of – but I will not knock a brother – let us go on with the story.

One evening Ramonti stopped in Helen's hall-office-reception-room and told his love with the tenderness and ardour of the enraptured artist. His words were a bright flame of the divine fire that glows in the heart of a man who is a dreamer and a doer combined.

'But before you give me an answer,' he went on, before she could accuse him of suddenness, 'I must tell you that "Ramonti" is the only name I have to offer you. My manager gave me that. I do not know who I am or where I came from. My first recollection is of opening my eyes in a hospital. I was a young man, and I had been there for weeks. My life before that is a blank to me. They told me that I was found lying in the street with a wound on my head and was brought there in an ambulance. They thought I must have fallen and struck my head upon the stones. There was nothing to show who I was. I have never been able to remember. After I was discharged from the hospital, I took up the violin. I have had success. Mrs. Barry – I do not know your name except that – I love you; the first time I saw you I realized that you were the one woman in the world for me – and' – oh, a lot of stuff like that

Helen felt young again. First a wave of pride and a sweet little thrill of vanity went all over her; and then she looked Ramonti in the eyes, and a tremendous throb went through her heart. She hadn't expected that throb. It took her by surprise. The musician had become a big factor in her life, and she hadn't been aware of it.

'Mr. Ramonti,' she said sorrowfully (this was not on the stage, remember; it was in the old home near Abingdon Square), 'I'm awfully sorry, but I'm a married woman.'

And then she told him the sad story of her life, as a heroine must do, sooner or later, either to a theatrical manager or to a reporter.

Ramonti took her hand, bowed low and kissed it, and went up to his room.

Helen sat down and looked mournfully at her hand. Well she might. Three suitors had kissed it, mounted their red roan steeds and ridden away.

In an hour entered the mysterious stranger with the haunting eyes. Helen was in the willow rocker, knitting a useless thing in cotton-wool. He ricocheted from the stairs and stopped for a chat. Sitting across the table from her, he also poured out his narrative of love. And then he said: 'Helen, do you not remember me? I think I have seen it in your eyes. Can you forgive the past and remember the love that has lasted for twenty years? I wronged you deeply – I was afraid to come back to you – but my love overpowered my reason. Can you, will you, forgive me?'

Helen stood up. The mysterious stranger held one of her hands in a strong and trembling clasp.

There she stood, and I pity the stage that it has not acquired a scene like that and her emotions to portray.

For she stood with a divided heart. The fresh, unforgettable, virginal love for her bridegroom was hers; the treasured, sacred, honoured memory of her first choice filled half her soul. She leaned to that pure feeling. Honour and faith and sweet, abiding romance bound her to it. But the other half of her heart and soul was filled with something else – a later, fuller, nearer influence. And so the old fought against the new.

And while she hesitated, from the room above came the soft,

racking, petitionary music of a violin The hag, music, bewitches some of the noblest The daws may peck upon one's sleeve without in injury, but whoever wears his heart upon his tympanum gets it not far from the neck.

This music and the musician called her, and at her side honour and the old love held her back.

'Forgive me,' he pleaded.

'Twenty years is a long time to remain away from the one you say you love,' she declared, with a purgatorial touch.

'How could I tell?' he begged. 'I will conceal nothing from you. That night when he left I followed him. I was mad with jealousy. On a dark street I struck him down. He did not rise. I examined him. His head had struck a stone. I did not intend to kill him. I was mad with love and jealousy. I hid near by and saw an ambulance take him away. Although you married him, Helen –'

'*Who are you?*' cried the woman, with wide-open eyes, snatching her hand away.

'Don't you remember me, Helen – the one who has always loved you the best? I am John Delaney. If you can forgive –'

But she was gone, leaping, stumbling, hurrying, flying up the stairs toward the music and him who had forgotten, but who had known her for his in each of his two existences, and as she climbed up she sobbed, cried and sang: 'Frank! Frank! Frank!'

Three mortals thus juggling with years as though they were billiard balls, and my friend, the reporter, couldn't see anything funny in it!

XLIX

A Ramble in Aphasia

MY WIFE AND I PARTED on that morning in precisely our usual manner. She left her second cup of tea to follow me to the front door. There she plucked from my lapel the invisible strand of lint (the universal act of woman to proclaim ownership) and bade me take care of my cold. I had no cold. Next came her kiss of parting – the level kiss of domesticity flavoured with Young Hyson. There was no fear of the extemporaneous, of variety spicing her infinite custom. With the deft touch of long malpractice, she dabbed awry my well-set scarf-pin; and then, as I closed the door, I heard her morning slippers pattering back to her cooling tea.

When I set out I had no thought or premonition of what was to occur. The attack came suddenly.

For many weeks I had been toiling, almost night and day, at a famous railroad law case that I won triumphantly but a few days previously. In fact, I had been digging away at the law almost without cessation for many years. Once or twice good Doctor Volney, my friend and physician, had warned me.

'If you don't slacken up, Bellford,' he said, 'you'll go suddenly to pieces. Either your nerves or your brain will give way. Tell me, does a week pass in which you do not read in the papers of a case of aphasia — of some man lost, wandering nameless, with his past and his identity blotted out — and all from that little brain-clot made by overwork or worry?'

'I always thought,' said I, 'that the clot in those instances was really to be found on the brains of the newspaper reporters.'

Dr. Volney shook his head.

'The disease exists,' he said. 'You need a change or a rest. Court-room, office and home — there is the only route you travel. For recreation you — read law books. Better take warning in time.'

'On Thursday nights,' I said defensively, 'my wife and I play cribbage. On Sundays she reads to me the weekly letter from her mother. That law books are not a recreation remains yet to be established.'

That morning as I walked I was thinking of Doctor Volney's words. I was feeling as well as I usually did — possibly in better spirits than usual.

I awoke with stiff and cramped muscles from having slept long on the incommodious seat of a day coach. I leaned my head against the seat and tried to think. After a long time I said to myself: 'I must have a name of some sort.' I searched my pockets. Not a card; not a letter; not a paper or monogram could I find. But I found in my coat pocket nearly $3,000 in bills of large denomination. 'I must be someone, of course,' I repeated to myself, and began again to consider.

The car was well crowded with men, among whom I told myself, there must have been some common interest, for they intermingled freely, and seemed in the best good-humour and spirits. One of them — a stout, spectacled gentleman enveloped in a decided odour of cinnamon and aloes — took the vacant half of my seat with a friendly nod, and unfolded a newspaper. In the intervals between his periods of reading, we conversed, as travellers will, on current affairs. I found myself able to sustain the conversation on such subjects with credit, at least to my memory. By and by my companion said:

'You are one of us, of course. Fine lot of men the West sends in this time. I'm glad they held the convention in New York; I've never been East before. My name's R. P. Bolder – Bolder & Son, of Hickory Grove, Missouri.'

Though unprepared, I rose to the emergency, as men will when put to it. Now must I hold a christening, and be at once babe, parson and parent. My senses came to the rescue of my slower brain. The insistent odour of drugs from my companion supplied one idea; a glance at his newspaper, where my eye met a conspicuous advertisement, assisted me further.

'My name,' said I glibly, 'is Edward Pinkhammer. I am a druggist, and my home is in Cornopolis, Kansas.'

'I knew you were a druggist,' said my fellow-traveller affably. 'I saw the callous spot on your right forefinger where the handle of the pestle rubs. Of course, you are a delegate to our National Convention.'

'Are all these men druggists?' I asked wonderingly.

'They are. This car came through from the West. And they're your old-time druggists, too – none of your patent tablet-and-granule pharmashootists that use slot machines instead of a prescription desk. We percolate our own paregoric and roll our own pills, and we ain't above handling a few garden seeds in the spring, and carrying a sideline of confectionery and shoes. I tell you, Hampinker, I've got an idea to spring on this convention – new ideas is what they want. Now, you know the shelf bottles of tartar emetic and Rochelle salt Ant. et Pot. Tart. and Sod. et Pot. Tart. – one's poison, you know, and the other's harmless. It's easy to mistake one label for the other. Where do druggists mostly keep 'em? Why, as far apart as possible, on different shelves. That's wrong. I say keep 'em side by side so when you want one you can always compare it with the other and avoid mistakes. Do you catch the idea?'

'It seems to me a very good one,' I said.

'All right! When I spring it on the convention you back it up. We'll make some of these Eastern orange-phosphate-and-massage-cream professors that think they're the only lozenges in the market look like hypodermic tablets.'

'If I can be of any aid,' I said, warming, 'the two bottles of – er –'

'Tartrate of antimony and potash, and tartrate of soda and potash.'

'Shall henceforth sit side by side,' I concluded firmly.

'Now, there's another thing,' said Mr. Bolder. 'For an excipient in manipulating a pill mass which do you prefer – the magnesia carbonate or the pulverized glycerrhiza radix?'

'The – er – magnesia,' I said. It was easier to say than the other word.

Mr. Bolder glanced at me distrustfully through his spectacles.

'Give me the glycerrhiza,' said he. 'Magnesia cakes.'

'Here's another one of these fake aphasia cases,' he said, presently, handing me his newspaper, and laying his finger upon an article. 'I don't believe in 'em. I put nine out of ten of 'em down as frauds. A man gets sick of his business and his folks and wants to have a good time. He skips out somewhere, and when they find him he pretends to have lost his memory – don't know his own name, and won't even recognize the strawberry mark on his wife's left shoulder. Aphasia! Tut! Why can't they stay at home and forget?'

I took the paper and read, after the pungent headlines, the following:

'DENVER, June 12. – Elwyn C. Bellford, a prominent lawyer, is mysteriously missing from his home since three days ago, and all efforts to locate him have been in vain. Mr. Bellford is a well-known citizen of the highest standing, and has enjoyed a large and lucrative law practice. He is married and owns a fine home and the most extensive private library in the State. On the day of his disappearance, he drew quite a large sum of money from his bank. No one can be found who saw him after he left the bank. Mr. Bellford was a man of singularly quiet and domestic tastes, and seemed to find his happiness in his home and profession. If any clue at all exists to his strange disappearance, it may be found in the fact that for some months he had been deeply absorbed in an important law case in connection with the Q. Y. and Z. Railroad Company. It is feared that overwork may have affected his mind. Every effort is being made to discover the whereabouts of the missing man.'

'It seems to me you are not altogether uncynical Mr. Bolder,' I said, after I had read the despatch. 'This has the sound, to me, of a genuine case. Why should this man, prosperous, happily married and respected, choose suddenly to abandon everything? I know that these lapses of memory do occur, and that men do find themselves adrift without a name, a history or a home.'

'Oh, gammon and jalap!' said Mr. Bolder. 'It's larks they're after. There's too much education nowadays. Men know about aphasia, and they use it for an excuse. The women are wise, too.'

When it's all over they look you in the eye, as scientific as you please, and say: "He hypnotized me." '

Thus Mr. Bolder diverted, but did not aid me with his comments and philosophy.

We arrived in New York about ten at night. I rode in a cab to an hotel, and I wrote my name 'Edward Pinkhammer' in the register. As I did so I felt pervade me a splendid, wild, intoxicating buoyancy — a sense of unlimited freedom, of newly attained possibilities. I was just born into the world. The old fetters — whatever they had been — were stricken from my hands and feet. The future lay before me a clear road such as an infant enters, and I could set out upon it equipped with a man's learning and experience.

I thought the hotel clerk looked at me five seconds too long. I had no baggage.

'The Druggists' Convention,' I said. 'My trunk has somehow failed to arrive.' I drew out a roll of money.

'Ah!' said he, showing an auriferous tooth, 'we have quite a number of the Western delegates stopping here.' He struck a bell for the boy.

I endeavoured to give colour to my rôle.

'There is an important movement on foot among us Westerners,' I said, 'in regard to a recommendation to the convention that the bottles containing the tartrate of antimony and potash, and the tartrate of sodium and potash, be kept in a contiguous position on the shelf.'

'Gentleman to three-fourteen,' said the clerk hastily. I was whisked away to my room.

The next day I bought a trunk and clothing, and began to live the life of Edward Pinkhammer. I did not tax my brain with endeavours to solve problems of the past.

It was a piquant and sparkling cup that the great island city held up to my lips. I drank of it gratefully. The keys of Manhattan belong to him who is able to bear them. You must be either the city's guest or its victim.

The following few days were as gold and silver. Edward Pinkhammer, yet counting back to his birth by hours only, knew the rare joy of having come upon so diverting a world full-fledged and unrestrained. I sat entranced on the magic carpets provided in theatres and roof-gardens, that transported one into strange and delightful lands full of frolicsome music, pretty girls and grotesque, drolly extravagant parodies upon humankind. I went here and there at my own dear will, bound by no limits of space,

time or comportment. I dined in weird cabarets, at weirder tables
d'hôte to the sound of Hungarian music and the wild shouts of
mercurial artists and sculptors. Or, again, where the night life
quivers in the electric glare like a kinetoscopic picture, and the
millinery of the world, and its jewels, and the ones whom they
adorn, and the men who make all three possible are met for good
cheer and the spectacular effect. And among all these scenes that I
have mentioned I learned one thing that I never knew before. And
that is that the key to liberty is not in the hands of Licence, but
Convention holds it. Comity has a toll-gate at which you must
pay, or you may not enter the land of Freedom. In all the glitter,
the seeming disorder, the parade, the abandon, I saw this law,
unobtrusive, yet like iron, prevail. Therefore, in Manhattan you
must obey these unwritten laws, and then you will be freest of the
free. If you decline to be bound by them, you put on shackles.

Sometimes, as my mood urged me, I would seek the stately,
softly murmuring palm-rooms, redolent with high-born life and
delicate restraint, in which to dine. Again I would go down to the
waterways in steamers packed with vociferous, bedecked,
unchecked, love-making clerks and shop-girls to their crude pleasures on the island shores. And there was always Broadway – glis-
tening, opulent, wily, varying, desirable Broadway – growing upon
one like an opium habit.

One afternoon as I entered my hotel a stout man with a big nose
and a black moustache blocked my way in the corridor. When I
would have passed around him, he greeted me with offensive
familiarity.

'Hallo, Bellford!' he cried loudly. 'What the deuce are you
doing in New York? Didn't know anything could drag you away
from that old book den of yours. Is Mrs. B. along or is this a little
business run alone, eh?'

'You have made a mistake, sir,' I said coldly, releasing my hand
from his grasp. 'My name is Pinkhammer. You will excuse me.'

The man dropped to one side, apparently astonished. As I
walked to the clerk's desk I heard him call to a bell-boy and say
something about telegraph blanks.

'You will give me my bill,' I said to the clerk, 'and have my baggage brought down in half an hour. I do not care to remain where
I am annoyed by confidence men.'

I moved that afternoon to another hotel, a sedate, old-fashioned
one on lower Fifth Avenue.

There was a restaurant a little way off Broadway where one

could be served almost *alfresco* in a tropic array of screening flora. Quiet and luxury and a perfect service made it an ideal place in which to take luncheon or refreshment. One afternoon I was there picking my way to a table among the ferns when I felt my sleeve caught.

'Mr. Bellford!' exclaimed an amazingly sweet voice.

I turned quickly to see a lady seated alone – a lady of about thirty, with exceedingly handsome eyes, who looked at me as though I had been her very dear friend.

'You were about to pass me,' she said accusingly. 'Don't tell me you did not know me. Why should we not shake hands – at least once in fifteen years?'

I shook hands with her at once. I took a chair opposite her at the table. I summoned with my eyebrows a hovering waiter. The lady was philandering with an orange ice. I ordered a *crème de menthe*. Her hair was reddish bronze. You could not look at it, because you could not look away from her eyes. But you were conscious of it as you are conscious of sunset while you look into the profundities of a wood at twilight.

'Are you sure you know me?' I asked.

'No,' she said, smiling, 'I was never sure of that.'

'What would you think,' I said, a little anxiously, 'if I were to tell you that my name is Edward Pinkhammer, from Cornopolis, Kansas.'

'What would I think?' she repeated, with a merry glance. 'Why, that you had not brought Mrs. Bellford to New York with you, of course. I do wish you had. I would have liked to see Marian.' Her voice lowered slightly – 'You haven't changed much, Elwyn.'

I felt her wonderful eyes searching mine and my face more closely.

'Yes, you have,' she amended, and there was a soft, exultant note in her latest tones; 'I see it now. You haven't forgotten. You haven't forgotten for a year or a day or an hour. I told you you never could.'

I poked my straw anxiously in the *crème de menthe*.

'I'm sure I beg your pardon,' I said, a little uneasy at her gaze. 'But that is just the trouble. I have forgotten. I've forgotten everything.'

She flouted my denial. She laughed deliciously at something she seemed to see in my face.

'I've heard of you at times,' she went on. 'You're quite a big lawyer out West – Denver, isn't it, or Los Angeles? Marian must be very proud of you. You knew, I suppose, that I married six months after you did. You may have seen it in the papers. The flowers alone cost two thousand dollars.'

She had mentioned fifteen years. Fifteen years is a long time.

'Would it be too late,' I asked somewhat timorously, 'to offer you congratulations?'

'Not if you dare do it,' she answered, with such fine intrepidity that I was silent, and began to crease patterns on the cloth with my thumb-nail.

'Tell me one thing,' she said, leaning toward me rather eagerly – 'a thing I have wanted to know for many years – just from a woman's curiosity, of course – have you ever dared since that night to touch, smell or look at white roses – at white roses wet with rain and dew?'

I took a sip of *crème de menthe*.

'It would be useless, I suppose,' I said, with a sigh, 'for me to repeat that I have no recollection at all about these things. My memory is completely at fault. I need not say how much I regret it.'

The lady rested her arms upon the table, and again her eyes disdained my words and went travelling by their own route direct to my soul. She laughed softly, with a strange quality in the sound – it was a laugh of happiness yes, and of content – and of misery. I tried to look away from her.

'You lie, Elwyn Bellford,' she breathed blissfully. 'Oh, I know you lie!'

I gazed dully into the ferns.

'My name is Edward Pinkhammer,' I said. 'I came with the delegates to the Druggists' National Convention. There is a movement on foot for arranging a new position for the bottles of tartrate of antimony and tartrate of potash, in which, very likely, you would take little interest.'

A shining landau stopped before the entrance. The lady rose. I took her hand, and bowed.

'I am deeply sorry,' I said to her, 'that I cannot remember. I could explain, but fear you would not understand. You will not concede Pinkhammer; and I really cannot at all conceive of the – the roses and other things.'

'Good-bye, Mr. Bellford,' she said, with her happy, sorrowful smile, as she stepped into her carriage.

I attended the theatre that night. When I returned to my hotel, a quiet man in dark clothes, who seemed interested in rubbing his finger-nails with a silk handkerchief, appeared, magically, at my side.

'Mr. Pinkhammer,' he said casually, giving the bulk of his attention to his forefinger, 'may I request you to step aside with me for a little conversation? There is a room here.'

'Certainly,' I answered.

He conducted me into a small, private parlour. A lady and a gentleman were there. The lady, I surmised, would have been unusually good-looking had her features not been clouded by an expression of keen worry and fatigue. She was of a style of figure and possessed colouring and features that were agreeable to my fancy. She was in a travellingdress; she fixed upon me an earnest look of extreme anxiety, and pressed an unsteady hand to her bosom. I think she would have started forward, but the gentleman arrested her movement with an authoritative motion of his hand. He then came, himself, to meet me. He was a man of forty, a little grey about the temples, and with a strong, thoughtful face.

'Bellford, old man,' he said cordially, 'I'm glad to see you again. Of course we know everything is all right. I warned you, you know, that you were overdoing it. Now, you'll go back with us, and be yourself again in no time.'

I smiled ironically.

'I have been "Bellforded" so often,' I said, 'that it has lost its edge. Still, in the end, it may grow wearisome. Would you be willing at all to entertain the hypothesis that my name is Edward Pinkhammer, and that I never saw you before in my life?'

Before the man could reply a wailing cry came from the woman. She sprang past his detaining arm. 'Elwyn!' she sobbed, and cast herself upon me, and clung tight. 'Elwyn,' she cried again, 'don't break my heart. I am your wife – call my name once – just once! I could see you dead rather than this way.'

I unwound her arms respectfully, but firmly.

'Madam,' I said severely, 'pardon me if I suggest that you accept a resemblance too precipitately. It is a pity,' I went on, with an amused laugh, as the thought occurred to me, 'that this Bellford and I could not be kept side by side upon the same shelf like tartrates of sodium and antimony for purposes of identification. In order to understand the allusion,' I concluded airily, 'it may be necessary for you to keep an eye on the proceedings of the Druggists' National Convention.'

The lady turned to her companion, and grasped his arm.

'What is it, Doctor Volney? Oh, what is it?' she moaned.

He led her to the door.

'Go to your room for awhile,' I heard him say. 'I will remain and talk with him. His mind? No, I think not – only a portion of the brain. Yes, I am sure he will recover. Go to your room and leave me with him.'

The lady disappeared. The man in dark clothes also went outside, still manicuring himself in a thoughtful way. I think he waited in the hall.

'I would like to talk with you a while, Mr. Pinkhammer, if I may,' said the gentleman who remained.

'Very well, if you care to,' I replied, 'and will excuse me if I take it comfortably; I am rather tired.' I stretched myself upon a couch by a window and lit a cigar. He drew a chair near by.

'Let us speak to the point,' he said soothingly. 'Your name is not Pinkhammer.'

'I know that as well as you do,' I said coolly. 'But a man must have a name of some sort. I can assure you that I do not extravagantly admire the name of Pinkhammer. But when one christens one's self, suddenly the fine names do not seem to suggest themselves. But suppose it had been Scheringhausen or Scroggins! I think I did very well with Pinkhammer.'

'Your name,' said the other man seriously, 'is Elwyn C. Bellford. You are one of the first lawyers in Denver. You are suffering from an attack of aphasia, which has caused you to forget your identity. The cause of it was over-application to your profession, and, perhaps, a life too bare of natural recreation and pleasures. The lady who has just left the room is your wife.'

'She is what I would call a fine-looking woman,' I said, after a judicial pause. 'I particularly admire the shade of brown in her hair.'

'She is a wife to be proud of. Since your disappearance, nearly two weeks ago, she has scarcely closed her eyes. We learned that you were in New York through a telegram sent by Isidore Newman, a travelling man from Denver. He said that he had met you in an hotel here, and that you did not recognize him.'

'I think I remember the occasion,' I said. 'The fellow called me "Bellford," if I am not mistaken. But don't you think it about time, now, for you to introduce yourself?'

'I am Robert Volney – Doctor Volney. I have been your close friend for twenty years, and your physician for fifteen. I came with Mrs. Bellford to trace you as soon as we got the telegram. Try, Elwyn, old man – try to remember!'

'What's the use to try!' I asked, with a little frown. 'You say you are a physician. Is aphasia curable? When a man loses his memory, does it return slowly, or suddenly?'

'Sometimes gradually and imperfectly; sometimes as suddenly as it went.'

'Will you undertake the treatment of my case, Doctor Volney?' I asked.

'Old friend,' said he, 'I'll do everything in my power, and will have done everything that science can do to cure you.'

'Very well,' said I. 'Then you will consider that I am your patient. Everything is in confidence now – professional confidence.'

'Of course,' said Doctor Volney.

I got up from the couch. Someone had set a vase of white roses on the centre table – a cluster of white roses freshly sprinkled and fragrant. I threw them far out of the window, and then I laid myself upon the couch again.

'It will be best, Bobby,' I said, 'to have this cure happen suddenly. I'm rather tired of it all, anyway. You may go now and bring Marian in. But, oh, Doc,' I said, with a sigh, as I kicked him on the shin – 'good old Doc – it was glorious!'

L

A Municipal Report

The cities are full of pride,
    Challenging each to each –
This from her mountainside,
    That from her burthened beach.
                              R. KIPLING.

Fancy a novel about Chicago or Buffalo, let us say, or Nashville, Tennessee! There are just three big cities in the United States that are 'story cities' – New York, of course, New Orleans, and, best of the lot, San Francisco. – FRANK NORRIS.

EAST IS EAST, and West is San Francisco, according to Californians. Californians are a race of people; they are not merely inhabitants of a State. They are the Southerners of the West. Now, Chicagoans are no less loyal to their city; but when you ask them why, they stammer and speak of lake fish and the new Odd Fellows Building. But Californians go into detail.

Of course they have, in the climate, an argument that is good
for half an hour while you are thinking of your coal bills and heavy
underwear. But as soon as they come to mistake your silence for
conviction, madness comes upon them, and they picture the city
of the Golden Gate as the Bagdad of the New World. So far, as a
matter of opinion, no refutation is necessary. But, dear cousins all
(from Adam and Eve descended), it is a rash one who will lay his
finger on the map and say: 'In this town there can be no romance
– what could happen here?' Yes, it is a bold and a rash deed to
challenge in one sentence history, romance, and Rand and
McNally.

NASHVILLE. – A city, port of delivery, and the capital of the State of Tennessee, is on the Cumberland River and on the N.C. & St. L. and the L. & N.
railroads. This city is regarded as the most important educational centre in the
South.

I stepped off the train at 8 p.m. Having searched the thesaurus in
vain for adjectives, I must, as a substitution, hie me to comparison
in the form of a recipe.

Take of London fog 30 parts; malaria 10 parts; gas leaks 20
parts; dewdrops, gathered in a brickyard at sunrise, 25 parts; odour
of honeysuckle 15 parts. Mix.

The mixture will give you an approximate conception of a
Nashville drizzle. It is not so fragrant as a moth-ball nor as thick
as pea-soup; but 'tis enough – 'twill serve.

I went to an hotel in a tumbril. It required strong self-suppres-
sion for me to keep from climbing to the top of it and giving an
imitation of Sidney Carton. The vehicle was drawn by beasts of a
bygone era and driven by something dark and emancipated.

I was sleepy and tired, so when I got to the hotel I hurriedly
paid it the fifty cents it demanded (with approximate lagniappe, I
assure you). I knew its habits; and I did not want to hear it prate
about its old 'marster' or anything that happened 'befo' de wah.'

The hotel was one of the kind described as 'renovated.' That
means $20,000 worth of new marble pillars, tiling, electric lights
and brass cuspidors in the lobby, and a new L. & N. time table
and a lithograph of Lookout Mountain in each one of the great
rooms above. The management was without reproach, the attention full of exquisite Southern courtesy, the service as slow as the
progress of a snail and as good-humoured as Rip Van Winkle.
The food was worth travelling a thousand miles for. There is no

other hotel in the world where you can get such chicken livers *en brochette*.

At dinner I asked a negro waiter if there was anything doing in town. He pondered gravely for a minute, and then replied: 'Well, boss, I don't really reckon there's anything at all doin' after sundown.'

Sundown had been accomplished; it had been drowned in the drizzle long before. So that spectacle was denied me. But I went forth upon the streets in the drizzle to see what might be there.

It is built on undulating grounds; and the streets are lighted by electricity at a cost of $32,470 per annum.

As I left the hotel there was a race riot. Down upon me charged a company of freedmen, or Arabs, or Zulus, armed with – no, I saw with relief that they were not rifles, but whips. And I saw dimly a caravan of black, clumsy vehicles; and at the reassuring shouts, 'Kyar you anywhere in the town, boss, fuh fifty cents,' I reasoned that I was merely a 'fare' instead of a victim.

I walked through long streets, all leading uphill. I wondered how those streets ever came down again. Perhaps they didn't until they were 'graded.' On a few of the 'main streets' I saw lights in stores here and there; saw street-cars go by conveying worthy burghers hither and yon, saw people pass engaged in the art of conversation, and heard a burst of semi-lively laughter issuing from a soda-water and ice-cream parlour. The streets other than 'main' seemed to have enticed upon their borders houses consecrated to peace and domesticity. In many of them lights shone behind discreetly drawn window shades; in a few pianos tinkled orderly and irreproachable music. There was, indeed, little 'doing.' I wished I had come before sundown. So I returned to my hotel.

In November, 1864, the Confederate General Hood advanced against Nashville, where he shut up a National force under General Thomas. The latter then sallied forth and defeated the confederates in a terrible conflict.

All my life I have heard of, admired, and witnessed the fine markmanship of the South in its peaceful conflicts in the tobacco-chewing regions. But in my hotel a surprise awaited me. There were twelve bright, new, imposing, capacious brass cuspidors in the great lobby, tall enough to be called urns and so wide-mouthed that the crack pitcher of a lady baseball team should

have been able to throw a ball into one of them at five paces distant. But, although a terrible battle had raged and was still raging,
the enemy had not suffered. Bright, new, imposing, capacious,
untouched, they stood. But shades of Jefferson Brick! the tile
floor – the beautiful tile floor! I could not avoid thinking of the
battle of Nashville, and trying to draw, as is my foolish habit,
some deductions about hereditary markmanship.

Here I first saw Major (by misplaced courtesy) Wentworth
Caswell. I knew him for a type the moment my eyes suffered from
the sight of him. A rat has no geographical habitat. My old friend,
A. Tennyson, said, as he so well said almost everything:

> 'Prophet, curse me the blabbing lip,
> And curse me the British vermin, the rat.'

Let us regard the word 'British' as interchangeable *ad lib*. A rat
is a rat.

This man was hunting about the hotel lobby like a starved dog
that had forgotten where he had buried a bone. He had a face of
great acreage, red, pulpy, and with a kind of sleepy massiveness
like that of Buddha. He possessed one single virtue – he was very
smoothly shaven. The mark of the beast is not indelible upon a
man until he goes about with a stubble. I think that if he had not
used his razor that day I would have repulsed his advances, and the
criminal calendar of the world would have been spared the addition of one murder.

I happened to be standing within five feet of a cuspidor when
Major Caswell opened fire upon it. I had been observant enough
to perceive that the attacking force was using Gatlings instead of
squirrel rifles; so I side-stepped so promptly that the major seized
the opportunity to apologize to a non-combatant. He had the
blabbing lip. In four minutes he had become my friend and had
dragged me to the bar.

I desire to interpolate here that I am a Southerner. But I am not
one by profession or trade. I eschew the string tie, the slouch hat,
the Prince Albert, the number of bales of cotton destroyed by
Sherman, and plug chewing. When the orchestra plays Dixie I do
not cheer. I slide a little lower on the leather-cornered seat and,
well, order another Würzburger and wish that Longstreet had –
but what's the use?

Major Caswell banged the bar with his fist, and the first gun at
Fort Sumter re-echoed. When he fired the last one at Appomattox

I began to hope. But then he began on family trees, and demonstrated that Adam was only a third cousin of a collateral branch of the Caswell family. Genealogy disposed of, he took up, to my distaste, his private family matters. He spoke of his wife, traced her descent back to Eve, and profanely denied any possible rumour that she may have had relations in the land of Nod.

By this time I began to suspect that he was trying to obscure by noise the fact that he had ordered the drinks, on the chance that I would be bewildered into paying for them. But when they were down he crashed a silver dollar loudly upon the bar. Then, of course, another serving was obligatory. And when I had paid for that I took leave of him brusquely; for I wanted no more of him. But before I had obtained my release he had prated loudly of an income that his wife received, and showed a handful of silver money.

When I got my key at the desk the clerk said to me courteously: 'If that man Caswell has annoyed you, and if you would like to make a complaint, we will have him ejected. He is a nuisance, a loafer, and without any known means of support, although he seems to have some money most the time. But we don't seem to be able to hit upon any means of throwing him out legally.'

'Why, no,' said I, after some reflection; 'I don't see my way clear to making a complaint. But I would like to place myself on record as asserting that I do not care for his company. Your town,' I continued, 'seems to be a quiet one. What manner of entertainment, adventure, or excitement have you to offer to the stranger within your gates?'

'Well, sir,' said the clerk, 'there will be a show here next Thursday. It is — I'll look it up and have the announcement sent up to your room with the ice water. Good night.'

After I went up to my room I looked out of the window. It was only about ten o'clock, but I looked upon a silent town. The drizzle continued, spangled with dim lights, as far apart as currants in a cake sold at the Ladies' Exchange.

'A quiet place,' I said to myself, as my first shoe struck the ceiling of the occupant of the room beneath mine. 'Nothing of the life here that gives colour and variety to the cities in the East and West. Just a good, ordinary, humdrum business town.'

Nashville occupies a foremost place among the manufacturing centres of the country. It is the fifth boot and shoe market in the United States, the largest candy and cracker manufacturing city in the South, and does an enormous wholesale dry goods, grocery and drug business.

I must tell you how I came to be in Nashville, and assure you the digression brings as much tedium to me as it does to you. I was travelling elsewhere on my own business, but I had a commission from a Northern literary magazine to stop over there and establish a personal connection between the publication and one of its contributors, Azalea Adair.

Adair (there was no clue to the personality except the handwriting) had sent in some essays (lost art!) and poems that had made the editors swear approvingly over their one o'clock luncheon. So they had commissioned me to round up said Adair and corner by contract his or her output at two cents a word before some other publisher offered her ten or twenty.

At nine o'clock the next morning, after my chicken livers *en brochette* (try them if you can find that hotel), I strayed out into the drizzle, which was still on for an unlimited run. At the first corner I came upon Uncle Cæsar. He was a stalwart negro, older than the pyramids, with grey wool and a face that reminded me of Brutus, and a second afterwards of the late King Cetewayo. He wore the most remarkable coat that I ever had seen or expect to see. It reached to his ankles and had once been a Confederate grey in colours. But rain and sun and age had so variegated it that Joseph's coat, beside it, would have faded to a pale monochrome. I must linger with that coat for it has to do with the story – the story that is so long in coming, because you can hardly expect anything to happen in Nashville.

Once it must have been the military coat of an officer. The cape of it had vanished, but all adown its front it had been frogged and tasselled magnificently. But now the frogs and tassels were gone. In their stead had been patiently stitched (I surmised by some surviving 'black mammy') new frogs made of cunningly twisted common hempen twine. This twine was frayed and dishevelled. It must have been added to the coat as a substitute for vanished splendours, with tasteless but painstaking devotion, for it followed faithfully the curves of the long-missing frogs. And, to complete the comedy and pathos of the garment, all its buttons were gone save one. The second button from the top alone remained. The coat was fastened by other twine strings tied through the buttonholes and other holes rudely pierced in the opposite side. There was never such a weird garment so fantastically bedecked and of so many mottled hues. The lone button was the size of a half-dollar, made of yellow horn and sewed on with coarse twine.

This negro stood by a carriage so old that Ham himself might have started a hack line with it after he left the ark with the two animals hitched to it. As I approached he threw open the door, drew out a leather duster, waved it, without using it, and said in deep, rumbling tones:

'Step right in, suh; ain't a speck of dust in it – jus' back from a funeral, suh.'

I inferred that on such gala occasions carriages were given an extra cleaning. I looked up and down the street and perceived that there was little choice among the vehicles for hire that lined the kerb. I looked in my memorandum book for the address of Azalea Adair.

'I want to go to 861 Jessamine Street,' I said, and was about to step into the hack. But for an instant the thick, long, gorilla-like arm of the old negro barred me. On his massive and saturnine face a look of sudden suspicion and enmity flashed for a moment. Then, with quickly returning conviction, he asked blandishingly:

'What are you gwine there for, boss?'

'What is that to you?' I asked a little sharply.

'Nothin', suh, jus' nothin'. Only it's a lonesome kind of part of town and few folks ever has business out there. Step right in. The seats is clean – jes' got back from a funeral, suh.'

A mile and a half it must have been to our journey's end. I could hear nothing but the fearful rattle of the ancient hack over the uneven brick paving; I could smell nothing but the drizzle, now further flavoured with coal smoke and something like a mixture of tar and oleander blossoms. All I could see through the streaming windows were two rows of dim houses.

The city has an area of 10 square miles; 181 miles of streets, of which 137 miles are paved; a system of waterworks that cost $2,000,000, with 77 miles of mains.

Eight-sixty-one Jessamine Street was a decayed mansion. Thirty yards back from the street it stood, outmerged in a splendid grove of trees and untrimmed shrubbery. A row of box bushes overflowed and almost hid the paling fence from sight; the gate was kept closed by a rope noose that encircled the gate post and the first paling of the gate. But when you got inside you saw that 861 was a shell, a shadow, a ghost of former grandeur and excellence. But in the story, I have not yet got inside.

When the hack had ceased from rattling and the weary quadrupeds came to a rest I handed my jehu his fifty cents with an additional quarter, feeling a glow of conscious generosity as I did so. He refused it.

'It's two dollars, suh,' he said.

'How's that?' I asked. 'I plainly heard you call out at the hotel: "Fifty cents to any part of the town." '

'It's two dollars, suh,' he repeated obstinately. 'It's a long ways from the hotel.'

'It is within the city limits and well within them,' I argued. 'Don't think that you have picked up a greenhorn Yankee. Do you see those hills over there?' I went on, pointing toward the east (I could not see them, myself, for the drizzle); 'well, I was born and raised on their other side. You old fool nigger, can't you tell people from other people when you see em?'

The grim face of King Cetewayo softened. 'Is you from the South, suh? I reckon it was them shoes of yourn fooied me. There is somethin' sharp in the toes for a Southern gen'l'man to wear.'

'Then the charge is fifty cents, I suppose?' said I inexorably.

His former expression, a mingling of cupidity and hostility, returned, remained ten minutes, and vanished.

'Boss,' he said, 'fifty cents is right; but *I needs* two dollars, suh; I'm *obleeged* to have two dollars. I ain't *demandin'* it now, suh; after I knows whar you's from; I'm jus' sayin' that I *has* to have two dollars to-night, and business is mighty po'.'

Peace and confidence settled upon his heavy features. He had been luckier than he had hoped. Instead of having picked up a greenhorn, ignorant of rates, he had come upon an inheritance.

'You confounded old rascal,' I said, reaching down into my pocket, 'you ought to be turned over to the police.'

For the first time I saw him smile. He knew; *he knew;* HE KNEW.

I gave him two one-dollar bills. As I handed them over I noticed that one of them had seen parlous times. Its upper right-hand corner was missing, and it had been torn through in the middle but joined again. A strip of blue tissue-paper, pasted over the split, preserved its negotiability.

Enough of the African bandit for the present: I left him happy, lifted the rope and opened the creaky gate.

The house, as I said, was a shell. A paint-brush had not touched it in twenty years. I could not see why a strong wind should not have bowled it over like a house of cards until I looked again at the trees that hugged it close − the trees that saw the battle of Nashville and still drew their protecting branches around it against storm and enemy and cold.

Azalea Adair, fifty years old, white-haired, a descendant of the cavaliers, as thin and frail as the house she lived in, robed in the cheapest and cleanest dress I ever saw, with an air as simple as a queen's, received me.

The reception-room seemed a mile square, because there was nothing in it except some rows of books, on unpainted, white-pine bookshelves, a cracked, marble-top table, a rag rug, a hairless horse-hair sofa and two or three chairs. Yes, there was a picture on the wall, a coloured crayon drawing of a cluster of pansies. I looked around for the portrait of Andrew Jackson and the pine-cone hanging basket, but they were not there.

Azalea Adair and I had conversation, a little of which will be repeated to you. She was a product of the old South, gently nur-tured in the sheltered life. Her learning was not broad, but was deep and of splendid originality in its somewhat narrow scope. She had been educated at home, and her knowledge of the world was derived from inference and by inspiration. Of such is the precious, small group of essayists made. While she talked to me, I kept brushing my fingers, trying, unconsciously, to rid them guiltily of the absent dust from the half-calf backs of Lamb, Chaucer, Hazlitt, Marcus Aurelius, Montaigne and Hood. She was exquis-ite, she was a valuable discovery. Nearly everybody nowadays knows too much — oh, so much too much — of real life.

I could perceive clearly that Azalea Adair was very poor. A house and a dress she had, not much else, I fancied. So, divided between my duty to the magazine and my loyalty to the poets and essayists who fought Thomas in the valley of the Cumberland, I listened to her voice, which was like a harpsichord's, and found that I could not speak of contracts. In the presence of the Nine Muses and the Three Graces one hesitated to lower the topic to two cents. There would have to be another colloquy after I had regained my commercialism. But I spoke of my mission, and three o'clock of the next afternoon was set for the discussion of the business proposition

'Your town,' I said, as I began to make ready to depart (which is the time for smooth generalities), 'seems to be a quiet, sedate place. A home town, I should say, where few things out of the ordinary ever happen.'

It carries on an extensive trade in stoves and hollow ware with the West and South, and its flouring mills have a daily capacity of more than 2,000 barrels.

Azalea Adair seemed to reflect.

'I have never thought of it that way,' she said, with a kind of sincere intensity that seemed to belong to her. 'Isn't it in the still, quiet places that things do happen? I fancy that when God began to create the earth on the first Monday morning one could have leaned out one's windows and heard the drop of mud splashing from His trowel as He built up the everlasting hills. What did the noisiest project in the world – I mean the building of the tower of Babel – result in finally? A page and a half of Esperanto in the *North American Review.*'

'Of course,' said I platitudinously, 'human nature is the same everywhere; but there is more colour – er – more drama and movement and – er – romance in some cities than in others.'

'On the surface,' said Azalea Adair. 'I have travelled many times around the world in a golden airship wafted on two wings – print and dreams. I have seen (on one of my imaginary tours) the Sultan of Turkey bow-string with his own hands one of his wives who had uncovered her face in public. I have seen a man in Nashville tear up his theatre tickets because his wife was going out with her face covered – with rice powder. In San Francisco's Chinatown I saw the slave girl Sing Yee dipped slowly, inch by inch, in boiling almond oil to make her swear she would never see her American lover again. She gave in when the boiling oil had reached three inches above her knee. At a euchre party in East Nashville the other night I saw Kitty Morgan cut dead by seven of her schoolmates and lifelong friends because she had married a house painter. The boiling oil was sizzling as high as her heart; but I wish you could have seen the fine little smile that she carried from table to table. Oh yes, it is a humdrum town. Just a few miles of redbrick houses and mud and stores and lumber yards.'

Someone knocked hollowly at the back of the house. Azalea Adair breathed a soft apology and went to investigate the sound. She came back in three minutes with brightened eyes, a faint flush on her cheeks, and ten years lifted from her shoulders.

'You must have a cup of tea before you go,' she said, 'and a sugar cake.'

She reached and shook a little iron bell. In shuffled a small negro girl about twelve, bare-foot, not very tidy, glowering at me with thumb in mouth and bulging eyes.

Azalea Adair opened a tiny, worn purse and drew out a dollar bill, a dollar bill with the upper right-hand corner missing, torn in two pieces and pasted together again with a strip of blue tissue-paper. It was one of the bills I had given the piratical negro – there was no doubt of it.

'Go up to Mr. Baker's store on the corner, Impy,' she said, handing the girl the dollar bill, 'and get a quarter of a pound of tea – the kind he always sends me – and ten cents worth of sugar cakes. Now, hurry. The supply of tea in the house happens to be exhausted,' she explained to me.

Impy left by the back way. Before the scrape of her hard, bare feet had died away on the back porch, a wild shriek – I was sure it was hers – filled the hollow house. Then the deep, gruff tones of an angry man's voice mingled with the girl's further squeals and unintelligible words.

Azalea Adair rose without surprise or emotion and disappeared. For two minutes I heard the hoarse rumble of the man's voice; then something like an oath and a light scuffle, and she returned calmly to her chair.

'This is a roomy house,' she said, 'and I have a tenant for part of it. I am sorry to have to rescind my invitation to tea. It was impossible to get the kind I always use at the store. Perhaps to-morrow Mr. Baker will be able to supply me.'

I was sure that Impy had not had time to leave the house. I inquired concerning street-car lines and took my leave. After I was well on my way I remembered that I had not learned Azalea Adair's name. But to-morrow would do.

That same day I started in on the course of iniquity that this uneventful city forced upon me. I was in the town only two days, but in that time I managed to lie shamelessly by telegraph, and to be an accomplice – after the fact, if that is the correct legal term – to a murder.

As I rounded the corner nearest my hotel the Afrite coachman of the polychromatic, nonpareil coat seized me, swung open the dungeony door of his peripatetic sarcophagus, flirted his feather duster and began his ritual: 'Step right in, boss. Carriage is clean – jus' got back from a funeral. Fifty cents to any –'

And then he knew me and grinned broadly. ' 'Scuse me, boss; you is de gen'l'man what rid out with me dis mawnin'. Thank you kindly, suh.'

'I am going out to 861 again to-morrow afternoon at three,' said I, 'and if you will be here, I'll let you drive me. So you know Miss Adair?' I concluded, thinking of my dollar bill.

'I belonged to her father, Judge Adair, suh,' he replied.

'I judge that she is pretty poor,' I said. 'She hasn't much money to speak of, has she?'

For an instant I looked again at the fierce countenance of King Cetewayo, and then he changed back to an extortionate old negro hack-driver.

'She a'n't gwine to starve, suh,' he said slowly. 'She has reso'ces, suh; she has reso'ces.'

'I shall pay you fifty cents for the trip,' said I.

'Dat is puffeckly correct, suh,' he answered humbly; 'I jus' *had* to have dat two dollars dis mawnin, boss.'

I went to the hotel and lied by electricity. I wired the magazine: 'A. Adair holds out for eight cents a word.'

The answer that came back was: 'Give it to her quick, you duffer.'

Just before dinner 'Major' Wentworth Caswell bore down upon me with the greetings of a long-lost friend. I have seen few men whom I have so instantaneously hated, and of whom it was so difficult to be rid. I was standing at the bar when he invaded me; therefore I could not wave the white ribbon in his face. I would have paid gladly for the drinks, hoping thereby to escape another, but he was one of those despicable, roaring, advertising bibbers who must have brass bands and fireworks attend upon every cent that they waste in their follies.

With an air of producing millions he drew two one-dollar bills from a pocket and dashed one of them upon the bar. I looked once more at the dollar bill with the upper right-hand corner missing, torn through the middle, and patched with a strip of blue tissue-paper. It was my dollar bill again. It could have been no other.

I went up to my room. The drizzle and the monotony of a dreary, eventless Southern town had made me tired and listless. I remember that just before I went to bed I mentally disposed of the mysterious dollar bill (which might have formed the clue to a tremendously fine detective story of San Francisco) by saying to myself sleepily: 'Seems as if a lot of people here own stock in the Hack-Driver's Trust. Pays dividends promptly, too. Wonder if –' Then I fell asleep.

King Cetewayo was at his post the next day, and rattled my bones over the stones out to 861. He was to wait and rattle me back again when I was ready.

Azalea Adair looked paler and cleaner and frailer than she had looked on the day before. After she had signed the contract at eight cents per word she grew still paler and began to slip out of her chair.

Without much trouble I managed to get her up on the antediluvian horsehair sofa and then I ran out to the sidewalk and yelled to the coffee-coloured Pirate to bring a doctor. With a wisdom that I had not suspected in him, he abandoned his team and struck off up the street afoot, realizing the value of speed. In ten minutes he returned with a grave, grey-haired and capable man of medicine. In a few words (worth much less than eight cents each) I explained to him my presence in the hollow house of mystery. He bowed with stately understanding, and turned to the old negro.

'Uncle Cæsar,' he said calmly, 'run up to my house and ask Miss Lucy to give you a cream pitcher full of fresh milk and half a tumbler of port wine. And hurry back. Don't drive – run. I want you to get back some time this week.'

It occurred to me that Dr. Merriman also felt a distrust as to the speeding powers of the landpirate's steeds. After Uncle Cæsar was gone, lumberingly, but swiftly, up the street, the doctor looked me over with great politeness and as much careful calculation until he had decided that I might do.

'It is only a case of insufficient nutrition,' he said. 'In other words, the result of poverty, pride, and starvation. Mrs. Caswell has many devoted friends who would be glad to aid her, but she will accept nothing except from that old negro, Uncle Cæsar, who was once owned by her family.'

'Mrs. Caswell!' said I, in surprise. And then I looked at the contract and saw that she had signed it 'Azalea Adair Caswell.'

'I thought she was Miss Adair,' I said.

'Married to a drunken, worthless loafer, sir,' said the doctor. 'It is said that he robs her even of the small sums that her old servant contributes toward her support.'

When the milk and wine had been brought, the doctor soon revived Azalea Adair. She sat up and talked of the beauty of the autumn leaves that were then in season, and their height of colour. She referred lightly to her fainting seizure as the outcome of an old palpitation of the heart. Impy fanned her as she lay on the sofa. The doctor was due elsewhere, and I followed him to the door. I told him that it was within my power and intentions to make a reasonable advance of money to Azalea Adair on future contributions to the magazine, and he seemed pleased.

'By the way,' he said, 'perhaps you would like to know that you have had royalty for a coachman. Old Cæsar's grandfather was a king in Congo. Cæsar himself has royal ways, as you may have observed.'

As the doctor was moving off I heard Uncle Cæsar's voice inside: 'Did he git bofe of dem two dollars from you, Mis' Zalea?'

'Yes, Cæsar,' I heard Azalea Adair answer weakly. And then I went in and concluded business negotiations with our contributor. I assumed the responsibility of advancing fifty dollars, putting it as a necessary formality in binding our bargain. And then Uncle Cæsar drove me back to the hotel.

Here ends all the story as far as I can testify as a witness. The rest must be only bare statements of facts.

At about six o'clock I went out for a stroll. Uncle Cæsar was at his corner. He threw open the door of his carriage, flourished his duster and began his depressing formula: 'Step right in, suh. Fifty cents to anywhere in the city – hack's puffickly clean, suh – jus' got back from a funeral –'

And then he recognized me. I think his eyesight was getting bad. His coat had taken on a few more faded shades of colour, the twine strings were more frayed and ragged, the last remaining button – the button of yellow horn – was gone. A motley descendant of kings was Uncle Cæsar.

About two hours later I saw an excited crowd besieging the front of a drug store. In a desert where nothing happens this was manna; so I edged my way inside. On an extemporized couch of empty boxes and chairs was stretched the mortal corporeality of Major Wentworth Caswell. A doctor was testing him for the immortal ingredient. His decision was that it was conspicuous by its absence.

The erstwhile Major had been found dead on a dark street and brought by curious and ennuied citizens to the drug store. The late human being had been engaged in terrific battle – the details showed that. Loafer and reprobate though he had been, he had been also a warrior. But he had lost. His hands were yet clenched so tightly that his fingers would not be opened. The gentle citizens who had known him stood about and searched their vocabularies to find some good words, if it were possible, to speak of him. One kind-looking man said, after much thought: 'When "Cas" was about fo'teen he was one of the best spellers in school.'

While I stood there the fingers of the right hand of 'the man that was,' which hung down the side of a white pine box, relaxed, and dropped something at my feet. I covered it with one foot quietly, and a little later on I picked it up and pocketed it. I reasoned that in his last struggle his hand must have seized that object unwittingly and held it in a death-grip.

O HENRY – 100 SELECTED STORIES   321

At the hotel that night the main topic of conversation, with the possible exceptions of politics and prohibition, was the demise of Major Caswell. I heard one man say to a group of listeners:

'In my opinion, gentlemen, Caswell was murdered by some of these no-account niggers for his money. He had fifty dollars this afternoon which he showed to several gentlemen in the hotel. When he was found the money was not on his person.'

I left the city the next morning at nine, and as the train was crossing the bridge over the Cumberland River I took out of my pocket a yellow, horn, overcoat button the size of a fifty-cent piece, with frayed ends of coarse twine hanging from it, and cast it out of the window into the slow, muddy waters below.

I wonder what's doing in Buffalo!

LI

Compliments of the Season

THERE ARE NO MORE Christmas stories to write. Fiction is exhausted; and newspaper items the next best, are manufactured by clever young Journalists who have married early and have an engagingly pessimistic view of life. Therefore, for seasonable diversion, we are reduced to two very questionable sources – facts and philosophy. We will begin with – whichever you choose to call it.

Children are pestilential little animals with which we have to cope under a bewildering variety of conditions. Especially when childish sorrows overwhelm them are we put to our wits' end. We exhaust our paltry store of consolation; and then beat them, sobbing, to sleep. Then we grovel in the dust of a million years, and ask God why. Thus we call out of the rat-trap. As for the children, no one understands them except old maids, hunchbacks, and shepherd dogs.

Now come the facts in the case of the Rag-Doll, the Tatterdemalion, and the Twenty-fifth of December.

On the tenth of that month the Child of the Millionaire lost her rag-doll. There were many servants in the Millionaire's palace on the Hudson, and these ransacked the house and grounds, but without finding the lost treasure. The Child was a girl of five, and one of those perverse little beasts that often wound the sensibilities of wealthy parents by fixing their affections upon some vulgar, inexpensive toy instead of upon diamond-studded automobiles and pony phætons.

The Child grieved sorely and truly, a thing inexplicable to the Millionaire, to whom the rag-doll market was about as interesting as Bay State Gas; and to the Lady, the Child's mother, who was all for form – that is, nearly all, as you shall see.

The Child cried inconsolably, and grew holloweyed, knock-kneed, spindling, and cory-kilverty in many other respects. The Millionaire smiled and tapped his coffers confidently. The pick of the output of the French and German toymakers was rushed by special delivery to the mansion; but Rachel refused to be comforted. She was weeping for her rag child, and was for a high protective tariff against all foreign foolishness. Then doctors with the finest bedside manners and stop-watches were called in. One by one they chattered futilely about peptomanganate of iron and sea voyages and hypophosphites until their stop-watches showed that Bill Rendered was under the wire for show or place. Then, as men, they advised that the rag-doll be found as soon as possible and restored to its mourning parent. The Child sniffed at therapeutics, chewed a thumb, and wailed for her Betsy. And all this time cablegrams were coming from Santa Claus saying that he would soon be here and enjoining us to show a true Christian spirit and let up on the pool-rooms and tontine policies and platoon systems long enough to give him a welcome. Everywhere the spirit of Christmas was diffusing itself. The banks were refusing loans, the pawnbrokers had doubled their gang of helpers, people bumped your shins on the streets with red sleds, Thomas and Jeremiah bubbled before you on the bars while you waited on one foot, hollywreaths of hospitality were hung in windows of the stores, they who had 'em were getting out their furs. You hardly knew which was the best bet in balls – three, high, moth, or snow. It was no time at which to lose the rag-doll of your heart.

If Doctor Watson's investigating friend had been called in to solve this mysterious disappearance, he might have observed on the Millionaire's wall a copy of 'The Vampire.' That would have quickly suggested, by induction, 'A rag and a bone and a hank of hair.' 'Flip,' a Scotch terrier, next to the ragdoll in the Child's heart, frisked through the halls. The hank of hair! Aha! X, the unfound quantity, represented the rag-doll. But, the bone? Well, when dogs find bones they – Done! It were an easy and a fruitful task to examine Flip's fore-feet. Look, Watson! Earth – dried earth between the toes. Of course, the dog – but Sherlock was not there. Therefore it devolves. But topography and architecture must intervene.

The millionaire's palace occupied a lordly space. In front of it was a lawn close-mowed as a South Ireland man's face two days after a shave. At one side of it, and fronting on another street, was a pleasaunce trimmed to a leaf, and the garage and stables. The Scotch pup had ravished the rag-doll from the nursery, dragged it to a corner of the lawn, dug a hole, and buried it after the manner of careless undertakers. There you have the mystery solved, and no cheques to write for the hypodermical wizard or fi'-pun notes to toss to the sergeant. Then let's get down to the heart of the thing, tiresome readers — the Christmas heart of the thing.

Fuzzy was drunk — not riotously or helplessly or loquaciously, as you or I might get, but decently, appropriately, and inoffensively, as becomes a gentleman down on his luck.

Fuzzy was a soldier of misfortune. The road, the haystack, the park bench, the kitchen door, the bitter round of eleemosynary beds-with-shower-bath-attachment, the petty pickings and ignobly garnered largesse of great cities — these formed the chapters of his history.

Fuzzy walked toward the river, down the street that bounded one side of the Millionaire's house and grounds. He saw a leg of Betsy, the lost rag-doll, protruding, like the clue to a Lilliputian murder mystery, from its untimely grave in a corner of the fence. He dragged forth the maltreated infant, tucked it under his arm, and went on his way crooning a road song of his brethren that no doll that has been brought up to the sheltered life should hear. Well for Betsy that she had no ears. And well that she had no eyes save unseeing circles of black; for the faces of Fuzzy and the Scotch terrier were those of brothers, and the heart of no rag-doll could withstand twice to become the prey of such fearsome monsters.

Though you may not know it, Grogan's saloon stands near the river and near the foot of the street down which Fuzzy travelled. In Grogan's, Christmas cheer was already rampant

Fuzzy entered with his doll. He fancied that as a mummer at the feast of Saturn he might earn a few drops from the wassail cup.

He set Betsy on the bar and addressed her loudly and humorously, seasoning his speech with exaggerated compliments and endearments, as one entertaining his lady friend. The loafers and bibbers around caught the farce of it, and roared. The bartender gave Fuzzy a drink. Oh, many of us carry rag-dolls.

'One for the lady?' suggested Fuzzy impudently, and tucked another contribution to Art beneath his waistcoat.

He began to see possibilities in Betsy. His first night had been a success. Visions of a vaudeville circuit about town dawned upon him.

In a group near the stove sat 'Pigeon' McCarthy, Black Riley, and 'One-ear' Mike, well and unfavourably known in the tough shoestring district that blackened the left bank of the river. They passed a newspaper back and forth among themselves. The item that each solid and blunt forefinger pointed out was an advertisement headed 'One Hundred Dollars Reward.' To earn it one must return the rag-doll, lost, strayed, or stolen from the Millionaire's mansion. It seemed that grief still ravaged, unchecked, in the bosom of the too faithful Child. Flip, the terrier, capered and shook his absurd whisker before her, powerless to distract. She wailed for her Betsy in the faces of walking, talking, mama-ing, and eye-closing French Mabelles and Violettes. The advertisement was a last resort.

Black Riley came from behind the stove and approached Fuzzy in his one-sided parabolic way.

The Christmas mummer, flushed with success, had tucked Betsy under his arm, and was about to depart to the filling of impromptu dates elsewhere.

'Say, Bo',' said Black Riley to him, 'where did you cop out dat doll?'

'This doll?' asked Fuzzy, touching Betsy with his forefinger to be sure that she was the one referred to. 'Why, this doll was presented to me by the Emperor of Beloochistan. I have seven hundred others in my country home in Newport. This doll –'

'Cheese the funny business,' said Riley. 'You swiped it or picked it up at de house on de hill where – but never mind dat. You want to take fifty cents for de rags, and take it quick. Me brother's kid at home might be wantin' to play wid it. Hey – what?'

He produced the coin.

Fuzzy laughed a gurgling, insolent, alcoholic laugh in his face. Go to the office of Sarah Bernhardt's manager and propose to him that she be released from a night's performance to entertain the Tackytown Lyceum and Literary Coterie. You will hear the duplicate of Fuzzy's laugh.

Black Riley gauged Fuzzy quickly with his blueberry eye as a wrestler does. His hand was itching to play the Roman and wrest the rag Sabine from the extemporaneous merry-andrew who was entertaining an angel unaware. But he refrained. Fuzzy was fat and solid and big. Three inches of well-nourished corporeity, defended from the winter winds by dingy linen, intervened between his vest and trousers. Countless small, circular wrinkles running around his coat-sleeves and knees guaranteed the quality of his bone and muscle. His small, blue eyes, bathed in the moisture of altruism and wooziness, looked upon you kindly, yet without abashment. He was whiskerly, whiskyly, fleshily formidable. So, Black Riley temporized.

'Wot'll you take for it, den?' he asked

'Money,' said Fuzzy, with husky firmness, 'cannot buy her.'

He was intoxicated with the artist's first sweet cup of attainment. To set a faded-blue, earthstained rag-doll on a bar, to hold mimic converse with it, and to find his heart leaping with the sense of plaudits earned and his throat scorching with free libations poured in his honour – could base coin buy him from such achievements? You will perceive that Fuzzy had the temperament.

Fuzzy walked out with the gait of a trained sealion in search of other cafés to conquer.

Though the dusk of twilight was hardly yet apparent, lights were beginning to spangle the city like pop-corn bursting in a deep skillet. Christmas Eve, impatiently expected, was peeping over the brink of the hour. Millions had prepared for its celebration. Towns would be painted red. You yourself, have heard the horns and dodged the capers of the Saturnalians.

'Pigeon' McCarthy, Black Riley, and 'One-ear' Mike held a hasty converse outside Grogan's. They were narrow-chested, pallid striplings, not fighters in the open, but more dangerous in their ways of warfare than the most terrible of Turks. Fuzzy, in a pitched battle, could have eaten the three of them. In a go-as-you-please encounter, he was already doomed.

They overtook him just as he and Betsy were entering Costigan's Casino. They deflected him, and shoved the newspaper under his nose. Fuzzy could read – and more.

'Boys,' said he, 'you are certainly damn true friends. Give me a week to think it over.'

The soul of a real artist is quenched with difficulty.

The boys carefully pointed out to him that advertisements were soulless, and that the deficiencies of the day might not be supplied by the morrow.

'A cool hundred,' said Fuzzy thoughtfully and mushily.

'Boys,' said he, 'you are true friends. I'll go up and claim the reward. The show business is not what it used to be.'

Night was falling more surely. The three tagged at his sides to the foot of the rise on which stood the Millionaire's house. There Fuzzy turned upon them acrimoniously.

'You are a pack of putty-faced beagle-hounds,' he roared. 'Go away.'

They went away – a little way.

In 'Pigeon' McCarthy's pocket was a section of one-inch gas-pipe, eight inches long. In one end of it and in the middle of it was a lead plug. One half of it was packed tight with solder. Black Riley carried a slung-shot, being a conventional thug. 'One-ear' Mike relied upon a pair of brass knucks – an heirloom in the family.

'Why fetch and carry,' said Black Riley, 'when someone will do it for ye? Let him bring it out to us. Hey – what?'

'We can chuck him in the river,' said 'Pigeon' McCarthy, 'with a stone tied to his feet.'

'Youse guys make me tired,' said 'One-ear' Mike sadly. 'Ain't progress ever appealed to none of yez? Sprinkle a little gasoline on 'im, and drop 'im on the Drive – well?'

Fuzzy entered the Millionaire's gate and zigzagged toward the softly glowing entrance of the mansion. The three goblins came up to the gate and lingered – one on each side of it, one beyond the roadway. They fingered their cold metal and leather, confident.

Fuzzy rang the door-bell, smiling foolishly and dreamily. An atavistic instinct prompted him to reach for the button of his right glove. But he wore no gloves; so his left hand dropped, embarrassed.

The particular menial whose duty it was to open doors to silks and laces shied at first sight of Fuzzy. But a second glance took in his passport, his card of admission, his surety of welcome – the lost ragdoll of the daughter of the house dangling under his arm.

Fuzzy was admitted into a great hall, dim with the glow from unseen lights. The hireling went away and returned with a maid and the Child. The doll was restored to the mourning one. She clasped her lost darling to her breast; and then, with the inordinate selfishness and candour of childhood, stamped her foot and whined hatred and fear of the odious being who had rescued her from the depths of sorrow and despair. Fuzzy wriggled himself into an ingratiatory attitude and essayed the idiotic smile and blattering small-talk that is supposed to charm the budding intellect of the young. The Child bawled, and was dragged away, hugging her Betsy close.

There came the Secretary, pale, poised, polished, gliding in pumps, and worshipping pomp and ceremony. He counted out into Fuzzy's hand ten ten-dollar bills; then dropped his eye upon the door, transferred it to James, its custodian, indicated the obnoxious earner of the reward with the other, and allowed his pumps to waft him away to secretarial regions.

James gathered Fuzzy with his own commanding optic and swept him as far as the front door.

When the money touched Fuzzy's dingy palm his first instinct was to take to his heels; but a second thought restrained him from that blunder of etiquette. It was his; it had been given him. It – and, oh, what an elysium it opened to the gaze of his mind's eye! He had tumbled to the foot of the ladder; he was hungry, home-less, friendless, ragged, cold, drifting; and he held in his hand the key to a paradise of the mud-honey that he craved. The fairy doll had waved a wand with her rag-stuffed hand; and now wherever he might go the enchanted palaces with shining foot-rests and magic red fluids in gleaming glassware would be open to him.

He followed James to the door.

He paused there as the flunkey drew open the great mahogany portal for him to pass into the vestibule.

Beyond the wrought-iron gates in the dark highway Black Riley and his two pals casually strolled, fingering under their coats the inevitably fatal weapons that were to make the reward of the rag-doll theirs.

Fuzzy stopped at the Millionaire's door and bethought himself. Like little sprigs of mistletoe on a dead tree, certain living green thoughts and memories began to decorate his confused mind. He was quite drunk, mind you, and the present was beginning to fade. Those wreaths and festoons of holly with their scarlet berries making the great hall gay – where had he seen such things before? Somewhere he had known polished floors and odours of fresh flowers in winter, and – and someone was singing a song in the house that he thought he had heard before. Someone was singing and playing a harp. Of course, it was Christmas – Fuzzy thought he must have been pretty drunk to have overlooked that.

And then he went out of the present, and there came back to him out of some impossible, vanished, and irrevocable past a little, pure white, transient, forgotten ghost – the spirit of *noblesse oblige*. Upon a gentleman certain things devolve.

James opened the outer door. A stream of light went down the gravelled walk to the iron gate. Black Riley, McCarthy, and 'One-

ear' Mike saw, and carelessly drew their sinister cordon closer
about the gate.

With a more imperious gesture than James's master had ever
used or ever could use, Fuzzy compelled the menial to close the
door. Upon a gentleman certain things devolve. Especially at the
Christmas season.

'It is cust – custormary,' he said to James, the flustered, 'when a
gentleman calls on Christmas Eve to pass the compliments of the
season with the lady of the house. You und'stand? I shall not move
shtep till I pass compl'ments season with lady the house.
Und'stand?'

There was an argument. James lost. Fuzzy raised his voice and
sent it through the house unpleasantly. I did not say he was a
gentleman. He was simply a tramp being visited by a ghost.

A sterling-silver bell rang. James went back to answer it, leaving
Fuzzy in the hall James explained somewhere to someone.

Then he came and conducted Fuzzy into the library.

The lady entered a moment later. She was more beautiful and
holy than any picture that Fuzzy had seen. She smiled, and said
something about a doll. Fuzzy didn't understand that; he
remembered nothing about a doll.

A footman brought in two small glasses of sparkling wine on a
stamped sterling-silver waiter. The Lady took one. The other was
handed to Fuzzy.

As his fingers closed on the slender glass stem his disabilities
dropped from him for one brief moment. He straightened himself;
and Time, so disobliging to most of us, turned backward to
accommodate Fuzzy.

Forgotten Christmas ghosts whiter than the false beards of the
most opulent Kriss Kringle were rising in the fumes of Grogan's
whisky. What had the millionaire's mansion to do with a long,
wainscoted Virginia hall, where the riders were grouped around a
silver punch-bowl, drinking the ancient toast of the House? And
why should the patter of the cabhorses' hoofs on the frozen street
be in anywise related to the sound of the saddled hunters stamping
under the shelter of the west veranda? And what had Fuzzy to do
with any of it?

The Lady, looking at him over her glass, let her condescending
smile fade away like a false dawn. Her eyes turned serious. She saw
something beneath the rags and Scotch-terrier whiskers that she
did not understand. But it did not matter.

Fuzzy lifted his glass and smiled vacantly.

'P-pardon, lady,' he said, 'but couldn't leave without exchangin' comp'ments sheason with lady th' house. "Gainst princ'ples gen'leman do sho.'

And then he began the ancient salutation that was a tradition in the House when men wore lace ruffles and powder.

'The blessings of another year –'

Fuzzy's memory failed him. The Lady prompted:

'– Be upon this hearth.'

'– The guest –' stammered Fuzzy.

'– And upon her who –' continued the Lady, with a leading smile.

'Oh, cut it out,' said Fuzzy ill-manneredly. 'I can't remember. Drink hearty.'

Fuzzy had shot his arrow. They drank. The Lady smiled again the smile of her caste. James enveloped Fuzzy and re-conducted him toward the front door. The harp music still softly drifted through the house.

Outside, Black Riley breathed on his cold hands and hugged the gate.

'I wonder,' said the Lady to herself, musing 'who – but there were so many who came. I wonder whether memory is a curse or a blessing to them after they have fallen so low.'

Fuzzy and his escort were nearly at the door The Lady called· 'James!'

James stalked back obsequiously, leaving Fuzzy waiting unsteadily, with his brief spark of the divine fire gone.

Outside, Black Riley stamped his cold feet and got a firmer grip on his section of gas-pipe.

'You will conduct this gentleman,' said the Lady, 'downstairs. Then tell Louis to get out the Mercedes and take him to whatever place he wishes to go.'

LII

Proof of the Pudding

SPRING WINKED a vitreous optic at Editor Westbrook, of the *Minerva Magazine*, and deflected him from his course. He had lunched in his favourite corner of a Broadway hotel, and was returning to his office when his feet became entangled in the lure of the vernal coquette. Which is by way of saying that he turned eastward in

Twenty-sixth Street, safely forded the spring freshet of vehicles in
Fifth Avenue, and meandered along the walks of budding Madison
Square.

The lenient air and the settings of the little park almost formed
a pastoral; the colour motif was green – the presiding shade at the
creation of man and vegetation.

The callow grass between the walks was the colour of verdigris,
a poisonous green, reminiscent of the horde of derelict humans
that had breathed upon the soil during the summer and autumn.
The bursting tree-buds looked strangely familiar to those who had
botanized among the garnishings of the fish course of a forty-cent
dinner. The sky above was of that pale aquamarine tint that hall-
room poets rhyme with 'true' and 'Sue' and 'coo.' The one natural
and frank colour visible was the ostensible green of the newly
painted benches – a shade between the colour of a pickled cucum-
ber and that of a last year's fast-back cravenette raincoat. But, to
the city-bred eye of Editor Westbrook, the landscape appeared a
masterpiece.

And now, whether you are of those who rush in, or of the gentle
concourse that fears to tread, you must follow in a brief invasion
of the editor's mind.

Editor Westbrook's spirit was contented and serene. The April
number of the *Minerva* had sold its entire edition before the tenth
day of the month – a newsdealer in Keokuk had written that he
could have sold fifty copies more if he had had 'em. The owners of
the magazine had raised his (the editor's) salary; he had just
installed in his home a jewel of a recently imported cook who was
afraid of policemen; and the morning papers had published in full
a speech he had made at a publishers' banquet. Also there were
echoing in his mind the jubilant notes of a splendid song that his
charming young wife had sung to him before he left his uptown
apartment that morning. She was taking enthusiastic interest in
her music of late, practising early and diligently. When he had
complimented her on the improvement in her voice she had fairly
hugged him for joy at his praise. He felt, too, the benign, tonic
medicament of the trained nurse, Spring, tripping softly adown
the wards of the convalescent city.

While Editor Westbrook was sauntering between rows of park
benches (already filling with vagrants and the guardians of lawless
childhood) he felt his sleeve grasped and held. Suspecting that he
was about to be panhandled, he turned a cold and unprofitable
face, and saw that his captor was – Dawe – Shackleford Dawe,

dingy, almost ragged, the genteel scarcely visible in him through the deeper lines of the shabby.

While the editor is pulling himself out of his surprise, a flash-light biography of Dawe is offered.

He was a fiction writer, and one of Westbrook's old acquaintances. At one time they might have called each other old friends. Dawe had some money in those days, and lived in a decent apartment-house near Westbrook's. The two families often went to theatres and dinners together. Mrs. Dawe and Mrs. Westbrook became 'dearest' friends. Then one day a little tentacle of the octopus, just to amuse itself, ingurgitated Dawe's capital, and he moved to the Gramercy Park neighbourhood, where one, for a few groats per week, may sit upon one's trunk under eight-branched chandeliers and opposite Carrara marble mantels and watch the mice play upon the floor. Dawe thought to live by writing fiction. Now and then he sold a story. He submitted many to Westbrook. The *Minerva* printed one or two of them; the rest were returned. Westbrook sent a careful and conscientious personal letter with each rejected manuscript, pointing out in detail his reasons for considering it unavailable. Editor Westbrook had his own clear conception of what constituted good fiction. So had Dawe. Mrs. Dawe was mainly concerned about the constituents of the scanty dishes of food that she managed to scrape together. One day Dawe had been spouting to her about the excellences of certain French writers. At dinner they sat down to a dish that a hungry schoolboy could have encompassed at a gulp. Dawe commented.

'It's Maupassant hash,' said Mrs. Dawe. 'It may not be art, but I do wish you would do a five course Marion Crawford serial with an Ella Wheeler Wilcox sonnet for dessert. I'm hungry.'

As far as this from success was Shackleford Dawe when he plucked Editor Westbrook's sleeve in Madison Square. That was the first time the editor had seen Dawe in several months.

'Why, Shack, is this you?' said Westbrook somewhat awkwardly, for the form of this phrase seemed to touch upon the other's changed appearance.

'Sit down for a minute,' said Dawe, tugging at his sleeve. 'This is my office. I can't come to yours, looking as I do. Oh, sit down – you won't be disgraced. Those half-plucked birds on the other benches will take you for a swell porch-climber. They won't know you are only an editor.'

'Smoke, Shack?' said Editor Westbrook, sinking cautiously

upon the virulent green bench. He always yielded gracefully when he did yield.

Dawe snapped at the cigar as a kingfisher darts at a sunperch, or a girl pecks at a chocolate cream.

'I have just –' began the editor.

'Oh, I know; don't finish,' said Dawe. 'Give me a match. You have just ten minutes to spare. How did you manage to get past my office-boy and invade my sanctum? There he goes now, throwing his club at a dog that couldn't read the "Keep off the Grass" signs.'

'How goes the writing?' asked the editor.

'Look at me,' said Dawe, 'for your answer. Now don't put on that embarrassed, friendly-but-honest look and ask me why I don't get a job as a wine agent or a cab-driver. I'm in the fight to a finish. I know I can write good fiction and I'll force you fellows to admit it yet. I'll make you change the spelling of "regrets" to "c-h-e-q-u-e" before I'm done with you.'

Editor Westbrook gazed through his nose-glasses with a sweetly sorrowful, omniscient, sympathetic, sceptical expression – the copyrighted expression of the editor beleaguered by the unavailable contributor.

'Have you read the last story I sent you – "The Alarum of the Soul"?' asked Dawe.

'Carefully. I hesitated over that story, Shack, really I did. It had some good points. I was writing you a letter to send with it when it goes back to you. I regret –'

'Never mind the regrets,' said Dawe grimly. 'There's neither salve nor sting in 'em any more. What I want to know is why. Come, now; out with the good points first.'

'The story,' said Westbrook deliberately, after a suppressed sigh, 'is written around an almost original plot. Characterization – the best you have done. Construction – almost as good, except for a few weak joints which might be strengthened by a few changes and touches. It was a good story, except –'

'I can write English, can't I?' interrupted Dawe.

'I have always told you,' said the editor, 'that you had a style.'

'Then the trouble is the –'

'Same old thing,' said Editor Westbrook. 'You work up to your climax like an artist. And then you turn yourself into a photographer. I don't know what form of obstinate madness possesses you, Shack, but that is what you do with everything that you write. No, I will retract the comparison with the photographer. Now and then photography, in spite of its impossible perspective, manages to record a fleeting glimpse of truth. But you spoil every denouement by those flat, drab, obliterating strokes of your brush that I have so often complained of. If you would rise to the literary pinnacle of your dramatic scenes, and paint them in the high colours that art requires, the postman would leave fewer bulky, self-addressed envelopes at your door.'

'Oh, fiddles and footlights!' cried Dawe derisively. 'You've got that old sawmill drama kink in your brain yet. When the man with the black moustache kidnaps golden-haired Bessie you are bound to have the mother kneel and raise her hands in the spotlight and say: "May high heaven witness that I will rest neither night nor day till the heartless villain that has stolen me child feels the weight of a mother's vengeance!" '

Editor Westbrook conceded a smile of impervious complacency.

'I think,' said he, 'that in real life the woman would express herself in those words or in very similar ones.'

'Not in a six hundred nights' run anywhere but on the stage,' said Dawe hotly. 'I'll tell you what she'd say in real life. She'd say: "What! Bessie led away by a strange man? Good Lord! It's one trouble after another! Get my other hat, I must hurry around to the police-station. Why wasn't somebody looking after her, I'd like to know? For God's sake, get out of my way or I'll never get ready. Not that hat - the brown one with the velvet bows. Bessie must have been crazy; she's usually shy of strangers. Is that too much powder? Lordy! How I'm upset!"

'That's the way she'd talk,' continued Dawe. 'People in real life don't fly into heroics and blank verse at emotional crises. They simply can't do it. If they talk at all on such occasions they draw from the same vocabulary that they use every day, and muddle up their words and ideas a little more, that's all.'

'Shack,' said Editor Westbrook impressively, 'did you ever pick up the mangled and lifeless form of a child from under the fender of a street-car, and carry it in your arms and lay it down before the distracted mother? Did you ever do that and listen to the words of grief and despair as they flowed spontaneously from her lips?'

'I never did,' said Dawe. 'Did you?'

'Well, no,' said Editor Westbrook, with a slight frown. 'But I can well imagine what she would say.'

'So can I,' said Dawe.

And now the fitting time had come for Editor Westbrook to play the oracle and silence his opinionated contributor. It was not for an unarrived fictionist to dictate words to be uttered by the heroes and heroines of the *Minerva Magazine*, contrary to the theories of the editor thereof.

'My dear Shack,' said he, 'if I know anything of life I know that every sudden, deep and tragic emotion in the human heart calls forth an apposite, concordant, conformable, and proportionate expression of feeling? How much of this inevitable accord between expression and feeling should be attributed to nature, and how much to the influence of art, it would be difficult to say. The sublimely terrible roar of the lioness that has been deprived of her cubs is dramatically as far above her customary whine and purr as the kingly and transcendent utterances of Lear are above the level of his senile vapourings. But it is also true that all men and women have what may be called a subconscious dramatic sense that is awakened by a sufficiently deep and powerful emotion – a sense unconsciously acquired from literature and the stage that prompts them to express those emotions in language befitting their importance and histrionic value.'

'And in the name of seven sacred saddle-blankets of Sagittarius, where did the stage and literature get the stunt?' asked Dawe.

'From life,' answered the editor triumphantly.

The story-writer rose from the bench and gesticulated eloquently but dumbly. He was beggared for words with which to formulate adequately his dissent.

On a bench near by a frowsy loafer opened his red eyes and perceived that his moral support was due to a down-trodden brother.

'Punch him one, Jack,' he called hoarsely to Dawe. 'W'at's he come makin' a noise like a penny arcade for amongst gen'lemen that comes in the Square to set and think?'

Editor Westbrook looked at his watch with an affected show of leisure.

'Tell me,' asked Dawe, with truculent anxiety, 'what especial faults in "The Alarum of the Soul" caused you to throw it down.'

'When Gabriel Murray,' said Westbrook, 'goes to his telephone and is told that his fiancée has been shot by a burglar, he says – I do not recall the exact words, but –'

'I do,' said Dawe. 'He says: "Damn Central; she always cuts me off." (And then to his friend): "Say, Tommy, does a thirty-two bullet make a big hole? It's kind of hard luck, ain't it? Could you get me a drink from the sideboard, Tommy? No; straight; nothing on the side." '

'And again,' continued the editor, without pausing for argument, 'when Berenice opens the letter from her husband informing her that he has fled with the manicure girl, her words are – let me see –'

'She says,' interposed the author: ' "Well, what do you think of that!" '

'Absurdly inappropriate words,' said Westbrook, 'presenting an anti-climax – plunging the story into hopeless bathos. Worse yet; they mirror life falsely. No human being ever uttered banal colloquialisms when confronted by sudden tragedy.'

'Wrong,' said Dawe, closing his unshaven jaws doggedly. 'I say no man or woman ever spouts highfalutin talk when they go up against a real climax. They talk naturally, and a little worse.'

The editor rose from the bench with his air of indulgence and inside information.

'Say, Westbrook,' said Dawe, pinning him by the lapel, 'would you have accepted "The Alarum of the Soul" if you had believed that the actions and words of the characters were true to life in the parts of the story that we discussed?'

'It is very likely that I would, if I believed that way,' said the editor. 'But I have explained to you that I do not.'

'If I could prove to you that I am right?'

'I'm sorry, Shack, but I'm afraid I haven't time to argue any further just now.'

'I don't want to argue,' said Dawe. 'I want to demonstrate to you from life itself that my view is the correct one.'

'How could you do that?' asked Westbrook in a surprised tone.

'Listen,' said the writer seriously. 'I have thought of a way. It is important to me that my theory of true-to-life fiction be recognized as correct by the magazines. I've fought for it for three years, and I'm down to my last dollar, with two months' rent due.'

'I have applied the opposite of your theory,' said the editor, 'in selecting the fiction for the *Minerva Magazine*. The circulation has gone up from ninety thousand to –'

'Four hundred thousand,' said Dawe. 'Whereas it should have been boosted to a million.'

'You said something to me just now about demonstrating your pet theory.'

'I will. If you'll give me about half an hour of your time I'll prove to you that I am right. I'll prove it by Louise.'

'Your wife!' exclaimed Westbrook. 'How?'

'Well, not exactly by her, but with her,' said Dawe. 'Now, you know how devoted and loving Louise has always been. She thinks I'm the only genuine preparation on the market that bears the old doctor's signature. She's been fonder and more faithful than ever, since I've been cast for the neglected genius part.'

'Indeed, she is a charming and admirable life companion,' agreed the editor. 'I remember what inseparable friends she and Mrs. Westbrook once were. We are both lucky chaps, Shack, to have such wives. You must bring Mrs. Dawe up some evening soon, and we'll have one of those informal chafing-dish suppers that we used to enjoy so much.'

'Later,' said Dawe. 'When I get another shirt. And now I'll tell you my scheme. When I was about to leave home after breakfast – if you can call tea and oatmeal breakfast – Louise told me she was going to visit her aunt in Eighty-ninth Street. She said she would return home at three o'clock. She is always on time to a minute. It is now –'

Dawe glanced toward the editor's watch pocket.

'Twenty-seven minutes to three,' said Westbrook, scanning his timepiece.

'We have just enough time,' said Dawe. 'We will go to my flat at once. I will write a note, address it to her and leave it on the table where she will see it as she enters the door. You and I will be in the dining-room concealed by the portieres. In that note I'll say that I have fled from her for ever with an affinity who understands the needs of my artistic soul as she never did. When she reads it we will observe her actions and hear her words. Then we will know which theory is the correct one – yours or mine.'

'Oh, never!' exclaimed the editor, shaking his head. 'That would be inexcusably cruel. I could not consent to have Mrs. Dawe's feelings played upon in such a manner.'

'Brace up,' said the writer. 'I guess I think as much of her as you do. It's for her benefit as well as mine. I've got to get a market for my stories in some way. It won't hurt Louise. She's healthy and sound. Her heart goes as strong as a ninety-eight-cent watch. It'll last for only a minute, and then I'll step out and explain to her. You really owe it to me to give me the chance, Westbrook.'

Editor Westbrook at length yielded, though but half willingly. And in the half of him that consented lurked the vivisectionist that is in all of us.

Let him who has not used the scalpel rise and stand in his place. Pity 'tis that there are not enough rabbits and guinea-pigs to go around.

The two experimenters in Art left the Square and hurried eastward and then to the south until they arrived in the Gramercy
neighbourhood. Within its high iron railings the little park had put
on its smart coat of vernal green, and was admiring itself in its fountain mirror. Outside the railings the hollow square of crumbling
houses, shells of a bygone gentry, leaned as if in ghostly gossip over
the forgotten doings of the vanished quality. *Sic transit gloria urbis.*

A block or two north of the Park, Dawe steered the editor again
eastward, then, after covering a short distance, into a lofty but
narrow flathouse burdened with a floridly over-decorated facade.
To the fifth story they toiled, and Dawe, panting, pushed his
latch-key into the door of one of the front flats.

When the door opened Editor Westbrook saw, with feelings of
pity, how meanly and meagrely the rooms were furnished.

'Get a chair, if you can find one,' said Dawe, 'while I hunt up
pen and ink. Hallo, what's this? Here's a note from Louise. She
must have left it there when she went out this morning.'

He picked up an envelope that lay on the centre-table and tore
it open. He began to read the letter that he drew out of it; and
once having begun it aloud he so read it through to the end.
These are the words that Editor Westbrook heard:

DEAR SHACKLEFORD, –
    'By the time you get this I will be about a hundred miles away
and still a-going. I've got a place in the chorus of the Occidental
Opera Co., and we start on the road to-day at twelve o'clock. I
didn't want to starve to death, and so I decided to make my own
living. I'm not coming back. Mrs. Westbrook is going with me.
She said she was tired of living with a combination phonograph,
iceberg and dictionary, and she's not coming back, either. We've
been practising the songs and dances for two months on the quiet.
I hope you will be successful, and get along all right. Good-bye.
                                                            'LOUISE.'

Dawe dropped the letter, covered his face with his trembling
hands, and cried out in a deep vibrating voice:

'*My God, why hast Thou given me this cup to drink? Since she is
false, then let Thy Heaven's fairest gifts, faith and love, become the
jesting bywords of traitors and friends!*'

Editor Westbrook's glasses fell to the floor. The fingers of one
hand fumbled with a button on his coat as he blurted between his
pale lips:

'*Say, Shack, ain't that a hell of a note? Wouldn't that knock you off your perch, Shack? Ain't it hell, now, Shack — ain't it?*'

LIII

Past One at Rooney's

ONLY ON THE LOWER East Side of New York do the Houses of Capulet and Montague survive. There they do not fight by the book of arithmetic. If you but bite your thumb at an upholder of your opposing house you have work cut out for your steel. On Broadway you may drag your man along a dozen blocks by his nose, and he will only bawl for the watch; but in the domain of the East Side Tybalts and Mercutios you must observe the niceties of deportment to the wink of an eyelash and to an inch of elbow-room at the bar when its patrons include foes of your house and kin.

So, when Eddie McManus, known to the Capulets as Cork McManus, drifted into Dutch Mike's for a stein of beer, and came upon a bunch of Montagues making merry with the suds, he began to observe the strictest parliamentary rules. Courtesy forbade his leaving the saloon with his thirst unslaked; caution steered him to a place at the bar where the mirror supplied the cognizance of the enemy's movements that his indifferent gaze seemed to disdain; experience whispered to him that the finger of trouble would be busy among the chattering steins at Dutch Mike's that night. Close by his side drew Brick Cleary, his Mercutio, companion of his perambulations. Thus they stood, four of the Mulberry Hill Gang and two of the Dry Dock Gang minding their P's and Q's so solicitously that Dutch Mike kept one eye on his customers and the other on an open space beneath his bar in which it was his custom to seek safety whenever the ominous politeness of the rival associations congealed into the shapes of bullets and cold steel.

But we have not to do with the wars of the Mulberry Hills and the Dry Docks. We must to Rooney's, where, on the most blighted dead branch of the tree of life, a little pale orchid shall bloom.

Overstrained etiquette at last gave way. It is not known who first overstepped the bounds of punctilio; but the consequences were immediate. Buck Malone, of the Mulberry Hills, with a Dewey-like swiftness, got an eight-inch gun swung round from his hurricane deck. But McManus's simile must be the torpedo. He glided in under the guns and slipped a scant three inches of knife-blade between the ribs of the Mulberry Hill cruiser. Meanwhile Brick Cleary, a devotee to strategy, had skimmed across the lunch-counter and thrown the switch of the electrics, leaving the combat to be waged by the light of gunfire alone. Dutch Mike crawled from his haven and ran into the street crying for the watch instead of for a Shakespeare to immortalize the Cimmerian shindy.

The cop came, and found a prostrate, bleeding Montague sup-ported by three distrait and reticent followers of the House. Faith-ful to the ethics of the gangs, no one knew whence the hurt came. There was no Capulet to be seen.

'Raus mit der interrogatories,' said Buck Malone to the officer. 'Sure I know who done it. I always manages to get a bird's-eye view of any guy that comes up an' makes a show-case for a hard-ware store out of me. No. I'm not telling you his name. I'll settle with um meself. Wow – ouch! Easy, boys! Yes, I'll attend to his case meself. I'm not making any complaint.'

At midnight McManus strolled around a pile of lumber near an East Side dock, and lingered in the vicinity of a certain water-plug. Brick Cleary drifted casually to the trysting-place ten min-utes later. 'He'll maybe not croak,' said Brick; 'and he won't tell, of course. But Dutch Mike did. He told the police he was tired of having his place shot up. It's unhandy just now, because Tim Cor-rigan's in Europe for a week's end with Kings. He'll be back on the *Kaiser Williams* next Friday. You'll have to duck out of sight till then. Tim'll fix it up all right for us when he comes back.'

This goes to explain why Cork McManus went into Rooney's one night and there looked upon the bright, stranger face of Romance for the first time in his precarious career.

Until Tim Corrigan should return from his jaunt among Kings and Princes and hold up his big white finger in private offices, it was unsafe for Cork in any of the old haunts of his gang. So he lay, perdu, in the high rear room of a Capulet, reading pink sporting sheets and cursing the slow paddle-wheels of the *Kaiser Wilhelm*.

It was on Thursday evening that Cork's seclusion became intolerable to him. Never a hart panted for water fountain as he did for the cool touch of a drifting stein, for the firm security of a foot-rail in the hollow of his shoe and the quiet, hearty challenges of friendship and repartee along and across the shining bars. But he must avoid the district where he was known. The cops were looking for him everywhere, for news was scarce, and the newspapers were harping again on the failure of the police to suppress the gangs. If they got him before Corrigan came back, the big white finger could not be uplifted; it would be too late then. But Corrigan would be home the next day, so he felt sure there would be small danger in a little excursion that night among the crass pleasures that represented life to him.

At half-past twelve McManus stood in a darkish cross-town street looking up at the name 'Rooney's,' picked out by incandescent lights against a signboard over a second-story window. He had heard of the place as a tough 'hang-out'; with its frequenters and its locality he was unfamiliar. Guided by certain unerring indications common to all such resorts, he ascended the stairs and entered the large room over the café.

Here were some twenty or thirty tables, at this time about half filled with Rooney's guests. Waiters served drinks. At one end a human pianola with drugged eyes hammered the keys with automatic and furious unprecision. At merciful intervals a waiter would roar or squeak a song – songs full of 'Mr. Johnsons' and 'babes' and 'coons' – historical word guarantees of the genuineness of African melodies composed by red-waistcoated young gentlemen, natives of the cotton fields and rice swamps of West Twenty-eighth Street.

For one brief moment you must admire Rooney with me as he receives, seats, manipulates, and chaffs his guests. He is twenty-nine. He has Wellington's nose, Dante's chin, the cheek-bones of an Iroquois, the smile of Talleyrand, Corbett's footwork, and the poise of an eleven-year-old East Side Central Park Queen of the May. He is assisted by a lieutenant known as Frank, a pudgy, easy chap, swell-dressed, who goes among the tables seeing that dull care does not intrude. Now, what is there about Rooney's to inspire all this pother? It is more than respectable by daylight; stout ladies with children and mittens and bundles and unpedigreed dogs drop up of afternoons for a stein and a chat. Even by gaslight the diversions are melancholy i' the mouth – drink and ragtime, and an occasional surprise when the waiter swabs the suds from under your sticky glass. There is an answer. Transmigration! The soul of Sir Walter Raleigh has travelled from beneath his slashed doublet to a kindred home under Rooney's visible plaid waist- coat. Rooney's is twenty years ahead of the times. Rooney has removed the embargo. Rooney has spread his cloak upon the soggy crossing of public opinion, and any Elizabeth who treads upon it is as much a queen as another. Attend to the revelation of the secret. In Rooney's ladies may smoke!

McManus sat down at a vacant table. He paid for the glass of beer that he ordered, tilted his narrow-brimmed derby to the back of his brick-dust head, twined his feet among the rungs of his chair, and heaved a sigh of contentment from the breathing spaces of his innermost soul; for this mud honey was clarified sweetness to his taste. The sham gaiety, the hectic glow of counterfeit hospitality, the self-conscious, joyless laughter, the wine-born warmth, the loud music retrieving the hour from frequent whiles of awful and corroding silence, the presence of well-clothed and frank-eyed beneficiaries of Rooney's removal of the restrictions laid upon the weed, the familiar blended odours of soaked lemonpeel, flat beer, and *peau d'Espagne* – all these were manna to Cork McManus, hungry from his week in the desert of the Capulet's high rear room.

A girl, alone, entered Rooney's, glanced around with leisurely swiftness, and sat opposite McManus at his table. Her eyes rested upon him for two seconds in the look with which woman reconnoitres all men whom she for the first time confronts. In that space of time she will decide upon one of two things – either to scream for the police, or that she may marry him later on.

Her brief inspection concluded, the girl laid on the table a worn red morocco shopping-bag with the inevitable topgallant sail of frayed lace handkerchief flying from a corner of it. After she had ordered a small beer from the immediate waiter she took from her bag a box of cigarettes and lighted one with slightly exaggerated ease of manner. Then she looked again in the eyes of Cork McManus and smiled.

Instantly the doom of each was sealed.

The unqualified desire of a man to buy clothes and build fires for a woman for a whole lifetime at first sight of her is not uncommon among that humble portion of humanity that does not care for Bradstreet or coats-of-arms or Shaw's plays. Love at first sight has occurred a time or two in high life; but, as a rule, the extempore mania is to be found among unsophisticated creatures such as the dove, the blue-tailed dingbat, and the ten-dollar-a-week clerk. Poets, subscribers to all fiction magazines, and schatchens, take notice.

With the exchange of the mysterious magnetic current came to each of them the instant desire to lie, pretend, dazzle, and deceive, which is the worst thing about the hypocritical disorder known as love.

'Have another beer?' suggested Cork. In his circle the phrase was considered to be a card, accompanied by a letter of introduction and references.

'No, thanks,' said the girl, raising her eyebrows and choosing her conventional words carefully. 'I – merely dropped in for – a slight refreshment.' The cigarette between her fingers seemed to require explanation. 'My aunt is a Russian lady,' she concluded, 'and we often have a post perannual cigarette after dinner at home.'

'Cheese it!' said Cork, whom society airs oppressed. 'Your fingers are as yellow as mine.'

'Say,' said the girl, blazing upon him with low-voiced indignation, 'what do you think I am? Say, who do you think you are talking to? What?'

She was pretty to look at. Her eyes were big, brown, intrepid and bright. Under her flat sailor hat, planted jauntily on one side, her crinkly, tawny hair parted and was drawn back, low and massy, in a thick, pendent knot behind. The roundness of girlhood still lingered in her chin and neck, but her cheeks and fingers were thinning slightly. She looked upon the world with defiance, suspicion, and sullen wonder. Her smart, short tan coat was soiled and expensive. Two inches below her black dress dropped the lowest flounce of a heliotrope silk underskirt.

'Beg your pardon,' said Cork, looking at her admiringly. 'I didn't mean anything. Sure, it's no harm to smoke, Maudy.'

'Rooney's,' said the girl, softened at once by his amends, 'is the only place I know where a lady can smoke. Maybe it ain't a nice habit, but aunty lets us at home. And my name ain't Maudy, if you please; it's Ruby Delamere.'

'That's a swell handle,' said Cork approvingly. 'Mine's McManus – Cor er – Eddie McManus.'

'Oh, you can't help that,' laughed Ruby. 'Don t apologize.'

Cork looked seriously at the big clock on Rooney's wall. The girl's ubiquitous eyes took in the movement.

'I know it's late,' she said, reaching for her bag; 'but you know how you want a smoke when you want one. Ain't Rooney's all right? I never saw anything wrong here. This is twice I've been in. I work in a bookbindery on Third Avenue. A lot of us girls have been working overtime three nights a week. They won't let you smoke there, of course. I just dropped in here on my way home for a puff. Ain't it all right in here? If it ain't, I won't come any more.'

'It's a little bit late for you to be out alone anywhere,' said Cork. 'I'm not wise to this particular joint; but anyhow you don't want to have your picture taken in it for a present to your Sunday-school teacher. Have one more beer, and then say I take you home.'

'But I don't know you,' said the girl, with fine scrupulosity. 'I don't accept the company of gentlemen I ain't acquainted with. My aunt never would allow that.'

'Why,' said Cork McManus, pulling his ear, 'I'm the latest thing in suitings with side vents and bell skirt when it comes to escortin' a lady. You bet you'll find me all right, Ruby. And I'll give you a tip as to who I am. My governor is one of the hottest cross-buns of the Wall Street push. Morgan's cab-horse casts a shoe every time the old man sticks his head out of the window. Me! Well, I'm in trainin' down the Street. The old man's goin' to put a seat on the Stock Exchange in my stockin' my next birthday. But it all sounds like a lemon to me. What I like is golf and yachtin' and – er – well, say a corkin' fast ten-round bout between welter-weights with walkin' gloves.'

'I guess you can walk to the door with me,' said the girl hesitatingly, but with a certain pleased flutter. 'Still I never heard anything extra good about Wall Street brokers, or sports who go to prize-fights, either. Ain't you got any other recommendations?'

'I think you're the swellest looker I've had my lamps on in little old New York,' said Cork impressively.

'That'll be about enough of that, now. Ain't you the kidder!' She modified her chiding words by a deep, long, beaming, smile-embellished look at her cavalier. 'We'll drink our beer before we go, ha?'

A waiter sang. The tobacco smoke grew denser, drifting and rising in spirals, waves, tilted layers, cumulus clouds, cataracts and suspended fogs like some fifth element created from the ribs of the ancient four. Laughter and chat grew louder, stimulated by Rooney's liquids and Rooney's gallant hospitality to Lady Nicotine.

One o'clock struck. Downstairs there was a sound of closing and locking doors. Frank pulled down the green shades of the front windows carefully. Rooney went below in the dark hall and stood at the front door, his cigarette cached in the hollow of his hand. Thenceforth whoever might seek admittance must present a countenance familiar to Rooney's hawk's eye – the countenance of a true sport.

Cork McManus and the bookbindery girl conversed absorbedly, with their elbows on the table. Their glasses of beer were pushed to one side, scarcely touched, with the foam on them sunken to a thin, white scum. Since the stroke of one the stale pleasures of Rooney's had become renovated and spiced; not by any addition to the list of distractions, but because from that moment the sweets became stolen ones. The flattest glass of beer acquired the tang of illegality; the mildest claret punch struck a knock-out blow at law and order; the harmless and genial company became outlaws, defying authority and rule. For after the stroke of one in such places as Rooney's, where neither bed nor board is to be had, drink may not be set before the thirsty of the city of the four million. It is the law.

'Say,' said Cork McManus, almost covering the table with his eloquent chest and elbows, 'was that dead straight about you workin' in a bookbindery and livin' at home – and just happenin' in here – and – and all that spiel you gave me?'

'Sure it was,' answered the girl with spirit. 'Why, what do you think? Do you suppose I'd lie to you? Go down to the shop and ask 'em. I handed it to you on the level.'

'On the dead level?' said Cork. 'That's the way I want it; because –'

'Because what?'

'I throw up my hands,' said Cork. 'You've got me goin'. You're the girl I've been lookin' for. Will you keep company with me, Ruby?'

'Would you like me to – Eddie?'

'Surest thing. But I wanted a straight story about – about yourself, you know. When a fellow has a girl – a steady girl – she's got to be all right, you know. She's got to be straight goods.'

'You'll find I'll be straight goods, Eddie.'

'Of course you will. I believe what you told me. But you can't blame me for wantin' to find out. You don't see many girls smokin' cigarettes in a place like Rooney's after midnight that are like you.'

The girl flushed a little and lowered her eyes. 'I see that now,' she said meekly. 'I didn't know how bad it looked. But I won't do it any more. And I'll go straight home every night and stay there. And I'll give up cigarettes if you say so, Eddie – I'll cut 'em out from this minute on.'

Cork's air became judicial, proprietary, condemnatory, yet sympathetic. 'A lady can smoke,' he decided slowly, 'at times and places. Why? Because it's being a lady that helps her to pull it off.'

'I'm going to quit. There's nothing to it,' said the girl. She flicked the stub of her cigarette to the floor.

'At times and places,' repeated Cork. 'When I call round for you of evenin's we'll hunt out a dark bench in Stuyvesant Square and have a puff or two. But no more Rooney's at one o'clock – see?'

'Eddie, do you really like me?' The girl searched his hard but frank features eagerly with anxious eyes.

'On the dead level.'

'When are you coming to see me – where I live?'

'Thursday – day after to-morrow evenin'. That suit you?'

'Fine. I'll be ready for you. Come about seven. Walk to the door with me to-night and I'll show you where I live. Don't forget, now. And don't you go to see any other girls before then, mister! I bet you will, though.'

'On the dead level,' said Cork, 'you make 'em all look like rag-dolls to me. Honest, you do. I know when I'm suited. On the dead level, I do.'

Against the front door downstairs repeated heavy blows were delivered. The loud crashes resounded in the room above. Only a trip-hammer or a policeman's boot could have been the author of those sounds. Rooney jumped like a bullfrog to a corner of the room, turned off the electric lights and hurried swiftly below. The room was left utterly dark except for the winking, red glow of cigars and cigarettes. A second volley of crashes came up from the assaulted door. A little, rustling, murmuring panic moved among the besieged guests. Frank, cool, smooth, reassuring, could be seen in the rosy glow of the burning tobacco, going from table to table.

'All keep still!' was his caution. 'Don't talk or make any noise! Everything will be all right. Now, don't feel the slightest alarm. We'll take care of you all.'

Ruby felt across the table until Cork's firm hand closed upon hers. 'Are you afraid, Eddie?' she whispered. 'Are you afraid you'll get a free ride?'

'Nothin' doin' in the teeth-chatterin' line,' said Cork. 'I guess Rooney's been slow with his envelope. Don't you worry, girly; I'll look out for you all right.'

Yet Mr. McManus's ease was only skin and muscle-deep. With the police looking everywhere for Buck Malone's assailant, and with Corrigan still on the ocean wave, he felt that to be caught in a police raid would mean an ended career for him. And just when he had met Ruby, too! He wished he had remained in the high rear room of the true Capulet reading the pink extras.

Rooney seemed to have opened the front door below and engaged the police in conference in the dark hall. The wordless, low growl of their voices came up the stairway. Frank made a wireless news station of himself at the upper door. Suddenly he closed the door, hurried to the extreme rear of the room and lighted a dim gas-jet.

'This way, everybody,' he called sharply. 'In a hurry, but no noise, please!'

The guests crowded in confusion to the rear. Rooney's lieutenant swung open a panel in the wall, overlooking the back yard, revealing a ladder placed already for the escape.

'Down and out, everybody!' he commanded. 'Ladies first! Less talking, please! Don't crowd. There's no danger.'

Among the last, Cork and Ruby waited their turn at the open panel. Suddenly she swept him aside and clung to his arm fiercely.

'Before we go out,' she whispered in his ear – 'before anything happens, tell me again, Eddie, do you – do you really like me?'

'On the dead level,' said Cork, holding her close with one arm, 'when it comes to you, I'm all in.'

When they turned they found they were lost and in darkness. The last of the fleeing customers had descended. Half-way across the yard they bore the ladder, stumbling, giggling? hurrying to place it against an adjoining low building over the roof of which lay their only route to safety.

'We may as well sit down,' said Cork grimly. 'Maybe Rooney will stand the cops off, anyhow.'

They sat at a table; and their hands came together again.

A number of men then entered the dark room, feeling their way about. One of them, Rooney himself, found the switch and turned on the electric light. The other man was a cop of the old regime – a big cop, a thick cop, a fuming, abrupt cop – not a pretty cop. He went up to the pair at the table and sneered familiarly at the girl.

'What are youse doing" ' in here?' he asked.

'Dropped in for a smoke,' said Cork mildly.

'Had any drinks?'

'Not later than one o'clock.'

'Get out – quick!' ordered the cop. Then, 'Sit down!' he countermanded.

He took of Cork's hat roughly and scrutinized him shrewdly. 'Your name's McManus."?

'Bad guess,' said Cork. 'It's Peterson.'

'Cork McManus, or something like that,' said the cop. 'You put a knife into a man in Dutch Mike's saloon a week ago.'

'Aw, forget it!' said Cork, who perceived a shade of doubt in the officer's tones. 'You've got my mug mixed with somebody else's.'

'Have I? Well, you'll come to the station with me, anyhow, and be looked over. The description fits you all right.' The cop twisted his fingers under Cork's collar. 'Come on!' he ordered roughly.

Cork glanced at Ruby. She was pale, and her thin nostrils quivered. Her quick eye glanced from one man's face to the other's as they spoke or moved. What hard luck! Cork was thinking – Corrigan on the briny; and Ruby met and lost almost within an hour! Somebody at the police-station would recognize him, without a doubt. Hard luck!

But suddenly the girl sprang up and hurled herself with both arms extended against the cop. His hold on Cork's collar was loosened and he stumbled back two or three paces.

'Don't go so fast, Maguire!' she cried in shrill fury. 'Keep your hands off my man! You know me, and you know I'm givin' you good advice. Don't you touch him again! He's not the guy you are lookin' for – I'll stand for that.'

'See here, Fanny,' said the cop, red and angry, 'I'll take you, too, if you don't look out! How do you know this ain't the man I want? What are you doing in here with him?'

'How do I know?' said the girl, flaming red and white by turns. 'Because I've known him a year. He's mine. Oughtn't I to know? And what am I doin' here with him? That's easy.'

She stooped low and reached down somewhere into a swirl of flirted draperies, heliotrope and black. An elastic snapped, she threw on the table toward Cork a folded wad of bills. The money slowly straightened itself with little leisurely jerks.

'Take that, Jimmy, and let's go,' said the girl. 'I'm declaring the usual dividends, Maguire,' she said to the officer. 'You had your usual five-dollar graft at the usual corner at ten.'

'A lie!' said the cop, turning purple. 'You go on my beat again and I'll arrest you every time I see you.

'No you won't,' said the girl. 'And I'll tell you why. Witnesses saw me give you the money tonight, and last week, too. I've been getting fixed for you.'

Cork put the wad of money carefully into his pocket, and said: 'Come on, Fanny; let's have some chop suey before we go home.'

'Clear out, quick, both of you, or I'll –'

The cop's bluster trailed away into inconsequentiality.

At the corner of the street the two halted. Cork handed back the money without a word. The girl took it and slipped it slowly into her hand-bag. Her expression was the same she had worn when she entered Rooney's that night – she looked upon the world with defiance, suspicion and sullen wonder.

'I guess I might as well say good-bye here,' she said dully. 'You won't want to see me again, of course. Will you – shake hands – Mr. McManus?'

'I mightn't have got wise if you hadn't give the snap away,' said Cork. 'Why did you do it?'

'You'd have been pinched if I hadn't. That's why. Ain't that reason enough?' Then she began to cry. 'Honest, Eddie, I was goin' to be the best girl in the world. I hated to be what I am; I hated men: I was ready almost to die when I saw you. And you seemed different from everybody else. And when I found you liked me, too, why, I thought I'd make you believe I was good, and I was goin' to be good. When you asked to come to my house and see me, why, I'd have died rather than do anything wrong after that. But what's the use of talking about it? I'll say good-bye, if you will, Mr. McManus.'

Cork was pulling at his ear. 'I knifed Malone,' said he. 'I was the one the cop wanted.'

'Oh, that's all right,' said the girl listlessly. 'It didn't make any difference about that.'

'That was all hot air about Wall Street. I don't do nothin' but hang out with a tough gang on the East Side.'

'That was all right, too,' repeated the girl. 'It didn't make any difference.'

Cork straightened himself, and pulled his hat down low. 'I could get a job at O'Brien's,' he said aloud, but to himself.

'Good-bye,' said the girl.

'Come on,' said Cork, taking her arm. 'I know a place.'

Two blocks away he turned with her up the steps of a red-brick house facing a little park.

'What house is this?' she asked, drawing back. 'Why are you going in there?'

A street lamp shone brightly in front. There was a brass name-plate on one side of the closed front doors. Cork drew her firmly up the steps. 'Read that,' said he.

She looked at the name on the plate, and gave a cry between a moan and a scream. 'No, no, no, Eddie! Oh, my God, no! I won't let you do that – not now! Let me go! You shan't do that! You can't – you mustn't! Not after you know! No, no! Come away quick! Oh, my God! Please, Eddie, come!'

Half fainting, she reeled, and was caught in the bend of his arm. Cork's right hand felt for the electric button and pressed it long.

Another cop – how quickly they scent trouble when trouble is on the wing! – came along, saw them, and ran up the steps. 'Here I What are you doing with that girl?' he called gruffly.

'She'll be all right in a minute,' said Cork. 'It's a straight deal.'

'Reverend Jeremiah Jones,' read the cop from the door-plate with true detective cunning.

'Correct,' said Cork. 'On the dead level, we're going to get married.'

LIV

'The Rose of Dixie'

WHEN *The Rose of Dixie* magazine was started by a stock company in Toombs City, Georgia, there was never but one candidate for its chief editorial position in the minds of its owners. Col. Aquila Telfair was the man for the place. By all the rights of learning, family, reputation, and Southern traditions, he was its foreordained, fit, and logical editor. So, a committee of the patriotic Georgia citizens who had subscribed the founding fund of $100,000 called upon Colonel Telfair at his residence, Cedar Heights, fearful lest the enterprise and the South should suffer by his possible refusal.

The colonel received them in his great library, where he spent most of his days. The library had descended to him from his father. It contained ten thousand volumes, some of which had been published as late as the year 1861. When the deputation arrived, Colonel Telfair was seated at his massive white-pine centre-table, reading Burton's *Anatomy of Melancholy*. He arose and shook hands punctiliously with each member of the committee. If you were familiar with *The Rose of Dixie* you will remember the colonel's portrait, which appeared in it from time to time. You could not forget the long, carefully brushed white hair; the hooked, high-bridged nose, slightly twisted to the left; the keen eyes under the still black eyebrows; the classic mouth beneath the drooping white moustache, slightly frazzled at the ends.

The committee solicitously offered him the position of managing editor, humbly presenting an outline of the field that the publication was designed to cover and mentioning a comfortable salary. The colonel's lands were growing poorer each year and were much cut up by red gullies. Besides, the honour was not one to be refused.

In a forty-minute speech of acceptance, Colonel Telfair gave an outline of English literature from Chaucer to Macaulay, re-fought the battle of Chancellorsville, and said that, God helping him, he would so conduct *The Rose of Dixie* that its fragrance and beauty would permeate the entire world hurling back into the teeth of the Northern minions their belief that no genius or good could exist in the brains and hearts of the people whose property they had destroyed and whose rights they had curtailed.

Offices for the magazine were partitioned off and furnished in the second floor of the first National Bank Building; and it was for the colonel to cause *The Rose of Dixie* to blossom and flourish or to wilt in the balmy air of the land of flowers.

The staff of assistants and contributors that Editor-Colonel Telfair drew about him was a peach. It was a whole crate of Georgia peaches. The first assistant editor, Tolliver Lee Fairfax, had had a father killed during Pickett's charge. The second assistant, Keats Unthank, was the nephew of one of Morgan's Raiders. The book reviewer, Jackson Rockingham, had been the youngest soldier in the Confederate army, having appeared on the field of battle with a sword in one hand and a milk-bottle in the other. The art editor, Roncesvalles Sykes, was a third cousin to a nephew of Jefferson Davis. Miss Lavinia Terhune, the colonel's stenographer and typewriter, had an aunt who had once been kissed by Stonewall Jackson. Tommy Webster, the head office boy, got his job by having recited Father Ryan's poems, complete, at the commencement exercises of the Toombs City High School. The girls who wrapped and addressed the magazines were members of old Southern families in Reduced Circumstances. The cashier was a scrub named Hawkins from Ann Arbor, Michigan, who had recommendations and a bond from a guarantee company filed with the owners. Even Georgia stock companies sometimes realize that it takes live ones to bury the dead.

Well, sir, if you believe me, *The Rose of Dixie* blossomed five times before anybody heard of it except the people who buy their hooks and eyes in Toombs City. Then Hawkins climbed off his stool and told on 'em to the stock company. Even in Ann Arbor he had been used to having his business propositions heard of at least as far away as Detroit. So an advertising manager was engaged – Beauregard Fitzhugh Banks – a young man in a lavender necktie, whose grandfather had been the Exalted High Pillow-slip of the Ku-Klux-Klan.

In spite of which *The Rose of Dixie* kept coming out every month.

Although in every issue it ran photos of either the Taj Mahal or the Luxembourg Gardens, or Carmencita or La Follette, a certain number of people bought it and subscribed for it. As a boom for it, Editor-Colonel Telfair ran three different views of Andrew Jackson's old home, 'The Hermitage,' a full-page engraving of the second battle of Manassas, entitled 'Lee to the Rear!' and a five-thousand-word biography of Belle Boyd in the same number. The subscription list that month advanced 118. Also there were poems in the same issue by Leonina Vashti Haricot (pen-name), related to the Haricots of Charleston, South Carolina, and Bill Thompson, nephew of one of the stockholders. And an article from a special society correspondent describing a tea-party given by the swell Boston and English set, where a lot of tea was spilled overboard by some of the guests masquerading as Indians.

One day a person whose breath would easily cloud a mirror, he was so much alive, entered the office of *The Rose of Dixie*. He was a man about the size or a real estate agent, with a self-tied tie and a manner that he must have borrowed conjointly from W. J. Bryan, Hackenschmidt, and Hetty Green. He was shown into the editor-colonel's *pons asinorum*. Colonel Telfair rose and began a Prince Albert bow.

'I'm Thacker,' said the intruder, taking the editor's chair – 'T. T. Thacker, of New York.'

He dribbled hastily upon the colonel's desk some cards, a bulky manila envelope, and a letter from the owners of *The Rose of Dixie*. This letter introduced Mr. Thacker, and politely requested Colonel Telfair to give him a conference and whatever information about the magazine he might desire.

'I've been corresponding with the secretary of the magazine owners for some time,' said Thacker, briskly. 'I'm a practical magazine man myself, and a circulation booster as good as any, if I do say it. I'll guarantee an increase of anywhere from ten thousand to a hundred thousand a year for any publication that isn't printed in a dead language. I've had my eye on *The Rose of Dixie* ever since it started. I know every end of the business from editing to setting up the classified ads. Now, I've come down here to put a good bunch of money in the magazine, if I can see my way clear. It ought to be made to pay. The secretary tells me it's losing money. I don't see why a magazine in the South, if it's properly handled, shouldn't get a good circulation in the North too.'

Colonel Telfair leaned back in his chair and polished his gold-rimmed glasses.

'Mr. Thacker,' said he, courteously but firmly, 'The Rose of Dixie is a publication devoted to the fostering and the voicing of Southern genius. Its watchword, which you may have seen on the cover, is "Of, For, and By the South." '

'But you wouldn't object to a Northern circulation, would you?' asked Thacker.

'I suppose,' said the editor-colonel, 'that it is customary to open the circulation to all. I do not know. I have nothing to do with the business affairs of the magazine. I was called upon to assume editorial control of it, and I have devoted to its conduct such poor literary talents as I possess and whatever store or erudition I may have acquired.'

'Sure,' said Thacker. 'But a dollar is a dollar anywhere, North, South, or West – whether you're buying codfish, goober peas, or Rocky Ford cantaloupes. Now, I've been looking over your November number. I see one here on your desk. You don't mind running over it with me?

'Well, your leading article is all right. A good write-up of the cotton-belt with plenty of photographs is a winner any time. New York is always interested in the cotton crop. And this sensational account of the Hatfield-McCoy feud, by a schoolmate of a niece of the Governor of Kentucky, isn't such a bad idea. It happened so long ago that most people have forgotten it. Now, here's a poem three pages long called "The Tyrant's Foot," by Lorella Lascelles. I've pawed around a good deal over manuscripts, but I never saw her name on a rejection slip.'

'Miss Lascelles,' said the editor, 'is one of our most widely recognized Southern poetesses. She is closely related to the Alabama Lascelles family, and made with her own hands the silken Confederate banner that was presented to the governor of that state at his inauguration.'

'But why,' persisted Thacker, 'is the poem illustrated with a view of the M. & O. Railroad freight depot at Tuscaloosa?'

'The illustration,' said the colonel, with dignity, 'shows a corner of the fence surrounding the old homestead where Miss Lascelles was born.'

'All right,' said Thacker. 'I read the poem, but I couldn't tell whether it was about the depot or the battle of Bull Run. Now, here's a short story called "Rosie's Temptation," by Fosdyke Piggott. It's rotten. What is a Piggott, anyway?

'Mr. Piggott,' said the editor, 'is a brother of the principal stockholder of the magazine.'

'All's right with the world – Piggot passes,' said Thacker. 'Well, this article on Arctic exploration and the one on tarpon fishing might go. But how about this write-up of the Atlanta, New Orleans, Nashville, and Savannah breweries? It seems to consist mainly of statistics about their output and the quality of their beer. What's the chip over the bug?'

'If I understand your figurative language,' answered Colonel Telfair, 'it is this: the article you refer to was handed to me by the owners of the magazine with instructions to publish it. The literary quality of it did not appeal to me. But, in a measure, I feel impelled to conform, in certain matters, to the wishes of the gentlemen who are interested in the financial side of *The Rose*.'

'I see,' said Thacker. 'Next we have two pages of selections from "Lalla Rookh," by Thomas Moore. Now, what Federal prison did Moore escape from, or what's the name of the F. F. V. family that he carries as a handicap?'

'Moore was an Irish poet who died in 1852,' said Colonel Telfair pityingly. 'He is a classic. I have been thinking of reprinting his translation of Anacreon serially in the magazine.

'Look out for the copyright laws,' said Thacker flippantly. 'Who's Bessie Belleclair, who contributes the essay on the newly completed water works plant in Milledgeville?'

'The name, sir,' said Colonel Telfair, 'is the *nom de guewe* of Miss Elvira Simpkins. I have not the honour of knowing the lady; but her contribution was sent us by Congressman Brower, of her native state. Congressman Brower's mother was related to the Polks of Tennessee.'

'Now, see here, Colonel,' said Thacker, throwing down the magazine, 'this won't do. You can't successfully run a magazine for one particular section of the country. You've got to make a universal appeal. Look how the Northern publications have catered to the South and encouraged the Southern writers. And you've got to go far and wide for your contributors. You've got to buy stuff according to its quality, without any regard to the pedigree of the author. Now, I'll bet a quart of ink that this Southern parlour organ you've been running has never played a note that originated above Mason & Hamlin's line. Am I right?'

'I have carefully and conscientiously rejected all contributions from that section of the country – if I understand your figurative language aright,' replied the colonel.

'All right. Now I'll show you something!'

Thacker reached for his thick manila envelope and dumped a mass of typewritten manuscript on the editor's desk.

'Here's some truck,' said he, 'that I paid cash for and brought along with me.'

.One by one he folded back the manuscripts and showed their first pages to the colonel.

'Here are four short stories by four of he highest priced authors in the United States – three of 'em living in New York, and one commuting. Here's a special article on Vienna-bred society by Tom Vampson. Here's an Italian serial by Captain Jack – no – it's the other Crawford. Here are three separate exposes of city governments by Sniffings, and here's a dandy entitled "What Women Carry in Dress-Suit Cases' – a Chicago newspaper woman hired herself out for five years as a lady's maid to get that information. And here's a Synopsis of Preceding Chapters of Hall Caine's new serial to appear next June. And here's a couple of pounds of *vers de société* that I got at a rate from the clever magazines. That's the stuff that people everywhere want. And now here's a write-up with photographs at the ages of four, twelve, twenty-two, and thirty of George B. McClellan. It's a prognostication. He's bound to be elected Mayor of New York. It'll make a big hit all over the country. He –'

'I beg your pardon,' said Colonel Telfair, stiffening in his chair. 'What was the name?'

'Oh, I see,' said Thacker, with half a grin. 'Yes, he's a son of the General. We'll pass that manuscript up. But, if you'll excuse me, Colonel, it's a magazine we're trying to make go off – not the first gun at Fort Sumter. Now, here's a thing that's bound to get next to you. It's an original poem by James Whitcomb Riley. J. W. himself. You know what that means to a magazine. I won't tell you what I had to pay for that poem; but I'll tell you this – Riley can make more money writing with a fountain-pen than you or I can with one that lets the ink run. I'll read you the last two stanzas:

' "Pa lays around 'n' loafs all day,
    'N' reads and makes us leave him be,
He lets me do just like I please,
    'N' when I'm bad he laughs at me,
'N' when I holler loud 'n' say
    Bad words 'n' then begin to tease
The cat, 'n' pa just smiles, ma's mad
    'N' gives me Jesse crost her knees.
    I always wondered why that wuz
      I guess it's 'cause
      Pa never does.

'N' after all the lights are out
I'm sorry 'bout it; so I creep
Out of my trundle bed to ma's
'N' say I love her a whole heap,
'N' kiss her, 'n' I hug her tight.
'N' it's too dark to see her eyes,
But every time I do I know
She cries 'n' cries 'n' cries 'n' cries.
I always wondered why that wuz –
I guess it's 'cause
Pa never does."

'That's the stuff,' continued Thacker. 'What do you think of that?'

'I am not unfamiliar with the works of Mr. Riley,' said the colonel, deliberately. 'I believe he lives in Indiana. For the last ten years I have been somewhat of a literary recluse, and am familar with nearly all the books in the Cedar Heights library. I am also of the opinion that a magazine should contain a certain amount of poetry. Many of the sweetest singers of the South have already contributed to the pages of *The Rose of Dixie*. I, myself, have thought of translating from the original for publication in its pages the works of the great Italian poet Tasso. Have you ever drunk from the fountain of this immortal poet's lines, Mr. Thacker?'

'Not even a demi-Tasso,' said Thacker. 'Now, let's come to the point, Colonel Telfair. I've already invested some money in this as a flyer. That bunch of manuscripts cost me $4,000. My object was to try a number of them in the next issue – I believe you make up less than a month ahead – and see what effect it has on the circulation. I believe that by printing the best stuff we can get in the North, South, East, or West we can make the magazine go. You have there the letter from the owning company asking you to co-operate with me in the plan. Let's chuck out some of this slush that you've been publishing just because the writers are related to the Skoopdoodles of Skoopdoodle County. Are you with me?'

'As long as I continue to be the editor of *The Rose*,' said Colonel Telfair, with dignity, 'I shall be its editor. But I desire also to conform to the wishes of its owners if I can do so conscientiously.'

'That's the talk,' said Thacker, briskly. 'Now, how much of this stuff I've brought can we get into the January number? We want to begin right away.

'There is yet space in the January number,' said the editor, 'for about eight thousand words, roughly estimated.'

'Great!' said Thacker. 'It isn't much, but it'll give the readers some change from goobers, governors, and Gettysburg. I'll leave the selection of the stuff I brought to fill the space to you, as it's all good. I've got to run back to New York, and I'll be down again in a couple of weeks.'

Colonel Telfair slowly swung his eye-glasses by their broad black ribbon.

'The space in the January number that I referred to,' said he, measuredly, 'has been held open purposely, pending a decision that I have not yet made. A short time ago a contribution was submitted to *The Rose of Dixie* that is one of the most remarkable literary efforts that has ever come under my observation. None but a master mind and talent could have produced it. It would about fill the space that I have reserved for its possible use.'

Thacker looked anxious.

'What kind of stuff is it?' he asked. 'Eight thousand words sounds suspicious. The oldest families must have been collaborating. Is there going to be another secession?'

'The author of the article,' continued the colonel, ignoring Thacker's allusions, 'is a writer of some reputation. He has also distinguished himself in other ways. I do not feel at liberty to reveal to you his name – at least not until I have decided whether or not to accept his contribution.'

'Well,' said Thacker, nervously, 'is it a continued story, or an account of the unveiling of the new town pump in Whitmire, South Carolina, or a revised list of General Lee's body-servants, or what?'

'You are disposed to be facetious,' said Colonel Telfair calmly. 'The article is from the pen of a thinker, a philosopher, a lover of mankind, a student, and a rhetorician of high degree.'

'It must have been written by a syndicate,' said Thacker. 'But, honestly, Colonel, you want to go slow. I don't know of any eight-thousand-word single doses of written matter that are read by anybody these days, except Supreme Court briefs and reports of murder trials. You haven't by any accident gotten hold of a copy of one of Daniel Webster's speeches, have you?'

Colonel Telfair swung a little in his chair and looked steadily from under his bushy eyebrows at the magazine promoter.

'Mr. Thacker,' he said, gravely, 'I am willing to segregate the somewhat crude expression of your sense of humour from the solicitude that your business investments undoubtedly have conferred upon you. But I must ask you to cease your gibes and derogatory comments upon the South and the Southern people. They, sir, will not be tolerated in the office of *The Rose of Dixie* for one moment. And before you proceed with more of your covert insinuations that I, the editor of this magazine, am not a competent judge of the merits of the matter submitted to its consideration, I beg that you will first present some evidence or proof that you are my superior in any way, shape, or form relative to the question in hand.'

'Oh, come, Colonel,' said Thacker, good-naturedly. 'I didn't do anything like that to you. It sounds like an indictment by the fourth assistant attorney-general. Let's get back to business. What's this 8,000 to I shot about?'

'The article,' said Colonel Telfair, acknowledging the apology by a slight bow, 'covers a wide area of knowledge. It takes up theories and questions that have puzzled the world for centuries, and disposes of them logically and concisely. One by one it holds up to view the evils of the world, points out the way of eradicating them, and then conscientiously and in detail commends the good. There is hardly a phase of human life that it does not discuss wisely, calmly, and equitably. The great policies of governments, the duties of private citizens, the obligations of home life, law, ethics, morality – all these important subjects are handled with a calm wisdom and confidence that I must confess has captured my admiration.'

'It must be a crackerjack,' said Thacker, impressed.

'It is a great contribution to the world's wisdom,' said the colonel. 'The only doubt remaining in my mind as to the tremendous advantage it would be to us to give it publication in *The Rose of Dixie* is that I have not yet sufficient information about the author to give his work publicity in our magazine.'

'I thought you said he is a distinguished man,' said Thacker.

'He is,' replied the colonel, 'both in literary and in other more diversified and extraneous fields. But I am extremely careful about the matter that I accept for publication. My contributors are people of unquestionable repute and connections, which fact can be verified at any time. As I said, I am holding this article until I can acquire more information about its author. I do not know whether I will publish it or not. If I decide against it, I shall be much pleased, Mr. Thacker, to substitute the matter that you are leaving with me in its place.'

Thacker was somewhat at sea.

'I don't seem to gather,' said he, 'much about the gist of this inspired piece of literature. It sounds more like a dark horse than Pegasus to me.'

'It is a human document,' said the colonel-editor, confidently, 'from a man of great accomplishments who, in my opinion, has obtained a stronger grasp on the world and its outcomes than that of any man living to-day.'

Thacker rose to his feet excitedly.

'Say!' he said. 'It isn't possible that you've cornered John D. Rockefeller's memoirs, is it? Don't tell me that all at once.'

'No, sir,' said Colonel Telfair. 'I am speaking of mentality and literature, not of the less worthy intricacies of trade.'

'Well, what's the trouble about running the article,' asked Thacker, a little impatiently, 'if the man's well known and has got the stuff?'

Colonel Telfair sighed.

'Mr. Thacker,' said he, 'for once I have been tempted. Nothing has yet appeared in *The Rose of Dixie* that has not been from the pen of one of its sons or daughters. I know little about the author of this article except that he has acquired prominence in a section of the country that has always been inimical to my heart and mind. But I recognize his genius; and, as I have told you, I have instituted an investigation of his personality. Perhaps it will be futile. But I shall pursue the inquiry. Until that is finished, I must leave open the question of filling the vacant space in our January number.'

Thacker arose to leave.

'All right, Colonel,' he said, as cordially as he could. 'You use your own judgment. If you've really got a scoop or something that will make 'em sit up, run it instead of my stuff. I'll drop in again in about two weeks. Good luck!'

Colonel Telfair and the magazine promoter shook hands.

Returning a fortnight later, Thacker dropped off a very rocky Pullman at Toombs City. He found the January number of the magazine made up and the forms closed.

The vacant space that had been yawning for type was filled by an article that was headed thus:

SECOND MESSAGE TO CONGRESS

Written for

THE ROSE OF DIXIE

BY

A Member of the Well-known

BULLOCH FAMILY, OF GEORGIA

T. ROOSEVELT

LV

The Third Ingredient

THE (SO-CALLED) Vallambrosa Apartment House is not an apartment-house. It is composed of two old-fashioned, brownstone-front residences welded into one. The parlour floor of one side is gay with the wraps and headgear of a modiste; the other is lugubrious with the sophistical promises and grisly display of a painless dentist. You may have a room there for two dollars a week or you may have one for twenty dollars. Among the Vallambrosa's roomers are stenographers, musicians, brokers, shop-girls, space-rate writers, art students, wire-tappers, and other people who lean far over the banister-rail when the door-bell rings.

This treatise shall have to do with two of the Vallambrosians — though meaning no disrespect to the others.

At six o'clock one afternoon Hetty Pepper came back to her third-floor rear $3.50 room in the Vallambrosa with her nose and chin more sharply pointed than usual. To be discharged from the department store where you have been working four years, and with only fifteen cents in your purse, does have a tendency to make your features appear more finely chiselled.

And now for Hetty's thumb-nail biography while she climbs the two flights of stairs.

She walked into the Biggest Store one morning four years before, with seventy-five other girls, applying for a job behind the waist department counter. The phalanx of wage-earners formed a bewildering scene of beauty, carrying a total mass of blonde hair sufficient to have justified the horseback gallops of a hundred Lady Godivas.

The capable, cool-eyed, impersonal, young, baldheaded man, whose task it was to engage six of the contestants, was aware of a feeling of suffocation as if he were drowning in a sea of frangipanni, while white clouds, hand-embroidered, floated about him. And then a sail hove in sight. Hetty Pepper, homely of countenance, with small, contemptuous, green eyes and chocolate-coloured hair, dressed in a suit of plain burlap and a common-sense hat, stood before him with every one of her twenty-nine years of life unmistakably in sight.

'You're on!' shouted the bald-headed young man, and was saved. And that is how Hetty came to be employed in the Biggest Store. The story of her rise to an eight-dollar-a-week salary is the combined stories of Hercules, Joan of Arc, Una, Job, and Little-Red-Riding-Hood. You shall not learn from me the salary that was paid her as a beginner. There is a sentiment growing about such things, and I want no millionaire store-proprietors climbing the fire-escape of my tenement-house to throw dynamite bombs into my skylight boudoir.

The story of Hetty's discharge from the Biggest Store is so nearly a repetition of her engagement as to be monotonous.

In each department of the store there is an omniscient, omnipresent, and omnivorous person carrying always a mileage book and a red necktie, and referred to as a 'buyer.' The destinies of the girls in his department who live on (see Bureau of Victual Statistics) – so much per week are in his hands.

This particular buyer was a capable, cool-eyed, impersonal, young, bald-headed man. As he walked along the aisles of his department he seemed to be sailing on a sea of frangipanni, while white clouds, machine-embroidered, floated around him. Too many sweets bring surfeit. He looked upon Hetty Pepper's homely countenance, emerald eyes, and chocolate-coloured hair as a welcome oasis of green in a desert of cloying beauty. In a quiet angle of a counter he pinched her arm kindly, three inches above the elbow. She slapped him three feet away with one good blow of her muscular and not especially lily-white right. So, now you know why Hetty Pepper came to leave the Biggest Store at thirty minutes' notice, with one dime and a nickel in her purse.

This morning's quotations list the price of rib beef at six cents per (butcher's) pound. But on the day that Hetty was 'released' by the B.S. the price was seven and one-half cents. That fact is what makes this story possible. Otherwise the extra four cents would have –

But the plot of nearly all the good stories in the world is concerned with shorts who were unable to cover; so you can find no fault with this one.

Hetty mounted with her rib beef to her $3.50 third-floor back. One hot, savoury beef-stew for supper, a night's good sleep, and she would be fit in the morning to apply again for the tasks of Hercules, Joan of Arc, Una, Job, and Little-Red-Riding-Hood.

In her room she got the graniteware stew-pan out of the 2 by 4-foot china – er – I mean earthenware closet, and began to dig down in a rat's-nest of paper bags for the potatoes and onions. She came out with her nose and chin just a little sharper pointed.

There was neither a potato nor an onion. Now, what kind of beef-stew can you make out of simply beef? You can make oyster-soup without oysters, turtle-soup without turtles, coffee-cake without coffee, but you can't make beef-stew without potatoes and onions.

But rib beef alone, in an emergency, can make an ordinary pine door look like a wrought-iron gambling-house portal to the wolf. With salt and pepper and a tablespoonful of flour (first well stirred in a little cold water) 'twill serve – 'tis not so deep as a lobster a la New-burgh, nor so wide as a church festival doughnut; but 'twill serve.

Hetty took her stew-pan to the rear of the third-floor hall. According to the advertisements of the Vallambrosa there was running water to be found there. Between you and me and the water-meter, it only ambled or walked through the faucets; but technicalities have no place here. There was also a sink where housekeeping roomers often met to dump their coffee grounds and glare at one another's kimonos.

At this sink Hetty found a girl with heavy, gold-brown artistic hair and plaintive eyes, washing two large 'Irish' potatoes. Hetty knew the Vallambrosa as well as anyone not owning 'double hextra-magnifying eyes' could compass its mysteries. The kimonos were her encyclopaedia, her 'Who's What?' her clearing-house of news, of goers and comers. From a rose-pink kimono edged with Nile green she had learned that the girl with the potatoes was a miniature-painter living in a kind of attic – or 'studio,' as they prefer to call it – on the top-floor. Hetty was not certain in her mind what a miniature was; but it certainly wasn't a house; because house-painters, although they wear splashy overalls and poke ladders in your face on the street, are known to indulge in a riotous profusion of food at home.

The potato girl was quite slim and small, and handled her pota-toes as an old bachelor uncle handles a baby who is cutting teeth. She had a dull shoemaker's knife in her right hand, and she had begun to peel one of the potatoes with it.

Hetty addressed her in the punctiliously formal tone of one who intends to be cheerfully familar with you in the second round.

'Beg pardon,' she said, 'for butting into what's not my business, but if you peel them potatoes you lose out. They're new Bermudas. You want to scrape 'em. Lemme show you.'

She took a potato and the knife and began to demonstrate.

'Oh, thank you,' breathed the artist. 'I didn't know. And I *did* hate to see the thick peeling go; it seemed such a waste. But I thought they always had to be peeled. When you've got only potatoes to eat, the peelings count, you know.'

'Say, kid,' said Hetty, staying her knife, 'you ain't up against it, too, are you?'

The miniature artist smiled stonedly.

'I suppose I am. Art – or, at least, the way I interpret it – doesn't seem to be much in demand. I have only these potatoes for my dinner. But they aren't so bad boiled and hot, with a little butter and salt.'

'Child,' said Hetty, letting a brief smile soften her rigid features, 'Fate has sent me and you together. I've had it handed to me in the neck, too; but I've got a chunk of meat in my room as big as a lap-dog. And I've done everything to get potatoes except pray for 'em. Let's me and you bunch our commissary departments and make a stew of 'em. We'll cook it in my room. If we only had an onion to go in it! Say, kid, you haven't got a couple of pennies that've slipped down into the lining of your last winter's sealskin, have you? I could step down to the corner and get one at old Giuseppe's stand. A stew without an onion is worse'n a matinee without candy.'

'You may call me Cecilia,' said the artist. 'No; I spent my last penny three days ago.'

'Then we'll have to cut the onion out instead of slicing it in,' said Hetty. 'I'd ask the janitress for one, but I don't want 'em hep just yet to the fact that I'm pounding the asphalt for another job. But I wish we did have an onion.'

In the shop-girl's room the two began to prepare their supper. Cecilia's part was to sit on the couch helplessly and beg to be allowed to do something in the voice of a cooing ringdove. Hetty prepared the rib beef, putting it in cold salted water in the stew-pan and setting it on the one-burner gas-stove.

'I wish we had an onion,' said Hetty, as she scraped the two potatoes.

On the wall opposite the couch was pinned a flaming, gorgeous advertising picture of one of the new ferry-boats of the P.U.F.F. Railroad that had been built to cut down the time between Los Angeles and New York City one eighth of a minute.

Hetty turned her head during her continuous monologue, saw tears running from her guest's eyes as she gazed on the idealized presentment of the speeding, foam-girdled transport.

'Why, say, Cecilia, kid,' said Hetty, poising her knife, 'is it as bad art as that? I ain't a critic, but I thought it kind of brightened up the room. Of course, a manicure-painter could tell it was a bum picture in a minute. I'll take it down, if you say so; I wish to the holy Saint Pot-luck we had an onion.'

But the miniature miniature-painter had tumbled down, sobbing, with her nose indenting the hard-woven drapery of the couch. Something was here deeper than the artistic temperament offended at crude lithography.

Hetty knew. She had accepted her rôle long ago. How scant the words with which we try to describe a single quality of a human being! When we reach the abstract we are lost. The nearer to Nature that the babbling of our lips comes, the better do we understand. Figuratively (let us say), some people are Bosoms, some are Hands, some are Heads, some are Muscles, some are Feet, some are Backs for burdens.

Hetty was a Shoulder. Hers was a sharp, sinewy shoulder; but all her life people had laid their heads upon it, metaphorically or actually and had left there all or half their troubles. Looking at Life anatomically, which is as good a way as any, she was pre-ordained to be a Shoulder. There were few truer collar-bones anywhere than hers.

Hetty was only thirty-three, and she had not yet outlived the little pang that visited her whenever the head of youth and beauty leaned upon her for consolation. But one glance in her mirror always served as an instantaneous pain-killer. So she gave one pale look into the crinkly old looking-glass on the wall above the gas-stove, turned down the flame a little lower from the bubbling beef and potatoes, went over to the couch, and lifted Cecilia's head to its confessional.

'Go on and tell me, honey,' she said. 'I know now that it ain't art that's worrying you. You met him on a ferry-boat, didn't you? Go on, Cecilia, kid, and tell your – your Aunt Hetty about it.'

But youth and melancholy must first spend the surplus of sighs and tears that waft and float the barque of romance to its harbour in the delectable isles. Presently, through the stringy tendons that formed the bars of the confessional, the penitent – or was it the glorified communicant of the sacred flame? – told her story without art or illumination.

'It was only three days ago. I was coming back on the ferry from Jersey City. Old Mr. Schrum, an art dealer, told me of a rich man in Newark who wanted a miniature of his daughter painted. I went to see him and showed him some of my work. When I told him the price would be fifty dollars he laughed at me like a hyena. He said an enlarged crayon twenty times the size would cost him only eight dollars.

'I had just enough money to buy my ferry ticket back to New York. I felt as if I didn't want to live another day. I must have looked as I felt, for I saw him on the row of seats opposite me, looking at me as if he understood. He was nice-looking, but, oh, above everything else, he looked kind. When one is tired or unhappy or hopeless, kindness counts more than anything else.

'When I got so miserable that I couldn't fight against it any longer, I got up and walked out of the rear door of the ferry-boat cabin. No one was there, and I slipped quickly over the rail, and dropped into the water. Oh, friend Hetty, it was cold, cold!

'For just one moment I wished I was back in the old Vallambrosa, starving and hoping. And then I got numb, and didn't care. And then I felt that somebody else was in the water close by me, holding me up. *He* had followed me, and jumped in to save me.

'Somebody threw a thing like a big, white doughnut at us, and he made me put my arms through the hole. Then the ferry-boat backed, and they pulled us on board. Oh, Hetty, I was so ashamed of my wickedness in trying to drown myself; and, besides, my hair had all tumbled down and was sopping wet, and I was such a sight.

'And then some men in blue clothes came around; and *he* gave them his card, and I heard him tell them he had seen me drop my purse on the edge of the boat outside the rail, and in leaning over to get it I had fallen overboard. And then I remembered having read in the papers that people who try to kill themselves are locked up in cells with people who try to kill other people, and I was afraid.

'But some ladies on the boat took me downstairs to the furnace-room and got me nearly dry and did up my hair. When the boat landed, *he* came and put me in a cab. He was all dripping himself, but laughed as if he thought it was all a joke. He begged me, but I wouldn't tell him my name nor where I lived, I was so ashamed.'

'You were a fool, child,' said Hetty, kindly. 'Wait till I turn up the light a bit. I wish to Heaven we had an onion.'

'Then he raised his hat,' went on Cecilia, 'and said: "Very well. But I'll find you, anyhow. I'm going to claim my rights of salvage." Then he gave money to the cab-driver and told him to take me where I wanted to go, and walked away. What is "salvage," Hetty?'

'The edge of a piece of goods that ain't hemmed,' said the shop-girl. 'You must have looked pretty well frazzled out to the little hero boy.'

'It's been three days,' moaned the miniature-painter, 'and he hasn't found me yet.'

'Extend the time,' said Hetty. 'This is a big town. Think of how many girls he might have to see soaked in water with their hair down before he would recognize you. The stew's getting on fine – but, oh, for an onion! I'd even use a piece of garlic, if I had it.'

The beef and potatoes bubbled merrily, exhaling a mouth-watering savour that yet lacked something leaving a hunger on the palate, a haunting, wistful desire for some lost and needful ingredient.

'I came near drowning in that awful river,' said Cecilia, shuddering.

'It ought to have more water in it,' said Hetty; 'the stew, I mean. I'll go get some at the sink.'

'It smells good,' said the artist.

'That nasty old North River?' objected Hetty. 'It smells to me like soap factories and wet setter-dogs – oh, you mean the stew. Well, I wish we had an onion for it. Did he look like he had money?'

'First he looked kind,' said Cecilia. 'I'm sure he was rich; but that matters so little. When he drew out his bill-folder to pay the cabman you couldn't help seeing hundreds and thousands of dollars in it. And I looked over the cab doors and saw him leave the ferry station in a motor-car; and the chauffeur gave him his bearskin to put on, for he was sopping wet. And it was only three days ago.

'What a fool!' said Hetty shortly.

'Oh, the chauffeur wasn't wet,' breathed Cecilia. 'And he drove the car away very nicely.'

'I mean you,' said Hetty. 'For not giving him your address.'

'I never give my address to chauffeurs,' said Cecilia, haughtily.

'I wish we had one,' said Hetty, disconsolately.

'What for?'

'For the stew, of course – oh, I mean an onion.'

Hetty took a pitcher and started to the sink at the end of the hall. A young man came down the steps from above just as she was opposite the lower step. He was decently dressed, but pale and haggard. His eyes were dull with the stress of some burden of physical or mental woe. In his hand he bore an onion – a pink, smooth, solid, shining onion, as large around as a ninety-eight-cent alarm clock.

Hetty stopped. So did the young man. There was something Joan of Arc-ish, Herculean, and Una-ish in the look and pose of the shop-lady – she had cast off the roles of Job and Little-Red-Riding Hood. The young man stopped at the foot of the stairs and coughed distractedly. He felt marooned, held up, attacked, assailed, levied upon, sacked, assessed, panhandled, brow-beaten, though he knew not why. It was the look in Hetty's eyes that did it. In them he saw the Jolly Roger fly to the masthead and an able seaman with a dirk between his teeth scurry up the ratlines and nail it there. But as yet he did not know that the cargo he carried was the thing that had caused him to be so nearly blown out of the water without even a parley.

'*Beg* your pardon,' said Hetty, as sweetly as her dilute acetic acid tones permitted, 'but did you find that onion on the stairs? There was a hole in the paper bag; and I've just come out to look for it.'

The young man coughed for half a minute. The interval may have given him the courage to defend his own property. Also, he clutched his pungent prize greedily, and, with a show of spirit, faced his grim waylayer.

'No,' he said huskily, 'I didn't find it on the stairs. It was given to me by Jack Bevens, on the top floor. If you don't believe it, ask him. I'll wait until you do.'

'I know about Bevens,' said Hetty, sourly. 'He writes books and things up there for the paper-and-rags man. We can hear the postman guy him all over the house when he brings them thick envelopes back. Say – do you live in the Vallambrosa?'

'I do not,' said the young man. 'I come to see Bevens sometimes. He's my friend. I live two blocks west.'

'What are you going to do with the onion? – *begging* your pardon,' said Hetty.

'I'm going to eat it.'

'Raw?'

'Yes: as soon as I get home.'

'Haven't you got anything else to eat with it?'

The young man considered briefly.

'No,' he confessed; 'there's not another scrap of anything in my diggings to eat. I think old Jack is pretty hard up for grub in his shack, too. He hated to give up the onion, but I worried him into parting with it.'

'Man,' said Hetty, fixing him with her world-sapient eyes, and laying a bony but impressive finger on his sleeve, 'you've known trouble, too, haven't you?'

'Lots,' said the onion owner, promptly. 'But this onion is my own property, honestly come by. If you will excuse me, I must be going.'

'Listen,' said Hetty, paling a little with anxiety. 'Raw onion is a mighty poor diet. And so is a beef-steak without one. Now, if you're Jack Bevens' friend, I guess you're nearly right. There's a little lady — a friend of mine — in my room there at the end of the hall. Both of us are out of luck; and we had just potatoes and meat between us. They're stewing now. But it ain't got any soul. There's something lacking to it. There's certain things in life that are naturally intended to fit and belong together. One is pink cheese-cloth and green roses, and one is ham and eggs, and one is Irish and trouble. And the other one is beef and potatoes *with* onions. And still another one is people who are up against it and other people in the same fix.'

The young man went into a protracted paroxysm of coughing. With one hand he hugged his onion to his bosom.

'No doubt; no doubt,' said he, at length. 'But, as I said, I must be going because —'

Hetty clutched his sleeve firmly.

'Don't be a Dago, Little Brother. Don't eat raw onions. Chip it in toward the dinner and line yourself inside with the best stew you ever licked a spoon over. Must two ladies knock a young gentleman down and drag him inside for the honour of dining with 'em? No harm shall befall you, Little Brother. Loosen up and fall into line.'

The young man's pale face relaxed into a grim.

'Believe I'll go you,' he said, brightening. 'If my onion is good as a credential, I'll accept the invitation gladly.'

'It's good as that, but better as seasoning,' said Hetty. 'You come and stand outside the door till I ask my lady friend if she has any objections. And don't run away with that letter of recommendation before I come out.'

Hetty went into her room and closed the door. The young man waited outside.

'Cecilia, kid,' said the shop-girl, oiling the sharp saw of her voice as well as she could, 'there's an onion outside. With a young man attached. I've asked him in to dinner. You ain't going to kick, are you?'

'Oh, dear!' said Cecilia, sitting up and patting her artistic hair. She cast a mournful glance at the ferry-boat poster on the wall.

'Nit,' said Hetty. 'It ain't him. You're up against real life now. I believe you said your hero friend had money and automobiles. This is a poor skeezicks that's got nothing to eat but an onion. But he's easy spoken and not a freshy. I imagine he's been a gentleman, he's so low down now. And we need the onion. Shall I bring him in? I'll guarantee his behaviour.'

'Hetty, dear,' sighed Cecilia, 'I'm so hungry. What difference does it make whether he's a prince or a burglar? I don't care. Bring him in if he's got anything to eat with him.'

Hetty went back into the hall. The onion man was gone. Her heart missed a beat, and a grey look settled over her face except her nose and cheekbones. And then the times of life flowed in again, for she saw him leaning out of the front window at the other end of the hall. She hurried there. He was shouting to someone below. The noise of the street overpowered the sound of her footsteps. She looked down over his shoulder, saw whom he was speaking to, and heard his words. He pulled himself in from the window-sill and saw her standing over him.

Hetty's eyes bored into him like two steel gimlets.

'Don't lie to me,' she said, calmly. 'What were you going to do with that onion?'

The young man suppressed a cough and faced her resolutely. His manner was that of one who had been bearded sufficiently.

'I was going to eat it,' said he, with emphatic slowness; 'just as I told you before.'

'And you have nothing else to eat at home?'

'Not a thing.'

'What kind of work do you do?'

'I am not working at anything just now.'

Then why, said Hetty, with her voice set on its sharpest edge, 'do you lean out of windows and give orders to chauffeurs in green automobiles in the street below?'

The young man flushed, and his dull eyes began to sparkle.

'Because, madam,' said he, in *accelerando* tones, 'I pay the chauffeur's wages and I own the automobile – and also this onion – this onion, madam.'

He flourished the onion within an inch of Hetty's nose. The shop-lady did not retreat a hair's-breadth.

'Then why do you eat onions,' she said, with biting contempt, 'and nothing else?'

'I never said I did,' retorted the young man, heatedly. 'I said I had nothing else to eat where I live. I am not a delicatessen storekeeper.'

'Then why,' pursued Hetty, inflexibly, 'were you going to eat a raw onion?'

'My mother,' said the young man, 'always made me eat one for a cold. Pardon my referring to a physical infirmity; but you have noticed that I have a very, very severe cold. I was going to eat the onion and go to bed. I wonder why I am standing here and apologizing to you for it.'

'How did you catch this cold?' went on Hetty, suspiciously.

The young man seemed to have arrived at some extreme height of feeling. There were two modes of descent open to him – a burst of rage or a surrender to the ridiculous. He chose wisely; and the empty hall echoed his hoarse laughter.

'You're a dandy,' said he. 'And I don't blame you for being careful. I don't mind telling you. I got wet. I was on a North River ferry a few days ago when a girl jumped overboard. Of course, I –'

Hetty extended her hand, interrupting his story.

'Give me the onion,' she said.

The young man set his jaw a trifle harder.

'Give me the onion,' she repeated.

He grinned and laid it in her hand.

Then Hetty's infrequent, grim, melancholy smile showed itself. She took the young man's arm and pointed with her other hand to the door of her room.

'Little Brother,' she said, 'go in there. The little fool you fished out of the river is there waiting for you. Go on in. I'll give you three minutes before I come. Potatoes is in there, waiting. Go on in, Onions.'

After he had tapped at the door and entered Hetty began to peel and wash the onion at the sink. She gave a grey look at the grey roofs outside, and the smile on her face vanished by little jerks and twitches.

'But it's us,' she said, grimly, to herself, 'it's *us* that furnished the beef.'

LVI

Thimble, Thimble

THESE ARE THE DIRECTIONS for finding the office of Carteret & Carteret, Mill Supplies and Leather Belting:

You follow the Broadway trail down until you pass the Crosstown Line, the Bread Line, and the Dead Line, and come to the Big Cañons of the Moneygrubber Tribe. Then you turn to the left, to the right, dodge a push-cart and the tongue of a two-ton four-horse dray, and hop, skip, and jump to a granite ledge on the side of a twenty-one-story synthetic mountain of stone and iron. In the twelfth story is the office of Carteret & Carteret. The factory where they make the mill supplies and leather belting is in Brooklyn. Those commodities – to say nothing of Brooklyn – not being of interest to you, let us hold the incidents within the confines of a one-act, one-scene play, thereby lessening the toil of the reader and the expenditure of the publisher. So, if you have the courage to face four pages of type and Carteret & Carteret's office boy, Percival, you shall sit on a varnished chair in the inner office and peep at the little comedy of the Old Nigger Man, the Hunting-Case Watch, and the Open-faced Question – mostly borrowed from the late Mr. Frank Stockton, as you will conclude.

First, biography (but pared to the quick) must intervene. I am for the inverted sugar-coated quinine pill – the bitter on the outside.

The Carterets were, or was (Columbia College professors please rule), an old Virginia family. Long time ago the gentlemen of the family had worn lace ruffles and carried tinless foils and owned plantations and had slaves to burn. But the war had greatly reduced their holdings. (Of course you can perceive at once that this flavour has been shoplifted from Mr. F. Hopkinson Smith, in spite of the 'et' after 'Carter.') Well, anyhow:

In digging up the Carteret history I shall not take you farther back than the year 1620. The two original American Carterets came over in that year, but by different means of transportation. One brother, named John, came in the *Mayflower* and became a Pilgrim Father. You've seen his picture on the covers of the Thanksgiving magazines, hunting turkeys in the deep snow with a blunderbuss. Blandford Carteret, the other brother, crossed the pond in his own brigantine, landed on the Virginia coast, and became an F. F. V. John became distinguished for piety and shrewdness in business; Blandford for his pride, juleps, marksmanship and vast slave-cultivated plantations.

Then came the Civil War. (I must condense this historical interpolation.) Stonewall Jackson was shot; Lee surrendered; Grant toured the world; cotton went to nine cents; Old Crow whisky and Jim Crown cars were invented; the Seventy-ninth Massachusetts Volunteers returned to the Ninety-seventh Alabama Zouaves the battle flag of Lundy's Lane which they bought at a second-hand store in Chelsea, kept by a man named Skzchnzski; Georgia sent the President a sixty-pound watermelon – and that brings us up to the time when the story begins. My! but that was sparring for an opening! I really must brush up on my Aristotle.

The Yankee Carterets went into business in New York long before the war. Their house, as far as Leather Belting and Mill Supplies was concerned, was as musty and arrogant and solid as one of those old East India tea-importing concerns that you read about in Dickens. There were some rumours of a war behind its counters, but not enough to affect the business.

During and after the war, Blandford Carteret, F.F.V., lost his plantations, juleps, marksmanship and life. He bequeathed little more than his pride to his surviving family. So it came to pass that Blandford Carteret, the Fifth, aged fifteen, was invited by the leather-and-mill-supplies branch of that name to come North and learn business instead of hunting foxes and boasting of the glory of his fathers on the reduced acres of his impoverished family. The boy jumped at the chance, and, at the age of twenty-five, sat in the office of the firm equal partner with John, the Fifth, of the blunderbuss-and-turkey branch. Here the story begins again.

The young men were about the same age, smooth of face, alert, easy of manner, and with an air that promised mental and physical quickness. They were razored, blue-serged, strawhatted, and pearl stick-pinned like other young New Yorkers who might be millionaires or bill clerks.

One afternoon at four o'clock, in the private office of the firm, Blandford Carteret opened a letter that a clerk had just brought to his desk. After reading it, he chuckled audibly for nearly a minute. John looked around from his desk inquiringly.

'It's from mother,' said Blandford; 'I'll read you the funny part of it. She tells me all the neighbourhood news first, of course, and then cautions me against getting my feet wet and musical comedies. After that come vital statistics about calves and pigs and an estimate of the wheat crop. And now I'll quote some:

' "And what do you think! Old Uncle Jake, who was seventy-six last Wednesday, must go travelling. Nothing would do but he must go to New York and see his 'young Marster Blandford.' Old as he is, he has a deal of common sense, so I've let him go. I couldn't refuse him – he seemed to have concentrated all his hopes and desires into this one adventure into the wide world. You know he was born on the plantation, and has never been ten miles away from it in his life. And he was your father's body servant during the war, and has been always a faithful vassal and servant of the family. He has often seen the gold watch – the watch that was your father's and your father's father's. I told him it was to be yours, and he begged me to allow him to take it to you and to put it into your hands himself.

' "So he has it, carefully enclosed in a buckskin case, and is bringing it to you with all the pride and importance of a king's messenger. I gave him money for the round trip and for a two weeks' stay in the city. I wish you would see to it that he gets comfortable quarters – Jake won't need much looking after – he's able to take care of himself. But I have read in the papers that African bishops and coloured potentates generally have much trouble in obtaining food and lodging in the Yankee metropolis. That may be all right; but I don't see why the best hotel there shouldn't take Jake in. Still, I suppose it's a rule.

' "I gave him full directions about finding you, and packed his valise myself. You won't have to bother with him; but I do hope you'll see that he is made comfortable. Take the watch that he brings you – it's almost a decoration. It has been worn by true Carterets, and there isn't a stain upon it nor a false movement of the wheels. Bringing it to you is the crowning joy of old Jake's life. I wanted him to have that little outing and that happiness before it is too late. You have often heard us talk about how Jake, pretty badly wounded himself, crawled through the reddened grass at Chancellorsville to where your father lay with the bullet in his dear heart, and took the watch from his pocket to keep it from the 'Yanks.'

' "So, my son, when the old man comes consider him as a frail but worthy messenger from the old-time life and home.

' "You have been so long away from home, and so long among the people that we have always regarded as aliens, that I'm not sure that Jake will know you when he sees you. But Jake has a keen perception, and I rather believe that he will know a Virginia Carteret at sight. I can't conceive that even ten years in Yankee-land could change a boy of mine. Anyway, I'm sure you will know Jake. I put eighteen collars in his valise. If he should have to buy others, he wears a number 15 1/2. Please see that he gets the right ones. He will be no trouble to you at all.

' "If you are not too busy, I'd like for you to find him a place to board where they have white-meal corn-bread, and try to keep him from taking his shoes off in your office or on the street. His right foot swells a little, and he likes to be comfortable.

' "If you can spare the time, count his handkerchiefs when they come back from the wash. I bought him a dozen new ones before he left. He should be there about the time this letter reaches you. I told him to go straight to your office when he arrives." '

As soon as Blandford had finished the reading of this, something happened (as there should happen in stories and must happen on the stage).

Percival, the office boy, with his air of despising the world's output of mill supplies and leather belting, came in to announce that a coloured gentleman was outside to see Mr. Blandford Carteret.

'Bring him in,' said Blandford, rising.

John Carteret swung around in his chair and said to Percival: 'Ask him to wait a few minutes outside. We'll let you know when to bring him in.'

Then he turned to his cousin with one of those broad slow smiles that was an inheritance of all the Carterets, and said:

'Bland, I've always had a consuming curiosity to understand the differences that you haughty Southerners believe to exist between "you all" and the people of the North. Of course, I know that you consider yourselves made out of finer clay and look upon Adam as only a collateral branch of your ancestry; but I don't know why. I never could understand the differences between us.'

'Well, John,' said Blandford, laughing, 'what you don't understand about it is just the difference, of course. I suppose it was the feudal way in which we lived that gave us our lordly baronial airs and feeling of superiority.'

'But you are not feudal, now,' went on John. 'Since we licked you and stole your cotton and mules you've had to go to work just as we "dam-yankees," as you call us, have always been doing. And you're just as proud and exclusive and upperclassy as you were before the war. So it wasn't your money that caused it.'

'Maybe it was the climate,' said Blandford, lightly, 'or maybe our negroes spoiled us. I'll call old Jake in now. I'll be glad to see the old villain again.'

'Wait just a moment,' said John. 'I've got a little theory I want to test. You and I are pretty much alike in our general appearance. Old Jake hasn't seen you since you were fifteen. Let's have him in and play fair and see which of us gets the watch. The old darky surely ought to be able to pick out his "young marster" without any trouble. The alleged aristocratic superiority of a "reb" ought to be visible to him at once. He couldn't make the mistake of handing over the timepiece to a Yankee, of course. The loser buys the dinner this evening and two dozen 15 ½ collars for Jake. Is it a go?'

Blandford agreed heartily. Percival was summoned, and told to usher the 'coloured gentleman' in.

Uncle Jake stepped inside the private office cautiously. He was a little old man, as black as soot, wrinkled and bald except for a fringe of white wool, cut decorously short, that ran over his ears and around his head. There was nothing of the stage 'uncle' about him: his black suit nearly fitted him; his shoes shone, and his straw hat was banded with a gaudy ribbon. In his right hand he carried something carefully concealed by his closed fingers.

Uncle Jake stopped a few steps from the door. Two young men sat in their revolving desk-chairs ten feet apart and looked at him in friendly silence. His gaze slowly shifted many times from one to the other. He felt sure that he was in the presence of one, at least, of the revered family among whose fortunes his life had begun and was to end.

One had the pleasing but haughty Carteret air; the other had the unmistakable straight, long family nose. Both had the keen black eyes, horizontal brows, and thin, smiling lips that had distinguished both the Carteret of the *Mayflower* and him of the brigantine. Old Jake had thought that he could have picked out his young master instantly from a thousand Northerners; but he found himself in difficulties. The best he could do was to use strategy.

'Howdy, Marse Blandford – howdy, suh?' he said, looking midway between the two young men.

'Howdy, Uncle Jake?' they both answered pleasantly and in unison. 'Sit down. Have you brought the watch?'

Uncle Jake chose a hard-bottom chair at a respectful distance, sat on the edge of it, and laid his hat carefully on the floor. The watch in its buckskin case he gripped tightly. He had not risked his life on the battlefield to rescue that watch from his 'old marster's' foes to hand it over to the enemy again without a struggle.

'Yes, suh; I got it in my hand, suh. I'm gwine give it to you right away in jus' a minute. Old Missus told me to put it in young Marse Blandford's hand and tell him to wear it for the family pride and honour. It was a mighty longsome trip for an old nigger man to make – ten thousand miles, it must be, back to Old Vi'ginia, suh. You've growed mightily, young marster. I wouldn't have recognized you but for yo' powerful resemblance to the old marster.'

With admirable diplomacy the old man kept his eyes roaming in the space between the two men. His words might have been addressed to either. Though neither wicked nor perverse, he was seeking for a sign.

Blandford and John exchanged winks.

'I reckon you done got you ma's letter,' went on Uncle Jake. 'She said she was gwine to write to you bout my comin' along up this er-way.'

'Yes, yes, Uncle Jake,' said John briskly. 'My cousin and I have just been notified to expect you. We are both Carterets, you know.'

'Although one of us,' said Blandford, 'was born and raised in the North.'

'So if you will hand over the watch ' said John.

'My cousin and I –' said Blandford.

'Will then see to it –' said John

'That comfortable quarters are found for you,' said Blandford.

With credible ingenuity, old Jake set up a cackling, high-pitched, protracted laugh. He beat his knee, picked up his hat and bent the brim in an apparent paroxysm of humorous appreciation. The seizure afforded him a mask behind which he could roll his eye impartially between, above, and beyond his two tormentors.

'I sees what!' he chuckled, after awhile. 'You gen'lemen is tryin' to have fun with the po' old nigger. But you can't fool old Jake. I knowed you, Marse Blandford, the minute I set eyes on you. You was a po' skimpy little boy no mo' than about fo-teen when you lef' home to come No'th; but I knowed you the minute I sot eyes on you. You is the mawtal image of old marster. The other gen'lemen resembles you mightily, suh; but you can't fool old Jake on a member of the Old Vi'ginia family. No, suh.'

At exactly the same time both Carterets smiled and extended a hand for the watch.

Uncle Jake's wrinkled, black face lost the expression of amusement into which he had vainly twisted it. He knew that he was being teased, and that it made little real difference, as far as its safety went, into which of those outstretched hands he placed the family treasure. But it seemed to him that not only his own pride and loyalty but much of the Virginia Carterets' was at stake. He had heard down South during the war about that other branch of the family that lived in the North and fought on 'the yuther side,' and it had always grieved him. He had followed his 'old marster's' fortunes from stately luxury through war to almost poverty. And now, with the last relic and reminder of him, blessed by 'old missus,' and entrusted implicitly to his care, he had come ten thousand miles (as it seemed) to deliver it into the hands of the one who was to wear it and wind it and cherish it and listen to it tick off the unsullied hours that marked the lives of the Carterets – of Virginia.

His experience and conception of the Yankees had been an impression of tyrants – 'low-down, common trash' – in blue, laying waste with fire and sword. He had seen the smoke of many burning homesteads almost as grand as Carteret Hall ascending to the drowsy Southern skies. And now he was face to face with one of them – and he could not distinguish him from his 'young marster' whom he had come to find and bestow upon him the emblem of his kingship – even as the arm 'clothed in white samite, mystic, wonderful' laid Excalibur in the right hand of Arthur. He saw before him two young men, easy, kind, courteous, welcoming, either of whom might have been the one he sought. Troubled, bewildered, sorely grieved at his weakness of judgment, old Jake abandoned his loyal subterfuges. His right hand sweated against the buckskin cover of the watch. He was deeply humiliated and chastened. Seriously, now, his prominent, yellow-white eyes closely scanned the two young men. At the end of his scrutiny he was conscious of but one difference between them. One wore a narrow black tie with a white pearl stick-pin. The other's 'four-hand' was a narrow blue one pinned with a black pearl.

And then, to old Jake's relief, there came a sudden distraction. Drama knocked at the door with imperious knuckles, and forced Comedy to the wings, and Drama peeped with a smiling but set face over the footlights.

Percival, the hater of mill supplies, brought in a card, which he handed, with the manner of one bearing a cartel, to Blue-Tie.

' "Olivia De Ormond," ' read Blue-Tie from the card. He looked inquiringly at his cousin.

'Why not have her in,' said Black-Tie, 'and bring matters to a conclusion?'

'Uncle Jake,' said one of the young men, 'would you mind taking that chair over there in the corner for a while? A lady is coming in – on some business. We'll take up your case afterward.'

The lady whom Percival ushered in was young and petulantly, decidedly, freshly, consciously, and intentionally pretty. She was dressed with such expensive plainness that she made you consider lace and ruffles as mere tatters and rags. But one great ostrich plume that she wore would have marked her anywhere in the army of beauty as the wearer of the merry helmet of Navarre.

Miss De Ormond accepted the swivel chair at Blue-Tie's desk. Then the gentlemen drew leather-upholstered seats conveniently near, and spoke of the weather.

'Yes,' said she, 'I noticed it was warmer. But I mustn't take up too much of your time during business hours. That is,' she continued, 'unless we talk business.'

She addressed her words to Blue-Tie, with a charming smile.

'Very well,' said he. 'You don't mind my cousin being present, do you? We are generally rather confidential with each other – especially in business matters.'

'Oh, no,' carolled Miss De Ormond. 'I'd rather he did hear. He knows all about it, anyhow. In fact, he's quite a material witness because he was present when you – when it happened. I thought you might want to talk things over before – well, before any action is taken, as I believe the lawyers say.'

'Have you anything in the way of a proposition to make?' asked Blue-Tie.

Miss De Ormond looked reflectively at the neat toe of one of her dull kid pumps.

'I had a proposal made to me,' she said. 'If the proposal sticks it cuts out the proposition. Let's have that settled first.'

'Well, as far as –' began Blue-Tie.

'Excuse me, cousin,' interrupted Black-Tie, 'if you don't mind my cutting in.' And then he turned, with a good-natured air, toward the lady.

'Now, let's recapitulate a bit,' he said cheerfully 'All three of us, besides other mutual acquaintances, have been out on a good many larks together.'

'I'm afraid I'll have to call the birds by another name,' said Miss De Ormond.

'All right,' responded Black-Tie, with unimpaired cheerfulness;

'suppose we say "squabs" when we talk about the "proposal" and "larks" when we discuss the "proposition." You have a quick mind, Miss De Ormond. Two months ago, some half-dozen of us went in a motor-car for a day's run into the country. We stopped at a road-house for dinner. My cousin proposed marriage to you then and there. He was influenced to do so, of course, by the beauty and charm which no one can deny that you possess.'

'I wish I had you for a press agent, Mr. Carteret,' said the beauty, with a dazzling smile.

'You are on the stage, Miss De Ormond,' went on Black-Tie. 'You have had, doubtless, many admirers, and perhaps other proposals. You must remember, too, that we were a party of merry-makers on that occasion. There were a good many corks pulled. That the proposal of marriage was made to you by my cousin we cannot deny. But hasn't it been your experience that, by common consent, such things lose their seriousness when viewed in the next day's sunlight? Isn't there something of a "code" among good "sports" – I use the word in its best sense – that wipes out each day the follies of the evening previous?'

'Oh, yes,' said Miss De Ormond. 'I know that very well. And I've always played up to it. But as you seem to be conducting the case – with the silent consent of the defendant – I'll tell you something more. I've got letters from him repeating the proposal. And they're signed, too.'

'I understand,' said Black-Tie, gravely. 'What's your price for the letters?'

'I'm not a cheap one,' said Miss De Ormond. 'But I had decided to make you a rate. You both belong to a swell family. Well, if I am on the stage nobody can say a word against me truthfully. And the money is only a secondary consideration. It isn't the money I was after. I – I believed him – and – and I liked him.'

She cast a soft, entrancing glance at Blue-Tie from under her long eyelashes.

'And the price?' went on Black-Tie, inexorably.

'Ten thousand dollars,' said the lady, sweetly.

'Or –'

'Or the fulfilment of the engagement to marry.'

'I think it is time,' interrupted Blue-Tie, 'for me to be allowed to say a word or two. You and I, cousin, belong to a family that has held its head pretty high. You have been brought up in a section of the country very different from the one where our branch of the family lived. Yet both of us are Carterets, even if some of our ways and theories differ. You remember it is a tradition of the family, that no Carteret ever failed in chivalry to a lady or failed to keep his word when it was given.'

Then Blue-Tie, with frank decision showing on his countenance, turned to Miss De Ormond.

'Olivia,' said he, 'on what date will you marry me?'

Before she could answer, Black-Tie again interposed.

'It is a long journey,' said he, 'from Plymouth Rock to Norfolk Bay. Between the two points we find the changes that nearly three centuries have brought. In that time the old order has changed. We no longer burn witches or torture slaves. And to-day we neither spread our cloaks on the mud for ladies to walk over nor treat them to the ducking-stool. It is the age of common sense, adjustment, and proportion. All of us – ladies, gentlemen, women, men, Northerners, Southerners, lords, caitiffs, actors, hardware-drummers, senators, hodcarriers and politicians – are coming to a better understanding. Chivalry is one of our words that changes its meaning every day. Family pride is a thing of many constructions – it may show itself by maintaining a moth-eaten arrogance in a cobwebbed Colonial mansion or by the prompt paying of one's debts.

'Now, I suppose you've had enough of my monologue. I've learned something of business and a little of life; and I somehow believe, cousin, that our great-great-grandfathers, the original Carterets, would endorse my view of this matter.'

Black-Tie wheeled around to his desk, wrote in a cheque-book and tore out the cheque, the sharp rasp of the perforated leaf making the only sound in the room. He laid the cheque within easy reach of Miss De Ormond's hand.

'Business is business,' said he. 'We live in a business age. There is my personal cheque for $10,000. What do you say, Miss De Ormond – will it be orange blossoms or cash?'

Miss De Ormond picked up the cheque carelessly, folded it indifferently, and stuffed it into her glove.

'Oh, this'll do,' she said, calmly. 'I just thought I'd call and put it up to you. I guess you people are all right. But a girl has feelings, you know. I've heard one of you was a Southerner – I wonder which one of you it is?'

She arose, smiled sweetly, and walked to the door. There, with a flash of white teeth and a dip of the heavy plume, she disappeared.

Both of the cousins had forgotten Uncle Jake for the time. But now they heard the shuffling of his shoes as he came across the rug toward them from his seat in the corner.

'Young marster,' he said, 'take yo' watch.'

And without hesitation he laid the ancient timepiece in the hand of its rightful owner.

LVII

Buried Treasure

THERE ARE MANY KINDS OF FOOLS. Now, will everybody please sit still until they are called upon specifically to rise?

I had been every kind of fool except one. I had expended my patrimony, pretended my matrimony, played poker, lawn-tennis, and bucket shops – parted soon with my money in many ways. But there remained one role of the wearer of cap and bells that I had not played. That was the Seeker after Buried Treasure. To few does the delectable furor come. But of all the would-be followers in the hoof-prints of King Midas none has found a pursuit so rich in pleasurable promise.

But, going back from my theme a while – as lame pens must do – I was a fool of the sentimental sort. I saw May Martha Mangum, and was hers. She was eighteen, the colour of the white ivory keys of a new piano, beautiful, and possessed by the exquisite solemnity and pathetic witchery of an unsophisticated angel doomed to live in a small, dull, Texas prairie-town. She had a spirit and charm that could have enabled her to pluck rubies like raspberries from the crown of Belgium or any other sporty kingdom, but she did not know it, and I did not paint the picture for her.

You see, I wanted May Martha Mangum for to have and to hold. I wanted her to abide with me, and put my slippers and pipe away every day in places where they cannot be found of evenings.

May Martha's father was a man hidden behind whiskers and spectacles. He lived for bugs and butterflies and all insects that fly or crawl or buzz to get down your back or in the butter. He was an etymologist, or words to that effect. He spent his life seining the air for flying fish of the June-bug order, and then sticking pins through 'em and calling 'em names.

He and May Martha were the whole family. He prized her highly as a fine specimen of the *racibus humanus* because she saw that he had food at times, and put his clothes on right side before, and kept his alcohol-bottles filled. Scientists, they say, are apt to be absent-minded.

There was another beside myself who thought May Martha Mangum one to be desired. That was Goodloe Banks, a young man just home from college. He had all the attainments to be found in books — Latin, Greek, philosophy, and especially the higher branches of mathematics and logic.

If it hadn't been for his habit of pouring out this information and learning on every one that he addressed, I'd have liked him pretty well. But, even as it was, he and I were, you would have thought, great pals.

We got together every time we could because each of us wanted to pump the other for whatever straws we could find which way the wind blew from the heart of May Martha Mangum — rather a mixed metaphor; Goodloe Banks would never have been guilty of that. That is the way of rivals.

You might say that Goodloe ran to books, manners, culture, rowing, intellect, and clothes. I would have put you in mind more of baseball and Friday-night debating societies — by way of culture — and maybe of a good horse-back rider.

But in our talks together, and in our visits and conversation with May Martha, neither Goodloe Banks nor I could find out which one of us she preferred. May Martha was a natural-born noncommittal, and knew in her cradle how to keep people guessing.

As I said, old man Mangum was absent-minded. After a long time he found out one day — a little butterfly must have told him — that two young men were trying to throw a net over the head of the young person, a daughter, or some such technical appendage, who looked after his comforts.

I never knew scientists could rise to such occasions. Old Mangum orally labelled and classified Goodloe and myself easily among the lowest orders of the vertebrates; and in English, too, without going any further into Latin than the simple references to *Orgetorix, Rex Helvetii* — which is as far as I ever went myself. And he told us that if he ever caught us around his house again he would add us to his collection.

Goodloe Banks and I remained away five days, expecting the storm to subside. When we dared to call at the house again May Martha Mangum and her father were gone. Gone! The house they had rented was closed. Their little store of goods and chattels was gone also.

And not a word of farewell to either of us from May Martha — not a white, fluttering note pinned to the hawthorn-bush; not a chalk-mark on the gate-post nor a post card in the post office to give us a clue.

For two months Goodloe Banks and I – separately – tried every scheme we could think of to trace the runaways. We used our friendship and influence with the ticket agent, with livery-stable men, railroad conductors, and our one lone, lorn constable, but without results.

Then we became better friends and worse enemies than ever. We forgathered in the back room of Snyder's saloon every afternoon after work, and played dominoes, and laid conversational traps to find out from each other if anything had been discovered. That is the way of rivals.

Now, Goodloe Banks had a sarcastic way of displaying his own learning and putting me in the class that was reading 'Poor Jane Ray, her bird is dead, she cannot play.' Well, I rather liked Goodloe, and I had a contempt for his college learning, and I was always regarded as good-natured, so I kept my temper. And I was trying to find out if he knew anything about May Martha, so I endured his society.

In talking things over one afternoon he said to me:

'Suppose you do find her, Ed, whereby would you profit? Miss Mangum has a mind. Perhaps it is yet uncultured, but she is destined for higher things than you could give her. I have talked with no one who seemed to appreciate more the enchantment of the ancient poets and writers and the modern cults that have assimilated and expended their philosophy of life. Don't you think you are wasting your time looking for her?'

'My idea,' said I, 'of a happy home is an eight-room house in a grove of live-oaks by the side of a *charco* on a Texas prairie. A piano,' I went on, 'with an automatic player in the sitting-room, three thousand head of cattle under fence for a starter, a buckboard and ponies always hitched at a post for "the missus" – and May Martha Mangum to spend the profits of the ranch as she pleases, and to abide with me, and put my slippers and pipe away every day in places where they cannot be found of evenings. That,' said I, 'is what is to be; and a fig – a dried, Smyrna, Dagostand fig – for your curriculums, cults, and philosophy.'

'She is meant for higher things,' repeated Goodloe Banks.

'Whatever she is meant for,' I answered, 'just now she is out of pocket. And I shall find her as soon as I can without aid of the colleges.'

'The game is blocked,' said Goodloe, putting down a dominoe; and we had the beer.

Shortly after that a young farmer whom I knew came into town and brought me a folded blue paper. He said his grandfather had just died. I concealed a tear, and he went on to say that the old man had jealously guarded this paper for twenty years. He left it to his family as part of his estate, the rest of which consisted of two mules and a hypotenuse of non-arable land.

The sheet of paper was of the old, blue kind used during the rebellion of the abolitionists against the secessionists. It was dated June 14, 1863, and it described the hiding-place of ten burro-loads of gold and silver coin valued at three hundred thousand dollars. Old Rundle – grandfather of his grandson, Sam – was given the information by a Spanish priest who was in on the treasure-burying, and who died many years before – no, afterward – in old Rundle's house. Old Rundle wrote it down from dictation.

'Why didn't your father look this up?' I asked young Rundle.

'He went blind before he could do so,' he replied.

'Why didn't you hunt for it yourself?' I asked.

'Well,' said he, 'I've only known about the paper for ten years. First there was the spring ploughin' to do, and then choppin' the weeds out of the corn; and then come takin' fodder; and mighty soon winter was on us. It seemed to run along that way year after year.'

That sounded perfectly reasonable to me, so I took it up with young Lee Rundle at once.

The directions on the paper were simple. The whole burro cavalcade laden with the treasure started from an old Spanish mission in Dolores County. They travelled due south by the compass until they reached the Alamito River. They forded this, and buried the treasure on the top of a little mountain shaped like a pack-saddle standing in a row between two higher ones. A heap of stones marked the place of the buried treasure. All the party except the Spanish priest were killed by Indians a few days later. The secret was a monopoly. It looked good to me.

Lee Rundle suggested that we rig out a camping outfit, hire a surveyor to run out the line from the Spanish mission, and then spend the three hundred thousand dollars seeing the sights in Fort Worth. But, without being highly educated, I knew a way to save time and expense.

We went to the State land-office and had a practical, what they call a 'working,' sketch made of all the surveys of land from the old mission to the Alamito River. On this map I drew a line due southward to the river. The length of lines of each survey and section of land was accurately given on the sketch. By these we found the point on the river and had a 'connection' made with it and an important well-identified corner of the Los Animos five-league survey – a grant made by King Philip of Spain.

By doing this we did not need to have the line run out by a surveyor. It was a great saving of expense and time.

So, Lee Rundle and I fitted out a two-horse wagon team with all the accessories, and drove a hundred and forty-nine miles to Chico, the nearest town to the point we wished to reach. There we picked up a deputy county surveyor. He found the corner of the Los Animos survey for us, ran out the five thousand seven hundred and twenty varas west that our sketch called for, laid a stone on the spot, had coffee and bacon, and caught the mail-stage back to Chico.

I was pretty sure we would get that three hundred thousand dollars. Lee Rundle's was to be only one third, because I was paying all the expenses. With that two hundred thousand dollars I knew I could find May Martha Mangum if she was on earth. And with it I could flutter the butterflies in old man Mangum's dovecot, too. If I could find that treasure!

But Lee and I established camp. Across the river were a dozen little mountains densely covered by cedar-brakes, but not one shaped like a packsaddle. That did not deter us. Appearances are deceptive. A pack-saddle, like beauty, may exist only in the eye of the beholder.

I and the grandson of the treasure examined those cedar-covered hills with the care of a lady hunting for the wicked flea. We explored every side, top, circumference, mean elevation, angle, slope, and concavity of every one for two miles up and down the river. We spent four days doing so. Then we hitched up the roan and the dun, and hauled the remains of the coffee and bacon the one hundred and forty-nine miles back to Concho City.

Lee Rundle chewed much tobacco on the return trip. I was busy driving, because I was in a hurry.

As shortly as could be after our empty return, Goodloe Banks and I forgathered in the back room of Snyder's saloon to play dominoes and fish for information. I told Goodloe about my expedition after the buried treasure.

'If I could have found that three hundred thousand dollars,' I said to him, 'I could have scoured and sifted the surface of the earth to find May Martha Mangum.'

'She is meant for higher things,' said Goodloe. 'I shall find her myself. But, tell me how you went about discovering the spot where this unearthed increment was imprudently buried.'

I told him in the smallest detail. I showed him the draughtsman's sketch with the distances marked plainly upon it.

After glancing over it in a masterly way, he leaned back in his chair and bestowed upon me an explosion of sardonic, superior, collegiate laughter.

'Well, you *are* a fool, Jim,' he said, when he could speak.

'It's your play,' said I, patiently, fingering my double six.

'Twenty,' said Goodloe, making two crosses on the table with his chalk.

'Why am I a fool?' I asked. 'Buried treasure has been found before in many places.'

'Because,' said he, 'in calculating the point on the river where your line would strike you neglected to allow for the variation. The variation there would be nine degrees west. Let me have your pencil.'

Goodloe Banks figured rapidly on the back of an envelope.

'The distance, from north to south, of the line run from the Spanish mission,' said he, 'is exactly twenty-two miles. It was run by a pocket-compass, according to your story. Allowing for the variation, the point on the Alamito River where you should have searched for your treasure is exactly six miles and nine hundred and forty-five varas farther west than the place you hit upon. Oh, what a fool you are, Jim!'

'What is this variation that you speak of?' I asked. 'I thought figures never lied.'

'The variation of the magnetic compass,' said Goodloe, 'from the true meridian.'

He smiled in his superior way; and then I saw come out in his face the singular, eager, consuming cupidity of the seeker after buried treasure.

'Sometimes,' he said, with the air of the oracle, 'these old traditions of hidden money are not without foundation. Suppose you let me look over that paper describing the location. Perhaps together we might –'

The result was that Goodloe Banks and I, rivals in love, became companions in adventure. We went to Chico by stage from Huntersburg, the nearest railroad town. In Chico we hired a team drawing a covered spring-wagon and camping paraphernalia. We had the same surveyor run out our distance, as revised by Goodloe and his variations, and then dismissed him and sent him on his homeward road.

It was night when we arrived. I fed the horses and made a fire near the bank of the river and cooked supper. Goodloe would have helped, but his education had not fitted him for practical things.

But while I worked he cheered me with the expression of great thoughts handed down from the dead ones of old. He quoted some translations from the Greek at much length.

'Anacreon,' he explained. 'That was a favourite passage with Miss Mangum – as I recited it.'

'She is meant for higher things,' said I, repeating his phrase.

'Can there be anything higher,' asked Goodloe, 'than to dwell in the society of the classics, to live in the atmosphere of learning and culture? You have often decried education. What of your wasted efforts through your ignorance of simple mathematics? How soon would you have found your treasure if my knowledge had not shown you your error?'

'We'll take a look at those hills across the river first,' said I, 'and see what we find. I am still doubtful about variations. I have been brought up to believe that the needle is true to the pole.'

The next morning was a bright June one. We were up early and had breakfast. Goodloe was charmed. He recited – Keats, I think it was, and Kelly or Shelley – while I broiled the bacon. We were getting ready to cross the river, which was little more than a shallow creek there, and explore the many sharp-peaked, cedar-covered hills on the other side.

'My good Ulysses,' said Goodloe, slapping me on the shoulder while I was washing the tin breakfast plates, 'let me see the enchanted document once more. I believe it gives directions for climbing the hill shaped like a pack-saddle. I never saw a pack-saddle. What is it like, Jim?'

'Score one against culture,' said I. 'I'll know it when I see it.'

Goodloe was looking at old Rundle's document when he ripped out a most uncollegiate swearword.

'Come here,' he said, holding the paper up against the sunlight. 'Look at that,' he said, laying his finger against it.

On the blue paper – a thing I had never noticed before – I saw stand out in white letters the word and figures: 'Malvern, 1898.'

'What about it?' I asked.

'It's the water-mark,' said Goodloe. 'The paper was manufactured in 1898. The writing on the paper is dated 1863. This is a palpable fraud.'

'Oh, I don't know,' said I. 'The Rundles are pretty reliable, plain, uneducated country people. Maybe the paper manufacturers tried to perpetrate a swindle.'

And then Goodloe Banks went as wild as his education permitted. He dropped the glasses off his nose and glared at me.

'I've often told you you were a fool,' he said. 'You have let yourself be imposed upon by a clodhopper. And you have imposed upon me.'

'How,' I asked, 'have I imposed upon you?'

'By your ignorance,' said he. 'Twice I have discovered serious flaws in your plans that a common-school education should have enabled you to avoid. And,' he continued, 'I have been put to expense that I could ill afford in pursuing this swindling quest. I am done with it.'

I rose and pointed a large pewter spoon at him, fresh from the dish-water.

'Goodloe Banks,' I said, 'I care not one parboiled navy bean for your education. I always barely tolerated it in anyone, and I despised it in you. What has your learning done for you? It is a curse to yourself and a bore to your friends. Away,' I said – 'away with your water-marks and variations! They are nothing to me. They shall not deflect me from the quest.'

I pointed with my spoon across the river to a small mountain shaped like a pack-saddle.

'I am going to search that mountain,' I went on, 'for the treasure. Decide now whether you are in it or not. If you wish to let a water-mark or a variation shake your soul, you are no true adventurer. Decide.'

A white cloud of dust began to rise far down the river road. It was the mail-wagon from Hesperus to Chico. Goodloe flagged it.

'I am done with the swindle,' said he, sourly. 'No one but a fool would pay any attention to that paper now. Well, you always were a fool, Jim. I leave you to your fate.'

He gathered his personal traps, climbed into the mail-wagon, adjusted his glasses nervously, and flew away in a cloud of dust.

After I had washed the dishes and staked the horses on new grass, I crossed the shallow river and made my way slowly through the cedar-brakes up to the top of the hill shaped like a pack-saddle.

It was a wonderful June day. Never in my life had I seen so many birds, so many butterflies, dragon-flies, grasshoppers, and such winged and stinged beasts of the air and fields.

I investigated the hill shaped like a pack-saddle from base to summit. I found an absolute absence of signs relating to buried treasure. There was no pile of stones, no ancient blazes on the trees, none of the evidences of the three hundred thousand dollars, as set forth in the document of old man Rundle.

I came down the hill in the cool of the afternoon. Suddenly, out of the cedar-brake I stepped into a beautiful green valley where a tributary small stream ran into the Alamito River.

And there I was startled to see what I took to be a wild man, with unkempt beard and ragged hair, pursuing a giant butterfly with brilliant wings.

'Perhaps he is an escaped madman,' I thought; and wondered how he had strayed so far from seats of education and learning.

And then I took a few more steps and saw a vine-covered cottage near the small stream. And in a little grassy glade I saw May Martha Mangum plucking wild flowers.

She straightened up and looked at me. For the first time since I knew her I saw her face – which was the colour of the white keys of a new piano – turn pink. I walked toward her without a word. She let the gathered flowers trickle slowly from her hand to the grass.

'I knew you would come, Jim,' she said clearly. 'Father wouldn't let me write, but I knew you would come.'

What followed, you may guess – there was my wagon and team just across the river.

I've often wondered what good too much education is to a man if he can't use it for himself. If all the benefits of it are to go to others, where does it come in?

For May Martha Mangum abides with me. There is an eight-room house in a live-oak grove, and a piano with an automatic player, and a good start toward the three thousand head of cattle is under fence.

And when I ride home at night my pipe and slippers are in places put away where they cannot be found.

But who cares for that? Who cares – who cares?

LVIII

The Moment of Victory

BEN GRANGER IS A WAR VETERAN aged twenty-nine – which should enable you to guess the war. He is also principal merchant and postmaster of Cadiz, a little town over which the breezes from the Gulf of Mexico perpetually blow.

Ben helped to hurl the Don from his stronghold in the Greater Antilles; and then, hiking across half the world, he marched as a corporal-usher up and down the blazing tropic aisles of the open-air college in which the Filipino was schooled. Now, with his bay-onet beaten into a cheese slicer, he rallies his corporal's guard of cronies in the shade of his well-whittled porch, instead of in the matted jungles of Mindanao. Always have his interest and choice been for deeds rather than for words; but the consideration and digestion of motives is not beyond him, as this story, which is his, will attest.

'What is it,' he asked me one moonlit eve, as we sat among his boxes and barrels, 'that generally makes men go through dangers, and fire, and trouble, and starvation, and battle, and such recourses? What does a man do it for? Why does he try to outdo his fellow-humans, and be braver and stronger and more daring and showy than even his best friends are? What's his game? What does he expect to get out of it? He don't do it just for the fresh air and exercise. What would you say, now, Bill, that an ordinary man expects, generally speaking, for his efforts along the line of ambi-tion and extraordinary hustling in the market-places, forums, shooting-galleries, lyceums, battlefields, links, cinder-paths, and arenas of the civilized and vice versa places of the world?'

'Well, Ben,' said I, with judicious seriousness, 'I think we might safely limit the number of motives of a man who seeks fame to three — to ambition, which is a desire for popular applause; to avarice, which looks to the material side of success; and to love of some woman whom he either possesses or desires to possess.'

Ben pondered over my words while a mockingbird on the top of a mesquite by the porch trilled a dozen bars.

'I reckon,' said he, 'that your diagnosis about covers the case according to the rules laid down in the copybooks and historical readers. But what I had in my mind was the case of Willie Rob-bins, a person I used to know. I'll tell you about him before I close up the store, if you don't mind listening.

'Willie was one of our social set up in San Augustine. I was clerking there then for Brady & Murchison, wholesale dry-goods and ranch supplies. Willie and I belonged to the same german club and athletic association and military company. He played the triangle in our serenading and quartet crowd that used to ring the welkin three nights a week somewhere in town.

'Willie jibed with his name considerable. He weighed about as much as a hundred pounds of veal in his summer suitings, and he had a "Where-is-Mary?" expression on his features so plain that you could almost see the wool growing on him.

'And yet you couldn't fence him away from the girls with barbed wire. You know that kind of young fellows – a kind of a mixture of fools and angels – they rush in and fear to tread at the same time; but they never fail to tread when they get the chance. He was always on hand when "a joyful occasion was had," as the morning paper would say, looking as happy as a king full, and at the same time as uncomfortable as a raw oyster served with sweet pickles. He danced like he had hind hobbles on; and he had a vocabulary of about three hundred and fifty words that he made stretch over four germans a week, and plagiarized from to get him through two ice-cream suppers and a Sunday-night call. He seemed to me to be a sort of a mixture of Maltese kitten, sensitive plant, and a member of a stranded "Two Orphans" company.

'I'll give you an estimate of his physiological and pictorial make-up and then I'll stick spurs into the sides of my narrative.

'Willie inclined to the Caucasian in his colouring and manner of style. His hair was opalescent and his conversation fragmentary. His eyes were the same blue shade as the china dog's on the right-hand corner of your Aunt Ellen's mantelpiece. He took things as they came, and I never felt any hostility against him. I let him live, and so did others.

'But what does this Willie do but coax his heart out of his boots and lose it to Myra Allison, the liveliest, brightest, keenest, smartest, and prettiest girl in San Augustine. I tell you, she had the blackest eyes, the shiniest curls, and the most tantalizing – Oh, no, you're off – I wasn't a victim. I might have been, but I knew better. I kept out. Joe Granberry was It from the start. He had everybody else beat a couple of leagues and thence east to a stake and mound. But, anyhow, Myra was a nine-pound, full-merino, fall-clip fleece, sacked and loaded on a four-horse team for San Antone.

'One night there was an ice-cream sociable at Mrs. Colonel Spraggins', in San Augustine. We fellows had a big room upstairs opened up for us to put our hats and things in, and to comb our hair and put on the clean collars we brought along inside the sweat-bands of our hats – in short, a room to fix up in just like they have everywhere at high-toned doings. A little farther down the hall was the girls' room, which they used to powder up in, and so forth. Downstairs we – that is, the San Augustine Social Cotillion and Merrymakers' Club – had a stretcher put down in the parlour where our dance was going on.

'Willie Robbins and me happened to be up in our – cloak-room, I believe we called it – when Myra Allison skipped through the hall on her way downstairs from the girls' room. Willie was standing before the mirror, deeply interested in smoothing down the blond grass-plot on his head, which seemed to give him lots of trouble. Myra was always full of life and devilment. She stopped and stuck her head in our door. She certainly was good-looking. But I knew how Joe Granberry stood with her. So did Willie; but he kept on ba-a-a-ing after her and following her around. He had a system of persistence that didn't coincide with pale hair and light eyes.

' "Hello, Willie!" says Myra. "What are you doing to yourself in the glass?"

' "I'm trying to look fly," says Willie.

' "Well, you never could *be* fly,' says Myra with her special laugh, which was the provokingest sound I ever heard except the rattle of an empty canteen against my saddle-horn.

'I looked around at Willie after Myra had gone. He had a kind of a lily-white look on him which seemed to show that her remark had, as you might say, disrupted his soul. I never noticed anything in what she said that sounded particularly destructive to a man's ideas of self-consciousness; but he was set back to an extent you could scarcely imagine.

'After we went downstairs with our clean collars on, Willie never went near Myra again that night. After all, he seemed to be a diluted kind of a skimmilk sort of a chap, and I never wondered that Joe Granberry beat him out.

'The next day the battleship *Maine* was blown up, and then pretty soon somebody – I reckon it was Joe Bailey, or Ben Tillman, or maybe the Government – declared war against Spain.

'Well, everybody south of Mason & Hamlin's line knew that the North by itself couldn't whip a whole country the size of Spain. So the Yankees commenced to holler for help, and the Johnny Rebs answered the call. "We're coming, Father William, a hundred thousand strong – and then some," was the way they sang it. And the old party lines drawn by Sherman's march and the Ku-Klux and nine-cent cotton and the Jim Crow street-car ordinances faded away. We became one undivided country, with no North, very little East, a good-sized chunk of West, and a South that loomed up as big as the first foreign label in a new eight dollar suit-case.

'Of course the dogs of war weren't a complete pack without a

yelp from the San Augustine Rifles, Company D, of the Fourteenth Texas Regiment. Our company was among the first to land
in Cuba and strike terror into the hearts of the foe. I'm not going
to give you a history of the war; I'm just dragging it in to fill out
my story about Willie Robbins, just as the Republican party
dragged it in to help out the election in 1898.

'If anybody ever had heroitis, it was that Willie Robbins. From
the minute he set foot on the soil of the tyrants of Castile he
seemed to engulf danger as a cat laps up cream. He certainly
astonished every man in our company, from the captain up. You'd
have expected him to gravitate naturally to the job of an orderly to
the colonel, or typewriter in the commissary – but not any. He
created the part of the flaxen-haired boy hero who lives and gets
back home with the goods, instead of dying with an important
despatch in his hands at his colonel's feet.

'Our company got into a section of Cuban scenery where one of
the messiest and most unsung portions of the campaign occurred.
We were out every day capering around in the bushes, and having
little skirmishes with the Spanish troops that looked more like
kind of tired-out feuds than anything else. The war was a joke to
us, and of no interest to them. We never could see it any other
way than as a howling farce-comedy that the San Augustine Rifles
were actually fighting to uphold the Stars and Stripes. And the
blamed little señors didn't get enough pay to make them care
whether they were patriots or traitors. Now and then somebody
would get killed. It seemed like a waste of life to me. I was at
Coney Island when I went to New York once, and one of them
down-hill skidding apparatuses they call "roller-coasters" flew
the track and killed a man in a brown sack-suit. Whenever
the Spaniards shot one of our men it struck me as just about as
unnecessary and regrettable as that was.

'But I'm dropping Willie Robbins out of the conversation.

'He was out for bloodshed, laurels, ambition, medals, recommendations, and all other forms of military glory. And he didn't
seem to be afraid of any of the recognized forms of military danger,
such as Spaniards, cannon-balls, canned beef, gunpowder, or nepo-
tism. He went forth with his pallid hair and china-blue eyes and ate
up Spaniards like you would sardines *a la* canopy. Wars and rum-
bles of wars never flustered him. He would stand guard-duty, mosquitoes, hard-tack, treat, and fire with equally perfect unanimity.
No blondes in history ever come in comparison distance of him
except the Jack of Diamonds and Queen Catherine of Russia.

'I remember, one time, a little *caballard* of Spanish men sauntered out from behind a patch of sugar-cane and shot Bob Turner,
the first sergeant of our company, while we were eating dinner. As
required by the army regulations, we fellows went through the
usual tactics of falling into line, saluting the enemy, and loading
and firing, kneeling.

'That wasn't the Texas way of scrapping; but, being a very
important addendum and annex to the regular army, the San
Augustine Rifles had to conform to the red-tape system of getting
even.

'By the time we had got out our *Upton's Tactics*, turned to page
fifty-seven, said "one – two – three – one – two – three" a couple
of times, and got blank cartridges into our Springfields, the Spanish outfit had smiled repeatedly, rolled and lit cigarettes by squads
and walked away contemptuously.

'I went straight to Captain Floyd, and says to him: "Sam, I don't
think this war is a straight game. You know as well as I do that
Bob Turner was one of the whitest fellows that ever threw a leg
over a saddle, and now these wire-pullers in Washington have
fixed his clock. He's politically and ostensibly dead. It ain't fair.
Why should they keep this thing up? If they want Spain licked,
why don't they turn the San Augustine Rifles and Joe Seely's
ranger company and a carload of West Texas deputy-sheriffs on to
these Spaniards, and let us exonerate them from the face of the
earth? I never did," says I, "care much about fighting by the Lord
Chesterfield ring rules. I'm going to hand in my resignation and
go home if anybody else I am personally acquainted with gets hurt
in this war. If you can get somebody in my place, Sam," says I, "I'll
quit the first of next week. I don't want to work in an army that
don't give its help a chance. Never mind my wages," says I; "let
the Secretary of the Treasury keep 'em."

' "Well, Ben," says the captain to me, "your allegations and esti-
mations of the tactics of war, government, patriotism, guard-
mounting, and democracy are all right. But I've looked into the
system of international arbitration and the ethics of justifiable
slaughter a little closer, maybe, than you have. Now, you can hand
in your resignation the first of next week if you are so minded. But
if you do," says Sam, "I'll order a corporal's guard to take you over
by that limestone bluff on the creek and shoot enough lead into
you to ballast a submarine airship. I'm captain of this company,
and I've swore allegiance to the Amalgamated States regardless of
sectional, secessional, and Congressional differences. Have you

got any smoking-tobacco?" winds up Sam. "Mine got wet when I swum the creek this morning."

'The reason I drag all this *non ex parte* evidence in is because Willie Robbins was standing there listening to us. I was a second sergeant and he was a private then, but among us Texans and Westerners there never was as much tactics and subordination as there was in the regular army. We never called our captain anything but "Sam" except when there was a lot of major-generals and admirals around, so as to preserve the discipline.

'And says Willie Robbins to me, in a sharp construction of voice much unbecoming to his light hair and previous record:

' "You ought to be shot, Ben, for emitting any such sentiments. A man that won't fight for his country is worse than a horse-thief. If I was the cap, I'd put you in the guard-house for thirty days on round steak and tamales. War," says Willie, "is great and glorious. I didn't know you were a coward."

' "I'm not," says I. "If I was, I'd knock some of the pallidness off of your marble brow. I'm lenient with you," I says, "just as I am with the Spaniards, because you have always reminded me of something with mushrooms on the side. Why, you little Lady of Shalott," says I, "you underdone leader of cotillions, you glassy fashion and moulded form, you whitepine soldier made in the Cisalpine Alps in Germany for the late New-Year trade, do you know of whom you are talking to? We've been in the same social circle," says I, "and I've put up with you because you seemed so meek and self-unsatisfying. I don't understand why you have so sudden taken a personal interest in chivalrousness and murder. Your nature's undergone a complete revelation. Now, how is it?"

' "Well, you wouldn't understand, Ben," says Willie, giving one of his refined smiles and turning away.

' "Come back here!" says I, catching him by the tail of his khaki coat. "You've made me kind of mad in spite of the aloofness in which I have heretofore held you. You are out for making a success in this hero business, and I believe I know what for. You are doing it either because you are crazy or because you expect to catch some girl by it. Now, if it's a girl, I've got something here to show you."

'I wouldn't have done it, but I was plumb mad. I pulled a San Augustine paper out of my hip-pocket, and showed him an item. It was a half a column about the marriage of Myra Allison and Joe Granberry.

'Willie laughed, and I saw I hadn't touched him.

' "Oh," says he, "everybody knew that was going to happen. I heard about that a week ago." And then he gave me the laugh again.

' "All right," says I. "Then why do you so recklessly chase the bright rainbow of fame? Do you expect to be elected President, or do you belong to a suicide club?"

And then Captain Sam interferes.

' "You gentlemen quit jawing and go back to your quarters," says he, "or I'll have you escorted to the guard-house. Now, scat, both of you! Before you go, which one of you has got any chewing-tobacco?"

' "We're off, Sam," says I. "It's supper-time, anyhow. But what do you think of what we was talking about? I've noticed you throwing out a good many grappling-hooks for this here balloon called fame What's ambition, anyhow? What does a man risk his life day after day for? Do you know of anything he gets in the end that can pay him for the trouble? I want to go back home," says I. "I don't care whether Cuba sinks or swims, and I don't give a pipeful of rabbit tobacco whether Queen Sophia Christina or Charlie Culberson rules these fairy isles; and I don't want my name on any list except the list of survivors. But I've noticed you, Sam," says I, "seeking the bubble notoriety in the cannon's larynx a number of times. Now, what do you do it for? Is it ambition, business, or some freckle-faced Phœbe at home that you are heroing for?"

' "Well, Ben," says Sam, kind of hefting his sword out from between his knees, "as your superior officer I could court-martial you for attempted cowardice and desertion. But I won't. And I'll tell you why I'm trying for promotion and the usual honours of war and conquest. A major gets more pay than a captain, and I need the money."

' "Correct for you!" says I. "I can understand that. Your system of fame-seeking is rooted in the deepest soil of patriotism. But I can't comprehend," says I, "why Willie Robbins, whose folks at home are well off, and who used to be as meek and undesirous of notice as a cat with cream on his whiskers, should all at once develop into a warrior bold with the most fire-eating kind of proclivities. And the girl in his case seems to have been eliminated by marriage to another fellow. I reckon," says I, "it's a plain case of just common ambition. He wants his name, maybe, to go thundering down the coroners of time. It must be that."

'Well, without itemizing his deeds, Willie sure made good as a hero. He simply spent most of his time on his knees begging our captain to send him on forlorn hopes and dangerous scouting expeditions. In every fight he was the first man to mix it at close quarters with the Don Alfonsos. He got three or four bullets planted in various parts of his autonomy. Once he went off with a detail of eight men and captured a whole company of Spanish. He kept Captain Floyd busy writing out recommendations of his bravery to send in to headquarters; and he began to accumulate medals for all kinds of things – heroism and target-shooting and valour and tactics and uninsubordination, and all the little accomplishments that look good to the third assistant secretaries of the War Department.

'Finally, Cap Floyd got promoted to be a major-general, or a knight commander of the main herd, or something like that. He pounded around on a white horse, all desecrated up with gold-leaf and hen-feathers and a Good Templar's hat, and wasn't allowed by the regulations to speak to us. And Willie Robbins was made captain of our company.

'And maybe he didn't go after the wreath of fame then! As far as I could see it was him that ended the war. He got eighteen of us boys – friends of his, too – killed in battles that he stirred up himself and that didn't seem to me necessary at all. One night he took twelve of us and waded through a little rill about a hundred and ninety yards wide, and climbed a couple of mountains, and sneaked through a mile of neglected shrubbery and a couple of rock-quarries and into a rye-straw village, and captured a Spanish general named, as they said, Benny Veedus. Benny seemed to me hardly worth the trouble, being a blackish man without shoes or cuffs, and anxious to surrender and throw himself on the commissary of his foe.

'But that job gave Willie the big boost he wanted. The San Augustine News and the Galveston, St. Louis, New York, and Kansas City papers printed his picture and columns of stuff about him. Old San Augustine simply went crazy over its "gallant son." The News had an editorial tearfully begging the Government to call off the regular army and the national guard, and let Willie carry on the rest of the war single-handed. It said that a refusal to do so would be regarded as a proof that the Northern jealousy of the South was still as rampant as ever.

'If the war hadn't ended pretty soon, I don't know to what heights of gold braid and encomiums Willie would have climbed; but it did. There was a secession of hostilities just three days after

he was appointed a colonel, and got in three more medals by registered mail, and shot two Spaniards while they were drinking
lemonade in an ambuscade.

'Our company went back to San Augustine when the war was
over. There wasn't anywhere else for it to go. And what do you
think? The old town notified us in print, by wire cable, special
delivery, and a nigger named Saul sent on a grey mule to San
Antone, that they was going to give us the biggest blow-out, complimentary, alimentary, and elementary, that ever disturbed the
kildees on the sandflats outside of the immediate contiguity of the
city.

'I say "we," but it was all meant for ex-Private Captain *de facto*,
and Colonel-elect Willie Robbins. The town was crazy about him.
They notified us that the reception they were going to put up
would make the Mardi Gras in New Orleans look like an afternoon
tea in Bury St. Edmunds with a curate s aunt.

'Well, the San Augustine Rifles got back home on schedule
time. Everybody was at the depot giving forth Roosevelt-Democ-
rat — they used to be called Rebel — yells. There was two brass-
bands, and the mayor, and schoolgirls in white frightening the
street-car horses by throwing Cherokee roses in the streets, and —
well, maybe you've seen a celebration by a town that was inland
and out of water.

'They wanted Brevet-Colonel Willie to get into a carriage and
be drawn by prominent citizens and some of the city aldermen to
the armoury, but he stuck to his company and marched at the head
of it up Sam Houston Avenue. The buildings on both sides was
covered with flags and audiences, and everybody hollered "Robbins!" or "Hello, Willie!" as we marched up in files of fours. I
never saw a illustriouser-looking human in my life than Willie
was. He had at least seven or eight medals and diplomas and decorations on the breast of his khaki coat; he was sunburnt the colour
of a saddle, and he certainly done himself proud.

'They told us at the depot that the courthouse was to be illuminated at half-past seven, and there would be speeches and chili-
con-carne at the Palace Hotel. Miss Delphine Thompson was to
read an original poem by James Whitcomb Ryan, and Constable
Hooker had promised us a salute of nine guns from Chicago that
he had arrested that day.

'After we had disbanded in the armoury, Willie says to me:
' "Want to walk out a piece with me?"
' "Why, yes," says I, "if it ain't so far that we can't hear the

tumult and the shouting die away. I'm hungry myself," says I, "and I'm pining for some home grub, but I'll go with you."

'Willie steered me down some side streets till we came to a little white cottage in a new lot with a twenty-by-thirty-foot lawn decorated with brickbats and old barrel-staves.

' "Halt and give the countersign," says I to Willie. "Don't you know this dugout? It's the bird's nest that Joe Granberry built before he married Myra Allison. What you going there for?"

'But Willie already had the gate open. He walked up the brick walk to the steps, and I went with him. Myra was sitting in a rocking-chair on the porch, sewing. Her hair was smoothed back kind of hasty and tied in a knot. I never noticed till then that she had freckles. Joe was at one side of the porch, in his shirt-sleeves, with no collar on, and no signs of a shave, trying to scrape out a hole among the brickbats and tin cans to plant a little fruit-tree in. He looked up but never said a word, and neither did Myra.

'Willie was sure dandy-looking in his uniform, with medals strung on his breast and his new gold-handled sword. You'd never have taken him for the little white-headed snipe that the girls used to order about and make fun of. He just stood there for a minute, looking at Myra with a peculiar little smile on his face; and then he says to her, slow and kind of holding on to his words with his teeth.

' *"Oh, I don't know. Maybe I could if I tried!"*

'That was all that was said. Willie raised his hat, and we walked away.

'And, somehow, when he said that, I remembered, all of a sudden, the night of that dance and Willie brushing his hair before the looking-glass, and Myra sticking her head in the door to guy him.

'When we got back to Sam Houston Avenue, Willie says:

' "Well, so long, Ben. I'm going down home and get off my shoes and take a rest."

' "You?" says I. "What's the matter with you? Ain't the courthouse jammed with everybody in town waiting to honour the hero? And two brass-bands, and recitations and flags and jags, and grub to follow waiting for you?

'Willie sighs.

' "All right, Ben," says he. "Darned if I didn't forget all about that."

'And that's why I say,' concluded Ben Grainger, 'that you can't tell where ambition begins any more than you can tell where it is going to wind up.'

LIX

The Head-Hunter

WHEN THE WAR between Spain and George Dewey was over, I went to the Philippine Islands. There I remained as bush-whacker correspondent for my paper until its managing editor notified me that an eight-hundred-word cablegram describing the grief of a pet carabao over the death of an infant Moro was not considered by the office to be war news. So I resigned, and came home.

On board the trading-vessel that brought me back I pondered much upon the strange things I had sensed in the weird archipelago of the yellow-brown people. The manœuvres and skirmishings of the petty war interested me not: I was spellbound by the outlandish and unreadable countenance of that race that had turned its expressionless gaze upon us out of an unguessable past.

Particularly during my stay in Mindanao had I been fascinated and attracted by that delightfully original tribe of heathen known as the head-hunters. Those grim, flinty, relentless little men, never seen, but chilling the warmest noonday by the subtle terror of their concealed presence, paralleling the trail of their prey through unmapped forests, across perilous mountain-tops, adown bottomless chasms, into uninhabitable jungles, always near with the invisible hand of death uplifted, betraying their pursuit only by such signs as a beast or a bird or a gliding serpent might make – a twig crackling in the awful sweat-soaked night, a drench of dew showering from the screening foliage of a giant tree, a whisper at even from the rushes of a water-level – a hint of death for every mile and every hour – they amused me greatly, those little fellows of one idea.

When you think of it, their method is beautifully and almost hilariously effective and simple.

You have your hut in which you live and carry out the destiny that was decreed for you. Spiked to the jamb of your bamboo doorway is a basket made of green withies, plaited. From time to time as vanity or ennui or love or jealousy or ambition may move you, you creep forth with your snickersnee and take up the silent trail. Back from it you come, triumphant, bearing the severed, gory head of your victim, which you deposit with pardonable pride in the basket at the side of your door. It may be the head of your enemy, your friend, or a stranger, according as competition, Jealousy, or simple sportiveness has been your incentive to labour.

In any case, your reward is certain. The village men, in passing, stop to congratulate you, as your neighbour on weaker planes of life stops to admire and praise the begonias in your front yard. Your particular brown maid lingers, with fluttering bosom, casting soft tiger's eyes at the evidence of your love for her. You chew betel-nut and listen, content, to the intermittent soft drip from the ends of the severed neck arteries. And you show your teeth and grunt like a water-buffalo – which is as near as you can come to laughing – at the thought that the cold, acephalous body of your door ornament is being spotted by wheeling vultures in the Mindanaoan wilds.

Truly, the life of the merry head-hunter captivated me. He had reduced art and philosophy to a simple code. To take your adversary's head, to basket it at the portal of your castle, to see it lying there, a dead thing, with its cunning and stratagems and power gone – Is there a better way to foil his plots, to refute his arguments, to establish your superiority over his skill and wisdom?

The ship that brought me home was captained by an erratic Swede, who changed his course and deposited me, with genuine compassion, in a small town on the Pacific coast of one of the Central American republics, a few hundred miles south of the port to which he had engaged to convey me. But I was wearied of movement and exotic fancies; so I leaped contentedly upon the firm sands of the village of Mojada, telling myself I should be sure to find there the rest that I craved. After all, far better to linger there (I thought), lulled by the sedative plash of the waves and the rust]ing of palm-fronds, than to sit upon the horsehair sofa of my parental home in the East, and there, cast down by currant wine and cake, and scourged by fatuous relatives, drivel into the ears of gaping neighbours sad stories of the death of colonial governors.

When I first saw Chloe Greene she was standing, all in white, in the doorway of her father's tileroofed dobe house. She was polishing a silver cup with a cloth, and she looked like a pearl laid against black velvet. She turned on me a flatteringly protracted but a wiltingly disapproving gaze, and then went inside, humming a light song to indicate the value she placed upon my existence.

Small wonder: for Dr. Stamford (the most disreputable professional man between Juneau and Valparaiso) and I were zigzagging along the turfy street, tunelessly singing the words of 'Auld Lang

Syne' to the air of 'Muzzer's Little Coal-Black Coon.' We had come from the ice factory, which was Mojada's palace of wickedness, where we had been playing billiards and opening black bottles, white with frost, that we dragged with strings out of old Sandoval's ice-cold vats.

I turned in sudden rage to Dr. Stamford, as sober as the verger of a cathedral. In a moment I had become aware that we were swine cast before a pearl.

'You beast,' I said, 'this is half your doing. And the other half is the fault of this cursed country I'd better have gone back to Sleepytown and died in a wild orgy of currant wine and buns than to have had this happen.'

Stamford filled the empty street with his roaring laughter.

'You, too!' he cried. 'And all as quick as the popping of a cork. Well, she does seem to strike agreeably upon the retina. But don't burn your fingers. All Mojada will tell you that Louis Devoe is the man.'

'We will see about that,' said I. 'And, perhaps, whether he is a man as well as *the* man.'

I lost no time in meeting Louis Devoe. That was easily accomplished, for the foreign colony in Mojada numbered scarce a dozen; and they gathered daily at a half decent hotel kept by a Turk, where they managed to patch together the fluttering rags of country and civilization that were left them. I sought Devoe before I did my pearl of the doorway, because I had learned a little of the game of war, and knew better than to strike for a prize before testing the strength of the enemy.

A sort of cold dismay – something akin to fear – filled me when I had estimated him. I found a man so perfectly poised, so charming, so deeply learned in the world's rituals, so full of tact, courtesy, and hospitality, so endowed with grace and ease and a kind of careless, haughty power that I almost overstepped the bounds in probing him, in turning him on the spit to find the weak point that I so craved for him to have. But I left him whole – I had to make bitter acknowledgment to myself that Louis Devoe was a gentleman worthy of my best blows; and I swore to give him them. He was a great merchant of the country, a wealthy importer and exporter. All day he sat in a fastidiously appointed office surrounded by works of art and evidences of his high culture, directing through glass doors and windows the affairs of his house.

In person he was slender and hardly tall. His small, well-shaped head was covered with thick brown hair, trimmed short, and he wore a thick brown beard also cut close and to a fine point. His manners were a pattern.

Before long I had become a regular and a welcome visitor at the Greene home. I shook my wild habits from me like a worn-out cloak. I trained for the conflict with the care of a prize-fighter and the self-denial of a Brahmin.

As for Chloe Greene, I shall weary you with no sonnets to her eyebrow. She was a splendidly feminine girl, as wholesome as a November pippin, and no more mysterious than a window-pane. She had whimsical little theories that she had deduced from life, and that fitted the maxims of Epictetus like princess gowns. I wonder, after all, if that old duffer wasn't rather wise!

Chloe had a father, the Reverend Homer Greene, and an intermittent mother, who sometimes palely presided over a twilight teapot. The Reverend Homer was a burr-like man with a lifework. He was writing a concordance to the Scriptures, and had arrived as far as Kings. Being, presumably, a suitor for his daughter's hand, I was timber for his literary outpourings. I had the family tree of Israel drilled into my head until I used to cry aloud in my sleep: 'And Aminadab begat Jay Eye See,' and so forth, until he had tackled another book. I once made a calculation that the Reverend Homer's concordance would be worked up as far as the Seven Vials mentioned in Revelations about the third day after they were opened.

Louis Devoe, as well as I, was a visitor and an intimate friend of the Greenes. It was there I met him the oftenest, and a more agreeable man or a more accomplished I have never hated in my life.

Luckily or unfortunately, I came to be accepted as a Boy. My appearance was youthful, and I suppose I had that pleading and homeless air that always draws the motherliness that is in women and the cursed theories and hobbies of paterfamilias.

Chloe called me 'Tommy,' and made sisterly fun of my attempts to woo her. With Devoe she was vastly more reserved. He was the man of romance, one to stir her imagination and deepest feelings had her fancy leaned toward him. I was closer to her, but standing in no glamour; I had the task before me of winning her in what seems to me the American way of fighting – with cleanness and pluck and everyday devotion to break away the barriers of friendship that divided us, and to take her, if I could, between sunrise and dark, abetted by neither moonlight nor music nor foreign wiles.

Chloe gave no sign of bestowing her blithe affections upon either of us. But one day she let out to me an inkling of what she preferred in a man. It was tremendously interesting to me, but not illuminating as to its application. I had been tormenting her for the dozenth time with the statement and catalogue of my sentiments toward her.

'Tommy,' said she, 'I don't want a man to show his love for me by leading an army against another country and blowing people off the earth with cannons.'

'If you mean that the opposite way,' I answered, 'as they say women do, I'll see what I can do. The papers are full of this diplomatic row in Russia. My people know some big people in Washington who are right next to the army people, and I could get an artillery commission and –'

'I'm not that way,' interrupted Chloe. 'I mean what I say. It isn't the big things that are done in the world, Tommy, that count with a woman. When the knights were riding abroad in their armour to slay dragons, many a stay-at-home page won a lonesome lady's hand by being on the spot to pick up her glove and be quick with her cloak when the wind blew. The man I am to like best, whoever he shall be, must show his love in little ways. He must never forget, after hearing it once, that I do not like to have anyone walk at my left side; that I detest bright-coloured neckties; that I prefer to sit with my back to a light; that I like candied violets; that I must not be talked to when I am looking at the moonlight shining on water, and that I very, very often long for dates stuffed with English walnuts.'

'Frivolity,' I said, with a frown. 'Any well-trained servant would be equal to such details.'

'And he must remember,' went on Chloe, 'to remind me of what I want when I do not know, myself, what I want.'

'You're rising in the scale,' I said. 'What you seem to need is a first-class clairvoyant.'

'And if I say that I am dying to hear a Beethoven sonata, and stamp my foot when I say it, he must know by that that what my soul craves is salted almonds; and he will have them ready in his pocket.'

'Now,' said I, 'I am at a loss. I do not know whether your soul's affinity is to be an impresario or a fancy grocer.'

Chloe turned her pearly smile upon me.

'Take less than half of what I said as a jest,' she went on. 'And don't think too lightly of the little things, Boy. Be a paladin if you must, but don't let it show on you. Most women are only very big children, and most men are only very little ones. Please us; don't try to overpower us. When we want a hero we can make one out of even a plain grocer the third time he catches our handkerchief before it falls to the ground.'

That evening I was taken down with pernicious fever. That is a kind of coast fever with improvements and high-geared attachments. Your temperature goes up among the threes and fours and remains there, laughing scornfully and feverishly at the cinchona trees and the coal-tar derivatives. Pernicious fever is a case for a simple mathematician instead of a doctor. It is merely this formula: Vitality + the desire to live – the duration of the fever = the result.

I took to my bed in the two-roomed thatched hut where I had been comfortably established, and sent for a gallon of rum. That was not for myself. Drunk, Stamford was the best doctor between the Andes and the Pacific. He came, sat at my bedside, and drank himself into condition.

'My boy,' said he, 'my lily-white and reformed Romeo, medicine will do you no good. But I will give you quinine, which, being bitter, will arouse in you hatred and anger – two stimulants that will add ten per cent. to your chances. You are as strong as a caribou calf, and you will get well if the fever doesn't get in a knockout blow when you're off your guard.'

For two weeks I lay on my back feeling like a Hindu widow on a burning ghat. Old Atasca, an untrained Indian nurse, sat near the door like a petrified statue of What's-the-Use, attending to her duties, which were, mainly, to see that time went by without slipping a cog. Sometimes I would fancy myself back in the Philippines, or, at worse times, sliding off the horsehair sofa in Sleepytown.

One afternoon I ordered Atasca to vamose, and got up and dressed carefully. I took my temperature, which I was pleased to find 104. I paid almost dainty attention to my dress, choosing solicitously a necktie of a dull and subdued hue. The mirror showed that I was looking little the worse from my illness. The fever gave brightness to my eyes and colour to my face. And while I looked at my reflection my colour went and came again as I thought of Chloe Greene and the millions of eons that had passed since I'd seen her, and of Louis Devoe and the time he had gained on me.

I went straight to her house. I seemed to float rather than walk; I hardly felt the ground under my feet; I thought pernicious fever must be a great boon to make one feel so strong.

I found Chloe and Louis Devoe sitting under the awning in front of the house. She jumped up and met me with a double handshake.

'I'm glad, glad, glad to see you out again!' she cried, every word a pearl strung on the string of her sentence. 'You are well, Tommy – or better, of course. I wanted to come to see you, but they wouldn't let me.'

'Oh, yes,' said I, carelessly, 'it was nothing. Merely a little fever. I am out again, as you see.'

We three sat there and talked for half an hour or so. Then Chloe looked out yearningly and almost piteously across the ocean. I could see in her sea-blue eyes some deep and intense desire. Devoe, curse him! saw it too.

'What is it?' we asked in unison

'Coco-nut pudding,' said Chloe, pathetically. 'I've wanted some – oh, so badly, for two days. It's got beyond a wish; it's an obsession.'

'The coco-nut season is over,' said Devoe, in that voice of his that gave thrilling interest to his most commonplace words. 'I hardly think one could be found in Mojada. The natives never use them except when they are green and the milk is fresh. They sell all the ripe ones to the fruiterers.'

'Wouldn't a broiled lobster or a Welsh rabbit do as well?' I remarked, with the engaging idiocy of a pernicious-fever convalescent.

Chloe came as near pouting as a sweet disposition and a perfect profile would allow her to come.

The Reverend Homer poked his ermine-lined face through the doorway and added a concordance to the conversation.

'Sometimes,' said he, 'Old Campos keeps the dried nuts in his little store on the hill. But it would be far better, my daughter, to restrain unusual desires, and partake thankfully of the daily dishes that the Lord has set before us.'

'Stuff!' said I.

'How was that?' asked the Reverend Homer, sharply.

'I say it's tough,' said I, 'to drop into the vernacular, that Miss Greene should be deprived of the food she desires – a simple thing like kalsomine-pudding. Perhaps,' I continued, solicitously, 'some pickled walnuts or a fricassee of Hungarian butternuts would do as well.'

Every one looked at me with a slight exhibition of curiosity.

Louis Devoe arose and made his adieus. I watched him until he had sauntered slowly and grandiosely to the corner, around which he turned to reach his great warehouse and store. Chloe made her excuses, and went inside for a few minutes to attend to some detail affecting the seven-o'clock dinner. She was a past mistress in housekeeping. I had tasted her puddings and bread with beatitude.

When all had gone, I turned casually and saw a basket made of plaited green withes hanging by a nail outside the doorjamb. With a rush that made my hot temples throb there came vividly to my mind recollections of the head-hunters – *those grim, flinty, relentless little men, never seen, but chilling the warmest noonday by the subtle terror of their concealed presence. . . . From time to time, as vanity or ennui or love or jealousy or ambition may move him, one creeps forth with his snickersnee and takes up the silent trail. . . . Back he comes, triumphant, bearing the severed, gory head of his victim. . . . His particular brown or white maid lingers, with fluttering bosom, casting soft tigers eyes at the evidence of his love for her.*

I stole softly from the house and returned to my hut. From its supporting nails in the wall I took a machete as heavy as a butcher's cleaver and sharper than a safety-razor. And then I chuckled softly to myself, and set out to the fastidiously appointed private office of Monsieur Louis Devoe, usurper to the hand of the Pearl of the Pacific.

He was never slow at thinking; he gave one look at my face and another at the weapon in my hand as I entered his door, and then he seemed to fade from my sight. I ran to the back door, kicked it open, and saw him running like a deer up the road toward the wood that began two hundred yards away. I was after him with a shout. I remember hearing children and women screaming, and seeing them flying from the road.

He was fleet, but I was stronger. A mile, and I had almost come up with him. He doubled cunningly and dashed into a brake that extended into a small coñon. I crashed through this after him, and in five minutes had him cornered in an angle of insurmountable cliffs. There his instinct of self-preservation steadied him, as it will steady even animals at bay. He turned to me, quite calm, with a ghastly smile.

'Oh, Rayburn!' he said, with such an awful effort at ease that I was impolite enough to laugh rudely in his face. 'Oh, Rayburn!' said he, 'come, let's have done with this nonsense! Of course, I know it's the fever and you're not yourself; but collect yourself, man – give me that ridiculous weapon, now, and let's go back and talk it over.'

'I will go back,' said I, 'carrying your head with me. We will see how charmingly it can discourse when it lies in the basket at her door.'

'Come,' said he, persuasively, 'I think better of you than to suppose that you try this sort of thing as a joke. But even the vagaries of a fever-crazed lunatic come some time to a limit. What is this talk about heads and baskets? Get yourself together and throw away that absurd cane-chopper. What would Miss Greene think of you?' he ended, with the silky cajolery that one would use towards a fretful child.

'Listen,' said I. 'At last you have struck upon the right note. What would she think of me? Listen,' I repeated.

'There are women,' I said, 'who look upon horsehair sofas and currant wine as dross. To them even the calculated modulation of your well-trimmed talk sounds like the dropping of rotten plums from a tree in the night. They are the maidens who walk back and forth in the villages, scorning the emptiness of the baskets at the doors of the young men who would win them. One, such as they,' I said, 'is waiting. Only a fool would try to win a woman by drooling like a braggart in her doorway or by waiting upon her whims like a footman. They are all daughters of Herodias, and to gain their hearts one must lay the heads of his enemies before them with his own hands. Now, bend your neck, Louis Devoe. Do not be a coward as well as a chatterer at a lady's tea-table.'

'There, there!' said Devoe, falteringly. 'You know me, don't you, Rayburn?'

'Oh, yes,' I said, 'I know you. I know you. I know you. But the basket is empty. The old men of the village and the young men, and both the dark maidens and the ones who are as fair as pearls, walk back and forth and see its emptiness. Will you kneel now, or must we have a scuffle? It is not like you to make things go roughly and with bad form. But the basket is waiting for your head.'

With that he went to pieces. I had to catch him as he tried to scamper past me like a scared rabbit. I stretched him out and got a foot on his chest, but he squirmed like a worm, although I appealed repeatedly to his sense of propriety and the duty he owed to himself as a gentleman not to make a row.

But at last he gave me the chance, and I swung the machete.

It was not hard work. He flopped like a chicken during the six or seven blows that it took to sever his head; but finally he lay still, and I tied his head in my handkerchief. The eyes opened and shut thrice while I walked a hundred yards. I was red to my feet with the drip, but what did that matter? With delight I felt under my hands the crisp touch of his short, thick, brown hair and close-trimmed beard.

I reached the house of the Greenes and dumped the head of Louis Devoe into the basket that still hung by the nail in the door-jamb. I sat in a chair under the awning and waited. The sun was within two hours of setting. Chloe came out and looked surprised.

'Where have you been, Tommy?' she asked. 'You were gone when I came out.'

'Look in the basket,' I said, rising to my feet. She looked and gave a little scream – of delight, I was pleased to note.

'Oh, Tommy!' she said. 'It was just what I wanted you to do. It's leaking a little, but that doesn't matter. Wasn't I telling you? It's the little things that count. And you remembered.'

Little things! She held the ensanguined head of Louis Devoe in her white apron. Tiny streams of red widened on her apron and dripped upon the floor. Her face was bright and tender.

'Little things, indeed!' I thought again. 'The head-hunters are right. These are the things that women like you to do for them.'

Chloe came close to me. There was no one in sight. She looked up at me with sea-blue eyes that said things they had never said before.

'You think of me,' she said. 'You are the man I was describing. You think of the little things, and they are what make the world worth living in. The man for me must consider my little wishes, and make me happy in small ways. He must bring me little red peaches in December if I wish for them, and then I will love him till June. I will have no knight in armour slaying his rival or killing dragons for me. You please me very well, Tommy.'

I stooped and kissed her. Then a moisture broke out on my forehead, and I began to feel weak. I saw the red stains vanish from Chloe's apron, and the head of Louis Devoe turn to a brown, dried coco-nut.

'There will be coco-nut pudding for dinner, Tommy, boy,' said Chloe gaily, 'and you must come. I must go in for a little while.'

She vanished in a delightful flutter.

Dr. Stamford tramped up hurriedly. He seized my pulse as though it were his own property that I had escaped with.

'You are the biggest fool outside of any asylum!' he said, angrily. 'Why did you leave your bed? And the idiotic things you've been doing! – and no wonder, with your pulse going like a sledge-hammer.'

'Name some of them,' said I.

'Devoe sent for me,' said Stamford. 'He saw you from his window go to old Campos' store, chase him up the hill with his own yardstick, and then come back and make off with his biggest coco-nut.'

'It's the little things that count, after all,' said I.

'It's your little bed that counts with you just now,' said the doctor. 'You come with me at once, or I'll throw up the case. You're as loony as a loon.'

So I got no coco-nut pudding that evening, but I conceived a distrust as to the value of the method of the head-hunters. Perhaps for many centuries the maidens of the villages may have been looking wistfully at the heads in the baskets at the doorways, longing for other and lesser trophies.

LX

The Last of the Troubadours

INEXORABLY SAM GALLOWAY saddled his pony. He was going away from the Rancho Altito at the end of a three-months' visit. It is not to be expected that a guest should put up with wheat coffee and biscuits yellow-streaked with saleratus for longer than that. Nick Napoleon, the big negro man cook, had never been able to make good biscuits. Once before, when Nick was cooking at the Willow Ranch, Sam had been forced to fly from his *cuisine*, after only a six-weeks' sojourn.

On Sam's face was an expression of sorrow, deepened with regret and slightly tempered by the patient forgiveness of a connoisseur who cannot be understood. But very firmly and inexorably he buckled his saddle-cinches, looped his stake-rope and hung it to his saddle-horn, tied his slicker and coat on the cantle, and looped his quirt on his right wrist. The Merrydews (householders of the Rancho Altito), men, women, children, and servants, vassals, visitors, employes, dogs, and casual callers were grouped in the 'gallery' of the ranch house, all with faces set to the tune of melancholy and grief. For, as the coming of Sam Galloway to any ranch, camp, or cabin between the rivers Frio and Bravo del Norte aroused joy, so his departure caused mourning and distress.

And then, during absolute silence, except for the bumping of a hind elbow of a hound dog as he pursued a wicked flea, Sam tenderly and carefully tied his guitar across his saddle on top of his slicker and coat. The guitar was in a green duck bag; and if you catch the significance of it, it explains Sam.

Sam Galloway was the Last of the Troubadours. Of course you know about the troubadours. The encyclopaedia says they flourished between the eleventh and the thirteenth centuries. What they flourished doesn't seem clear – you may be pretty sure it wasn't a sword: maybe it was a fiddlebow, or a forkful of spaghetti, or a lady's scarf. Anyhow, Sam Galloway was one of 'em.

Sam put on a martyred expression as he mounted his pony. But the expression on his face was hilarious compared with the one on his pony's. You see, a pony gets to know his rider mighty well, and it is not unlikely that cow ponies in pastures and at hitching racks had often guyed Sam's pony for being ridden by a guitar player instead of by a rollicking, cussing, all-wool cowboy. No man is a hero to his saddle-horse. And even an escalator in a department store might be excused for tripping up a troubadour.

Oh, I know I'm one; and so are you. You remember the stories you memorize and the card tricks you study and that little piece on the piano – how does it go – ti-tum-te-tum-ti-tum – those little Arabian Ten Minute Entertainments that you furnish when you go up to call on your rich Aunt Jane. You should know that *omnæ personæ in tres partes divisæ sunt* Namely: Barons, Troubadours and Workers. Barons have no inclination to read such folderol as this; and Workers have no time: so I know you must be a Troubadour, and that you will understand Sam Galloway. Whether we sing, act, dance, write, lecture, or paint, we are only troubadours; so let us make the worst of it.

The pony with the Dante Alighieri face, guided by the pressure of Sam's knees, bore that wandering minstrel sixteen miles southeastward. Nature was in her most benignant mood. League after league of delicate, sweet flowerets made fragrant the gently undulating prairie. The east wind tempered the spring warmth; woolwhite clouds flying in from the Mexican Gulf hindered the direct rays of the April sun. Sam sang songs as he rode. Under his pony's bridle he had tucked some sprigs of chaparral to keep away the deer flies. Thus crowned, the long-faced quadruped looked more Dantesque than before, and, judging by his countenance, seemed to think of Beatrice.

Straight as topography permitted, Sam rode to the sheep ranch of old man Ellison. A visit to a sheep ranch seemed to him desirable just then. There had been too many people, too much noise, argument, competition, confusion at Rancho Altito. He had never conferred upon old man Ellison the favour of sojourning at his ranch; but he knew he would be welcome. The troubadour is his own passport everywhere. The Workers in the castle let down the drawbridge to him, and the Baron sets him at his left hand at table in the banquet hall. There ladies smile upon him and applaud his songs and stories, while the Workers bring boars' heads and flagons. If the Baron nods once or twice in his carved oaken chair, he does not do it maliciously.

Old man Ellison welcomes the troubadour flatteringly. He had often heard praises of Sam Galloway from other ranchmen who had been complimented by his visits, but had never aspired to such an honour for his own humble barony. I say barony because old man Ellison was the Last of the Barons. Of course, Bulwer-Lytton lived too early to know him, or he wouldn't have conferred that sobriquet upon Warwick. In life it is the duty and the function of the Baron to provide work for the Workers and lodging and shelter for the Troubadours.

Old man Ellison was a shrunken old man, with a short, yellow-white beard and a face lined and seamed by past-and-gone smiles. His ranch was a little two-room box house in a grove of hackberry trees in the lonesomest part of the sheep country. His household consisted of a Kiowa Indian man cook, four hounds, a pet sheep, and a half-tamed coyote chained to a fence-post. He owned 3,000 sheep, which he ran on two sections of leased land and many thousands of acres neither leased nor owned. Three or four times a year someone who spoke his language would ride up to his gate and exchange a few bald ideas with him. Those were red-letter days to old man Ellison. Then in what illuminated, embossed, and gorgeously decorated capitals must have been written the day on which a troubadour – a troubadour who, according to the encyclopaedia, should have flourished between the eleventh and the thirteenth centuries – drew rein at the gates of his baronial castle!

Old man Ellison's smiles came back and filled his wrinkles when he saw Sam. He hurried out of the house in his shuffling, limping way to greet him.

'Hallo, Mr. Ellison,' called Sam cheerfully. 'Thought I'd drop over and see you awhile. Notice you've had fine rains on your range. They ought to make good grazing for your spring lambs.'

'Well, well, well,' said old man Ellison. 'I'm mighty glad to see you, Sam. I never thought you'd take the trouble to ride over to as out-of-the-way an old ranch as this. But you're mighty welcome.

'Light. I've got a sack of new oats in the kitchen – shall I bring out a feed for your hoss?'

'Oats for him?' said Sam derisively. 'No, sir-ee. He's as fat as a pig now on grass. He don't get rode enough to keep him in condition. I'll just turn him in the horse pasture with a drag rope on if you don't mind.'

I am positive that never during the eleventh and thirteenth centuries did Baron, Troubadour, and Worker amalgamate as harmoniously as their parallels did that evening at old man Ellison's sheep ranch. The Kiowa's biscuits were light and tasty and his coffee strong. Ineradicable hospitality and appreciation glowed on old man Ellison's weather-tanned face. As for the troubadour, he said to himself that he had stumbled upon pleasant places indeed. A well-cooked, abundant meal, a host whom his lightest attempt to entertain seemed to delight far beyond the merits of the exertion, and the reposeful atmosphere that his sensitive soul at that time craved united to confer upon him a satisfaction and luxurious ease that he had seldom found on his tours of the ranches.

After the delectable supper, Sam untied the green duck bag and took out his guitar. Not by way of payment, mind you – neither Sam Galloway nor any other of the true troubadours are lineal descendants of the late Tommy Tucker. You have read of Tommy Tucker in the works of the esteemed but often obscure Mother Goose. Tommy Tucker sang for his supper. No true troubadour would do that. He would have his supper, and then sing for Art's sake.

Sam Galloway's repertoire comprised about fifty funny stories and between thirty and forty songs. He by no means stopped there. He could talk through twenty cigarettes on any topic that you brought up. And he never sat up when he could lie down; and never stood when he could sit. I am strongly disposed to linger with him, for I am drawing a portrait as well as a blunt pencil and a tattered thesaurus will allow.

I wish you could have seen him: he was small and tough and inactive beyond the power of imagination to conceive. He wore an ultramarine-blue woollen shirt laced down the front with a pearl-grey exaggerated sort of shoe-string, indestructible brown duck clothes, inevitable high-heeled boots with Mexican spurs, and a Mexican straw sombrero.

That evening Sam and old man Ellison dragged their chairs out under the hackberry trees. They lighted cigarettes, and the troubadour gaily touched his guitar. Many of the songs he sang were the weird, melancholy, minor-keyed *canciones* that he had learned from the Mexican sheep herders and *vaqueros*. One, in particular, charmed and soothed the soul of the lonely baron. It was a favourite song of the sheep herders, beginning 'Huile, huile, palomita,' which being translated means, 'Fly, fly, little dove.' Sam sang it for old man Ellison many times that evening.

The troubadour stayed on at the old man's ranch. There was peace and quiet and appreciation there such as he had not found in the noisy camps of the cattle kings. No audience in the world could have crowned the work of poet, musician, or artist with more worshipful and unflagging approval than that bestowed upon his efforts by old man Ellison. No visit by a royal personage to a humble wood-chopper or peasant could have been received with more flattering thankfulness and joy.

On a cool, canvas-covered cot in the shade of the hackberry trees, Sam Galloway passed the greater part of his time. There he rolled his brown-paper cigarettes, read such tedious literature as the ranch afforded, and added to his repertoire of improvisations that he played so expertly on his guitar. To him, as a slave ministering to a great lord, the Kiowa brought cool water from the red jar hanging under the brush shelter, and food when he called for it. The prairie zephyrs fanned him mildly; mocking-birds at morn and eve competed with, but scarce equalled, the sweet melodies of his lyre; a perfumed stillness seemed to fill all his world. While old man Ellison was pottering among his flocks of sheep on his mile-an-hour pony, and while the Kiowa took his siesta in the burning sunshine at the end of the kitchen, Sam would lie on his cot thinking what a happy world he lived in, and how kind it is to the ones whose mission in life it is to give entertainment and pleasure. Here he had food and lodging as good as he had ever longed for; absolute immunity from care or exertion or strife; an endless welcome, and a host whose delight at the sixteenth repetition of a song or a story was as keen as at its initial giving. Was there ever a troubadour of old who struck upon as royal a castle in his wanderings? While he lay thus, meditating upon his blessings, little brown cottontails would shyly frolic through the yard; a covey of white-topknotted blue quail would run past, in single file, twenty yards away; a *paisano* bird, out hunting for tarantulas, would hop upon the fence and salute him with sweeping flourishes of its long tail. In the eighty-acre horse pasture the pony with the Dantesque face grew fat and almost smiling. The troubadour was at the end of his wanderings.

Old man Ellison was his own *vaciero*. That means that he supplied his sheep camps with wood, water, and rations by his own labours instead of hiring a *vaciero*. On small ranches it is often done.

One morning he started for the camp of Incarnacion Felipe de la Cruz y Monte Piedras (one of his sheep herders) with the week's usual rations of brown beans, coffee, meal, and sugar. Two miles away on the trail from old Fort Ewing he met, face to face, a terrible being called King James, mounted on a fiery, prancing, Kentucky-bred horse.

King James's real name was James King; but people reversed it because it seemed to fit him better, and also because it seemed to please his majesty. King James was the biggest cattleman between the Alamo plaza in San Antone and Bill Hopper's saloon in Brownsville. Also he was the loudest and most offensive bully and braggart and bad man in south-west Texas. And he always made good whenever he bragged; and the more noise he made the more dangerous he was. In the story papers it is always the quiet, mild-mannered man with light-blue eyes and a low voice who turns out to be really dangerous; but in real life and in this story such is not the case. Give me my choice between assaulting a large, loud-mouthed rough-houser and an inoffensive stranger with blue eyes sitting quietly in a corner, and you will see something doing in the corner every time.

King James, as I intended to say earlier, was a fierce, two-hundred-pound, sunburned, blond man, as pink as an October strawberry, and with two horizontal slits under shaggy red eyebrows for eyes. On that day he wore a flannel shirt that was tan-coloured, with the exception of certain large areas which were darkened by transudations due to the summer sun. There seemed to be other clothing and garnishings about him, such as brown duck trousers stuffed into immense boots, and red handkerchiefs and revolvers; and a shot-gun laid across his saddle and a leather belt with millions of cartridges shining in it – but your mind skidded off such accessories; what held your gaze was just the two little horizontal slits that he used for eyes.

This was the man that old man Ellison met on the trail; and when you count up in the baron's favour that he was sixty-five and weighed ninety-eight pounds and had heard of King James's record and that he (the baron) had a hankering for the *vita simplex* and had no gun with him and wouldn't have used it if he had, you can't censure him if I tell you that the smiles with which the troubadour had filled his wrinkles went out of them and left them plain wrinkles again. But he was not the kind of baron that flies from danger. He reined in the mile-an-hour pony (no difficult feat), and saluted the formidable monarch.

King James expressed himself with royal directness.

'You're that old snoozer that's running sheep on this range, ain't you?' said he. 'What right have you got to do it? Do you own any land, or lease any?'

'I have two sections leased from the state,' said old man Ellison mildly.

'Not by no means you haven't,' said King James. Your lease expired yesterday; and I had a man at the land office on the minute to take it up. You don't control a foot of grass in Texas. You sheep men have got to git. Your time's up. It's a cattle country, and there ain't any room in it for snoozers. This range you've got your sheep on is mine. I'm putting up a wire fence, forty by sixty miles; and if there's a sheep inside of it when it's done it'll be a dead one. I'll give you a week to move yours away. If they ain't gone by then, I'll send six men over here with Winchesters to make mutton out of the whole lot. And if I find you here at the same time this is what you'll get.'

King James patted the breech of his shot-gun warningly.

Old man Ellison rode on to the camp of Incarnación. He sighed many times, and the wrinkles in his face grew deeper. Rumours that the old order was about to change had reached him before. The end of Free Grass was in sight. Other troubles, too, had been accumulating upon his shoulders. His flocks were decreasing instead of growing; the price of wool was declining at every clip; even Bradshaw, the storekeeper at Frio City, at whose store he bought his ranch supplies, was dunning him for his last six months' bill and threatening to cut him off. And so this last greatest calamity suddenly dealt out to him by the terrible King James was a crusher.

When the old man got back to the ranch at sunset he found Sam Galloway lying on his cot, propped against a roll of blankets and wool sacks, fingering his guitar.

'Hallo, Uncle Ben,' the troubadour called cheerfully. 'You rolled in early this evening. I been trying a new twist on the Spanish Fandango today. I just about got it. Here's how she goes — listen.'

'That's fine, that's mighty fine,' said old man Ellison, sitting on the kitchen step and rubbing his white Scotch-terrier whiskers. 'I reckon you've got all the musicians beat east and west, Sam, as far as the roads are cut out.'

'Oh, I don't know,' said Sam reflectively. 'But I certainly do get there on variations. I guess I can handle anything in five flats about as well as any of 'em. But you look kind of fagged out, Uncle Ben – ain't you feeling right well this evening?'

'Little tired; that's all, Sam. If you ain't played yourself out, let's have that Mexican piece that starts off with *"Huile, huile, palomita."* It seems that that song always kind of soothes and comforts me after I've been riding far or anything bothers me.'

'Why, *seguramente, señor,*' said Sam. 'I'll hit her up for you as often as you like. And before I forget about it, Uncle Ben, you want to jerk Bradshaw up about them last hams he sent us. They're just a little bit strong.'

A man sixty-five years old, living on a sheep ranch and beset by a complication of disasters, cannot successfully and continuously dissemble. Moreover, a troubadour has eyes quick to see unhappiness in others around him – because it disturbs his own ease. So, on the next day, Sam again questioned the old man about his air of sadness and abstraction. Then old man Ellison told him the story of King James's threats and orders and that pale melancholy and red ruin appeared to have marked him for their own. The troubadour took the news thoughtfully. He had heard much about King James.

On the third day of the seven days of grace allowed him by the autocrat of the range, old man Ellison drove his buckboard to Frio City to fetch some necessary supplies for the ranch. Bradshaw was hard but not implacable. He divided the old man's order by two, and let him have a little more time. One article secured was a new, fine ham for the pleasure of the troubadour.

Five miles out of Frio City on his way home the old man met King James riding into town. His majesty could never look anything but fierce and menacing, but to-day his slits of eyes appeared to be a little wider than they usually were.

'Good day,' said the king gruffly. 'I've been wanting to see you. I hear it said by a cowman from Sandy yesterday that you was from Jackson County, Mississippi, originally. I want to know if that's a fact.'

'Born there,' said old man Ellison, 'and raised there till I was twenty-one.'

'This man says,' went on King James, 'that he thinks you was related to the Jackson County Reeveses. Was he right?'

'Aunt Caroline Reeves,' said the old man, 'was my half-sister.'

'She was my aunt,' said King James. 'I run away from home when I was sixteen. Now, let's re-talk over some things that we discussed a few days ago. They call me a bad man; and they're only half right. There's plenty of room in my pasture for your bunch of sheep and their increase for a long time to come. Aunt Caroline used to cut out sheep in cake dough and bake 'em for me. You keep your sheep where they are, and use all the range you want. How s your finances?'

The old man related his woes in detail, dignifiedly, with restraint and candour.

'She used to smuggle extra grub into my school basket — I'm speaking of Aunt Caroline,' said King James. 'I'm going over to Frio City to-day, and I'll ride back by your ranch to-morrow. I'll draw $2,000 out of the bank there and bring it over to you; and I'll tell Bradshaw to let you have everything you want on credit. You are bound to have heard the old saying at home that the Jackson County Reeveses and Kings would stick closer by each other than chestnut burrs. Well, I'm a King yet whenever I run across a Reeves. So you look out for me along about sundown to-morrow, and don't worry about nothing. Shouldn't wonder if the dry spell don't kill out the young grass.'

Old man Ellison drove happily ranchward. Once more the smiles filled out his wrinkles. Very suddenly, by the magic of kinship and the good that lies somewhere in all hearts, his troubles had been removed.

On reaching the ranch he found that Sam Galloway was not there. His guitar hung by its buckskin string to a hackberry limb, moaning as the gulf breeze blew across its masterless strings.

The Kiowa endeavoured to explain.

'Sam, he catch pony,' said he, 'and say he ride to Frio City. What for no can damn sabe. Say he come back to-night. Maybe so. That all.'

As the first stars came out the troubadour rode back to his haven. He pastured his pony and went into the house, his spurs jingling martially.

Old man Ellison sat at the kitchen table, having a tin cup of before-supper coffee. He looked contented and pleased.

'Hallo, Sam,' said he, 'I'm darned glad to see ye back. I don't know how I managed to get along on this ranch, anyhow, before ye dropped in to cheer things up. I'll bet ye've been skylarking around with some of them Frio City gals, now, that's kept ye so late.'

And, then old man Ellison took another look at Sam's face and saw that the minstrel had changed to the man of action.

And while Sam is unbuckling from his waist old man Ellison's six-shooter, that the latter had left behind when he drove to town, we may well pause to remark that anywhere and whenever a troubadour lays down the guitar and takes up the sword trouble is sure to follow. It is not the expert thrust of Athos nor the cold skill of Aramis nor the iron wrist of Porthos that we have to fear – it is the Gascon's fury – the wild and unacademic attack of the troubadour – the sword of D'Artagnan.

'I done it,' said Sam. 'I went over to Frio City to do it. I couldn't let him put the skibunk on you, Uncle Ben. I met him in Summers's saloon. I knowed what to do. I said a few things to him that nobody else heard. He reached for his gun first – half a dozen fellows saw him do it – but I got mine unlimbered first. Three doses I gave him – right around the lungs, and a saucer could have covered up all of 'em. He won't bother you no more.'

'This – is – King – James – you speak – of?' asked old man Ellison, while he sipped his coffee.

'You bet it was. And they took me before the county judge; and the witnesses what saw him draw his gun first was all there. Well, of course, they put me under $300 bond to appear before the court, but there was four or five boys on the spot ready to sign the bail. He won't bother you no more, Uncle Ben. You ought to have seen how close them bullet holes was together. I reckon playing a guitar as much as I do must kind of limber a fellow's trigger finger up a little, don't you think, Uncle Ben?'

Then there was a little silence in the castle, except for the spluttering of a venison steak that the Kiowa was cooking.

'Sam,' said old man Ellison, stroking his white whiskers with a tremulous hand, 'would you mind getting the guitar and playing that *"Huile, huile, palomita"* piece once or twice? It always seems to be kind of soothing and comforting when a man's tired and fagged out.'

There is no more to be said, except that the title of the story is wrong. It should have been called *The Last of the Barons*. There never will be an end to the troubadours; and now and then it does seem that the jingle of their guitars will drown the sound of the muffled blows of the pickaxes and trip-hammers of all the Workers in the world.

LXI

The Sleuths

IN THE BIG CITY a man will disappear with the suddenness and completeness of the flame of a candle that is blown out. All the agencies of inquisition – the hounds of the trail, the sleuths of the city's labyrinths, the closet detectives of theory and induction – will be invoked to the search. Most often the man's face will be seen no more. Sometimes he will reappear in Sheboygan or in the wilds of Terre Haute, calling himself one of the synonyms of 'Smith,' and without memory of events up to a certain time, including his grocer's bill. Sometimes it will be found, after dragging the rivers, and polling the restaurants to see if he may be waiting for a well-done sirloin, that he has moved next door.

This snuffing out of a human being like the erasure of a chalk man from a blackboard, is one of the most impressive themes in dramaturgy.

The case of Mary Snyder, in point, should not be without interest.

A man of middle age, of the name of Meeks, came from the West to New York to find his sister, Mrs. Mary Snyder, a widow, aged fifty-two, who had been living for a year in a tenement house in a crowded neighbourhood.

At her address he was told that Mary Snyder had moved away longer than a month before. No one could tell him her new address.

On coming out Mr. Meeks addressed a policeman who was standing on the corner, and explained his dilemma.

'My sister is very poor,' he said, 'and I am anxious to find her. I have recently made quite a lot of money in a lead mine, and I want her to share my prosperity. There is no use in advertising her, because she cannot read.'

The policeman pulled his moustache and looked so thoughtful and mighty that Meeks could almost feel the joyful tears of his sister Mary dropping upon his bright blue tie.

'You go down in the Canal Street neighbourhood,' said the policeman, 'and get a job drivin' the biggest dray you can find. There's old women always gettin' knocked over by drays down there. You might see 'er among 'em. If you don't want to do that you better go 'round to head-quarters and get 'em to put a fly cop on to the dame.'

At police head-quarters Meeks received ready assistance. A general alarm was sent out, and copies of a photograph of Mary Snyder that her brother had were distributed among the stations. In Mulberry Street the chief assigned Detective Mullins to the case.

The detective took Meeks aside and said:

'This is not a very difficult case to unravel. Shave off your whiskers, fill your pockets with good cigars, and meet me in the café of the Waldorf at three o'clock this afternoon.'

Meeks obeyed. He found Mullins there. They had a bottle of wine, while the detective asked questions concerning the missing woman.

'Now,' said Mullins, 'New York is a big city, but we've got the detective business systematized. There are two ways we can go about finding your sister. We will try one of 'em first. You say she's fifty-two?'

'A little past,' said Meeks.

The detective conducted the Westerner to a branch advertising office of one of the largest dailies. There he wrote the following 'ad' and submitted it to Meeks.

'Wanted, at once – one hundred attractive chorus girls for a new musical comedy. Apply all day at No. – Broadway.'

Meeks was indignant.

'My sister,' said he, 'is a poor, hard-working, elderly woman. I do not see what aid an advertisement of this kind would be toward finding her.'

'All right,' said the detective. 'I guess you don't know New York. But if you've got a grouch against this scheme we'll try the other one. It's a sure thing. But it'll cost you more.'

'Never mind the expense,' said Meeks; 'we'll try it.'

The sleuth led him back to the Waldorf. 'Engage a couple of bedrooms and a parlour,' he advised, 'and let's go up.'

This was done, and the two were shown to a superb suite on the fourth floor. Meeks looked puzzled. The detective sank into a velvet armchair, and pulled out his cigar case

'I forgot to suggest, old man,' he said, 'that you should have taken the rooms by the month. They wouldn't have stuck you so much for 'em.'

'By the month!' exclaimed Meeks. 'What do you mean?'

'Oh, it'll take time to work the game this way. I told you it would cost you more. We'll have to wait till spring. There'll be a new city directory out then. Very likely your sister's name and address will be in it.'

Meeks rid himself of the city detective at once. On the next day someone advised him to consult Shamrock Jolnes, New York's famous private detective, who demanded fabulous fees, but performed miracles in the way of solving mysteries and crimes.

After waiting for two hours in the ante-room of the great detective's apartment, Meeks was shown into his presence. Jolnes sat in a purple dressing-gown at an inlaid ivory chess table, with a magazine before him, trying to solve the mystery of 'They.' The famous sleuth's thin, intellectual face, piercing eyes, and rate per word are too well known to need description.

Meeks set forth his errand. 'My fee, if successful, will be $500,' said Shamrock Jolnes.

Meeks bowed his agreement to the price.

'I will undertake your case, Mr. Meeks,' said Jolnes, finally. 'The disappearance of people in this city has always been an interesting problem to me. I remember a case that I brought to a successful outcome a year ago. A family bearing the name of Clark disappeared suddenly from a small flat in which they were living. I watched the flat building for two months for a clue. One day it struck me that a certain milkman and a grocer's boy always walked backward when they carried their wares upstairs. Following out by induction the idea that this observation gave me, I at once located the missing family. They had moved into the flat across the hall and changed their name to Kralc.'

Shamrock Jolnes and his client went to the tenement house where Mary Snyder had lived, and the detective demanded to be shown the room in which she had lived. It had been occupied by no tenant since her disappearance.

The room was small, dingy, and poorly furnished. Meeks seated himself dejectedly on a broken chair, while the great detective searched the walls and floor and the few sticks of old, rickety furniture for a clue.

At the end of half an hour Jolnes had collected a few seemingly unintelligible articles – a cheap black hat-pin, a piece torn off a theatre programme, and the end of a small torn card on which was the word 'left' and the characters 'C 12.'

Shamrock Jolnes leaned against the mantel for ten minutes, with his head resting upon his hand, and an absorbed look upon his intellectual face. At the end of that time he exclaimed, with animation:

'Come, Mr. Meeks; the problem is solved. I can take you directly to the house where your sister is living. And you may have no fears concerning her welfare, for she is amply provided with funds – for the present at least.'

Meeks felt joy and wonder in equal proportions.

'How did you manage it?' he asked, with admiration in his tones.

Perhaps Jolnes's only weakness was a professional pride in his wonderful achievements in induction. He was ever ready to astound and charm his listeners by describing his methods.

'By elimination,' said Jolnes, spreading his clues upon a little table, 'I got rid of certain parts of the city to which Mrs. Snyder might have removed. You see this hat-pin? That eliminates Brooklyn. No woman attempts to board a car at the Brooklyn Bridge without being sure that she carries a hat-pin with which to fight her way into a seat. And now I will demonstrate to you that she could not have gone to Harlem. Behind this door are two hooks in the wall. Upon one of these Mrs. Snyder has hung her bonnet, and upon the other her shawl. You will observe that the bottom of the hanging shawl has gradually made a soiled streak against the plastered wall. The mark is clean-cut, proving that there is no fringe on the shawl. Now, was there ever a case where a middle-aged woman, wearing a shawl, boarded a Harlem train without there being a fringe on the shawl to catch in the gate and delay the passengers behind her? So we eliminate Harlem.

'Therefore I conclude that Mrs. Snyder has not moved very far away. On this torn piece of card you see the word "left," the letter "C," and the number "12." Now, I happen to know that No. 12 Avenue C is a first-class boarding-house, far beyond your sister's means – as we suppose. But then I find this piece of a theatre programme, crumpled into an odd shape. What meaning does it convey? None to you, very likely, Mr. Meeks; but it is eloquent to one whose habits and training take cognizance of the smallest things.

'You have told me that your sister was a scrub woman. She scrubbed the floors of offices and hallways. Let us assume that she procured such work to perform in a theatre. Where is valuable jewellery lost the oftenest, Mr. Meeks? In the theatres, of course. Look at that piece of programme, Mr. Meeks. Observe the round impression on it. It has been wrapped around a ring – perhaps a ring of great value. Mrs. Snyder found the ring while at work in the theatre. She hastily tore off a piece of a programme, wrapped the ring carefully, and thrust it into her bosom. The next day she disposed of it, and, with her increased means, looked about her for a more comfortable place in which to live. When I reach thus far in the chain I see nothing impossible about No. 12 Avenue C. It is there we will find your sister, Mr. Meeks.'

Shamrock Jolnes concluded his convincing speech with the smile of a successful artist. Meeks's admiration was too great for words. Together they went to No. 12 Avenue C. It was an old-fashioned, brown-stone house in a prosperous and respectable neighbourhood.

They rang the bell, and on inquiring were told that no Mrs. Snyder was known there, and that not within six months had a new occupant come to the house.

When they reached the sidewalk again, Meeks examined the clues which he had brought away from his sister's old room.

'I am no detective,' he remarked to Jolnes as he raised the piece of theatre programme to his nose, 'but it seems to me that instead of a ring having been wrapped in this paper, it was one of those round peppermint drops. And this piece with the address on it looks to me like the end of a seat coupon – No. 12, row C, left aisle.'

Shamrock Jolnes had a far-away look in his eyes.

'I think you would do well to consult Juggins,' said he.

'Who is Juggins?' asked Meeks.

'He is the leader,' said Jolnes, 'of a new modern school of detectives. Their methods are different from ours, but it is said that Juggins has solved some extremely puzzling cases. I will take you to him.'

They found the greater Juggins in his office. He was a small man with light hair, deeply absorbed in reading one of the bourgeois works of Nathaniel Hawthorne.

The two great detectives of different schools shook hands with ceremony, and Meeks was introduced.

'State the facts,' said Juggins, going on with his reading.

When Meeks ceased, the greater one closed his book and said:

'Do I understand that your sister is fifty-two years of age, with a large mole on the side of her nose, and that she is a very poor widow, making a scanty living by scrubbing, and with a very homely face and figure?'

'That describes her exactly,' admitted Meeks. Juggins rose and put on his hat.

'In fifteen minutes,' he said, 'I will return, bringing you her present address.'

Shamrock Jolnes turned pale, but forced a smile.

Within the specified time Juggins returned and consulted a little slip of paper held in his hand.

'Your sister, Mary Snyder,' he announced calmly, 'will be found at No. 162 Chilton Street. She is living in the back hall-bedroom, five flights up. The house is only four blocks from here,' he continued, addressing Meeks. 'Suppose you go and verify the statement and then return here. Mr. Jolnes will await you, I dare say.'

Meeks hurried away. In twenty minutes he was back again, with a beaming face.

'She is there and well!' he cried. 'Name your fee!'

'Two dollars,' said Juggins.

When Meeks had settled his bill and departed, Shamrock Jolnes stood with his hat in his hand before Juggins.

'If it would not be asking too much,' he stammered – 'if you would favour me so far – would you object to –'

'Certainly not,' said Juggins pleasantly. 'I will tell you how I did it. You remember the description of Mrs. Snyder? Did you ever know a woman like that who wasn't paying weekly instalments on an enlarged crayon portrait of herself? The biggest factory of that kind in the country is just around the corner. I went there and got her address off the books. That's all.'

LXII

Witches' Loaves

MISS MARTHA MEACHAM kept the little bakery on the corner (the one where you go up three steps, and the bell tinkles when you open the door).

Miss Martha was forty, her bank-book showed a credit of two thousand dollars, and she possessed two false teeth and a sympathetic heart. Many people have married whose chances to do so were much inferior to Miss Martha's.

Two or three times a week a customer came in in whom she began to take an interest. He was a middle-aged man, wearing spectacles and a brown beard trimmed to a careful point.

He spoke English with a strong German accent. His clothes were worn and darned in places, and wrinkled and baggy in others. But he looked neat, and had very good manners.

He always bought two loaves of stale bread. Fresh bread was five cents a loaf. Stale ones were two for five. Never did he call for anything but stale bread.

Once Miss Martha saw a red and brown stain on his fingers. She was sure then that he was an artist and very poor. No doubt he lived in a garret, where he painted pictures and ate stale bread and thought of the good things to eat in Miss Martha's bakery.

Often when Miss Martha sat down to her chops and light rolls and jam and tea she would sigh, and wish that the gentle-mannered artist might share her tasty meal instead of eating his dry crust in that draughty attic.

Miss Martha's heart, as you have been told, was a sympathetic one.

In order to test her theory as to his occupation, she brought from her room one day a painting that she had bought at a sale, and set it against the shelves behind the bread counter.

It was a Venetian scene. A splendid marble palazzio (so it said on the picture) stood in the foreground – or rather forewater. For the rest there were gondolas (with the lady trailing her hand in the water), clouds, sky, and chiaroscuro in plenty. No artist could fail to notice it.

Two days afterward the customer came in.

'Two loafs of stale bread, if you blease.

'You haf here a fine bicture, madame,' he said while she was wrapping up the bread.

'Yes?' says Miss Martha, revelling in her own cunning. 'I do so admire art and' (no, it would not do to say 'artists' thus early) 'and paintings,' she substituted. 'You think it is a good picture?'

'Der balace,' said the customer, 'is not in good drawing. Der bairspective of it is not true Goot morning, madame.'

He took his bread, bowed, and hurried out.

Yes, he must be an artist. Miss Martha took the picture back to her room.

How gentle and kindly his eyes shone behind his spectacles! What a broad brow he had! To be able to judge perspective at a glance – and to live on stale bread! But genius often has to struggle before it is recognized.

What a thing it would be for art and perspective if genius were backed by two thousand dollars in the bank, a bakery, and a sympathetic heart to – But these were day-dreams, Miss Martha.

Often now when he came he would chat for awhile across the showcase. He seemed to crave Miss Martha's cheerful words.

He kept on buying stale bread. Never a cake, never a pie, never one of her delicious Sally Lunns.

She thought he began to look thinner and discouraged. Her heart ached to add something good to eat to his meagre purchase, but her courage failed at the act. She did not dare affront him. She knew the pride of artists.

Miss Martha took to wearing her blue-dotted silk waist behind the counter. In the back room she cooked a mysterious compound of quince seeds and borax. Ever so many people use it for the complexion.

One day the customer came in as usual, laid his nickel on the showcase, and called for his stale loaves. While Miss Martha was reaching for them there was a great tooting and clanging, and a fire-engine came lumbering past.

The customer hurried to the door to look, as anyone will. Suddenly inspired, Miss Martha seized the opportunity.

On the bottom shelf behind the counter was a pound of fresh butter that the dairyman had left ten minutes before. With a bread-knife Miss Martha made a deep slash in each of the stale loaves, inserted a generous quantity of butter, and pressed the loaves tight again.

When the customer turned once more she was tying the paper around them.

When he had gone, after an unusually pleasant little chat, Miss Martha smiled to herself, but not without a slight fluttering of the heart.

Had she been too bold? Would he take offence? But surely not. There was no language of edibles. Butter was no emblem of unmaidenly forwardness.

For a long time that day her mind dwelt on the subject. She imagined the scene when he should discover her little deception.

He would lay down his brushes and palette. There would stand his easel with the picture he was painting in which the perspective was beyond criticism.

He would prepare for his luncheon of dry bread and water. He would slice into a loaf – ah!

Miss Martha blushed. Would he think of the hand that placed it there as he ate? Would he –

The front door bell jangled viciously. Somebody was coming in, making a great deal of noise.

Miss Martha hurried to the front. Two men were there. One was a young man smoking a pipe – a man she had never seen before. The other was her artist.

His face was very red, his hat was on the back of his head, his hair was wildly rumpled. He clinched his two fists and shook them ferociously at Miss Martha. *At Miss Martha.*

'*Dummkopf!*' he shouted with extreme loudness; and then '*Tausendonfer!*' or something like it, in German.

The young man tried to draw him away.

'I vill not go,' he said angrily, 'else I shall told her.'

He made a bass drum of Miss Martha's counter.

'You haf shpoilt me,' he cried, his blue eyes blazing behind his spectacles. 'I vill tell you. You vas von *meddingsome old cat!*'

Miss Martha leaned weakly against the shelves and laid one hand on her blue-dotted silk waist. The young man took his companion by the collar.

'Come on,' he said, 'you've said enough.' He dragged the angry one out at the door to the sidewalk, and then came back.

'Guess you ought to be told, ma'am,' he said, 'what the row is about. That's Blumberger. He's an architectural draughtsman. I work in the same office with him.

'He's been working hard for three months drawing a plan for a new city hall. It was a prize competition. He finished inking the lines yesterday. You know, a draughtsman always makes his drawing in pencil first. When it's done he rubs out the pencil lines with handfuls of stale breadcrumbs. That's better than india-rubber.

'Blumberger's been buying the bread here. Well, to-day — well, you know, ma'am, that butter isn't — well, Blumberger's plan isn't good for anything now except to cut up into railroad sandwiches.'

Miss Martha went into the back room. She took off the blue-dotted silk waist and put on the old brown serge she used to wear. Then she poured the quince seed and borax mixture out of the window into the ash can.

LXIII

Holding up a Train

NOTE. The man who told me these things was for several years an outlaw in the South-west and a follower of the pursuit he so frankly describes. His description of the *modus operandi* should prove interesting, his counsel of value to the potential passenger in some future 'hold-up,' while his estimate of the pleasures of train robbing will hardly induce anyone to adopt it as a profession. I give the story in almost exactly his own words.

O. H.

MOST PEOPLE WOULD SAY, if their opinion was asked for, that holding up a train would be a hard job. Well, it isn't; it's easy. I have contributed some to the uneasiness of railroads and the insomnia of express companies, and the most trouble I ever had about a hold-up was in being swindled by unscrupulous people while spending the money I got. The danger wasn't anything to speak of, and we didn't mind the trouble.

One man has come pretty near robbing a train by himself; two have succeeded a few times; three can do it if they are hustlers, but five is about the right number. The time to do it and the place depend upon several things.

The first 'stick-up' I was ever in happened in 1890. Maybe the way I got into it will explain how most train robbers start in the business. Five out of six Western outlaws are just cowboys out of a job and gone wrong. The sixth is a tough from the East who dresses up like a bad man and plays some low-down trick that gives the boys a bad name. Wire fences and 'nesters' made five of them; a bad heart made the sixth.

Jim S – and I were working on the 101 Ranch in Colorado. The nesters had the cowman on the go. They had taken up the land and elected officers who were hard to get along with. Jim and I rode into La Junta one day, going south from a round-up. We were having a little fun without malice toward anybody when a farmer administration cut in and tried to harvest us. Jim shot a deputy-marshal, and I kind of corroborated his side of the argument. We skirmished up and down the main street, the boomers having bad luck all the time. After awhile we leaned forward and shoved for the ranch down on the Ceriso. We were riding a couple of horses that couldn't fly, but they could catch birds.

A few days after that, a gang of the La Junta boomers came to the ranch and wanted us to go back with them. Naturally, we declined. We had the house on them, and before we were done refusing, the old 'dobe was plumb full of lead. When dark came we fagged 'em a batch of bullets and shoved out the back door for the rocks. They sure smoked us as we went. We had to drift, which we did, and rounded up down in Oklahoma.

Well, there wasn't anything we could get there, and, being mighty hard up, we decided to transact a little business with the railroads. Jim and I joined forces with Tom and Ike Moore – two brothers who had plenty of sand they were willing to convert into dust. I can call their names, for both of them are dead. Tom was shot while robbing a bank in Arkansas; Ike was killed during the more dangerous pastime of attending a dance in the Creek Nation.

We selected a place on the Santa Fé where there was a bridge across a deep creek surrounded by heavy timber. All passenger trains took water at the tank close to one end of the bridge. It was a quiet place, the nearest house being five miles away. The day before it happened, we rested our horses and 'made medicine' as to how we should get about it. Our plans were not at all elaborate, as none of us had ever engaged in a hold-up before.

The Santa Fé flyer was due at the tank at 11.15 p.m. At eleven, Tom and I lay down on one side of the track, and Jim and Ike took the other. As the train rolled up, the headlight flashing far down the track and the steam hissing from the engine, I turned weak all over. I would have worked a whole year on the ranch for nothing to have been out of that affair right then. Some of the nervicst men in the business have told me that they felt the same way the first time.

The engine had hardly stopped when I jumped on the running-board on one side, while Jim mounted the other. As soon as the engineer and fireman saw our guns they threw up their hands without being told and begged us not to shoot, saying they would do anything we wanted them to.

'Hit the ground,' I ordered, and they both jumped off. We drove them before us down the side of the train. While this was happening, Tom and Ike had been blazing away, one on each side of the train, yelling like Apaches so as to keep the passengers herded in the cars. Some fellow stuck a little ??-calibre out one of the coach windows and fired it straight up in the air. I let drive and smashed the glass just over his head. That settled everything like resistance from that direction.

By this time all my nervousness was gone. I felt a kind of pleasant excitement as if I were at a dance or a frolic of some sort. The lights were all out in the coaches, and, as Tom and Ike gradually quit firing and yelling, it got to be almost as still as a graveyard. I remember hearing a little bird chirping in a bush at the side of the track, as if it were complaining at being waked up.

I made the fireman get a lantern, and then I went to the express car and yelled to the messenger to open up or get perforated. He slid the door back and stood in it with his hands up. 'Jump overboard, son,' I said, and he hit the dirt like a lump of lead. There were two safes in the car – a big one and a little one. By the way, I first located the messenger's arsenal – a double-barrelled shot-gun with buck-shot cartridges and a thirty-eight in a drawer. I drew the cartridges from the shot-gun, pocketed the pistol, and called the messenger inside. I shoved my gun against his nose,

and put him to work. He couldn't open the big safe, but he did
the little one. There was only nine hundred dollars in it. That
was mighty small winnings for our trouble, so we decided to go
through the passengers. We took our prisoners to the smoking-
car, and from there sent the engineer through the train to light
up the coaches. Beginning with the first one, we placed a man at
each door and ordered the passengers to stand between the seats
with their hands up.

If you want to find out what cowards the majority of men are,
all you have to do is rob a passenger train. I don't mean because
they don't resist – I'll tell you later on why they can't do that – but
it makes a man feel sorry for them the way they lose their heads.
Big, burly drummers and farmers and ex-soldiers and high-collared dudes and sports that, a few moments before, were filling the
car with noise and bragging, get so scared that their ears flop.

There were very few people in the day coaches at that time of
night, so we made a slim haul until we got to the sleeper. The
Pullman conductor met me at one door while Jim was going
round to the other one. He very politely informed me that I could
not go into that car, as it did not belong to the railroad company,
and, besides, the passengers had already been greatly disturbed by
the shouting and firing. Never in all my life have I met with a finer
instance of official dignity and reliance upon the power of Mr.
Pullman's great name. I jabbed my six-shooter so hard against Mr.
Conductor's front that I afterward found one of his vest-buttons
so firmly wedged in the end of the barrel that I had to shoot it out.
He just shut up like a weak-springed knife and rolled down the car
steps.

I opened the door of the sleeper and stepped inside. A big, fat
old man came wabbling up to me, puffing and blowing. He had
one coat-sleeve on and was trying to put his vest on over that. I
don't know who he thought I was.

'Young man, young man,' says he, 'you must keep cool and not
get excited. Above everything keep cool.'

'I can't,' says I. 'Excitement's just eating me up.' And then I let
out a yell and turned loose my forty-five through the skylight.

That old man tried to dive into one of the lower berths, but a
screech came out of it and a bare foot that took him in the bread-
basket and landed him on the floor. I saw Jim coming in the other
door, and I hollered for everybody to climb out and line up.

They commenced to scramble down, and for awhile we had a
three-ringed circus. The men looked as frightened and tame as a

lot of rabbits in a deep snow. They had on, on an average, about a quarter of a suit of clothes and one shoe apiece. One chap was sitting on the floor of the aisle, looking as if he were working a hard sum in arithmetic. He was trying, very solemn, to pull a lady's number two shoe on his number nine foot.

The ladies didn't stop to dress. They were so curious to see a real, live train robber, bless 'em, that they just wrapped blankets and sheets around themselves and came out, squeaky and fidgety looking. They always show more curiosity and sand than the men do.

We got them all lined up and pretty quiet, and I went through the bunch. I found very little on them – I mean in the way of valuables. One man in the line was a sight. He was one of those big, overgrown, solemn snoozers that sit on the platform at lectures and look wise. Before crawling out he had managed to put on his long, frock-tailed coat and his high silk hat. The rest of him was nothing but pyjamas and bunions. When I dug into that Prince Albert, I expected to drag out at least a block of gold mine stock or an armful of Government bonds, but all I found was a little boy's French harp about four inches long. What it was there for, I don't know. I felt a little mad because he had fooled me so. I stuck the harp up against his mouth

'If you can't pay – play,' I says.

'I can't play,' says he.

'Then learn right off quick,' says I, letting him smell the end of my gun-barrel.

He caught hold of the harp, turned red as a beet, and commenced to blow. He blew a dinky little tune I remembered hearing when I was a kid:

> Prettiest little gal in the country – oh!
> Mammy and Daddy told me so.

I made him keep on playing it all the time we were in the car. Now and then he'd get weak and off the key, and I'd turn my gun on him and ask what was the matter with that little gal, and whether he had any intention of going back on her, which would make him start up again like sixty. I think that old boy standing there in his silk hat and bare feet playing his little French harp, was the funniest sight I ever saw. One little red-headed woman in the line broke out laughing at him. You could have heard her in the next car.

Then Jim held them steady while I searched the berths. I grappled around in those beds and filled a pillow-case with the strangest assortment of stuff you ever saw. Now and then I'd come across a little pop-gun pistol, just about right for plugging teeth with, which I'd throw out the window. When I finished with the collection, I dumped the pillowcase load in the middle of the aisle. There were a good many watches, bracelets, rings, and pocket-books, with a sprinkling of false teeth, whisky flasks, face-powder boxes, chocolate caramels, and heads of hair of various colours and lengths. There were also about a dozen ladies' stockings into which jewellery, watches, and rolls of bills had been stuffed and then wadded up tight and stuck under the mattresses. I offered to return what I called the 'scalps,' saying that we were not Indians on the war-path, but none of the ladies seemed to know to whom the hair belonged.

One of the women — and a good-looker she was — wrapped in a striped blanket, saw me pick up one of the stockings that was pretty chunky and heavy about the toe, and she snapped out:

'That's mine, sir. You're not in the business of robbing women, are you?'

Now, as this was our first hold-up, we hadn't agreed upon any code of ethics, so I hardly knew what to answer. But, anyway, I replied: 'Well, not as a speciality. If this contains your personal property you can have it back.'

'It just does,' she declared eagerly, and reached out her hand for it.

'You'll excuse my taking a look at the contents,' I said, holding the stocking up by the toe. Out dumped a big gent's gold watch, worth two hundred, a gent's leather pocket-book that we afterward found to contain six hundred dollars, a 32-calibre revolver; and the only thing of the lot that could have been a lady's personal property was a silver bracelet worth about fifty cents.

I said, 'Madame, here's your property,' and handed her the bracelet. 'Now,' I went on, 'how can you expect us to act square with you when you try to deceive us in this manner? I'm surprised at such conduct.'

The young woman flushed up as if she had been caught doing something dishonest. Some other woman down the line called out: 'The mean thing!' I never knew whether she meant the other lady or me.

When we finished our job we ordered everybody back to bed, told 'em good night very politely at the door and left. We rode forty miles before daylight and then divided the stuff. Each one of us got $1,752-85 in money. We lumped the jewellery around. Then we scattered, each man for himself.

That was my first train robbery, and it was about as easily done as any of the ones that followed. But that was the last and only time I ever went through the passengers. I don't like that part of the business. Afterwards I stuck strictly to the express car. During the next eight years I handled a good deal of money.

The best haul I made was just seven years after the first one. We found out about a train that was going to bring out a lot of money to pay off the soldiers at a Government post. We stuck that train up in broad daylight. Five of us lay in the sandhills near a little station. Ten soldiers were guarding the money on the train, but they might just as well have been at home on a furlough. We didn't even allow them to stick their heads out the windows to see the fun. We had no trouble at all in getting the money, which was all in gold. Of course, a big howl was raised at the time about the robbery. It was Government stuff, and the Government got sarcastic and wanted to know what the convoy of soldiers went along for. The only excuse given was that nobody was expecting an attack among those bare sand-hills in daytime. I don't know what the Government thought about the excuse, but I know that it was a good one. The surprise - that is the keynote of the train-robbing business. The papers published all kinds of stories about the loss, finally agreeing that it was between nine thousand and ten thousand dollars. The Government sawed wood. Here are the correct figures, printed for the first time - forty-eight thousand dollars. If anybody will take the trouble to look over Uncle Sam's private accounts for that little debit to profit and loss, he will find that I am right to a cent.

By that time we were expert enough to know what to do. We rode due west twenty miles, making a trail that a Broadway policeman could have followed, and then we doubled back, hiding our tracks. On the second night after the hold-up, while posses were scouring the country in every direction, Jim and I were eating supper in the second story of a friend's house in the town where the alarm started from. Our friend pointed out to us, in an office across the street, a printing-press at work striking off handbills offering a reward for our capture.

I have been asked what we do with the money we get. Well, I never could account for a tenth part of it after it was spent. It goes fast and freely. An outlaw has to have a good many friends. A highly respected citizen may, and often does, get along with very few, but a man on the dodge has got to have 'side-kickers.' With angry posses and reward-hungry officers cutting out a hot trail for him, he must have a few places scattered about the country where he can stop and feed himself and his horse and get a few hours' sleep without having to keep both eyes open. When he makes a haul he feels like dropping some of the coin with these friends, and he does it liberally. Sometimes I have, at the end of a hasty visit at one of these havens of refuge, flung a handful of gold and bills into the laps of the kids playing on the floor, without knowing whether my contribution was a hundred dollars or a thousand.

When old-timers make a big haul they generally go far away to one of the big cities to spend their money. Green hands, however successful a hold-up they make, nearly always give themselves away by showing too much money near the place where they got it.

I was in a job in '94 where we got twenty thousand dollars. We followed our favourite plan for a getaway — that is, doubled on our trail — and laid low for a time near the scene of the train's bad luck. One morning I picked up a newspaper and read an article with big headlines stating that the marshal, with eight deputies and a posse of thirty armed citizens, had the train robbers surrounded in a mesquite thicket on the Cimarron and that it was a question of only a few hours when they would be dead men or prisoners. While I was reading that article I was sitting at breakfast in one of the most elegant private residences in Washington City, with a flunky in knee pants standing behind my chair. Jim was sitting across the table talking to his half-uncle, a retired naval officer, whose name you have often seen in the accounts of doings in the capital. We had gone there and bought rattling outfits of good clothes, and were resting from our labours among the nabobs. We must have been killed in that mesquite thicket, for I can make an affidavit that we didn't surrender.

Now I propose to tell why it is easy to hold up a train, and, then, why no one should ever do it.

In the first place, the attacking party has all the advantage. That is, of course, supposing that they are old-timers with the necessary experience and courage. They have the outside and are protected by the darkness, while the others are in the light, hemmed into a small space, and exposed, the moment they show a head at a window or door, to the aim of a man who is a dead shot and who won't hesitate to shoot.

But, in my opinion, the main condition that makes train robbing easy is the element of *surprise* in connection with the imagination of the passengers. If you have ever seen a horse that has
eaten loco weed you will understand what I mean when I say that
the passengers get locoed. That horse gets the awfullest imagination on him in the world. You can't coax him to cross a little
branch stream two feet wide. It looks as big to him as the Mississippi River. That's just the way with the passenger. He thinks
there are a hundred men yelling and shooting outside, when
maybe there are only two or three. And the muzzle of a forty-five
looks like the entrance to a tunnel. The passenger is all right,
although he may do mean little tricks, like hiding a wad of money
in his shoe and forgetting to dig up until you jostle his ribs some
with the end of your six-shooter; but there's no harm in him.

As to the train crew, we never had any more trouble with them
than if they had been so many sheep. I don't mean that they are
cowards; I mean that they have got sense. They know they're not
up against a bluff. It's the same way with the officers. I've seen
secret-service men, marshals, and railroad detectives fork over
their change as meek as Moses. I saw one of the bravest marshals I
ever knew hide his gun under his seat and dig up along with the
rest while I was taking toll. He wasn't afraid; he simply knew that
we had the drop on the whole outfit. Besides, many of those officers have families and they feel that they oughtn't to take chances;
whereas death has no terrors for the man who holds up a train. He
expects to get killed some day, and he generally does. My advice to
you, if you should ever be in a hold-up, is to line up with the cowards and save your bravery for an occasion when it may be of some
benefit to you. Another reason why officers are backward about
mixing things with a train robber is a financial one. Every time
there is a scrimmage and somebody gets killed, the officers lose
money. If the train robber gets away they swear out a warrant
against John Doe et *al.* and travel hundreds of miles and sign
vouchers for thousands on the trail of the fugitives, and the Government foots the bills. So, with them, it is a question of mileage
rather than courage.

I will give one instance to support my statement that the surprise
is the best card in playing for a hold-up.

Along in '92 the Daltons were cutting out a hot trail for the
officers down in the Cherokee Nation. Those were their lucky
days, and they got so reckless and sandy that they used to
announce beforehand what job they were going to undertake.

Once they gave it out that they were going to hold up the M. K. & T. flyer on a certain night at the station of Pryor Creek, in Indian Territory.

That night the railroad company got fifteen deputy marshals in Muscogee and put them on the train. Beside them they had fifty armed men hid in the depot at Pryor Creek.

When the Katy Flyer pulled in not a Dalton showed up. The next station was Adair, six miles away. When the train reached there and the deputies were having a good time explaining what they would have done to the Dalton gang if they had turned up, all at once it sounded like an army firing outside. The conductor and brake-man came running into the car yelling, 'Train robbers!'

Some of those deputies lit out of the door, hit the ground, and kept on running. Some of them hid their Winchesters under the seats. Two of them made a fight and were both killed.

It took the Daltons just ten minutes to capture the train and whip the escort. In twenty minutes more they robbed the express car of twenty-seven thousand dollars and made a clean get-away.

My opinion is that those deputies would have put up a stiff fight at Pryor Creek, where they were expecting trouble, but they were taken by surprise and 'locoed' at Adair, just as the Daltons, who knew their business, expected they would.

I don't think I ought to close without giving some deductions from my experience of eight years 'on the dodge.' It doesn't pay to rob trains. Leaving out the question of right and morals, which I don't think I ought to tackle, there is very little to envy in the life of an outlaw. After awhile money ceases to have any value in his eyes. He gets to looking upon the railroads and express companies as his bankers, and his six-shooter as a cheque-book good for any amount. He throws away money right and left. Most of the time he is on the jump, riding day and night, and he lives so hard between times that he doesn't enjoy the taste of high life when he gets it. He knows that his time is bound to come to lose his life or liberty, and that the accuracy of his aim, the speed of his horse, and the fidelity of his 'sider,' are all that postpone the inevitable.

It isn't that he loses any sleep over danger from the officers of the law. In all my experience I never knew officers to attack a band of outlaws unless they outnumbered them at least three to one.

But the outlaw carries one thought constantly in his mind – and that is what makes him so sore against life, more than anything else – he knows where the marshals get their recruits of deputies. He knows that the majority of these upholders of the law were once lawbreakers, horse thieves, rustlers, highwaymen, and outlaws like himself, and that they gained their positions and immunity by turning state's evidence, by turning traitor and delivering up their comrades to imprisonment and death. He knows that some day – unless he is shot first – his Judas will set to work, the trap will be laid, and he will be the surprised instead of a surpriser at a stick-up.

That is why the man who holds up trains picks his company with a thousand times the care with which a careful girl chooses a sweetheart. That is why he raises himself from his blanket of nights and listens to the tread of every horse's hoofs on the distant road. That is why he broods suspiciously for days upon a jesting remark or an unusual movement of a tried comrade, or the broken mutterings of his closest friend, sleeping by his side.

And it is one of the reasons why the train-robbing profession is not so pleasant a one as either of its collateral branches – politics or cornering the market.

LXIV

Ulysses and the Dogman

Do you know the time of the dogmen?

When the forefinger of twilight begins to smudge the clear-drawn lines of the Big City, there is inaugurated an hour devoted to one of the most melancholy sights of urban life.

Out from the towering flat crags and apartment peaks of the cliff-dwellers of New York steals an army of beings that were once men. Even yet they go upright upon two limbs and retain human form and speech; but you will observe that they are behind animals in progress. Each of these beings follows a dog, to which he is fastened by an artificial ligament.

These men are all victims to Circe. Not willingly do they become flunkeys to Fido, bell-boys to bull terriers, and toddlers after Towzer. Modern Circe, instead of turning them into animals, has kindly left the difference of a six-foot leash between them. Every one of these dogmen has been either cajoled, bribed, or commanded by his own particular Circe to take the dear household pet out for an airing.

By their faces and manner you can tell that the dogmen are bound in a hopeless enchantment. Never will there come even a dog-catcher Ulysses to remove the spell.

The faces of some are stonily set. They are past the commiseration, the curiosity, or the jeers of their fellow-beings. Years of
matrimony, of continuous compulsory canine constitutionals, have
made them callous. They unwind their beasts from lamp-posts, or
the ensnared legs of profane pedestrians, with the stolidity of
mandarins manipulating the strings of their kites.

Others, more recently reduced to the ranks of Rover's retinue,
take their medicine sulkily and fiercely. They play the dog on the
end of their line with the pleasure felt by the girl out fishing when
she catches a sea-robin on her hook. They glare at you threateningly if you look at them, as if it would be their delight to let slip
the dogs of war. These are half-mutinous dogmen, not quite
Circe-ized, and you will do well not to kick their charges, should
they sniff around your ankles.

Others of the tribe do not seem to feel so keenly. They are
mostly unfresh youths, with gold caps and drooping cigarettes,
who do not harmonize with their dogs. The animals they attend
wear satin bows in their collars; and the young men steer them so
assiduously that you are tempted to the theory that some personal
advantage, contingent upon satisfactory service, waits upon the
execution of their duties.

The dogs thus personally conducted are of many varieties: but
they are one in fatness, in pampered, diseased vileness of temper,
in insolent, snarling capriciousness of behaviour. They tug at the
leash fractiously, they make leisurely nasal inventory of every
doorstep, railing, and post. They sit down to rest when they
choose; they wheeze like the winner of a Third Avenue beefsteak-
eating contest; they blunder clumsily into open cellars and coal
holes; they lead the dogmen a merry dance.

These unfortunate dry nurses of dogdom, the cur cuddlers,
mongrel managers, Spitz stalkers, poodle pullers, Skye scrapers,
dachshund dandlers, terrier trailers and Pomeranian pushers of the
cliff-dwelling Circes follow their charges meekly. The doggies neither fear nor respect them. Masters of the house these men whom
they hold in leash may be, but they are not masters of them. From
cosy corner to fire-escape, from divan to dumb-waiter, doggy's
snarl easily drives this two-legged being who is commissioned to
walk at the other end of his string during his outing.

One twilight the dogmen came forth as usual at their Circes'
pleading, guerdon, or crack of the whip. One among them was a
strong man, apparently of too solid virtues for this airy vocation.
His expression was melancholic, his manner depressed. He was

leashed to a vile, white dog, loathsomely fat, fiendishly ill-natured, gloatingly intractable toward his despised conductor.

At a corner nearest to his apartment-house the dogman turned down a side-street, hoping for fewer witnesses to his ignominy. The surfeited beast waddled before him, panting with spleen and the labour of motion.

Suddenly the dog stopped. A tall, brown, longcoated, wide-brimmed man stood like a Colossus blocking the sidewalk and declaring:

'Well, I'm a son of a gun!'

'Jim Berry!' breathed the dogman, with exclamation points in his voice.

'Sam Telfair,' cried Wide-Brim again, 'you ding-basted old willywalloo, give us your hoof!'

Their hands clasped in the brief, tight greeting of the West that is death to the handshake microbe.

'You old fat rascal!' continued Wide-Brim, with a wrinkled, brown smile; 'it's been five years since I seen you. I been in this town a week, but you can't find nobody in such a place. Well, you dinged old married man, how are they coming?'

Something mushy and heavily soft like raised dough leaned against Jim's leg and chewed his trousers with a yeasty growl.

'Get to work,' said Jim, 'and explain this yard-wide hydrophobia yearling you've throwed your lasso over. Are you the pound-master of this burg? Do you call that a dog or what?'

'I need a drink,' said the dogman, dejected at the reminder of his old dog of the sea. 'Come on.'

Hard by was a café. 'Tis ever so in the big city. They sat at a table, and the bloated monster yelped and scrambled at the end of his leash to get at the café cat.

'Whisky,' said Jim to the waiter.

'Make it two,' said the dogman.

'You're fatter,' said Jim, 'and you look subjugated. I don't know about the East agreeing with you. All the boys asked me to hunt you up when I started. Sandy King, he went to the Klondike. Watson Burrel, he married the oldest Peters girl. I made some money buying beeves, and I bought a lot of wild land up on the Little Powder. Going to fence next fall. Bill Rawlins, he's gone to farming. You remember Bill, of course – he was courting Marcella – excuse me, Sam – I mean the lady you married, while she was teaching school at Prairie View. But you was the lucky man. How is Missis Telfair?'

'S-h-h-h!' said the dogman, signalling the waiter; 'give it a name.'

'Whisky,' said Jim.

'Make it two,' said the dogman.

'She's well,' he continued, after his chaser. 'She refused to live anywhere but in New York, where she came from. We live in a flat. Every evening at six I take that dog out for a walk. It's Marcella's pet. There never were two animals on earth, Jim, that hated one another like me and that dog does. His name's Lovekins. Marcella dresses for dinner while we're out. We eat tabble dote. Ever tried one of them, Jim?'

'No, I never,' said Jim. 'I seen the signs, but I thought they said "table de hole." I thought it was French for pool tables. How does it taste?'

'If you're going to be in the city for awhile we will –'

'No, sir-ee. I'm starting for home this evening on the 7.25. Like to stay longer, but I can't.'

'I'll walk down to the ferry with you,' said the dogman.

The dog had bound a leg each of Jim and the chair together, and had sunk into a comatose slumber. Jim stumbled and the leash was slightly wrenched. The shrieks of the awakened beast rang for a block around.

'If that's your dog,' said Jim, when they were on the street again, 'what's to hinder you from running that habeas corpus you've got around his neck over a limb and walking off and forgetting him?'

'I'd never dare to,' said the dogman, awed at the bold proposition. 'He sleeps in the bed. I sleep on a lounge. He runs howling to Marcella if I look at him. Some night, Jim, I'm going to get even with that dog. I've made up my mind to do it. I'm going to creep over with a knife and cut a hole in his mosquito bar so they can get in to him. See if I don't do it!'

'You ain't yourself, Sam Telfair. You ain't what you was once. I don't know about these cities and fiats over here. With my own eyes I seen you stand off both the Tillotson boys in Prairie View with the brass faucet out of a molasses barrel. And I seen you rope and tie the wildest steer on little Powder in 39 1–2.'

'I did, didn't I?' said the other, with a temporary gleam in his eye. 'But that was before I was dogmatized.'

'Does Missis Telfair –' began Jim.

'Hush!' said the dogman. 'Here's another café.'

They lined up at the bar. The dog fell asleep at their feet.

'Whisky,' said Jim.

'Make it two,' said the dogman.

'I thought about you,' said Jim, 'when I bought that wild land. I wished you was out there to help me with the stock.'

'Last Tuesday,' said the dogman, 'he bit me on the ankle because I asked for cream in my coffee. He always gets the cream.'

'You'd like Prairie View now,' said Jim. 'The boys from the round-ups for fifty miles around ride in there. One corner of my pasture is in sixteen miles of the town. There's a straight forty miles of wire on one side of it.'

'You pass through the kitchen to get to the bedroom,' said the dogman, 'and you pass through the parlour to get to the bath-room, and you back out through the dining-room to get into the bedroom so you can turn around and leave by the kitchen. And he snores and barks in his sleep, and I have to smoke in the park on account of his asthma.'

'Don't Missis Telfair —' began Jim.

'Oh, shut up!' said the dogman. 'What is it this time?'

'Whisky,' said Jim.

'Make it two,' said the dogman.

'Well, I'll be racking along down toward the ferry,' said the other.

'Come on, there, you mangy, turtle-backed, snake-headed, bench-legged ton-and-a-half of soap-grease!' shouted the dogman, with a new note in his voice and a new hand on the leash. The dog scrambled after them, with an angry whine at such unusual language from his guardian.

At the foot of Twenty-third Street the dogman led the way through swinging doors.

'Last chance,' said he. 'Speak up.'

'Whisky,' said Jim.

'Make it two,' said the dogman.

'I don't know,' said the ranchman, 'where I'll find the man I want to take charge of the Little Powder outfit. I want somebody I know something about. Finest stretch of prairie and timber you ever squinted your eye over, Sam. Now, if you was —'

'Speaking of hydrophobia,' said the dogman, 'the other night he chewed a piece out of my leg because I knocked a fly off of Marcella's arm. "It ought to be cauterized," says Marcella, and I was thinking so myself. I telephones for the doctor, and when he comes Marcella says to me: "Help me hold the poor dear while the doctor fixes his mouth. Oh, I hope he got no virus on any of his toofies when he bit you." Now what do you think of that?'

'Does Missis Telfair –' began Jim.

'Oh, drop it,' said the dogman. 'Come again!'

'Whisky,' said Jim.

'Make it two,' said the dogman.

They walked on to the ferry. The ranchman stepped to the ticket-window.

Suddenly the swift landing of three or four heavy kicks was heard, the air was rent by piercing canine shrieks, and a pained, outraged, lubberly, bow-legged pudding of a dog ran frenziedly up the street alone.

'Ticket to Denver,' said Jim.

'Make it two,' shouted the ex-dogman, reaching for his inside pocket.

LXV

At Arms with Morpheus

I NEVER COULD QUITE UNDERSTAND how Tom Hopkins came to make that blunder, for he had been through a whole term at a medical college – before he inherited his aunt's fortune – and had been considered strong in therapeutics.

We had been making a call together that evening, and afterwards Tom ran up to my rooms for a pipe and a chat before going on to his own luxurious apartments. I had stepped into the other room for a moment when I heard Tom sing out:

'Oh, Billy, I'm going to take about four grains of quinine, if you don't mind – I'm feeling all blue and shivery. Guess I'm taking cold.'

'All right,' I called back. 'The bottle is on the second shelf. Take it in a spoonful of that elixir of eucalyptus. It knocks the bitter out.'

After I came back we sat by the fire and got our briars going. In about eight minutes Tom sank back into a gentle collapse.

I went straight to the medicine cabinet and looked.

'You unmitigated hayseed!' I growled. 'See what money will do for a man's brains!'

There stood the morphine bottle with the stopper out, just as Tom had left it.

I routed out another young M.D. who roomed on the floor above, and sent him for old Doctor Gales, two squares away. Tom

Hopkins has too much money to be attended by rising young practitioners alone.

When Gales came we put Tom through as expensive a course of treatment as the resources of the profession permit. After the more drastic remedies we gave him citrate of caffeine in frequent doses and strong coffee, and walked him up and down the floor between two of us. Old Gales pinched him and slapped his face and worked hard for the big cheque he could see in the distance. The young M.D. from the next floor gave Tom a most hearty, rousing kick, and then apologized to me.

'Couldn't help it,' he said. 'I never kicked a millionaire before in my life. I may never have another opportunity.'

'Now,' said Doctor Gales, after a couple of hours, 'he'll do. But keep him awake for another hour. You can do that by talking to him and shaking him up occasionally. When his pulse and respiration are normal then let him sleep. I'll leave him with you now.'

I was left alone with Tom, whom we had laid on a couch. He lay very still, and his eyes were half closed. I began my work of keeping him awake.

'Well, old man,' I said, 'you've had a narrow squeak, but we've pulled you through. When you were attending lectures, Tom, didn't any of the professors ever casually remark that m-o-r-p-h-i-a never spells "quinia," especially in four-grain doses? But I won't pile it up on you until you get on your feet. But you ought to have been a druggist, Tom; you're splendidly qualified to fill prescriptions.'

Tom looked at me with a faint and foolish smile.

'B'ly,' he murmured, 'I feel jus' like a hum'n bird flyin' around a jolly lot of most 'shpensive roses. Don' bozzer me. Goin' sleep now.'

And he went to sleep in two seconds. I shook him by the shoulder.

'Now, Tom,' I said severely, 'this won't do. The big doctor said you must stay awake for at least an hour. Open your eyes. You're not entirely safe yet, you know. Wake up.'

Tom Hopkins weighs one hundred and ninety-eight. He gave me another somnolent grin, and fell into deeper slumber. I would have made him move about, but I might as well have tried to make Cleopatra's Needle waltz around the room with me. Tom's breathing became stertorous, and that, in connection with morphia poisoning, means danger.

Then I began to think. I could not rouse his body; I must strive to excite his mind. 'Make him angry,' was an idea that suggested itself! Good! I thought; but how? There was not a joint in Tom's armour. Dear old fellow! He was good-nature itself, and a gallant gentleman, fine and true and clean as sunlight. He came from somewhere down South, where they still have ideals and a code. New York had charmed, but had not spoiled him. He had that old-fashioned chivalrous reverence for women, that – Eureka! – there was my idea! I worked the thing up for a minute or two in my imagination. I chuckled to myself at the thought of springing a thing like that on old Tom Hopkins. Then I took him by the shoulder and shook him till his ears flopped. He opened his eyes lazily. I assumed an expression of scorn and contempt, and pointed my finger within two inches of his nose.

'Listen to me, Hopkins,' I said, in cutting and distinct tones, 'you and I have been good friends, but I want you to understand that in the future my doors are closed against any man who acts as much like a scoundrel as you have.'

Tom looked the least bit interested.

'What's the matter, Billy?' he muttered composedly. 'Don't your clothes fit you?'

'If I were in your place,' I went on, 'which, thank God, I'm not, I think I would be afraid to close my eyes. How about that girl you left waiting for you down among those lonesome Southern pines – the girl that you've forgotten since you came into your con-founded money? Oh, I know what I'm talking about. While you were a poor medical student she was good enough for you. But now, since you are a millionaire, it's different. I wonder what she thinks of the performances of that peculiar class of people which she has been taught to worship – the Southern gentlemen? I'm sorry, Hopkins, that I was forced to speak about these matters, but you've covered it up so well and played your part so nicely that I would have sworn you were above such unmanly tricks.'

Poor Tom. I could scarcely keep from laughing outright to see him struggling against the effects of the opiate. He was distinctly angry, and I didn't blame him. Tom had a Southern temper. His eyes were open now, and they showed a gleam or two of fire. But the drug still clouded his mind and bound his tongue.

'C-c-confound you,' he stammered, 'I'll s-smash you.'

He tried to rise from the couch. With all his size he was very weak now. I thrust him back with one arm. He lay there glaring like a lion in a trap.

'That will hold you for awhile, you old loony,' I said to myself. I

got up and lit my pipe, for I was needing a smoke. I walked around
a bit, congratulating myself on my brilliant idea.

I heard a snore. I looked around. Tom was asleep again. I walked
over and punched him on the jaw. He looked at me as pleasant and
ungrudging as an idiot. I chewed my pipe and gave it to him hard.

'I want you to recover yourself and get out of my rooms as soon
as you can,' I said insultingly. 'I've told you what I think of you. If
you have any honour or honesty left you will think twice before
you attempt again to associate with gentlemen. She's a poor girl,
isn't she?' I sneered. 'Somewhat too plain and unfashionable for us
since we got our money. Be ashamed to walk on Fifth Avenue with
her, wouldn't you? Hopkins, you're forty-seven times worse than a
cad. Who cares for your money? I don't. I'll bet that girl don't.
Perhaps if you didn't have it you'd be more of a man. As it is
you've made a cur of yourself, and' – I thought that quite dramatic
– 'perhaps broken a faithful heart.' (Old Tom Hopkins breaking a
faithful heart!) 'Let me be rid of you as soon as possible.'

I turned my back on Tom, and winked at myself in a mirror. I
heard him moving, and I turned again quickly. I didn't want a
hundred and ninety-eight pounds falling on me from the rear. But
Tom had only turned partly over, and laid one arm across his face.
He spoke a few words rather more distinctly than before.

'I couldn't have – talked this way – to you, Billy, even if I'd
heard people – lyin' 'bout you. But jus' soon's I can s-stand up –
I'll break your neck – don' f'get it.'

I did feel a little ashamed then. But it was to save Tom. In the
morning, when I explained it, we would have a good laugh over it
together.

In about twenty minutes Tom dropped into a sound, easy slumber. I felt his pulse, listened to his respiration, and let him sleep.
Everything was normal, and Tom was safe. I went into the other
room and tumbled into bed.

I found Tom up and dressed when I awoke the next morning.
He was entirely himself again with the exception of shaky nerves
and a tongue like a white-oak chip.

'What an idiot I was,' he said thoughtfully. 'I remember thinking that quinine bottle looked queer while I was taking the dose.
Have much trouble in bringing me round?'

I told him no. His memory seemed bad about the entire affair. I
concluded that he had no recollection of my efforts to keep him
awake, and decided not to enlighten him. Some other time, I thought,
when he was feeling better, we would have some fun over it.

When Tom was ready to go he stopped, with the door open, and shook my hand.

'Much obliged, old fellow,' he said quietly, 'for taking so much trouble with me – and for what you said; I'm going down now to telegraph to the little girl.'

LXVI

A Ghost of a Chance

'ACTUALLY A *hod!*' repeated Mrs. Kinsolving pathetically.

Mrs. Bellamy Bellmore arched a sympathetic eyebrow. Thus she expressed condolence and a generous amount of apparent surprise.

'Fancy her telling everywhere,' recapitulated Mrs. Kinsolving, 'that she saw a ghost in the apartment she occupied here – our choicest guest-room – a ghost, carrying a hod on its shoulder – the ghost of an old man in overalls, smoking a pipe and carrying a hod! The very absurdity of the thing shows her malicious intent. There never was a Kinsolving that carried a hod. Every one knows that Mr. Kinsolving's father accumulated his money by large building contracts, but he never worked a day with his own hands. He had this house built from his own plans; but – oh, a hod! Why need she have been so cruel and malicious?'

'It is really too bad,' murmured Mrs. Bellmore, with an approving glance of her fine eyes about the vast chamber done in lilac and old gold. 'And it was in this room she saw it! Oh, no, I'm not afraid of ghosts. Don't have the least fear on my account. I'm glad you put me in here. I think family ghosts so interesting! But, really, the story does sound a little inconsistent. I should have expected something better from Mrs. Fischer-Suympkins. Don't they carry bricks in hods? Why should a ghost bring bricks into a villa built of marble and stone? I'm so sorry, but it makes me think that age is beginning to tell upon Mrs. Fischer-Suympkins.'

'This house,' continued Mrs. Kinsolving, 'was built upon the site of an old one used by the family during the Revolution. There wouldn't be anything strange in its having a ghost. And there was a Captain Kinsolving who fought in General Greene's army, though we've never been able to secure any papers to vouch for it. If there is to be a family ghost, why couldn't it have been his, instead of a bricklayer's?'

'The ghost of a Revolutionary ancestor wouldn't be a bad idea,' agreed Mrs. Bellmore; 'but you know how arbitrary and inconsiderate ghosts can be. Maybe, like love, they are "engendered in the eye." One advantage of those who see ghosts is that their stories can't be disproved. By a spiteful eye, a Revolutionary knapsack might easily be construed to be a hod. Dear Mrs. Kinsolving, think no more of it. I am sure it was a knapsack.'

'But she told everybody!' mourned Mrs. Kinsolving, inconsolable. 'She insisted upon the details. There is the pipe. And how are you going to get out of the overalls?'

'Shan't get into them,' said Mrs. Bellmore, with a prettily suppressed yawn; 'too stiff and wrinkly. Is that you, Felice? Prepare my bath, please. Do you dine at seven at Clifftop, Mrs. Kinsolving? So kind of you to run in for a chat before dinner! I love those little touches of informality with a guest. They give such a home flavour to a visit. So sorry; I must be dressing. I am so indolent I always postpone it until the last moment.'

Mrs. Fischer-Suympkins had been the first large plum that the Kinsolvings had drawn from the social pie. For a long time the pie itself had been out of reach on a top shelf. But the purse and the pursuit had at last lowered it. Mrs. Fischer-Suympkins was the heliograph of the smart society parading corps. The glitter of her wit and actions passed along the line, transmitting whatever was latest and most daring in the game of peep-show. Formerly, her fame and leadership had been secure enough not to need the support of such artifices as handing around live frogs for favours at a cotillon. But, now, these things were necessary to the holding of her throne. Beside, middle age had come to preside, incongruous, at her capers. The sensational papers had cut her space from a page to two columns. Her wit developed a sting; her manners became more rough and inconsiderate, as if she felt the royal necessity of establishing her autocracy by scorning the conventionalities that bound lesser potentates.

To some pressure at the command of the Kinsolvings, she had yielded so far as to honour their house by her presence, for an evening and night. She had her revenge upon her hostess by relating, with grim enjoyment and sarcastic humour, her story of the vision carrying the hod. To that lady, in raptures at having penetrated thus far toward the coveted inner circle, the result came as a crushing disappointment. Everybody either sympathized or laughed, and there was little to choose between the two modes of expression.

But, later on, Mrs. Kinsolving's hopes and spirits were revived by the capture of a second and greater prize.

Mrs. Bellamy Bellmore had accepted an invitation to visit at Clifftop, and would remain for three days. Mrs. Bellmore was one of the younger matrons, whose beauty, descent, and wealth gave her a reserved seat in the holy of holies that required no strenuous bolstering. She was generous enough thus to give Mrs. Kinsolving the accolade that was so poignantly desired; and, at the same time, she thought how much it would please Terence. Perhaps it would end by solving him.

Terence was Mrs. Kinsolving's son, aged twenty-nine, quite good-looking enough, and with two or three attractive and mysterious traits. For one, he was very devoted to his mother, and that was sufficiently odd to deserve notice. For others, he talked so little that it was irritating, and he seemed either very shy or very deep. Terence interested Mrs. Bellmore, because she was not sure which it was. She intended to study him a little longer, unless she forgot the matter. If he was only shy, she would abandon him, for shyness is a bore. If he was deep, she would also abandon him, for depth is precarious.

On the afternoon of the third day of her visit, Terence hunted up Mrs. Bellmore, and found her in a nook actually looking at an album.

'It's so good of you,' said he, 'to come down here and retrieve the day for us. I suppose you have heard that Mrs. Fischer-Suympkins scuttled the ship before she left. She knocked a whole plank out of the bottom with a hod. My mother is grieving herself ill about it. Can't you manage to see a ghost for us while you are here, Mrs. Bellmore – a bangup, swell ghost, with a coronet on his head and a cheque-book under his arm?'

'That was a naughty old lady, Terence,' said Mrs. Bellmore, 'to tell such stories. Perhaps you gave her too much supper. Your mother doesn't really take it seriously, does she?'

'I think she does,' answered Terence. 'One would think every brick in the hod had dropped on her. It's a good mammy, and I don't like to see her worried. It's to be hoped that the ghost belongs to the hod-carriers' union, and will go out on a strike. If he doesn't, there will be no peace in this family.'

'I'm sleeping in the ghost-chamber,' said Mrs. Bellmore pensively. 'But it's so nice I wouldn't change it, even if I were afraid, which I'm not. It wouldn't do for me to submit a counter story of a desirable, aristocratic shade, would it? I would do so, with pleasure, but it seems to me it would be too obviously an antidote for the other narrative to be effective.'

'True,' said Terence, running two fingers thoughtfully into his crisp brown hair; 'that would never do. How would it work to see the same ghost again, minus the overalls, and have gold bricks in the hod? That would elevate the spectre from degrading toil to a financial plane. Don't you think that would be respectable enough?'

'There was an ancestor who fought against the Britishers, wasn't there? Your mother said something to that effect.'

'I believe so; one of those old chaps in raglan vests and golf trousers. I don't care a continental for a continental, myself. But the mother has set her heart on pomp and heraldry and pyrotechnics, and I want her to be happy.'

'You are a good boy, Terence,' said Mrs. Bellmore, sweeping her silks close to one side of her, 'not to beat your mother. Sit here by me, and let's look at the album, just as people used to do twenty years ago. Now, tell me about every one of them. Who is this tall, dignified gentleman leaning against the horizon, with one arm on the Corinthian column?'

'That old chap with the big feet?' inquired Terence, craning his neck. 'That's great-uncle O'Brannigan. He used to keep a rath-skeller on the Bowery.'

'I asked you to sit down, Terence. If you are not going to amuse, or obey me, I shall report in the morning that I saw a ghost wearing an apron and carrying schooners of beer. Now, that is better. To be shy, at your age, Terence, is a thing that you should blush to acknowledge.'

At breakfast on the last morning of her visit, Mrs. Bellmore startled and entranced every one present by announcing positively that she had seen the ghost.

'Did it have a – a – a –?' Mrs. Kinsolving, in her suspense and agitation, could not bring out the word.

'No, indeed – far from it.'

There was a chorus of questions from others at the table. 'Weren't you frightened?' 'What did it do?' 'How did it look?' 'How was it dressed?' 'Did it say anything?' 'Didn't you scream?'

'I'll try to answer everything at once,' said Mrs. Bellmore heroically, 'although I'm frightfully hungry. Something awakened me – I'm not sure whether it was a noise or a touch – and there stood the phantom. I never burn a light at night, so the room was quite dark, but I saw it plainly. I wasn't dreaming. It was a tall man, all misty white from head to foot. It wore the full dress of the old Colonial days – powdered hair, baggy coat skirts, lace ruffles, and a sword. It looked intangible and luminous in the dark, and moved without a sound. Yes, I was a little frightened at first – or startled, I should say. It was the first ghost I had ever seen. No, it didn't say anything. I didn't scream. I raised up on my elbow, and then it glided silently away, and disappeared when it reached the door.'

Mrs. Kinsolving was in the seventh heaven. 'The description is that of Captain Kinsolving, of General Greene's army, one of our ancestors,' she said, in a voice that trembled with pride and relief. 'I really think I must apologize for our ghostly relative, Mrs. Bellmore. I am afraid he must have badly disturbed your rest.'

Terence sent a smile of pleased congratulation toward his mother. Attainment was Mrs. Kinsolving's, at last, and he loved to see her happy.

'I suppose I ought to be ashamed to confess,' said Mrs. Bellmore, who was now enjoying her breakfast, 'that I wasn't very much disturbed. I presume it would have been the customary thing to scream and faint and have all of you running about in picturesque costumes. But, after the first alarm was over, I really couldn't work myself up to a panic. The ghost retired from the stage quietly and peacefully, after doing its little turn, and I went to sleep again.'

Nearly all listened, politely accepted Mrs. Bellmore's story as a made-up affair, charitably offered as an offset to the unkind vision seen by Mrs. Fischer-Suympkins. But one or two present perceived that her assertions bore the genuine stamp of her own convictions. Truth and candour seemed to attend upon every word. Even a scoffer at ghosts – if he were very observant – would have been forced to admit that she had, at least in a very vivid dream, been honestly aware of the weird visitor.

Soon Mrs. Bellmore's maid was packing. In two hours the auto would come to convey her to the station. As Terence was strolling upon the east piazza, Mrs. Bellmore came up to him, with a confidential sparkle in her eye.

'I didn't wish to tell the others all of it,' she said, 'but I will tell you. In a way, I think you should be held responsible. Can you guess in what manner that ghost awakened me last night?'

'Rattled chains,' suggested Terence, after some thought, 'or groaned? They usually do one or the other.'

'Do you happen to know,' continued Mrs. Bellmore with sudden irrelevancy, 'if I resemble any one of the female relatives of your restless ancestor, Captain Kinsolving?'

'Don't think so,' said Terence with an extremely puzzled air. 'Never heard of any of them being noted beauties.'

'Then, why,' said Mrs. Bellmore, looking the young man gravely in the eye, 'should that ghost have kissed me, as I'm sure it did?'

'Heavens!' exclaimed Terence, in wide-eyed amazement; 'you don't mean that, Mrs. Bellmore! Did he actually kiss you?'

'I said it,' corrected Mrs. Bellmore. 'I hope the impersonal pronoun is correctly used.'

'But why did you say I was responsible?'

'Because you are the only living male relative of the ghost.'

'I see. "Unto the third and fourth generation." But, seriously, did he – did it – how do you –?'

'Know? How does anyone know? I was asleep, and that is what awakened me, I'm almost certain.'

'Almost?'

'Well, I awoke just as – oh, can't you understand what I mean? When anything arouses you suddenly, you are not positive whether you dreamed, or – and yet you know that Dear me, Terence, must I dissect the most elementary sensations in order to accommodate your extremely practical intelligence?'

'But about kissing ghosts, you know,' said Terence humbly, 'I require the most primary instruction. I never kissed a ghost. Is it – is it?'

'The sensation,' said Mrs. Bellmore, with deliberate, but slightly smiling emphasis, 'since you are seeking instruction, is a mingling of the material and the spiritual.'

'Of course,' said Terence, suddenly growing serious, 'it was a dream or some kind of an hallucination. Nobody believes in spirits, these days. If you told the tale out of kindness of heart, Mrs. Bellmore, I can't express how grateful I am to you. It has made my mother supremely happy. That Revolutionary ancestor was a stunning idea.'

Mrs. Bellmore sighed. 'The usual fate of ghostseers is mine,' she said resignedly. 'My privileged encounter with a spirit is attributed to lobster salad or mendacity. Well, I have, at least, one memory left from the wreck – a kiss from the unseen world. Was Captain Kinsolving a very brave man, do you know, Terence?'

'He was licked at Yorktown, I believe,' said Terence, reflecting. 'They say he skedaddled with his company, after the first battle there.'

'I thought he must have been timid,' said Mrs. Bellmore absently. 'He might have had another.'

'Another battle?' asked Terence dully.

'What else could I mean? I must go and get ready now; the auto will be here in an hour. I've enjoyed Clifftop immensely. Such a lovely morning, isn't it, Terence?'

On her way to the station, Mrs. Bellmore took from her bag a silk handkerchief, and looked at it with a little peculiar smile. Then she tied it in several very hard knots, and threw it, at a convenient moment, over the edge of the cliff along which the road ran.

In his room, Terence was giving some directions to his man, Brooks. 'Have this stuff done up in a parcel,' he said, 'and ship it to the address on that card.'

The card was that of a New York costumer. The 'stuff' was a gentleman's costume of the days of '76, made of white satin, with silver buckles, white silk stockings, and white kid shoes. A powdered wig and a sword completed the dress.

'And look about, Brooks,' added Terence a little anxiously, 'for a silk handkerchief with my initials in one corner. I must have dropped it somewhere.'

It was a month later when Mrs. Bellmore and one or two others of the smart crowd were making up a list of names for a coaching trip through the Catskills. Mrs. Bellmore looked over the list for a final censoring. The name of Terence Kinsolving was there. Mrs. Bellmore ran her prohibitive pencil lightly through the name.

'Too shy!' she murmured sweetly, in explanation.

LXVII

Jimmy Hayes and Muriel

I

SUPPER WAS OVER, and there had fallen upon the camp the silence that accompanies the rolling of corn-husk cigarettes. The water-hole shone from the dark earth like a patch of fallen sky. Coyotes yelped. Dull thumps indicated the rocking-horse movements of the hobbled ponies as they moved to fresh grass. A half-troop of the Frontier Battalion of Texas Rangers were distributed about the fire.

A well-known sound – the fluttering and scraping of chaparral against wooden stirrups – came from the thick brush above the camp. The rangers listened cautiously. They heard a loud and cheerful voice call out reassuringly:

'Brace up, Muriel, old gal, we're 'most there now! Been a long ride for ye, ain't it, ye old antediluvian handful of animated carpet-tacks? Hey, now, quit a tryin' to kiss me! Don't hold on to my neck so tight – this here paint hoss ain't any too shore-footed, let me tell ye. He's liable to dump us both off if we don't watch out.'

Two minutes of waiting brought a tired 'paint' pony single-footing into camp. A gangling youth of twenty lolled in the saddle. Of the 'Muriel,' whom he had been addressing, nothing was to be seen.

'Hi, fellows!' shouted the rider cheerfully. 'This here's a letter fer Lieutenant Manning.'

He dismounted, unsaddled, dropped the coils of his stake-rope, and got his hobbles from the saddle-horn. While Lieutenant Manning, in command, was reading the letter, the new-comer rubbed solicitously at some dried mud in the loops of the hobbles, showing a consideration for the forelegs of his mount.

'Boys,' said the lieutenant, waving his hand to the rangers, 'this is Mr. James Hayes. He's a new member of the company. Captain McLean sends him down from El Paso. The boys will see that you have some supper, Hayes, as soon as you get your pony hobbled.'

The recruit was received cordially by the rangers. Still, they observed him shrewdly and with suspended judgment. Picking a comrade on the border is done with ten times the care and discretion with which a girl chooses a sweetheart. On your 'side-kicker's' nerve, loyalty, aim, and coolness your own life may depend many times.

After a hearty supper Hayes joined the smokers about the fire. His appearance did not settle all the questions in the minds of his brother-rangers. They saw simply a loose, lank youth with tow-coloured, sun-burned hair and a berry-brown, ingenuous face that wore a quizzical, good-natured smile.

'Fellows,' said the new ranger, 'I'm goin' to interduce to you a lady friend of mine. Ain't ever heard anybody call her a beauty, but you'll all admit, she's got some fine points about her. Come along, Muriel!'

He held open the front of his blue flannel shirt. Out of it crawled a horned frog. A bright red ribbon was tied jauntily around its spiky neck. It crawled to its owner's knee and sat there, motionless.

'This here Muriel,' says Hayes, with an oratorical wave of his hand, 'has got qualities. She never talks back, she always stays at home, and she's satisfied with one red dress for every day and Sunday, too.'

'Look at that blame insect!' said one of the rangers with a grin.
'I've seen plenty of them horny frogs, but I never knew anybody to
have one for a side-partner. Does the blame thing know you from
anybody else?'

'Take it over there and see,' said Hayes.

The stumpy little lizard known as the horned frog is harmless.
He has the hideousness of the prehistoric monsters whose reduced
descendant he is, but he is gentler than the dove.

The ranger took Muriel from Hayes's knee and went back to his
seat on a roll of blankets. The captive twisted and clawed and
struggled vigorously in his hand. After holding it for a moment or
two, the ranger set it upon the ground. Awkwardly but swiftly, the
frog worked its four oddly moving legs until it stopped close by
Hayes's foot.

'Well, dang my hide!' said the other ranger. 'The little cuss
knows you. Never thought them insects had that much sense!'

II

Jimmy Hayes became a favourite in the ranger camp. He had an
endless store of good-nature, and a mild, perennial quality of
humour that is well adapted to camp life. He was never without
his horned frog. In the bosom of his shirt during rides, on his knee
or shoulder in camp, under his blankets at night, the ugly little
beast never left him.

Jimmy was a humorist of a type that prevails in the rural South
and West. Unskilled in originating methods of amusing or in witty
conceptions, he had hit upon a comical idea and clung to it reverently. It had seemed to Jimmy a very funny thing to have about his
person, with which to amuse his friends, a tame horned frog with a
red ribbon around its neck.

As it was a happy idea, why not perpetuate it?

The sentiments existing between Jimmy and the frog cannot be
exactly determined. The capability of the horned frog for lasting
affection is a subject upon which we have had no symposiums. It is
easier to guess Jimmy's feelings. Muriel was his *chef d'œuvre* of wit,
and as such he cherished her. He caught flies for her, and shielded
her from sudden northers. Yet his care was half selfish, and when
the time came she repaid him a thousand-fold. Other Muriels have
thus overbalanced the light attentions of other Jimmies.

Not at once did Jimmy Hayes attain full brotherhood with his
comrades. They loved him for his simplicity and drollness, but
there hung above him a great sword of suspended judgment. To

make merry in camp is not all of a ranger's life. There are horse-thieves to trail, desperate criminals to run down, bravos to battle with, bandits to rout out of the chaparral, peace and order to be compelled at the muzzle of a six-shooter. Jimmy had been ' 'most generally a cow-puncher,' he said; he was inexperienced in ranger methods of warfare. Therefore the rangers speculated apart and solemnly as to how he would stand fire. For, let it be known, the honour and pride of each ranger company is the individual bravery of its members.

For two months the border was quiet. The rangers lolled, list-less, in camp. And then – bringing joy to the rusting guardians of the frontier – Sebastiano Saldar, an eminent Mexican desperado and cattle-thief, crossed the Rio Grande with his gang and began to lay waste the Texas side. There were indications that Jimmy Hayes would soon have the opportunity to show his mettle. The rangers patrolled with alacrity, but Saldar's men were mounted like Lochinvar, and were hard to catch.

One evening, about sundown, the rangers halted for supper after a long ride. Their horses stood panting, with their saddles on. The men were frying bacon and boiling coffee. Suddenly, out of the brush, Sebastiano Saldar and his gang dashed upon them with blazing six-shooters and high voiced yells. It was a neat sur-prise. The rangers swore in annoyed tones, and got their Win-chesters busy; but the attack was only a spectacular dash of the purest Mexican type. After the florid demonstration the raiders galloped away, yelling, down the river. The rangers mounted and pursued, but in less than two miles the fagged ponies laboured so that Lieutenant Manning gave the word to abandon the chase and return to the camp.

Then it was discovered that Jimmy Hayes was missing. Someone remembered having seen him run for his pony when the attack began, but no one had set eyes on him since. Morning came, but no Jimmy. They searched the country around, on the theory that he had been killed or wounded, but without success. Then they followed after Saldar's gang, but it seemed to have disappeared. Man-ning concluded that the wily Mexican had recrossed the river after his theatric farewell. And, indeed, no further depredations from him were reported.

This gave the rangers time to nurse a soreness they had. As has been said, the pride and honour of the company is the individual bravery of its members. And now they believed that Jimmy Hayes had turned coward at the whiz of Mexican bullets. There was no other deduction. Buck Davis pointed out that not a shot was fired by Saldar's gang after Jimmy was seen running for his horse. There was no way for him to have been shot. No, he had fled from his first fight, and afterward he would not return, aware that the scorn of his comrades would be a worse thing to face than the muzzles of many rifles.

So Manning's detachment of McLean's company, Frontier Battalion, was gloomy. It was the first blot on its escutcheon. Never before in the history of the service had a ranger shown the white feather. All of them had liked Jimmy Hayes, and that made it worse.

Days, weeks, and months went by, and still that little cloud of unforgotten cowardice hung above the camp.

III

Nearly a year afterward – after many camping-grounds and many hundreds of miles guarded and defended – Lieutenant Manning, with almost the same detachment of men, was sent to a point only a few miles below their old camp on the river to look after some smuggling there. One afternoon, while they were riding through a dense mesquite flat, they came upon a patch of open hog-wallow prairie. There they rode upon the scene of an unwritten tragedy.

In a big hog-wallow lay the skeletons of three Mexicans. Their clothing alone served to identify them. The largest of the figures had once been Sebastiano Saldar. His great, costly sombrero, heavy with gold ornamentation – a hat famous all along the Rio Grande – lay there pierced by three bullets. Along the ridge of the hog-wallow rested the rusting Winchesters of the Mexicans – all pointing in the same direction.

The rangers rode in that direction for fifty yards. There, in a little depression of the ground, with his rifle still bearing upon the three, lay another skeleton. It had been a battle of extermination. There was nothing to identify the solitary defender. His clothing – such as the elements had left distinguishable – seemed to be of the kind that any ranchman or cowboy might have worn.

'Some cow-puncher,' said Manning, 'that they caught out alone. Good boy! He put up a dandy scrap before they got him. So that's why we didn't hear from Don Sebastiano any more!'

And then, from beneath the weather-beaten rags of the dead man, there wriggled out a horned frog with a faded red ribbon around its neck, and sat upon the shoulder of its long-quiet master. Mutely it told the story of the untried youth and the swift 'paint' pony – how they had outstripped all their comrades that day in the pursuit of the Mexican raiders and how the boy had gone down upholding the honour of the company.

The ranger troop herded close, and a simultaneous wild yell arose from their lips. The outburst was at once a dirge, an apology, an epitaph, and a pæan of triumph. A strange requiem, you may say, over the body of a fallen comrade; but if Jimmy Hayes could have heard it he would have understood.

LXVIII

The Door of Unrest

I SAT AN HOUR BY SUN, in the editor's room of the Montopolis *Weekly Bugle*. I was the editor.

The saffron rays of the declining sunlight filtered through the cornstalks in Micajah Widdup's garden-patch, and cast an amber glory upon my paste-pot. I sat at the editorial desk in my non-rotary revolving chair, and prepared my editorial against the oligarchies. The room, with its one window, was already a prey to the twilight. One by one, with my trenchant sentences, I lopped off the heads of the political hydra, while I listened, full of kindly peace, to the home-coming cow-bells and wondered what Mrs. Flanagan was going to have for supper.

Then in from the dusky, quiet street there drifted and perched himself upon a corner of my desk old Father Time's younger brother. His face was beardless and as gnarled as an English walnut. I never saw clothes such as he wore. They would have reduced Joseph's coat to a monochrome. But the colours were not the dyer's. Stains and patches and the work of sun and rust were responsible for the diversity. On his coarse shoes was the dust, conceivably, of a thousand leagues. I can describe him no further, except to say that he was little and weird and old – old I began to estimate in centuries when I saw him. Yes, and I remember that there was an odour, a faint odour like aloes, or possibly like myrrh or leather; and I thought of museums.

And then I reached for a pad and pencil, for a business is business, and visits of the oldest inhabitants are sacred and honourable, requiring to be chronicled.

'I am glad to see you, sir,' I said. 'I would offer you a chair, but –

you see, sir,' I went on, 'I have lived in Montopolis only three weeks, and I have not met many of our citizens.' I turned a doubtful eye upon his dust-stained shoes, and concluded with a newspaper phrase, 'I suppose that you reside in our midst?'

My visitor fumbled in his raiment, drew forth a soiled card, and handed it to me. Upon it was written, in plain but unsteadily formed characters, the name 'Michob Ader.'

'I am glad you called, Mr. Ader,' I said. 'As one of our older citizens, you must view with pride the recent growth and enterprise of Montopolis. Among other improvements, I think I can promise that the town will now be provided with a live, enterprising newspa –'

'Do ye know the name on that card?' asked my caller, interrupting me.

'It is not a familiar one to me,' I said.

Again he visited the depths of his ancient vestments. This time he brought out a torn leaf of some book or journal, brown and flimsy with age. The heading of the page was the *Turkish Spy* in old-style type; the printing upon it was this:

'There is a man come to Paris in this year 1643 who pretends to have lived these sixteen hundred years. He says of himself that he was a shoemaker in Jerusalem at the time of the Crucifixion: that his name is Micob Ader; and that when Jesus, the Christian Messias, was condemned by Pontius Pilate, the Roman president, he paused to rest while bearing his cross to the place of crucifixion before the door of Michob Ader. The shoemaker struck Jesus with his fist, saying, "Go; why tarriest thou?" The Messias answered him: "I indeed am going; but thou shalt tarry until I come"; thereby condemning him to live until the day of judgment. He lives for ever, but at the end of every hundred years he falls into a fit or trance, on recovering from which he finds himself in the same state of youth in which he was when Jesus suffered, being then about thirty years of age.

'Such is the story of the Wandering Jew, as told by Michob Ader, who relates –'

Here the printing ended.

I must have muttered aloud something to myself about the Wandering Jew, for the old man spake up, bitterly and loudly.

' 'Tis a lie,' said he, 'like nine-tenths of what ye call history. 'Tis a Gentile I am, and no Jew. I am after footing it out of Jerusalem, my son; but if that makes me a Jew, then everything that comes out of a bottle is babies' milk. Ye have my name on the card ye hold; and ye have read the bit of paper they call the *Turkish Spy* that printed the news when I stepped into their office on the 12th day of June, in the year 1643, just as I have called upon ye to-day.'

I laid down my pencil and pad. Clearly it would not do. Here was an item for the local column of the *Bugle* that – but it would not do. Still, fragments of the impossible 'personal' began to flit through my conventionalized brain. 'Uncle Michob is as spry on his legs as a young chap of only a thousand or so.' 'Our venerable caller relates with pride that George Wash – no, Ptolemy the Great – once dandled him on his knee at his father's house.' 'Uncle Michob says that our wet spring was nothing in comparison with the dampness that ruined the crops around Mount Ararat when he was a boy –' But no, no – it would not do.

I was trying to think of some conversational subject with which to interest my visitor, and was hesitating between walking matches and the Pliocene Age, when the old man suddenly began to weep poignantly and distressfully.

'Cheer up, Mr. Ader,' I said a little awkwardly; 'this matter may blow over in a few hundred years more. There has already been a decided reaction in favour of Judas Iscariot and Colonel Burr and the celebrated violinist, Signor Nero. This is the age of white-wash. You must not allow yourself to become downhearted.'

Unknowingly, I had struck a chord. The old man blinked belligerently through his senile tears.

' 'Tis time,' he said, 'that the liars be doin' justice to somebody. Yer historians are no more than a pack of old women gabblin' at a wake. A finer man than the Imperor Nero niver wore sandals. Man, I was at the burnin' of Rome. I knowed the Imperor well, for in them days I was a well-known character. In thim days they had rayspect for a man that lived for ever.

'But 'twas of the Imperor Nero I was goin' to tell ye. I struck into Rome, up the Appian Way, on the night of July the 16th, the year 64. I had just stepped down by way of Siberia and Afghanistan; and one foot of me had a frost-bite, and the other a blister burned by the sand of the desert; and I was feelin' a bit blue from doin' patrol duty from the North Pole down to the Last Chance corner in Patagonia, and bein' miscalled a Jew into the bargain. Well, I'm tellin' ye I was passin' the Circus Maximus, and it was dark as pitch over the way, and then I heard somebody sing out, "Is that you, Michob?"

'Over ag'inst the wall, hid out amongst a pile of barrels and old dry-goods boxes, was the Imperor Nero wid his togy wrapped around his toes, smokin' a long, black cigar.

' "Have one, Michob?" says he.

' "None of the weeds for me," says I – "nayther pipe nor cigar. What's the use," says I, "of smokin' when ye've not got the ghost of a chance of killin' yeself by doin' it?"

' "True for ye, Michob Ader, my perpetual Jew," says the Imperor; "ye're not always wandering. Sure, 'tis danger gives the spice of our pleasures – next to their bein' forbidden."

' "And for what," says I, "do ye smoke be night in dark places widout even a cinturion in plain clothes to attend ye?"

' "Have ye ever heard, Michob," says the Imperor, "of predestinarianism?"

' "I've had the cousin of it," says I. "I've been on the trot with pedestrianism for many a year, and more to come, as ye well know."

' "The longer word," says me friend Nero, "is the tachin' of this new sect of people they call the Christians. 'Tis them that's raysponsible for me smokin' be night in holes and corners of the dark."

'And then I sets down and takes off a shoe and rubs me foot that is frosted, and the Imperor tells me about it. It seems that since I passed that way before, the Imperor had mandamused the Impress wid a divorce suit, and Misses Poppæa, a cilibrated lady, was ingaged, widout riferences, as housekeeper at the palace. "All in one day," says the Imperor, "she puts up new lace windy-curtains in the palace and joins the anti-tobacco society, and whin I feels the need of a smoke I must be after sneakin' out to these piles of lumber in the dark." So there in the dark me and the Imperor sat, and I told him of me travels. And when they say the Imperor was an incindiary, they lie. 'Twas that night the fire started that burnt the city. 'Tis my opinion that it began from a stump of cigar that he threw down among the boxes. And 'tis a lie that he fiddled. He did all he could for six days to stop it, sir.'

And now I detected a new flavour to Mr. Michob Ader. It had not been myrrh or balm or hyssop that I had smelled. The emanation was the odour of bad whisky – and, worse still, of low comedy – the sort that small humorists manufacture by clothing the grave and reverend things of legend and history in the vulgar, topical frippery that passes for a certain kind of wit. Michob Ader as an impostor, claiming nineteen hundred years, and playing his part with the decency of respectable lunacy, I could endure; but as a tedious wag, cheapening his egregious story with song-book levity, his importance as an entertainer grew less.

And then, as if he suspected my thoughts, he suddenly shifted his key.

'You'll excuse me, sir,' he whined, 'but sometimes I get a little mixed in my head. I am a very old man; and it is hard to remember everything.'

I knew that he was right, and that I should not try to reconcile him with Roman history; so I asked for news concerning other ancients with whom he had walked familiar.

Above my desk hung an engraving of Raphael's cherubs. You could yet make out their forms, though the dust blurred their outlines strangely.

'Ye calls them "cher-rubs,"' cackled the old man. 'Babes, ye fancy they are, with wings. And there's one wid legs and a bow and arrow that ye call Cupid — I know where they was found. The great-great-great-grandfather of thim all was a billy-goat. Bein' an editor, sir, do ye happen to know where Solomon's Temple stood?'

I fancied that it was in — in Persia? Well, I did not know.

' 'Tis not in history nor in the Bible where it was. But I saw it, meself. The first pictures of cher-rubs and cupids was sculptured upon thim walls and pillars. Two of the biggest, sir, stood in the adytum to form the baldachin over the Ark. But the wings of thim sculptures was intindid for horns. And the faces was the faces of goats. Ten thousand goats there was in and about the temple. And your cher-rubs was billy-goats in the days of King Solomon, but the painters misconstrued the horns into wings.

'And I knew Tamerlane, the lame Timour, sir, very well. I saw him at Keghut and at Zaranj. He was a little man no larger than yerself, with hair the colour of an amber pipe-stem. They buried him at Samarkand. I was at the wake, sir. Oh, he was a fine-built man in his coffin, six feet long, with black whiskers to his face. And I see 'em throw turnips at the Imperor Vispacian in Africa. All over the world I have tramped, sir, without the body of me findin' any rest. 'Twas so commanded. I saw Jerusalem destroyed, and Pompeii go up in the fireworks; and I was at the coronation of Charlemagne and the lynchin' of Joan of Arc. And everywhere I go there comes storms and revolutions and plagues and fires. 'Twas so commanded. Ye have heard of the Wandering Jew. 'Tis all so, except that divil a bit am I a Jew. But history lies, as I have told ye. Are ye quite sure, sir, that ye haven't a drop of whisky convenient? Ye well know that I have many miles of walking before me.'

'I have none,' said I, 'and, if you please, I am about to leave for my supper.'

I pushed my chair back creakingly. This ancient landlubber was becoming as great an affliction as any cross-bowed mariner. He shook a musty effluvium from his piebald clothes, overturned my inkstand, and went on with his insufferable nonsense.

'I wouldn't mind it so much,' he complained, 'if it wasn't for the work I must do on Good Fridays. Ye know about Pontius Pilate, sir, of course. His body, whin he killed himself, was pitched into a lake on the Alps mountains. Now, listen to the job that 'tis mine to perform on the night of ivery Good Friday. The ould divil goes down in the pool and drags up Pontius, and the water is bilin' and spewin' like a wash pot. And the ould divil sets the body on top of a throne on the rocks, and thin comes me share of the job. Oh, sir, ye would pity me thin – ye would pray for the poor Wandering Jew that niver was a Jew if ye could see the horror of the thing that I must do. 'Tis I that must fetch a bowl of water and kneel down before it till it washes its hands. I declare to ye that Pontius Pilate, a man dead two hundred years, dragged up with the lake slime coverin' him and fishes wrigglin' inside of him widout eyes, and in the discomposition of the body, sits there, sir, and washes his hands in the bowl I hold for him on Good Fridays. 'Twas so commanded.'

Clearly, the matter had progressed far beyond the scope of the *Bugle's* local column. There might have been employment here for the alienist or for those who circufate the pledge; but I had had enough of it. I got up, and repeated that I must go.

At this he seized my coat, grovelled upon my desk, and burst again into distressful weeping. Whatever it was about, I said to myself that his grief was genuine.

'Come now, Mr. Ader,' I said soothingly; 'what is the matter?'

The answer came brokenly through his racking sobs: 'Because I would not . . . let the poor Christ . . . rest . . . upon the step.'

His hallucination seemed beyond all reasonable answer; yet the effect of it upon him scarcely merited disrespect. But I knew nothing that might assuage it; and I told him once more that both of us should be leaving the office at once.

Obedient at last, he raised himself from my dishevelled desk, and permitted me to half lift him to the floor. The gale of his grief had blown away his words; his freshet of tears had soaked away the crust of his grief. Reminiscence died in him – at least, the coherent part of it.

' 'Twas me that did it,' he muttered, as I led him toward the door – 'me, the shoemaker of Jerusalem.'

I got him to the sidewalk, and in the augmented light I saw that his face was seared and lined and warped by a sadness almost incredibly the product of a single lifetime.

And then high up in the firmamental darkness we heard the clamant cries of some great, passing birds. My Wandering Jew lifted his hand, with side-tilted head.

'The Seven Whistlers!' he said, as one introduces well-known friends.

'Wild geese,' said I; 'but I confess that their number is beyond me.'

'They follow me everywhere,' he said. ' 'Twas so commanded. What ye hear is the souls of the seven Jews that helped with the Crucifixion. Sometimes they're plovers and sometimes geese, but ye'll find them always flyin' where I go.'

I stood, uncertain how to take my leave. I looked down the street, shuffled my feet, looked back again – and felt my hair rise. The old man had disappeared.

And then my capillaries relaxed, for I dimly saw him footing it away through the darkness. But he walked so swiftly and silently and contrary to the gait promised by his age that my composure was not all restored, though I knew not why.

That night I was foolish enough to take down some dust-covered volumes from my modest shelves. I searched *Hermippus Redivivus* and *Salathiel* and the *Pepys Collection* in vain. And then, in a book called *The Citizen of the World*, and in one two centuries old, I came upon what I desired. Michob Ader had indeed come to Paris in the year 1643, and related to the *Turkish Spy* an extraordinary story. He claimed to be the Wandering Jew, and that –

But here I fell asleep, for my editorial duties had not been light that day.

Judge Hoover was the *Bugle's* candidate for congress. Having to confer with him, I sought his home early the next morning; and we walked together down town through a little street with which I was unfamiliar.

'Did you ever hear of Michob Ader?' I asked him, smiling.

'Why, yes,' said the judge. 'And that reminds me of my shoes he has for mending. Here is his shop now.'

Judge Hoover stepped into a dingy, small shop. I looked up at the sign, and saw 'Mike O'Bader, Boot and Shoe Maker,' on it. Some wild geese passed above, honking clearly. I scratched my ear and frowned, and then trailed into the shop.

There sat my Wandering Jew on his shoemaker's bench, trimming a half-sole. He was drabbled with dew, grass-stained, unkempt, and miserable; and on his face was still the unexplained wretchedness, the problematic sorrow, the esoteric woe, that had been written there by nothing less, it seemed, than the stylus of the centuries.

Judge Hoover inquired kindly concerning his shoes. The old shoemaker looked up, and spoke sanely enough. He had been ill, he said, for a few days. The next day the shoes would be ready. He looked at me, and I could see that I had no place in his memory. So out we went, and on our way.

'Old Mike,' remarked the candidate, 'has been on one of his sprees. He gets crazy drunk regularly once a month. But he's a good shoemaker.'

'What is his history?' I inquired.

'Whisky,' epitomized Judge Hoover. 'That explains him.'

I was silent, but I did not accept the explanation. And so, when I had the chance, I asked old man Sellers, who browsed daily on my exchanges.

'Mike O'Bader,' said he, 'was makin' shoes in Montopolis when I come here goin' on fifteen year ago. I guess whisky's his trouble. Once a month he gets off the track, and stays so aweek. He's got a rigmarole somethin' about his bein' a Jew pedler that he tells ev'rybody. Nobody won't listen to him any more. When he's sober he ain't sich a fool – he's got a sight of books in the back room of his shop that he reads. I guess you can lay all his trouble to whisky.'

But again I would not. Not yet was my Wandering Jew rightly construed for me. I trust that woman may not be allowed a title to all the curiosity in the world. So when Montopolis's oldest inhabitant (some ninety score years younger than Michob Ader) dropped in to acquire promulgation in print, I siphoned his perpetual trickle of reminiscence in the direction of the uninterpreted maker of shoes.

Uncle Abner was the Complete History of Montopolis, bound in butternut.

'O'Bader,' he quavered, 'come here in '69. He was the first shoemaker in the place. Folks generally considers him crazy at times now. But he don't harm nobody. I s'pose drinkin' upset his mind – yes, drinkin' very likely done it. It's a powerful bad thing, drinkin'. I'm an old, old man, sir, and I never see no good in drinkin'.'

I felt disappointment. I was willing to admit drink in the case of my shoemaker, but I preferred it as a recourse instead of a cause.

Why had he pitched upon his perpetual, strange note of the Wandering Jew? Why his unutterable grief during his aberration? I could not yet accept whiskey as an explanation.

'Did Mike O'Bader ever have a great loss or trouble of any kind?' I asked.

'Lemme see! About thirty year ago there was somethin' of the kind, I recollect. Montopolis, sir, in them days used to be a mighty strict place.

'Well, Mike O'Bader had a daughter then – a right pretty girl. She was too gay a sort for Montopolis, so one day she slips off to another town and runs away with a circus. It was two years before she comes back, all fixed up in fine clothes and rings and jewellery, to see Mike. He wouldn't have nothin' to do with her, so she stays around town, awhile, anyway. I reckon the men folks wouldn't have raised no objections, but the women egged 'em on to order her to leave town. But she had plenty of spunk, and told 'em to mind their own business.

'So one night they decided to run her away. A crowd of men and women drove her out of her house, and chased her with sticks and stones. She run to her father's door, callin' for help. Mike opens it, and when he sees who it is he hits her with his fist and knocks her down and shuts the door.

'And then the crowd kept on chunkin' her till she run clear out of town. And the next day they finds her drowned dead in Hunter's mill pond. I mind it all now. That was thirty year ago.'

I leaned back in my non-rotary revolving chair and nodded gently, like a mandarin, at my paste-pot.

'When old Mike has a spell,' went on Uncle Abner, tepidly garrulous, 'he thinks he's the Wanderin' Jew.'

'He is,' said I, nodding away.

And Uncle Abner cackled insinuatingly at the editor's remark, for he was expecting at least a 'stickful' in the 'Personal Notes' of the *Bugle*.

LXIX

The Duplicity of Hargraves

WHEN MAJOR PENDLETON TALBOT, of Mobile, sir, and his daughter, Miss Lydia Talbot came to Washington to reside, they selected for a boarding place a house that stood fifty yards back from one of the quietest avenues. It was an old-fashioned, brick building, with a portico upheld by tall white pillars The yard was shaded by stately locusts and elms, and a catalpa tree in season rained its pink and white blossoms upon the grass. Rows of high box bushes lined the fence and walks. It was the Southern style and aspect of the place that pleased the eyes of the Talbots.

In this pleasant, private boarding-house they engaged rooms, including a study for Major Talbot who was adding the finishing chapters to his book, *Anecdotes and Reminiscences of the Alabama Army, Bench, and Bar.*

Major Talbot was of the old, old South. The present day had little interest or excellence in his eyes. His mind lived in that period before the Civil War, when the Talbots owned thousands of acres of fine cotton land and the slaves to till them; when the family mansion was the scene of princely hospitality, and drew its guests from the aristocracy of the South. Out of that period he had brought all its old pride and scruples of honour, an antiquated and punctilious politeness, and (you would think) its wardrobe.

Such clothes were surely never made within fifty years. The major was tall, but whenever he made that wonderful archaic genuflexion he called a bow, the corners of his frock-coat swept the floor. That garment was a surprise even to Washington, which has long ago ceased to shy at the frocks and broad-brimmed hats of Southern Congressmen. One of the boarders christened it a 'Father Hubbard,' and it certainly was high in the waist and full in the skirt.

But the major, with all his queer clothes, his immense area of plaited, ravelling shirt bosom, and the little black string tie with the bow always slipping on one side, both was smiled at and liked in Mrs. Vardeman's select boarding-house. Some of the young department clerks would often 'string him,' as they called it, getting him started upon the subject dearest to him – the traditions and history of his beloved Southland. During his talks he would quote freely from the *Anecdotes and Reminiscences.* But they were very careful not to let him see their designs, for in spite of his sixty-eight years, he could make the boldest of them uncomfortable under the steady regard of his piercing grey eyes.

Miss Lydia was a plump, little old maid of thirty-five, with smoothly drawn, tightly twisted hair that made her look still older. Old-fashioned, too, she was; but ante-bellum glory did not radiate from her as it did from the major. She possessed a thrifty common sense; and it was she who handled the finances of the family, and met all comers when there were bills to pay. The major regarded board bills and wash bills as contemptible nuisances. They kept coming in so persistently and so often. Why, the major wanted to know, could they not be filed and paid in a lump sum at some convenient period – say when the *Anecdotes and Reminiscences* had been published and paid for? Miss Lydia would calmly go on with her sewing and say, 'We'll pay as we go as long as the money lasts, and then perhaps they'll have to lump it.'

Most of Mrs. Vardeman's boarders were away during the day, being nearly all department clerks and business men; but there was one of them who was about the house a great deal from morning to night. This was a young man named Henry Hopkins Hargraves – every one in the house addressed him by his full name – who was engaged at one of the popular vaudeville theatres. Vaudeville has risen to such a respectable plane in the last few years, and Mr. Hargraves was such a modest and well-mannered person, that Mrs. Vardeman could find no objection to enrolling him upon her list of boarders.

At the theatre Hargraves was known as an allround dialect comedian, having a large repertoire of German, Irish, Swede, and black-face specialities. But Mr. Hargraves was ambitious, and often spoke of his great desire to succeed in legitimate comedy.

This young man appeared to conceive a strong fancy for Major Talbot. Whenever that gentleman would begin his Southern reminiscences, or repeat some of the liveliest of the anecdotes, Hargraves could always be found, the most attentive among his listeners.

For a time the major showed an inclination to discourage the advances of the 'play actor,' as he privately termed him; but soon the young man's agreeable manner and indubitable appreciation of the old gentleman's stories completely won him over.

It was not long before the two were like old chums. The major set apart each afternoon to read to him the manuscript of his book. During the anecdotes Hargraves never failed to laugh at exactly the right point. The major was moved to declare to Miss Lydia one day that young Hargraves possessed remarkable perception and a gratifying respect for the old regime. And when it came to talking of those old days – if Major Talbot liked to talk – Mr. Hargraves was entranced to listen.

Like almost all old people who talk of the past, the major loved to linger over details. In describing the splendid, almost royal, days of the old planters, he would hesitate until he had recalled the name of

the negro who held his horse, or the exact date of certain minor
happenings, or the number of bales of cotton raised in such a year;
but Hargraves never grew impatient or lost interest. On the contrary, he would advance questions on a variety of subjects connected
with the life of that time, and he never failed to extract ready replies.

The fox hunts, the 'possum suppers, the hoe downs and jubilees
in the negro quarters, the banquets in the plantation-house hall,
when invitations went for fifty miles around; the occasional feuds
with the neighbouring gentry; the major's duel with Rathbone
Culbertson about Kitty Chalmers, who afterward married a
Thwaite of South Carolina; private yacht races for fabulous sums
on Mobile Bay; the quaint beliefs, improvident habits, and loyal
virtues of the old slaves – all these were subjects that held both the
major and Hargraves absorbed for hours at a time.

Sometimes, at night, when the young man would be coming
upstairs to his room after his turn at the theatre was over, the
major would appear at the door of his study and beckon archly to
him. Going in Hargraves would find a little table set with a
decanter, sugar-bowl, fruit, and a big bunch of fresh green mint.

'It occurred to me,' the major would begin – he was always cere-
monious – 'that perhaps you might have found your duties at the –
at your place of occupation – sufficiently arduous to enable you,
Mr. Hargraves, to appreciate what the poet might well have had in
his mind when he wrote, "tired Nature's sweet restorer," – one of
our Southern juleps.'

It was a fascination to Hargraves to watch him make it. He took
rank among artists when he began, and he never varied the
process. With what delicacy he bruised the mint; with what
exquisite nicety he estimated the ingredients; with what solicitous
care he capped the compound with the scarlet fruit glowing
against the dark green fringe! And then the hospitality and grace
with which he offered it, after the selected oat straws had been
plunged into its tinkling depths!

After about four months in Washington, Miss Lydia discovered
one morning that they were almost without money. The *Anecdotes
and Reminiscences* was completed, but publishers had not jumped at
the collected gems of Alabama sense and wit. The rental of a small
house which they still owned in Mobile was two months in arrears.
Their board money for the month would be due in three days.
Miss Lydia called her father to a consultation.

'No money?' said he with a surprised look. 'It is quite annoying
to be called on so frequently for these petty sums. Really, I –'

The major searched his pockets. He found only a two-dollar bill, which he returned to his vest pocket.

'I must attend to this at once, Lydia,' he said. 'Kindly get me my umbrella and I will go down town immediately. The Congressman from our district, General Fulghum, assured me some days ago that he would use his influence to get my book published at an early date. I will go to his hotel at once and see what arrangement has been made.'

With a sad little smile Miss Lydia watched him button his 'Father Hubbard,' and depart, pausing at the door, as he always did, to bow profoundly.

That evening at dark, he returned. It seemed that Congressman Fulghum had seen the publisher who had the major's manuscript for reading. That person had said that if the anecdotes, etc., were carefully pruned down about one half, in order to eliminate the sectional and class prejudice with which the book was dyed from end to end, he might consider its publication.

The major was in a white heat of anger, but regained his equanimity, according to his code of manners, as soon as he was in Miss Lydia's presence.

'We must have money,' said Miss Lydia, with a little wrinkle above her nose. 'Give me the two dollars, and I will telegraph to Uncle Ralph for some to night.'

The major drew a small envelope from his upper vest pocket and tossed it on the table.

'Perhaps it was injudicious,' he said mildly, 'but the sum was so merely nominal that I bought tickets to the theatre to-night. It's a new war drama, Lydia. I thought you would be pleased to witness its first production in Washington. I am told that the South has very fair treatment in the play. I confess I should like to see the performance myself.'

Miss Lydia threw up her hands in silent despair.

Still, as the tickets were bought, they might as well be used. So that evening, as they sat in the theatre listening to the lively overture, even Miss Lydia was minded to relegate their troubles, for the hour, to second place. The major, in spotless linen, with his extraordinary coat showing only where it was closely buttoned, and his white hair smoothly roached, looked really fine and distinguished. The curtain went up on the first act of *A Magnolia Flower*, revealing a typical Southern plantation scene. Major Talbot betrayed some interest.

'Oh, see!' exclaimed Miss Lydia, nudging his arm, and pointing to her programme.

The major put on his glasses and read the line in the cast of characters that her finger indicated.

Col. Webster Calhoun ... H. Hopkins Hargraves.

'It's our Mr. Hargraves,' said Miss Lydia. 'It must be his first appearance in what he calls "the legitimate." I'm so glad for him.'

Not until the second act did Col. Webster Calhoun appear upon the stage. When he made his entry Major Talbot gave an audible sniff, glared at him, and seemed to freeze solid. Miss Lydia uttered a little, ambiguous squeak and crumpled her programme in her hand. For Colonel Calhoun was made up as nearly resembling Major Talbot as one pea does another. The long, thin, white hair, curly at the ends, the aristocratic beak of a nose, the crumpled, wide, ravelling shirt front, the string tie, with the bow nearly under one ear, were almost exactly duplicated. And then, to clinch the imitation, he wore the twin to the major's supposed to be unparalleled coat. High-collared, baggy, empire-waisted, ample-skirted, hanging a foot lower in front than behind, the garment could have been designed from no other pattern. From then on, the major and Miss Lydia sat bewitched, and saw the counterfeit presentment of a haughty Talbot 'dragged,' as the major afterwards expressed it, 'through the slanderous mire of a corrupt stage.'

Mr. Hargraves had used his opportunities well. He had caught the major's little idiosyncrasies of speech, accent, and intonation and his pompous courtliness to perfection – exaggerating all for the purposes of the stage. When he performed that marvellous bow that the major fondly imagined to be the pink of all salutations, the audience sent forth a sudden round of hearty applause.

Miss Lydia sat immovable, not daring to glance toward her father. Sometimes her hand next to him would be laid against her cheek, as if to conceal the smile which, in spite of her disapproval, she could not entirely suppress.

The culmination of Hargraves's audacious imitation took place in the third act. The scene is where Colonel Calhoun entertains a few of the neighbouring planters in his 'den.'

Standing at a table in the centre of the stage, with his friends grouped about him, he delivers that inimitable, rambling, character monologue so famous in *A Magnolia Flower*, at the same time that he deftly makes juleps for the party.

Major Talbot, sitting quietly, but white with indignation, heard his best stories retold, his pet theories and hobbies advanced and expanded, and the dream of the *Anecdotes and Reminiscences* served, exaggerated and garbled. His favourite narrative – that of his duel with Rathbone Culbertson – was not omitted, and it was delivered with more fire, egotism, and gusto than the major himself put into it.

The monologue concluded with a quaint, delicious, witty little lecture on the art of concocting a julep, illustrated by the act. Here Major Talbot's delicate but showy science was reproduced to a hair's breadth – from his dainty handling of the fragrant weed – 'the one-thousandth part of a grain too much pressure, gentlemen, and you extract the bitterness, instead of the aroma, of this heaven-bestowed plant' – to his solicitous selection of the oaten straws.

At the close of the scene the audience raised a tumultuous roar of appreciation. The portrayal of the type was so exact, so sure and thorough, that the leading characters in the play were forgotten. After repeated calls, Hargraves came before the curtain and bowed, his rather boyish face bright and flushed with the knowledge of success.

At last Miss Lydia turned and looked at the major. His thin nostrils were working like the gills of a fish. He laid both shaking hands upon the arms of his chair to rise.

'We will go, Lydia,' he said chokingly. 'This is an abominable – desecration.

Before he could rise, she pulled him back into his seat.

'We will stay it out,' she declared. 'Do you want to advertise the copy by exhibiting the original coat?' So they remained to the end.

Hargraves's success must have kept him up late that night, for neither at the breakfast nor at the dinner-table did he appear.

About three in the afternoon he tapped at the door of Major Talbot's study. The major opened it, and Hargraves walked in with his hands full of the morning papers – too full of his triumph to notice anything unusual in the major's demeanour.

'I put it all over 'em last night, major,' he began exultantly. 'I had my innings, and, I think, scored. Here's what the *Post* says:

His conception and portrayal of the old-time Southern colonel, with his absurd grandiloquence, his eccentric garb, his quaint idioms and phrases, his moth-eaten pride of family, and his really kind heart, fastidious sense of honour, and lovable simplicity, is the best delineation of a character rôle on the boards today. The coat worn by Colonel Calhoun is itself nothing less than an evolution of genius. Mr. Hargraves has captured his public.

'How does that sound, major, for a first nighter?'

'I had the honour' – the major's voice sounded ominously frigid

− 'of witnessing your very remarkable performance, sir, last night.'

Hargraves looked disconcerted.

'You were there? I didn't know you ever − I didn't know you cared for the theatre. Oh, I say, Major Talbot,' he exclaimed frankly, 'don't you be offended. I admit I did get a lot of pointers from you that helped me out wonderfully in the part. But it's a type, you know − not individual. The way the audience caught on shows that. Half the patrons of that theatre are Southerners. They recognized it.'

'Mr. Hargraves,' said the major, who had remained standing, 'you have put upon me an unpardonable insult. You have burlesqued my person, grossly betrayed my confidence, and misused my hospitality. If I thought you possessed the faintest conception of what is the sign manual of a gentleman, or what is due one, I would call you out, sir, old as I am. I will ask you to leave the room, sir.

The actor appeared to be slightly bewildered, and seemed hardly to take in the full meaning of the old gentleman's words.

'I am truly sorry you took offence,' he said regretfully. 'Up here we don't look at things just as you people do. I know men who would buy out half the house to have their personality put on the stage so the public would recognize it.'

'They are not from Alabama, sir,' said the major haughtily.

'Perhaps not. I have a pretty good memory, major; let me quote a few lines from your book. In response to a toast at a banquet given in − Milledgeville, I believe − you uttered, and intend to have printed, these words:

The Northern man is utterly without sentiment or warmth except in so far as the feelings may be turned to his own commercial profit. He will suffer without resentment any imputation cast upon the honour of himself or his loved ones that does not bear with it the consequence of pecuniary loss. In his charity, he gives with a liberal hand; but it must be heralded with the trumpet and chronicled in brass.

'Do you think that picture is fairer than the one you saw of Colonel Calhoun last night?'

'The description,' said the major, frowning, 'is − not without grounds. Some exag − latitude must be allowed in public speaking.'

'And in public acting,' replied Hargraves.

'That is not the point,' persisted the major, unrelenting. 'It was a personal caricature. I positively decline to overlook it, sir.'

'Major Talbot,' said Hargraves, with a winning smile, 'I wish you would understand me. I want you to know that I never dreamed of insulting you. In my profession, all life belongs to me. I take what I want, and what I can, and return it over the foot-lights. Now, if you will, let's let it go at that. We've been pretty good friends for some months, and I'm going to take the risk of offending you again. I know you are hard up for money – never mind how I found out; a boarding-house is no place to keep such matters secret – and I want you to let me help you out of the pinch. I've been there often enough myself. I've been getting a fair salary all the season, and I've saved some money. You're welcome to a couple hundred – or even more – until you get –'

'Stop!' commanded the major, with his arm outstretched. 'It seems that my book didn't lie, after all. You think your money salve will heal all the hurts of honour. Under no circumstances would I accept a loan from a casual acquaintance; and as to you, sir, I would starve before I would consider your insulting offer of a financial adjustment of the circumstances we have discussed. I beg to repeat my request relative to your quitting the apartment.'

Hargraves took his departure without another word. He also left the house the same day, moving, as Mrs. Vardeman explained at the supper-table, nearer the vicinity of the down-town theatre, where *Magnolia Flower* was booked for a week's run.

Critical was the situation with Major Talbot and Miss Lydia. There was no one in Washington to whom the major's scruples allowed him to apply for a loan. Miss Lydia wrote a letter to Uncle Ralph, but it was doubtful whether that relative's constricted affairs would permit him to furnish help. The major was forced to make an apologetic address to Mrs. Vardeman regarding the delayed payment for board, referring to 'delinquent rentals' and 'delayed remittances' in a rather confused strain.

Deliverance came from an entirely unexpected source.

Late one afternoon the door maid came up and announced an old coloured man who wanted to see Major Talbot. The major asked that he be sent up to his study. Soon an old darkey appeared in the doorway, with his hat in hand, bowing, and scraping with one clumsy foot. He was quite decently dressed in a baggy suit of black. His big, coarse shoes shone with a metallic lustre suggestive of stove polish. His bushy wool was grey – almost white. After middle life, it is difficult to estimate the age of a negro. This one might have seen as many years as had Major Talbot.

'I be bound you don't know me, Mars' Pendleton,' were his first words.

The major rose and came forward at the old, familiar style of

address. It was one of the old plantation darkeys without a doubt;
but they had been widely scattered, and he could not recall the
voice or face.

'I don't believe I do,' he said kindly - 'unless you will assist my
memory.'

'Don't you 'member Cindy's Mose, Mars' Pendleton, what
'migrated 'mediately after de war?'

'Wait a moment,' said the major, rubbing his forehead with the
tips of his fingers. He loved to recall everything connected with
those beloved days. 'Cindy's Mose,' he reflected. 'You worked
among the horses - breaking the colts. Yes, I remember now.
After the surrender, you took the name of - don't prompt me -
Mitchell, and went to the West - to Nebraska.'

'Yassir, yassir,' - the old man's face stretched with a delighted
grin - 'dat's him, dat's it. Newbraska. Dat's me - Mose Mitchell.
Old Uncle Mose Mitchell, dey calls me now. Old mars', your pa,
gimme a pah of dem mule colts when I lef' fur to staht me goin'
with. You 'member dem colts, Mars' Pendleton?'

'I don't seem to recall the colts,' said the major. 'You know I
was married the first year of the war and living at the old Follins-
bee place. But sit down, sit down, Uncle Mose. I'm glad to see
you. I hope you have prospered.'

Uncle Mose took a chair and laid his hat carefully on the floor
beside it.

'Yassir; of late I done mouty famous. When I first got to Newbraska, dey folks come all roun' me to see dem mule colts. Dey
ain't see no mules like dem in Newbraska. I sold dem mules for
three hundred dollars. Yassir - three hundred.

'Den I open a blacksmith shop, suh, and made some money and
bought some lan'. He and my old 'oman done raised up seb'm
chillun, and all doin' well 'cept two of 'em what died. Fo' year ago a
railroad come along and staht a town slam ag'inst my lan', and, suh,
Mars' Pendleton, Uncle Mose am worth leb'm thousand dollars in
money, property, and lan'.'

'I'm glad to hear it,' said the major heartily. 'Glad to hear it.'

'And dat little baby of yo'n, Mars' Pendleton - one what you
name Miss Lyddy - I be bound dat little tad done growed up tell
nobody wouldn't know her.'

The major stepped to the door and called: 'Lydia, dear, will you
come?'

Miss Lydia, looking quite grown up and a little worried, came in
from her room.

'Dar, now! What'd I tell you? I knowed dat baby be plum growed up. You don't 'member Uncle Mose, child?'

'This is Aunt Cindy's Mose, Lydia,' explained the major. 'He left Sunnymead for the West when you were two years old.'

'Well,' said Lydia, 'I can hardly be expected to remember you, Uncle Mose, at that age. And, as you say, I'm "plum growed up," and was a blessed long time ago. But I'm glad to see you, even if I can't remember you.'

And she was. And so was the major. Something alive and tangible had come to link them with the happy past. The three sat and talked over the olden times, the major and Uncle Mose correcting or prompting each other as they reviewed the plantation scenes and days.

The major inquired what the old man was doing so far from his home.

'Uncle Mose am a delicate,' he explained, 'to de grand Baptis' convention in dis city. I never preached none, but being a residin' elder in de church, and able fur to pay my own expenses, dey sent me along.'

'And how did you know we were in Washington?' inquired Miss Lydia.

'Dey's a cullud man works in de hotel whar I stops, what comes from Mobile. He told me he seen Mars' Pendleton comin' outen dish here house one mawnin'.'

'What I come fur,' continued Uncle Mose, reaching into his pocket – 'besides de sight of home folks – was to pay Mars' Pendleton what I owes him.'

'Owe me?' said the major, in surprise.

'Yassir – three hundred dollars.' He handed the major a roll of bills. 'When I lef' old mars' says: "Take dem mule colts, Mose, and, if it be so you gits able, pay fur 'em." Yassir – dem was his words. De war had done lef' old mars' po' hisself. Old mars' bein' long ago dead, de debt descends to Mars' Pendleton. Three hundred dollars. Uncle Mose is plenty able to pay now. When dat railroad buy my lan' I laid off to pay fur dem mules. Count de money, Mars' Pendleton. Dat's what I sold dem mules fur. Yassir.'

Tears were in Major Talbot's eyes. He took Uncle Mose's hand and laid his other upon his shoulder.

'Dear faithful, old servitor,' he said in an unsteady voice, 'I don't mind saying to you that "Mars" Pendleton' spent his last dollar in the world a week ago. We will accept this money, Uncle Mose, since in a way, it is a sort of payment, as well as a token of the loyalty and devotion of the old regime. Lydia, my dear, take the money. You are better fitted than I to manage its expenditure.'

'Take it, honey,' said Uncle Mose. 'Hit belongs to you. Hit's Talbot money.'

After Uncle Mose had gone, Miss Lydia had a good cry – for joy; and the major turned his face to a corner, and smoked his clay pipe volcanically.

The succeeding days saw the Talbots restored to peace and ease. Miss Lydia's face lost its worried look. The major appeared in a new frock-coat, in which he looked like a wax figure personifying the memory of his golden age. Another publisher who read the manuscript of the *Anecdotes and Reministences* thought that, with a little retouching and toning down of the high lights, he could make a really bright and saleable volume of it. Altogether, the situation was comfortable, and not without the touch of hope that is often sweeter than arrived blessings.

One day, about a week after their piece of good luck, a maid brought a letter for Miss Lydia to her room. The post-mark showed that it was from New York. Not knowing anyone there, Miss Lydia, in a mild flutter of wonder, sat down by her table and opened the letter with her scissors. This was what she read:

DEAR MISS TALBOT:

I thought you might be glad to learn of my good fortune. I have received and accepted an offer of two hundred dollars per week by a New York stock company to play Colonel Calhoun in *A Magnolia Flower*.

There is something else I wanted you to know. I guess you'd better not tell Major Talbot. I was anxious to make him some amends for the great help he was to me in studying the part, and for the bad humour he was in about it. He refused to let me, so I did it anyhow. I could easily spare the three hundred.

Sincerely yours,

H. HOPKINS HARGRAVES.

P.S. How did I play Uncle Mose?

Major Talbot, passing through the hall, saw Miss Lydia s door open and stopped.

'Any mail for us this morning, Lydia, dear?' he asked.

Miss Lydia slid the letter beneath a fold of her dress.

'The *Mobile Chronicle* came,' she said promptly. 'It's on the table in your study.'

LXX

Let me Feel Your Pulse

So I WENT TO A DOCTOR.

'How long has it been since you took any alcohol into your system?' he asked.

Turning my head sideways, I answered, 'Oh, quite a while.'

He was a young doctor, somewhere between twenty and forty. He wore heliotrope socks, but he looked like Napoleon. I liked him immensely.

'Now,' said he, 'I am going to show you the effect of alcohol upon your circulation.' I think it was 'circulation' he said; though it may have been 'advertising.'

He bared my left arm to the elbow, brought out a bottle of whisky, and gave me a drink. He began to look more like Napoleon. I began to like him better.

Then he put a tight compress on my upper arm, stopped my pulse with the fingers, and squeezed a rubber bulb connected with an apparatus on a stand that looked like a thermometer. The mercury jumped up and down without seeming to stop anywhere; but the doctor said it registered two hundred and thirty-seven or one hundred and sixty-five or some such number.

'Now,' said he, 'you see what alcohol does to the blood-pressure.'

'It's marvellous,' said I, 'but do you think it a sufficient test? Have one on me, and let's try the other arm.' But, no!

Then he grasped my hand. I thought I was doomed and he was saying good-bye. But all he wanted to do was to jab a needle into the end of a finger and compare the red drop with a lot of fifty-cent. poker chips that he had fastened to a card.

'It's the hæmoglobin test,' he explained. 'The colour of your blood is wrong.'

'Well,' said I, 'I know it should be blue; but this is a country of mix-ups. Some of my ancestors were cavaliers; but they got thick with some people on Nantucket Island, so —'

'I mean,' said the doctor, 'that the shade of red is too light.'

'Oh,' said I, 'it's a case of matching instead of matches.'

The doctor then pounded me severely in the region of the chest. When he did that I don't know whether he reminded me most of Napoleon or Battling or Lord Nelson. Then he looked grave and mentioned a string of grievances that the flesh is heir to – most ending in 'itis.' I immediately paid him fifteen dollars on account.

'Is or are it or some or any of them necessarily fatal?' I asked. I thought my connection with the matter justified my manifesting a certain amount of interest.

'All of them,' he answered cheerfully. 'But their progress may be arrested. With care and proper continuous treatment you may live to be eighty-five or ninety.'

I began to think of the doctor's bill. 'Eighty-five would be sufficient, I am sure,' was my comment. I paid him ten dollars more on account.

'The first thing to do,' he said, with renewed animation, 'is to find a sanatorium where you will get a complete rest for awhile, and allow your nerves to get into a better condition. I myself will go with you and select a suitable one.'

So he took me to a mad-house in the Catskills. It was on a bare mountain frequented only by infrequent frequenters. You could see nothing but stones and boulders, some patches of snow, and scattered pine trees. The young physician in charge was most agreeable. He gave me a stimulant without applying a compress to the arm. It was luncheon time, and we were invited to partake. There were about twenty inmates at little tables in the dining-room. The young physician in charge came to our table and said: 'It is a custom with our guests not to regard themselves as patients, but merely as tired ladies and gentlemen taking a rest. Whatever slight maladies they may have are never alluded to in conversation.'

My doctor called loudly to a waitress to bring some phospho-glycerate of lime hash, dog-bread, bromo-seltzer pancakes, and nux vomica tea for my repast. Then a sound arose like a sudden wind storm among pine trees. It was produced by every guest in the room whispering loudly, 'Neurasthenia!' – except one man with a nose, whom I distinctly heard say, 'Chronic alcoholism.' I hope to meet him again. The physician in charge turned and walked away.

An hour or so after luncheon he conducted us to the workshop – say fifty yards from the house. Thither the guests had been conducted by the physician in charge's understudy and sponge-holder – a man with feet and a blue sweater. He was so tall that I was not sure he had a face; but the Armour Packing Company would have been delighted with his hands.

'Here,' said the physician in charge, 'our guests find relaxation from past mental worries by devoting themselves to physical labour – reaction, in reality.'

There were turning-lathes, carpenter's outfits, clay-modelling tools, spinning-wheels, weaving-frames, treadmills, bass drums, enlarged-crayon-portrait apparatuses, blacksmith forges, and everything seemingly, that could interest the paying lunatic guests of a first-rate sanatorium.

'The lady making mud-pies in the corner,' whispered the physician in charge, 'is no other than – Lula Lulington, the authoress of the novel entitled *Why Love Loves*. What she is doing now is simply to rest her mind after performing that piece of work.'

I had seen the book. 'Why doesn't she do it by writing another one instead?' I asked.

As you see, I wasn't as far gone as they thought I was.

'The gentleman pouring water through the funnel,' continued the physician in charge, 'is a Wall Street broker broken down from overwork.'

I buttoned my coat.

Others, he pointed out, were architects playing with Noah's arks, ministers reading Darwin's *Theory of Evolution*, lawyers sawing wood, tired-out society ladies talking Ibsen to the blue-sweatered spongeholder, a neurotic millionaire lying asleep on the floor, and a prominent artist drawing a little red wagon around the room.

'You look pretty strong,' said the physician in charge to me. 'I think the best mental relaxation for you would be throwing small boulders over the mountain-side and then bringing them up again.'

I was a hundred yards away before my doctor overtook me.

'What's the matter?' he asked.

'The matter is,' said I, 'that there are no aeroplanes handy. So I am going to merrily and hastily jog the foot-pathway to yon station and catch the first unlimited-soft-coal express back to town.'

'Well,' said the doctor, 'perhaps you are right. This seems hardly the place suitable for you. But what you need is rest – absolute rest and exercise.'

That night I went to an hotel in the city, and said to the clerk: 'What I need is absolute rest and exercise. Can you give me a room with one of those tall folding-beds in it, and a relay of bell-boys to work it up and down while I rest?'

The clerk rubbed a speck off one of his fingernails and glanced sideways at a tall man in a white hat sitting in the lobby. That man came over and asked me politely if I had seen the shrubbery at the west entrance. I had not, so he showed it to me and then looked me over.

'I thought you had 'em,' he said, not unkindly, 'but I guess you're all right. You'd better go see a doctor, old man.'

A week afterward my doctor tested my blood-pressure again without the preliminary stimulant. He looked to me a little less like Napoleon. And his socks were of a shade of tan that did not appeal to me.

'What you need,' he decided, 'is sea air and companionship.'

'Would a mermaid –' I began; but he slipped on his professional manner.

'I myself,' he said, 'will take you to the Hotel Bonair off the coast of Long Island and see that you get in good shape. It is a quiet, comfortable resort where you will soon recuperate.'

The Hotel Bonair proved to be a nine-hundred room fashionable hostelry on an island off the main shore. Everybody who did not dress for dinner was shoved into a side dining-room and given only a terrapin and champagne table d'hôte. The bay was a great stamping-ground for wealthy yachtsmen. The *Corsair* anchored there the day we arrived. I saw Mr. Morgan standing on deck eating a cheese sandwich and gazing longingly at the hotel. Still, it was a very inexpensive place. Nobody could afford to pay their prices. When you went away you simply left your baggage, stole a skiff, and beat it for the mainland in the night.

When I had been there one day I got a pad of monogrammed telegraph blanks at the clerk's desk and began to wire to all my friends for get-away money. My doctor and I played one game of croquet on the golf links and went to sleep on the lawn.

When we got back to town a thought seemed to occur to him suddenly. 'By the way,' he asked, 'how do you feel?'

'Relieved of very much,' I replied.

Now a consulting physician is different. He isn't exactly sure whether he is to be paid or not, and this uncertainty ensures you either the most careful or the most careless attention. My doctor took me to see a consulting physician. He made a poor guess and gave me careful attention. I liked him immensely. He put me through some co-ordination exercises.

'Have you a pain in the back of your head?' he asked. I told him I had not.

'Shut your eyes,' he ordered, 'put your feet close together, and jump backwards as far as you can.'

I was always a good backward jumper with my eyes shut, so I obeyed. My head struck the edge of the bathroom door, which had been left open and was only three feet away. The doctor was very sorry. He had overlooked the fact that the door was open. He closed it.

'Now touch your nose with your right forefinger,' he said.

'Where is it?' I asked.

'On your face,' said he.

'I mean my right forefinger,' I explained.

'Oh, excuse me,' said he. He reopened the bathroom door, and I took my finger out of the crack of it. After I had performed the marvellous digitonasal feat I said:

'I do not wish to deceive you as to symptoms, doctor; I really have something like a pain in the back of my head.' He ignored the symptom and examined my heart carefully with a latest-popular-air-penny-in-the-slot ear-trumpet. I felt like a ballad.

'Now,' he said, 'gallop like a horse for about five minutes around the room.'

I gave the best imitation I could of a disqualified Percheron being led out of Madison Square Garden. Then, without dropping in a penny, he listened to my chest again.

'No glanders in our family, Doc,' I said.

The consulting physician held up his forefinger within three inches of my nose. 'Look at my finger,' he commanded.

'Did you ever try Pears' –' I began; but he went on with his test rapidly.

'Now look across the bay. At my finger. Across the bay. At my finger. At my finger. Across the bay. Across the bay. At my finger. Across the bay.' This for about three minutes.

He explained that this was a test of the action of the brain. It seemed easy to me. I never once mistook his finger for the bay. I'll bet that if he had used the phrases: 'Gaze, as it were, unpre-occupied, outward – or rather laterally – in the direction of the horizon, underlaid, so to speak, with the adjacent fluid inlet,' and 'Now, returning – or rather, in a manner, withdrawing your attention, bestow it upon my upraised digit' – I'll bet, I say, that Harry James himself could have passed the examination.

After asking me if I had ever had a grand uncle with curvature of the spine or a cousin with swelled ankles, the two doctors retired to the bathroom and sat on the edge of the bath tub for their consultation. I ate an apple, and gazed first at my finger and then across the bay.

The doctors came out looking grave. More: they looked tomb-stones and Tennessee-papers-please-copy. They wrote out a diet list to which I was to be restricted. It had everything that I had ever heard of to eat on it, except snails. And I never eat a snail unless it overtakes me and bites me first.

'You must follow this diet strictly,' said the doctors.

'I'd follow it a mile if I could get one-tenth of what's on it,' I answered.

'Of next importance,' they went on, 'is outdoor air and exercise. And here is a prescription that will be of great benefit to you.'

Then all of us took something. They took their hats, and I took my departure.

I went to a druggist and showed him the prescription.

'It will be $2.87 for an ounce bottle,' he said.

'Will you give me a piece of your wrapping cord?' said I.

I made a hole in the prescription, ran the cord through it, tied it around my neck, and tucked it inside. All of us have a little super-stition, and mine runs to a confidence in amulets.

Of course there was nothing the matter with me, but I was very ill. I couldn't work, sleep, eat, or bowl. The only way I could get any sympathy was to go without shaving for four days. Even then somebody would say: 'Old man, you look as hardy as a pine-knot. Been up for a jaunt in the Maine woods, eh?'

Then, suddenly, I remembered that I must have outdoor air and exercise. So I went down South to John's. John is an approximate relative by verdict of a preacher standing with a little book in his hands in a bower of chrysanthemums while a hundred thousand people looked on. John has a country house seven miles from Pineville. It is at an altitude and on the Blue Ridge Mountains in a state too dignified to be dragged into this controversy. John is mica, which is more valuable and clearer than gold.

He met me at Pineville, and we took the trolley car to his home. It is a big neighbourless cottage on a hill surrounded by a hundred mountains. We got off at his little private station, where John's family and Amaryllis met and greeted us. Amaryllis looked at me a trifle anxiously.

A rabbit came bounding across the hill between us and the house. I threw down my suit-case and pursued it hot-foot. After I had run twenty yards and seen it disappear, I sat down on the grass and wept disconsolately.

'I can't catch a rabbit any more,' I sobbed. 'I'm of no further use in the world. I may as well be dead.'

'Oh, what is it – what is it, Brother John?' I heard Amaryllis say. 'Nerves a little unstrung,' said John in his calm way. 'Don't worry. Get up, you rabbit-chaser, and come on to the house before the biscuits get cold.' It was about twilight, and the mountains came up nobly to Miss Murfree's descriptions of them.

Soon after dinner I announced that I believed I could sleep for a year or two, including legal holidays. So I was shown to a room as big and cool as a flower garden, where there was a bed as broad as a lawn. Soon afterward the remainder of the household retired, and then there fell upon the land a silence.

I had not heard a silence before in years. It was absolute. I raised myself on my elbow and listened to it. Sleep! I thought that if I only could hear a star twinkle or a blade of grass sharpen itself I could compose myself to rest. I thought once that I heard a sound like the sail of a catboat flapping as it veered about in a breeze, but I decided that it was probably only a tack in the carpet. Still I listened.

Suddenly some belated little bird alighted upon the window-sill, and, in what he no doubt considered sleepy tones, enunciated the noise generally translated as 'cheep!'

I leaped into the air.

'Hey! what's the matter down there?' called John from his room above mine.

'Oh, nothing,' I answered, 'except that I accidentally bumped my head against the ceiling.'

The next morning I went out on the porch and looked at the mountains. There were forty-seven of them in sight. I shuddered, went into the big hall sitting-room of the house, selected *Pancoast's Family Practice of Medicine* from a bookcase, and began to read. John came in, took the book away from me, and led me outside. He has a farm of three hundred acres furnished with the usual complement of barns, mules, peasantry, and harrows with three front teeth broken off. I had seen such things in my childhood, and my heart began to sink.

Then John spoke of alfalfa, and I brightened at once. 'Oh, yes,' said I, 'wasn't she in the chorus of – let's see –'

'Green, you know,' said John, 'and tender, and you plough it under after the first season.'

'I know,' said I, 'and the grass grows over her.'

'Right,' said John. 'You know something about farming, after all.'

'I know something of some farmers,' said I, 'and a sure scythe will mow them down some day.'

On the way back to the house a beautiful and inexplicable creature walked across our path. I stopped irresistibly fascinated, gazing at it. John waited patiently, smoking his cigarette. He is a modern farmer. After ten minutes he said: 'Are you going to stand there looking at that chicken all day? Breakfast is nearly ready.'

'A chicken?' said I.

'A White Orpington hen, if you want to particularize.'

'A White Orpington hen?' I repeated, with intense interest. The fowl walked slowly away with graceful dignity, and I followed like a child after the Pied Piper. Five minutes more were allowed me by John, and then he took me by the sleeve and conducted me to breakfast.

After I had been there a week I began to grow alarmed. I was sleeping and eating well and actually beginning to enjoy life. For a man in my desperate condition that would never do. So I sneaked down to the trolley-station, took the car for Pineville, and went to see one of the best physicians in town. By this time I knew exactly what to do when I needed medical treatment. I hung my hat on the back of a chair, and said rapidly:

'Doctor, I have cirrhosis of the heart, indurated arteries, neurasthenia, neuritis, acute indigestion, and convalescence. I am going to live on a strict diet. I shall also take a tepid bath at night and a cold one in the morning. I shall endeavour to be cheerful, and fix my mind on pleasant subjects. In the way of drugs I intend to take a phosphorus pill three times a day, preferably after meals, and a tonic composed of the tinctures of gentian, cinchona, calisaya, and cardamom compound. Into each tablespoonful of this I shall mix tincture of nux vomica, beginning with one drop and increasing it a drop each day until the maximum dose is reached. I shall drop this with a medicine-dropper, which can be procured at a trifling cost at any pharmacy. Good morning.'

I took my hat and walked out. After I had closed the door I remembered something that I had forgotten to say. I opened it again. The doctor had not moved from where he had been sitting, but he gave a slightly nervous start when he saw me again.

'I forgot to mention,' said I, 'that I shall also take absolute rest and exercise.'

After this consultation I felt much better. The re-establishing in my mind of the fact that I was hopelessly ill gave me so much satisfaction that I almost became gloomy again. There is nothing more alarming to a neurasthenic than to feel himself growing well and cheerful.

John looked after me carefully. After I had evinced so much interest in his White Orpington chicken he tried his best to divert my mind, and was particular to lock his hen house of nights. Gradually the tonic mountain air, the wholesome food, and the daily walks among the hills so alleviated my malady that I became utterly wretched and despondent. I heard of a country doctor who lived in the mountains near-by. I went to see him and told him the whole story. He was a grey-bearded man with clear, blue, wrinkled eyes, in a home-made suit of grey jeans.

In order to save time I diagnosed my case, touched my nose with my right forefinger, struck myself below the knee to make my foot kick, sounded my chest, stuck out my tongue, and asked him the price of cemetery lots in Pineville.

He lit his pipe and looked at me for about three minutes. 'Brother,' he said, after awhile, 'you are in a mighty bad way. There's a chance for you to pull through, but it's a mighty slim one.'

'What can it be?' I asked eagerly. 'I have taken arsenic and gold, phosphorus, exercise, nux vomica, hydrotherapeutic baths, rest, excitement, codein, and aromatic spirits of ammonia. Is there anything left in the pharmacopœia?'

'Somewhere in these mountains,' said the doctor, 'there's a plant growing – a flowering plant that'll cure you, and it's about the only thing that will. It's of a kind that's as old as the world; but of late it's powerful scarce and hard to find You and I will have to hunt it up. I'm not engaged in active practice now; I'm getting along in years; but I'll take your case. You'll have to come every day in the afternoon and help me hunt for this plant till we find it. The city doctors may know a lot about new scientific things, but they don't know much about the cures that Nature carries around in her saddlebags.'

So every day the old doctor and I hunted the cure-all plant among the mountains and valleys of the Blue Ridge. Together we toiled up steep heights so slippery with fallen autumn leaves that we had to catch every sapling and branch within our reach to save us from falling. We waded through forges and chasms, breast-deep with laurel and ferns; we followed the banks of mountain streams for miles; we wound our way like Indians through brakes of pine – road-side, hill-side, river-side, mountain side we explored in our search for the miraculous plant.

As the old doctor said, it must have grown scarce and hard to find. But we followed our quest. Day by day we plumbed the valleys, scaled the heights, and tramped the plateaux in search of the miraculous plant. Mountain bred, he never seemed to tire. I often reached home too fatigued to do anything except fall into bed and sleep until morning. This we kept up for a month.

One evening after I had returned from a six-mile tramp with the old doctor, Amaryllis and I took a little walk under the trees near the road. We looked at the mountains drawing their royal-purple robes around them for their night's repose.

'I'm glad you're well again,' she said. 'When you first came you frightened me. I thought you were really ill.'

'Well again!' I almost shrieked. 'Do you know that I have only one chance in a thousand to live?'

Amaryllis looked at me in surprise. 'Why,' said she, 'you are as strong as one of the plough-mules, you sleep ten or twelve hours every night, and you are eating us out of house and home. What more do you want?'

'I tell you,' said I, 'that unless we find the magic – that is, the plant we are looking for – in time, nothing can save me. The doctor tells me so.'

'What doctor?'

'Doctor Tatum – the old doctor who lives halfway up Black Oak Mountain. Do you know him?'

'I have known him since I was able to talk. And is that where you go every day – is it he who takes you on these long walks and climbs that have brought back your health and strength? God bless the old doctor.'

Just then the old doctor himself drove slowly down the road in his rickety old buggy. I waved my hand at him and shouted that I would be on hand the next day at the usual time. He stopped his horse and called to Amaryllis to come to him. They talked for five minutes while I waited. Then the old doctor drove on.

When we got to the house Amaryllis lugged out an encyclopaedia and sought a word in it. 'The doctor said,' she told me, 'that you needn't call any more as a patient, but he'd be glad to see you any time as a friend. And then he told me to look up my name in the encyclopædia and tell you what it means. It seems to be the name of a genus of flowering plants, and also the name of a country girl in Theocritus and Virgil. What do you suppose the doctor meant by that?'

'I know what he meant,' said I. 'I know now.'

A word to a brother who may have come under the spell of the unquiet Lady Neurasthenia.

The formula was true. Even though gropingly at times, the

physicians of the walled cities had put their fingers upon the specific medicament.

And so for the exercise one is referred to good Doctor Tatum on Black Oak Mountain – take the road to your right at the Methodist meeting-house in the pine-grove.

Absolute rest and exercise.

What rest more remedial than to sit with Amaryllis in the shade, and, with a sixth sense, read the wordless Theocritan idyll of the gold-bannered blue mountains marching orderly into the dormitories of the night?

LXXI

Law and Order

I FOUND MYSELF IN TEXAS RECENTLY, revisiting old places and vistas. At a sheep ranch where I had sojourned many years ago, I stopped for a week. And, as all visitors do, I heartily plunged into the business at hand, which happened to be that of dipping the sheep.

Now, this process is so different from ordinary human baptism that it deserves a word of itself. A vast iron cauldron with half the fires of Avernus beneath it is partly filled with water that soon boils furiously. Into that is cast concentrated lye, lime, and sulphur, which is allowed to stew and fume until the witches' broth is strong enough to scorch the third arm of Palladino herself.

Then this concentrated brew is mixed in a long, deep vat with cubic gallons of hot water, and the sheep are caught by their hind legs and flung into the compound. After being thoroughly ducked by means of a forked pole in the hands of a gentleman detailed for that purpose, they are allowed to clamber up an incline into a corral and dry or die, as the state of their constitutions may decree. If you ever caught an able-bodied, two-year-old mutton by the hind legs and felt the 750 volts of kicking that he can send through your arm seventeen times before you can hurl him into the vat, you will, of course, hope that he may die instead of dry.

But this is merely to explain why Bud Oakley and I gladly stretched ourselves on the bank of the near-by *charco* after the dipping, glad for the welcome inanition and pure contact with the earth after our muscle-racking labours. The flock was a small one, and we finished at three in the afternoon; so Bud brought from the *morral* on his saddle-horn, coffee and a coffee-pot and a big hunk of bread and some side bacon. Mr. Mills, the ranch owner and my old friend, rode away to the ranch with his force of Mexican *trabajadores*.

While the bacon was frizzling nicely, there was the sound of horses' hoofs behind us. Bud's six-shooter lay in its scabbard ten feet away from his hand. He paid not the slightest heed to the approaching horseman. This attitude of a Texas ranchman was so different from the old-time custom that I marvelled. Instinctively I turned to inspect the possible foe that menaced us in the rear. I saw a horseman dressed in black, who might have been a lawyer or a parson or an undertaker trotting peaceably along the road by the *arroyo*.

Bud noticed my precautionary movement and smiled sarcastically and sorrowfully.

'You've been away too long,' said he. 'You don't need to look around any more when anybody gallops up behind you in this state, unless something hits you in the back; and even then it's liable to be only a bunch of tracts or a petition to sign against the trusts. I never looked at that *hombre* that rode by; but I'll bet a quart of sheep dip that he's some double-dyed son of a popgun out rounding up prohibition votes.'

'Times have changed, Bud,' said I oracularly. 'Law and order is the rule now in the South and the South-west.'

I caught a cold gleam from Bud's pale blue eyes.

'Not that I –' I began hastily.

'Of course you don't,' said Bud warmly. 'You know better. You've lived here before. Law and order, you say? Twenty years ago we had 'em here. We only had two or three laws, such as against murder before witnesses, and being caught stealing horses, and voting the Republican ticket. But how is it now? All we get is orders; and the laws go out of the state. Them legislators set up there at Austin and don't do nothing but makes laws against kerosene oil and schoolbooks being brought into the state. I reckon they was afraid some man would go home some evening after work and light up and get an education and go to work and make laws to repeal aforesaid laws. Me, I'm for the old days when law and order meant what they said. A law was a law, and a order was a order.'

'But –' I began.

'I was going on,' continued Bud, 'while this coffee is boiling, to describe to you a case of genuine law and order that I knew of once in the times when cases was decided in the chambers of a six-shooter instead of a supreme court.

'You've heard of old Ben Kirkman, the cattle king? His ranch run from the Nueces to the Rio Grande. In them days, as you know, there was cattle barons and cattle kings. The difference was this; when a cattleman went to San Antone and bought beer for the newspaper reporters and only give them the number of cattle he actually owned, they wrote him up for a baron. When he bought 'em champagne wine and added in the amount of cattle he had stole, they called him a king.

'Luke Summers was one of his range bosses. And down to the king's ranch comes one day a bunch of these Oriental people from New York or Kansas City or thereabouts. Luke was detailed with a squad to ride about with 'em, and see that the rattlesnakes got fair warning when they was coming, and drive the deer out of their way. Among the bunch was a black-eyed girl that wore a number two shoe. That's all I noticed about her. But Luke must have seen more, for he married her one day before the *cabballard* started back, and went over on Canada Verde and set up a ranch of his own. I'm skipping over the sentimental stuff on purpose, because I never saw or wanted to see any of it. And Luke takes me along with him because we was old friends and I handled cattle to suit him.

'I'm skipping over much what followed, because I never saw or wanted to see any of it — but three years afterward there was a boy kid stumbling and blubbering around the galleries and floors of Luke's ranch. I never had no use for kids; but it seems they did. And I'm skipping over much what followed until one day out to the ranch drives in hacks and buckboards a lot of Mrs. Summers's friends from the East — a sister or so and two or three men. One looked like an uncle to somebody; and one looked like nothing; and the other one had on corkscrew pants and spoke in a tone of voice. I never liked a man who spoke in a tone of voice.

'I'm skipping over much what followed; but one afternoon when I rides up to the ranch house to get some orders about a drove of beeves that was to be shipped, I hears something like a popgun go off. I waits at the hitching-rack, not wishing to intrude on private affairs. In a little while Luke comes out and gives some orders to some of his Mexican hands, and they go and hitch up sundry and divers vehicles; and mighty soon out comes one of the sisters or so and some of the two or three men. But two of the two or three men carries between 'em the corkscrew man who spoke in a tone of voice, and lays him flat down in one of the wagons. And they all might have been seen wending their way away.

' "Bud," says Luke to me, "I want you to fix up a little and go up to San Antone with me."

' "Let me get on my Mexican spurs," says I, "and I'm your company."

'One of the sisters or so seems to have stayed at the ranch with Mrs. Summers and the kid. We rides to Encinal and catches the International, and hits San Antone in the morning. After breakfast Luke steers me straight to the office of a lawyer. They go in a room and talk and then come out.

' "Oh, there won't be any trouble, Mr. Summers," says the lawyer. "I'll acquaint Judge Simmons with the facts to-day; and the matter will be put through as promptly as possible. Law and order reigns in this state as swift and sure as any in the country."

' "I'll wait for the decree if it won't take over half an hour," says Luke.

' "Tut, tut," says the lawyer man. "Law must take its course. Come back day after to-morrow at half-past nine."

'At that time me and Luke shows up, and the lawyer hands him a folded document. And Luke writes him out a cheque.

'On the sidewalk Luke holds up the paper to me and puts a finger the size of a kitchen door latch on it and says:

' "Decree of ab-so-lute divorce with cus-to-dy of the child."

' "Skipping over much what has happened of which I know nothing," says I, "it looks to me like a split. Couldn't the lawyer man have made it a strike for you?"

' "Bud," says he, in a pained style, "that child is the one thing I have to live for. *She* may go; but the boy is mine! – think of it – I have custody of the child."

' "All right," says I. "If it's the law, let's abide by it. But I think," says I, "that Judge Simmons might have used exemplary clemency, or whatever is the legal term, in our case."

'You see, I wasn't inveigled much into the desirableness of having infants around a ranch except the kind that feed themselves and sell for so much on the hoof when they grow up. But Luke was struck with that sort of parental foolishness that I never could understand. All the way riding from the station back to the ranch, he kept pulling that decree out of his pocket and laying his finger on the back of it, and reading off to me the sum and substance of it. "Cus-to-dy of the child, Bud," says he. "Don't forget it – cus-to-dy of the child."

'But when we hits the ranch we finds our decree of court obviated, *nolle prossed*, and remanded for trial. Mrs. Summers and the kid was gone. They tell us that an hour after me and Luke had started for San Antone she had a team hitched and lit out for the nearest station with her trunks and the youngster.

'Luke takes out his decree once more and reads off its emoluments.

' "It ain't possible, Bud," says he, "for this to be. It's contrary to law and order. It's wrote as plain as day here – 'Cus-to-dy of the child.' "

' "There is what you might call a human leaning," says I, "toward smashing 'em both – not to mention the child."

' "Judge Simmons," goes on Luke, "is a incorporated officer of the law. She can't take the boy away. He belongs to me by statutes passed and approved by the state of Texas."

' "And he's removed from the jurisdiction of mundane mandamuses," says I, "by the unearthly statutes of female partiality. Let us praise the Lord and be thankful for whatever small mercies –" I begins; but I see Luke don't listen to me. Tired as he was, he calls for a fresh horse and starts back again for the station.

'He comes back two weeks afterward, not saying much.

' "We can't get the trail," says he; "but we've done all the telegraphing that the wires'll stand, and we've got these city rangers they call detectives on the lookout. In the meantime, Bud," says he, "we'll round up them cows on Brush Creek, and wait for the law to take its course."

'And after that we never alluded to allusions, as you might say.

'Skipping over much what happened in the next twelve years, Luke was made sheriff of Mojada County. He made me his office deputy. Now, don't get in your mind no wrong apparitions of an office deputy doing sums in a book or mashing letters in a cider press. In them days his job was to watch the back windows so nobody didn't plug the sheriff in the rear while he was adding up mileage at his desk in front. And in them days I had qualifications for the job. And there was law and order in Mojada County, and school-books, and all the whisky you wanted, and the Government built its own battleships instead of collecting nickels from the school children to do it with. And, as I say, there was law and order instead of enactments and restrictions such as disfigure our umpire state to-day. We had our office at Bildad, the county seat, from which we emerged forth on necessary occasions to soothe whatever fracases and unrest that might occur in our jurisdiction.

'Skipping over much what happened while me and Luke was sheriff, I want to give you an idea of how the law was respected in them days. Luke was what you would call one of the most conscious men in the world. He never knew much book law, but he had the inner emoluments of justice and mercy inculcated into his system. If a respectable citizen shot a Mexican or held up a train and cleaned out the safe in the express car, and Luke ever got hold of him, he'd give the guilty party such a reprimand and a cussin' out that he'd probable never do it again. But once let somebody steal a horse (unless it was a Spanish pony), or cut a wire fence, or otherwise impair the peace and indignity of Mojada County, Luke and me would be on 'em with habeas corpuses and smokeless powder and all the modern inventions of equity and etiquette.

'We certainly had our county on a basis of lawfulness. I've known persons of Eastern classification with little spotted caps and buttoned-up shoes to get off the train at Bildad and eat sandwiches at the railroad station without being shot at or even roped and drug about by the citizens of the town.

'Luke had his own ideas of legality and justice. He was kind of training me to succeed him when he went out of office. He was always looking ahead to the time when he'd quit sheriffing. What he wanted to do was to build a yellow house with latticework under the porch and have hens scratching in the yard. The one main thing in his mind seemed to be the yard.

' "Bud," he says to me, "by instinct and sentiment I'm a contractor. I want to be a contractor. That's what I'll be when I get out of office."

' "What kind of a contractor?" says I. "It sounds like a kind of a business to me. You ain't going to haul cement or establish branches or work on a railroad, are you?"

' "You don't understand," says Luke. "I'm tired of space and horizons and territory and distances and things like that. What I want is reasonable contraction. I want a yard with a fence around it that you can go out and set on after supper and listen to whip-poor-wills," says Luke.

'That's the kind of a man he was. He was homelike, although he'd had bad luck in such investments. But he never talked about them times on the ranch. It seemed like he'd forgotten about it. I wondered how, with his ideas of yards and chickens and notions of lattice-work, he'd seemed to have got out of his mind that kid of his that had been taken away from him, unlawful, in spite of his decree of court. But he wasn't a man you could ask about such things as he didn't refer to in his own conversation.

'I reckon he'd put all his emotions and ideas into being sheriff. I've read in books about men that was disappointed in these poetic and fine-haired and high-collared affairs with ladies renouncing truck of that kind and wrapping themselves up into some occupation like painting pictures, or herding sheep, or science, or teaching school – something to make 'em forget. Well, I guess that was the way with Luke. But, as he couldn't paint pictures, he took it out in rounding up horse-thieves and in making Mojada County a safe place to sleep in if you was well armed and not afraid of requisitions or tarantulas.

'One day there passes through Bildad a bunch of these money investors from the East, and they stopped off there, Bildad being the dinner station on the I. & G.N. They was just coming back from Mexico looking after mines and such. There was five of 'em – four solid parties, with gold watch-chains, that would grade up over two hundred pounds on the hoof, and one kid about seventeen or eighteen.

'This youngster had on one of them cowboy suits such as tenderfoots bring West with 'em; and you could see he was aching to wing a couple of Indians or bag a grizzly or two with the little pearl-handled gun he had buckled around his waist.

'I walked down to the depot to keep an eye on the outfit and see that they didn't locate any land or scare the cow ponies hitched in front of Murchison's store or act otherwise unseemly. Luke was away after a gang of cattle-thieves down on the Frio, and I always looked after the law and order when he wasn't there.

'After dinner this boy comes out of the dining-room while the train was waiting, and prances up and down the platform ready to shoot all antelope, lions, or private citizens that might endeavour to molest or come too near him. He was a good-looking kid; only he was like all them tenderfoots – he didn't know a law-and-order town when he saw it.

'By and by along comes Pedro Johnson, the proprietor of the Crystal Palace *chili-con-carne* stand in Bildad. Pedro was a man who liked to amuse himself; so he kind of herd rides this youngster laughing at him, tickled to death. I was too far away to hear, but the kid seems to mention some remarks to Pedro, and Pedro goes up and slaps him about nine feet away, and laughs harder than ever. And then the boy gets up quicker than he fell and jerks out his little pearl-handle, and – bing! bing! bing! Pedro gets it three times in special and treasured portions of his carcass. I saw the dust fly off his clothes every time the bullets hit. Sometimes them little thirty-twos cause worry at close range.

'The engine bell was ringing, and the train starting off slow. I goes up to the kid and places him under arrest, and takes away his gun. But the first thing I knew that *caballard* of capitalists makes a break for the train. One of 'em hesitates in front of me for a second, and kind of smiles and shoves his hand up against my chin, and I sort of laid down on the platform and took a nap. I never was afraid of guns; but I don't want any person except a barber to take liberties like that with my face again When I woke up, the whole outfit – train, boy, and all – was gone. I asked about Pedro, and they told me the doctor said he would recover provided his wounds didn't turn out to be fatal.

'When Luke got back three days later, and I told him about it, he was mad all over.

' "Why'n't you telegraph to San Antone," he asks, "and have the bunch arrested there?"

' "Oh, well," says I, "I always did admire telegraphy; but astronomy was what I had took up just then." That capitalist sure knew how to gesticulate with his hands.

'Luke got madder and madder. He investigates and finds in the depot a card one of the men had dropped that gives the address of some *hombre* called Scudder in New York City.

' "Bud," says Luke, "I'm going after that bunch. I'm going there and get the man or boy, as you say he was, and bring him back. I'm sheriff of Mojada County, and I shall keep law and order in its precincts while I'm able to draw a gun. And I want you to go with me. No Eastern Yankee can shoot up a respectable and well-known citizen of Bildad, "specially with a 32-calibre, and escape the law. Pedro Johnson," says Luke, "is one of our most prominent citizens and business men. I'll appoint Sam Bell acting sheriff with penitentiary powers while I'm away, and you and me will take the six-forty-five northbound to-morrow evening and follow up this trail."

' "I'm your company," says I. "I never see this New York, but I'd like to. But, Luke," says I, "don't you have to have a dispensation or a habeas corpus or something from the state, when you reach out that far for rich men and malefactors?"

' "Did I have a requisition," says Luke, "when I went over into the Brazos bottoms and brought back Bill Grimes and two more for holding up the International? Did me and you have a search warrant or a posse comitatus when we rounded up them six Mexican cow-thieves down in Hidalgo? It's my business to keep order in Mojada County."

' "And it's my business as office deputy," says I, "to see that business is carried on according to law. Between us both we ought to keep things pretty well cleaned up.

'So, the next day, Luke packs a blanket and some collars and his mileage book in a haversack, and him and me hits the breeze for New York. It was a powerful long ride. The seats in the cars was too short for six-footers like us to sleep comfortable on; and the conductor had to keep us from getting off at every town that had five-story houses in it. But we got there finally; and we seemed to see right away that he was right about it.

' "Luke," says I, "as office deputy and from a law standpoint, it don't look to me like this place is properly and legally in the jurisdiction of Mojada County, Texas."

' "From the standpoint of order," says he, "it's amenable to answer for its sins to the properly appointed authorities from Bildad to Jerusalem."

' "Amen," says I. "But let's turn our trick sudden, and ride. I don't like the looks of this place."

' "Think of Pedro Johnson," says Luke, "a friend of mine and yours shot down by one of these gilded abolitionists at his very door!"

' "It was at the door of the freight depot," says I. "But the law will not be balked at a quibble like that."

'We put up at one of them big hotels on Broadway. The next morning I goes down about two miles of stairsteps to the bottom and hunts for Luke. It ain't no use. It looks like San Jacinto day in San Antone. There's a thousand folks milling around in a kind of a roofed-over plaza with marble pavements and trees growing right out of 'em, and I see no more chance of finding Luke than if we was hunting each other in the big pear flat down below Old Fort Ewell. But soon Luke and me runs together in one of the turns of them marble alleys.

' "It ain't no use, Bud," says he. "I can't find no place to eat at. I've been looking for restaurant signs and smelling for ham all over the camp. But I'm used to going hungry when I have to. Now," says he, "I'm going out and get a hack and ride down to the address on this Scudder card. You stay here and try to hustle some grub. But I doubt if you'll find it. I wish we'd brought along some corn-meal and bacon and beans. I'll be back when I see this Scudder, if the trail ain't wiped out."

'So I starts foraging for breakfast. For the honour of the old Mojada County I didn't want to seem green to them abolitionists, so every time I turned a corner in them marble halls I went up to the first desk or counter I see and looks around for grub. If I didn't see what I wanted I asked for something else. In about half an hour I had a dozen cigars, five story magazines, and seven or eight railroad time-tables in my pockets, and never a smell of coffee or bacon to point out the trail.

'Once a lady sitting at a table and playing a game kind of like pushpin told me to go into a closet that she called Number 3. I went in and shut the door, and the blamed thing lit itself up. I set down on a stool before a shelf and waited. Thinks I, "This is a private dining-room." But no waiter never came. When I got to sweating good and hard, I goes out again.

' "Did you get what you wanted?" says she.

' "No, ma'am," says I. "Not a bite."

' "Then there's no charge," says she.

' "Thanky, ma'am," says I, and I takes up the trail again.

'By and by I thinks I'll shed etiquette; and I picks up one of them boys with blue clothes and yellow buttons in front, and he leads me to what he calls the caffay breakfast room. And the first thing I lays my eyes on when I go in is that boy that had shot Pedro Johnson. He was setting all alone at a little table, hitting a egg with a spoon like he was afraid he'd break it.

'I takes the chair across the table from him; and he looks insulted and makes a move like he was going to get up.

' "Keep still, son," says I. "You're apprehended, arrested, and in charge of the Texas authorities. Go on and hammer that egg some more if it's the inside of it you want. Now, what did you shoot Mr. Johnson, of Bildad, for?"

' "And may I ask who you are?" says he.

' "You may," says I. "Go ahead."

' "I suppose you're on," says this kid, without batting his eyes. "But what are you eating? Here, waiter!" he calls out, raising his finger. "Take this gentleman's order."

' "A beefsteak," says I, "and some fried eggs and a can of peaches and a quart of coffee will about suffice."

'We talk awhile about the sundries of life and then he says:

' "What are you going to do about that shooting? I had a right to shoot that man," says he. "He called me names that I couldn't overlook, and then he struck me. He carried a gun, too. What else could I do?"

' "We'll have to take you back to Texas," says I.

' "I'd like to go back," says the boy, with a kind of a grin – "if it wasn't on an occasion of this kind. It's the life I like. I've always wanted to ride and shoot and live in the open air ever since I can remember."

' "Who was this gang of stout parties you took this trip with?" I asks.

' "My stepfather," says he, "and some business partners of his in some Mexican mining and land schemes."

' "I saw you shoot Pedro Johnson," says I, "and I took that little popgun away from you that you did it with. And when I did so I noticed three or four little scars in a row over your right eyebrow. You've been in rookus before, haven't you?"

' "I've had these scars ever since I can remember," says he. "I don't know how they came there."

' "Was you ever in Texas before? says I.

' "Not that I remember of," says he. "But I thought I had when we struck the prairie country. But I guess I hadn't."

' "Have you got a mother?" I asks.

' "She died five years ago," says he.

'Skipping over the most of what followed – when Luke came back I turned the kid over to him. He had seen Scudder and told him what he granted; and it seems that Scudder got active with one of these telephones as soon as he left. For in about an hour afterwards there comes to our hotel some of these city rangers in everyday clothes that they call detectives, and marches the whole outfit of us to what they call a magistrate's court. They accuse Luke of attempted kidnapping, and ask him what he has to say.

' "This snipe," says Luke to the Judge, "shot and wilfully punctured with malice and forethought one of the most respected and prominent citizens of the town of Bildad, Texas, Your Honour. And in so doing laid himself liable to the penitence of law and order. And I hereby make claim and demand restitution of the state of New York City for the said alleged criminal; and I know he done it."

' "Have you the usual and necessary requisition papers from the governor of your state?" asks the judge.

' "My usual papers," says Luke, "was taken away from me at the hotel by these gentlemen who represent law and order in your city. They was two Colt's 45's that I've packed for nine years; and if I don't get 'em back, there'll be more trouble. You can ask anybody in Mojada County about Luke Summers. I don't usually need any other kind of papers for what I do."

'I see the judge looks mad, so I steps up and says:

' "Your Honour, the aforesaid defendant, Mr. Luke Summers, sheriff of Mojada County, Texas, is as fine a man as ever threw a rope or upheld the statutes and codicils of the greatest state in the Union. But he –"

'The judge hits his table with a wooden hammer and asks who I am.

' "Bud Oakley," says I. "Office deputy of the sheriff's office of Mojada County, Texas. Representing," says I, "the Law. Luke Summers," I goes on, "represents Order. And if Your Honour will give me about ten minutes in private talk, I'll explain the whole thing to you, and show you the equitable and legal requisition papers which I carry in my pocket."

'The judge kind of half smiles and says he will talk with me in his private room. In there I put the whole up to him in such language as I had, and when we goes outside, he announces the verdict that the young man is delivered into the hands of the Texas authorities; and calls the next case.

'Skipping over much of what happened on the way back, I'll tell you how the thing wound up in Bildad.

'When we got the prisoner in the sheriff's office I says to Luke:

' "You remember that kid of yours – that two-year-old that they stole away from you when the bust-up come?"

'Luke looks black and angry. He'd never let anybody talk to him about that business, and he never mentioned it himself.

' "Toe the mark," says I. "Do you remember when he was toddling around on the porch and fell down on a pair of Mexican spurs and cut four little holes over his right eye? Look at the prisoner," says I, look at his nose and the shape of his head and – why, you old fool, don't you know your own son? – I knew him," says I, "when he perforated Mr Johnson at the depot."

'Luke comes over to me shaking all over. I never saw him lose his nerve before

' "Bud," says he, "I've never had that boy out of my mind one day or one night since he was took away. But I never let on. But can we hold him? – Can we make him stay? – I'll make the best man of him that ever put his foot in a stirrup. Wait a minute," says he, all excited and out of his mind – I ve got something here in my desk – I reckon it'll hold legal yet – I've looked at it a thousand times – 'Cus-to-dy of the child,' " says Luke – " 'Cus-to-dy of the child.' We can hold him on that, can't we? Le'me see if I can find that decree."

'Luke begins to tear his desk to pieces.

' "Hold on," says I. "You are Order and I'm Law. You needn't look for that paper, Luke. It ain't a decree any more. It's requisition papers. It's on file in that Magistrates' office in New York. I took it along when we went, because I was office deputy and knew the law."

' "I've got him back," says Luke. "He's mine again. I never thought –'

' "Wait a minute," says I. "We've got to have law and order. You and me have got to preserve 'em both in Mojada County according to our oath and conscience. The kid shot Pedro Johnson, one of Bildad's most prominent and –"

' "Oh, hell!" says Luke. "That don't amount to anything. That fellow was half Mexican, anyhow." '

LXXII

The Transformation of Martin Burney

IN BEHALF OF SIR WALTER'S soothing plant let us look into the case of Martin Burney.

They were constructing the Speedway along the west bank of the Harlem River. The grub-boat of Dennis Corrigan, sub-contractor, was moored to a tree on the bank. Twenty-two men belonging to the little green island toiled there at the sinew-cracking labour. One among them, who wrought in the kitchen of the grub-boat, was of the race of the Goths. Over them all stood the exorbitant Corrigan, harrying them like the captain of a galley crew. He paid them so little that most of the gang, work as they might, earned little more than food and tobacco; many of them were in debt to him. Corrigan boarded them all in the grub-boat, and gave them good grub, for he got it back in work.

Martin Burney was farthest behind of all. He was a little man, all muscles and hands and feet, with a grey-red, stubbly beard. He was too light for the work, which would have glutted the capacity of a steam shovel.

The work was hard. Besides that, the banks of the river were humming with mosquitoes. As a child in a dark room fixes his regard on the pale light of a comforting window, these toilers watched the sun that brought around the one hour of the day that tasted less bitter. After the sundown supper they would huddle together on the river bank, and send the mosquitoes whining and

eddying back from the malignant puffs of twenty-three reeking
pipes. Thus socially banded against the foe, they wrenched out of
the hour a few well-smoked drops from the cup of joy.

Each week Burney grew deeper in debt. Corrigan kept a small
stock of goods on the boat, which he sold to the men at prices that
brought him no loss. Burney was a good customer at the tobacco
counter. One sack when he went to work in the morning and one
when he came in at night, so much was his account swelled daily.
Burney was something of a smoker. Yet it was not true that he ate
his meals with a pipe in his mouth, which had been said of him. The
little man was not discontented. He had plenty to eat, plenty of
tobacco, and a tyrant to curse; so why should not he, an Irishman,
be well satisfied?

One morning as he was starting with the others for work he
stopped at the pine counter for his usual sack of tobacco.

'There's no more for ye,' said Corrigan. 'Your account's closed.
Ye are a losing investment. No, not even tobaccy, my son. No more
tobaccy on account. If ye want to work on and eat, do so, but the
smoke of ye has all ascended. 'Tis my advice that ye hunt a new job.'

'I have no tobaccy to smoke in my pipe this day, Mr. Corrigan,'
said Burney, not quite understanding that such a thing could
happen to him.

'Earn it,' said Corrigan, 'and then buy it.'

Burney stayed on. He knew of no other job. At first he did not realize that tobacco had got to be his father and mother, his confessor
and sweetheart, and wife and child.

For three days he managed to fill his pipe from the other men's
sacks, and then they shut him off, one and all. They told him,
rough but friendly, that of all things in the world tobacco must be
quickest forthcoming to a fellow-man desiring it, but that beyond
the immediate temporary need requisition upon the store of a
comrade is pressed with great danger to friendship.

Then the blackness of the pit arose and filled the heart of
Burney. Sucking the corpse of his deceased dudheen, he staggered
through his duties with his barrowful of stones and dirt, feeling for
the first time that the curse of Adam was upon him. Other men
bereft of a pleasure might have recourse to other delights, but
Burney had only two comforts in life. One was his pipe, the other
was an ecstatic hope that there would be no Speedways to build on
the other side of Jordan.

At meal times he would let the other men go first into the grub-
boat, and then he would go down on his hands and knees, grovelling

fiercely upon the ground where they had been sitting, trying to find some stray crumbs of tobacco. Once he sneaked down the river bank and filled his pipe with dead willow leaves. At the first whiff of the smoke he spat in the direction of the boat and put the finest curse he knew on Corrigan – one that began with the first Corrigans born on earth and ended with the Corrigans that shall hear the trumpet of Gabriel blow. He began to hate Corrigan with all his shaking nerves and soul. Even murder occurred to him in a vague sort of way. Five days he went without the taste of tobacco – he who had smoked all day and thought the night misspent in which he had not awakened for a pipeful or two under the bedclothes.

One day a man stopped at the boat to say that there was work to be had in the Bronx Park, where a large number of labourers were required in making some improvements.

After dinner Burney walked thirty yards down the river bank away from the maddening smell of the others' pipes. He sat down upon a stone. He was thinking he would set out for the Bronx. At least he could earn tobacco there. What if the books did say he owed Corrigan? Any man's work was worth his keep. But then he hated to go without getting even with the hard-hearted screw who had put his pipe out. Was there any way to do it?

Softly stepping among the clods came Tony, he of the race of Goths, who worked in the kitchen. He grinned at Burney's elbow, and that unhappy man, full of race animosity and holding urbanity in contempt, growled at him: 'What d'ye want, ye – Dago?'

Tony also contained a grievance – and a plot. He, too, was a Corrigan hater, and had been primed to see it in others.

'How you like-a Mr. Corrigan?' he asked. 'You think-a him a nice-a man?'

'To hell with 'm,' he said. 'May his liver turn to water, and the bones of him crack in the cold of his heart. May dog fennel grow upon his ancestors' graves, and the grandsons of his children be born without eyes. May whisky turn to clabber in his mouth, and every time he sneezes may he blister the soles of his feet. And the smoke of his pipe – may it make his eyes water, and the drops fall on the grass that his cows eat and poison the butter that he spreads on his bread.'

Though Tony remained a stranger to the beauties of this imagery, he gathered from it the conviction that it was sufficiently anti-Corrigan in its tendency. So, with the confidence of a fellow-conspirator, he sat by Burney upon the stone and unfolded his plot.

It was very simple in design. Every day after dinner it was Corrigan's habit to sleep for an hour in his bunk. At such times it was the duty of the cook and his helper, Tony, to leave the boat so that no noise might disturb the autocrat. The cook always spent this hour in walking exercise. Tony's plan was this: After Corrigan should be asleep he (Tony) and Burney would cut the mooring ropes that held the boat to the shore. Tony lacked the nerve to do the deed alone. Then the awkward boat would swing out into a swift current and surely overturn against a rock there was below.

'Come on and do it,' said Burney. 'If the back of ye aches from the lick he give ye as the pit of me stomach does for the taste of a bit of smoke, we can't cut the ropes too quick.'

'All a-right,' said Tony. 'But better wait 'bout-a ten minute more. Give-a Corrigan plenty time get good-a sleep.'

They waited, sitting upon the stone. The rest of the men were at work out of sight around a bend in the road. Everything would have gone well – except, perhaps, with Corrigan, had not Tony been moved to decorate the plot with its conventional accompaniment. He was of dramatic blood, and perhaps he intuitively divined the appendage to villainous machinations as prescribed by the stage. He pulled from his shirt bosom a long, black, beautiful, venomous cigar, and handed it to Burney.

'You like-a smoke while we wait?' he asked.

Burney clutched it and snapped off the end as a terrier bites at a rat. He laid it to his lips like a long-lost sweetheart. When the smoke began to draw he gave a long, deep sigh, and the bristles of his grey-red moustache curled down over the cigar like the talons of an eagle. Slowly the red faded from the whites of his eyes. He fixed his gaze dreamily upon the hills across the river. The minutes came and went.

' "Bout time to go now,' said Tony. 'That damn-a Corrigan he be in the reever very quick.'

Burney started out of his trance with a grunt. He turned his head and gazed with a surprised and pained severity at his accomplice. He took the cigar partly from his mouth, but sucked it back again immediately, chewed it lovingly once or twice, and spoke, in virulent puffs, from the corner of his mouth:

'What is it, ye yaller haythen? Would ye lay contrivances against the enlightened races of the earth, ye instigator of illegal crimes? Would ye seek to persuade Martin Burney into the dirty tricks of an indecent Dago? Would ye be for murderin' your benefactor, the good man that gives ye food and work? Take that, ye punkin-coloured assassin!'

The torrent of Burney's indignation carried with it bodily assault. The toe of his shoe sent the would-be cutter of ropes tumbling from his seat.

Tony arose and fled. His vendetta he again relegated to the files of things that might have been. Beyond the boat he fled and away-away; he was afraid to remain.

Burney, with expanded chest, watched his late co-plotter disappear. Then he, too, departed, setting his face in the direction of the Bronx.

In his wake was a rank and pernicious trail of noisome smoke that brought peace to his heart and drove the birds from the roadside into the deepest thickets.

LXXIII

Roads of Destiny

I go to seek on many roads
            What is to be. True heart and strong, with love to light –
Will they not bear me in the fight
To order, shun or wield or mould
            My Destiny?
                              Unpublished Poems of David Mignot.

THE SONG WAS OVER. The words were David's; the air, one of the countryside. The company about the inn table applauded heartily, for the young poet paid for the wine. Only the notary, M. Papineau, shook his head a little at the lines, for he was a man of books, and he had not drunk with the rest.

David went out into the village street, where the night air drove the wine vapour from his head. And then he remembered that he and Yvonne had quarrelled that day, and that he had resolved to leave his home that night to seek fame and honour in the great world outside.

'When my poems are on every man's tongue,' he told himself, in a fine exhilaration, 'she will, perhaps, think of the hard words she spoke this day.'

Except the roysterers in the tavern, the village folk were abed. David crept softly into his room in the shed of his father's cottage and made a bundle of his small store of clothing. With this upon a staff he set his face outward upon the road that ran from Vernoy.

He passed his father's herd of sheep huddled in their nightly pen – the sheep he herded daily, leaving them to scatter while he wrote verses on scraps of paper. He saw a light yet shining in Yvonne s window, and a weakness shook his purpose of a sudden. Perhaps that light meant that she rued, sleepless, her anger, and that morning might – But, no! His decision was made. Vernoy was no place for him. Not one soul there could share his thoughts. Out along that road lay his fate and his future.

Three leagues across the dim, moonlit champaign ran the road, straight as a ploughman's furrow. It was believed in the village that the road ran to Paris, at least; and this name the poet whispered often to himself as he walked. Never so far from Vernoy had David travelled before.

THE LEFT BRANCH

Three leagues, then, the road ran, and turned into a puzzle. It joined with another and a larger road at right angles. David stood, uncertain, for a while, and then took the road to the left.

Upon this more important highway were, imprinted in the dust, wheel tracks left by the recent passage of some vehicle. Some half an hour later these traces were verified by the sight of a ponderous carriage mired in a little brook at the bottom of a steep hill. The driver and postilions were shouting and tugging at the horses' bridles. On the road at one side stood a huge, black-clothed man and a slender lady wrapped in a long, light cloak.

David saw the lack of skill in the efforts of the servants. He quietly assumed control of the work. He directed the outriders to cease their clamour at the horses and to exercise their strength upon the wheels. The driver alone urged the animals with his familiar voice; David himself heaved a powerful shoulder at the rear of the carriage, and with one harmonious tug the great vehicle rolled up on solid ground. The outriders climbed to their places.

David stood for a moment upon one foot. The huge gentleman waved a hand. 'You will enter the carriage,' he said, in a voice large, like himself, but smoothed by art and habit. Obedience belonged in the path of such a voice. Brief as was the young poet's hesitation, it was cut shorter still by a renewal of the command. David's foot went to the step. In the darkness he perceived dimly the form of the lady upon the rear seat. He was about to seat himself opposite, when the voice again swayed him to its will: 'You will sit at the lady's side.'

The gentleman swung his great weight to the forward seat. The carriage proceeded up the hill. The lady was shrunk, silent, into her corner. David could not estimate whether she was old or young, but a delicate, mild perfume from her clothes stirred his poet's fancy to the belief that there was loveliness beneath the mystery. Here was an adventure such as he had often imagined. But as yet he held no key to it, for no word was spoken while he sat with his impenetrable companions.

In an hour's time David perceived through the window that the vehicle traversed the street of some town. Then it stopped in front of a closed and darkened house, and a postilion alighted to hammer impatiently upon the door. A latticed window above flew wide and a night-capped head popped out.

'Who are ye that disturb honest folk at this time of night? My house is closed. 'Tis too late for profitable travellers to be abroad. Cease knocking at my door, and be off.'

'Open!' spluttered the postilion, loudly; 'open for Monseigneur the Marquis de Beaupertuys.'

'Ah!' cried the voice above. 'Ten thousand pardons, my lord. I did not know – the hour is so late – at once shall the door be opened, and the house placed at my lord's disposal.'

Inside was heard the clink of chain and bar, and the door was flung open. Shivering with chill and apprehension, the landlord of the Silver Flagon stood, half clad, candle in hand, upon the threshold.

David followed the marquis out of the carriage. 'Assist the lady,' he was ordered. The poet obeyed. He felt her small hand tremble as he guided her descent. 'Into the house,' was the next command.

The room was the long dining-hall of the tavern. A great oak table ran down its length. The huge gentlemen seated himself in a chair at the nearer end. The lady sank into another against the wall, with an air of great weariness. David stood, considering how best he might now take his leave and continue upon his way.

'My lord,' said the landlord, bowing to the floor, 'h-had I ex-expected this honour, entertainment would have been ready. T t-there is wine and cold fowl and m-m-maybe –'

'Candles,' said the marquis, spreading the fingers of one plump white hand in a gesture he had.

'Y-yes, my lord.' He fetched half a dozen candles, lighted them, and set them upon the table.

'If monsieur would, perhaps, deign to taste a certain Burgundy – there is a cask –'

'Candles,' said monsieur, spreading his fingers.

'Assuredly – quickly – I fly, my lord.'

A dozen more lighted candles shone in the hall. The great bulk of the marquis overflowed his chair. He was dressed in fine black from head to foot save for the snowy ruffles at his wrists and throat. Even the hilt and scabbard of his sword were black. His expression was one of sneering pride. The ends of an upturned moustache reached nearly to his mocking eyes.

The lady sat motionless, and now David perceived that she was young, and possessed of pathetic and appealing beauty. He was startled from the contemplation of her forlorn loveliness by the booming voice of the marquis.

'What is your name and pursuit?'

'David Mignot. I am a poet.'

The moustache of the marquis curled nearer to his eyes.

'How do you live?'

'I am also a shepherd; I guarded my father's flock,' David answered, with his head high, but a flush upon his cheek.

'Then listen, master shepherd and poet, to the fortune you have blundered upon to-night. This lady is my niece, Mademoiselle Lucie de Varennes. She is of noble descent and is possessed of ten thousand francs a year in her own right. As to her charms, you have but to observe for yourself. If the inventory pleases your shepherd's heart, she becomes your wife at a word. Do not interrupt me. To-night I conveyed her to the château of the Comte de Villemaur, to whom her hand had been promised. Guests were present; the priest was waiting; her marriage to one eligible in rank and fortune was ready to be accomplished. At the altar this demoiselle, so meek and dutiful, turned upon me like a leopardess, charged me with cruelty and crimes, and broke, before the gaping priest, the troth I had plighted for her. I swore there and then, by ten thousand devils, that she should marry the first man we met after leaving the château, be he prince, charcoal-burner, or thief. You, shepherd, are the first. Mademoiselle must be wed this night. If not you, then another. You have ten minutes in which to make your decision. Do not vex me with words or questions. Ten minutes, shepherd; and they are speeding.'

The marquis drummed loudly with his white fingers upon the table. He sank into a veiled attitude of waiting. It was as if some great house had shut its doors and windows against approach. David would have spoken, but the huge man's bearing stopped his tongue. Instead he stood by the lady's chair and bowed.

'Mademoiselle,' he said, and he marvelled to find his words flowing easily before so much elegance and beauty. 'You have heard me say I was a shepherd. I have also had the fancy, at times, that I am a poet. If it be the test of a poet to adore and cherish the beautiful that fancy is now strengthened. Can I serve you in any way, mademoiselle?'

The young woman looked up at him with eyes dry and mournful. His frank, glowing face, made serious by the gravity of the adventure, his strong, straight figure and the liquid sympathy in his blue eyes, perhaps, also, her imminent need of long-denied help and kindness, thawed her to sudden tears.

'Monsieur,' she said, in low tones, 'you look to be true and kind. He is my uncle, the brother of my father, and my only relative. He loved my mother, and he hates me because I am like her. He has made my life one long terror. I am afraid of his very looks, and never before dared to disobey him. But to-night he would have married me to a man three times my age. You will forgive me for bringing this vexation upon you, monsieur. You will, of course, decline this mad act he tries to force upon you. But let me thank you for your generous words, at least. I have had none spoken to me in so long.'

There was now something more than generosity in the poet's eye. Poet he must have been, for Yvonne was forgotten; this fine, new loveliness held him with its freshness and grace. The subtle perfume from her filled him with strange emotions. His tender look fell warmly upon her. She leaned to it, thirstily.

'Ten minutes,' said David, 'is given me in which to do what I would devote years to achieve. I will not say I pity you, mademoiselle; it would not be true — I love you. I cannot ask love from you yet, but let me rescue you from this cruel man, and, in time, love may come. I think I have a future; I will not always be a shepherd. For the present I will cherish you with all my heart and make your life less sad. Will you trust your fate to me, mademoiselle?'

'Ah, you would sacrifice yourself from pity!'

'From love. The time is almost up, mademoiselle.'

'You will regret it, and despise me.'

'I will live only to make you happy, and myself worthy of you.'

Her fine small hand crept into his from beneath her cloak.

'I will trust you,' she breathed, 'with my life. And — and love — may not be so far off as you think. Tell him. Once away from the power of his eyes I may forget.'

David went and stood before the marquis. The black figure stirred, and the mocking eyes glanced at the great hall clock.

'Two minutes to spare. A shepherd requires eight minutes to decide whether he will accept a bride of beauty and income! Speak up, shepherd; do you consent to become mademoiselle's husband?'

'Mademoiselle,' said David, standing proudly, 'has done me the honour to yield to my request that she become my wife.'

'Well said!' said the marquis. 'You have yet the making of a courtier in you, master shepherd. Mademoiselle could have drawn a worse prize, after all. And now to be done with the affair as quick as the Church and the devil will allow!'

He struck the table soundly with his sword hilt. The landlord came, knee-shaking, bringing more candles in the hope of anticipating the great lord's whims. 'Fetch a priest,' said the marquis, 'a priest; do you understand? In ten minutes have a priest here, or –'

The landlord dropped his candles and flew.

The priest came, heavy-eyed and ruffled. He made David Mignot and Lucie de Varennes man and wife, pocketed a gold piece that the marquis tossed him, and shuffled out again into the night.

'Wine,' ordered the marquis, spreading his ominous fingers at the host.

'Fill glasses,' he said, when it was brought. He stood up at the head of the table in the candlelight, a black mountain of venom and conceit with something like the memory of an old love turned to poison in his eye, as it fell upon his niece.

'Monsieur Mignot,' he said, raising his wineglass, 'drink after I say this to you: You have taken to be your wife one who will make your life a foul and wretched thing. The blood in her is an inheritance running black lies and red ruin. She will bring you shame and anxiety. The devil that descended to her is there in her eyes and skin and mouth that stoop even to beguile a peasant. There is your promise, monsieur poet, for a happy life. Drink your wine. At last, mademoiselle, I am rid of you.'

The marquis drank. A little grievous cry, as if from a sudden wound, came from the girl's lips. David, with his glass in his hand, stepped forward three paces and faced the marquis. There was little of a shepherd in his bearing.

'Just now,' he said, calmly, 'you did me the honour to call me "monsieur." May I hope, therefore, that my marriage to mademoiselle has placed me somewhat nearer to you in – let us say, reflected rank – has given me the right to stand more as an equal to monseigneur in a certain little piece of business I have in my mind?'

'You may hope, shepherd,' sneered the marquis.

'Then,' said David, dashing his glass of wine into the contemptuous eyes that mocked him, 'perhaps you will condescend to fight me.'

The fury of the great lord outbroke in one sudden curse like a blast from a horn. He tore his sword from its black sheath; he called to the hovering landlord: "A sword there, for this lout!' He turned to the lady, with a laugh that chilled her heart, and said: 'You put much labour upon me, madame. It seems I must find you a husband and make you a widow in the same night.'

'I know not sword-play,' said David. He flushed to make the confession before his lady.

' "I know not sword-play," ' mimicked the marquis. 'Shall we fight like peasants with oaken cudgels? *Hola!* François, my pistols!'

A postilion brought two shining great pistols ornamented with carven silver, from the carriage holsters. The marquis tossed one upon the table near David's hand. 'To the other end of the table,' he cried; 'even a shepherd may pull a trigger. Few of them attain the honour to die by the weapon of a De Beaupertuys.'

The shepherd and the marquis faced each other from the ends of the long table. The landlord, in an ague of terror, clutched the air and stammered; 'M-M-Monseigneur, for the love of Christ! not in my house! – do not spill blood – it will ruin my custom –' The look of the marquis, threatening him, paralysed his tongue.

'Coward,' cried the lord of Beaupertuys, 'cease chattering your teeth long enough to give the word for us, if you can.'

Mine host's knees smote the floor. He was without a vocabulary. Even sounds were beyond him. Still, by gestures he seemed to beseech peace in the name of his house and custom

'I will give the word,' said the lady, in a clear voice. She went up to David and kissed him sweetly. Her eyes were sparkling bright, and colour had come to her cheek. She stood against the wall, and the two men levelled their pistols for her count.

'*Un – deux – trois!*'

The two reports came so nearly together that the candles flickered but once. The marquis stood, smiling, the fingers of his left hand resting, outspread, upon the end of the table. David remained erect, and turned his head very slowly, searching for his wife with his eyes. Then, as a garment falls from where it is hung, he sank, crumpled, upon the floor.

With a little cry of terror and despair, the widowed maid ran and stooped above him. She found his wound, and then looked up with her old look of pale melancholy. 'Through his heart,' she whispered. 'Oh, his heart!'

'Come,' boomed the great voice of the marquis, 'out with you to the carriage! Daybreak shall not find you on my hands. Wed you shall be again, and to a living husband, this night. The next we come upon, my lady, highwayman or peasant. If the road yields no other, then the churl that opens my gates. Out with you to the carriage!'

The marquis, implacable and huge, the lady wrapped again in the mystery of her cloak, the postilion bearing the weapons – all moved out to the waiting carriage. The sound of its ponderous wheels rolling away echoed through the slumbering village. In the hall of the Silver Flagon the distracted landlord wrung his hands above the slain poet's body, while the flames of the four and twenty candles danced and flickered on the table.

THE RIGHT BRANCH

Three leagues, then, the road ran, and turned into a puzzle. It joined with another and larger road at right angles. David stood, uncertain, for a while, and then took the road to the right.

Whither it led he knew not, but he was resolved to leave Vernoy far behind that night. He travelled a league and then passed a large chateau which showed testimony of recent entertainment. Lights shone from every window; from the great stone gateway ran a tracery of wheel tracks drawn in the dust by the vehicles of the guests.

Three leagues farther and David was weary. He rested and slept for a while on a bed of pine boughs at the roadside. Then up and on again along the unknown way.

Thus for five days he travelled the great road, sleeping upon Nature's balsamic beds or in peasants' ricks, eating of their black, hospitable bread, drinking from streams or the willing cup of the goatherd.

At length he crossed a great bridge and set his foot within the smiling city that has crushed or crowned more poets than all the rest of the world. His breath came quickly as Paris sang to him in a little undertone her vital chant of greeting – the hum of voice and foot and wheel.

High up under the eaves of an old house in the Rue Conti, David paid for lodging, and set himself, in a wooden chair, to his poems. The street, once sheltering citizens of import and consequence, was now given over to those who ever follow in the wake of decline.

The houses were tall and still possessed of a ruined dignity, but many of them were empty save for dust and the spider. By night there was the clash of steel and the cries of brawlers straying restlessly from inn to inn. Where once gentility abode was now but a rancid and rude incontinence. But here David found housing commensurate to his scant purse. Daylight and candlelight found him at pen and paper.

One afternoon he was returning from a foraging trip to the lower world, with bread and curds and a bottle of thin wine. Halfway up his dark stairway he met — or rather came upon, for she rested on the stair — a young woman of a beauty that should balk even the justice of a poet's imagination. A loose, dark cloak, flung open, showed a rich gown beneath. Her eyes changed swiftly with every little shade of thought. Within one moment they would be round and artless like a child's, and long and cozening like a gipsy's. One hand raised her gown, undraping a little shoe, highheeled, with its ribbons dangling, untied. So heavenly she was, so unfitted to stoop, so qualified to charm and command! Perhaps she had seen David coming, and had waited for his help there.

Ah, would monsieur pardon that she occupied the stairway, but the shoe! — the naughty shoe! Alas! it would not remain tied. Ah! if monsieur *would* be so gracious!

The poet's fingers trembled as he tied the contrary ribbons. Then he would have fled from the danger of her presence, but the eyes grew long and cozening, like a gipsy's, and held him. He leaned against the balustrade, clutching his bottle of sour wine.

'You have been so good,' she said, smiling. 'Does monsieur, perhaps, live in the house?'

'Yes, madame. I — I think so, madame.'

'Perhaps in the third story, then?'

'No, madame; higher up.'

The lady fluttered her fingers with the least possible gesture of impatience.

'Pardon. Certainly I am not discreet in asking. Monsieur will forgive me? It is surely not becoming that I should inquire where he lodges.'

'Madame, do not say so. I live in the —'

'No, no, no; do not tell me. Now I see that I erred. But I cannot lose the interest I feel in this house and all that is in it. Once it was my home. Often I come here but to dream of those happy days again. Will you let that be my excuse?'

'Let me tell you, then, for you need no excuse,' stammered the poet. 'I live in the top floor − the small room where the stairs turn.'

'In the front room?' asked the lady, turning her head sideways.

'The rear, madame.'

The lady sighed, as if with relief.

'I will detain you no longer then, monsieur,' she said, employing the round and artless eye. Take good care of my house. Alas! only the memories of it are mine now. Adieu, and accept my thanks for your courtesy.'

She was gone, leaving but a smile and a trace of sweet perfume. David climbed the stairs as one in slumber. But he awoke from it, and the smile and the perfume lingered with him and never afterward did either seem quite to leave him. This lady of whom he knew nothing drove him to lyrics of eyes, chansons of swiftly conceived love, odes to curling hair, and sonnets to slippers on slender feet.

Poet he must have been, for Yvonne was forgotten; this fine, new loveliness held him with its freshness and grace. The subtle perfume about her filled him with strange emotions.

On a certain night three persons were gathered about a table in a room on the third floor of the same house. Three chairs and the table and a lighted candle upon it was all the furniture. One of the persons was a huge man, dressed in black. His expression was one of sneering pride. The ends of his upturned moustache reached nearly to his mocking eyes. Another was a lady, young and beautiful, with eyes that could be round and artless, like a child's, or long and cozening, like a gipsy's, but were now keen and ambitious, like any other conspirator's. The third man was a man of action, a combatant, a bold and impatient executive, breathing fire and steel. He was addressed by the others as Captain Desrolles.

This man struck the table with his fist, and said, with controlled violence:

'To-night. To-night as he goes to midnight mass. I am tired of the plotting that get's nowhere. I am sick of signals and ciphers and secret meetings and such *baragouin*. Let us be honest traitors. If France is to be rid of him, let us kill in the open, and not hunt with snares and traps. To-night, I say. I back my words. My hand will do the deed. To-night, as he goes to mass.'

The lady turned upon him a cordial look. Woman, however wedded to plots, must ever thus bow to rash courage. The big man stroked his upturned moustache.

'Dear captain,' he said, in a great voice, softened by habit, 'this time I agree with you. Nothing is to be gained by waiting. Enough of the palace guards belong to us to make the endeavour a safe one.'

'To-night,' repeated Captain Desrolles, again striking the table. 'You have heard me, marquis; my hand will do the deed.'

'But now,' said the huge man, softly, 'comes a question. Word must be sent to our partisans in the palace, and a signal agreed upon. Our staunchest men must accompany the royal carriage. At this hour what messenger can penetrate so far as the south door-way? Ribout is stationed there; once a message is placed in his hands, all will go well.'

'I will send the message,' said the lady.

'You, countess?' said the marquis, raising his eyebrows. 'Your devotion is great, we know, but –'

'Listen!' exclaimed the lady, rising and resting her hands upon the table; 'in a garret of this house lives a youth from the provinces as guileless and tender as the lambs he tended there. I have met him twice or thrice upon the stairs. I questioned him, fearing that he might dwell too near the room in which we are accustomed to meet. He is mine if I will. He writes poems in his garret, and I think he dreams of me. He will do what I say. He shall take the message to the palace.'

The marquis rose from his chair and bowed. 'You did not permit me to finish my sentence countess,' he said. 'I would have said: "Your devotion is great, but your wit and charm are infinitely greater."'

While the conspirators were thus engaged David was polishing some lines addressed to his *amorette d'escalier*. He heard a timorous knock at the door, and opened it, with a great throb, to behold her there, panting as one in straits, with eyes wide open and artless, like a child's.

'Monsieur,' she breathed, 'I come to you in distress. I believe you to be good and true, and I know of no other help. How I flew through the streets among the swaggering men! Monsieur, my mother is dying. My uncle is a captain of guards in the palace of the king. Someone must fly to bring him. May I hope –'

'Mademoiselle,' interrupted David, his eyes shining with the desire to do her service, 'your hopes shall be my wings. Tell me how I may reach him.'

The lady thrust a sealed paper into his hand.

'Go to the south gate – the south gate, mind – and say to the guards there, "The falcon has left his nest." They will pass you, and you will go to the south entrance to the palace. Repeat the words, and give this letter to the man who will reply "Let him strike when he will." This is the password, monsieur, entrusted to me by my uncle, for now when the country is disturbed and men plot against the king's life, no one without it can gain entrance to the palace grounds after nightfall. If you will, monsieur, take him this letter so that my mother may see him before she closes her eyes.'

'Give it me,' said David eagerly. 'But shall I let you return home through the streets alone so late? I –'

'No, no – fly. Each moment is like a precious jewel. Some time,' said the lady, with eyes long and cozening, like a gipsy's, 'I will try to thank you for your goodness.'

The poet thrust the letter into his breast, and bounded down the stairway. The lady, when he was gone, returned to the room below.

The eloquent eyebrows of the marquis interrogated her.

'He is gone,' she said, 'as fleet and stupid as one of his own sheep, to deliver it.'

The table shook again from the batter of Captain Desrolles's fist.

'Sacred name!' he cried; 'I have left my pistols behind! I can trust no others.'

'Take this,' said the marquis, drawing from beneath his cloak a shining, great weapon, ornamented with carven silver. 'There are none truer. But guard it closely, for it bears my arms and crest, and already I am suspected. Me, I must put many leagues between myself and Paris this night. To-morrow must find me in my chateau. After you, dear countess.'

The marquis puffed out the candle. The lady, well cloaked, and the two gentlemen softly descended the stairway and flowed into the crowd that roamed along the narrow pavements of the Rue Conti.

David sped. At the south gate of the king's residence a halberd was laid to his breast, but he turned its point with the words: 'The falcon has left his nest.'

'Pass, brother,' said the guard, 'and go quickly.'

On the south steps of the palace they moved to seize him, but again the mot *de passe* charmed the watchers. One among them stepped forward and began: 'Let him strike –' but a flurry among the guards told of a surprise. A man of keen look and soldierly

stride suddenly pressed through them and seized the letter which
David held in his hand. 'Come with me,' he said and led him
inside the great hall. Then he tore open the letter and read it. He
beckoned to a man uniformed as an officer of musketeers, who
was passing. 'Captain Tetreau, you will have the guards at the
south entrance and the south gate arrested and confined. Place
men known to be loyal in their places.' To David he said 'Come
with me.'

He conducted him through a corridor and an ante-room into a
spacious chamber, where a melancholy man, sombrely dressed, sat
brooding in a great, leather-covered chair. To that man he said-

'Sire, I have told you that the palace is as full of traitors and
spies as a sewer is of rats. You have thought, sire, that it was my
fancy. This man penetrated to your very door by their connivance.
He bore a letter which I have intercepted. I have brought him
here that your majesty may no longer think my zeal excessive.'

'I will question him,' said the king, stirring in his chair. He
looked at David with heavy eyes dulled by an opaque film. The
poet bent his knee.

'From where do you come?' asked the king.

'From the village of Vernoy, in the province of Eure-et-Loir,
sire.'

'What do you follow in Paris?'

'I – I would be a poet, sire.'

'What did you in Vernoy?'

'I minded my father's flock of sheep.'

The king stirred again, and the film lifted from his eyes.

'Ah! in the fields!'

'Yes, sire.'

'You lived in the fields; you went out in the cool of the morning
and lay among the hedges in the grass. The flock distributed itself
upon the hill-side; you drank of the living stream; you ate your
sweet, brown bread in the shade, and you listened, doubtless, to
blackbirds piping in the grove. Is not that so, the shepherd?'

'It is, sire,' answered David, with a sigh; 'and to the bees at the
flowers, and, maybe, to the grape gatherers singing on the hill.'

'Yes, yes,' said the king, impatiently; 'maybe to them; but surely
to the blackbirds. They whistled often in the grove, did they not?'

'Nowhere, sire, so sweetly as in Eure-et-Loir. I have endeavoured
to express their song in some verses that I have written.'

'Can you repeat those verses?' asked the king, eagerly. 'A long
time ago I listened to the blackbirds. It would be something better

than a kingdom if one could rightly construe their song. And at
night you drove the sheep to the fold and then sat, in peace and
tranquillity, to your pleasant bread. Can you repeat those verses,
shepherd?'

'They run this way, sire,' said David, with respectful ardour:

> ' "Lazy shepherd, see your lambkins
>   Skip, ecstatic, on the mead;
> See the firs dance in the breezes,
>   Hear Pan blowing at his reed.

> ' "Hear us calling from the tree-tops,
>   See us swoop upon your flock;
> Yield us wool to make our nests warm
>   In the branches of the –" '

'If it please your majesty,' interrupted a harsh voice, 'I will ask a
question or two of this rhymester. There is little time to spare. I
crave pardon, sire, if my anxiety for your safety offends.'

'The loyalty,' said the king, 'of the Duke D'Aumale is too well
proven to give offence.' He sank into his chair, and the film came
again over his eyes.

'First,' said the duke, 'I will read you the letter he brought:

> ' "To-night is the anniversary of the dauphin's death. If he goes,
> as is his custom, to midnight mass to pray for the soul of his son,
> the falcon will strike, at the corner of the Rue Esplanade. If this be
> his intention, set a red light in the upper room at the south-west
> corner of the palace, that the falcon may take heed."

'Peasant,' said the duke, sternly, 'you have heard these words.
Who gave you this message to bring?'

'My lord duke,' said David, sincerely, 'I will tell you. A lady gave
it me. She said her mother was ill, and that this writing would
fetch her uncle to her bedside. I do not know the meaning of the
letter, but I will swear that she is beautiful and good.'

'Describe the woman,' commanded the duke, 'and how you
came to be her dupe.'

'Describe her!' said David, with a tender smile. 'You would
command words to perform miracles. Well, she is made of sunshine and deep shade. She is slender, like the alders, and moves
with their grace. Her eyes change while you gaze into them; now
round, and then half shut as the sun peeps between two clouds.
When she comes, heaven is all about her; when she leaves there is

chaos and a scent of hawthorn blossoms. She came to me in the Rue Conti, number twenty-nine.'

'It is the house,' said the duke, turning to the king, 'that we have been watching. Thanks to the poet's tongue, we have a picture of the infamous Countess Quebedaux.'

'Sire and my lord duke,' said David, earnestly, 'I hope my poor words have done no injustice. I have looked into that lady's eyes. I will stake my life that she is an angel, letter or no letter.'

The duke looked at him steadily. 'I will put you to the proof,' he said, slowly. 'Dressed as the king, you shall, yourself, attend mass in his carriage at midnight. Do you accept the test?'

David smiled. 'I have looked into her eyes,' he said. 'I had my proof there. Take yours how you will.'

Half an hour before twelve the Duke D'Aumale with his own hands set a red lamp in a south-west window of the palace. At ten minutes to the hour, David, leaning on his arm, dressed as the king, from top to toe, with his head bowed in his cloak, walked slowly from the royal apartments to the waiting carriage. The duke assisted him inside and closed the door. The carriage whirled away along its route to the cathedral.

On the qui vive at a house at the corner of the Rue Esplanade was Captain Tetreau with twenty men, ready to pounce upon the conspirators when they should appear.

But it seemed that, for some reason, the plotters had slightly altered their plans. When the royal carriage had reached the Rue Christopher, one square nearer than the Rue Esplanade, forth from it burst Captain Desrolles, with his band of would-be regicides, and assailed the equipage. The guards upon the carriage, though surprised at the premature attack, descended and fought valiantly. The noise of conflict attracted the force of Captain Tetreau, and they came pelting down the street to the rescue. But, in the meantime, the desperate Desrolles had torn open the door of the king's carriage, thrust his weapon against the body of the dark figure inside, and fired.

Now, with loyal reinforcements at hand, the street rang with cries and the rasp of steel, but the frightened horses had dashed away. Upon the cushions lay the dead body of the poor mock king and poet, slain by a ball from the pistol of Monseigneur, the Marquis de Beaupertuys.

THE MAIN ROAD
Three leagues, then, the road ran, and turned into a puzzle. It joined

*with another and larger road at right angles. David stood, uncertain, for
a while, and then sat himself to rest upon its side.*

Whither those roads led he knew not. Either way there seemed
to lie a great world full of chance and peril. And then, sitting
there, his eye fell upon a bright star, one that he and Yvonne had
named for theirs. That set him thinking of Yvonne, and he wondered if he had not been too hasty. Why should he leave her and
his home because a few hot words had come between them? Was
love so brittle a thing that jealousy, the very proof of it, could
break it? Mornings always brought a cure for the little heartaches
of evening. There was yet time for him to return home without
anyone in the sweetly-sleeping village of Vernoy being the wiser.
His heart was Yvonne's; there where he had lived always he could
write his poems and find his happiness.

David rose, and shook off his unrest and the wild mood that had
tempted him. He set his face steadfastly back along the road he
had come. By the time he had re-travelled the road to Vernoy his
desire to rove was gone. He passed the sheepfold, and the sheep
scurried, with a drumming flutter, at his late footsteps, warming
his heart by the homely sound. He crept without noise into his
little room and lay there, thankful that his feet had escaped the
distress of new roads that night.

How well he knew woman's heart! The next evening Yvonne was
at the well in the road where the young congregated in order that
the *cure* might have business. The corner of her eye was engaged in
a search for David, albeit her set mouth seemed unrelenting. He
saw the look; braved the mouth, drew from it a recantation, and,
later, a kiss as they walked homeward together.

Three months afterward they were married. David's father was
shrewd and prosperous. He gave them a wedding that was heard
of three leagues away. Both the young people were favourites in
the village. There was a procession in the streets, a dance on the
green; they had the marionettes and a tumbler out from Dreux to
delight the guests.

Then a year, and David's father died. The sheep and the cottage
descended to him. He already had the seemliest wife in the village.
Yvonne's milk pails and her brass kettles were bright – *ouf!* they
blinded you in the sun when you passed that way. But you must
keep your eyes upon her yard, for her flower beds were so neat
and gay they restored to you your sight. And you might hear her
sing, aye, as far as the double chestnut tree above Père Gruneau's
blacksmith forge.

But a day came when David drew out paper from a long-shut drawer, and began to bite the end of a pencil. Spring had come again and touched his heart. Poet he must have been, for now Yvonne was well-nigh forgotten. This fine new loveliness of earth held him with its witchery and grace. The perfume from her woods and meadows stirred him strangely. Daily had he gone forth with his flock, and brought it safe at night. But now he stretched himself under the hedge and pieced words together on his bits of paper. The sheep strayed, and the wolves, perceiving that difficult poems make easy mutton, ventured from the woods and stole his lambs.

David's stock of poems grew larger and his flock smaller. Yvonne's nose and temper waxed sharp and her talk blunt. Her pans and kettles grew dull, but her eyes had caught their flash. She pointed out to the poet that his neglect was reducing the flock and bringing woe upon the household. David hired a boy to guard the sheep, locked himself in the little room in the top of the cottage, and wrote more poems. The boy, being a poet by nature, but not furnished with an outlet in the way of writing, spent his time in slumber. The wolves lost no time in discovering that poetry and sleep are practically the same; so the flock steadily grew smaller. Yvonne's ill temper increased at an equal rate. Sometimes she would stand in the yard and rail at David through his high window. Then you could hear her as far as the double chestnut tree above Père Gruneau's forge.

M. Papineau, the kind, wise, meddling old notary, saw this, as he saw everything at which his nose pointed. He went to David, fortified himself with a great pinch of snuff, and said:

'Friend Mignot, I affixed the seal upon the marriage certificate of your father. It would distress me to be obliged to attest a paper signifying the bankruptcy of his son. But that is what you are coming to. I speak as an old friend. Now, listen to what I have to say. You have your heart set, I perceive, upon poetry. At Dreux I have a friend, one Monsieur Bril – Georges Bril. He lives in a little cleared space in a houseful of books. He is a learned man; he visits Paris each year; he himself has written books. He will tell you when the catacombs were made, how they found out the names of the stars, and why the plover has a long bill. The meaning and the form of poetry is to him as intelligent as the baa of a sheep is to you. I will give you a letter to him, and you shall take him your poems and let him read them. Then you will know if you shall write more, or give your attention to your wife and business.'

'Write the letter,' said David; 'I am sorry you did not speak of this sooner.'

At sunrise next morning he was on the road to Dreux with the precious roll of poems under his arm. At noon he wiped the dust from his feet at the door of Monsieur Bril. That learned man broke the seal of M. Papineau's letter, and sucked up its contents through his gleaming spectacles as the sun draws water. He took David inside to his study and sat him down upon a little island beat upon by a sea of books.

Monsieur Bril had a conscience. He flinched not even at a mass of manuscript the thickness of a finger length and rolled to an incorrigible curve. He broke the back of the roll against his knee and began to read. He slighted nothing; he bored into the lump as a worm into a nut, seeking for a kernel.

Meanwhile, David sat, marooned, trembling in the spray of so much literature. It roared in his ears. He held no chart or compass for voyaging in that sea. Half the world, he thought, must be writing books.

Monsieur Bril bored to the last page of the poems. Then he took off his spectacles and wiped them with his handkerchief.

'My old friend, Papineau, is well?' he asked

'In the best of health,' said David.

'How many sheep have you, Monsieur Mignot?'

'Three hundred and nine, when I counted them yesterday. The flock has had ill fortune. To that number it has decreased from eight hundred and fifty.'

'You have a wife and a home, and lived in comfort. The sheep brought you plenty. You went into the fields with them and lived in the keen air and ate the sweet bread of contentment. You had but to be vigilant and recline there upon Nature's breast, listening to the whistle of the blackbirds in the grove. Am I right thus far?'

'It was so,' said David.

'I have read all your verses,' continued Monsieur Bril, his eyes wandering about his sea of books as if he conned the horizon for a sail. 'Look yonder, through that window, Monsieur Mignot; tell me what you see in that tree.'

'I see a crow,' said David, looking.

'There is a bird,' said Monsieur Bril, 'that shall assist me where I am disposed to shirk a duty. You know that bird, Monsieur Mignot; he is the philosopher of the air. He is happy through submission to his lot. None so merry or full-crawed as he with his whimsical eye and rollicking step. The fields yield him what he desires. He never grieves that his plumage is not gay, like the oriole's. And you have heard, Monsieur Mignot, the notes that Nature has given him? Is the nightingale any happier, do you think?'

David rose to his feet. The crow cawed harshly from his tree.

'I thank you, Monsieur Bril,' he said, slowly. 'There was not, then, one nightingale note among all those croaks?'

'I could not have missed it,' said Monsieur Bril, with a sigh. 'I read every word. Live your poetry, man; do not try to write it any more.'

'I thank you,' said David, again. 'And now I will be going back to my sheep.'

'If you would dine with me,' said the man of books, 'and overlook the smart of it, I will give you reasons at length.'

'No,' said the poet, 'I must be back in the fields cawing at my sheep.'

Back along the road to Vernoy he trudged with his poems under his arm. When he reached his village he turned into the shop of one Zeigler, a Jew out of Armenia, who sold anything that came to his hand.

'Friend,' said David, 'wolves from the forest harass my sheep on the hills. I must purchase firearms to protect them. What have you?'

'A bad day, this, for me, friend Mignot,' said Zeigler, spreading his hands, 'for I perceive that I must sell you a weapon that will not fetch a tenth of its value. Only last week I bought from a peddler a wagon full of goods that he procured at a sale by a *commissionaire* of the crown. The sale was of the chateau and belongings of a great lord – I know not his title – who has been banished for conspiracy against the king. There are some choice firearms in the lot. This pistol – oh, a weapon fit for a prince! – it shall be only forty francs to you, friend Mignot, if I lose ten by the sale. But perhaps an arquebuse –'

'This will do,' said David, throwing the money on the counter. 'Is it charged?'

'I will charge it,' said Zeigler. 'And, for ten francs more, add a store of powder and ball.'

David laid his pistol under his coat and walked to his cottage. Yvonne was not there. Of late she had taken to gadding much among the neighbours. But a fire was glowing in the kitchen stove. David opened the door of it and thrust his poems in upon the coals. As they blazed up they made a singing, harsh sound in the flue.

'The song of the crow!' said the poet.

He went up to his attic room and closed the door. So quiet was the village that a score of people heard the roar of the great pistol. They flocked thither, and up the stairs where the smoke, issuing, drew their notice.

The men laid the body of the poet upon his bed, awkwardly arranging it to conceal the torn plumage of the poor black crow. The women chattered in a luxury of zealous pity. Some of them ran to tell Yvonne.

M. Papineau, whose nose had brought him there among the first, picked up the weapon and ran his eye over its silver mountings with a mingled air of connoisseurship and grief.

'The arms,' he explained, aside, to the *cure*, "and crest of Monseigneur, the Marquis de Beaupertuys.'

LXXIV

The Guardian of the Accolade

NOT THE LEAST IMPORTANT of the force of the Weymouth Bank was Uncle Bushrod. Sixty years had Uncle Bushrod given of faithful service to the house of Weymouth as chattel, servitor, and friend. Of the colour of the mahogany bank furniture was Uncle Bushrod – thus dark was he externally; white as the uninked pages of the bank ledgers was his soul. Eminently pleasing to Uncle Bushrod would the comparison have been; for to him the only institution in existence worth considering was the Weymouth Bank, of which he was something between porter and generalissimo-in-charge.

Weymouthville lay, dreamy and umbrageous, among the low foothills along the brow of a Southern valley. Three banks there were in Weymouthville. Two were hopeless, misguided enterprises, lacking the presence and prestige of a Weymouth to give them glory. The third was The Bank, managed by the Weymouths – and Uncle Bushrod. In the old Weymouth homestead – the red brick, white-porticoed mansion, the first to your right as you crossed Elder Creek, coming into town – lived Mr. Robert Weymouth (the president of the bank), his widowed daughter, Mrs. Vesey – called 'Miss Letty' by every one – and her two children, Nan and Guy. There, also, in a cottage on the grounds resided Uncle Bushrod and Aunt Malindy, his wife. Mr. William

Weymouth (the cashier of the bank) lived in a modern, fine house on the principal avenue.

Mr. Robert was a large, stout man, sixty-two years of age, with a smooth plump face, long iron-grey hair and fiery blue eyes. He was high-tempered, kind, and generous, with a youthful smile and a formidable, stern voice that did not always mean what it sounded like. Mr. William was a milder man, correct in deportment and absorbed in business. The Weymouths formed The Family of Weymouthville, and were looked up to, as was their right of heritage.

Uncle Bushrod was the bank's trusted porter, messenger, vassal and guardian. He carried a key to the vault, just as Mr. Robert and Mr. William did. Sometimes there was ten, fifteen, or twenty thousand dollars in sacked silver stacked on the vault floor. It was safe with Uncle Bushrod. He was a Weymouth in heart, honesty and pride.

Of late Uncle Bushrod had not been without worry. It was on account of Marse Robert. For nearly a year Mr. Robert had been known to indulge in too much drink. Not enough, understand, to become tipsy, but the habit was getting a hold upon him, and every one was beginning to notice it. Half a dozen times a day he would leave the bank and step around to the Merchants and Planters' Hotel to take a drink. Mr. Robert's usual keen judgment and business capacity became a little impaired. Mr. William, a Weymouth, but not so rich in experience, tried to dam the inevitable backflow of the tide, but with incomplete success. The deposits in the Weymouth Bank dropped from six figures to five. Past-due paper began to accumulate, owing to injudicious loans. No one cared to address Mr. Robert on the subject of temperance. Many of his friends said that the cause of it had been the death of his wife some two years before. Others hesitated on account of Mr. Robert's quick temper, which was extremely apt to resent personal interference of such a nature. Miss Letty and the children noticed the change and grieved about it. Uncle Bushrod also worried, but he was one of those who would not have dared to remonstrate, although he and Marse Robert had been raised almost as companions. But there was a heavier shock coming to Uncle Bushrod than that caused by the bank president's toddies and juleps.

Mr. Robert had a passion for fishing, which he usually indulged whenever the season and business permitted. One day, when reports had been coming in relating to the bass and perch, he announced his intention of making a two or three days' visit to the lakes. He was going down, he said, to Reedy Lake with Judge Archinard, an old friend.

Now, Uncle Bushrod was treasurer of the Sons and Daughters of the Burning Bush. Every association he belonged to made him treasurer without hesitation. He stood AA1 in coloured circles. He was understood among them to be Mr. Bushrod Weymouth, of the Weymouth Bank.

The night following the day on which Mr. Robert mentioned his intended fishing-trip the old man woke up and rose from his bed at twelve o'clock, declaring he must go down to the bank and fetch the pass-book of the Sons and Daughters, which he had forgotten to bring home. The bookkeeper had balanced it for him that day, put the cancelled checks in it, and snapped two elastic bands around it. He put but one band around other pass-books.

Aunt Malindy objected to the mission at so late an hour, denouncing it as foolish and unnecessary, but Uncle Bushrod was not to be deflected from a duty.

'I done told Sister Adaline Hoskins,' he said, 'to come by here for dat book to-morrer mawnin' at sebin o'clock, for to kyar' it to de meetin' of de bo'd of 'rangements, and dat book gwine to be here when she come.'

So Uncle Bushrod put on his old brown suit, got his thick hickory stick, and meandered through the almost deserted streets of Weymouthville. He entered the bank, unlocking the side door, and found the pass-book where he had left it, in the little back room used for private consultations, where he always hung his coat. Looking about casually, he saw that everything was as he had left it, and was about to start for home when he was brought to a standstill by the sudden rattle of a key in the front door. Someone came quickly in, closed the door softly, and entered the counting-room through the door in the iron railing.

That division of the bank's space was connected with the back room by a narrow passage-way, now in deep darkness.

Uncle Bushrod, firmly gripping his hickory stick, tip-toed gently up this passage until he could see the midnight intruder into the sacred precincts of the Weymouth Bank. One dim gas-jet burned there, but even in its nebulous light he perceived at once that the prowler was the bank's president.

Wondering, fearful, undecided what to do, the old coloured man stood motionless in the gloomy strip of hall-way, and waited developments.

The vault, with its big iron door, was opposite him. Inside that was the safe, holding the papers of value, the gold and currency of the bank. On the floor of the vault was, perhaps, eighteen thousand dollars in silver.

The president took his key from his pocket, opened the vault and went inside, nearly closing the door behind him. Uncle Bushrod saw, through the narrow aperture, the flicker of a candle. In a minute or two – it seemed an hour to the watcher – Mr. Robert came out, bringing with him a large hand-satchel, handling it in a careful but hurried manner, as if fearful that he might be observed. With one hand he closed and locked the vault door.

With a reluctant theory forming itself beneath his wool, Uncle Bushrod waited and watched, shaking in his concealing shadow.

Mr. Robert set the satchel softly upon a desk, and turned his coat collar up about his neck and ears. He was dressed in a rough suit of grey, as if for travelling. He glanced with frowning intentness at the big office clock above the burning gas-jet, and then looked lingeringly about the bank – lingeringly and fondly, Uncle Bushrod thought, as one who bids farewell to dear and familiar scenes.

Now he caught up his burden again and moved promptly and softly out of the bank by the way he had come, locking the front door behind him.

For a minute or longer Uncle Bushrod was as stone in his tracks. Had that midnight rifler of safes and vaults been any other on earth than the man he was, the old retainer would have rushed upon him and struck to save the Weymouth property. But now the watcher's soul was tortured by the poignant dread of something worse than mere robbery. He was seized by an accusing terror that said the Weymouth name and the Weymouth honour were about to be lost. Marse Robert robbing the bank! What else could it mean? The hour of the night, the stealthy visit to the vault, the satchel brought forth full and with expedition and silence, the prowler's rough dress, his solicitous reading of the clock, and noiseless departure – what else could it mean?

And then to the turmoil of Uncle Bushrod's thoughts came the corroborating recollection of preceding events – Mr. Robert's increasing intemperance and consequent many moods of royal high spirits and stern tempers; the casual talk he had heard in the bank of the decrease in business and difficulty in collecting loans. What else could it all mean but that Mr. Robert Weymouth was an absconder – was about to fly with the bank's remaining funds,

leaving Mr. William, Miss Letty, little Nan, Guy and Uncle
Bushrod to bear the disgrace?

During one minute Uncle Bushrod considered these things, and
then he awoke to sudden determination and action.

'Lawd! Lawd!' he moaned aloud, as he hobbled hastily toward the
side door. 'Sech a come-off after all dese here years of big doin's an
fine doin's. Scan'lous sights upon de yearth when de Weymouth
fambly done turn out robbers and 'bezzlers! Time for Uncle
Bushrod to clean out somebody's chicken-coop and eben matters up.
Oh, Lawd! Marse Robert, you ain't gwine do dat. 'N Miss Letty an'
dem chillun so proud and talkin' "Weymouth, Weymouth," all de
time! I'm gwine to stop you ef I can. 'Spec you shoot Mr. Nigger's
head off ef he fool wid you, but I'm gwine stop you ef I can.'

Uncle Bushrod, aided by his hickory stick, impeded by his
rheumatism, hurried down the street toward the railroad station,
where the two lines touching Weymouthville met. As he had
expected and feared, he saw there Mr. Robert, standing in the
shadow of the building, waiting for the train. He held the satchel
in his hand.

When Uncle Bushrod came within twenty yards of the bank
president, standing like a huge, grey ghost by the station wall,
sudden perturbation seized him. The rashness and audacity of the
thing he had come to do struck him fully. He would have been
happy could he have turned and fled from the possibilities of the
famous Weymouth wrath. But again he saw, in his fancy, the
white, reproachful face of Miss Letty, and the distressed looks of
Nan and Guy, should he fail in his duty and they question him as
to his stewardship.

Braced by the thought, he approached in a straight line, clearing
his throat and pounding with his stick so that he might be early
recognized. Thus he might avoid the likely danger of too suddenly
surprising the sometimes hasty Mr. Robert.

'Is that you, Bushrod?' called the clamant, clear voice of the
grey ghost.

'Yes, suh, Marse Robert.'

'What the devil are you doing out at this time of night?'

For the first time in his life, Uncle Bushrod told Marse Robert a
falsehood. He could not repress it. He would have to circumlocute
a little. His nerve was not equal to a direct attack.

'I done been down, suh, to see ol' Aunt M'ria Patterson. She
taken sick in de night, and I kyar'ed her a bottle of M'lindy's
medercine. Yes, suh.'

'Humph!' said Robert. 'You better get home out of the night air. It's damp. You'll hardly be worth killing to-morrow on account of your rheumatism. Think it'll be a clear day, Bushrod?'

'I 'low it will, suh. De sun sot red las' night.'

Mr. Robert lit a cigar in the shadow, and the smoke looked like his grey ghost expanding and escaping into the night air. Somehow, Uncle Bushrod could barely force his reluctant tongue to the dreadful subject. He stood, awkward, shambling, with his feet upon the gravel and fumbling with his stick. But then, afar off – three miles away, at the Jimtown switch – he heard the faint whistle of the coming train, the one that was to transport the Weymouth name into the regions of dishonour and shame. All fear left him. He took off his hat and faced the chief of the clan he served, the great, royal, kind, lofty, terrible Weymouth – he bearded him there at the brink of the awful thing that was about to happen.

'Marse Robert,' he began, his voice quavering a little with the stress of his feelings, 'you 'member de day dey all rode de tunnament at Oak Lawn? De day, suh, dat you win in de ridin', and you crown Miss Lucy de queen?'

'Tournament?' said Mr. Robert, taking his cigar from his mouth. 'Yes, I remember very well the but what the deuce are you talking about tournaments here at midnight for? Go 'long home, Bushrod. I believe you're sleepwalking.'

'Miss Lucy tetch you on de shoulder,' continued the old man, never heeding, 'wid a s'ord, and say: "I mek you a knight, Suh Robert – rise up, pure and fearless and widout reproach." Dat what Miss Lucy say. Dat's been a long time ago, but me nor you ain't forgot it. And den dar's another time we ain't forgot – de time when Miss Lucy lay on her las' bed. She sent for Uncle Bushrod, and she say: "Uncle Bushrod, when I die, I want you to take good care of Mr. Robert. Seem like" – so Miss Lucy say – "he listen to you mo' dan to anybody else. He apt to be mighty fractious sometimes, and maybe he cuss you when you try to 'suade him, but he need somebody what understand him to be "round wid him. He am like a little child sometimes" – so Miss Lucy say, wid her eyes shinin' in her po', thin face – "but he always been" – dem was her words – "my knight, pure and fearless and widout reproach." '

Mr. Robert began to mask, as was his habit, a tendency to soft-heartedness with a spurious anger.

'You – you old windbag!' he growled, through a cloud of swirling cigar smoke. 'I believe you are crazy. I told you to go

home, Bushrod. Miss Lucy said that, did she? Well, we haven't
kept the scutcheon very clear. Two years ago last week, wasn't it,
Bushrod, when she died? Confound it! Are you going to stand
there all night gabbing like a coffee-coloured gander?'

The train whistled again. Now it was at the water tank, a mile
away.

'Marse Robert,' said Uncle Bushrod, laying his hand on the
satchel that the banker held, 'for Gawd's sake, don' take dis wid
you. I knows what's in it. I knows where you got it in de bank.
Don' kyar' it wid you. Dey's big trouble in dat valise for Miss
Lucy and Miss Lucy's child's chillun. Hit's bound to destroy de
name of Weymouth and bow down dem dat own it wid shame and
triberlation. Marse Robert, you can kill dis ole nigger ef you will,
but don't take away dis 'er' valise. If I ever crosses over the Jordan,
what I gwine to say to Miss Lucy when she ax me: "Uncle
Bushrod, wharfo' didn' you take good care of Mr. Robert?"'

Mr. Robert Weymouth threw away his cigar and shook free one
arm with that peculiar gesture that always preceded his outbursts
of irascibility. Uncle Bushrod bowed his head to the expected
storm, but he did not flinch. If the house of Weymouth was to fall,
he would fall with it. The banker spoke, and Uncle Bushrod
blinked with surprise. The storm was there, but it was suppressed
to the quietness of a summer breeze.

'Bushrod,' said Mr. Robert, in a lower voice than he usually
employed, 'you have overstepped all bounds. You have presumed
upon the leniency with which you have been treated to meddle
unpardonably. So you know what is in this satchel! Your long and
faithful service is some excuse, but – go home, Bushrod – not
another word!'

But Bushrod grasped the satchel with a firmer hand. The head-
lights of the train was now lightening the shadows about the station. The roar was increasing, and folks were stirring about at the
track side.

'Marse Robert, gimme dis 'er' valise. I got a right, suh, to talk to
you dis 'er' way. I slaved for you and 'tended to you from a child
up. I went th'ough de war as yo' body-servant tell we whipped de
Yankees and sent 'em back to de No'th. I was at yo' weddin', and I
wasn' fur away when yo' Miss Letty was bawn. And Miss Letty's
chillun, dey watches to-day for Uncle Bushrod when he come
home ever' evenin'. I been a Weymouth, all 'cept in colour and
entitlements. Both of us is old, Marse Robert. 'Tain't goin' to be
long tell we gwine to see Miss Lucy and has to give an account of

our doin's. De ole nigger man won't be 'spected to say much mo' dan he done all he could by de fambly dat owned him. But de Weymouths, dey must say dey been livin' pure and fearless and widout reproach. Gimme dis valise, Marse Robert – I'm gwine to hab it. I'm gwine to take it back to de bank and lock it up in de vault. I'm gwine to do Miss Lucy's biddin'. Turn 'er loose, Marse Robert.'

The train was standing at the station. Some men were pushing trucks along the side. Two or three sleepy passengers got off and wandered away into the night. The conductor stepped to the gravel, swung his lantern and called: 'Hello, Frank!' at someone invisible. The bell clanged, the brakes hissed, the conductor drawled, 'All aboard!'

Mr. Robert released his hold on the satchel. Uncle Bushrod hugged it to his breast with both arms, as a lover clasps his first beloved.

'Take it back with you, Bushrod,' said Mr. Robert, thrusting his hands into his pockets. 'And let the subject drop – now mind! You've said quite enough. I'm going to take this train. Tell Mr. William I will be back on Saturday. Good night.'

The banker climbed the steps of the moving train and disappeared in a coach. Uncle Bushrod stood motionless, still embracing the precious satchel. His eyes were closed and his lips were moving in thanks to the Master above for the salvation of the Weymouth honour. He knew Mr. Robert would return when he said he would. The Weymouths never lied. Nor now, thank the Lord! could it be said that they embezzled the money in banks.

Then, awake to the necessity for further guardianship of Weymouth trust funds, the old man started for the bank with the redeemed satchel.

Three hours from Weymouthville, in the grey dawn, Mr. Robert alighted from the train at a lonely flag-station. Dimly he could see the figure of a man waiting on the platform, and the shape of a spring-waggon, team and driver. Half a dozen lengthy fishing-poles projected from the waggon's rear

'You're here, Bob,' said Judge Archinard, Mr. Robert's old friend and schoolmate. 'It's going to be a royal day for fishing. I thought you said – why, didn't you bring along the stuff?'

The president of the Weymouth Bank took off his hat and rumpled his grey locks.

'Well, Ben, to tell you the truth, there's an infernally presumptuous old nigger belonging in my family that broke up the arrangement. He came down to the depot and vetoed the whole proceeding. He means all right, and – well, I reckon he is right. Somehow, he had found out what I had along – though I hid it in the bank vault and sneaked it out at midnight. I reckon he has noticed that I've been indulging a little more than a gentleman should, and he laid for me with some reaching arguments.

'I'm going to quit drinking,' Mr. Robert concluded. 'I've come to the conclusion that a man can't keep it up and be quite what he'd like to be – "pure and fearless and without reproach" – that's the way old Bushrod quoted it.'

'Well, I'll have to admit,' said the judge, thoughtfully, as they climbed into the waggon, 'that the old darky's argument can't conscientiously be overruled.'

'Still,' said Mr. Robert, with a ghost of a sigh, 'there was two quarts of the finest old silk-velvet Bourbon in that satchel you ever wet your lips with.'

LXXV

The Enchanted Profile

THERE ARE FEW CALIPHESSES. Women are Scheherazades by birth, predilection, instinct, and arrangement of the vocal cords. The thousand and one stories are being told every day by hundreds of thousands of viziers' daughters to their respective sultans. But the bowstring will get some of 'em yet if they don't watch out

I heard a story, though, of one lady Caliph. It isn't precisely an Arabian Nights story, because it brings in Cinderella, who flourished her dishrag in another epoch and country. So, if you don't mind the mixed dates (which seem to give it an Eastern flavour, after all), we'll get along.

In New York there is an old, old hotel. You have seen woodcuts of it in the magazines. It was built – let's see – at a time when there was nothing above Fourteenth Street except the old Indian trail to Boston and Hammerstein's office. Soon the old hostelry will be torn down. And, as the stout walls are riven apart and the bricks go roaring down the chutes, crowds of citizens will gather at the nearest corners and weep over the destruction of a dear old landmark. Civic pride is strong in New Bagdad; and the wettest weeper and the loudest howler against the iconoclasts will be the man (originally from Terre Haute) whose fond memories of the old hotel are limited to his having been kicked out from its free-lunch counter in 1873.

At this hotel always stopped Mrs. Maggie Brown. Mrs. Brown was a bony woman of sixty, dressed in the rustiest black, and carrying a handbag made, apparently, from the hide of the original animal that Adam decided to call an alligator. She always occupied a small parlour and bedroom at the top of the hotel at a rental of two dollars per day. And always, while she was there, each day came hurrying to see her many men, sharp-faced, anxious-looking, with only seconds to spare. For Maggie Brown was said to be the third richest woman in the world; and these solicitous gentlemen were only the city's wealthiest brokers and business men seeking trifling loans of half a dozen millions or so from the dingy old lady with the prehistoric handbag.

The stenographer and typewriter of the Acropolis Hotel (there! I've let the name of it out!) was Miss Ida Bates. She was a holdover from the Greek classics. There wasn't a flaw in her looks. Some old-timer in paying his regards to a lady said: 'To have loved her was a liberal education.' Well, even to have looked over the back hair and neat white shirt-waist of Miss Bates was equal to a full course in any correspondence school in the country. She sometimes did a little typewriting for me, and, as she refused to take the money in advance, she came to look upon me as something of a friend and protégé. She had unfailing kindliness and good nature; and not even a white-lead drummer or a fur importer had ever dared to cross the dead line of good behaviour in her presence. The entire force of the Acropolis, from the owner, who lived in Vienna, down to the head porter, who had been bedridden for sixteen years, would have sprung to her defence in a moment.

One day I walked past Miss Bates's little sanctum Remingtorium, and saw in her place a black-haired unit – unmistakably a person – pounding with each of her forefingers upon the keys. Musing on the mutability of temporal affairs, I passed on. The next day I went on a two weeks' vacation. Returning, I strolled through the lobby of the Acropolis, and saw, with a little warm glow of auld lang syne, Miss Bates, as Grecian and kind and flawless as ever, just putting the cover on her machine. The hour for closing had come; but she asked me in to sit for a few minutes in the dictation chair. Miss Bates explained her absence from and return to the Acropolis Hotel in words identical with or similar to these following:

'Well, Man, how are the stories coming?'

'Pretty regularly,' said I. 'About equal to their going.'

'I'm sorry,' said she. 'Good typewriting is the main thing in a story. You've missed me, haven't you?'

'No one,' said I, 'whom I have ever known knows as well as you do how to place properly belt buckles, semi-colons, hotel guests, and hairpins. But you've been away, too. I saw a package of peppermint-pepsin in your place the other day.'

'I was going to tell you about it,' said Miss Bates, 'if you hadn't interrupted me.

'Of course, you know about Maggie Brown, who stops here. Well, she's worth $40,000,000. She lives in Jersey in a ten-dollar flat. She's always got more cash on hand than half a dozen business candidates for vice-president. I don't know whether she carries it in her stocking or not, but I know she's mighty popular down in the part of the town where they worship the golden calf.

'Well, about two weeks ago, Mrs. Brown stops at the door and rubbers at me for ten minutes. I'm sitting with my side to her, striking off some manifold copies of a copper-mine proposition for a nice old man from Tonopah. But I always see everything all around me. When I'm hard at work I can see things through my side-combs; and I can leave one button unbuttoned in the back of my shirt-waist and see who's behind me. I didn't look around, because I make from eighteen to twenty dollars a week, and I didn't have to.

'That evening at knocking-off time she sends for me to come up to her apartment. I expected to have to typewrite about two thousand words of notes-of-hand, liens and contracts, with a ten-cent tip in sight; but I went. Well, Man, I was certainly surprised. Old Maggie Brown had turned human.

' "Child," says she, "you're the most beautiful creature I ever saw in my life. I want you to quit your work and come and live with me. I've no kith or kin," says she, "except a husband and a son or two, and I hold no communication with any of 'em. They're extravagant burdens on a hard-working woman. I want you to be a daughter to me. They say I'm stingy and mean, and the papers print lies about my doing my own cooking and washing. It s a lie, she goes on. "I put my washing out, except the handkerchiefs and stockings and petticoats and collars, and light stuff like that. I've got forty million dollars in cash and stocks and bonds that are as negotiable as Standard Oil, preferred, at a church fair. I'm a lonely old woman, and I need companionship.

You're the most beautiful human being I ever saw," says she. "Will you come and live with me? I'll show 'em whether I can spend money or not," she says.

'Well, Man, what would you have done? Of course, I fell to it. And, to tell you the truth, I began to like old Maggie. It wasn't all on account of the forty millions and what she could do for me. I was kind of lonesome in the world, too. Everybody's got to have somebody they can explain to about the pain in their left shoulder and how fast patent-leather shoes wear out when they begin to crack. And you can't talk about such things to men you meet in hotels — they're looking for just such openings.

'So I gave up my job in the hotel and went with Mrs. Brown. I certainly seemed to have a mash on her. She'd look at me for half an hour at a time when I was sitting, reading, or looking at the magazines.

'One time I says to her: "Do I remind you of some deceased relative or friend of your childhood, Mrs. Brown? I've noticed you give me a pretty good optical inspection from time to time."

' "You have a face," she says, "exactly like a dear friend of mine — the best friend I ever had. But I like you for yourself, child, too," she says.

'And say, Man, what do you suppose she did? Loosened up like a Marcel wave in the surf at Coney. She took me to a swell dressmaker and gave her d la carte to fit me out — money no object They were rush orders, and madame locked the front door and put the whole force to work.

'Then we moved to — where do you think? — no: guess again — that's right — the Hotel Bonton. We had a six-room apartment; and it cost $100 a day. I saw the bill. I began to love that old lady.

'And then, Man, when my dresses began to come in — oh, I won't tell you about 'em! you couldn't understand. And I began to call her Aunt Maggie. You've read about Cinderella, of course. Well, what Cinderella said when the prince fitted that 3½ A on her foot was a hard-luck story compared to the things I told myself.

'Then Aunt Maggie says she is going to give me a coming-out banquet in the Bonton that'll make moving Vans of all the old Dutch families on Fifth Avenue.

' "I've been out before, Aunt Maggie," says I. "But I'll come out again. But you know," says I, "that this is one of the swellest hotels in the city. And you know — pardon me — that it's hard to get a bunch of notables together unless you've trained for it."

' "Don't fret about that, child," says Aunt Maggie. "I don't send out invitations – I issue orders. I'll have fifty guests here that couldn't be brought together again at any reception unless it were given by King Edward or William Travers Jerome. They are men, of course, and all of 'em either owe me money or intend to. Some of their wives won't come, but a good many will."

'Well, I wish you could have been at the banquet. The dinner service was all gold and cut glass. There were about forty men and eight ladies present besides Aunt Maggie and I. You'd never have known the third richest woman in the world. She had on a new black silk dress with so much passementerie on it that it sounded exactly like a hailstorm I heard once when I was staying all night with a girl that lived in a top-floor studio.

'And my dress! – say, Man, I can't waste the words on you. It was all hand-made lace – where there was any of it at all – and it cost $300. I saw the bill. The men were all bald-headed or white-side-whiskered, and they kept up a running fire of light repartee about three per cents. and Bryan and the cotton crop.

'On the left of me was something that talked like a banker, and on my right was a young fellow who said he was a newspaper artist. He was the only – well, I was going to tell you.

'After the dinner was over Mrs. Brown and I went up to the apartment. We had to squeeze our way through a mob of reporters all the way through the halls. That's one of the things money does for you. Say, do you happen to know a newspaper artist named Lathrop – a tall man with nice eyes and an easy way of talking? No, I don't remember what paper he works *on*. Well, all right.

'When we got upstairs Mrs. Brown telephones for the bill right away. It came, and it was $600. I saw the bill. Aunt Maggie fainted. I got her on a lounge and opened the bead-work.

' "Child," says she, when she got back to the world, "what was it? A raise of rent or an income tax?"

' "Just a little dinner," says I. "Nothing to worry about – hardly a drop in the bucket-shop. Sit up and take notice – a dispossess notice, if there's no other kind."

'But say, Man, do you know what Aunt Maggie did? She got cold feet! She hustled me out of that Hotel Bonton at nine the next morning. We went to a rooming-house on the lower West Side. She rented one room that had water on the floor below and light on the floor above. After we got moved all you could see in the room was about $1,500 worth of new swell dresses and a one-burner gas-stove.

'Aunt Maggie had had a sudden attack of the hedges. I guess everybody has got to go on a spree once in their life. A man spends his on highballs, and a woman gets woozy on clothes. But with forty million dollars – say! I'd like to have a picture of – but, speaking of pictures, did you ever run across a newspaper artist named Lathrop – a tall – oh, I asked you that before, didn't I? He was mighty nice to me at the dinner. His voice just suited me. I guess he must have thought I was to inherit some of Aunt Maggie's money.

'Well, Mr. Man, three days of that lighthouse-keeping was plenty for me. Aunt Maggie was affectionate as ever. She'd hardly let me get out of her sight. But let me tell you. She was a hedger from Hedgersville, Hedger County. Seventy-five cents a day was the limit she set. We cooked our own meals in the room. There I was, with a thousand dollars worth of the latest things in clothes, doing stunts over a one-burner gas-stove.

'As I say, on the third day I flew the coop. I couldn't stand for throwing together a fifteen-cent kidney stew while wearing, at the same time, a $150 house-dress, with Valenciennes lace insertion. So I goes into the closet and puts on the cheapest dress Mrs. Brown had bought for me – it's the one I've got on now – not so bad for $75, is it? I'd left all my own clothes in my sister's flat in Brooklyn.

' "Mrs. Brown, formerly 'Aunt Maggie,' " says I to her, "I am going to extend my feet alternately, one after the other, in such a manner and direction that this tenement will recede from me in the quickest possible time. I am no worshipper of money," says I, "but there are some things I can't stand. I can stand the fabulous monster that I've read about that blows hot birds and cold bottles with the same breath. But I can't stand a quitter," says I. "They say you've got forty million dollars – well, you'll never have any less. And I was beginning to like you, too," says I.

'Well, the late Aunt Maggie kicks till the tears flow. She offers to move into a swell room with a two-burner stove and running water.

' "I've spent an awful lot of money, child," says she. "We'll have to economize for a while. You're the most beautiful creature I ever laid eyes on," she says, "and I don't want you to leave me."

'Well, you see me, don't you? I walked straight to the Acropolis and asked for my job back, and I got it. How did you say your writings were getting along? I know you've lost out some by not having me to typewrite 'em. Do you ever have 'em illustrated?

And, by the way, did you ever happen to know a newspaper artist – oh, shut up! I know I asked you before. I wonder what paper he works on? It's funny, but I couldn't help thinking that he wasn't thinking about the money he might have been thinking I was thinking I'd get from old Maggie Brown. If I only knew some of the newspaper editors I'd –'

The sound of an easy footstep came from the doorway. Ida Bates saw who it was with her back-hair comb. I saw her turn pink, perfect statue that she was – a miracle that I share with Pygmalion only.

'Am I excusable?' she said to me – adorable petitioner that she became. 'It's – it's Mr. Lathrop. I wonder if it really wasn't the money – I wonder, if after all, he –'

Of course, I was invited to the wedding. After the ceremony I dragged Lathrop aside.

'You an artist,' said I, 'and haven't figured out why Maggie Brown conceived such a strong liking for Miss Bates – that was? Let me show you.'

The bride wore a simple white dress as beautifully draped as the costumes of the ancient Greeks. I took some leaves from one of the decorative wreaths in the little parlour, and made a chaplet of them, and placed them on *née* Bates's shining chestnut hair, and made her turn her profile to her husband.

'By jingo!' said he. 'Isn't Ida's a dead ringer for the lady's head on the silver dollar?'

LXXVI

'Next to Reading Matter'

HE COMPELLED MY INTEREST as he stepped from the ferry at Desbrosses Street. He had the air of being familiar with hemispheres and worlds, and of entering New York as the lord of a demesne who revisited it after years of absence. But I thought that, with all his air, he had never before set foot on the slippery cobble-stones of the City of Too Many Caliphs.

He wore loose clothes of a strange bluish-drab colour, and a conservative, round Panama hat without the cock-a-hoop indentations and cants with which Northern fanciers disfigure the tropic head-gear. Moreover he was the homeliest man I have ever seen. His ugliness was less repellent than startling – arising from a sort of

Lincolnian ruggedness and irregularity of feature that spellbound you with wonder and dismay. So may have looked afrites or the shapes metamorphosed from the vapour of the fisherman's vase. As he afterward told me, his name was Judson Tate; and he may as well be called so at once. He wore his green silk tie through a topaz ring; and he carried a cane made of the vertebræ of a shark.

Judson Tate accosted me with some large and casual inquiries about the city's streets and hotels, in the manner of one who had but for the moment forgotten the trifling details. I could think of no reason for dispraising my own quiet hotel in the down-town district; so the mid-morning of the night found us already vict-ualled and drinked (at my expense), and ready to be chaired and tobaccoed in a quiet corner of the lobby.

There was something on Judson Tate's mind, and, such as it was, he tried to convey it to me. Already he had accepted me as his friend; and when I looked at his great, snuff-brown, firstmate's hand, with which he brought emphasis to his periods, within six inches of my nose, I wondered if, by any chance, he was as sudden in conceiving enmity against strangers.

When this man began to talk I perceived in him a certain power. His voice was a persuasive instrument, upon which he played with a somewhat specious but effective art. He did not try to make you forget his ugliness; he flaunted it in your face and made it part of the charm of his speech. Shutting your eyes, you would have trailed after this rat-catcher's pipes at least to the walls of Hamelin. Beyond that you would have had to be more childish to follow. But let him play his own tune to the words set down, so that if all is too dull, the art of music may bear the blame.

'Women,' said Judson Tate, 'are mysterious creatures.'

My spirits sank. I was not there to listen to such a world-old hypothesis – to such a timeworn, long-ago-refuted, bald, feeble, illogical, vicious, patent sophistry – to an ancient, baseless, weari-some, ragged, unfounded, insidious falsehood originated by women themselves, and by them insinuated, foisted, thrust, spread, and ingeniously promulgated into the ears of mankind by underhanded, secret, and deceptive methods, for the purpose of augmenting, furthering, and reinforcing their own charms and designs:

'Oh, I don't know!' said I, vernacularly.

'Have you ever heard of Oratama?' he asked.

'Possibly,' I answered. 'I seem to recall a toe dancer – or a suburban addition – or was it a perfume? – of some such name.'

'It is a town,' said Judson Tate, 'on the coast of a foreign country of which you know nothing and could understand less. It is a
country governed by a dictator and controlled by revolutions and
insubordination. It was there that a great life-drama was played,
with Judson Tate, the homeliest man in America, and Fergus
McMahan, the handsomest adventurer in history or fiction, and
Señorita Anabela Zamora, the beautiful daughter of the alcalde of
Oratama, as chief actors. And another thing – nowhere else on the
globe except in the department of Trienta y tres in Uruguay does
the *chuchula* plant grow. The products of the country I speak of
are valuable woods, dyestuffs, gold, rubber, ivory and cocoa.'

'I was not aware,' said I, 'that South America produced any
ivory.'

'There you are twice mistaken,' said Judson Tate, distributing
the words over at least an octave of his wonderful voice. 'I did not
say that the country I spoke of was in South America – I must be
careful, my dear man; I have been in politics there, you know. But,
even so – I have played chess against its president with a set carved
from the nasal bones of the tapir – one of our native specimens of
the order of *Perissodactyle ungulates* inhabiting the Cordilleras –
which was as pretty ivory as you would care to see.

'But it was of romance and adventure and the ways of woman
that I was going to tell you, and not of zoological animals.

'For fifteen years I was the ruling power behind old Sancho
Benavides, the Royal High Thumbscrew of the republic. You've
seen his picture in the papers – a mushy black man with whiskers
like the notes on a Swiss music-box cylinder, and a scroll in his
right hand like the ones they write births on in the family Bible.
Well, that chocolate potentate used to be the biggest item of
interest anywhere between the colour line and the parallels of latitude. It was three throws horses, whether he was to wind up in the
Hall of Fame or the Bureau of Combustibles. He'd have been sure
called the Roosevelt of the Southern Continent if it hadn't been
that Grover Cleveland was President at the time. he'd hold office
a couple of terms, then he'd sit out for a hand – always after
appointing his own successor for the interims.

'But it was not Benavides, the Liberator, who was making all
this fame for himself. Not him. It was Judson Tate. Benavides was
only the chip over the bug. I gave him the tip when to declare war
and increase import duties and wear his state trousers. But that
wasn't what I wanted to tell you. How did I get to be It? I'll tell
you. Because I'm the most gifted talker that ever made vocal

sounds since Adam first opened his eyes, pushed aside the smelling-salts, and asked: "Where am I?"

'As you observe, I am about the ugliest man you ever saw outside of the gallery of photographs of the New England early Christian Scientists. So, at an early age I perceived that what I lacked in looks I must make up in eloquence. That I've done. I get what I go after. As the backstop and still small voice of old Benavides I made all the great historical powers-behind-the-throne, such as Talleyrand, Mrs. de Pompadour, and Loeb, look as small as the minority report of a Duma. I could talk nations into or out of debt, harangue armies to sleep on the battlefield, reduce insurrections, inflammations, taxes, appropriations, or surpluses with a few words, and call up the dogs of war or the dove of peace with the same birdlike whistle. Beauty and epaulettes and curly moustaches and Grecian profiles in other men were never in my way. When people first look at me they shudder. Unless they are in the last stages of *angina pectoris* they are mine in ten minutes after I begin to talk. Women and men — I win 'em as they come. Now, you wouldn't think women would fancy a man with a face like mine, would you?'

'Oh, yes, Mr. Tate,' said I. 'History is bright and fiction dull with homely men who have charmed women. There seems —'

'Pardon me,' interrupted Judson Tate, 'but you don't quite understand. You have yet to hear my story.

'Fergus McMahan was a friend of mine in the capital. For a handsome man I'll admit he was the duty-free merchandise. He had blond curls and laughing blue eyes and was featured regular. They said he was a ringer for the statue they call Herr Mees, the god of speech and eloquence resting in some museum at Rome. Some German anarchist, I suppose. They are always resting and talking.

'But Fergus was no talker. He was brought up with the idea that to be beautiful was to make good. His conversation was about as edifying as listening to a leak dropping in a tin dish-pan at the head of the bed when you want to go to sleep. But he and me got to be friends — maybe because he was so opposite, don't you think? Looking at the Hallowe'en mask that I call my face when I'm shaving seemed to give Fergus pleasure; and I'm sure that whenever I heard the feeble output of throat noises that he called conversation I felt contented to be a gargoyle with a silver tongue.

'One time I found it necessary to go down to this coast town of Oratama to straighten out a lot of political unrest and chop off a few heads in the customs and military departments. Fergus, who owned the ice and sulphur-match concessions of the republic, says he'll keep me company.

'So, in a jangle of mule-train bells, we gallops into Oratama, and the town belonged to us as much as Long Island Sound doesn't belong to Japan when T. R. is at Oyster Bay. I say us; but I mean me. Everybody for four nations, two oceans, one bay and isthmus, and five archipelagos around had heard of Judson Tate. Gentleman adventurer, they call me. I had been written up in five columns of the yellow journals, 40,000 words (with marginal decorations), in a monthly magazine, and a stickful on the twelfth page of the New York *Times*. If the beauty of Fergus McMahan gained any part of our reception in Oratama I'll eat the price-tag in my Panama. It was me that they hung out paper flowers and palm branches for. I am not a jealous man; I am stating facts. The people were Nebuchadnezzars; they bit the grass before me; there was no dust in the town for them to bite. They bowed down to Judson Tate. They knew that I was the power behind Sancho Benavides. A word from me was more to them than a whole deckle-edged library from East Aurora in sectional bookcases was from anybody else. And yet there are people who spend hours fixing their faces – rubbing in cold cream and massaging the muscles (always toward the eyes) and taking in the slack with tincture of benzoin and electrolysing moles to what end? Looking handsome. Oh, what a mistake! It's the larynx that the beauty doctors ought to work on. It's words more than warts, talk more than talcum, palaver more than powder, blarney more than bloom that counts – the phonograph instead of the photograph. But I was going to tell you.

'The local Astors put me and Fergus up at the Centipede Club, a frame building built on posts sunk in the surf. The tide's only nine inches. The Little Big High Low Jacks-in-the game of the town came around and kowtowed. Oh, it wasn't to Herr Mees. They had heard about Judson Tate.

'One afternoon me and Fergus McMahan was sitting on the seaward gallery of the Centipede, drinking iced rum and talking.

' "Judson," says Fergus, "there's an angel in Oratama."

' "So long," says I, "as it ain't Gabriel, why talk as if you had heard a trump blow?"

' "It's the Señiorita Anabela Zamora," says Fergus. "She's – she's – she's as lovely as – as hell!"

' "Bravo!" says I, laughing heartily. "You have a true lover's eloquence to paint the beauties of your inamorata. You remind me," says I, "of Faust's wooing of Marguerite – that is, if he wooed her after he went down the trap-door of the stage."

' "Judson,' says Fergus, "you know you are as beautiless as a rhinoceros. You can't have any interest in women. I'm awfully gone on Miss Anabela. And that's why I'm telling you."

' "Oh, *seguramente*," says I. "I know I have a front elevation like an Aztec god that guards a buried treasure that never did exist in Jefferson County, Yucatan. But there are compensations. For instance, I am It in this country as far as the eye can reach, and then a few perches and poles. And again," says I, "when I engage people in a set-to of oral, vocal, and laryngeal utterances, I do not usually confine my side of the argument to what may be likened to a cheap phonographic reproduction of the ravings of a jellyfish."

' "Oh, I know," says Fergus, amiable, "that I'm not handy at small talk. Or large, either. That's why I'm telling you. I want you to help me."

' "How can I do it?" I asked.

' "I have subsidized," says Fergus, "the services of Señorita Anabela's duenna, whose name is Francesca. You have a reputation in this country, Judson," says Fergus, "of being a great man and a hero."

' "I have," says I. "And I deserve it."

' "And I," says Fergus, "am the best-looking man between the Arctic Circle and the Antarctic ice pack."

' "With limitations," says I, "as to physiognomy and geography, I freely concede you to be."

' "Between the two of us," says Fergus, "we ought to land the Señorita Anabela Zamora. The lady, as you know, is of an old Spanish family, and further than looking at her driving in the family *carruaje* of afternoons around the plaza, or catching a glimpse of her through a barred window of evenings, she is as unapproachable as a star."

' "Land her for which one of us?" says I.

' "For me, of course," says Fergus. "You've never seen her. Now, I've had Francesca point me out to her as being you on several occasions. When she sees me on the plaza, she thinks she's looking at Don Judson Tate, the greatest hero, statesman, and romantic figure in the country. With your reputation and my looks combined in one man, how can she resist him? She's heard all about your thrilling history, of course. And she's seen me. Can any woman want more?" asks Fergus McMahan.

' "Can she do with less?" I ask. "How can we separate our mutual attractions, and how shall we apportion the proceeds?"

'Then Fergus tells me his scheme

'The house of the alcalde, Don Luis Zamora, he says, has a *patio*, of course – a kind of inner courtyard opening from the street. In an angle of it is his daughter's window – as dark a place as you could find. And what do you think he wants me to do? Why, knowing my freedom charm, and skilfulness of tongue, he proposes that I go into that *patio* at midnight, when the hobgoblin face of me cannot be seen, and make love to her for him – for the pretty man that she has seen on the plaza, thinking him to be Don Judson Tate.

'Why shouldn't I do it for him – for my friend Fergus McMahan? For him to ask me was a compliment – an acknowledgment of his own shortcomings.

' "You little, lily-white, fine-haired, highly-polished piece of dumb sculpture," says I, "I'll help you. Make your arrangements and get me in the dark outside her window and my stream of conversation opened up with the moonlight tremolo stop turned on, and she's yours."

' "Keep your face hid, Jud," says Fergus. "For heaven's sake, keep your face hid. I'm a friend of yours in all kinds of sentiment, but this is a business deal. If I could talk I wouldn't ask you But seeing me and listening to you I don't see why she can't be landed."

' "By you?" says I.

' "By me," says Fergus.

'Well, Fergus and the duenna, Francesca, attended to the details. And one night they fetched me a long black cloak with a high collar, and led me to the house at midnight. I stood by the window in the *patio* until I heard a voice as soft and sweet as an angel's whisper on the other side of the bars. I could see only a faint white-clad shape inside; and, true to Fergus, I pulled the collar of my cloak high up, for it was July in the wet season, and the nights were chilly. And, smothering a laugh as I thought of the tongue-tied Fergus, I began to talk.

'Well, sir, I talked an hour at the Señorita Anabela. I say "at" because it was not "with." Now and then she would say: "Oh, Señor," or "Now, ain't you foolin'?" or "I know you don't mean that," and such things as women will when they are being rightly courted. Both of us knew English and Spanish; so in two languages I tried to win the heart of the lady for my friend Fergus.

But for the bars to the window I could have done it in one. At the end of the hour she dismissed me and gave me a big red rose. I handed it over to Fergus when I got home.

'For three weeks every third or fourth night I impersonated my friend in the *patio* at the window of Señorita Anabela. At last she admitted that her heart was mine, and spoke of having seen me every afternoon when she drove in the plaza. It was Fergus she had seen, of course. But it was my talk that won her. Suppose Fergus had gone there and tried to make a hit in the dark with his beauty all invisible, and not a word to say for himself!

'On the last night she promised to be mine – that is, Fergus's. And she put her hand between the bars for me to kiss. I bestowed the kiss and took the news to Fergus.

' "You might have left that for me to do," says he.

' "That'll be your job hereafter," says I. "Keep on doing that and don't try to talk. Maybe after she thinks she's in love she won't notice the difference between real conversation and the inarticulate sort of droning that you give forth.'

'Now, I had never seen Señorita Anabela. So, the next day Fergus asks me to walk with him through the plaza and view the daily promenade and exhibition of Oratama society, a sight that had no interest for me. But I went; and children and dogs took to the banana groves and mangrove swamps as soon as they had a look at my face.

' "Here she comes," said Fergus, twirling his moustache – "the one in white, in the open carriage with the black horse."

'I looked, and felt the ground rock under my feet. For Señorita Anabela Zamora was the most beautiful woman in the world, and the only one from that moment on, so far as Judson Tate was concerned. I saw at a glance that I must be hers and she mine for ever. I thought of my face and nearly fainted; and then I thought of my other talents and stood upright again. And I had been wooing her for three weeks for another man!

'As Señorita Anabela's carriage rolled slowly past, she gave Fergus a long, soft glance from the corners of her night-black eyes, a glance that would have sent Judson Tate up into heaven in a rubber-tyred chariot. But she never looked at me. And that handsome man only ruffles his curls and smirks and prances like a lady-killer at my side.

' "What do you think of her, Judson?" asks Fergus, with an air.

' "This much," says I. "She is to be Mrs. Judson Tate. I am no man to play tricks on a friend. So take your warning."

'I thought Fergus would die laughing.

' "Well, well, well," said he, "you old doughface! Struck too, are you? That's great! But you're too late. Francesca tells me that Anabela talks of nothing but me, day and night. Of course, I'm awfully obliged to you for making that chin-music to her of evenings. But, do you know, I've an idea that I could have done it as well myself."

' "Mrs. Judson Tate," says I. "Don't forget the name. You've had the use of my tongue to go with your good looks, my boy. You can't lend me your looks; but hereafter my tongue is my own. Keep your mind on the name that's to be on the visiting cards two inches by three and a half – 'Mrs. Judson Tate.' That's all."

' "All right," says Fergus, laughing again. "I've talked with her father, the alcalde, and he's willing. He's to give a *baile* to-morrow evening in his new warehouse. If you were a dancing man, Jud, I'd expect you around to meet the future Mrs. McMahan."

'But on the next evening when the music was playing loudest at the Alcalde Zamora's *baile*, into the room steps Judson Tate in new white linen clothes as if he were the biggest man in the whole nation, which he was.

'Some of the musicians jumped off the key when they saw my face, and one or two of the timidest señoritas let out a screech or two. But up prances the alcalde and almost wipes the dust off my shoes with his forehead. No mere good looks could have won me that sensational entrance.

' "I hear much, Señor Zamora," says I, "of the charm of your daughter. It would give me great pleasure to be presented to her."

'There were about six dozen willow rocking-chairs, with pink tidies tied on to them, arranged against the walls. In one of them sat Señorita Anabela in white Swiss and red slippers, with pearls and fireflies in her hair. Fergus was at the other end of the room trying to break away from two maroons and a claybank girl.

'The alcalde leads me up to Anabela and presents me. When she took the first look at my face she dropped her fan and nearly turned her chair over from the shock. But I'm used to that.

'I sat down by her and began to talk. When she heard me speak she jumped, and her eyes got as big as alligator pears. She couldn't strike a balance between the tones of my voice and the face I carried. But I kept on talking in the key of C, which is the ladies' key, and presently she sat still in her chair and a dreamy look came into her eyes. She was coming my way. She knew of Judson Tate, and what a big man he was, and the big things he had done; and that

was in my favour. But, of course, it was some shock to her to find
out that I was not the pretty man that had been pointed out to her
as the great Judson. And then I took the Spanish language, which
is better than English for certain purposes, and played on it like a
harp of a thousand strings. I ranged from the second G below the
staff up to F sharp above it. I set my voice to poetry, art, romance,
flowers and moonlight. I repeated some of the verses that I had
murmured to her in the dark at her window; and I knew from a
sudden soft sparkle in her eye that she recognized in my voice the
tones of her midnight mysterious wooer.

'Anyhow, I had Fergus McMahan going. Oh, the vocal is the
true art — no doubt about that. Handsome is as handsome palavers.
That's the renovated proverb.

'I took Señorita Anabela for a walk in the lemon grove while
Fergus, disfiguring himself with an ugly frown, was waltzing with
the claybank girl. Before we returned I had permission to come to
her window in the *patio* the next evening at midnight and talk
some more.

'Oh, it was easy enough. In two weeks Anabela was engaged to
me, and Fergus was out. He took it calm, for a handsome man,
and told me he wasn't going to give in.

' "Talk may be all right in its place, Judson," he says to me,
"although I've never thought it worth cultivating. But," says he,
"to expect mere words to back up successfully a face like yours in a
lady's good graces is like expecting a man to make a square meal
on the ringing of a dinner-bell."

'But I haven't begun on the story I was going to tell you yet.

'One day I took a long ride in the hot sunshine, and then took a
bath in the cold waters of a lagoon on the edge of the town before
I'd cooled off.

'That evening after dark I called at the alcalde's to see Anabela.
I was calling regularly every evening then, and we were to be married in a month. She was looking like a bulbul, a gazelle, and a tea-
rose, and her eyes were as soft and bright as two quarts of cream
skimmed off from the Milky Way. She looked at my rugged features without any expression of fear or repugnance. Indeed, I fancied that I saw a look of deep admiration and affection, such as she
had cast at Fergus on the plaza.

'I sat down, and opened my mouth to tell Anabela what she
loved to hear — that she was a trust, monopolizing all the loveliness
of earth I opened my mouth, and instead of the usual vibrating
words of love and compliment, there came forth a faint wheeze

such as a baby with croup might emit. Not a word – not a syllable – not an intelligible sound. I had caught cold in my laryngeal regions when I took my injudicious bath.

'For two hours I sat trying to entertain Anabela. She talked a certain amount, but it was perfunctory and diluted. The nearest approach I made to speech was to formulate a sound like a clam trying to sing "A Life on the Ocean Wave" at low tide. It seemed that Anabela's eyes did not rest upon me as often as usual. I had nothing with which to charm her ears. We looked at pictures and she played the guitar occasionally, very badly. When I left, her parting manner seemed cool – or at least thoughtful.

'This happened for five evenings consecutively.

'On the sixth day she ran away with Fergus McMahan.

'It was known that they fled in a sailing yacht bound for Belize. I was only eight hours behind them in a small steam launch belonging to the Revenue Department.

'Before I sailed, I rushed into the *botica* of old Manuel Iquito, a half-breed Indian druggist. I could not speak, but I pointed to my throat and made a sound like escaping steam. He began to yawn. In an hour, according to the customs of the country, I would have been waited on. I reached across the counter, seized him by the throat, and pointed again to my own. He yawned once more, and thrust into my hand a small bottle containing a black liquid.

' "Take one small spoonful every two hours," says he.

'I threw him a dollar and skinned for the steamer.

'I steamed into the harbour at Belize thirteen seconds behind the yacht that Anabela and Fergus were on. They started for the shore in a dory just as my skiff was lowered over the side. I tried to order my sailormen to row faster, but the sound died in my larynx before they came to the light. Then I thought of old Iquito's medicine, and I got out his bottle and took a swallow of it.

'The two boats landed at the same moment. I walked straight up to Anabela and Fergus. Her eyes rested upon me for an instant; then she turned them, full of feeling and confidence, upon Fergus. I knew I could not speak, but I was desperate. In speech lay my only hope. I could not stand beside Fergus and challenge comparison in the way of beauty. Purely involuntarily, my larynx and epiglottis attempted to reproduce the sound that my mind was calling upon my vocal organs to send forth.

'To my intense surprise and delight the words rolled forth beautifully clear, resonant, exquisitely modulated, full of power, expression and long-repressed emotion.

' "Señorita Anabela," says I, "may I speak with you aside for a moment?"

'You don't want details about that, do you? Thanks. The old eloquence had come back all right. I led her under a coco-nut palm and put my old verbal spell on her again.

' "Judson," says she, "when you are talking to me I can hear nothing else — I can see nothing else — there is nothing and nobody else in the world for me."

'Well, that's about all of the story. Anabela went back to Oratama in the steamer with me. I never heard what became of Fergus. I never saw him any more. Anabela is now Mrs. Judson Tate. Has my story bored you much?'

'No,' said I. 'I am always interested in psychological studies. A human heart — and especially a woman's — is a wonderful thing to contemplate.'

'It is,' said Judson Tate. 'And so are the trachea and the bronchial tubes of man. And the larynx, too. Did you ever make a study of the windpipe?'

'Never,' said I. 'But I have taken much pleasure in your story. May I ask after Mrs. Tate, and inquire of her present health and whereabouts?'

'Oh, sure,' said Judson Tate. 'We are living in Bergen Avenue, Jersey City. The climate down in Oratama didn't suit Mrs. T. I don't suppose you ever dissected the arytenoid cartilages of the epiglottis, did you?'

'Why, no,' said I, 'I am no surgeon.'

'Pardon me,' said Judson Tate, 'but every man should know enough of anatomy and therapeutics to safeguard his own health. A sudden cold may set up capillary bronchitis or inflammation of the pulmonary vesicles, which may result in a serious affection of the vocal organs.'

'Perhaps so,' said I, with some impatience, 'but that is neither here nor there. Speaking of the strange manifestations of the affection of women, I —'

'Yes, yes,' interrupted Judson Tate, 'they have peculiar ways. But, as I was going to tell you: when I went back to Oratama I found out from Manuel Iquito what was in that mixture he gave me for my lost voice. I told you how quick it cured me. He made that stuff from the *chuchula* plant. Now, look here.'

Judson Tate drew an oblong, white pasteboard box from his pocket.

'For any cough,' he said, 'or cold, or hoarseness, or bronchial affection whatsoever, I have here the greatest remedy in the world. You see the formula printed on the box. Each tablet contains licorice, 2 grains; balsam tolu, $1/10$ grain; oil of anise, $1/20$ minim; oil of tar, $1/60$ minim; oleoresin of cubebs, $1/60$ minim; fluid extract of *chuchula*, $1/10$ minim.

'I am in New York,' went on Judson Tate, 'for the purpose of organizing a company to market the greatest remedy for throat affections ever discovered. At present I am introducing the lozenges in a small way. I have here a box containing four dozen, which I am selling for the sum of fifty cents. If you are suffering –'

I got up, and went away without a word. I walked slowly up to the little park near my hotel, leaving Judson Tate alone with his conscience. My feelings were lacerated. He had poured gently upon me a story that I might have used. There was a little of the breath of life in it, and some of the synthetic atmosphere that passes, when cunningly tinkered, in the marts. And, at the last, it had proven to be a commercial pill, deftly coated with the sugar of fiction. The worst of it was that I could not over it for sale. Advertising departments and counting-rooms look down upon me. And it would never do for the literary. Therefore I sat upon a bench with other disappointed ones until my eyelids drooped.

I went to my room, and, as my custom is, read for an hour stories in my favourite magazines This was to get my mind back to art again.

And as I read each story, I threw the magazines sadly and hopelessly, one by one, upon the floor. Each author, without one exception, to bring balm to my heart, wrote liltingly and sprightly a story of some particular make of motor-car that seemed to control the sparking plug of his genius.

And when the last one was hurled from me I took heart.

'If readers can swallow so many proprietary automobiles,' I said to myself, 'they ought not to strain at one of Tate's Compound Magic Chuchula Bronchial Lozenges.'

And so if you see this story in print you will understand that business is business, and that if Art gets very far ahead of Commerce, she will have to get up and hustle.

I may as well add, to make a clean job of it, that you can't buy the *chuchula* plant in the drug stores.

LXXVII

A Double-Dyed Deceiver

THE TROUBLE BEGAN in Laredo. It was the Llano Kid's fault, for he should have confined his habit of manslaughter to Mexicans. But the Kid was past twenty; and to have only Mexicans to one's credit at twenty is to blush unseen on the Rio Grande border.

It happened in old Justo Valdos's gambling house. There was a poker game at which sat players who were not all friends, as happens often where men ride in from afar to shoot Folly as she gallops. There was a row over so small a matter as a pair of queens; and when the smoke had cleared away it was found that the Kid had committed an indiscretion, and his adversary had been guilty of a blunder. For the unfortunate combatant, instead of being a Greaser, was a high-blooded youth from the cow ranches, of about the Kid's own age and possessed of friends and champions. His blunder in missing the Kid's right ear only a sixteenth of an inch when he pulled his gun did not lessen the indiscretion of the better marksman.

The Kid, not being equipped with a retinue, nor bountifully supplied with personal admirers and supporters – on account of a rather umbrageous reputation, even for the border – considered it not incompatible with his indisputable gameness to perform that judicious tractional act known as 'pulling his freight.'

Quickly the avengers gathered and sought him. Three of them overtook him within a rod of the station. The Kid turned and showed his teeth in that brilliant but mirthless smile that usually preceded his deeds of insolence and violence, and his pursuers fell back without making it necessary for him even to reach for his weapon.

But in this affair the Kid had not felt the grim thirst for encounter that usually urged him on to battle. It had been a purely chance row, born of the cards and certain epithets impossible for a gentleman to brook that had passed between the two. The Kid had rather liked the slim, haughty, brown-faced young chap whom his bullet had cut off in the first pride of manhood. And now he wanted no more blood. He wanted to get away and have a good long sleep somewhere in the sun on the mesquit grass with his handkerchief over his face. Even a Mexican might have crossed his path in safety while he was in this mood.

The Kid openly boarded the north-bound passenger train that departed five minutes later. But at Webb, a few miles out, where it was flagged to take on a traveller, he abandoned that manner of escape. There were telegraph stations ahead; and the Kid looked askance at electricity and steam. Saddle and spur were his rocks of safety.

The man whom he had shot was a stranger to him. But the Kid knew that he was of the Coralitos outfit from Hidalgo; and that the punchers from that ranch were more relentless and vengeful than Kentucky feudists when wrong or harm was done to one of them. So, with the wisdom that has characterized many great fighters, the Kid decided to pile up as many leagues as possible of chaparral and pear between himself and the retaliation of the Coralitos bunch.

Near the station was a store; and near the store, scattered among the mesquits and elms, stood the saddle horses of the customers. Most of them waited, half asleep, with sagging limbs and drooping heads. But one, a long-legged roan with a curved neck, snorted and pawed the turf. Him the Kid mounted, gripped with his knees, and slapped gently with the owner's own quirt.

If the slaying of the temerarious card-player had cast a cloud over the Kid's standing as a good and true citizen, this last act of his veiled his figure in the darkest shadows of disrepute. On the Rio Grande border if you take a man's life you sometimes take trash; but if you take his horse, you take a thing the loss of which renders him poor indeed, and which enriches you not – if you are caught. For the Kid there was no turning back now.

With the springing roan under him he felt little care or uneasiness. After a five-mile gallop he drew in to the plainsman's jogging trot, and rode north-eastward toward the Nueces River bottoms. He knew the country well – its most tortuous and obscure trails through the great wilderness of brush and pear, and its camps and lonesome ranches where one might find safe entertainment. Always he bore to the east; for the Kid had never seen the ocean, and he had a fancy to lay his hand upon the mane of the great Gulf, the gamesome colt of the greater waters.

So after three days he stood on the shore at Corpus Christi, and looked out across the gentle ripples of a quiet sea.

Captain Boone, of the schooner *Flyaway*, stood near his skiff, which one of his crew was guarding in the surf. When ready to sail he had discovered that one of the necessaries of life, in the parallelogrammatic shape of plug tobacco, had been forgotten. A sailor had been dispatched for the missing cargo. Meanwhile the captain paced the sands, chewing profanely at his pocket store.

A slim, wiry youth in high-heeled boots came down to the water's edge. His face was boyish, but with a premature severity that hinted at a man's experience. His complexion was naturally dark; and the sun and wind of an outdoor life had burned it to a coffee-brown. His hair was as black and straight as an Indian's; his face had not yet been upturned to the humiliation of a razor; his eyes were a cold and steady blue. He carried his left arm somewhat away from his body, for pearl-handled 45's are frowned upon by town marshals, and are a little bulky when packed in the left arm-hole of one's vest. He looked beyond Captain Boone at the gulf with the impersonal and expressionless dignity of a Chinese emperor.

'Thinkin' of buyin' that 'ar gulf, buddy?' asked the captain, made sarcastic by his narrow escape from a tobaccoless voyage.

'Why, no,' said the Kid gently, 'I reckon not. I never saw it before. I was just looking at it. Not thinking of selling it, are you?'

'Not this trip,' said the captain. 'I'll send it to you C.O.D. when I get back to Buenas Tierras. Here comes that capstan-footed lubber with the chewin'. I ought to 've weighed anchor an hour ago.

'Is that your ship out there?' asked the Kid.

'Why, yes,' answered the captain, 'if you want to call a schooner a ship, and I don't mind lyin'. But you better say Miller and Gonzales, owners, and ordinary plain, Billy-be-damned old Samuel K. Boone, skipper.'

'Where are you going to?' asked the refugee.

'Buenas Tierras, coast of South America – I forget what they called the country the last time I was there. Cargo – lumber, corrugated iron, and machetes.'

'What kind of a country is it?' asked the Kid – 'hot or cold?'

'Warmish, buddy,' said the captain. 'But a regular Paradise Lost for elegance of scenery and be-yooty of geography. Ye're wakened every morning by the sweet singin' of red birds with seven purple tails, and the sighin' of breezes in the posies and roses. And the inhabitants never work, for they can reach out and pick steamer baskets of the choicest hothouse fruit without gettin' out of bed. And there's no Sunday and no ice and no rent and no troubles and no use and no nothin'. It's a great country for a man to go to sleep with, and wait for somethin' to turn up. The bananys and oranges and hurricanes and pineapples that ye eat comes from there.'

'That sounds to me!' said the Kid, at last betraying interest. 'What'll the expressage be to take me out there with you?'

'Twenty-four dollars,' said Captain Boone; 'grub and transportation. Second cabin. I haven't got a first cabin.'

'You've got my company,' said the Kid, pulling out a buckskin bag.

With three hundred dollars he had gone to Laredo for his regular 'blow-out.' The duel in Valdos's had cut short his season of hilarity, but it had left him with nearly two hundred dollars for aid in the flight that it had made necessary.

'All right, buddy,' said the captain. 'I hope your ma won't blame me for this little childish escapade of yours.' He beckoned to one of the boat's crew. 'Let Sanchez lift you out to the skiff so you won't get your feet wet.'

Thacker, the United States consul at Buenas Tierras, was not yet drunk. It was only eleven o'clock; and he never arrived at his desired state of beatitude – a state wherein he sang ancient maudlin vaudeville songs and pelted his screaming parrot with banana peels – until the middle of the afternoon. So, when he looked up from his hammock at the sound of a slight cough, and saw the Kid standing in the door of the consulate, he was still in a condition to extend the hospitality and courtesy due from the representative of a great nation. 'Don't disturb yourself,' said the Kid easily. 'I just dropped in. They told me it was customary to light at your camp before starting in to round up the town. I just came in on a ship from Texas.'

'Glad to see you, Mr. –,' said the consul.

The Kid laughed.

'Sprague Dalton,' he said. 'It sounds funny to me to hear it. I'm called the Llano Kid in the Rio Grande country.'

'I'm Thacker,' said the consul. 'Take that cane-bottom chair. Now if you've come to invest, you want somebody to advise you. These dingies will cheat you out of the gold in your teeth if you don't understand their ways. Try a cigar?'

'Much obliged,' said the Kid, 'but if it wasn't for my corn shucks and the little bag in my back pocket I couldn't live a minute.' He took out his 'makings,' and rolled a cigarette.

'They speak Spanish here,' said the consul. 'You'll need an interpreter. If there's anything I can do, why, I'd be delighted. If you're buying fruit lands or looking for a concession of any sort, you'll want somebody who knows the ropes to look out for you.'

'I speak Spanish,' said the Kid, 'about nine times better than I do English. Everybody speaks it on the range where I come from. And I'm not in the market for anything.'

'You speak Spanish?' said Thacker thoughtfully. He regarded the Kid absorbedly.

'You look like a Spaniard, too,' he continued. 'And you're from Texas. And you can't be more than twenty or twenty-one. I wonder if you've got any nerve.'

'You got a deal of some kind to put through?' asked the Texan, with unexpected shrewdness.

'Are you open to a proposition?' said Thacker.

'What's the use to deny it?' said the Kid. 'I got into a little gun frolic down in Laredo and plugged a white man. There wasn't any Mexican handy. And I come down to your parrot-and-monkey range just for to smell the morning-glories and marigolds. Now, do you *sabe?*'

Thacker got up and closed the door.

'Let me see your hand,' he said.

He took the Kid's left hand and examined the back of it closely.

'I can do it,' he said excitedly. 'Your flesh is as hard as wood and as healthy as a baby's. It will heal in a week.'

'If it's a fist fight you want to back me for,' said the Kid, 'don't put your money up yet. Make it gun work, and I'll keep you company. But no barehanded scrapping, like ladies at a tea-party, for me.'

'It's easier than that,' said Thacker. 'Just step here, will you?'

Through the window he pointed to a two-story white-stuccoed house with wide galleries rising amid the deep-green tropical foliage on a wooded hill that sloped gently from the sea.

'In that house,' said Thacker, 'a fine old Castilian gentleman and his wife are yearning to gather you into their arms and fill your pockets with money. Old Santos Urique lives there. He owns half the gold mines in the country.'

'You haven't been eating loco weed, have you?' asked the Kid.

'Sit down again,' said Thacker, 'and I'll tell you. Twelve years ago they lost a kid. No, he didn't die – although most of 'em here do from drinking the surface water. He was a wild little devil, even if he wasn't but eight years old. Everybody knows about it. Some Americans who were through here prospecting for gold had letters to Señor Urique, and the boy was a favourite with them. They filled his head with big stories about the States; and about a month after they left, the kid disappeared too. He was supposed to have stowed himself away among the banana bunches on a fruit steamer, and gone to New Orleans. He was seen once afterward in Texas, it was thought, but they never heard anything more of him. Old Urique has spent thousands of dollars having him looked for. The madam was broken up worst of all. The kid was her life. She wears mourning yet. But they say she believes he'll come back to her some day, and never gives up hope. On the back of the boy's left hand was tattooed a flying eagle carrying a spear in his claws. That's old Urique's coat-of-arms or something that he inherited in Spain.'

The Kid raised his left hand slowly and gazed at it curiously.

'That's it,' said Thacker, reaching behind the official desk for his bottle of smuggled brandy. 'You're not so slow. I can do it. What was I consul at Sandakan for? I never knew till now. In a week I'll have the eagle bird with the frog-sticker blended in so you'd think you were born with it. I brought a set of the needles and ink just because I was sure you'd drop in some day, Mr. Dalton.'

'Oh, hell,' said the Kid. 'I thought I told you my name!'

'All right, "Kid," then. It won't be that long. How does Señorito Urique sound, for a change?'

'I never played son any that I remember of,' said the Kid. 'If I had any parents to mention they went over the divide about the time I gave my first bleat. What is the plan of your roundup?'

Thacker leaned back against the wall and held his glass up to the light.

'We've come now,' said he, 'to the question of how far you're willing to go in a little matter of the sort.'

'I told you why I came down here,' said the Kid simply.

'A good answer,' said the consul. 'But you won't have to go that far. Here's the scheme. After I get the trade-mark tattooed on your hand I'll notify old Urique. In the meantime I'll furnish you with all of the family history I can find out, so you can be studying up points to talk about. You've got the looks, you speak the Spanish, you know the facts, you can tell about Texas, you've got the tattoo mark. When I notify them that the rightful heir has returned and is waiting to know whether he will be received and pardoned, what will happen? They'll simply rush down here and fall on your neck, and the curtain goes down for refreshments and a stroll in the lobby.'

'I'm waiting,' said the Kid. 'I haven't had my saddle off in your camp long, pardner, and I never met you before; but if you intend to let it go at a parental blessing, why, I'm mistaken in my man, that's all.'

'Thanks,' said the consul. 'I haven't met anybody in a long time that keeps up with an argument as well as you do. The rest of it is simple. If they take you in only for a while it's long enough. Don't give 'em time to hunt up the strawberry mark on your left shoulder. Old Urique keeps anywhere from $50,000 to $100,000 in his house all the time in a little safe that you could open with a shoe buttoner. Get it. My skill as a tattooer is worth half the boodle. We go halves and catch a tramp steamer for Rio de Janeiro. Let the United States go to pieces if it can't get along without my services. *Que dice, señor?*'

'It sounds to me!' said the Kid, nodding his head. 'I'm out for the dust.'

'All right, then,' said Thacker. 'You'll have to keep close until we get the bird on you. You can live in the back room here. I do my own cooking, and I'll make you as comfortable as a parsimonious Government will allow me.'

Thacker had set the time at a week, but it was two weeks before the design that he patiently tattooed upon the Kid's hand was to his notion. And then Thacker called a *muchacho*, and dispatched this note to the intended victim:

EL SEÑOR DON SANTOS URIQUE,
   La Casa Blanca.

MY DEAR SIR,
   I beg permission to inform you that there is in my house as a temporary guest a young man who arrived in Buenas Tierras from the United States some days ago. Without wishing to excite any hopes that may not be realized, I think there is a possibility of his being your long-absent son. It might be well for you to call and see him. If he is, it is my opinion that his intention was to return to his home, but upon arriving here, his courage failed him from doubts as to how he would be received.

                              Your true servant,
                              THOMPSON THACKER.

Half an hour afterward – quick time for Buenas Tierras – Señor Urique's ancient landau drove to the consul's door, with the barefooted coachman beating and shouting at the team of fat, awkward horses.

A tall man with a white moustache alighted, and assisted to the ground a lady who was dressed and veiled in unrelieved black.

The two hastened inside, and were met by Thacker with his best diplomatic bow. By his desk stood a slender young man with clear-cut sun-browned features and smoothly brushed black hair.

Señora Urique threw back her heavy veil with a quick gesture. She was past middle age, and her hair was beginning to silver, but her full, proud figure and clear olive skin retained traces of the beauty peculiar to the Basque province. But, once you have seen her eyes, and comprehended the great sadness that was revealed in their deep shadows and hopeless expression, you saw that the woman lived only in some memory.

She bent upon the young man a long look of the most agonized questioning. Then her great black eyes turned, and her gaze rested upon his left hand. And then with a sob, not loud, but seeming to shake the room, she cried, 'Hijo mio!' and caught the Llano Kid to her heart.

A month afterward the Kid came to the consulate in response to a message sent by Thacker.

He looked the young Spanish *caballero*. *His* clothes were imported, and the wiles of the jewellers had not been spent upon him in vain. A more than respectable diamond shone on his finger as he rolled a shuck cigarette.

'What's doing?' asked Thacker.

'Nothing much,' said the Kid calmly. 'I eat my first iguana steak to-day. They're them big lizards, you *sabe*? *I* reckon, though, that frijoles and side bacon would do me about as well. Do you care for iguanas, Thacker?'

'No, nor for some other kinds of reptiles,' said Thacker.

It was three in the afternoon, and in another hour he would be in his state of beatitude.

'It's time you were making good, sonny,' he went on, with an ugly look on his reddened face. 'You're not playing up to me square. You've been the prodigal son for four weeks now, and you could have had veal for every meal on a gold dish if you'd wanted to. Now, Mr. Kid, do you think it's right to leave me out so long on a husk diet? What's the trouble? Don't you get your filial eyes on anything that looks like cash in the Casa Blanca? Don't tell me you don't. Everybody knows where old Urique keeps his stuff. It's U.S. currency, too; he don't accept anything else. What's doing? Don't say "nothing" this time.'

'Why, sure,' said the Kid, admiring his diamond, 'there's plenty of money up there. I'm no judge of collateral in bunches, but I will undertake for to say that I've seen the rise of $50,000 at a time in that tin grub box that my adopted father calls his safe. And he lets me carry the key sometimes just to show me that he knows I'm the real little Francisco that strayed from the herd a long time ago.'

'Well, what are you waiting for?' asked Thacker angrily. 'Don't you forget that I can upset your apple-cart any day I want to. If old Urique knew you were an impostor, what sort of things would happen to you? Oh, you don't know this country, Mr. Texas Kid. The laws here have got mustard spread between 'em. These people here'd stretch you out like a frog that had been stepped on, and give you about fifty sticks at every corner of the plaza. And they'd wear every stick out, too. What was left of you they'd feed to alligators.'

'I might as well tell you now, pardner,' said the Kid, sliding down low on his steamer chair, 'that things are going to stay just as they are. They're about right now.'

'What do you mean?' asked Thatcher, rattling the bottom of his glass on his desk.

'The scheme's off,' said the Kid. 'And whenever you have the pleasure of speaking to me, address me as Don Francisco Urique. I'll guarantee I'll answer to it. We'll let Colonel Urique keep his money. His little tin safe is as good as the time-locker in the First National Bank of Laredo as far as you and me are concerned.'

'You're going to throw me down, then, are you?' said the consul.

'Sure,' said the Kid cheerfully. 'Throw you down. That's it. And now I'll tell you why. The first night I was up at the colonel's house they introduced me to a bedroom. No blankets on the floor – a real room, with a bed and things in it. And before I was asleep in comes this artificial mother of mine and tucks in the covers. "Panchito," she says, "my little lost one, God has brought you back to me. I bless His name for ever." It was that, or some truck like that, she said. And down comes a drop or two of rain and hits me on the nose. And all that stuck by me, Mr. Thacker. And it's been that way ever since. And it's got to stay that way. Don't you think that it's for what's in it for me, either, that I say so. If you have any such ideas, keep 'em to yourself. I haven't had much truck with women in my life, and no mothers to speak of, but here's a lady that we've got to keep fooled. Once she stood it; twice she won't. I'm a low-down wolf, and the devil may have sent me on this trail instead of God, but I'll travel it to the end. And

110W, don't forget that I'm Don Francisco Urique whenever you happen to mention my name.'

'I'll expose you to-day, you – you double-dyed traitor,' stammered Thacker.

The Kid arose' and, without violence, took Thacker by the throat with a hand of steel and shoved him slowly into a corner. Then he drew from under his left arm his pearl-handled .45 and poked the cold muzzle of it against the consul's mouth.

'I told you why I come here,' he said, with his old freezing smile. 'If I leave here, you'll be the reason. Never forget it, pardner. Now, what is my name?'

'Er – Don Francisco Urique,' gasped Thacker.

From outside came a sound of wheels, and the shouting of someone, and the sharp thwacks of a wooden whip-stock upon the backs of fat horses.

The Kid put up his gun, and walked toward the door. But he turned again and came back to the trembling Thacker, and held up his left hand with its back toward the consul.

'There's one more reason,' he said slowly, 'why things have got to stand as they are. The fellow I killed in Laredo had one of them same pictures on his left hand.'

Outside, the ancient landau of Don Santos Urique rattled to the door. The coachman ceased his bellowing. Señora Urique, in a voluminous gay gown of white lace and flying ribbons, leaned forward with a happy look in her great soft eyes.

'Are you within, dear son?' she called, in the rippling Castilian.

'*Madre mia, yo vengo* [mother, I come],' answered the young Don Francisco Urique.

LXXVIII

The Passing of Black Eagle

FOR SOME MONTHS of a certain year a grim bandit infested the Texas border along the Rio Grande. Peculiarly striking to the optic nerve was this notorious marauder. His personality secured him the title of 'Black Eagle, the Terror of the Border.' Many fearsome tales are on record concerning the doings of him and his followers. Suddenly, in the space of a single minute, Black Eagle vanished from earth. He was never heard of again. His own band never even guessed the mystery of his disappearance. The border ranches and settlements feared he would come again to ride and ravage the mesquite flats. He never will. It is to disclose the fate of Black Eagle that this narrative is written.

The initial movement of the story is furnished by the foot of a bartender in St. Louis. His discerning eye fell upon the form of Chicken Ruggles as he pecked with avidity at the free lunch. Chicken was a 'hobo.' He had a long nose like the bill of a fowl, an inordinate appetite for poultry, and a habit of gratifying it without expense, which accounts for the name given him by his fellow-vagrants.

Physicians agree that the partaking of liquids at meal times is not a healthy practice. The hygiene of the saloon promulgates the opposite. Chicken had neglected to purchase a drink to accompany his meal. The bartender rounded the counter, caught the injudicious diner by the ear with a lemon squeezer, led him to the door and kicked him into the street.

Thus the mind of Chicken was brought to realize the signs *of* coming winter. The night was cold; the stars shone with unkindly brilliance; people were hurrying along the streets in two egotistic, jostling streams. Men had donned their overcoats, and Chicken knew to an exact percentage the increased difficulty of coaxing dimes from those buttoned-in vest pockets. The time had come for his annual exodus to the south.

A little boy, five or six years old, stood looking with covetous eyes in a confectioner's window. In one small hand he held an empty two-ounce vial; in the other he grasped tightly something flat and round, with a shining milled edge. The scene presented a field of operations commensurate to Chicken's talents and daring. After sweeping the horizon to make sure that no official tug was cruising near, he insidiously accosted his prey. The boy, having been early taught by his household to regard altruistic advances with extreme suspicion, received the overtures coldly.

Then Chicken knew that he must make one of those desperate, nerve-shattering plunges into speculation that fortune sometimes requires of those who would win her favour. Five cents was his capital, and this he must risk against the chance of winning what lay within the close grasp of the youngster's chubby hand. It was a fearful lottery, Chicken knew. But he must accomplish his end by strategy, since he had a wholesome terror of plundering infants by force. Once, in a park, driven by hunger, he had committed an onslaught upon a bottle of peptonized infant's food in the possession of an occupant of a baby carriage. The outraged infant had so

promptly opened its mouth and pressed the button that communi-
cated with the welkin that help arrived, and Chicken did his thirty
days in a snug coop. Wherefore he was, as he said, 'leary of kids.'

Beginning artfully to question the boy concerning his choice of
sweets, he gradually drew out the information he wanted. Mamma
said he was to ask the drug store man for ten cents worth of paregoric in the bottle; he was to keep his hand shut tight over the
dollar; he must not stop to talk to anyone in the street; he must ask
the drug store man to wrap up the change and put it in the pocket
of his trousers. Indeed, they had pockets – two of them! And he
liked chocolate creams best.

Chicken went into the store and turned plunger. He invested
his entire capital in C. A. N. D. Y. stocks, simply to pave the way
to the greater risk following.

He gave the sweets to the youngster, and had the satisfaction of
perceiving that confidence was established. After that it was easy
to obtain leadership of the expedition; to take the investment by
the hand and lead it to a nice drug store he knew of in the same
block. There Chicken, with a parental air, passed over the dollar
and called for the medicine, while the boy crunched his candy,
glad to be relieved of the responsibility of the purchase. And then
the successful investor, searching his pockets, found an overcoat
button – the extent of his winter trousseau – and, wrapping it carefully, placed the ostensible change in the pocket of confiding juve-
nility. Setting the youngster's face homeward and patting him
benevolently on the back – for Chicken's heart was as soft as those
of his feathered namesakes – the speculator quit the market with a
profit of 1,700 per cent. on his invested capital.

Two hours later an Iron Mountain freight engine pulled out of
the railroad yards, Texas bound, with a string of empties. In one
of the cattle cars, half buried in excelsior, Chicken lay at ease.
Beside him in his nest was a quart bottle of very poor whisky and a
paper bag of bread and cheese. Mr. Ruggles, in his private car, was
on his trip south for the winter season.

For a week that car was trundled southward, shifted, laid over,
and manipulated after the manner of rolling stock, but Chicken
stuck to it, leaving it only at necessary times to satisfy his hunger
and thirst. He knew it must go down to the cattle country, and
San Antonio, in the heart of it, was his goal. There the air was
salubrious and mild; the people indulgent and long-suffering. The
bartenders there would not kick him. If he should eat too long or
too often at one place they would swear at him as if by rote and

without heat. They swore so drawlingly, and they rarely paused short of their full vocabulary, which was copious, so that Chicken had often gulped a good meal during the process of the vituperative prohibition. The season there was always spring-like; the plazas were pleasant at night, with music and gaiety; except during the slight and infrequent cold snaps one could sleep comfortably out of doors in case the interiors should develop inhospitality.

At Texarkana his car was switched to the I. and G.N. Then still southward it trailed until, at length, it crawled across the Colorado bridge at Austin, and lined out, straight as an arrow, for the run to San Antonio.

When the freight halted at that town Chicken was fast asleep. In ten minutes the train was off again for Laredo, the end of the road. Those empty cattle cars were for distribution along the line at points from which the ranches shipped their stock.

When Chicken awoke his car was stationary. Looking out between the slats he saw it was a bright, moonlit night. Scrambling out, he saw his car with three others abandoned on a little siding in a wild and lonesome country. A cattle pen and chute stood on one side of the track. The railroad bisected a vast, dim ocean of prairie, in the midst of which Chicken, with his futile rolling stock, was as completely stranded as was Robinson with his land locked boat.

A white post stood near the rails. Going up to it, Chicken read the letters at the top, S. A. 90. Laredo was nearly as far to the south. He was almost a hundred miles from any town. Coyotes began to yelp in the mysterious sea around him. Chicken felt lonesome. He had lived in Boston without an education, in Chicago without nerve, in Philadelphia without a sleeping-place, in New York without a pull, and in Pittsburg sober, and yet he had never felt so lonely as now.

Suddenly through the intense silence he heard the whicker of a horse. The sound came from the side of the track toward the east, and Chicken began to explore timorously in that direction. He stepped high along the mat of curly mesquit grass, for he was afraid of everything there might be in this wilderness – snakes, rats, brigands, centipedes, mirages, cowboys, fandangoes, tarantulas, tamales – he had read of them in the story-papers. Rounding a clump of prickly pear that reared high its fantastic and menacing array of rounded heads, he was struck to shivering terror by a snort and a thunderous plunge, as the horse, himself startled, bounded away some fifty yards, and then resumed his grazing. But here was the one thing in the desert that Chicken did not fear. He had been reared on a farm; he had handled horses, understood them, and could ride.

Approaching slowly and speaking soothingly, he followed the animal, which, after its first flight, seemed gentle enough, and secured the end of the twenty-foot lariat that dragged after him in the grass. It required him but a few moments to contrive the rope into an ingenious nose-bridle, after the style of the Mexican *borsal*. In another he was upon the horse's back and off at a splendid lope, giving the animal free choice of direction. 'He will take me somewhere,' said Chicken to himself.

It would have been a thing of joy, that untrammelled gallop over the moonlit prairie, even to Chicken, who loathed exertion, but that his mood was not for it. His head ached; a growing thirst was upon him; the 'somewhere' whither his lucky mount might convey him was full of dismal peradventure.

And now he noted that the horse moved to a definite goal. Where the prairie lay smooth he kept his course straight as an arrow's toward the east. Deflected by hill or arroyo or impracticable spinous brakes, he quickly flowed again into the current, charted by his unerring instinct. At last, upon the side of a gentle rise, he suddenly subsided to a complacent walk. A stone's cast away stood a little mott of coma trees; beneath it a *jacal* such as the Mexicans erect – a one-room house of upright poles daubed with clay and roofed with grass or tule reeds. An experienced eye would have estimated the spot as the headquarters of a small sheep ranch. In the moonlight the ground in the near-by corral showed pulverized to a level smoothness by the hoofs of the sheep Everywhere was carelessly distributed the paraphernalia of the place – ropes, bridles, saddles, sheep pelts, wool sacks, feed troughs, and camp litter. The barrel of drinking water stood in the end of the two-horse wagon near the door. The harness was piled, promiscuous, upon the wagon tongue, soaking up the dew.

Chicken slipped to earth, and tied the horse to a tree. He halloed again and again, but the house remained quiet. The door stood open, and he entered cautiously. The light was sufficient for him to see that no one was at home. He struck a match and lighted a lamp that stood on a table. The room was that of a bachelor ranchman who was content with the necessaries of life Chicken rummaged intelligently until he found what he had hardly dared hope for – a small, brown jug that still contained something near a quart of his desire.

Half an hour later, Chicken – now a gamecock of hostile aspect – emerged from the house with unsteady steps. He had drawn upon the absent ranchman's equipment to replace his own ragged attire. He wore a suit of coarse brown ducking, the coat being a sort of rakish bolero, jaunty to a degree. Boots he had donned, and spurs that whirred with every lurching step. Buckled around him was a belt full of cartridges with a big six-shooter in each of its two holsters.

Prowling about, he found blankets, a saddle and bridle with which he caparisoned his steed. Again mounting, he rode swiftly away, singing a loud and tuneless song.

Bud King's band of desperadoes, outlaws and horse and cattle thieves, were in camp at a secluded spot on the bank of the Frio. Their depredations in the Rio Grande country, while no bolder than usual, had been advertised more extensively, and Captain Kinney's company of rangers had been ordered down to look after them. Consequently, Bud King, who was a wise general, instead of cutting out a hot trail for the upholders of the law, as his men wished to do, retired for the time to the prickly fastnesses of the Frio valley.

Though the move was a prudent one, and not incompatible with Bud's well-known courage, it raised dissension among the members of the band. In fact, while they thus lay ingloriously *perdu* in the brush, the question of Bud King's fitness for the leadership was argued, with closed doors, as it were, by his followers. Never before had Bud's skill or efficiency been brought to criticism; but his glory was waning (and such is glory's fate) in the light of a newer star. The sentiment of the band was crystallizing into the opinion that Black Eagle could lead them with more lustre profit and distinction.

This Black Eagle – sub-titled the 'Terror of the Border' – had been a member of the gang about three months.

One night while they were in camp on the San Miguel water-hole a solitary horseman on the regulation fiery steed dashed in among them The new-comer was of a portentous and devastating aspect. A beak-like nose with a predatory curve projected above a mass of bristling blue-black whiskers. His eye was cavernous and fierce. He was spurred, sombreroed, booted, garnished with revolvers, abundantly drunk, and very much unafraid. Few people in the country drained by the Rio Bravo would have cared thus to invade alone the camp of Bud King. But this fell bird swooped fearlessly upon them and demanded to be fed.

Hospitality in the prairie country is not limited. Even if your enemy pass your way you must feed him before you shoot him. You must empty your larder into him before you empty your lead So the stranger of undeclared intentions was set down to a mighty feast.

A talkative bird he was, full of most marvellous loud tales and exploits, and speaking a language at times obscure but never colourless. He was a new sensation to Bud King's men, who rarely encountered new types. They hung, delighted, upon his vainglorious boasting, the spicy strangeness of his lingo, his contemptuous familiarity with life, the world, and remote places, and the extravagant frankness with which he conveyed his sentiments.

To their guest the band of outlaws seemed to be nothing more than a congregation of country bumpkins whom he was 'stringing for grub' just as he would have told his stories at the back door of a farmhouse to wheedle a meal. And, indeed, his ignorance was not without excuse, for the 'bad man' of the South-west does not run to extremes. Those brigands might justly have been taken for a little party of peaceable rustics assembled for a fish-fry or pecan gathering. Gentle of manner, slouching of gait, soft-voiced, unpicturesquely clothed; not one of them presented to the eye any witness of the desperate records they had earned.

For two days the glittering stranger within the camp was feasted. Then, by common consent, he was invited to become a member of the band. He consented, presenting for enrolment the prodigious name of 'Captain Montressor.' This name was immediately overruled by the band, and 'Piggy' substituted as a compliment to the awful and insatiate appetite of its owner.

Thus did the Texas border receive the most spectacular brigand that ever rode its chaparral.

For the next three months Bud King conducted business as usual, escaping encounters with law officers and being content with reasonable profits. The band ran off some very good companies of horses from the ranges, and a few bunches of fine cattle which they got safely across the Rio Grande and disposed of to fair advantage. Often the band would ride into the little villages and Mexican settlements, terrorizing the inhabitants and plundering for the provisions and ammunition they needed. It was during these bloodless raids that Piggy's ferocious aspect and frightful voice gained him a renown more widespread and glorious than those other gentle-voiced and sad-faced desperadoes could have acquired in a lifetime.

The Mexicans, most apt in nomenclature, first called him The Black Eagle, and used to frighten the babes by threatening them with tales of the dreadful robber who carried off little children in his great beak. Soon the name extended, and Black Eagle, the Terror of the Border, became a recognized factor in exaggerated newspaper reports and ranch gossip.

The country from the Nueces to the Rio Grande was a wild but fertile stretch, given over to the sheep and cattle ranches. Range was free; the inhabitants were few; the law was mainly a letter, and the pirates met with little opposition until the flaunting and garish Piggy gave the band undue advertisement. Then McKinney's ranger company headed for those precincts, and Bud King knew that it meant grim and sudden war or else temporary retirement. Regarding the risk to be unnecessary, he drew off his band to an almost inaccessible spot on the bank of the Frio. Wherefore, as has been said, dissatisfaction arose among the members, and impeachment proceedings against Bud were premeditated with Black Eagle in high favour for the succession. Bud King was not unaware of the sentiment, and he called aside Cactus Taylor, his trusted lieutenant, to discuss it.

'If the boys,' said Bud, 'ain't satisfied with me, I'm willin' to step out. They're buckin' against my way of handlin' 'em. And 'specially because I concludes to hit the brush while Sam Kinney is ridin' the line. I saves 'em from bein' shot or sent up on a state contract, and they up and says I'm no good.'

'It ain't so much that,' explained Cactus, 'as it is they're plum locoed about Piggy. They want them whiskers and that nose of his to split the wind at the head of the column.'

'There's somethin' mighty seldom about Piggy,' declared Bud, musingly. 'I never yet see anything on the hoof that he exactly grades up with. He can shore holler a plenty, and he straddles a hoss from where you laid the chunk. But he ain't never been smoked yet. You know, Cactus, we ain't had a row since he's been with us. Piggy's all right for skearin' the greaser kids and layin' waste a cross-roads store. I reckon he's the finest canned oyster buccaneer and cheese pirate that ever was, but how's his appetite for fightin'? I've knowed some citizens you'd think was starvin' for trouble get a bad case of dyspepsy the first dose of lead they had to take.'

'He talks all spraddled out,' said Cactus, ' 'bout the rookuses he's been in. He claims to have saw the elephant and hearn the owl.'

'I know,' replied Bud, using the cow-puncher's expressive phrase of scepticism, 'but it sounds to me!

This conversation was held one night in camp while the other members of the band – eight in number – were sprawling around the fire, lingering over their supper. When Bud and Cactus ceased talking they heard Piggy's formidable voice holding forth to the others as usual while he was engaged in checking, though never satisfying, his ravening appetite.

'Wat's de use,' he was saying, 'of chasin' little red cowses and hosses 'round for t'ousands of miles? Dere ain't nuttin' in it. Gallopin' t'rough dese bushes and briers, and gettin' a t'irst dat a brewery couldn't put out, and missin' meals! Say! You know what I'd do if I was main finger of dis bunch? I'd stick up a train. I'd blow de express car and make hard dollars where you guys gets wind. Youse makes me tired. Dis sook-cow kind of cheap sport gives me a pain.'

Later on, a deputation waited on Bud. They stood on one leg, chewed mesquit twigs and circumlocuted, for they hated to hurt his feelings. Bud foresaw their business, and made it easy for them. Bigger risks and larger profits was what they wanted.

The suggestion of Piggy's about holding up a train had fired their imagination and increased their admiration for the dash and boldness of the instigator. They were such simple, artless, and custom-bound bushrangers that they had never before thought of extending their habits beyond the running off of live-stock and the shooting of such of their acquaintances as ventured to interfere.

Bud acted 'on the level,' agreeing to take a subordinate place in the gang until Black Eagle should have been given a trial as leader.

After a great deal of consultation, studying of time-tables, and discussion of the country's topography, the time and place for carrying out their new enterprise was decided upon. At that time there was a feedstuff famine in Mexico and a cattle famine in certain parts of the United States, and there was a brisk international trade. Much money was being shipped along the railroads that connected the two republics. It was agreed that the most promising place for the contemplated robbery was at Espina, a little station on the I. and G.N., about forty miles north of Laredo. The train stopped there one minute; the country around was wild and unsettled; the station consisted of but one house in which the agent lived.

Black Eagle's band set out, riding by night. Arriving in the vicinity of Espina, they rested their horses all day in a thicket a few miles distant.

The train was due at Espina at 10.30 p.m. They could rob the train and be well over the Mexican border with their booty by daylight the next morning.

To do Black Eagle justice, he exhibited no signs of flinching from the responsible honours that had been conferred upon him.

He assigned his men to their respective posts with discretion, and coached them carefully as to their duties. On each side of the track four of the band were to lie concealed in the chaparral. Gotch-Ear Rodgers was to stick up the station agent. Bronco Charlie was to remain with the horses, holding them in readiness. At a spot where it was calculated the engine would be when the train stopped, Bud King was to lie hidden on one side, Black Eagle himself on the other. The two would get the drop on the engineer and fireman, force them to descend and proceed to the rear. Then the express car would be looted, and the escape made. No one was to move until Black Eagle gave the signal by firing his revolver. The plan was perfect.

At ten minutes to train time every man was at his post, effectually concealed by the thick chaparral that grew almost to the rails. The night was dark and lowering, with a fine drizzle falling from the flying gulf clouds. Black Eagle crouched behind a bush within five yards of the track. Two six-shooters were belted around him. Occasionally he drew a large black bottle from his pocket and raised it to his mouth.

A star appeared far down the track which soon waxed into the headlight of the approaching train. It came on with an increasing roar; the engine bore down upon the ambushing desperadoes with a glare and a shriek like some avenging monster come to deliver them to justice. Black Eagle flattened himself upon the ground. The engine, contrary to their calculations, instead of stopping between him and Bud King's place of concealment, passed fully forty yards farther before it came to a stand.

The bandit leader rose to his feet and peered around the bush. His men all lay quiet, awaiting the signal. Immediately opposite Black Eagle was a thing that drew his attention. Instead of being a regular passenger train it was a mixed one. Before him stood a box car, the door of which, by some means, had been left slightly open. Black Eagle went up to it and pushed the door farther open. An odour came forth – a damp, rancid, familiar, musty, intoxicating, beloved odour stirring strongly at old memories of happy days and travels. Black Eagle sniffed at the witching smell as the returned wanderer smells of the rose that twines his boyhood's cottage home. Nostalgia seized him. He put his hand inside. Excelsior – dry, springy, curly, soft, enticing, covered the floor. Outside the drizzle had turned to a chilling rain

The train bell clanged. The bandit chief unbuckled his belt and cast it, with its revolvers, upon the ground. His spurs followed quickly, and his broad sombrero. Black Eagle was moulting. The train started with a rattling jerk. The ex-Terror of the Border scrambled into the box car and closed the door. Stretched luxuriously upon the excelsior, with the black bottle clasped closely to his breast, his eyes closed, and a foolish, happy smile upon his terrible features, Chicken Ruggles started upon his return trip.

Undisturbed, with the band of desperate bandits lying motionless, awaiting the signal to attack, the train pulled out from Espina. As its speed increased and the black masses of chaparral went whizzing past on either side, the express messenger, lighting his pipe, looked through his window and remarked, feelingly:

'What a jim-dandy place for a hold-up!'

LXXIX

A Retrieved Reformation

A GUARD CAME to the prison shoe-shop, where Jimmy Valentine was assiduously stitching uppers, and escorted him to the front office. There the warden handed Jimmy his pardon, which had been signed that morning by the governor. Jimmy took it in a tired kind of way. He had served nearly ten months of a four-year sentence. He had expected to stay only about three months, at the longest. When a man with as many friends on the outside as Jimmy Valentine had is received in the 'stir' it is hardly worth while to cut his hair.

'Now, Valentine,' said the warden, 'you'll go out in the morning. Brace up, and make a man of yourself. You're not a bad fellow at heart. Stop cracking safes, and live straight.'

'Me?' said Jimmy in surprise. 'Why, I never cracked a safe in my life.'

'Oh, no,' laughed the warden. 'Of course not. Let's see, now. How was it you happened to get sent up on that Springfield job? Was it because you wouldn't prove an alibi for fear of compromising somebody in extremely high-toned society? Or was it simply a case of a mean old jury that had it in for you? It's always one or the other with you innocent victims.'

'Me?' said Jimmy, still blankly virtuous. 'Why, warden, I never was in Springfield in my life!'

'Take him back, Cronin,' smiled the warden, 'and fix him up with out-going clothes. Unlock him at seven in the morning, and let him come to the bull-pen. Better think over my advice, Valentine.'

At a quarter past seven on the next morning Jimmy stood in the warden's outer office. He had on a suit of the villainously fitting, ready-made clothes and a pair of the stiff, squeaky shoes that the state furnishes to its discharged compulsory guests.

The clerk handed him a railroad ticket and the five-dollar bill with which the law expected him to rehabilitate himself into good citizenship and prosperity. The warden gave him a cigar, and shook hands. Valentine, 9762, was chronicled on the books 'Pardoned by Governor,' and Mr. James Valentine walked out into the sunshine.

Disregarding the song of the birds, the waving green trees, and the smell of the flowers, Jimmy headed straight for a restaurant. There he tasted the first sweet joys of liberty in the shape of a broiled chicken and a bottle of white wine – followed by a cigar a grade better than the one the warden had given him. From there he proceeded leisurely to the depot. He tossed a quarter into the hat of a blind man sitting by the door, and boarded his train. Three hours set him down in a little town near the state line. He went to the café of one Mike Dolan and shook hands with Mike, who was alone behind the bar.

'Sorry we couldn't make it sooner, Jimmy, me boy,' said Mike. 'But we had that protest from Springfield to buck against, and the governor nearly balked. Feeling all right?'

'Fine,' said Jimmy. 'Got my key?'

He got his key and went upstairs, unlocking the door of a room at the rear. Everything was just as he had left it. There on the floor was still Ben Price's collar-button that had been torn from that eminent detective's shirt-band when they had overpowered Jimmy to arrest him.

Pulling out from the wall a folding-bed, Jimmy slid back a panel in the wall and dragged out a dust-covered suit-case. He opened this and gazed fondly at the finest set of burglar's tools in the East. It was a complete set, made of specially tempered steel, the latest designs in drills, punches, braces and bits, jimmies, clamps, and augers, with two or three novelties invented by Jimmy himself, in which he took pride. Over nine hundred dollars they had cost him to have made at –, a place where they make such things for the profession.

In half an hour Jimmy went downstairs and through the café. He was now dressed in tasteful and well-fitting clothes, and carried his dusted and cleaned suit-case in his hand.

'Got anything on?' asked Mike Dolan, genially.

'Me?' said Jimmy, in a puzzled tone. 'I don't understand. I'm representing the New York Amalgamated Short Snap Biscuit Cracker and Frazzled Wheat Company.'

This statement delighted Mike to such an extent that Jimmy had to take a seltzer-and-milk on the spot. He never touched 'hard' drinks.

A week after the release of Valentine, 9762, there was a neat job of safe-burglary done in Richmond, Indiana, with no clue to the author. A scant eight hundred dollars was all that was secured. Two weeks after that a patented, improved, burglar-proof safe in Logansport was opened like a cheese to the tune of fifteen hundred dollars, currency; securities and silver untouched. That began to interest the rogue-catchers. Then an old-fashioned bank-safe in Jefferson City became active and threw out of its crater an eruption of bank-notes amounting to five thousand dollars. The losses were now high enough to bring the matter up into Ben Price's class of work. By comparing notes, a remarkable similarity in the methods of the burglaries was noticed. Ben Price investigated the scenes of the robberies, and was heard to remark:

'That's Dandy Jim Valentine's autograph. He's resumed business. Look at that combination knob – jerked out as easy as pulling up a radish in wet weather. He's got the only clamps that can do it. And look how clean those tumblers were punched out! Jimmy never has to drill but one hole. Yes, I guess I want Mr. Valentine. He'll do his bit next time without any short-time or clemency foolishness.'

Ben Price knew Jimmy's habits. He had learned them while working up the Springfield case. Long jumps, quick get-aways, no confederates, and a taste for good society – these ways had helped Mr. Valentine to become noted as a successful dodger of retribution. It was given out that Ben Price had taken up the trail of the elusive cracksman, and other people with burglar-proof safes felt more at ease.

One afternoon Jimmy Valentine and his suitcase climbed out of the mail-hack in Elmore, a little town five miles off the railroad down in the blackjack country of Arkansas. Jimmy, looking like an athletic young senior just home from college, went down the board sidewalk toward the hotel.

A young lady crossed the street, passed him at the corner and entered a door over which was the sign 'The Elmore Bank.' Jimmy Valentine looked into her eyes, forgot what he was, and became another man. She lowered her eyes and coloured slightly. Young men of Jimmy's style and looks were scarce in Elmore.

Jimmy collared a boy that was loafing on the steps of the bank as if he were one of the stockholders, and began to ask him questions about the town, feeding him dimes at intervals. By and by the young lady came out, looking royally unconscious of the young man with the suit-case, and went her way.

'Isn't that young lady Miss Polly Simpson?' asked Jimmy, with specious guile.

'Naw,' said the boy. 'She's Annabel Adams. Her pa owns this bank. What'd you come to Elmore for? Is that a gold watch-chain? I'm going to get a bulldog. Got any more dimes?'

Jimmy went to the Planters' Hotel, registered as Ralph D. Spencer, and engaged a room. He leaned on the desk and declared his platform to the clerk. He said he had come to Elmore to look for a location to go into business. How was the shoe business, now, in the town? He had thought of the shoe business. Was there an opening?

The clerk was impressed by the clothes and manner of Jimmy. He, himself, was something of a pattern of fashion to the thinly gilded youth of Elmore, but he now perceived his shortcomings. While trying to figure out Jimmy's manner of tying his four-in-hand he cordially gave information.

Yes, there ought to be a good opening in the shoe line. There wasn't an exclusive shoe-store in the place. The dry-goods and general stores handled them. Business in all lines was fairly good. Hoped Mr. Spencer would decide to locate in Elmore. He would find it a pleasant town to live in, and the people very sociable.

Mr. Spencer thought he would stop over in the town a few days and look over the situation. No, the clerk needn't call the boy. He would carry up his suit-case himself; it was rather heavy.

Mr. Ralph Spencer, the phœnix that arose from Jimmy Valentine's ashes — ashes left by the flame of a sudden and alterative attack of love — remained in Elmore, and prospered. He opened a shoe-store and secured a good run of trade.

Socially he was also a success, and made many friends. And he accomplished the wish of his heart. He met Miss Annabel Adams, and became more and more captivated by her charms.

At the end of a year the situation of Mr. Ralph Spencer was this: he had won the respect of the community, his shoe-store was flourishing, and he and Annabel were engaged to be married in two weeks. Mr. Adams, the typical, plodding, country banker, approved of Spencer. Annabel's pride in him almost equalled her affection. He was as much at home in the family of Mr. Adams and that of Annabel's married sister as if he were already a member.

One day Jimmy sat down in his room and wrote this letter, which he mailed to the safe address of one of his old friends in St. Louis:

DEAR OLD PAL, –

I want you to be at Sullivan's place, in Little Rock, next Wednesday night, at nine o'clock. I want you to wind up some little matters for me. And, also, I want to make you a present of my kit of tools. I know you'll be glad to get them – you couldn't duplicate the lot for a thousand dollars. Say, Billy, I've quit the old business – a year ago. I've got a nice store. I'm making an honest living, and I'm going to marry the finest girl on earth two weeks from now. It's the only life, Billy – the straight one. I wouldn't touch a dollar of another man's money now for a million. After I get married I'm going to sell out and go West, where there won't be so much danger of having old scores brought up against me. I tell you, Billy, she's an angel. She believes in me; and I wouldn't do another crooked thing for the whole world. Be sure to be at Sully's, for I must see you. I'll bring along the tools with me.
                              Your old friend,
                                        JIMMY.

On the Monday night after Jimmy wrote this letter, Ben Price jogged unobtrusively into Elmore in a livery buggy. He lounged about town in his quiet way until he found out what he wanted to know. From the drug-store across the street from Spencer's shoe-store he got a good look at Ralph D. Spencer.

'Going to marry the banker's daughter, are you, Jimmy?' said Ben to himself, softly. 'Well, I don't know!'

The next morning Jimmy took breakfast at the Adamses. He was going to Little Rock that day to order his wedding-suit and buy something nice for Annabel. That would be the first time he had left town since he came to Elmore. It had been more than a year now since those last professional 'Jobs,' and he thought he could safely venture out.

After breakfast quite a family party went downtown together – Mr. Adams, Annabel, Jimmy and Annabel's married sister with her two little girls, aged five and nine. They came by the hotel where Jimmy still boarded, and he ran up to his room and brought along his suit-case. Then they went on to the bank. There stood Jimmy's horse and buggy and Dolph Gibson, who was going to drive him over to the railroad station.

All went inside the high, carved oak railings into the banking-room – Jimmy included, for Mr. Adams's future son-in-law was welcome anywhere. The clerks were pleased to be greeted by the good-looking, agreeable young man who was going to marry Miss Amabel. Jimmy set her suit-case down. Annabel, whose heart was bubbling with happiness and lively youth, put on Jimmy's hat, and picked up the suit-case. 'Wouldn't I make a nice drummer?' said Annabel. 'My! Ralph, how heavy it is? Feels like it was full of gold bricks.'

'Lot of nickel-plated shoe-horns in there,' said Jimmy coolly, 'that I'm going to return. Thought I'd save express charges by taking them up. I'm getting awfully economical.'

The Elmore Bank had just put in a new safe and vault. Mr. Adams was very proud of it, and insisted on an inspection by every one. The vault was a small one, but it had a new, patented door. It fastened with three solid steel bolts thrown simultaneously with a single handle, and had a time-lock. Mr. Adams beamingly explained its workings to Mr. Spencer, who showed a courteous but not too intelligent interest. The two children, May and Agatha, were delighted by the shining metal and funny clock and knobs.

While they were thus engaged Ben Price sauntered in and leaned on his elbow, looking casually inside between the railings. He told the teller that he didn't want anything; he was just waiting for a man he knew.

Suddenly there was a scream or two from the women, and a commotion. Unperceived by the elders, May, the nine-year-old girl, in a spirit of play, had shut Agatha in the vault. She had then shot the bolts and turned the knob of the combination as she had seen Mr. Adams do.

The old banker sprang to the handle and tugged at it for a moment. 'The door can't be opened,' he groaned. 'The clock hasn't been wound nor the combination set.'

Agatha's mother screamed again, hysterically.

'Hush!' said Mr. Adams, raising his trembling hand. 'All be

O HENRY – 100 SELECTED STORIES

quiet for a moment. Agatha!' he called as loudly as he could. 'Listen to me.' During the following silence they could just hear the faint sound of the child wildly shrieking in the dark vault in a panic of terror.

'My precious darling!' wailed the mother. 'She will die of fright! Open the door! Oh, break it open! Can't you men do something?'

'There isn't a man nearer than Little Rock who can open that door,' said Mr. Adams, in a shaky voice. 'My God! Spencer, what shall we do? That child – she can't stand it long in there. There isn't enough air, and, besides, she'll go into convulsions from fright.'

Agatha's mother, frantic now, beat the door of the vault with her hands. Somebody wildly suggested dynamite. Annabel turned to Jimmy, her large eyes full of anguish, but not yet despairing. To a woman nothing seems quite impossible to the powers of the man she worships.

'Can't you do something, Ralph – try, won't you?'

He looked at her with a queer, soft smile on his lips and in his keen eyes.

'Annabel,' he said, 'give me that rose you are wearing, will you?'

Hardly believing that she heard him aright, she unpinned the bud from the bosom of her dress, and placed it in his hand. Jimmy stuffed it into his vest-pocket, threw off his coat and pulled up his shirt-sleeves. With that act Ralph D. Spencer passed away and Jimmy Valentine took his place.

'Get away from the door, all of you,' he commanded, shortly.

He set his suit-case on the table, and opened it out flat. From that time on he seemed to be unconscious of the presence of anyone else. He laid out the shining, queer implements swiftly and orderly, whistling softly to himself as he always did when at work. In a deep silence and immovable, the others watched him as if under a spell.

In a minute Jimmy's pet drill was biting smoothly into the steel door. In ten minutes – breaking his own burglarious record – he threw back the bolts and opened the door.

Agatha, almost collapsed, but safe, was gathered into her mother's arms.

Jimmy Valentine put on his coat, and walked outside the railings toward the front door. As he went he thought he heard a far-away voice that he once knew call 'Ralph!' But he never hesitated.

At the door a big man stood somewhat in his way.

'Hello, Ben!' said Jimmy, still with his strange smile. 'Got around at last, have you? Well let's go. I don't know that it makes much difference, now.'

And then Ben Price acted rather strangely.

'Guess you're mistaken, Mr. Spencer,' he said. 'Don't believe I recognize you. Your buggy's waiting for you, ain't it?'

And Ben Price turned and strolled down the street.

LXXX

The Little Rheinschloss

GO SOMETIMES INTO THE *Bierhalle* and restaurant called Old Munich. Not long ago it was a resort of interesting Bohemians, but now only artists and musicians and literary folk frequent it But the Pilsner is yet good, and I take some diversion from the conversation of Waiter No. 18.

For many years the customers of Old Munich have accepted the place as a faithful copy from the ancient German town. The big hall with its smoky rafters, rows of imported steins, portrait of Goethe, and verses painted on the walls – translated into German from the original of the Cincinnati poets – seems atmospherically correct when viewed through the bottom of a glass.

But not long ago the proprietors added the room above, called it the Little Rheinschloss, and built in a stairway. Up there was an imitation stone parapet, ivy-covered, and the walls were painted to represent depth and distance, with the Rhine winding at the base of the vineyarded slopes, and the Castle of Ehrenbreitstein looming directly opposite the entrance. Of course, there were tables and chairs; and you could have beer and food brought you, as you naturally would on the top of a castle on the Rhine.

I went into Old Munich one afternoon when there were few customers, and sat at my usual table near the stairway. I was shocked and almost displeased to perceive that the glass cigarcase by the orchestra stand had been smashed to smithereens. I did not like things to happen in Old Munich. Nothing had ever happened there before.

Waiter No. 18 came and breathed on my neck. I was his by right of discovery. Eighteen's brain was built like a corral. It was full of ideas, which, when he opened the gate, came huddling out like a flock of sheep that might get together afterward or might not. I did not shine as a shepherd. As a type Eighteen fitted nowhere. I did not find out if he had a nationality, family creed, grievance, hobby, soul, preference, home or vote. He only came always to my table, and, as long as his leisure would permit, let words flutter from him like swallows leaving a barn at daylight.

'How did the cigar-case come to be broken, Eighteen?' I asked, with a certain feeling of personal grievance.

'I can tell you about that, sir,' said he, resting his foot on the chair next to mine. 'Did you ever have anybody hand you a double handful of good luck while both your hands was full of bad luck, and stop to notice how your fingers behaved?'

'No riddles, Eighteen,' said I. 'Leave out palmistry and manicuring.'

'You remember,' said Eighteen, 'the guy in the hammered brass Prince Albert and the oroide gold pants and the amalgamated copper hat, that carried the combination meat-axe, ice-pick, and liberty-pole, and used to stand on the first landing as you go up to the Little Rindslosh?'

'Why, yes,' said I. 'The halberdier. I never noticed him particularly. I remember I thought he was only a suit of armour. He had a perfect poise.'

'He had more than that,' said Eighteen. 'He was me friend. He was an advertisement. The boss hired him to stand on the stairs for a kind of scenery, to show there was something doing in the has-been line upstairs. What did you call him — a what kind of a beer?'

'A halberdier,' said I. 'That was an ancient man-at-arms of many hundred years ago.'

'Some mistake,' said Eighteen. 'This one wasn't that old. He wasn't over twenty-three or four.

'It was the boss's idea, rigging a man up in an antebellum suit of tinware and standing him on the landing of the slosh. He bought the goods at a Fourth Avenue antique store, and hung a sign out: "Able-bodied hal — halberdier wanted. Costume furnished."

'The same morning a young man with wrecked good clothes and a hungry look comes in, bringing the sign with him. I was filling the mustard-pots at my station.

' "I'm it," says he, "whatever it is. But I never halberdiered in a restaurant. Put me on. Is it a masquerade?"

' "I hear talk in the kitchen of a fishball," says I.

' "Bully for you, Eighteen," says he. "You and I'll get on. Show me the boss's desk."

'Well, the boss tries the Harveyized pajamas on him, and they fitted him like the scales on a baked redsnapper, and he gets the job. You've seen what it is – he stood straight up in the corner of the first landing with his halberd to his shoulder, looking right ahead and guarding the Portugals of the castle. The boss is nutty about having the true Old-World flavour to his joint. "Halberdiers goes with Rindsloshes," says he, "just as rats goes with rathskellers and white cotton stockings with Tyrolean villages." The boss is a kind of a antiologist, and is all posted up on data and such information.

'From 8 p.m. to two in the morning was the halberdier's hours. He got two meals with us help and a dollar a night. I eat with him at the table. He liked me. He never told his name. He was travelling impromptu, like kings, I guess. The first time at supper I says to him: "Have some more of the spuds, Mr. Frelinghuysen." "Oh, don't be so formal and offish, Eighteen," says he. "Call me Hal – that's short for halberdier." "Oh, don't think I wanted to pry for names," says I. "I know all about the dizzy fall from wealth and greatness. We've got a count washing dishes in the kitchen; and the third bartender used to be a Pullman conductor. And they *work*, Sir Percival," says I, sarcastic.

' "Eighteen," says he, "as a friendly devil in a cabbage-scented hell, would you mind cutting up this piece of steak for me? I don't say that it's got more muscle than I have, but –" And then he shows me the insides of his hands. They was blistered and cut and corned and swelled up till they looked like a couple of flank steaks criss-crossed with a knife   the kind the butchers hide and take home, knowing what is the best.

' "Shovelling coal," says he, "and piling bricks and loading drays. But they gave out, and I had to resign. I was born for a halberdier, and I've been educated for twenty-four years to fill the position. Now quit knocking my profession, and pass along a lot more of that ham. I'm holding the closing exercises," says he, "of a forty-eight-hour fast."

'The second night he was on the job he walks down from his corner to the cigar-case and calls for cigarettes. The customers at the tables all snicker out loud to show their acquaintance with history. The boss is on.

' "An" – let's see – oh, yes – an anarchism," says the boss. "Cigarettes was not made at the time when halberdiers was invented."

' "The ones you sell was," says Sir Percival. "Caporal wins from chronology by the length of a cork tip." So he gets 'em and lights one, and puts the box in his brass helmet, and goes back to patrolling the Rindslosh.

'He made a big hit, 'specially with the ladies. Some of 'em would poke him with their fingers to see if he was real, or only a kind of a stuffed figure like they burn in elegy. And when he'd move they'd squeak, and make eyes at him as they went up to the slosh. He looked fine in his halberdashery. He slept at $2 a week in a hallroom on Third Avenue. He invited me up there one night. He had a little book on the washstand that he read instead of shopping in the saloons after hours. "I'm on to that," says I, "from reading about it in novels. All the heroes on the bum carry the little book. It's either Tantalus or Liver or Horace, and it's printed in Latin, and you're a college man. And I wouldn't be surprised," says I, "if you wasn't educated, too." But it was only the batting averages of the League for the last ten years.

'One night, about half-past eleven, there comes in a party of these high-rollers that are always hunting up new places to eat in and poke fun at. There was a swell girl in a 40 h.p. auto tan coat and veil, and a fat old man with white side-whiskers, and a young chap that couldn't keep his feet off the tail of the girl's coat, and an oldish lady that looked upon life as immoral and unnecessary. "How perfectly delightful," they says, "to sup in a slosh." Up the stairs they go; and in half a minute back down comes the girl, her skirts swishing like the waves on the beach. She stops on the landing and looks our halberdier in the eye.

' "You!" she says, with a smile that reminded me of lemon sherbet. I was waiting upstairs in the slosh, then, and I was right down here by the door, putting some vinegar and cayenne into an empty bottle of tabasco, and I heard all they said.

' "It," says Sir Percival, without moving. "I'm only local colour. Are my hauberk, helmet, and halberd on straight?"

' "Is there an explanation to this?" says she. "Is it a practical joke such as men play in those Griddlecake and Lamb Clubs? I'm afraid I don't see the point. I heard, vaguely, that you were away. For three months I – we have not seen you or heard from you."

' "I'm halberdiering for my living," says the statue. "I'm working," says he. "I don't suppose you know what work means."

' "Have you – have you lost your money?" she asks.

'Sir Percival studies a minute.

' "I am poorer," says he, "than the poorest sandwich man on the streets – if I don't earn my living."

' "You call this work?" says she. "I thought a man worked with his hands or his head instead of becoming a mountebank."

' "The calling of a halberdier," says he, "is an ancient and honourable one. Sometimes," says he, "the man-at-arms at the door has saved the castle while the plumed knights were cake-walking in the banquet-halls above."

' "I see you're not ashamed," says she, "of your peculiar tastes. I wonder, though, that the manhood I used to think I saw in you didn't prompt you to draw water or hew wood instead of publicly flaunting your ignominy in this disgraceful masquerade.

'Sir Percival kind of rattles his armour and says: "Helen, will you suspend sentence in this matter for just a little while? You don't understand," says he. "I've got to hold this job down a bit longer."

' "You like being a harlequin – or halberdier, as you call it?" says she.

' "I wouldn't get thrown out of the job just now," says he, with a grin, "to be appointed Minister to the Court of St. James's."

'And then the 40 h.p. girl's eyes sparkled as hard as diamonds.

' "Very well," says she. "You shall have full run of your serving-man's tastes this night." And she swims over to the boss's desk and gives him a smile that knocks the specs off his nose.

' "I think your Rindslosh," says she, "is as beautiful as a dream. It is a little slice of the Old World set down in New York. We shall have a nice supper up there; but if you will grant us one favour the illusion will be perfect – give us your halberdier to wait on our table."

'That hit the boss's antiology hobby just right. "Sure," says he, "dot vill be fine. Und der orchestra shall blay 'Die Wacht am Rhein' all der time." And he goes over and tells the halberdier to go upstairs and hustle the grub at the swells' table.

' "I'm on the job," says Sir Percival, taking off his helmet and hanging it on his halberd and leaning 'em in the corner. The girl goes up and takes her seat, and I see her jaw squared tight under her smile. "We're going to be waited on by a real halberdier," says she, "one who is proud of his profession. Isn't it sweet?"

' "Ripping," says the swell young man. "Much prefer a waiter," says the fat old gent. "I hope he doesn't come from a cheap museum," says the old lady; "he might have microbes in his costume."

'Before he goes to the table, Sir Percival takes me by the arm. "Eighteen," says he, "I've got to pull off this job without a blunder. You coach me straight, or I'll take that halberd and make hash out of you." And then he goes up to the table with his coat of mail on and a napkin over his arm and waits for the order.

' "Why, it's Deering!" says the young swell. "Hello, old man. What the –'

' "Beg pardon, sir," interrupts the halberdier, "I'm waiting on the table."

'The old man looks at him grim, like a Boston bull. "So, Deering," he says, "you're at work yet."

' "Yes, sir," says Sir Percival, quiet and gentlemanly as I could have been myself, "for almost three months, now." "You haven't been discharged during the time?" asks the old man. "Not once, sir," says he, "though I've had to change my work several times."

' "Waiter," orders the girl, short and sharp, "another napkin." He brings her one, respectful.

'I never saw more devil, if I may say it, stirred up in a lady. There was two bright red spots on her cheeks, and her eyes looked exactly like a wild cat's I'd seen in the Zoo. Her foot kept slapping the floor all the time.

' "Waiter," she orders, "bring me filtered water without ice. Bring me a footstool. Take away this empty salt-cellar." She kept him on the jump. She was sure giving the halberdier his.

'There wasn't but a few customers up in the slosh at that time, so I hung out near the door so I could help Sir Percival serve.

'He got along fine with the olives and celery and the blue-points. They were easy. And then the consommé came up the dumb-waiter all in one big silver tureen. Instead of serving it from the side-table, he picks it up between his hands and starts to the dining-table with it. When nearly there he drops the tureen smash on the floor, and the soup soaks all the lower part of that girl's swell silk dress.

' "Stupid – incompetent," says she, giving him a look. "Standing in a corner with a halberd seems to be your mission in life."

' "Pardon me, lady," says he. "It was just a little bit hotter than blazes. I couldn't help it."

'The old man pulls out a memorandum book and hunts in it. "The 25th of April, Deering," says he. "I know it," says Sir Percival. "And ten minutes to twelve o'clock," says the old man. "By Jupiter! you haven't won yet." And he pounds the table with his fist and yells to me: "Waiter, call the manager at once – tell him to hurry here as fast as he can." I go after the boss, and old Brockmann hikes up to the slosh on the jump.

'I want this man discharged at once," roars the old guy. "Look what he's done. Ruined my daughter's dress. It cost at least $600. Discharge this awkward lout at once, or I'll sue you for the price of it."

' "Dis is bad pizness," says the boss. "Six hundred dollars is much. I reckon I vill haf to –'

' "Wait a minute, Herr Brockmann," says Sir Percival easy and smiling. But he was worked up under his tin suitings; I could see that. And then he made the finest, neatest little speech I ever listened to. I can't give you the words, of course. He gave the millionaires a lovely roast in a sarcastic way, describing their automobiles and opera-boxes and diamonds; and then he got around to the working-classes and the kind of grub they eat and the long hours they work – and all that sort of stuff – bunkum, of course. "The restless rich," says he, "never content with their luxuries, always prowling among the haunts of the poor and humble, amusing themselves with the imperfections and misfortunes of their fellow men and women. And even here, Herr Brockmann," he says, "in this beautiful Rindslosh, a grand and enlightening reproduction of Old-World history and architecture, they come to disturb its symmetry and picturesqueness by demanding in their arrogance that the halberdier of the castle wait upon their table! I have faithfully and conscientiously," says he, "performed my duties as a halberdier. I know nothing of a waiter's duties. It was the insolent whim of these transient, pampered aristocrats that I should be detailed to serve them food. Must I be blamed – must I be deprived of the means of a livelihood," he goes on, "on account of an accident that was the result of their own presumption and haughtiness? But what hurts me more than all," says Sir Percival, "is the desecration that has been done to this splendid Rindslosh – the confiscation of its halberdier to serve menially at the banquet board."

'Even I could see that this stuff was piffle; but it caught the boss.

' "Mein Gott," says he, "you vas right. Ein halberdier have not got der right to dish up soup. Him I vil not discharge. Have anoder waiter if you like, und let mein halberdier go back and stand mit his halberd. But, gendleman," he says, pointing to the old man, "you go ahead and sue mit der dress. Sue me for $600 or $6,000. I stand der suit." And the boss puffs off downstairs. Old Brockmann was an all-right Dutchman.

'Just then the clock strikes twelve, and the old guy laughs loud. "You win, Deering," says he. "Let me explain to all," he goes on. "Some time ago Mr. Deering asked me for something that I did not want to give him." (I looks at the girl, and she turns as red as a pickled beet.) "I told him," says the old guy, "if he would earn his own living for three months without once being discharged for incompetence, I would give him what he wanted. It seems that the time was up at twelve o'clock to-night. I came near fetching you, though, Deering, on that soup question," says the old boy, standing up and grabbing Sir Percival's hand.

'The halberdier lets out a yell and jumps three feet high.

' "Look out for those hands," says he, and he holds 'em up. You never saw such hands except on a labourer in a limestone quarry.

' "Heavens, boy!" says old side-whiskers, "what have you been doing to 'em?"

' "Oh," says Sir Percival, "little chores like hauling coal and excavating rock till they went back on me. And when I couldn't hold a pick or a whip I took up halberdiering to give 'em a rest. Tureens full of hot soup don't seem to be a particularly soothing treatment."

'I would have bet on that girl. That high-tempered kind always go as far the other way, according to my experience. She whizzes round the table like a cyclone and catches both his hands in hers. "Poor hands – dear hands," she sings out, and sheds tears on 'em and holds 'em close to her bosom. Well, sir, with all that Rindslosh scenery it was just like a play. And the halberdier sits down at the table at the girl's side, and I served the rest of the supper. And that was about all, except that when they left he shed his hardware store and went with 'em.'

I dislike to be side-tracked from an original proposition.

'But you haven't told me, Eighteen,' said I, 'how the cigar-case came to be broken.'

'Oh, that was last night,' said Eighteen. 'Sir Percival and the girl drove up in a cream-coloured motor-car, and had dinner in the Rindslosh. "The same table, Billy," I heard her say as they went up. I waited on 'em. We've got a new halberdier now, a bow-legged guy with a face like a sheep. As they came downstairs Sir Percival passes him a ten-case note. The new halberdier drops his halberd, and it falls on the cigar-case. That's how that happened.'

LXXXI

Two Renegades

IN THE GATE CITY of the South the Confederate Veterans were reuniting; and I stood to see them march, beneath the tangled flags of the great conflict, to the hall of their oratory and commemoration.

While the irregular and halting line was passing I made onslaught

O HENRY - 100 SELECTED STORIES   583

upon it and dragged forth from the ranks my friend Barnard
O'Keefe, who had no right to be there. For he was a Northerner
born and bred; and what should he be doing hallooing for the Stars
and Bars among those grey and moribund veterans? And why
should he be trudging, with his shining, martial, humorous, broad
face, among those warriors of a previous and alien generation?

I say I dragged him forth, and held him till the last hickory leg
and waving goatee had stumbled past. And then I hustled him out
of the crowd into a cool interior; for the Gate City was stirred that
day, and the hand-organs wisely eliminated 'Marching Through
Georgia' from their repertories.

'Now, what deviltry are you up to?' I asked of O'Keefe when
there were a table and things in glasses between us.

O'Keefe wiped his heated face and instigated a commotion
among the floating ice in his glass before he chose to answer.

'I am assisting at the wake,' said he, 'of the only nation on earth
that ever did me a good turn. As one gentleman to another, I am
ratifying and celebrating the foreign policy of the late Jefferson
Davis, as fine a statesman as ever settled the financial question of a
country. Equal ratio – that was his platform – a barrel of money
for a barrel of flour – a pair of $20 bills for a pair of boots – a
hatful of currency for a new hat – say, ain't that simple compared
with W. J. B.'s little old oxidized plank?'

'What talk is this?' I asked. 'Your financial digression is merely a
subterfuge. Why were you marching in the ranks of the Confederate
Veterans?'

'Because, my lad,' answered O'Keefe, 'the Confederate Government in its might and power interposed to protect and defend
Barnard O'Keefe against immediate and dangerous assassination
at the hands of a bloodthirsty foreign country, after the United
States of America had overruled his appeal for protection, and had
instructed Private Secretary Cortelyou to reduce his estimate of
the Republican majority for 1905 by one vote.'

'Come, Barney,' said I, 'the Confederate States of America has
been out of existence nearly forty years. You do not look older
yourself. When was it that the deceased government exerted its
foreign policy in your behalf?'

'Four months ago,' said O'Keefe promptly. 'The infamous foreign power I alluded to is still staggering from the official blow
dealt it by Mr. Davis's contraband aggregation of states. That's
why you see me cake-walking with the ex-rebs to the illegitimate
tune about 'simmon-seeds and cotton. I vote for the Great Father

in Washington but I am not going back on Mars, Jeff. You say the Confederacy has been dead forty years? Well, if it hadn't been for it, I'd have been breathing to-day with soul so dead I couldn't have whispered a single cuss-word about my native land. The O'Keefes are not overburdened with ingratitude.'

I must have looked bewildered. 'The war was over,' I said vacantly, 'in —'

O'Keefe laughed loudly, scattering my thoughts.

'Ask old Doc Millikin if the war is over!' he shouted, hugely diverted. 'Oh no! Doc hasn't surrendered yet. And the Confederate States! Well, I just told you they bucked officially and solidly and nationally against a foreign government four months ago and kept me from being shot. Old Jeff's country stepped in and brought me off under its wing while Roosevelt was having a gunboat repainted and waiting for the National Campaign Committee to look up whether I had ever scratched the ticket.'

'Isn't there a story in this, Barney?' I asked.

'No,' said O'Keefe; 'but I'll give you the facts. You know I went down to Panama when this irritation about a canal began. I thought I'd get in on the ground floor. I did, and had to sleep on it, and drink water with little zoos in it; so, of course, I got the Chagres fever. That was in a little town called San Juan on the coast.

'After I got the fever hard enough to kill a Port-au-Prince nigger, I had a relapse in the shape of Doc Millikin.

'There was a doctor to attend a sick man! If Doc Millikin had your case, he made the terrors of death seem like an invitation to a donkey-party. He had the bedside manners of a Piute medicine-man and the soothing presence of a dray loaded with iron bridge-girders. When he laid his hand on your fevered brow you felt like Cap John Smith just before Pocahontas went his bail.

'Well, this old medical outrage floated down to my shack when I sent for him. He was built like a shad, and his eyebrows was black, and his white whiskers trickled down from his chin like milk coming out of a sprinkling-pot. He had a nigger boy along carrying an old tomato-can full of calomel, and a saw.

'Doc felt my pulse, and then he began to mess up some calomel with an agricultural implement that belonged to the trowel class.

' "I don't want any death-mask made yet, Doc," I says, "nor my liver put in a plaster-of-Paris cast. I'm sick; and it's medicine I need, not frescoing."

' "You're a blame Yankee, ain't you?" asks Doc, going on mixing up his Portland cement.

' "I'm from the North," says I, "but I'm a plain man, and don't care for mural decorations. When you get the Isthmus all asphalted over with that boll-weevil prescription, would you mind giving me a dose of painkiller, or a little strychnine on toast to ease up this feeling of unhealthiness that I have got?"

' "They was all sassy, just like you," says old Doc, "but we lowered their temperature considerable. Yes, sir, I reckon we sent a good many of ye over to old *mortuis nisi bonum*. Look at Antietam and Bull Run and Seven Pines and around Nashville! There never was a battle where we didn't lick ye unless you was ten to our one. I knew you was a blame Yankee the minute I laid eyes on you.

' "Don't reopen the chasm, Doc," I begs him. "Any Yankeeness I may have is geographical; and, as far as I am concerned, a Southerner is as good as a Filipino any day. I'm feeling too bad to argue. Let's have secession without misrepresentation, if you say so; but what I need is more laudanum, and less Lundy's Lane. If you're mixing that compound gefloxide of gefloxicum for me, please fill my ears with it before you get around to the Battle of Gettysburg, for there is a subject full of talk."

'By this time Doc Millikin had thrown up a line of fortifications on square pieces of paper; and he says to me: "Yank, take one of these powders every two hours. They won't kill you. I'll be around again about sundown to see if you're alive."

'Old Doc's powders knocked the chagres. I stayed in San Juan, and got to knowing him better. He was from Mississippi, and the red-hottest Southerner that ever smelled mint. He made Stonewall Jackson and R. E. Lee look like Abolitionists. He had a family somewhere down near Yazoo City; but he stayed away from the States on account of an uncontrollable liking he had for the absence of a Yankee government. Him and me got as thick personally as the Emperor of Russia and the dove of peace, but sectionally we didn't amalgamate.

' 'Twas a beautiful system of medical practice introduced by old Doc into that isthmus of land. He'd take that bracket-saw and the mild chloride and his hypodermic, and treat anything from yellow fever to a personal friend.

'Besides his other liabilities Doc could play a flute for a minute or two. He was guilty of two tunes – "Dixie" and another one that was mighty close to the "Suwanee River" – you might say one of its tributaries. He used to come down and sit with me while I was getting well, and aggrieve his flute and say unreconstructed things

about the North. You'd have thought the smoke from the first gun
at Fort Sumter was still floating around in the air.

'You know that was about the time they staged them property
revolutions down there, that wound up in the fifth act with the
thrilling canal scene where Uncle Sam has nine curtain-calls holding Miss Panama by the hand, while the bloodhounds keep Senator
Morgan treed up in a coco-nut palm.

'That's the way it wound up: but at first it seemed as if Colom-
bia was going to make Panama look like one of the $3.98 kind,
with dents made in it in the factory, like they wear at North Beach
fish fries. For mine I played the straw-hat crowd to win; and they
gave me a colonel's commission over a brigade of twenty-seven
men in the left wing and second joint of the insurgent army.

'The Colombian troops were awfully rude to us. One day when
I had my brigade in a sandy spot, with its shoes off doing a battalion drill by squads, the Government army rushed from behind a
bush at us, acting as noisy and disagreeable as they could.

'My troops enfiladed, left-faced, and left the spot. After enticing
the enemy for three miles or so we struck a brier-patch and had to
sit down. When we were ordered to throw up our toes and surrender we obeyed. Five of my best staff-officers fell, suffering
extremely with stone-bruised heels.

'Then and there those Colombians took your friend Barney, sir,
stripped him of the insignia of his rank, consisting of a pair of
brass knuckles and a canteen of rum, and dragged him before a
military court. The presiding general went through the usual legal
formalities that sometimes cause a case to hang on the calendar of
a South American military court as long as ten minutes. He asked
me my age, and then sentenced me to be shot.

'They woke up the court interpreter, an American named Jenks,
who was in the rum business and vice versa, and told him to translate
the verdict.

'Jenks stretched himself and took a morphine tablet.

' "You've got to back up against th' 'dobe, old man," says he to
me. "Three weeks, I believe, you get. Haven't got a chew of fine-cut
on you, have you?"

' "Translate that again, with foot-notes and a glossary," says I.
"I don't know whether I'm discharged, condemned, or handed
over to the Gerry Society."

' "Oh," says Jenks, "don't you understand? You're to be stood
up against a 'dobe wall and shot in two or three weeks – three, I
think, they said."

' "Would you mind askin' 'em which?" says I. "A week don't amount to much after you are dead, but it seems a real nice long spell while you are alive."

' "It's two weeks," says the interpreter, after inquiring in Spanish of the court. "Shall I ask 'em again?"

' "Let be," says I. "Let's have a stationary verdict. If I keep on appealing this way they'll have me shot about ten days before I was captured. No, I haven't got any fine-cut."

'They sends me over to the *calaboza* with a detachment of coloured postal-telegraph boys carrying Enfield rifles, and I am locked up in a kind of brick bakery. The temperature in there was just about the kind mentioned in the cooking recipes that call for a quick oven.

'Then I gives a silver dollar to one of the guards to send for the United States consul. He comes around in pyjamas, with a pair of glasses on his nose and a dozen or two inside of him.

' "I'm to be shot in two weeks," says I. "And although I've made a memorandum of it, I don't seem to get it off my mind. You want to call up Uncle Sam on the cable as quick as you can and get him all worked up about it. Have 'em send the *Kentucky* and the *Kearsarge* and the *Oregon* down right away. That'll be about enough battleships; but it wouldn't hurt to have a couple of cruisers and a torpedo-boat destroyer, too. And — say, if Dewey isn't busy, better have him come along on the fastest one of the fleet."

' "Now, see here, O'Keefe," says the consul, getting the best of a hiccup, "what do you want to bother the State Department about this matter for?"

' "Didn't you hear me?" says I; "I'm to be shot in two weeks. Did you think I said I was going to a lawn-party? And it wouldn't hurt if Roosevelt could get the Japs to send down the *Yellowyamtiskookum* or the *Ogotosingsing* or some other first-class cruisers to help. It would make me feel safer."

' "Now, what you want," says the consul, "is not to get excited. I'll send you over some chewing tobacco and some banana fritters when I go back. The United States can't interfere in this. You know you were caught insurging against the government, and you're subject to the laws of this country. Tell you the truth, I've had an intimation from the State Department — unofficially of course — that whenever a soldier of fortune demands a fleet of gunboats in a case of revolutionary *katzenjammer*, I should cut the cable, give him all the tobacco he wants, and after he's shot take his clothes, if they fit me, for part payment of my salary."

' "Consul," says I to him, "this is a serious question. You are representing Uncle Sam. This ain't any little international tom-foolery, like a universal peace congress or the christening of the *Shamrock IV*. I'm an American citizen, and I demand protection. I demand the Mosquito fleet, and Schley, and the Atlantic Squadron, and Bob Evans, and General E. Byrd Grubb, and two or three protocols. What are you going to do about it?"

' "Nothing doing," says the consul.

' "Be off with you, then," says I, out of patience with him, "and send me Doc Millikin. Ask Doc to come and see me."

'Doc comes and looks through the bars at me, surrounded by dirty soldiers, with even my shoes and canteen confiscated, and he looks mightily pleased.

' "Hallo, Yank," says he, "getting a little taste of Johnson's Island, now, ain't ye?"

' "Doc," says I, "I've just had an interview with the U.S. consul. I gather from his remarks that I might just as well have been caught selling suspenders in Kishineff under the name of Rosen-stein as to be in my present condition. It seems that the only mar-itime aid I am to receive from the United States is some navy-plug to chew. Doc," says I, "can't you suspend hostilities on the slavery question long enough to do something for me?"

' "It ain't been my habit," Doc Millikin answers, "to do any painless dentistry when I find a Yank cutting an eye-tooth. So the Stars and Stripes ain't landing any marines to shell the huts of the Colombian cannibals, hey? Oh, say, can you see by the dawn's early light the star-spangled banner has fluked in the fight? What's the matter with the War Department, hey? It's a great thing to be a citizen of a gold-standard nation, ain't it?"

' "Rub it in, Doc, all you want," says I. "I guess we're weak on foreign policy."

' "For a Yank," says Doc, putting on his specs and talking more mild, "you ain't so bad. If you had come from below the line I reckon I would have liked you right smart. Now since your coun-try has gone back on you, you have to come to the old doctor, whose cotton you burned and whose mules you stole, and whose niggers you freed to help you. Ain't that so, Yank?"

' "It is," says I heartily, "and let's have a diagnosis of the case right away, for in two weeks' time all you can do is to hold an autopsy and I don't want to be amputated if I can help it."

' "Now," says Doc, businesslike, "it's easy enough for you to get out of this scrape. Money'll do it. You've got to pay a long string of 'em from General Pomposo down to this anthropoid ape guarding your door. About $10,000 will do the trick. Have you got the money?"

' "Me?" says I. "I've got one Chili dollar, two *real* pieces, and a *medio.*"

' "Then if you've any last words, utter 'em," says that old reb. "The roster of your financial budget sounds quite much to me like the noise of a requiem."

' "Change the treatment," says I. "I admit that I'm short. Call a consultation or use radium or smuggle me in some saws or something."

' "Yank," says Doc Millikin, "I've a good notion to help you. There's only one government in the world that can get you out of this difficulty; and that's the Confederate States of America, the grandest nation that ever existed."

'Just as you said to me I says to Doc: "Why, the Confederacy ain't a nation. It's been absolved forty years ago."

' "That's a campaign lie," says Doc. "She's running along as solid as the Roman Empire. She's the only hope you've got. Now, you, being a Yank, have got to go through with some preliminary obsequies before you can get official aid. You've got to take the oath of allegiance to the Confederate Government. Then I'll guarantee she does all she can for you. What do you say, Yank? – it's your last chance."

' "If you're fooling with me, Doc," I answers, "you're no better than the United States. But as you say it's the last chance, hurry up and swear me. I always did like corn whisky and 'possum, anyhow. I believe I'm half Southerner by nature. I'm willing to try the Ku-Klux in place of the khaki. Get brisk."

'Doc Millikin thinks awhile, and then he offers me this oath of allegiance to take without any kind of a chaser:

' "I, Barnard O'Keefe, Yank, being of sound body but a Republican mind, hereby swear to transfer my fealty, respect, and allegiance to the Confederate States of America, and the government thereof in consideration of said government, through its official acts and powers, obtaining my freedom and release from confinement and sentence of death brought about by the exuberance of my Irish proclivities and my general pizenness as a Yank."

'I repeated these words after Doc, but they seemed to me a kind of hocus-pocus; and I don't believe any life-insurance company in the country would have issued me a policy on the strength of 'em.

'Doc went away saying he would communicate with his government immediately.

'Say – you can imagine how I felt – me to be shot in two weeks, and my only hope for help being in a government that's been dead so long that it isn't even remembered except on Decoration Day and when Joe Wheeler signs the voucher for his pay-cheque. But it was all there was in sight; and somehow I thought Doc Millikin had something up his old alpaca sleeve that wasn't all foolishness.

'Around to the jail comes old Doc again in about a week. I was flea-bitten, a mite sarcastic, and fundamentally hungry.

' "Any Confederate ironclads in the offing?" I asks. "Do you notice any sounds resembling the approach of Jeb Stewart's cavalry overland or Stonewall Jackson sneaking up in the rear? If you do, I wish you'd say so."

' "It's too soon yet for help to come," says Doc.

' "The sooner the better," says I. "I don't care if it gets in fully fifteen minutes before I am shot; and if you happen to lay eyes on Beauregard or Albert Sidney Johnston or any of the relief corps, wig-wag 'em to hike along."

' "There's been no answer received yet," says Doc.

' "Don't forget," says I, "that there's only four days more. I don't know how you propose to work this thing, Doc," I says to him, "but it seems to me I'd sleep better if you had got a government that was alive and on the map – like Afghanistan or Great Britain, or old man Kruger's kingdom, to take this matter up. I don't mean any disrespect to your Confederate States, but I can't help feeling that my chances of being pulled out of this scrape was decidedly weakened when General Lee surrendered."

' "It's your only chance," said Doc; "don't quarrel with it. What did your own country do for you?"

'It was only two days before the morning I was to be shot, when Doc Millikin came around again.

' "All right, Yank," he says. "Help's come. The Confederate States of America is going to apply for your release. The representatives of the government arrived on a fruit-steamer last night."

' "Bully!" says I – "bully for you, Doc! suppose it's marines with a Gatling. I'm going to love your country all I can for this."

' "Negotiations," says old Doc, "will be opened between the two governments at once. You will know later on to-day if they are successful."

'About four in the afternoon a soldier in red trousers brings a paper round to the jail, and they unlocks the door and I walks out. The guard at the door bows and I bows, and I steps into the grass and wades around to Doc Millikin's shack.

'Doc was sitting in his hammock playing "Dixie," soft and low and out of tune, on his flute. I interrupted him at "Look away! look away!" and shook his hand for five minutes.

' "I never thought," says Doc, taking a chew fretfully, "that I'd ever try to save any blame Yank's life. But, Mr. O'Keefe, I don't see but what you are entitled to be considered part human, anyhow. I never thought Yanks had any of the rudiments of decorum and laudability about them. I reckon I might have been too aggregative in my tabulation. But it ain't me you want to thank – it's the Confederate States of America."

' "And I'm much obliged to 'em," says I. "It's a poor man that wouldn't be patriotic with a country that's saved his life. I'll drink to the Stars and Bars whenever there's a flag-staff and a glass convenient. But where," says I, "are the rescuing troops? If there was a gun fired or a shell burst, I didn't hear it."

'Doc Millikin raises up and points out the window with his flute at the banana-steamer loading with fruit.

' "Yank," says he, "there's a steamer that's going to sail in the morning. If I was you, I'd sail on it. The Confederate Government's done all it can for you. There wasn't a gun fired. The negotiations was carried on secretly between the two nations by the purser of that steamer. I got him to do it because I didn't want to appear in it. Twelve thousand dollars was paid to the officials in bribes to let you go."

' "Man!" says I, sitting down hard – "twelve thousand – how will I ever – who could have – where did the money come from?"

' "Yazoo City," says Doc Millikin; "I've got a little saved up there. Two barrels full. It looks good to these Colombians. 'Twas Confederate money, every dollar of it. Now do you see why you'd better leave before they try to pass some of it on an expert?"

' "I do," says I.

' "Now let's hear you give the password," says Doc Millikin.

' "Hurrah for Jeff Davis!" says I.

' "Correct," says Doc. "And let me tell you something: The next tune I learn on my flute is going to be 'Yankee Doodle.' I reckon there's some Yanks that are not so pizen. Or, if you was me, would you try 'The Red, White, and Blue'?" '

LXXXII

A Lickpenny Lover

THERE WERE 3,000 GIRLS in the Biggest Store. Masie was one of them. She was eighteen, and a saleslady in the gents' gloves. Here she became versed in two varieties of human beings – the kind of gents who buy their gloves in department stores and the kind of women who buy gloves for unfortunate gents. Besides this wide knowledge of the human species, Masie had acquired other information. She had listened to the promulgated wisdom of the 2,999 other girls, and had stored it in a brain that was as secretive and wary as that of a Maltese cat. Perhaps Nature, foreseeing that she would lack wise counsellors, had mingled the saving ingredient of shrewdness along with her beauty, as she has endowed the silver fox of the priceless fur above the other animals with cunning.

For Masie was beautiful. She was a deep-tinted blonde, with the calm poise of a lady who cooks butter-cakes in a window. She stood behind her counter in the Biggest Store; and as you closed your hand over the tape-line for your glove measure you thought of Hebe; and as you looked again you wondered how she had come by Minerva's eyes.

When the floor-walker was not looking Masie chewed tutti frutti; when he was looking she gazed up as if at the clouds and smiled wistfully.

That is the shop-girl smile, and I enjoin you to shun it unless you are well fortified with callosity of the heart, caramels, and a congeniality for the capers of Cupid. This smile belonged to Masie's recreation hours and not to the store; but the floorwalker must have his own. He is the Shylock of the stores. When he comes nosing around the bridge of his nose is a toll-bridge. It is goo-goo eyes or 'git' when he looks toward a pretty girl. Of course, not all floor-walkers are thus. Only a few days ago the papers printed news of one over eighty years of age.

One day, Irving Carter, painter, millionaire, traveller, poet, automobilist, happened to enter the Biggest Store. It is due to him to add that his visit was not voluntary. Filial duty took him by the collar and dragged him inside, while his mother philandered among the bronze and terra-cotta statuettes.

Carter strolled across to the glove counter in order to shoot a few minutes on the wing. His need for gloves was genuine; he had forgotten to bring a pair with him. But his action hardly calls for apology, because he had never heard of glove-counter flirtations.

As he neared the vicinity of his fate he hesitated, suddenly conscious of this unknown phase of Cupid's less worthy profession.

Three or four cheap fellows, sonorously garbed, were leaning over the counters, wrestling with the mediatorial hand-coverings, while giggling girls played vivacious seconds to their lead upon the strident string of coquetry. Carter would have retreated, but he had gone too far. Masie confronted him behind her counter with a questioning look in eyes as coldly, beautifully, warmly blue as the glint of summer sunshine on an iceberg drifting in southern seas.

And then Irving Carter, painter, millionaire, etc., felt a warm flush rise to this aristocratically pale face. But not from diffidence. The blush was intellectual in origin. He knew in a moment that he stood in the ranks of the ready-made youths who wooed the giggling girls at other counters. Himself leaned against the oaken trysting-place of a cockney Cupid with a desire in his heart for the favour of a glove salesgirl. He was no more than Bill and Jack and Mickey. And then he felt a sudden tolerance for them, and an elating, courageous contempt for the conventions upon which he had fed, and an unhesitating determination to have this perfect creature for his own.

When the gloves were paid for and wrapped Carter lingered for a moment. The dimples at the corners of Masie's damask mouth deepened. All gentlemen who bought gloves lingered in just that way. She curved an arm, showing like Psyche's through her shirt-waist sleeve, and rested an elbow upon the showcase edge.

Carter had never before encountered a situation of which he had not been perfect master. But now he stood far more awkward than Bill or Jack or Mickey. He had no chance of meeting this beautiful girl socially. His mind struggled to recall the nature and habits of shop-girls as he had read or heard of them. Somehow he had received the idea that they sometimes did not insist too strictly upon the regular channels of introduction. His heart beat loudly at the thought of proposing an unconventional meeting with this lovely and virginal being. But the tumult in his heart gave him courage.

After a few friendly and well-received remarks on general subjects, he laid his card by her hand on the counter.

'Will you please pardon me,' he said, 'if I seem too bold; but I earnestly hope you will allow me the pleasure of seeing you again.

There is my name; I assure you that it is with the greatest respect that I ask the favour of becoming one of your fr – acquaintances. May I not hope for the privilege?'

Masie knew men – especially men who buy gloves. Without hesitation she looked him frankly and smilingly in the eyes, and said:

'Sure. I guess you're all right. I don't usually go out with strange gentlemen, though. It ain't quite ladylike. When should you want to see me again?

'As soon as I may,' said Carter. 'If you would allow me to call at your home, I –'

Masie laughed musically. 'Oh, gee, no!' she said emphatically. 'If you could see our flat once! There's five of us in three rooms. I'd just like to see ma's face if I was to bring a gentleman friend there!'

'Anywhere, then,' said the enamoured Carter, 'that will be convenient to you.'

'Say,' suggested Masie, with a bright-idea look in her peach-blow face, 'I guess Thursday night will about suit me. Suppose you come to the corner of Eighth Avenue and Forty-eighth Street at 7.30. I live right near the corner. But I've got to be back home by eleven. Ma never lets me stay out after eleven.'

Carter promised gratefully to keep the tryst and then hastened to his mother, who was looking about for him to ratify her purchase of a bronze Diana.

A salesgirl, with small eyes and an obtuse nose, strolled near Masie, with a friendly leer.

'Did you make a hit with his nobs, Masie?' she asked familiarly.

'The gentleman asked permission to call,' answered Masie, with the grand air, as she slipped Carter's card into the bosom of her waist.

'Permission to call!' echoed small eyes, with a snigger. 'Did he say anything about dinner in the Waldorf and a spin in his auto afterward?'

'Oh, cheese it!' said Masie wearily. 'You've been used to swell things, I don't think. You've had a swelled head ever since that hose-cart driver took you out to a chop suey joint. No, he never mentioned the Waldorf; but there's a Fifth Avenue address on his card, and if he buys the supper you can bet your life there won't be no pigtail on the waiter what takes the order.'

As Carter glided away from the Biggest Store with his mother in his electric runabout, he bit his lip with a dull pain at his heart. He

knew that love had come to him for the first time in all the
twenty-nine years of his life. And that the object of it should make
so readily an appointment with him at a street corner, though it
was a step toward his desires, tortured him with misgivings.

Carter did not know the shop-girl. He did not know that her
home is often either a scarcely habitable, tiny room or a domicile
filled to overflowing with kith and kin. The street corner is her
parlour the park is her drawing-room, the avenue is her garden
walk; yet for the most part she is as inviolate mistress of herself in
them as is my lady inside her tapestried chamber.

One evening at dusk, two weeks after their first meeting, Carter
and Masie strolled arm-in-arm into a little, dimly lit park. They
found a bench, tree-shadowed and secluded, and sat there.

For the first time his arm stole gently around her. Her
golden-bronze head slid restfully against his shoulder.

'Gee!' sighed Masie thankfully. 'Why didn't you ever think of
that before?'

'Masie,' said Carter earnestly, 'you surely know that I love you. I
ask you sincerely to marry me. You know me well enough by this
time to have no doubts of me. I want you, and I must have you. I
care nothing for the difference in our stations.'

'What is the difference?' asked Masie curiously.

'Well, there isn't any,' said Carter, quickly, 'except in the minds
of foolish people. It is in my power to give you a life of luxury. My
social position is beyond dispute, and my means are ample.'

'They all say that,' remarked Masie. 'It's the kid they all give
you. I suppose you really work in a delicatessen or follow the
races. I ain't as green as I look.'

'I can furnish you all the proofs you want,' said Carter gently.
'And I want you, Masie. I loved you the first day I saw you.'

'They all do,' said Masie, with an amused laugh, 'to hear 'em
talk. If I could meet a man that got stuck on me the third time
he'd seen me I think I'd get mashed on him.'

'Please don't say such things,' pleaded Carter. 'Listen to me,
dear. Ever since I first looked into your eyes you have been the
only woman in the world for me.'

'Oh, ain't you the kidder!' smiled Masie. 'How many other girls
did you ever tell that?'

But Carter persisted. And at length he reached the flimsy, fluttering little soul of the shop-girl that existed somewhere deep
down in her lovely bosom. His words penetrated the heart whose
very lightness was its safest armour. She looked up at him with

eyes that saw. And a warm glow visited her cool cheeks. Tremblingly, awfully, her moth wings closed, and she seemed about to settle upon the flower of love. Some faint glimmer of life and its possibilities on the other side of her glove counter dawned upon her. Carter felt the change and crowded the opportunity.

'Marry me, Masie,' he whispered softly, 'and we will go away from this ugly city to beautiful ones. We will forget work and business, and life will be one long holiday. I know where I should take you – I have been there often. Just think of a shore where summer is eternal, where the waves are always rippling on the lovely beach and the people are happy and free as children. We will sail to those shores and remain there as long as you please. In one of those far-away cities there are grand and lovely palaces and towers full of beautiful pictures and statues. The streets of the city are water, and one travels about in –'

'I know,' said Masie, sitting up suddenly. 'Gondolas.'

'Yes,' smiled Carter.

'I thought so,' said Masie

'And then,' continued Carter, 'we will travel on and see whatever we wish in the world. After the European cities we will visit India and the ancient cities there, and ride on elephants and see the wonderful temples of the Hindus and Brahmins, and the Japanese gardens, and the camel trains and chariot races in Persia, and all the queer sights of foreign countries. Don't you think you would like it, Masie?'

Masie rose to her feet.

'I think we had better be going home,' she said coolly. 'It's getting late.'

Carter humoured her. He had come to know her varying, thistledown moods, and that it was useless to combat them. But he felt a certain happy triumph. He had held for a moment, though but by a silken thread, the soul of his wild Psyche, and hope was stronger within him. Once she had folded her wings and her cool hand had closed about his own.

At the Biggest Store the next day Masie's chum, Lulu, waylaid her in an angle of the counter.

'How are you and your swell friend making it?' she asked.

'Oh, him?' said Masie, patting her side-curls. He ain't in it any more. Say, Lu, what do you think that fellow wanted me to do?'

'Go on the stage?' guessed Lulu breathlessly.

'Nit; he's too cheap a guy for that. He wanted me to marry him and go down to Coney Island for a wedding tour!'

LXXXIII

Dougherty's Eye-opener

BIG JIM DOUGHERTY was a sport. He belonged to that race of men. In Manhattan it is a distinct race. They are the Caribs of the North – strong, artful, self-sufficient, clannish, honourable within the laws of their race, holding in lenient contempt neighbouring tribes who bow to the measure of Society's tape-line. I refer, of course, to the titled nobility of sportdom. There is a class which bears as a qualifying adjective the substantive belonging to a wind instrument made of a cheap and base metal. But the tin mines of Cornwall never produced the material for manufacturing descriptive nomenclature for 'Big Jim' Dougherty.

The habitat of the sport is the lobby or the outside corner of certain hotels and combination restaurants and cafés. They are mostly men of different sizes, running from small to large; but they are unanimous in the possession of a recently shaven, blue-black cheek and chin and dark overcoats (in season) with black velvet collars.

Of the domestic life of the sport little is known. It has been said that Cupid and Hymen sometimes take a hand in the game and copper the queen of hearts to lose. Daring theorists have averred – not content with simply saying – that a sport often contracts a spouse, and even incurs descendants. Sometimes he sits in the game of politics; and then at chowder picnics there is a revelation of a Mrs. Sport and little Sports in glazed hats with tin pails.

But mostly the sport is Oriental. He believes his women-folk should not be too patent. Somewhere behind grilles or flower-ornamented fire-escapes they await him. There, no doubt, they tread on rugs from Teheran and are diverted by the bulbul and play upon the dulcimer and feed upon sweetmeats. But away from his home the sport is an integer. He does not, as men of other races in Manhattan do, become the convoy in his unoccupied hours of fluttering laces and high heels that tick off delectably the happy seconds of the evening parade. He herds with his own race at corners, and delivers a commentary in his Carib lingo upon the passing show.

'Big Jim' Dougherty had a wife, but he did not wear a button portrait of her upon his lapel. He had a home in one of those brown-stone, iron-railed streets on the west side that look like a recently excavated bowling-alley of Pompeii.

To this home of his Mr. Dougherty repaired each night when the hour was so late as to promise no further diversion in the arch domains of sport. By that time the occupant of the monogamistic harem would be in dreamland, the bulbul silenced, and the hour propitious for slumber.

'Big Jim' always arose at twelve, meridian, for breakfast, and soon afterward he would return to the rendezvous of his 'crowd.'

He was always vaguely conscious that there was a Mrs. Dougherty. He would have received without denial the charge that the quiet, neat, comfortable little woman across the table at home was his wife. In fact, he remembered pretty well that they had been married for nearly four years. She would often tell him about the cute tricks of Spot, the canary, and the light-haired lady that lived in the window of the flat across the street.

'Big Jim' Dougherty even listened to this conversation of hers sometimes. He knew that she would have a nice dinner ready for him every evening at seven when he came for it. She sometimes went to matinees, and she had a talking machine with six dozen records. Once when her Uncle Amos blew in on a wind from up-state, she went with him to the Eden Musée. Surely these things were diversions enough for any woman.

One afternoon, Mr. Dougherty finished his breakfast, put on his hat, and got away fairly for the door. When his hand was on the knob he heard his wife's voice.

'Jim,' she said firmly, 'I wish you would take me out to dinner this evening. It has been three years since you have been outside the door with me.'

'Big Jim' was astounded. She had never asked anything like this before. It had the flavour of a totally new proposition. But he was a game sport.

'All right,' he said. 'You be ready when I come at seven. None of this "wait two minutes till I primp an hour or two" kind of business, now, Dele.'

'I'll be ready,' said his wife calmly.

At seven she descended the stone steps in the Pompeian bowl-ing-alley at the side of 'Big Jim' Dougherty. She wore a dinner gown made of a stuff that the spiders must have woven, and of a colour that a twilight sky must have contributed. A light coat with many admirably unnecessary capes and adorably inutile ribbons floated downward from her shoulders. Fine feathers do make fine birds; and the only reproach in the saying is for the man who refuses to give up his earnings to the ostrich-tip industry.

'Big Jim' Dougherty was troubled. There was a being at his side whom he did not know. He thought of the sober-hued plumage that this bird of paradise was accustomed to wear in her cage, and this winged revelation puzzled him. In some way she reminded him of the Delia Cullen that he had married four years before. Shyly and rather awkwardly he stalked at her right hand.

'After dinner I'll take you back home, Dele,' said Mr. Dougherty, 'and then I'll drop back up to Seltzer's with the boys. You can have swell chuck to-night if you want it. I made a winning on Anaconda yesterday; so you can go as far as you like.'

Mr. Dougherty had intended to make the outing with his unwonted wife an inconspicuous one. Uxoriousness was a weakness that the precepts of the Caribs did not countenance. If any of his friends of the track, the billiard cloth or the square circle had wives they had never complained of the fact in public. There were a number of table d'hôte places on the cross streets near the broad and shining way; and to one of these he had purposed to escort her so that the bushel might not be removed from the light of his domesticity.

But while on the way Mr. Dougherty altered those intentions. He had been casting stealthy glances at his attractive companion, and he was seized with the conviction that she was no selling-plater. He resolved to parade with his wife past Seltzer's café, where at this time a number of his tribe would be gathered to view the daily evening procession. Yes; and he would take her to dine at Hoogley's, the swellest slow-lunch warehouse on the line, he said to himself.

The congregation of smooth-faced tribal gentlemen were on watch at Seltzer's. As Mr. Dougherty and his reorganized Delia passed they stared, momentarily petrified, and then removed their hats – a performance as unusual to them as was the astonishing innovation presented to their gaze by 'Big Jim.' On the latter gentleman's impassive face there appeared a slight flicker of triumph – a faint flicker, no more to be observed than the expression called there by the draft of little casino to a four-card spade flush.

Hoogley's was animated. Electric lights shone – as, indeed, they were expected to do. And the napery, the glassware and the flowers also meritoriously performed the spectacular duties required of them. The guests were numerous, well-dressed and gay.

A waiter – not necessarily obsequious – conducted 'Big Jim' Dougherty and his wife to a table.

'Play that menu straight across for what you like, Dele,' said 'Big Jim.' 'It's you for a trough of the gilded oats to-night. It strikes me that maybe we've been sticking too fast to home fodder.'

'Big Jim's' wife gave her order. He looked at her with respect. She had mentioned truffles; and he had not known that she knew what truffles were. From the wine list she designated an appropriate and desirable brand. He looked at her with some admiration.

She was beaming with the innocent excitement that woman derives from the exercise of her gregariousness. She was talking to him about a hundred things with animation and delight. And as the meal progressed her cheeks, colourless from a life indoors, took on a delicate flush. 'Big Jim' looked around the room and saw that none of the women there had her charm. And then he thought of the three years she had suffered immurement, uncomplaining, and a flush of shame warmed him, for he carried fair play as an item in his creed.

But when the Honourable Patrick Corrigan, leader in Dougherty's district and a friend of his, saw them and came over to the table, matters got to the three-quarter stretch. The Honourable Patrick was a gallant man, both in deeds and words. As for the Blarney Stone, his previous actions toward it must have been pronounced. Heavy damages for breach of promise could surely have been obtained had the Blarney Stone seen fit to sue the Honourable Patrick.

'Jimmy, old man!' he called; he clapped Dougherty on the back; he shone like a midday sun upon Delia.

'Honourable Mr. Corrigan – Mrs. Dougherty,'

The Honourable Patrick became a fountain of entertainment and admiration. The waiter had to fetch a third chair for him; he made another at the table, and the wine-glasses were refilled. .

'You selfish old rascal!' he exclaimed, shaking an arch finger at 'Big Jim,' 'to have kept Mrs. Dougherty a secret from us.'

And then 'Big Jim' Dougherty, who was no talker, sat dumb, and saw the wife who had dined every evening for three years at home, blossom like a fairy flower. Quick, witty, charming, full of light and ready talk, she received the experienced attack of the Honourable Patrick on the field of repartee and surprised, vanquished, delighted him. She unfolded her long-closed petals, and around her the room became a garden. They tried to include 'Big Jim' in the conversation, but he was without a vocabulary.

And then a stray bunch of politicians and good fellows who lived for sport came into the room. They saw 'Big Jim' and the leader, and over they came and were made acquainted with Mrs. Dougherty. And in a few minutes she was holding a salon. Half a dozen men surrounded her, courtiers all, and six found her capable of charming. 'Big Jim' sat, grim, and kept saying to himself: 'Three years, three years!'

The dinner came to an end. The Honourable Patrick reached for Mrs. Dougherty's cloak; but that was a matter of action instead of words, and Dougherty's big hand got it first by two seconds.

While the farewells were being said at the door the Honourable Patrick smote Dougherty mightily between the shoulders.

'Jimmy, me boy,' he declared, in a giant whisper, 'the madam is a jewel of the first water. Ye're a lucky dog.'

'Big Jim' walked homeward with his wife. She seemed quite as pleased with the lights and show windows in the streets as with the admiration of the men in Hoogley's. As they passed Seltzer's they heard the sound of many voices in the café. The boys would be starting the drinks around now and discussing past performances.

At the door of their home Delia paused. The pleasure of the outing radiated softly from her countenance. She could not hope for Jim of evenings, but the glory of this one would lighten her lonely hours for a long time.

'Thank you for taking me out, Jim,' she said gratefully. 'You'll be going back up to Seltzer's now, of course.'

'To - with Seltzer's,' said 'Big Jim' emphatically. 'And d - Pat Corrigan! Does he think I haven't got any eyes?'

And the door closed behind both of them.

LXXXIV

'Little Speck in Garnered Fruit'

THE HONEYMOON was at its full. There was a flat with the reddest of new carpets, tasselled portieres and six steins with pewter lids arranged on a ledge above the wainscoting of the dining-room. The wonder of it was yet upon them. Neither of them had ever seen a yellow primrose by the river's brim; but if such a sight had met their eyes at that time it would have seemed like - well, whatever the poet expected the right kind of people to see in it besides a primrose.

The bride sat in the rocker with her feet resting upon the world. She was wrapt in rosy dreams and a kimono of the same hue. She wondered what the people in Greenland and Tasmania and Baluchistan were saying one to another about her marriage to Kid McGarry. Not that it made any difference. There was no welterweight from London to the Southern Cross that could stand up four hours — no, four rounds — with her bridegroom. And he had been hers for three weeks; and the crook of her little finger could sway him more than the fist of any 142-pounder in the world.

Love, when it is ours, is the other name for self-abnegation and sacrifice. When it belongs to people across the airshaft it means arrogance and self-conceit.

The bride crossed her Oxfords and looked thoughtfully at the distemper Cupids on the ceiling.

'Precious,' said she, with the air of Cleopatra asking Antony for Rome done up in tissue-paper and delivered at residence, 'I think I would like a peach.'

Kid McGarry arose and put on his coat and hat. He was serious, shaven, sentimental, and spry.

'All right,' said he, as coolly as though he were only agreeing to sign articles to fight the champion of England. 'I'll step down and cop one out for you — see?'

'Don't be long,' said the bride. 'I'll be lonesome without my naughty boy. Get a nice ripe one.'

After a series of farewells that would have befitted an imminent voyage to foreign parts, the Kid went down to the street.

Here he not unreasonably hesitated, for the season was yet early spring, and there seemed small chance of wrestling anywhere from those chill streets and stores the coveted luscious guerdon of summer's golden prime.

At the Italian's fruit-stand on the corner he stopped and cast a contemptuous eye over the display of papered oranges, highly polished apples and wan, sun-hungry bananas.

'Gotta da peach?' asked the Kid in the tongue of Dante, the lover of lovers.

'Ah, no,' sighed the vender. 'Not for one mont com-a da peach. Too soon. Gotta da nice-a orange. Like-a da orange?'

Scornful, the Kid pursued his quest. He entered the all-night chop-house, café, and bowling-alley of his friend and admirer, Justus O'Callahan. The O'Callahan was about in his institution, looking for leaks.

'I want it straight,' said the Kid to him. 'The old woman has got a hunch that she wants a peach. Now, if you've got a peach, Cal, get it out quick. I want it and others like it if you've got 'em in plural quantities.'

'The house is yours,' said O'Callahan. 'But there's no peach in it. It's too soon. I don't suppose you could even find 'em at one of the Broadway joints. That's too bad. When a lady fixes her mouth for a certain kind of fruit nothing else won't do. It's too late now to find any of the first-class fruiterers open. But if you think the missis would like some nice oranges, I've just got a box of fine ones in that she might –'

'Much obliged, Cal. It's a peach proposition right from the ring of the gong. I'll try farther.'

The time was nearly midnight as the Kid walked down the West-Side avenue. Few stores were open, and such as were practically hooted at the idea of a peach.

But in her moated flat the bride confidently awaited her Persian fruit. A champion welterweight not find a peach? – not stride triumphantly over the seasons and the zodiac and the almanac to fetch an Amsden's June or a Georgia cling to his owny-own?

The Kid's eye caught sight of a window that was lighted and gorgeous with Nature's most entrancing colours. The light suddenly went out. The Kid sprinted and caught the fruiterer locking his door.

'Peaches?' said he, with extreme deliberation.

'Well, no, sir. Not for three or four weeks yet. I haven't any idea where you might find some. There may be a few in town from under the glass, but they'd be hard to locate. Maybe at one of the more expensive hotels – some place where there's plenty of money to waste. I've got some very fine oranges, though – from a shipload that came in to-day.'

The Kid lingered on the corner for a moment, and then set out briskly toward a pair of green lights that flanked the steps of a building down a dark side-street.

'Captain around anywhere?' he asked of the desk sergeant of the police-station.

At that moment the Captain came briskly forward from the rear. He was in plain clothes, and had a busy air.

'Hello, Kid,' he said to the pugilist. 'Thought you were bridal-touring?'

'Got back yesterday. I'm a solid citizen now. Think I'll take an interest in municipal doings. How would it suit you to get into Denver Dick's place to-night, Cap?'

'Past performances,' said the Captain, twisting his moustache. 'Denver was closed up two months ago.'

'Correct,' said the Kid. 'Rafferty chased him out of the Forty-third. He's running in your precinct now, and his game's bigger than ever. I'm down on this gambling business. I can put you against his game.'

'In my precinct?' growled the Captain. 'Are you sure, Kid? I'll take it as a favour. Have you got the entree. How is it to be done?'

'Hammers,' said the Kid. 'They haven't got any steel on the doors yet. You'll need ten men. No; they won't let me in the place. Denver has been trying to do me. He thought I tipped him off for the other raid. I didn't though. You want to hurry. I've got to get back home. The house is only three blocks from here.'

Before ten minutes had sped the Captain with a dozen men stole with their guide into the hallway of a dark and virtuous-looking building in which many businesses were conducted by day.

'Third floor, rear,' said the Kid softly. 'I'll lead the way.'

Two axemen faced the door that he pointed out to them.

'It seems all quiet,' said the Captain doubtfully. 'Are you sure your tip is straight?'

'Cut away!' said the Kid. 'It's on me if it ain't.'

The axes crashed through the as yet unprotected door. A blaze of light from within poured through the smashed panels. The door fell, and the raiders sprang into the room with their guns handy.

The big room was furnished with the gaudy magnificence dear to Denver Dick's western ideas. Various well-patronized games were in progress. About fifty men who were in the room rushed upon the police in a grand break for personal liberty. The plain-clothes men had to do a little club-swinging. More than half the patrons escaped.

Denver Dick had graced his game with his own presence that night. He led the rush that was intended to sweep away the smaller body of raiders. But when he saw the Kid his manner became personal. Being in the heavy-weight class, he cast himself joyfully upon his slighter enemy, and they rolled down a flight of stairs in each other's arms. On the landing they separated and arose, and then the Kid was able to use some of his professional tactics, which had been useless to him while in the clutch of a 200-pound sporting gentleman who was about to lose $20,000 worth of paraphernalia.

After vanquishing his adversary, the Kid hurried upstairs and through the gambling-room into a smaller apartment connecting by an arched doorway.

Here was a long table set with choicest chinaware and silver, and lavishly furnished with food of that expensive and spectacular sort of which the devotees of sport are supposed to be fond. Here again was to be perceived the liberal and florid taste of the gentleman with the urban cognomenal prefix.

A No. 10 patent leather shoe protruded a few of its inches outside the tablecloth along the floor. The Kid seized this, and plucked forth a black man in a white tie and the garb of a servitor.

'Get up!' commanded the Kid. 'Are you in charge of this free lunch?'

'Yes, sah, I was. Has they done pinched us ag'in, boss?'

'Looks that way. Listen to me. Are there any peaches in this lay-out? If there ain't I'll have to throw up the sponge.'

'There was three dozen, sah, when the game opened this evinin'; but I reckon the gentlemen done eat 'em all up. If you'd like to eat a fust-rate orange, sah, I kin find you some.'

'Get busy,' ordered the Kid sternly, 'and move whatever peach crop you've got quick, or there'll be trouble. If anybody oranges me again to-night, I'll knock his face off.'

The raid on Denver Dick's high-priced and prodigal luncheon revealed one lone, last peach that had escaped the epicurean jaws of the followers of chance. Into the Kid's pocket it went, and that indefatigable forager departed immediately with his prize. With scarcely a glance at the scene on the sidewalk below, where the officers were loading their prisoners into the patrol wagons, he moved homeward with long, swift strides.

His heart was light as he went. So rode the knights back to Camelot after perils and high deeds done for their ladies fair. The Kid's lady had commanded him and he had obeyed. True, it was but a peach that she had craved; but it had been no small deed to glean a peach at midnight from that wintry city where yet the February snows lay like iron. She had asked for a peach; she was his bride; in his pocket the peach was warming in his hand that held it for fear that it might fall out and be lost.

On the way the Kid turned in at an all-night drug store and said to the spectacled clerk:

'Say, sport, I wish you'd size up this rib of mine and see if it s broke. I was in a little scrap, and bumped down a flight or two of stairs.'

The druggist made an examination.

'It isn't broken,' was his diagnosis; 'but you have a bruise there that looks like you'd fallen off the Flatiron twice.'

'That's all right,' said the Kid. 'Let's have your clothes-brush, please.'

The bride waited in the rosy glow of the pink lamp-shade. The miracles were not all passed away. By breathing a desire for some slight thing – a flower, a pomegranate, a – oh, yes, a peach – she could send forth her man into the night, into the world which could not withstand him, and he would do her bidding.

And now he stood by her chair and laid the peach in her hand.

'Naughty boy!' she said fondly. 'Did I say a peach? I think I would much rather have had an orange.'

Blest be the bride.

LXXXV

While the Auto Waits

PROMPTLY AT THE BEGINNING of twilight came again to that quiet corner of that quiet, small park the girl in grey. She sat upon a bench and read a book, for there was yet to come a half-hour in which print could be accomplished.

To repeat: Her dress was grey, and plain enough to mask its impeccancy of style and fit. A large-meshed veil imprisoned her turban hat and a face that shone through it with a calm and unconscious beauty. She had come there at the same hour on the day previous, and on the day before that, and there was one who knew it.

The young man who knew it hovered near, relying upon burnt sacrifices to the great joss Luck. His piety was rewarded, for, in turning a page, her book slipped from her fingers and bounded from the bench a full yard away.

The young man pounced upon it with instant avidity, returning it to its owner with that air that seems to flourish in parks and public places – a compound of gallantry and hope, tempered with respect for the policeman on the beat. In a pleasant voice, he risked an inconsequent remark upon the weather – that introductory topic responsible for so much of the world's unhappiness – and stood poised for a moment, awaiting his fate.

The girl looked him over leisurely; at his ordinary, neat dress and his features distinguished by nothing particular in the way of expression.

'You may sit down, if you like,' she said, in a full, deliberate contralto. 'Really, I would like to have you do so. The light is too bad for reading. I would prefer to talk.'

The vassal of Luck slid upon the seat by her side with complaisance.

'Do you know,' he said, speaking the formula with which park chairmen open their meetings 'that you are quite the stunningest girl I have seen in a long time? I had my eye on you yesterday. Didn't know somebody was bowled over by those pretty lamps of yours, did you, honeysuckle?'

'Whoever you are,' said the girl, in icy tones, you must remember that I am a lady. I will excuse the remark you have just made, because the mistake was, doubtless, not an unnatural one – in your circle. I asked you to sit down: if the invitation must constitute me your honeysuckle, consider it withdrawn.'

'I earnestly beg your pardon,' pleaded the young man. His expression of satisfaction had changed to one of penitence and humility. 'It was my fault, you know – I mean, there are girls, in parks, you know – that is, of course, you don't know, but –'

'Abandon the subject, if you please. Of course I know. Now, tell me about these people passing and crowding, each way, along these paths. Where are they going? Why do they hurry so? Are they happy?'

The young man had promptly abandoned his air of coquetry. His cue was now for a waiting part; he could not guess the rôle he would be expected to play.

'It is interesting to watch them,' he replied, postulating her mood. 'It is the wonderful drama of life. Some are going to supper and some to – er – other places. One wonders what their histories are.'

'I do not,' said the girl; 'I am not so inquisitive. I come here to sit because here, only, can I be near the great, common, throbbing heart of humanity. My part in life is cast where its beats are never felt. Can you surmise why I spoke to you, Mr – ?'

'Parkenstacker,' supplied the young man. Then he looked eager and hopeful.

'No,' said the girl, holding up a slender finger, and smiling slightly. 'You would recognize it immediately. It is impossible to keep one's name out of print. Or even one's portrait. This veil and this hat of my maid furnish me with an *incog*. You should have seen the chauffeur stare at it when he thought I did not see. Candidly, there are five or six names that belong in the holy of holies,

and mine, by the accident of birth, is one of them. I spoke to you,
Mr. Stackenpot –'

'Parkenstacker,' corrected the young man modestly.

'– Mr. Parkenstacker, because I wanted to talk, for once, with a
natural man – one unspoiled by the despicable gloss of wealth and
supposed social superiority. Oh! you do not know how weary I am
of it – money, money, money! And of the men who surround me,
dancing like little marionettes all cut by the same pattern. I am
sick of pleasure, of jewels, of travel, of society, of luxuries of all
kinds.'

'I always had an idea,' ventured the young man hesitatingly,
'that money must be a pretty good thing.

'A competence is to be desired. But when you have so many millions that!' She concluded the sentence with a gesture of despair.
'It is the monotony of it,' she continued, 'that palls. Drives, dinners, theatres, balls, suppers, with the gilding of superfluous
wealth over it all. Sometimes the very tinkle of the ice in my
champagne glass nearly drives me mad.'

Mr. Parkenstacker looked ingenuously interested.

'I have always liked,' he said, 'to read and hear about the ways of
wealthy and fashionable folks. I suppose I am a bit of a snob. But I
like to have my information accurate. Now, I had formed the
opinion that champagne is cooled in the bottle, and not by placing
ice in the glass.'

The girl gave a musical laugh of genuine amusement.

'You should know,' she explained, in an indulgent tone, 'that we
of the non-useful class depend for our amusement upon departure
from precedent. Just now it is a fad to put ice in champagne. The
idea was originated by a visiting Prince of Tartary while dining at
the Waldorf. It will soon give way to some other whim. Just as at a
dinner party this week on Madison Avenue a green kid glove was
laid by the plate of each guest to be put on and used while eating
olives.'

'I see,' admitted the young man humbly. 'These special diversions of the inner circle do not become familiar to the common
public.'

'Sometimes,' continued the girl, acknowledging his confession
of error by a slight bow, 'I have thought that if I ever should love a
man it would be one of lowly station. One who is a worker and not
a drone. But, doubtless, the claims of caste and wealth will prove
stronger than my inclination. Just now I am besieged by two. One
is a Grand Duke of a German principality. I think he has, or has

had, a wife, somewhere, driven mad by his intemperance and cruelty. The other is an English Marquis, so cold and mercenary that I even prefer the diabolism of the Duke. What is it that impels me to tell you these things, Mr. Packenstacker?'

'Parkenstackei,' breathed the young man. 'Indeed you cannot know how much I appreciate your confidences.'

The girl contemplated him with the calm, impersonal regard that befitted the difference in their stations.

'What is your line of business, Mr. Parkenstacker?' she asked.

'A very humble one. But I hope to rise in the world. Were you really in earnest when you said that you could love a man of lowly position?'

'Indeed I was. But I said "might." There is the Grand Duke and the Marquis, you know. Yes; no calling could be too humble were the man what I would wish him to be.'

'I work,' declared Mr. Parkenstacker, 'in a restaurant.'

The girl shrank slightly.

'Not as a waiter?' she said, a little imploringly. 'Labour is noble, but – personal attendance, you know – valets and –'

'I am not a waiter. I am cashier in' – on the street they faced that bounded the opposite side of the park was the brilliant electric sign 'RESTAURANT' – 'I am cashier in that restaurant you see there.'

The girl consulted a tiny watch set in a bracelet of rich design upon her left wrist, and rose hurriedly. She thrust her book into a glittering reticule suspended from her waist, for which, however, the book was too large.

'Why are you not at work?' she asked.

'I am on the night turn,' said the young man; 'it is yet an hour before my period begins. May I not hope to see you again?'

'I do not know. Perhaps – but the whim may not seize me again. I must go quickly now. There is a dinner, and a box at the play – and, oh! the same old round. Perhaps you noticed an automobile at the upper corner of the park as you came. One with a white body.'

'And red running gear?' asked the young man, knitting his brows reflectively.

'Yes. I always come in that. Pierre waits for me there. He supposes me to be shopping in the department store across the square. Conceive of the bondage of the life wherein we must deceive even our chauffeurs. Good night.'

'But it is dark now,' said Mr. Parkenstacker, 'and the park is full of rude men. May I not walk –?'

'If you have the slightest regard for my wishes,' said the girl firmly, 'you will remain at this bench for ten minutes after I have left. I do not mean to accuse you, but you are probably aware that autos generally bear the monogram of their owner. Again, good night.'

Swift and stately she moved away through the dusk. The young man watched her graceful form as she reached the pavement at the park's edge, and turned up along it toward the corner where stood the automobile. Then he treacherously and unhesitatingly began to dodge and skim among the park trees and shrubbery in a course parallel to her route, keeping her well in sight.

When she reached the corner she turned her head to glance at the motor-car, and then passed it, continuing on across the street. Sheltered behind a convenient standing cab, the young man followed her movements closely with his eyes. Passing down the sidewalk of the street opposite the park, she entered the restaurant with the blazing sign. The place was one of those frankly glaring establishments, all white paint and glass, where one may dine cheaply and conspicuously. The girl penetrated the restaurant to some retreat at its rear, whence she quickly emerged without her hat and veil.

The cashier's desk was well to the front. A red-haired girl on the stool climbed down, glancing pointedly at the clock as she did so. The girl in grey mounted in her place.

The young man thrust his hands into his pockets and walked slowly back along the sidewalk. At the corner his foot struck a small, paper-covered volume lying there, sending it sliding to the edge of the turf. By its picturesque cover he recognized it as the book the girl had been reading. He picked it up carelessly, and saw that its title was *New Arabian Nights*, the author being of the name of Stevenson. He dropped it again upon the grass, and lounged, irresolute, for a minute. Then he stepped into the automobile, reclined upon the cushions, and said two words to the chauffeur:

'Club, Henri.'

LXXXVI

A Comedy in Rubber

ONE MAY HOPE, in spite of the metaphorists, to avoid the breath of the deadly upas tree; one may, by great good fortune, succeed in blacking the eye of the basilisk; one might even dodge the attentions of Cerberus and Argus; but no man, alive or dead, can escape the gaze of the Rubberer.

New York is the Caoutchouc City. There are many, of course, who go their ways, making money, without turning to the right or the left, but there is a tribe abroad wonderfully composed, like the Martians, solely of eyes and means of locomotion.

These devotees of curiosity swarm like flies, in a moment in a struggling, breathless circle about the scene of an unusual occurrence. If a workman opens a manhole, if a street-car runs over a man from North Tarrytown, if a little boy drops an egg on his way home from the grocery, if a casual house or two drops into a subway, if a lady loses a nickel through a hole in the lisle thread, if the police drag a telephone and a racing chart forth from an Ibsen Society reading-room, if Senator Depew or Mr. Chuck Connors walks out to take the air — if any of these incidents or accidents takes place, you will see the mad, irresistible rush of the 'rubber' tribe to the spot.

The importance of the event does not count. They gaze with equal interest and absorption at a chorus girl or at a man painting a liver-pill sign. They will form as deep a cordon around a man with a club-foot as they will around a balked automobile. They have the *furor rubberendi*. They are optical gluttons, feasting and fattening on the misfortunes of their fellow-beings. They gloat and pore, and glare and squint and stare with their fishy eyes like goggle-eyed perch at the hook baited with calamity.

It would seem that Cupid would find these ocular vampires too cold game for his calorific shafts, but have we not yet to discover an immune even among the Protozoa? Yes, beautiful Romance descended upon two of this tribe, and love came into their hearts as they crowded about the prostrate form of a man who had been run over by a brewery wagon.

William Pry was the first on the spot. He was an expert at such gatherings. With an expression of intense happiness on his features, he stood over the victim of the accident, listening to his groans as if to the sweetest music. When the crowd of spectators had swelled to a closely packed circle, William saw a violent commotion in the crowd opposite him. Men were hurled aside like ninepins by the impact of some moving body that clove them like the rush of a tornado. With elbows, umbrella, hat-pin, tongue and fingernails doing their duty, Violet Seymour forced her way through the mob of onlookers to the first row. Strong men who even had been able to secure a seat on the 5.30 Harlem express staggered back like children as she bucked centre. Two large lady spectators who had seen the Duke of Roxburgh married and had often blocked traffic on Twenty-third Street fell back into the second row with ripped shirt-waists when Violet had finished with them. William Pry loved her at first sight.

The ambulance removed the unconscious agent of Cupid. William and Violet remained after the crowd had dispersed. They were true Rubberers. People who leave the scene of an accident with the ambulance have not genuine caoutchouc in the cosmogony of their necks. The delicate, fine flavour of the affair is to be had only in the aftertaste − in gloating over the spot, in gazing fixedly at the houses opposite, in hovering there in a dream more exquisite than the opium-eater's ecstasy. William Pry and Violet Seymour were connoisseurs in casualties. They knew how to extract full enjoyment from every incident.

Presently they looked at each other. Violet had a brown birthmark on her neck as large as a silver half-dollar. William fixed his eyes upon it. William Pry had inordinately bowed legs. Violet allowed her gaze to linger unswervingly upon them. Face to face they stood thus for moments, each staring at the other. Etiquette would not allow them to speak; but in the Caoutchouc City it is permitted to gaze, without stint, at the trees in the parks and at the physical blemishes of a fellow-creature.

At length with a sigh they parted. But Cupid had been the driver of the brewery wagon, and the wheel that broke a leg united two fond hearts.

The next meeting of the hero and heroine was in front of a board fence near Broadway. The day had been a disappointing one. There had been no fights on the street, children had kept from under the wheels of the street-cars, cripples and fat men in negligee shirts were scarce; nobody seemed to be inclined to slip on banana peels or fall down with heart disease. Even the sport from Kokomo, Ind., who claims to be a cousin of ex-Mayor Low and scatters nickels from a cab window, had not put in his appearance. There was nothing to stare at, and William Pry had premonitions of ennui.

But he saw a large crowd scrambling and pushing excitedly in front of a bill-board. Sprinting for it, he knocked down an old woman and a child carrying a bottle of milk, and fought his way like a demon into the mass of spectators. Already in the inner line stood Violet Seymour with one sleeve and two gold fillings gone, a corset steel puncture and a sprained wrist, but happy. She was looking at what there was to see. A man was painting upon the fence: 'Eat Bricklets – They Fill Your Face.'

Violet blushed when she saw William Pry. William jabbed a lady in a black silk raglan in the ribs, kicked a boy in the shin, hit an old gentleman on the left ear, and managed to crowd nearer to Violet. They stood for an hour looking at the man paint the letters. Then William's love could be repressed no longer. He touched her on the arm.

'Come with me,' he said. 'I know where there is a bootblack without an Adam's apple.'

She looked up at him shyly, yet with unmistakable love transfiguring her countenance.

'And you have saved it for me?' she asked, trembling with the first dim ecstasy of a woman beloved.

Together they hurried to the bootblack's stand. An hour they spent there gazing at the malformed youth.

A window-cleaner fell from the fifth story to the sidewalk beside them. As the ambulance came clanging up William pressed her hand joyously. 'Four ribs at least and a compound fracture,' he whispered swiftly. 'You are not sorry that you met me, are you, dearest?'

'Me?' said Violet, returning the pressure. 'Sure not. I could stand all day rubbering with you.'

The climax of the romance occurred a few days later. Perhaps the reader will remember the intense excitement into which the city was thrown when Eliza Jane, a coloured woman, was served with a subpœna. The Rubber Tribe encamped on the spot. With his own hands William Pry placed a board upon two beer kegs in the street opposite Eliza Jane's residence. He and Violet sat there for three days and nights. Then it occurred to a detective to open the door and serve the subpœna. He sent for a kinetoscope and did so.

Two souls with such congenial tastes could not long remain apart. As a policeman drove them away with his night-stick that evening they plighted their troth. The seeds of love had been well sown, and had grown up, hardy and vigorous, into a – let us call it a rubber plant

The wedding of William Pry and Violet Seymour was set for June 10. The Big Church in the Middle of the Block was banked high with flowers. The populous tribe of Rubberers the world over is rampant over weddings. They are the pessimists of the pews. They are the guyers of the groom and the banterers of the bride. They come to laugh at your marriage, and should you escape from Hymen's tower on the back of death's pale steed they will come to the funeral and sit in the same pew and cry over your luck. Rubber will stretch.

The church was lighted. A grosgrain carpet lay over the asphalt to the edge of the sidewalk. Bridesmaids were patting one another's sashes awry and speaking of the Bride's freckles. Coachmen tied white ribbons on their whips and bewailed the space of time between drinks. The minister was musing over his possible fee, essaying conjecture whether it would suffice to purchase a new broadcloth suit for himself and a photograph of Laura Jane Libbey for his wife. Yea, Cupid was in the air.

And outside the church, oh, my brothers, surged and heaved the rank and file of the tribe of Rubberers. In two bodies they were, with the grosgrain carpet and cops with clubs between. They crowded like cattle, they fought, they pressed and surged, and swayed and trampled one another to see a bit of a girl in a white veil acquire licence to go through a man's pockets while he sleeps.

But the hour for the wedding came and went, and the bride and bridegroom came not. And impatience gave way to alarm, and alarm brought about search, and they were not found. And then two big policemen took a hand, and dragged out of the furious mob of onlookers a crushed and trampled thing, with a wedding-ring in its vest pocket, and a shredded and hysterical woman beating her way to the carpet's edge, ragged, bruised and obstreperous.

William Pry and Violet Seymour, creatures of habit, had joined in the seething game of the spectators, unable to resist the overwhelming desire to gaze upon themselves entering, as bride and bridegroom, the rose-decked church.

Rubber will out.

LXXXVII

One Thousand Dollars

'ONE THOUSAND DOLLARS,' repeated Lawyer Tolman solemnly and severely, 'and here is the money.'

Young Gillian gave a decidedly amused laugh as he fingered the thin package of new fifty-dollar notes.

'It's such a confoundedly awkward amount,' he explained, genially, to the lawyer. 'If it had been ten thousand a fellow might wind up with a lot of fireworks and do himself credit. Even fifty dollars would have been less trouble.'

'You heard the reading of your uncle's will,' continued Lawyer Tolman, professionally dry in his tones. 'I do not know if you paid much attention to its details. I must remind you of one. You are required to render to us an account of the manner of expenditure of this $1,000 as soon as you have disposed of it. The will stipulates that. I trust that you will so far comply with the late Mr. Gillian's wishes.'

'You may depend upon it,' said the young man politely, 'in spite of the extra expense it will entail. I may have to engage a secretary. I was never good at accounts.'

Gillian went to his club. There he hunted out one whom he called Old Bryson.

Old Bryson was calm and forty and sequestered. He was in a corner reading a book, and when he saw Gillian approaching he sighed, laid down his book and took off his glasses.

'Old Bryson, wake up,' said Gillian. 'I've a funny story to tell you.'

'I wish you would tell it to someone in the billiard-room,' said Old Bryson. 'You know how I hate your stories.'

'This is a better one than usual,' said Gillian, rolling a cigarette, 'and I'm glad to tell it to you. It's too sad and funny to go with the rattling of billiard balls. I've just come from my late uncle's firm of legal corsairs. He leaves me an even thousand dollars. Now, what can a man possibly do with a thousand dollars?'

'I thought,' said Old Bryson, showing as much interest as a bee shows in a vinegar cruet, 'that the late Septimus Gillian was worth something like half a million.'

'He was,' assented Gillian joyously, 'and that's where the joke comes in. He's left his whole cargo of doubloons to a microbe. That is, part of it goes to the man who invents a new bacillus, and the rest to establish a hospital for doing away with it again. There are one or two trifling bequests on the side. The butler and the housekeeper get a seal ring and $10 each. His nephew gets $1,000.'

'You've always had plenty of money to spend,' observed Old Bryson.

'Tons,' said Gillian. 'Uncle was the fairy godmother as far as an allowance was concerned.'

'Any other heirs?' asked Old Bryson.

'None.' Gillian frowned at his cigarette and kicked the upholstered leather of a divan uneasily. 'There is a Miss Hayden, a ward
of my uncle who lived in his house. She's a quiet thing – musical –
the daughter of somebody who was unlucky enough to be his
friend. I forgot to say that she was in on the seal ring and $10 joke,
too. I wish I had been. Then I could have had two bottles of brut,
tipped the waiter with the ring, and had the whole business off my
hands. Don't be superior and insulting, Old Bryson – tell me what
a fellow can do with a thousand dollars.'

Old Bryson rubbed his glasses and smiled. And when Old Bryson
smiled, Gillian knew that he intended to be more offensive than ever.

'A thousand dollars,' he said, 'means much or little. One man may
buy a happy home with it and laugh at Rockefeller. Another could
send his wife South with it and save her life. A thousand dollars
would buy pure milk for one hundred babies during June, July, and
August, and save fifty of their lives. You could Count upon a half-
hour's diversion with it at faro in one of the fortified art galleries. It
would furnish an education to an ambitious boy. I am told that a
genuine Corot was secured for that amount in an auction room yesterday. You could move to a New Hampshire town and live
respectably two years on it. You could rent Madison Square Garden
for one evening with it, and lecture your audience, if you should have
one, on the precariousness of the profession of heir-presumptive.'

'People might like you, Old Bryson,' said Gillian, always unruf-
fled, 'if you wouldn't moralize. I asked you to tell me what I could
do with a thousand dollars.'

'You?' said Bryson, with a gentle laugh. 'Why, Bobby Gillian,
there's only one logical thing you could do. You can go buy Miss
Lotta Lauriere a diamond pendant with the money, and then take
yourself off to Idaho and inflict your presence upon a ranch. I
advise a sheep ranch, as I have a particular dislike for sheep.'

'Thanks,' said Gillian, rising, 'I thought I could depend upon
you, Old Bryson. You've hit on the very scheme. I wanted to
chuck the money in a lump, for I've got to turn in an account for
it, and I hate itemizing.'

Gillian phoned for a cab and said to the driver:

'The stage entrance of the Columbine Theatre.'

Miss Lotta Lauriere was assisting Nature with a powder puff,
almost ready for her call at a crowded matinee, when her dresser
mentioned the name of Mr. Gillian.

'Let it in,' said Miss Lauriere. 'Now, what is it, Bobby? I'm
going on in two minutes.'

'Rabbit-foot your right ear a little,' suggested Gillian critically. 'That's better. It won't take two minutes for me. What do you say to a little thing in the pendant line? I can stand three ciphers with a figure one in front of 'em.'

'Oh, just as you say,' carolled Miss Lauriere. 'My right glove, Adams. Say, Bobby, did you see that necklace Della Stacey had on the other night? Twenty-two hundred dollars it cost at Tiffany's. But of course – pull my sash a little to the left, Adams.'

'Miss Lauriere for the opening chorus!' cried the call-boy without.

Gillian strolled out to where his cab was waiting. 'What would you do with a thousand dollars if you had it?' he asked the driver.

'Open a s'loon,' said the cabby promptly and huskily. 'I know a place I could take money in with both hands. It's a four-story brick on a corner. I've got it figured out. Second story – Chinks and chop suey; third floor – manicures and foreign missions; fourth floor – poolroom. If you was thinking of putting up the cap –'

'Oh, no,' said Gillian, 'I merely asked from curiosity. I take you by the hour. Drive till I tell you to stop.'

Eight blocks down Broadway Gillian poked up the trap with his cane and got out. A blind man sat upon a stool on the sidewalk selling pencils. Gillian went out and stood before him.

'Excuse me,' he said, 'but would you mind telling me what you would do if you had a thousand dollars?'

'You got out of that cab that just drove up, didn't you?' asked the blind man.

'I did,' said Gillian.

'I guess you are all right,' said the pencil dealer, 'to ride in a cab by daylight. Take a look at that, if you like.'

He drew a small book from his coat-pocket and held it out. Gillian opened it, and saw that it was a bank deposit book. It showed a balance of $1,785 to the blind man's credit.

Gillian returned the book and got into the cab.

'I forgot something,' he said. 'You may drive to the law offices of Tolman & Sharp, at – Broadway.'

Lawyer Tolman looked at him hostilely and inquiringly through his gold-rimmed glasses.

'I beg your pardon,' said Gillian cheerfully, 'but may I ask you a question? It is not an impertinent one, I hope. Was Miss Hayden left anything by my uncle's will besides the ring and the $10?'

'Nothing,' said Mr. Tolman.

'I thank you very much, sir,' said Gillian, and out he went to his cab. He gave the driver the address of his late uncle's home.

Miss Hayden was writing letters in the library. She was small and slender and clothed in black. But you would have noticed her eyes. Gillian drifted in with his air of regarding the world as inconsequent.

'I've just come from old Tolman's,' he explained. 'They've been going over the papers down there They found a' – Gillian searched his memory for a legal term – 'they found an amendment or a postscript or something to the will. It seemed that the old boy loosened up a little on second thoughts and willed you a thousand dollars. I was driving up this way, and Tolman asked me to bring you the money. Here it is. You'd better count it to see if it's right.' Gillian laid the money beside her hand on the desk.

Miss Hayden turned white. 'Oh!' she said, and again 'Oh!'

Gillian half turned and looked out the window.

'I suppose, of course,' he said, in a low voice, 'that you know I love you.'

'I am sorry,' said Miss Hayden, taking up her money.

'There is no use?' asked Gillian, almost lightheartedly.

'I am sorry,' she said again.

'May I write a note?' asked Gillian, with a smile. He seated himself at the big library table. She supplied him with paper and pen, and then went back to her secretaire.

Gillian made out his account of his expenditure of the thousand dollars in these words:

'Paid by the black sheep, Robert Gillian, $1,000 on account of the eternal happiness, owed by Heaven to the best and dearest woman on earth.'

Gillian slipped his writing into an envelope, bowed, and went his way.

His cab-stopped again at the offices of Tolman & Sharp.

'I have expended the thousand dollars,' he said, cheerily, to Tolman of the gold glasses, 'and I have come to render account of it as I agreed. There is quite a feeling of summer in the air – do you not think so, Mr. Tolman?' He tossed a white envelope on the lawyer's table. 'You will find there a memorandum, sir, of the *modus operandi* of the vanishing of the dollars.'

Without touching the envelope, Mr. Tolman went to a door and called his partner, Sharp. Together they explored the caverns of an immense safe. Forth they dragged as trophy of their search a big envelope sealed with wax. This they forcibly invaded, and wagged their venerable heads together over its contents. Then Tolman became spokesman.

'Mr. Gillian,' he said formally, 'there was a codicil to your uncle's will. It was intrusted to us privately, with instructions that it be not opened until you had furnished us with a full account of your handling of the $1,000 bequest in the will. As you have fulfilled the conditions, my partner and I have read the codicil. I do not wish to encumber your understanding with its legal phraseology, but I will acquaint you with the spirit of its contents.

'In the event that your disposition of the $1,000 demonstrates that you possess any of the qualifications that deserve reward, much benefit will accrue to you. Mr. Sharp and I are named as the judges, and I assure you that we will do our duty strictly according to justice – with liberality. We are not at all unfavourably disposed toward you, Mr. Gillian. But let us return to the letter of the codicil. If your disposal of the money in question has been prudent, wise, or unselfish, it is in our power to hand you over bonds to the value of $50,000, which have been placed in our hands for that purpose. But if – as our client, the late Mr. Gillian, explicitly provides – you have used this money as you have used money in the past – I quote the late Mr. Gillian – in reprehensible dissipation among disreputable associates – the $50,000 is to be paid to Miriam Hayden, ward of the late Mr. Gillian, without delay. Now, Mr. Gillian, Mr. Sharp and I will examine your account in regard to the $1,000. You submit it in writing, I believe. I hope you will repose confidence in our decision.

Mr. Tolman reached for the envelope. Gillian was a little the quicker in taking it up. He tore the account and its cover leisurely into strips and dropped them into his pocket.

'It's all right,' he said smilingly. 'There isn't a bit of need to bother you with this. I don't suppose you'd understand these itemized bets, anyway. I lost the thousand dollars on the races. Good day to you, gentlemen.'

Tolman & Sharp shook their heads mournfully at each other when Gillian left, for they heard him whistling gaily in the hallway as he waited for the elevator.

LXXXIII

The Shocks of Doom

THERE IS AN ARISTOCRACY of the public parks and even of the vagabonds who use them for their private apartments. Vallance felt rather than knew this, but when he stepped down out of his world into chaos his feet brought him directly to Madison Square.

Raw and astringent as a schoolgirl – of the old order – young May breathed austerely among the budding trees. Vallance buttoned his coat, lighted his last cigarette, and took a seat upon a bench. For three minutes he mildly regretted the last hundred of his last thousand that it had cost him when the bicycle cop put an end to his last automobile ride. Then he felt in every pocket and found not a single penny. He had given up his apartment that morning. His furniture had gone toward certain debts. His clothes, save what were upon him, had descended to his man-servant for back wages. As he sat there was not in the whole city for him a bed or a broiled lobster or a street-car fare or a carnation for his buttonhole unless he should obtain them by sponging on his friends or by false pretences. Therefore he had chosen the park.

And all this was because an uncle had disinherited him, and cut down his allowance from liberality to nothing. And all that was because his nephew had disobeyed him concerning a certain girl, who comes not into this story – therefore, all readers who brush their hair toward its roots may be warned to read no further. There was another nephew, of a different branch, who had once been the prospective heir and favourite. Being without grace or hope, he had long ago disappeared in the mire. Now drag-nets were out for him; he was to be rehabilitated and restored. And so Vallance fell grandly as Lucifer to the lowest pit, joining the tattered ghosts in the little park.

Sitting there, he leaned far back on the hard bench and laughed a jet of cigarette smoke up to the lowest tree branches. The sudden severing of all his life's ties had brought him a free, thrilling, almost joyous elation. He felt precisely the sensation of the aeronaut when he cuts loose his parachute and lets his balloon drift away.

The hour was nearly ten. Not many loungers were on the benches. The park-dweller, though a stubborn fighter against autumnal coolness, is slow to attack the advance line of spring's chilly cohorts.

Then arose one from a seat near the leaping fountain, and came and sat himself at Vallance's side. He was either young or old; cheap lodging-houses had flavoured him mustily; razors and combs had passed him by; in him drink had been bottled and sealed in the devil's bond. He begged a match, which is the form of introduction among park benchers, and then began to talk.

'You're not one of the regulars,' he said to Vallance. 'I know tai-
lored clothes when I see 'em. You just stopped for a moment on
your way through the park. Don't mind my talking to you for
awhile? I've got to be with somebody. I'm afraid – I'm afraid. I've
told two or three of those bummers over there about it. They
think I'm crazy. Say – let me tell you – all I've had to eat to-day
was a couple of bretzels and an apple. To-morrow I'll stand in line
to inherit three millions; and that restaurant you see over there
with the autos around it will be too cheap for me to eat in. Don't
believe it, do you?'

'Without the slightest trouble,' said Vallance, with a laugh. 'I
lunched there yesterday. Tonight I couldn't buy a five-cent cup of
coffee.'

'You don't look like one of us. Well, I guess those things
happen. I used to be a high-flyer myself – some years ago. What
knocked you out of the game?'

'I – oh, I lost my job,' said Vallance.

'It's undiluted Hades, this city,' went on the other. 'One day
you're eating from china, the next you are eating in China – a
chop-suey joint. I've had more than my share of hard luck. For
five years I've been little better than a panhandler. I was raised up
to live expensively and do nothing. Say – I don't mind telling you
– I've got to talk to somebody, you see, because I'm afraid – I'm
afraid. My name's Ide. You wouldn't think that old Paulding, one
of the millionaires on Riverside Drive, was my uncle, would you?
Well, he is. I lived in his house once, and had all the money I
wanted. Say, haven't you got the price of a couple of drinks about
you – er – what's your name –'

'Dawson,' said Vallance. 'No; I'm sorry to say that I'm all in,
financially.'

'I've been living for a week in a coal cellar on Division Street,'
went on Ide, 'with a crook they called "Blinky" Morris. I didn't
have anywhere else to go. While I was out to-day a chap with
some papers in his pocket was there, asking for me. I didn't know
but what he was a fly cop, so I didn't go around again until after
dark. There was a letter there he had left for me. Say – Dawson, it
was from a big down-town lawyer, Mead. I've seen his sign on
Ann Street. Paulding wants me to play the prodigal nephew –
wants me to come back and be his heir again and blow in his
money. I'm to call at the lawyer's office at ten to-morrow and step
into my old shoes again – heir to three million, Dawson, and
$10,000 a year pocket money. And – I'm afraid – I'm afraid.'

The vagrant leaped to his feet and raised both trembling arms above his head. He caught his breath and moaned hysterically.

Vallance seized his arm and forced him back to the bench.

'Be quiet!' he commanded, with something like disgust in his tones. 'One would think you had lost a fortune, instead of being about to acquire one. Of what are you afraid?'

Ide cowered and shivered on the bench. He clung to Vallance's sleeve, and even in the dim glow of the Broadway lights the latest disinherited one could see drops on the other's brow wrung out by some strange terror.

'Why, I'm afraid something will happen to me before morning. I don't know what – something to keep me from coming into that money. I'm afraid a tree will fall on me – I'm afraid a cab will run over me, or a stone drop on me from a housetop, or something. I never was afraid before. I've sat in this park a hundred nights as calm as a graven image without knowing where my breakfast was to come from. But now it's different. I love money, Dawson – I'm happy as a god when it's trickling through my fingers, and people are bowing to me, with the music and the flowers and fine clothes all around. As long as I knew I was out of the game I didn't mind. I was even happy sitting here ragged and hungry, listening to the fountain jump and watching the carriages go up the avenue. But it's in reach of my hand again now – almost – and I can't stand it to wait twelve hours, Dawson – I can't stand it. There are fifty things that could happen to me – I could go blind – I might be attacked with heart disease – the world might come to an end before I could –'

Ide sprang to his feet again, with a shriek. People stirred on the benches and began to look. Vallance took his arm.

'Come and walk,' he said soothingly. 'And try to calm yourself. There is no need to become excited or alarmed. Nothing is going to happen to you. One night is like another.'

'That's right,' said Ide. 'Stay with me, Dawson – that's a good fellow. Walk around with me awhile. I never went to pieces like this before, and I've had a good many hard knocks. Do you think you could hustle something in the way of a little lunch, old man? I'm afraid my nerve's too far gone to try any panhandling.'

Vallance led his companion up almost deserted Fifth Avenue, and then westward along the Thirties toward Broadway. 'Wait here a few minutes,' he said, leaving Ide in a quiet and shadowed spot. He entered a familiar hotel, and strolled toward the bar quite in his old assured way.

'There's a poor devil outside, Jimmy,' he said to the bartender, 'who says he's hungry, and looks it. You know what they do when you give them money. Fix up a sandwich or two for him; and I'll see that he doesn't throw it away.'

'Certainly, Mr. Vallance,' said the bartender. 'They ain't all fakes. Don't like to see anybody go hungry.'

He folded a liberal supply of the free lunch into a napkin. Vallance went with it and joined his companion. Ide pounced upon the food ravenously. 'I haven't had any free lunch as good as this in a year,' he said. 'Aren't you going to eat any, Dawson?'

'I'm not hungry — thanks,' said Vallance.

'We'll go back to the Square,' said Ide. 'The cops won't bother us there. I'll roll up the rest of this ham and stuff for our breakfast. I won't eat any more. I'm afraid I'll get sick. Suppose I'd die of cramps or something to-night, and never get to touch that money again! It's eleven hours yet till time to see that lawyer. You won't leave me, will you, Dawson? I'm afraid something might happen. You haven't any place to go, have you?'

'No,' said Vallance, 'nowhere to-night. I'll have a bench with you.'

'You take it cool,' said Ide, 'if you've told it to me straight. I should think a man put on the bum from a good job just in one day would be tearing his hair.'

'I believe I've already remarked,' said Vallance, laughing, 'that I would have thought that a man who was expecting to come into a fortune on the next day would be feeling pretty easy and quiet.'

'It's funny business,' philosophized Ide, 'about the way people take things, anyhow. Here's your bench, Dawson, right next to mine. The light don't shine in your eyes here. Say, Dawson, I'll get the old man to give you a letter to somebody about a job when I get back home. You've helped me a lot to-night. I don't believe I could have gone through the night if I hadn't struck you.'

'Thank you,' said Vallance. 'Do you lie down or sit up on these when you sleep?'

For hours Vallance gazed almost without winking at the stars through the branches of the trees, and listened to the sharp slapping of horses' hoofs on the sea of asphalt to the south. His mind was active, but his feelings were dormant. Every emotion seemed to have been eradicated. He felt no regrets, no fears, no pain or discomfort. Even when he thought of the girl, it was as of an inhabitant of one of those remote stars at which he gazed. He remembered the absurd antics of his companion and laughed softly, yet without a feeling of mirth. Soon the daily army of milk wagons made of the city a roaring drum to which they marched. Vallance fell asleep on his comfortless bench.

At ten o'clock the next day the two stood at the door of Lawyer Mead's office in Ann Street.

Ide's nerves fluttered worse than ever when the hour approached; and Vallance could not decide to leave him a possible prey to the dangers he dreaded.

When they entered the office, Lawyer Mead looked at them wonderingly. He and Vallance were old friends. After his greeting, he turned to Ide, who stood with white face and trembling limbs before the expected crisis.

'I sent a second letter to your address last night, Mr. Ide,' he said. 'I learned this morning that you were not there to receive it. It will inform you that Mr. Paulding has reconsidered his offer to take you back into favour. He has decided not to do so, and desires you to understand that no change will be made in the relations existing between you and him.'

Ide's trembling suddenly ceased. The colour came back to his face, and he straightened his back. His jaw went forward half an inch, and a gleam came into his eye. He pushed back his battered hat with one hand, and extended the other, with levelled fingers, toward the lawyer. He took a long breath and then laughed sardonically.

'Tell old Paulding he may go to the devil,' he said loudly and clearly, and turned and walked out of the office with a firm and lively step.

Lawyer Mead turned on his heel to Vallance and smiled.

'I am glad you came in,' he said genially. 'Your uncle wants you to return home at once. He is reconciled to the situation that led to his hasty action, and desires to say that all will be as –'

'Hey, Adams!' cried Lawyer Mead, breaking his sentence, and calling to his clerk. 'Bring a glass of water – Mr. Vallance has fainted.'

LXXXIX

Nemesis and the Candy Man

'WE SAIL AT EIGHT IN THE MORNING on the *Celtic*,' said Honoria, plucking a loose thread from her lace sleeve.

'I heard so,' said young Ives, dropping his hat, and muffing it as he tried to catch it, 'and I came around to wish you a pleasant voyage.'

'Of course you heard it,' said Honoria, coldly sweet, 'since we have had no opportunity of informing you ourselves.'

Ives looked at her pleadingly, but with little hope.

Outside in the street a high-pitched voice chanted, not unmusically, a commercial gamut of 'Cand-eeee-ee-s! Nice, fresh cand-ee-ee-ee-ees!'

'It's our old candy man,' said Honoria, leaning out the window and beckoning. 'I want some of his motto kisses. There's nothing in the Broadway shops half so good.'

The candyman stopped his push-cart in front of the old Madison Avenue home. He had a holiday and festival air unusual to street pedlars. His tie was new and bright red, and a horseshoe pin, almost life-size, glittered speciously from its folds. His brown, thin face was crinkled into a semi-foolish smile. Striped cuffs with dog-head buttons covered the tan on his wrists.

'I do believe he's going to get married,' said Honoria pityingly. 'I never saw him taken that way before. And to-day is the first time in months that he has cried his wares, I am sure.'

Ives threw a coin to the sidewalk. The candy man knows his customers. He filled a paper bag, climbed the old-fashioned stoop, and handed it in.

'I remember —' said Ives.

'Wait,' said Honoria.

She took a small portfolio from the drawer of a writing-desk, and from the portfolio a slip of flimsy paper one-quarter of an inch by two inches in size.

'This,' said Honoria inflexibly, 'was wrapped about the first one we opened.'

'It was a year ago,' apologized Ives, as he held out his hand for it —

'As long as skies above are blue
To you, my love, I will be true.'

This he read from the slip of flimsy paper.

'We were to have sailed a fortnight ago,' said Honoria gossipingly. 'It has been such a warm summer. The town is quite deserted. There is nowhere to go. Yet I am told that one or two of the roof gardens are amusing. The singing — and the dancing — on one or two seem to have met with approval.'

Ives did not wince. When you are in the ring you are not surprised when your adversary taps you on the ribs.

'I followed the candy man that time,' said Ives irrelevantly, 'and gave him five dollars at the corner of Broadway.'

He reached for the paper bag in Honoria's lap, took out one of the square, wrapped confections, and slowly unrolled it.

'Sara Chillingworth's father,' said Honoria, 'has given her an automobile.'

'Read that,' said Ives, handing over the slip that had been wrapped around the square of candy,

> 'Life teaches us – how to live,
> Love teaches us – to forgive.'

Honoria's cheeks turned pink.

'Honoria!' cried Ives, starting up from his chair.

'Miss Clinton,' corrected Honoria, rising like Venus from the bead on the surf. 'I warned you not to speak that name again.'

'Honoria,' repeated Ives, 'you must hear me. I know I do not deserve your forgiveness, but I must have it. There is a madness that possesses one sometimes for which his better nature is not responsible. I throw everything else but you to the winds. I strike off the chains that have bound me. I renounce the siren that lured me from you. Let the bought verse of that street pedlar plead for me. It is you only whom I can love. Let your love forgive, and I swear to you that mine will be true "as long as skies above are blue." '

•   •   •   •   •

On the west side, between Sixth and Seventh Avenues, an alley cuts the block in the middle. It perishes in a little court in the centre of the block. The district is theatrical; the inhabitants the bubbling froth of half a dozen nations. The atmosphere is Bohemian, the language polyglot, the locality precarious.

In the court at the rear of the alley lived the candy man. At seven o'clock he pushed his cart into the narrow entrance, rested it upon the irregular stone slats, and sat upon one of the handles to cool himself. There was a great draught of cool wind through the alley.

There was a window above the spot where he always stopped his push-cart. In the cool of the afternoon Mlle. Adele, drawing card of the Aerial Roof Garden, sat at the window and took the air. Generally her ponderous mass of dark, auburn hair was down, that the breeze might have the felicity of aiding Sidonie, the maid, in drying and airing it. About her shoulders – the point of her that the photographers always made the most of – was loosely draped a heliotrope scarf. Her arms to the elbow were bare – there were no sculptors there to rave over them – but even the stolid bricks in the walls of the alley should not have been so insensate as to disapprove. While she sat thus Felice, another maid, anointed and bathed the small feet that twinkled and so charmed the nightly Aerial audiences.

Gradually Mademoiselle began to notice the candy man stopping to mop his brow and cool himself beneath her window. In the hands of her maids she was deprived for the time of her vocation – the charming and binding chariot of man. To lose time was displeasing to Mademoiselle. Here was the candy man – no fit game for her darts, truly – but of the sex upon which she had been born to make war.

After casting upon him looks of unseeing coldness for a dozen times, one afternoon she suddenly thawed, and poured down upon him a smile that put to shame the sweets upon his cart.

'Candy man,' she said, cooingly, while Sidonie followed her impulsive dive, brushing the heavy, auburn hair, 'don't you think I am beautiful?'

The candy man laughed harshly, and looked up, with his thin jaw set, while he wiped his forehead with a red-and-blue handkerchief.

'Yer'd make a dandy magazine cover,' he said grudgingly. 'Beautiful or not is for them that cares. It's not my line. If yer lookin' for bouquets apply elsewhere between nine and twelve. I think we'll have rain.'

Truly, fascinating a candy man is like killing rabbits in a deep snow; but the hunter's blood is widely diffused. Mademoiselle tugged a great coil of hair from Sidonie's hands and let it fall out the window.

'Candy man, have you a sweetheart anywhere with hair as long and soft as that? And with an arm so round?' She flexed an arm like Galatea's after the miracle across the window-sill

The candy man cackled shrilly as he arranged a stock of butter-scotch that had tumbled down.

'Smoke up!' said he vulgarly. 'Nothin' doin' in the complimentary line. I'm too wise to be bamboozled by a switch of hair and a newly massaged arm. Oh, I guess you'll make good in the calcium, all right, with plenty of powder and paint on and the orchestra playing "Under the Old Apple Tree." But don't put on your hat and chase downstairs to fly to the Little Church Around the Corner with me. I've been up against peroxide and make-up boxes before. Say, all joking aside – don't you think we'll have rain?'

'Candy man,' said Mademoiselle softly, with her lips curving and her chin dimpling, 'don't you think I'm pretty?'

The candy man grinned.

'Savin' money, ain't yer?' said he, 'by bein' yer own press agent. I smoke, but I haven't seen yer mug on any of the five-cent cigar boxes. It'd take a new brand of woman to get me goin', anyway. I know 'em from side-combs to shoe-laces. Gimme a good day's sales and steak-and-onions at seven, and a pipe and an evenin' paper back there in the court, and I'll not trouble Lillian Russell herself to wink at me, if you please.'

Mademoiselle pouted.

'Candy man,' she said softly and deeply, 'yet you shall say that I am beautiful. All men say so, and so shall you.'

The candy man laughed and pulled out his pipe.

'Well,' said he, 'I must be goin' in. There is a story in the evenin' paper that I am readin'. Men are divin' in the seas for a treasure, and pirates are watchin' them from behind a reef. And there ain't a woman on land or water or in the air. Good evenin'.'

And he trundled his push-cart down the alley and back to the musty court where he lived.

Incredibly to him who has not learned woman, Mademoiselle sat at the window each day and spread her nets for the ignominious game. Once she kept a grand cavalier waiting in her reception chamber for half an hour while she battered in vain the candy man's tough philosophy. His rough laugh chafed her vanity to its core. Daily he sat on his cart in the breeze of the alley while her hair was being ministered to, and daily the shafts of her beauty rebounded from his dull bosom pointless and ineffectual. Unworthy pique brightened her eyes. Pride-hurt, she glowed upon him in a way that would have sent her higher adorers into an egoistic paradise. The candy man's hard eyes looked upon her with a half-concealed derision that urged her to the use of the sharpest arrow in her beauty's quiver.

One afternoon she leaned far over the sill, and she did not challenge and torment him as usual.

'Candy man,' said she, 'stand up and look into my eyes.'

He stood up and looked into her eyes, with his harsh laugh like the sawing of wood. He took out his pipe, fumbled with it, and put it back into his pocket with a trembling hand.

'That will do,' said Mademoiselle, with a slow smile. 'I must go now to my *masseuse*. Good evening.'

The next evening at seven the candy man came and rested his cart under the window. But was it the candy man? His clothes were a bright new check. His necktie was a flaming red, adorned by a glittering horseshoe pin, almost life-size. His shoes were polished; the tan of his cheeks had paled – his hands had been washed. The window was empty, and he waited under it with his nose upward, like a hound hoping for a bone.

Mademoiselle came, with Sidonie, carrying her load of hair. She looked at the candy man and smiled, a slow smile that faded away into ennui. Instantly she knew that the game was bagged; and so quickly she wearied of the chase. She began to talk to Sidonie.

'Been a fine day,' said the candy man hollowly. 'First time in a month I've felt first-class. Hit it up down old Madison, hollering out like I useter. Think it'll rain to-morrow?'

Mademoiselle laid two round arms on the cushion on the window-sill, and a dimpled chin upon them.

'Candy man,' said she softly, 'do you not love me?'

The candy man stood up and leaned against the brick wall.

'Lady,' said he chokingly, 'I've got $800 saved up. Did I say you wasn't beautiful? Take it, every bit of it, and buy a collar for your dog with it.'

A sound as of a hundred silvery bells tinkled in the room of Mademoiselle. The laughter filled the alley and trickled back into the court, as strange a thing to enter there as sunlight itself. Mademoiselle was amused. Sidonie, a wise echo, added a sepulchral but faithful contralto. The laughter of the two seemed at last to penetrate the candy man. He fumbled with his horseshoe pin. At length Mademoiselle, exhausted, turned her flushed, beautiful face to the window.

'Candy man,' said she, 'go away. When I laugh Sidonie pulls my hair. I can but laugh while you remain there.'

'Here is a note for Mademoiselle,' said Felice, coming to the window in the room.

'There is no justice,' said the candy man, lifting the handle of his cart and moving away.

Three yards he moved, and stopped. Loud shriek after shriek came from the window of Mademoiselle. Quickly he ran back. He heard a body thumping upon the floor and a sound as though heels beat alternately upon it.

'What is it?' he called.

Sidonie's severe head came into the window.

'Mademoiselle is overcome by bad news,' she said. 'One whom she loved with all her soul has gone – you may have heard of him – he is Monsieur Ives. He sails across the ocean to-morrow. Oh, you men!'

XC

The Memento

MISS LYNNETTE D'ARMANDE turned her back on Broadway. This was but tit for tat, because Broadway had often done the same thing to Miss D'Armande. Still, the 'tats' seemed to have it, for the ex-leading lady of the 'Reaping the Whirlwind' Company had everything to ask of Broadway, while there was no vice versa.

So Miss Lynnette D'Armande turned the back of her chair to her window that overlooked Broadway, and sat down to stitch in time the lisle-thread heel of a black silk stocking. The tumult and glitter of the roaring Broadway beneath her window had no charm for her; what she greatly desired was the stifling air of a dressing-room on that fairyland street and the roar of an audience gathered in that capricious quarter. In the meantime, those stockings must not be neglected. Silk does wear out so, but – after all, isn't it just the only goods there is?

The Hotel Thalia looks on Broadway as Marathon looks on the sea. It stands like a gloomy cliff above the whirlpool where the tides of two great thoroughfares clash. Here the player-bands gather at the end of their wanderings, to loosen the buskin and dust the sock. Thick in the streets around it are booking-offices, theatres, agents, schools, and the lobster-palaces to which those thorny paths lead.

Wandering through the eccentric halls of the dim and fusty Thalia, you seem to have found yourself in some great ark or caravan about to sail, or fly, or roll away on wheels. About the house lingers a sense of unrest, of expectation, of transientness, even of anxiety and apprehension. The halls are a labyrinth. Without a guide you wander like a lost soul in a Sam Loyd puzzle.

Turning any corner, a dressing-sack or a *cul-de-sac* may bring you up short. You meet alarming tragedians stalking in bath-robes in search of rumoured bath-rooms. From hundreds of rooms come the buzz of talk, scraps of new and old songs, and the ready laughter of the convened players.

Summer has come; their companies have disbanded, and they take their rest in their favourite caravansary, while they besiege the managers for engagements for the coming season.

At this hour of the afternoon the day's work of tramping the rounds of the agents' offices is over. Past you, as you ramble distractedly through the mossy halls, flit audible visions of houris, with veiled, starry eyes, flying tag-ends of things, and a swish of silk, bequeathing to the dull hallways an odour of gaiety and a memory of *frangipanni*. Serious young comedians, with versatile Adam's apples, gather in doorways and talk of Booth. Far-reaching from somewhere comes the smell of ham and red cabbage, and the crash of dishes on the American plan.

The indeterminate hum of life in the Thalia is enlivened by the discreet popping – at reasonable and salubrious intervals – of beer-bottle corks. Thus punctuated, life in the genial hostel scans easily – the comma being the favourite mark, semicolons frowned upon, and periods barred.

Miss D'Armande's room was a small one. There was room for her rocker between the dresser and the wash-stand if it were placed longitudinally. On the dresser were its usual accoutrements, plus the ex-leading lady's collected souvenirs of road engagements and photographs of her dearest and best professional friends.

At one of these photographs she looked twice or thrice as she darned, and smiled friendlily.

'I'd like to know where Lee is just this minute,' she said, half-aloud.

If you had been privileged to view the photograph thus flattered, you would have thought at the first glance that you saw the picture of a many-petalled, white flower, blown through the air by a storm.

But the floral kingdom was not responsible for that swirl of petalous whiteness.

You saw the filmy, brief skirt of Miss Rosalie Ray as she made a complete heels-over-head turn in her wistaria-entwined swing, far out from the stage, high above the heads of the audience. You saw the camera's inadequate representation of the graceful, strong kick, with which she, at this exciting moment, sent flying, high and far, the yellow silk garter that each evening spun from her agile limb and descended upon the delighted audience below.

You saw, too, amid the black-clothed, mainly masculine patrons of select vaudeville a hundred hands raised with the hope of staying the flight of the brilliant aerial token.

Forty weeks of the best circuits this act had brought Miss Rosalie Ray for each of two years. She did other things during her twelve minutes — a song and dance, imitations of two or three actors who are but imitations of themselves, and a balancing feat with a step-ladder and feather-duster; but when the blossom-decked swing was let down from the flies, and Miss Rosalie sprang smiling into the seat, with the golden circlet conspicuous in the place whence it was soon to slide and become a soaring and coveted guerdon — then it was that the audience rose in its seat as a single man — or presumably so — and endorsed the speciality that made Miss Ray's name a favourite in the booking-offices.

At the end of the two years Miss Ray suddenly announced to her dear friend, Miss D'Armande, that she was going to spend the summer at an antediluvian village on the north shore of Long Island, and that the stage would see her no more. Seventeen minutes after Miss Lynnette D'Armande had expressed her wish to know the whereabouts of her old chum, there were sharp raps at her door.

Doubt not that it was Rosalie Ray. At the shrill command to enter she did so, with something of a tired flutter, and dropped a heavy handbag on the floor. Upon my word, it was Rosalie, in a loose, travel-stained automobileless coat, closely tied brown veil with yard-long flying ends, grey walking-suit and tan Oxfords with lavender over-gaiters.

When she threw off her veil and hat, you saw a pretty enough face, now flushed and disturbed by some unusual emotion, and restless, large eyes with discontent marring their brightness. A heavy pile of dull auburn hair, hastily put up, was escaping in crinkly waving strands and curling small locks from the confining combs and pins.

The meeting of the two was not marked by the effusion vocal, gymnastical, osculatory, and catechetical that distinguishes the greetings of their unprofessional sisters in society. There was a brief clinch, two simultaneous labial dabs, and they stood on the same footing of the old days. Very much like the short salutations of soldiers or of travellers in foreign wilds are the welcomes between the strollers at the corners of their criss-cross roads.

'I've got the hall-room two flights up above yours,' said Rosalie, 'but I came straight to see you before going up. I didn't know you were here till they told me.'

'I've been in since the last of April,' said Lynnette. 'And I'm going on the road with a "Fatal Inheritance" Company. We open next week in Elizabath. I thought you'd quit the stage, Lee. Tell me about yourself.'

Rosalie settled herself with a skilful wriggle on the top of Miss D'Armande's wardrobe trunk, and leaned her head against the papered wall. From long habit, thus can peripatetic leading ladies and their sisters make themselves as comfortable as though the deepest arm-chairs embraced them.

'I'm going to tell you, Lynn,' she said, with a strangely sardonic and yet carelessly resigned look on her youthful face. 'And then to-morrow I'll strike the old Broadway trail again, and wear some more paint off the chairs in the agents' offices. If anybody had told me any time in the last three months up to four o'clock this afternoon that I'd ever listen to that "Leave-your-name-and-address" rot of the booking bunch again, I'd have given 'em the real Mrs. Fiske laugh. Loan me a handkerchief, Lynn. Gee! but those Long Island trains are fierce. I've got enough soft coal cinders on my face to go on and play *Topsy* without using the cork. And, speaking of corks — got anything to drink, Lynn?'

Miss D'Armande opened a door of the washstand and took out a bottle.

'There's nearly a pint of Manhattan. There's a cluster of carnations in the drinking-glass, but —'

'Oh, pass the bottle. Save the glass for company. Thanks! That hits the spot. The same to you. My first drink in three months!'

'Yes, Lynn, I quit the stage at the end of last season. I quit it because I was sick of the life. And especially because my heart and soul were sick of men — of the kind of men we stage people have to be up against. You know what the game is to us — it's a fight against 'em all the way down the line, from the manager who wants us to try his new motor-car to the bill-posters who want to call us by our front names.

'And the men we have to meet after the show are the worst of all. The stage-door kind, and the manager's friends who take us to supper, and show their diamonds, and talk about seeing "Dan" and "Dave" and "Charlie" for us. They're beasts, and I hate 'em.

'I tell you, Lynn, it's the girls like us on the stage that ought to be pitied. It's girls from good homes that are honestly ambitious and work hard to rise in the profession, but never do get there. You hear a lot of sympathy sloshed around on chorus girls and their fifteen dollars a week. Piffle! There ain't a sorrow in the chorus that a lobster cannot heal.

'If there's any tears to shed, let 'em fall for the actress that gets a salary of from thirty to forty-five dollars a week for taking a leading part in a bum show. She knows she'll never do any better; but she hangs on for years, hoping for the "chance" that never comes.

'And the fool plays we have to work in! Having another girl roll you around the stage by the hind legs in a "Wheelbarrow Chorus" in a musical comedy is dignified drama compared with the idiotic things I've had to do in the thirty-centers.

'But what I hated most was the men – the men leering and blathering at you across tables, trying to buy you with Würzburger or Extra Dry, according to their estimate of your price. And the men in the audiences, clapping, yelling, snarling, crowding, writhing, gloating – like a lot of wild beasts, with their eyes fixed on you, ready to eat you up if you come in reach of their claws. Oh, how I hate 'em!

'Well, I'm not telling you much about myself, am I, Lynn?

'I had two hundred dollars saved up, and I cut the stage the first of the summer. I went over on Long Island, and found the sweetest little village that ever was, called Soundport, right on the water. I was going to spend the summer there, and study up on elocution, and try to get a class in the fall. There was an old widow lady with a cottage near the beach who sometimes rented a room or two just for company, and she took me in. She had another boarder, too – the Reverend Arthur Lyle.

'Yes, he was the head-liner. You're on, Lynn. I'll tell you all of it in a minute. It's only a one-act play.

'The first time he walked on, Lynn, I felt myself going; the first lines he spoke, he had me. He was different from the men in audiences. He was tall and slim, and you never heard him come in the room, but you *felt* him. He had a face like a picture of a knight – like one of that Round Table bunch – and a voice like a 'cello solo. And his manners!

'Lynn, if you'd take John Drew in his best drawing-room scene and compare the two you'd have John arrested for disturbing the peace.

'I'll spare you the particulars; but in less than a month Arthur and I were engaged. He preached at a little one-night stand of a Methodist church. There was to be a parsonage the size of a lunch-wagon, and hens and honeysuckles when we were married.

Arthur used to preach to me a good deal about Heaven, but he never could get my mind quite off those honeysuckles and hens.

'No; I didn't tell him I'd been on the stage. I hated the business and all that went with it; I'd cut it out for ever, and I didn't see any use of stirring things up. I was a good girl, and I didn't have anything to confess, except being an elocutionist, and that was about all the strain my conscience would stand.

'Oh, I tell you, Lynn, I was happy. I sang in the choir and attended the sewing society, and recited that "Annie Laurie" thing with the whistling stunt in it, "in a manner bordering upon the professional," as the weekly village paper reported it. And Arthur and I went rowing, and walking in the woods, and clamming, and that poky little village seemed to me the best place in the world. I'd have been happy to live there always, too, if —

'But one morning old Mrs. Gurley, the widow lady, got gossipy while I was helping her string beans on the back porch, and began to gush information, as folks who rent out their rooms usually do. Mr. Lyle was her idea of a saint on earth — as he was mine, too. She went over all his virtues and graces, and wound up by telling me that Arthur had had an extremely romantic love-affair, not long before, that had ended unhappily. She didn't seem to be on to the details, but she knew that he had been hit pretty hard. He was paler and thinner, she said, and he had some kind of a remembrance or keepsake of the lady in a little rosewood box that he kept locked in his desk drawer in his study.

' "Several times," says she, "I've seen him gloomerin' over that box of evenings, and he always locks it up right away if anybody comes into the room."

'Well, you can imagine how long it was before I got Arthur by the wrist and led him down stage and hissed in his ear.

'That same afternoon we were lazying around in a boat among the water-lilies at the edge of the bay.

' "Arthur," says I, "you never told me you'd had another love-affair. But Mrs. Gurley did," I went on, to let him know I knew. I hate to hear a man lie.

' "Before you came," says he, looking me frankly in the eye, "there was a previous affection — a strong one. Since you know of it, I will be perfectly candid with you.'

' "I am waiting," says I.

' "My dear Ida," says Arthur — of course, I went by my real name while I was in Soundport — "this former affection was a spiritual one, in fact. Although the lady aroused my deepest sentiments, and was, as I thought, my ideal woman, I never met her, and never spoke to her. It was an ideal love. My love for you, while no less ideal, is different. You wouldn't let that come between us.'

' "Was she pretty?" I asked.

' "She was very beautiful," said Arthur.

' "Did you see her often?" I asked.

' "Something like a dozen times," says he

' "Always from a distance?" says I.

' "Always from quite a distance," says he.

' "And you loved her?" I asked.

' "She seemed my ideal of beauty and grace — and soul," says Arthur.

' "And this keepsake that you keep under lock and key, and moon over at times, is that a remembrance from her?"

' "A memento," says Arthur, "that I have treasured."

' "Did she send it to you?"

' "It came to me from her," says he.

' "In a roundabout way?" I asked.

' "Somewhat roundabout," says he, "and yet rather direct."

' "Why didn't you ever meet her?" I asked. "Were your positions in life so different?"

' "She was far above me," says Arthur. "Now, Ida," he goes on, "this is all of the past. You're not going to be jealous, are you?

' "Jealous!" says I. "Why, man, what are you talking about? It makes me think ten times as much of you as I did before I knew about it."

'And it did, Lynn — if you can understand it. That ideal love was a new one on me, but it struck me as being the most beautiful and glorious thing I'd ever heard of. Think of a man loving a woman he'd never even spoken to, and being faithful just to what his mind and heart pictured her. Oh, it sounded great to me. The men I'd always known come at you with either diamonds, knock-out-drops or a raise of salary — and their ideals! — well, we'll say no more.

'Yes, it made me think more of Arthur than I did before. I couldn't be jealous of that far-away divinity that he used to worship, for I was going to have him myself. And I began to look upon him as a saint on earth, just as old lady Gurley did.

'About four o'clock this afternoon a man came to the house for Arthur to go and see somebody that was sick among his church bunch. Old lady Gurley was taking her afternoon snore on a couch, so that left me pretty much alone.

'In passing by Arthur's study I looked in, and saw his bunch of keys hanging in the drawer of his desk, where he'd forgotten 'em. Well, I guess we're all to the Mrs. Bluebeard now and then, ain't we, Lynn? I made up my mind I'd have a look at that memento he kept so secret. Not that I cared where it was - it was just curiosity.

'While I was opening the drawer I imagined one or two things it might be. I thought it might be a dried rosebud she'd dropped down to him from a balcony, or maybe a picture of her he'd cut out of a magazine, she being so high up in the world.

'I opened the drawer, and there was the rosewood casket about the size of a gent's collar box I found the little key in the bunch that fitted it and unlocked it and raised the lid.

'I took one look at that memento, and then I went to my room and packed my trunk. I threw a few things into my grip, gave my hair a flirt or two with a side-comb, put on my hat, and went in and gave the old lady's foot a kick. I'd tried awfully hard to use proper and correct language while I was there for Arthur's sake, and I had the habit down pat, but it left me then.

' "Stop sawing gourds," says I, "and sit up and take notice. The ghost's about to walk. I'm going away from here, and I owe you eight dollars. The expressman will call for my trunk."

'I handed her the money.

' "Dear me, Miss Crosby!" says she. "Is anything wrong? I thought you were pleased here. Dear me, young women are so hard to understand, and so different from what you expect 'em to be."

' "You're damn right," says I. "Some of 'em are. But you can't say that about men. *When you know one man you know 'em all!* That settles the human-race question."

'And then I caught the four-thirty-eight, softcoal unlimited; and here I am.'

'You didn't tell me what was in the box, Lee,' said Miss D'Armande anxiously.

'One of those yellow silk garters that I used to kick off my leg into the audience during that old vaudeville swing act of mine. Is there any of the cocktail left, Lynn!'

XCI

The Hypotheses of Failure

LAWYER GOOCH BESTOWED his undivided attention upon the engrossing arts of his profession. But one flight of fancy did he allow his mind to entertain. He was fond of likening his suite of office rooms to the bottom of a ship. The rooms were three in number, with a door opening from one to another. These doors could also be closed.

'Ships,' Lawyer Gooch would say, 'are constructed for safety, with separate, water-tight compartments in their bottoms. If one compartment springs a leak it fills with water; but the good ship goes on unhurt. Were it not for the separating bulkheads one leak would sink the vessel. Now it often happens that while I am occupied with clients, other clients with conflicting interests call. With the assistance of Archibald – an office boy with a future – I cause the dangerous influx to be diverted into separate compartments, while I sound with my legal plummet the depth of each. If necessary they may be baled into the hallway and permitted to escape by way of the stairs, which we may term the lee scuppers. Thus the good ship of business is kept afloat; whereas if the element that supports her were allowed to mingle freely in her hold we might be swamped – ha, ha, ha!'

The law is dry. Good jokes are few. Surely it might be permitted Lawyer Gooch to mitigate the bore of briefs, the tedium of torts, and the prosiness of processes with even so light a levy upon the good property of humour.

Lawyer Gooch's practice leaned largely to the settlement of marital infelicities. Did matrimony languish through complications, he mediated, soothed and arbitrated. Did it suffer from implications, he readjusted, defended and championed. Did it arrive at the extremity of duplications, he always got light sentences for his clients.

But not always was Lawyer Gooch the keen, armed, wily belligerent, ready with his two-edged sword to lop off the shackles of Hymen. He had been known to build up instead of demolishing, to reunite instead of severing, to lead erring and foolish ones back into the fold instead of scattering the flock. Often had he by his eloquent and moving appeals sent husband and wife, weeping, back into each other's arms. Frequently he had coached childhood so successfully that, at the psychological moment (and at a given signal) the plaintive pipe of 'Papa, won't you tum home adain to me and muvver?' had won the day and upheld the pillars of a tottering home.

Unprejudiced persons admitted that Lawyer Gooch received as big fees from these revoked clients as would have been paid him had the cases been contested in court. Prejudiced ones intimated that his fees were doubled, because the penitent couples always came back later for the divorce, anyhow.

There came a season in June when the legal ship of Lawyer Gooch (to borrow his own figure) was nearly becalmed. The divorce mill grinds slowly in June. It is the month of Cupid and Hymen.

Lawyer Gooch, then, sat idle in the middle room of his client-less suite. A small anteroom connected — or rather separated — this apartment from the hallway. Here was stationed Archibald, who wrested from visitors their cards or oral nomenclature which he bore to his master while they waited.

Suddenly, on this day, there came a great knocking at the outermost door.

Archibald, opening it, was thrust aside as superfluous by the visitor, who without due reverence at once penetrated to the office of Lawyer Gooch and threw himself with good-natured insolence into a comfortable chair facing that gentleman.

'You are Phineas C. Gooch, attorney-at-law?' said the visitor, his tone of voice and inflection making his words at once a question, an assertion and an accusation.

Before committing himself by a reply, the lawyer estimated his possible client in one of his brief but shrewd and calculating glances.

The man was of the emphatic type — large-sized, active, bold and debonair in demeanour, vain beyond a doubt, slightly swaggering, ready and at ease. He was well-clothed, but with a shade too much ornateness. He was seeking a lawyer; but if that fact would seem to saddle him with troubles they were not patent in his beaming eye and courageous air.

'My name is Gooch,' at length the lawyer admitted. Upon pressure he would also have confessed to the Phineas C. But he did not consider it good practice to volunteer information. 'I did not receive your card,' he continued, by way of rebuke, 'so I —'

'I know you didn't,' remarked the visitor coolly 'and you won't just yet. Light up?' He threw a leg over an arm of his chair, and tossed a handful of rich-hued cigars upon the table. Lawyer Gooch knew the brand. He thawed just enough to accept the invitation to smoke.

'You are a divorce lawyer,' said the cardless visitor. This time there was no interrogation in his voice. Nor did his words constitute a simple assertion. They formed a charge — a denunciation — as one would say to a dog: 'You are a dog.' Lawyer Gooch was silent under the imputation.

'You handle,' continued the visitor, 'all the various ramifications of busted-up connubiality. You are a surgeon, we might say, who extracts Cupid's darts when he shoots 'em into the wrong parties. You furnish patent, incandescent lights for premises where the torch of Hymen has burned so low you can't light a cigar at it. Am I right, Mr. Gooch?'

'I have undertaken cases,' said the lawyer guardedly, 'in the line to which your figurative speech seems to refer. Do you wish to consult me professionally, Mr. –' The lawyer paused, with significance.

'Not yet,' said the other, with an arch wave of his cigar, 'not just yet. Let us approach the subject with the caution that should have been used in the original act that makes this pow-wow necessary. There exists a matrimonial jumble, to be straightened out. But before I give you names I want your honest – well, anyhow, your professional opinion on the merits of the mix-up. I want you to size up the catastrophe – abstractly – you understand? I'm Mr. Nobody: and I've got a story to tell you. Then you say what's what. Do you get my wireless?'

'You want to state a hypothetical case?' suggested Lawyer Gooch.

'That's the word I was after. "Apothecary" was the best shot I could make at it in my mind. The hypothetical goes. I'll state the case. Suppose there's a woman – a deuced fine-looking woman – who has run away from her husband and home? She's badly mashed on another man who went to her town to work up some real estate business. Now, we may as well call this woman's husband Thomas R. Billings, for that's his name. I'm giving you straight tips on the cognomens. The Lothario chap is Henry K. Jessup. The Billingses lived in a little town called Susanville – a good many miles from here. Now, Jessup leaves Susanville two weeks ago. The next day Mrs. Billings follows him. She's dead gone on this man Jessup; you can bet your law library on that.'

Lawyer Gooch's client said this with such unctuous satisfaction that even the callous lawyer experienced a slight ripple of repulsion. He now saw clearly in his fatuous visitor the conceit of the lady-killer, the egoistic complacency of the successful trifler.

'Now,' continued the visitor, 'suppose this Mrs. Billings wasn't happy at home? We'll say she and her husband didn't gee worth a cent. They've got incompatibility to burn. The things she likes, Billings wouldn't have as a gift with trading-stamps. It's Tabby and Rover with them all the time. She's an educated woman in science and culture, and she reads things out loud at meetings. Billings is not on. He don't appreciate progress and obelisks and ethics, and things of that sort. Old Billings is simply a blink when it comes to such things. The lady is out and out above his class. Now, lawyer, don't it look like a fair equalization of rights and wrongs that a woman like that should be allowed to throw down Billings and take the man that can appreciate her?'

'Incompatibility,' said Lawyer Gooch, 'is undoubtedly the source of much marital discord and unhappiness. Where it is positively proved, divorce would seem to be the equitable remedy. Are you – excuse me – is this man Jessup one to whom the lady may safely trust her future?'

'Oh, you can bet on Jessup,' said the client, with a confident wag of his head. 'Jessup's all right He'll do the square thing. Why, he left Susanville just to keep people from talking about Mrs. Billings. But she followed him up, and now, of course, he'll stick to her. When she gets a divorce, all legal and proper, Jessup will do the proper thing.'

'And now,' said Lawyer Gooch, 'continuing the hypothesis, if you prefer, and supposing that my services should be desired in the case, what –'

The client rose impulsively to his feet.

'Oh, dang the hypothetical business,' he exclaimed impatiently. 'Let's let her drop, and get down to straight talk. You ought to know who I am by this time. I want that woman to have her divorce. I'll pay for it. The day you set Mrs. Billings free I'll pay you five hundred dollars.'

Lawyer Gooch's client banged his fist upon the table to punctuate his generosity.

'If that is the case –' began the lawyer.

'Lady to see you, sir,' bawled Archibald, bouncing in from his anteroom. He had orders to always announce immediately any client that might come. There was no sense in turning business away.

Lawyer Gooch took client number one by the arm and led him suavely into one of the adjoining rooms. 'Favour me by remaining here a few minutes, sir,' said he. 'I will return and resume our consultation with the least possible delay. I am rather expecting a visit from a very wealthy old lady in connection with a will. I will not keep you waiting long.'

The breezy gentleman seated himself with obliging acquiescence, and took up a magazine. The lawyer returned to the middle office, carefully closing behind him the connecting door.

'Show the lady in, Archibald,' he said to the office boy, who was awaiting his order.

A tall lady, of commanding presence and sternly handsome, entered the room. She wore robes – robes; not clothes – ample and fluent. In her eye could be perceived the lambent flame of genius and soul. In her hand was a green bag of the capacity of a bushel, and an umbrella that also seemed to wear a robe, ample and fluent. She accepted a chair.

'Are you Mr. Phineas C. Gooch, the lawyer?' she asked, in formal and unconciliatory tones.

'I am,' answered Lawyer Gooch, without circum-locution. He never circumlocuted when dealing with a woman. Women circumlocute. Time is wasted when both sides in debate employ the same tactics.

'As a lawyer, sir,' began the lady, 'you may have acquired some knowledge of the human heart. Do you believe that the pusillanimous and petty conventions of our artificial social life should stand as an obstacle in the way of a noble and affectionate heart when it finds its true mate among the miserable and worthless wretches in the world that are called men?'

'Madam,' said Lawyer Gooch, in the tone that he used in curbing his female clients, 'this is an office for conducting the practice of law. I am a lawyer, not a philosopher, nor the editor of an "Answers to the Lovelorn" column of a newspaper. I have other clients waiting. I will ask you kindly to come to the point.'

'Well, you needn't get so stiff around the gills about it,' said the lady, with a snap of her luminous eyes and a startling gyration of her umbrella. 'Business is what I've come for. I want your opinion in the matter of a suit for divorce, as the vulgar would call it, but which is really only the readjustment of the false and ignoble conditions that the short-sighted laws of man have interposed between a loving –'

'I beg your pardon, madam,' interrupted Lawyer Gooch, with some impatience, 'for reminding you again that this is a law office. Perhaps Mrs. Wilcox –'

'Mrs. Wilcox is all right,' cut in the lady, with a hint of asperity. 'And so are Tolstoi, and Mrs. Gertrude Atherton, and Omar Khayyám, and Mr. Edward Bok. I've read 'em all. I would like to discuss with you the divine right of the soul as opposed to the freedom-destroying restrictions of a bigoted and narrow-minded society. But I will proceed to business. I would prefer to lay the matter before you in an impersonal way until you pass upon its merits. That is to describe it as a supposable instance, without –'

'You wish to state a hypothetical case?' said Lawyer Gooch.

'I was going to say that,' said the lady sharply. 'Now, suppose there is a woman who is all soul and heart and aspirations for a complete existence. This woman has a husband who is far below her in intellect, in taste — in everything. Bah! he is a brute. He despises literature. He sneers at the lofty thoughts of the world's great thinkers. He thinks only of real estate and such sordid things. He is no mate for a woman with soul. We will say that this unfortunate wife one day meets with her ideal — a man with brain and heart and force. She loves him. Although this man feels the thrill of a new-found affinity he is too noble, too honourable to declare himself. He flies from the presence of his beloved. She flies after him, trampling, with superb indifference, upon the fetters with which an unenlightened social system would bind her. Now, what will a divorce cost? Eliza Ann Timmins, the poetess of Sycamore Gap, got one for three hundred and forty dollars. Can I — I mean can this lady I speak of — get one that cheap?'

'Madam,' said Lawyer Gooch, 'your last two or three sentences delight me with their intelligence and clearness. Can we not now abandon the hypothetical and come down to names and business?'

'I should say so,' exclaimed the lady, adopting the practical with admirable readiness. 'Thomas R. Billings is the name of the low brute who stands between the happiness of his legal — his legal, but not his spiritual — wife and Henry K. Jessup, the noble man whom nature intended for her mate. I,' concluded the client, with an air of dramatic revelation 'am Mrs. Billings!'

'Gentleman to see you, sir,' shouted Archibald, invading the room almost at a handspring. Lawyer Gooch arose from his chair.

'Mrs. Billings,' he said courteously, 'allow me to conduct you into the adjoining office apartment for a few minutes. I am expecting a very wealthy old gentleman on business connected with a will. In a very short while I will join you, and continue our consultation.'

With his accustomed chivalrous manner, Lawyer Gooch ushered his soulful client into the remaining unoccupied room, and came out, closing the door with circumspection.

The next visitor introduced by Archibald was a thin, nervous, irritable-looking man of middle age, with a worried and apprehensive expression of countenance. He carried in one hand a small satchel, which he set down upon the floor beside the chair which the lawyer placed for him. His clothing was of good quality, but it was worn without regard to neatness or style, and appeared to be covered with the dust of travel.

'You make a speciality of divorce cases,' he said, in an agitated but business-like tone.

'I may say,' began Lawyer Gooch, 'that my practice has not altogether avoided –'

'I know you do,' interrupted client number three 'You needn't tell me. I've heard all about you. I have a case to lay before you without necessarily disclosing any connection that I might have with it – that is –'

'You wish,' said Lawyer Gooch, 'to state a hypothetical case.'

'You may call it that. I am a plain man of business. I will be as brief as possible. We will first take up the hypothetical woman. We will say she is married uncongenially. In many ways she is a superior woman. Physically she is considered to be handsome. She is devoted to what she calls literature – poetry, and prose, and such stuff. Her husband is a plain man in the business walks of life. Their home has not been happy, although the husband has tried to make it so. Some time ago a man – a stranger – came to the peaceful town in which they lived and engaged in some real estate operations. This woman met him, and became unaccountably infatuated with him. Her attentions became so open that the man felt the community to be no safe place for him, so he left it. She abandoned husband and home, and followed him. She forsook her home, where she was provided with every comfort, to follow this man who had inspired her with such a strange affection. Is there anything more to be deplored,' concluded the client, in a trembling voice, 'than the wrecking of a home by a woman's uncalculating folly?'

Lawyer Gooch delivered the cautious opinion that there was not.

'This man she has gone to join,' resumed the visitor, 'is not the man to make her happy. It is a wild and foolish self-deception that makes her think he will. Her husband, in spite of their many disagreements, is the only one capable of dealing with her sensitive and peculiar nature. But this she does not realize now.'

'Would you consider a divorce the logical cure in the case you present?' asked Lawyer Gooch, who felt that the conversation was wandering too far from the field of business.

'A divorce!' exclaimed the client feelingly – almost tearfully.

'No, no – not that. I have read Mr. Gooch, of many instances where your sympathy and kindly interest led you to act as a mediator between estranged husband and wife, and brought them together again. Let us drop the hypothetical case – I need conceal no longer that it is I who am the sufferer in this sad affair – the names you shall have – Thomas R. Billings and wife – and Henry K. Jessup, the man with whom she is infatuated.'

Client number three laid his hand upon Mr. Gooch's arm. Deep emotion was written upon his careworn face. 'For Heaven's sake,' he said fervently, 'help me in this hour of trouble. Seek out Mrs. Billings, and persuade her to abandon this distressing pursuit of her lamentable folly. Tell her, Mr. Gooch, that her husband is willing to receive her back to his heart and home – promise her anything that will induce her to return. I have heard of your success in these matters. Mrs. Billings cannot be very far away. I am worn out with travel and weariness. Twice during the pursuit I saw her, but various circumstances prevented our having an interview. Will you undertake this mission for me, Mr. Gooch, and earn my everlasting gratitude?'

'It is true,' said Lawyer Gooch, frowning slightly at the other's last words, but immediately calling up an expression of virtuous benevolence, 'that on a number of occasions I have been successful in persuading couples who sought the severing of their matrimonial bonds to think better of their rash intentions and return to their homes reconciled. But I assure you that the work is often exceedingly difficult. The amount of argument, perseverence, and, if I may be allowed to say it, eloquence that it requires would astonish you. But this is a case in which my sympathies would be wholly enlisted. I feel deeply for you, sir, and I would be most happy to see husband and wife reunited. But my time,' concluded the lawyer, looking at his watch as if suddenly reminded of the fact, 'is valuable.'

'I am aware of that,' said the client, 'and if you will take the case and persuade Mrs. Billings to return home and leave the man alone that she is following – on that day I will pay you the sum of one thousand dollars. I have made a little money in real estate during the recent boom in Susanville, and I will not begrudge that amount.'

'Retain your seat for a few minutes, please,' said Lawyer Gooch, arising, and again consulting his watch. 'I have another client waiting in an adjoining room whom I had very nearly forgotten. I will return in the briefest possible space.'

The situation was now one that fully satisfied Lawyer Gooch's love of intricacy and complication. He revelled in cases that presented such subtle problems and possibilities. It pleased him to think that he was master of the happiness and fate of the three individuals, who sat unconscious of one another's presence, within his reach. His old figure of the ship glided into his mind. But now the figure failed, for to have filled every compartment of an actual vessel would have been to endanger her safety; while here, with his compartments full, his ship of affairs could but sail on to the advantageous port of a fine, fat fee. The thing for him to do, of course, was to wring the best bargain he could from someone of his anxious cargo.

First he called to the office boy: 'Lock the outer door, Archibald, and admit no one.' Then he moved with long, silent strides into the room in which client number one waited. That gentleman sat, patiently scanning the pictures in the magazine with a cigar in his mouth and his feet upon a table.

'Well,' he remarked cheerfully, as the lawyer entered, 'have you made up your mind? Does five hundred dollars go for getting the fair lady a divorce?

'You mean that as a retainer?' asked Lawyer Gooch, softly interrogative.

'Hey? No; for the whole job. It's enough ain't it?'

'My fee,' said Lawyer Gooch, 'would be one thousand five hundred dollars. Five hundred dollars down, and the remainder upon issuance of the divorce.'

A loud whistle came from client number one. His feet descended to the floor.

'Guess we can't close the deal,' he said, arising. 'I clinked up five hundred dollars in a little real estate dicker down in Susanville. I'd do anything I could to free the lady, but it outsizes my pile.'

'Could you stand one thousand two hundred dollars?' asked the lawyer insinuatingly.

'Five hundred is my limit, I tell you. Guess I'll have to hunt up a cheaper lawyer.' The client put on his hat.

'Out this way, please,' said Lawyer Gooch, opening the door that led into the hallway.

As the gentleman flowed out of the compartment and down the stairs, Lawyer Gooch smiled to himself. 'Exit Mr. Jessup,' he murmured, as he fingered the Henry Clay tuft of hair at his ear. 'And now for the forsaken husband.' He returned to the middle office, and assumed a businesslike manner.

'I understand,' he said to client number three, 'that you agree to pay one thousand dollars if I bring about, or am instrumental in bringing about, the return of Mrs. Billings to her home, and her abandonment of her infatuated pursuit of the man for whom she has conceived such a violent fancy. Also that the case is now unreservedly in my hands on that basis. Is that correct?'

'Entirely,' said the other eagerly. 'And I can produce the cash any time at two hours' notice.'

Lawyer Gooch stood up at his full height. His thin figure seemed to expand. His thumbs sought the arm-holes of his vest. Upon his face was a look of sympathetic benignity that he always wore during such undertakings.

'Then, sir,' he said, in kindly tones, 'I think I can promise you an early relief from your troubles. I have that much confidence in my powers of argument and persuasion, in the natural impulses of the human heart toward good, and in the strong influence of a husband's unfaltering love. Mrs. Billings, sir, is here – in that room –' The lawyer's long arm pointed to the door. 'I will call her in at once; and our united pleadings –'

Lawyer Gooch paused, for client number three had leaped from his chair as if propelled by steel springs, and clutched his satchel.

'What the devil,' he exclaimed harshly, 'do you mean? That woman in there! I thought I shook her off forty miles back '

He ran to the open window, looked out below, and threw one leg over the sill.

'Stop!' cried Lawyer Gooch, in amazement. 'What would you do? Come, Mr. Billings, and face your erring but innocent wife. Our combined entreaties cannot fail to –'

'Billings!' shouted the now thoroughly moved client; 'I'll Billings you, you old idiot!'

Turning, he hurled his satchel with fury at the lawyer's head. It struck that astounded peacemaker between the eyes, causing him to stagger backward a pace or two. When Lawyer Gooch recovered his wits he saw that his client had disappeared. Rushing to the window, he leaned out, and saw the recreant gathering himself up from the top of a shed upon which he had dropped from the second-story window. Without stopping to collect his hat he then plunged downward the remaining ten feet to the alley, up which he flew with prodigious celerity until the surrounding building swallowed him up from view.

Lawyer Gooch passed his hand tremblingly across his brow. It was an habitual act with him, serving to clear his thoughts. Perhaps also it now seemed to soothe the spot where a very hard alligator-hide satchel had struck.

The satchel lay upon the floor, wide open, with its contents spilled about. Mechanically Lawyer Gooch stooped to gather up the articles. The first was a collar; and the omniscient eye of the man of law perceived, wonderingly, the initial H. K. J. marked upon it. Then came a comb, a brush, a folded map and a piece of soap. Lastly a handful of old business letters, addressed – every one of them – to 'Henry K. Jessup, Esq.'

Lawyer Gooch closed the satchel, and set it upon the table. He hesitated for a moment, and then put on his hat and walked into the office boy's anteroom.

'Archibald,' he said mildly, as he opened the hall door, 'I am going around to the Supreme Court rooms. In five minutes you may step into the inner office, and inform the lady who is waiting there that' – here Lawyer Gooch made use of the vernacular – 'that there's nothing doing.'

XCII

Calloway's Code

THE NEW YORK *Enterprise* sent H. B. Calloway as special correspondent to the Russo-Japanese-Portsmouth war.

For two months Calloway hung about Yokohama and Tokio, shaking dice with the other correspondents for drinks of 'rick-shaws – oh, no, that's something to ride in; anyhow, he wasn't earning the salary that his paper was paying him. But that was not Calloway's fault. The little brown men who held the strings of Fate between their fingers were not ready for the readers of the *Enterprise* to season their breakfast bacon and eggs with the battles of the descendants of the gods.

But soon the column of correspondents that were to go out with the First Army tightened their field-glass belts and went down to the Yalu with Kuroki. Calloway was one of these.

Now, this is no history of the battle of the Yalu River. That has been told in detail by the correspondents who gazed at the shrapnel smoke rings from a distance of three miles. But, for justice's sake, let it be understood that the Japanese commander prohibited a nearer view.

Calloway's feat was accomplished before the battle. What he did was to furnish the *Enterprise* with the biggest beat of the war. That paper published exclusively and in detail the news of the attack on the lines of the Russian General Zassulitch on the same day that it was made. No other paper printed a word about it for two days afterward, except a London paper, whose account was absolutely incorrect and untrue.

Calloway did this in face of the fact that General Kuroki was making his moves and laying his plans with the profoundest secrecy as far as the world outside his camps was concerned. The correspondents were forbidden to send out any news whatever of his plans; and every message that was allowed on the wires was censored with rigid severity.

The correspondent for the London paper handed in a cablegram describing Kuroki's plans; but as it was wrong from beginning to end the censor grinned and let it go through.

So, there they were – Kuroki on one side of the Yalu with forty-two thousand infantry, five thousand cavalry, and one hundred and twenty-four guns. On the other side, Zassulitch waited for him with only twenty-three thousand men, and with a long stretch of river to guard. And Calloway had got hold of some important inside information that he knew would bring the *Enterprise* staff around a cablegram as thick as flies around a Park Row lemonade stand. If he could only get that message past the censor – the new censor who had arrived and taken his post that day.

Calloway did the obviously proper thing. He lit his pipe and sat down on a gun carriage to think it over. And there we must leave him; for the rest of the story belongs to Vesey, a sixteen-dollar-a-week reporter on the *Enterprise*.

Calloway's cablegram was handed to the managing editor at four o'clock in the afternoon. He read it three times; and then drew a pocket mirror from a pigeon-hole in his desk, and looked at his reflection carefully. Then he went over to the desk of Boyd, his assistant (he usually called Boyd when he wanted him), and laid the cablegram before him.

'It's from Calloway,' he said. 'See what you make of it.'

The message was dated at Wi-ju, and these were the words of it:

'Foregone preconcerted rash witching goes muffled rumour mine dark silent unfortunate richmond existing great hotly brute select mooted parlous beggars ye angel incontrovertible.'

Boyd read it twice.

'It's either a cipher or a sunstroke,' said he.

'Ever hear of anything like a code in the office – a secret code?' asked the m. e., who had held his desk for only two years. Managing editors come and go.

'None except the vernacular that the lady specials write in,' said Boyd. 'Couldn't be an acrostic, could it?'

'I thought of that,' said the m. e., 'but the beginning letters contain only four vowels. It must be a code of some sort.'

'Try 'em in groups,' suggested Boyd. 'Let's see – "Rash witching goes" – not with me it doesn't. "Muffled rumour mine" – must have an underground wire. "Dark silent unfortunate richmond" – no reason why he should knock that town so hard. "Existing great hotly" – no, it doesn't pan out. I'll call Scott.'

The city editor came in a hurry, and tried his luck. A city editor must know something about everything; so Scott knew a little about cipher-writing.

'It may be what is called an inverted alphabet cipher,' said he. 'I'll try that. "R" seems to be the oftenest used initial letter, with the exception of "m." Assuming "r" to mean "e," the most frequently used vowel, we transpose the letters – so.'

Scott worked rapidly with his pencil for two minutes; and then showed the first word according to his reading – the word 'Scejtzez.'

'Great!' cried Boyd. 'It's a charade. My first is a Russian general. Go on, Scott.'

'No, that won't work,' said the city editor. 'It's undoubtedly a code. It's impossible to read it without the key. Has the office ever used a cipher code?'

'Just what I was asking,' said the m. e. 'Hustle everybody up that ought to know. We must get at it some way. Calloway has evidently got hold of something big, and the censor has put the screws on, or he wouldn't have cabled in a lot of chop suey like this.'

Throughout the office of the *Enterprise* a drag-net was sent, hauling in such members of the staff as would be likely to know of a code, past or present, by reason of their wisdom, information, natural intelligence, or length of servitude. They got together in a group in the city room, with the m. e. in the centre. No one had heard of a code. All began to explain to the head investigator that newspapers never use a code, anyhow – that is, a cipher code. Of course the Associated Press stuff is a sort of code – an abbreviation, rather – but –

The m. e. knew all that, and said so. He asked each man how long he had worked on the paper. Not one of them had drawn pay from an *Enterprise* envelope for longer than six years.

Calloway had been on the paper twelve years.

'Try old Heffelbauer,' said the m. e. 'He was here when Park Row was a potato patch.'

Heffelbauer was an institution. He was half janitor, half handyman about the office, and half watchman – thus becoming the peer of thirteen and one-half tailors. Sent for, he came, radiating his nationality.

'Heffelbauer,' said the m. e., 'did you ever hear of a code belonging to the office a long time ago – a private code? You know what a code is, don't you?'

'Yah,' said Heffelbauer. 'Sure I know vat a code is. Yah, apout dwelf or fifteen year ago der office had a code. Der reborters in der city-room haf it here.'

'Ah!' said the m. e. 'We're getting on the trail now. Where was it kept, Heffelbauer? What do you know about it?'

'Somedimes,' said the retainer, 'dey keep it in der little room behind der library room.'

'Can you find it?' asked the m. e. eagerly. 'Do you know where it is?'

'Mein Gott!' said Heffelbauer. 'How long you dink a code live? Der reborters call him a maskeet. But von day he butt mit his head der editor, und –'

'Oh, he's talking about a goat,' said Boyd. 'Get out, Heffelbauer.'

Again discomfited, the concerted wit and resource of the *Enterprise* huddled around Calloway's puzzle, considering its mysterious words in vain.

Then Vesey came in.

Vesey was the youngest reporter. He had a thirty-two-inch chest and wore a number fourteen collar; but his bright Scotch plaid suit gave him presence and conferred no obscurity upon his whereabouts. He wore his hat in such a position that people followed him about to see him take it off, convinced that it must be hung upon a peg driven into the back of his head. He was never without an immense, knotted, hard-wood cane with a German-silver tip on its crooked handle. Vesey was the best photograph hustler in the office. Scott said it was because no living human being could resist the personal triumph it was to hand his picture over to Vesey. Vesey always wrote his own news stories, except the big ones, which were sent to the re-write men. Add to this fact that among all the inhabitants, temples, and groves of the earth nothing existed that could abash Vesey, and his dim sketch is concluded.

Vesey butted into the circle of cipher readers very much as Heffelbauer's 'code' would have done, and asked what was up. Someone explained, with the touch of half-familiar condescension that they always used toward him. Vesey reached out and took the cablegram from the m. e.'s hand. Under the protection of some special Providence, he was always doing appalling things like that, and coming off unscathed.

'It's a code,' said Vesey. 'Anybody got the key?'

'The office has no code,' said Boyd, reaching for the message. Vesey held to it.

'Then old Calloway expects us to read it, anyhow,' said he. 'He's up a tree, or something, and he's made this up so as to get it by the censor. It's up to us. Gee! I wish they had sent me, too. Say − we can't afford to fall down on our end of it. "Foregone, preconcerted rash, witching" − h'm.'

Vesey sat down on a table corner and began to whistle softly, frowning at the cablegram.

'Let's have it, please,' said the m. e. 'We've got to get to work on it.'

'I believe I've got a line on it,' said Vesey. 'Give me ten minutes.'

He walked to his desk, threw his hat into a wastebasket, spread out flat on his chest like a gorgeous lizard, and started his pencil going. The wit and wisdom of the *Enterprise* remained in a loose group, and smiled at one another, nodding their heads toward Vesey. Then they began to exchange their theories about the cipher.

It took Vesey exactly fifteen minutes. He brought to the m. e. a pad with the code-key written on it.

'I felt the swing of it as soon as I saw it,' said Vesey. 'Hurrah for old Calloway! He's done the Japs and every paper in town that prints literature instead of news. Take a look at that.'

Thus had Vesey set forth the reading of the code:

> Foregone − conclusion
> Preconcerted − arrangement
> Rash − act
> Witching − hour of midnight

Goes – without saying
Muffled – report
Rumour – hath it
Mine – host
Dark – horse
Silent – majority
Unfortunate – pedestrians[1]
Richmond – in the field
Existing – conditions
Great – White Way
Hotly – contested
Brute – force
Select – few
Mooted – question
Parlous – times
Beggars – description
Ye – correspondent
Angel – unawares
Incontrovertible – fact

'It's simply newspaper English,' explained Vesey. 'I've been reporting on the *Enterprise* long enough to know it by heart. Old Calloway gives us the cue word, and we use the word that naturally follows it just as we use 'em in the paper. Read it over, and you'll see how pat they drop into their places. Now, here's the message he intended us to get.'

Vesey handed out another sheet of paper.

Concluded arrangement to act at hour of midnight without saying. Report hath it that a large body of cavalry and an overwhelming force of infantry will be thrown into the field. Conditions white. Way contested by only a small force. Question the *Times* description. Its correspondent is unaware of the facts.

'Great stuff!' cried Boyd excitedly. 'Kuroki crosses the Yalu tonight and attacks. Oh, we won't do a thing to the sheets that make up with Addison's essays, real estate transfers, and bowling scores!'

---

[1]Mr. Vesey afterwards explained that the logical journalistic complement of the word 'unfortunate' was once the word 'victim.' But, since the automobile became so popular, the correct following word is now 'pedestrians.' Of course, in Calloway's code it meant infantry.

'Mr. Vesey,' said the m. e., with his jollying-which-you-should-regard-as-a-favour manner, 'you have cast a serious reflection upon the literary standards of the paper that employs you. You have also assisted materially in giving us the biggest "beat" of the year. I will let you know in a day or two whether you are to be discharged or retained at a larger salary. Somebody send Ames to me.'

Ames was the king-pin, the snowy-petalled marguerite, the star-bright looloo of the rewrite men. He saw attempted murder in the pains of green-apple colic, cyclones in the summer zephyr, lost children in every top-spinning urchin, an uprising of the down-trodden masses in every hurling of a derelict potato at a passing automobile. When not rewriting, Ames sat on the porch of his Brooklyn villa playing checkers with his ten-year-old son.

Ames and the 'war editor' shut themselves in a room. There was a map in there stuck full of little pins that represented armies and divisions. Their fingers had been itching for days to move those pins along the crooked line of the Yalu. They did so now; and in words of fire Ames translated Calloway's brief message into a front-page masterpiece that set the world talking. He told of the secret councils of the Japanese officers; gave Kuroki's flaming speeches in full; counted the cavalry and infantry to a man and a horse; described the quick and silent building of the bridge at Suikauchen, across which the Mikado's legions were hurled upon the surprised Zassulitch, whose troops were widely scattered along the river. And the battle! – well, you know what Ames can do with a battle if you give him just one smell of smoke for a foundation. And in the same story, with seemingly supernatural knowledge, he gleefully scored the most profound and ponderous paper in England for the false and misleading account of the intended movements of the Japanese First Army printed in its issue of *the same date*.

Only one error was made; and that was the fault of the cable operator at Wi-ju. Calloway pointed it out after he came back. The word 'great' in his code should have been 'gauge,' and its complemental words 'of battle.' But it went to Ames 'conditions white,' and of course he took that to mean snow. His description of the Japanese army struggling through the snow-storm, blinded by the whirling flakes, was thrillingly vivid. The artists turned out some effective illustrations that made a hit as pictures of the artillery dragging their guns through the drifts. But, as the attack was made on the first day of May, the 'conditions white' excited some amusement. But it made no difference to the *Enterprise*, anyway.

It was wonderful. And Calloway was wonderful in having made the new censor believe that his jargon of words meant no more than a complaint of the dearth of news and a petition for more expense money. And Vesey was wonderful. And most wonderful of all are words, and how they make friends one with another, being oft associated, until not even obituary notices them do part.

On the second day following, the city editor halted at Vesey's desk where the reporter was writing the story of a man who had broken his leg by falling into a coal-hole – Ames having failed to find a murder motive in it.

'The old man says your salary is to be raised to twenty a week,' said Scott.

'All right,' said Vesey. 'Every little helps. Say – Mr. Scott, which would you say – "We can state without fear of successful contradiction," or "On the whole it can be safely asserted"?'

XCIII

'Girl'

IN GILT letters on the ground glass of the door of room No. 962 were the words: 'Robbins & Hartley, Brokers.' The clerks had gone. It was past five, and with the solid tramp of a drove of prize Percherons, scrub-women were invading the cloud-capped twenty-story office building. A puff of red-hot air flavoured with lemon peelings, soft-coal smoke and train oil came in through the half-open windows.

Robbins, fifty, something of an overweight beau, and addicted to first nights and hotel palm-rooms, pretended to be envious of his partner's commuter's joys.

'Going to be something doing in the humidity line to-night,' he said. 'You out-of-town chaps will be the people, with your katy-dids and moonlight and long drinks and things out on the front porch.'

Hartley, twenty-nine, serious, thin, good-looking, nervous, sighed and frowned a little.

'Yes,' said he, 'we always have cool nights in Floralhurst, especially in the winter.'

A man with an air of mystery came in the door and went up to Hartley.

'I've found where she lives,' he announced in the portentous half-whisper that makes the detective at work a marked being to his fellow-men.

Hartley scowled him into a state of dramatic silence and quietude. But by that time Robbins had got his cane and set his tie-pin to his liking, and with a debonair nod went out to his metropolitan amusements.

'Here is the address,' said the detective in a natural tone, being deprived of an audience to foil.

Hartley took the leaf torn out of the sleuth's dingy memorandum book. On it were pencilled the words 'Vivienne Arlington, No. 341 East – th Street, care of Mrs. McComus.'

'Moved there a week ago,' said the detective. 'Now, if you want any shadowing done, Mr. Hartley, I can do you as fine a job in that line as anybody in the city. It will be only $7 a day and expenses. Can send in a daily typewritten report, covering –'

'You needn't go on,' interrupted the broker. 'It isn't a case of that kind. I merely wanted the address. How much shall I pay you?'

'One day's work,' said the sleuth. 'A tenner will cover it.'

Hartley paid the man and dismissed him. Then he left the office and boarded a Broadway car. At the first large cross-town artery of travel he took an eastbound car that deposited him in a decaying avenue, whose ancient structures once sheltered the pride and glory of the town.

Walking a few squares, he came to the building that he sought. It was a new flat-house, bearing carved upon its cheap stone portal its sonorous name, 'The Vallambrosa.' Fire-escapes zigzagged down its front – these laden with household goods, drying clothes, and squalling children evicted by the midsummer heat. Here and there a pale rubber plant peeped from the miscellaneous mass, as if wondering to what kingdom it belonged – vegetable, animal or artificial.

Hartley pressed the 'McComus' button. The door latch clicked spasmodically – now hospitably, now doubtfully, as though in anxiety whether it might be admitting friends or duns. Hartley entered and began to climb the stairs after the manner of those who seek their friends in city flathouses – which is the manner of a boy who climbs an apple-tree, stopping when he comes upon what he wants.

On the fourth floor he saw Vivienne standing in an open door.

She invited him inside, with a nod and a bright, genuine smile. She placed a chair for him near a window, and poised herself gracefully upon the edge of one of those Jekyll-and-Hyde pieces of furniture that are masked and mysteriously hooded, unguessable bulks by day and inquisitorial racks of torture by night.

Hartley cast a quick, critical, appreciative glance at her before speaking, and told himself that his taste in choosing had been flawless.

Vivienne was about twenty-one. She was of the purest Saxon type. Her hair was a ruddy golden, each filament of the neatly gathered mass shining with its own lustre and delicate graduation of colour. In perfect harmony were her ivory-clear complexion and deep sea-blue eyes that looked upon the world with the ingenuous calmness of a mermaid or the pixie of an undiscovered mountain stream. Her frame was strong and yet possessed the grace of absolute naturalness. And yet with all her Northern clearness and frankness of line and colouring there seemed to be something of the tropics in her – something of languor in the droop of her pose, of love of ease in her ingenious complacency of satisfaction and comfort in the mere act of breathing – something that seemed to claim for her a right as a perfect work of nature to exist and be admired equally with a rare flower or some beautiful, milk-white dove among its sober-hued companions.

She was dressed in a white waist and dark skirt – that discreet masquerade of goose-girl and duchess.

'Vivienne,' said Hartley, looking at her pleadingly, 'you did not answer my last letter. It was only by nearly a week's search that I found where you had moved to. Why have you kept me in suspense when you knew how anxiously I was waiting to see you and hear from you?'

The girl looked out the window dreamily.

'Mr. Hartley,' she said hesitatingly, 'I hardly know what to say to you. I realize all the advantages of your offer, and sometimes I feel sure that I could be contented with you. But, again, I am doubtful. I was born a city girl, and I am afraid to bind myself to a quiet surburban life.'

'My dear girl,' said Hartley ardently, 'have I not told you that you shall have everything that your heart can desire that is in my power to give you? You shall come to the city for the theatres, for shopping and to visit your friends as often as you care to. You can trust me, can you not?'

'To the fullest,' she said, turning her frank eyes upon him with a smile. 'I know you are the kindest of men, and that the girl you get will be a lucky one. I learned all about you when I was at the Montgomerys'.'

'Ah!' exclaimed Hartley, with a tender, reminiscent light in his eye; 'I remember well the evening I first saw you at the Montgomerys'. Mrs. Montgomery was sounding your praises to me all the evening. And she hardly did you justice. I shall never forget that supper. Come, Vivienne, promise me. I want you. You'll never regret coming with me. No one else will ever give you as pleasant a home.'

The girl sighed and looked down at her folded hands.

A sudden jealous suspicion seized Hartley.

'Tell me, Vivienne,' he asked, regarding her keenly, 'is there another – is there someone else?'

A rosy flush crept slowly over her fair cheeks and neck.

'You shouldn't ask that, Mr. Hartley,' she said, in some confusion. 'But I will tell you. There is one other – but he has no right – I have promised him nothing.'

'His name?' demanded Hartley sternly.

'Townsend.'

'Rafford Townsend!' exclaimed Hartley, with a grim tightening of his jaw. 'How did that man come to know you? After all I've done for him –'

'His auto has just stopped below,' said Vivienne, bending over the window-sill. 'He's coming for his answer. Oh, I don't know what to do!'

The bell in the flat kitchen whirred. Vivienne hurried to press the latch button.

'Stay here,' said Hartley. 'I will meet him in the hall.'

Townsend, looking like a Spanish grandee in his light tweeds, Panama hat and curling black moustache, came up the stairs three at a time. He stopped at sight of Hartley and looked foolish.

'Go back,' said Hartley firmly, pointing downstairs with his forefinger.

'Hullo!' said Townsend, feigning surprise. 'What's up? What are you doing here, old man?'

'Go back,' repeated Hartley inflexibly. 'The Law of the Jungle? Do you want the Pack to tear you to pieces? The kill is mine.'

'I came here to see a plumber about the bath-room connections,' said Townsend bravely.

'All right,' said Hartley. 'You shall have that lying plaster to stick upon your traitorous soul. But, go back.'

Townsend went downstairs, leaving a bitter word to be wafted up the draught of the staircase. Hartley went back to his wooing.

'Vivienne,' said he masterfully. 'I have got to have you. I will take no more refusals or dilly-dallying.'

'When do you want me?' she asked.

'Now. As soon as you can get ready.'

She stood calmly before him and looked him in the eye.

'Do you think for one moment,' she said, 'that I would enter your home while Héloise is there?'

Hartley cringed as if from an unexpected blow. He folded his arms and paced the carpet once or twice.

'She shall go,' he declared grimly. Drops stood upon his brow. 'Why should I let that woman make my life miserable? Never have I seen one day of freedom from trouble since I have known her. You are right, Vivienne. Héloise must be sent away before I can take you home. But she shall go. I have decided. I will turn her from my doors.'

'When will you do this?' asked the girl.

Hartley clinched his teeth and bent his brows together.

'To-night,' he said resolutely. 'I will send her away to-night.'

'Then,' said Vivienne, 'my answer is "yes." Come for me when you will.'

She looked into his eyes with a sweet, sincere light in her own. Hartley could scarcely believe that her surrender was true, it was so swift and complete.

'Promise me,' he said feelingly, 'on your word and honour.'

'On my word and honour,' repeated Vivienne softly.

At the door he turned and gazed at her happily, but yet as one who scarcely trusts the foundations of his joy.

'To-morrow,' he said, with a forefinger of reminder uplifted.

'To-morrow,' she repeated, with a smile of truth and candour.

In an hour and forty minutes Hartley stepped off the train at Floralhurst. A brisk walk of ten minutes brought him to the gate of a handsome two-story cottage set upon a wide and well-tended lawn. Half-way to the house he was met by a woman with jet-black braided hair and flowing white summer gown, who half strangled him without apparent cause.

When they stepped into the hall she said:

'Mamma's here. The auto is coming for her in half an hour. She came to dinner, but there's no dinner.'

'I've something to tell you,' said Hartley. 'I thought to break it to you gently, but since your mother is here we may as well out with it.'

He stooped and whispered something in her ear.

His wife screamed. Her mother came running into the hall.
The dark-haired woman screamed again – the joyful scream of a
well-beloved and petted woman.

'Oh, mamma!' she cried ecstatically, 'what do you think? Vivienne is coming to cook for us. She is the one that stayed with the
Montgomerys' a whole year. And now, Billy, dear,' she concluded,
'you must go right down into the kitchen and discharge Héloise.
She has been drunk again the whole day long.'

XCIV

A Technical Error

I NEVER CARED ESPECIALLY FOR FEUDS, believing them to be even
more overrated products of our country than grape-fruit, scrap-
ple, or honeymoons. Nevertheless, if I may be allowed, I will tell
you of an Indian Territory feud of which I was press-agent,
camp-follower, and inaccessory during the fact.

I was on a visit to Sam Durkee's ranch, where I had a great time
falling off unmanicured ponies and waving my bare hand at the
lower jaws of wolves about two miles away. Sam was a hardened
person of about twenty-five, with a reputation for going home in
the dark with perfect equanimity, though often with reluctance.

Over in the Creek Nation was a family bearing the name of
Tatum. I was told that the Durkees and Tatums had been feuding
for years. Several of each family had bitten the grass, and it was
expected that more Nebuchadnezzars would follow. A younger
generation of each family was growing up, and the grass was keeping pace with them. But I gathered that they had fought fairly;
that they had not lain in cornfields and aimed at the division of
their enemies' suspenders in the back – partly, perhaps, because
there were no cornfields, and nobody wore more than one suspender. Nor had any woman or child of either house ever been
harmed. In those days – and you will find it so yet – their women
were safe.

Sam Durkee had a girl. (If it were an all-fiction magazine that I
expect to sell this story to, I should say, 'Mr. Durkee rejoiced in a
fiancée.') Her name was Ella Baynes. They appeared to be devoted
to each other, and to have perfect confidence in each other, as all
couples do who are and have or aren't and haven't. She was tolerably
pretty, with a heavy mass of brown hair that helped her along. He

introduced me to her, which seemed not to lessen her preference for him; so I reasoned that they were surely soul-mates.

Miss Baynes lived in Kingfisher, twenty miles from the ranch. Sam lived on a gallop between the two places.

One day there came to Kingfisher a courageous young man, rather small, with smooth face and regular features. He made many inquiries about the business of the town, and especially of the inhabitants cognominally. He said he was from Muscogee, and he looked it, with his yellow shoes and crocheted four-in-hand. I met him once when I rode in for the mail. He said his name was Beverly Travers, which seemed rather improbable.

There were active times on the ranch, just then, and Sam was too busy to go to town often. As an incompetent and generally worthless guest, it devolved upon me to ride in for little things such as post cards, barrels of flour, baking-powder, smoking-tobacco, and – letters from Ella.

One day, when I was messenger for half a gross of cigarette papers and a couple of wagon tyres, I saw the alleged Beverly Travers in a yellow-wheeled buggy with Ella Baynes, driving about town as ostentatiously as the black, waxy mud would permit. I knew that this information would bring no balm of Gilead to Sam's soul, so I refrained from including it in the news of the city that I retailed on my return. But on the next afternoon an elongated ox cowboy of the name of Simmons, an old-time pal of Sam's, who kept a feed store in Kingfisher, rode out to the ranch and rolled and burned many cigarettes before he would talk. When he did make oration, his words were these:

'Say, Sam, there's been a description of a galoot miscallin' himself Bevel-edged Travels impairing the atmospheric air of Kingfisher for the past two weeks. You know who he was? He was not otherwise than Ben Tatum, from the Creek Nation, son of old Gopher Tatum that your Uncle Newt shot last February. You know what he done this morning? He killed your brother Lester – shot him in the co't-house yard.'

I wondered if Sam had heard. He pulled a twig from a mesquite bush, chewed it gravely, and said:

'He did, did he? He killed Lester?'

'The same,' said Simmons. 'And he did more. He run away with your girl, the same as to say Miss Ella Baynes. I thought you might like to know, so I rode out to impart the information.'

'I am much obliged, Jim,' said Sam, taking the chewed twig from his mouth. 'Yes, I'm glad you rode out. Yes, I'm right glad.'

'Well, I'll be ridin' back, I reckon. That boy I left in the feed store don't know hay from oats. He shot Lester in the *back*.'

'Shot him in the back?'

'Yes, while he was hitchin' his hoss.'

'I'm much obliged, Jim.'

'I kind of thought you'd like to know as soon as you could.'

'Come in and have some coffee before you ride back, Jim?'

'Why, no, I reckon not; I must get back to the store.'

'And you say —'

'Yes, Sam. Everybody seen 'em drive away together in a buckboard, with a big bundle, like clothes, tied up in the back of it. He was drivin' the team he brought over with him from Muscogee. They'll be hard to overtake right away.'

'And which —'

'I was goin' on to tell you. They left on the Guthrie road; but there's no tellin' which forks they'll take — you know that.'

'All right, Jim; much obliged.'

'You're welcome, Sam.'

Simmons rolled a cigarette and stabbed his pony with both heels. Twenty yards away he reined up and called back:

'You don't want no — assistance, as you might say?'

'Not any, thanks.'

'I didn't think you would. Well, so long!'

Sam took out and opened a bone-handled pocket-knife and scraped a dried piece of mud from his left boot. I thought at first he was going to swear a vendetta on the blade of it, or recite 'The Gipsy's Curse.' The few feuds I had ever seen or read about usually opened that way. This one seemed to be presented with a new treatment. Thus offered on the stage, it would have been hissed off, and one of Belasco's thrilling melodramas demanded instead.

'I wonder,' said Sam, with a profoundly thoughtful expression, 'if the cook has any cold beans left over!'

He called Wash, the Negro cook, and finding that he had some, ordered him to heat up the pot and make some strong coffee. Then we went into Sam's private room, where he slept, and kept his armoury, dogs, and the saddles of his favourite mounts. He took three or four six-shooters out of a bookcase and began to look them over, whistling 'The Cowboy's Lament' abstractedly. Afterward he ordered the two best horses on the ranch saddled and tied to the hitching-post.

Now, in the feud business, in all sections of the country, I have observed that in one particular there is a delicate but strict etiquette belonging. You must not mention the word or refer to the subject in the presence of a feudist. It would be more reprehensible than commenting upon the mole on the chin of your rich aunt. I found, later on, that there is another unwritten rule, but I think that belongs solely to the West.

It yet lacked two hours to supper-time; but in twenty minutes Sam and I were plunging deep into the reheated beans, hot coffee, and cold beef.

'Nothing like a good meal before a long ride,' said Sam. 'Eat hearty.'

I had a sudden suspicion.

'Why did you have two horses saddled?' I asked.

'One, two — one, two,' said Sam. 'You can count, can't you?'

His mathematics carried with it a momentary qualm and a lesson. The thought had not occurred to him that the thought could possibly occur to me not to ride at his side on that red road to revenge and justice. It was the higher calculus. I was booked for the trail. I began to eat more beans.

In an hour we set forth at a steady gallop eastward. Our horses were Kentucky-bred, strengthened by the mesquite grass of the west. Ben Tatum's steeds may have been swifter, and he had a good lead; but if he had heard the punctual thuds of the hoofs of those trailers of ours, born in the heart of feudland, he might have felt that retribution was creeping up on the hoof-prints of his dapper nags.

I knew that Ben Tatum's card to play was flight — flight until he came within the safer territory of his own henchmen and supporters. He knew that the man pursuing him would follow the trail to any end where it might lead.

During the ride Sam talked of the prospect for rain, of the price of beef, and of the musical glasses. You would have thought he had never had a brother or a sweetheart or an enemy on earth. There are some subjects too big even for the words in the 'Unabridged.' Knowing this phase of the feud code, but not having practised it sufficiently, I overdid the thing by telling some slightly funny anecdotes. Sam laughed at exactly the right place — laughed with his mouth. When I caught sight of his mouth, I wished I had been blessed with enough sense of humour to have suppressed those anecdotes.

Our first sight of them we had in Guthrie. Tired and hungry, we stumbled, unwashed, into a little yellow-pine hotel and sat at a table. In the opposite corner we saw the fugitives. They were bent upon their meal, but looked around at times uneasily.

The girl was dressed in brown — one of those smooth, half-shiny, silky-looking affairs with lace collar and cuffs, and what I believe they call an accordion-plaited skirt. She wore a thick brown veil down to her nose, and a broad-brimmed straw hat with some kind of feathers adorning it. The man wore plain, dark clothes, and his hair was trimmed very short. He was such a man as you might see anywhere.

There they were — the murderer and the woman he had stolen. There we were — the rightful avenger, according to the code, and the supernumerary who writes these words.

For one time, at least, in the heart of the supernumerary there rose the killing instinct. For one moment he joined the force of combatants — orally

'What are you waiting for, Sam?' I said in a whisper. 'Let him have it now!'

Sam gave a melancholy sigh.

'You don't understand; but *he* does,' he said. '*He* knows. Mr. Tenderfoot, there's a rule out here among white men in the Nation that you can't shoot a man when he's with a woman. I never knew it to be broke yet. You *can't* do it. You've got to get him in a gang of men or by himself. That's why. He knows it, too. We all know. So, that's Mr. Ben Tatum! One of the "pretty men"! I'll cut him out of the herd before they leave the hotel, and regulate his account!'

After supper the flying pair disappeared quickly. Although Sam haunted lobby and stairway and halls half the night, in some mysterious way the fugitives eluded him; and in the morning the veiled lady in the brown dress with the accordion-plaited skirt and the dapper young man with the close-clipped hair, and the buckboard with the prancing nags, were gone.

It is a monotonous story, that of the ride; so it shall be curtailed. Once again we overtook them on a road. We were about fifty yards behind. They turned in the buckboard and looked at us; then drove on without whipping up their horses. Their safety no longer lay in speed. Ben Tatum knew. He knew that the only rock of safety left to him was the code. There is no doubt that, had he been alone, the matter would have been settled quickly with Sam Durkee in the usual way; but he had something at his side that kept still the trigger-finger of both. It seemed likely that he was no coward.

So, you may perceive that woman, on occasions, may postpone

instead of precipitating conflict between man and man. But not willingly or consciously. She is oblivious of codes.

Five miles farther, we came upon the future great Western city of Chandler. The horses of pursuers and pursued were starved and weary. There was one hotel that offered danger to man and entertainment to beast; so the four of us met again in the dining-room at the ringing of a bell so resonant and large that it had cracked the welkin long ago. The dining-room was not as large as the one at Guthrie.

Just as we were eating apple pie – how Ben Davises and tragedy impinge upon each other! – I noticed Sam looking with keen intentness at our quarry where they were seated at a table across the room. The girl still wore the brown dress with lace collar and cuffs, and the veil drawn down to her nose. The man bent over his plate, with his close-cropped head held low.

'There's a code,' I heard Sam say, either to me or to himself, 'that won't let you shoot a man in the company of a woman; but, by thunder, there ain't one to keep you from killing a woman in the company of a man!'

And, quicker than my mind could follow his argument, he whipped a Colt's automatic from under his left arm and pumped six bullets into the body that the brown dress covered – the brown dress with the lace collar and cuffs and the accordion-plaited skirt.

The young person in the dark sack suit, from whose head and from whose life a woman's glory had been clipped, laid her head on her arms stretched upon the table; while people came running to raise Ben Tatum from the floor in his feminine masquerade that had given Sam the opportunity to set aside, technically, the obligations of the code.

XCV

A Blackjack Bargainer

THE MOST DISREPUTABLE THING in Yancey Goree's law office was Goree himself, sprawled in his creaky old arm-chair. The rickety little office, built of red brick, was set flush with the street – the main street of the town of Bethel.

Bethel rested upon the foot-hills of the Blue Ridge. Above it the mountains were piled to the sky. Far below it the turbid Catawba gleamed yellow along its disconsolate valley.

The June day was at its sultriest hour. Bethel dozed in the tepid shade. Trade was not. It was so still that Goree, reclining in his chair, distinctly heard the clicking of the chips in the grand-jury room, where the 'court-house gang' was playing poker. From the open back door of the office a well-worn path meandered across the grassy lot to the court-house. The treading out of that path had cost Goree all he ever had — first, inheritance of a few thousand dollars; next, the old family home; and, latterly, the last shreds of his self-respect and manhood. The 'gang' had cleaned him out. The broken gambler had turned drunkard and parasite; he had lived to see this day come when the men who had stripped him denied him a seat at the game. His word was no longer to be taken. The daily bouts at cards had arranged itself accordingly, and to him was assigned the ignoble part of the onlooker. The sheriff, the county clerk, a sportive deputy, a gay attorney, and a chalk-faced man hailing 'from the valley,' sat at table, and the sheared one was thus tacitly advised to go and grow more wool.

Soon wearying of his ostracism, Goree had departed for his office, muttering to himself as he unsteadily traversed the unlucky pathway. After a drink of corn whisky from a demijohn under the table, he had flung himself into the chair, staring, in a sort of maudlin apathy, out at the mountains immersed in the summer haze. The little white patch he saw away up on the side of Black-jack was Laurel, the village near which he had been born and bred. There, also, was the birthplace of the feud between the Gorees and the Coltranes. Now no direct heir of the Gorees survived except this plucked and singed bird of misfortune. To the Coltranes, also, but one male supporter was left — Colonel Abner Coltrane, a man of substance and standing, a member of the State Legislature, and a contemporary with Goree's father. The feud had been a typical one of the region; it had left a red record of hate, wrong and slaughter.

But Yancey Goree was not thinking of feuds. His befuddled brain was hopelessly attacking the problem of the future maintenance of himself and his favourite follies. Of late, old friends of the family had seen to it that he had whereof to eat and a place to sleep, but whisky they would not buy for him, and he must have whisky. His law business was extinct; no case had been entrusted to him in two years. He had been a borrower and a sponge, and it seemed that if he fell no lower it would be from lack of opportunity. One more chance — he was saying to himself — if he had one more stake at the game, he thought he could win; but he had nothing left to sell, and his credit was more than exhausted.

He could not help smiling, even in his misery, as he thought of the man to whom, six months before, he had sold the old Goree homestead. There had come from 'back yan' ' in the mountains two of the strangest creatures – a man named Pike Garvey and his wife. 'Back yan',' with a wave of the hand toward the hills, was understood among the mountaineers to designate the remotest fastnesses, the unplumbed gorges, the haunts of lawbreakers, the wolf's den, and the boudoir of the bear. In the cabin far up on Blackjack's shoulder, in the wildest part of these retreats, this odd couple had lived for twenty years. They had neither dog nor children to mitigate the heavy silence of the hills. Pike Garvey was little known in the settlements, but all who had dealt with him pronounced him 'crazy as a loon.' He acknowledged no occupation save that of a squirrel hunter, but he 'moonshined' occasionally by way of diversion. Once the 'revenues' had dragged him from his lair, fighting silently and desperately like a terrier, and he had been sent to state's prison for two years. Released, he popped back into his hole like an angry weasel.

Fortune, passing over many anxious wooers, made a freakish flight into Blackjack's bosky pockets to smile upon Pike and his faithful partner.

One day a party of spectacled, knickerbockered, and altogether absurd prospectors invaded the vicinity of the Garveys' cabin. Pike lifted his squirrel rifle off the hooks and took a shot at them at long range on the chance of their being revenues. Happily he missed, and the unconscious agents of good luck drew nearer, disclosing their innocence of anything resembling law or justice. Later on, they offered the Garveys an enormous quantity of ready, green, crisp money for their thirty-acre patch of cleared land, mentioning, as an excuse for such a mad action, some irrelevant and inadequate nonsense about a bed of mica underlying the said property.

When the Garveys became possessed of so many dollars that they faltered in computing them, the deficiencies of life on Blackjack began to grow prominent. Pike began to talk of new shoes, a hogshead of tobacco to set in the corner, a new lock to his rifle; and, leading Martella to a certain spot on the mountain-side, he pointed out to her how a small cannon – doubtless a thing not beyond the scope of their fortune in price – might be planted so as to command and defend the sole accessible trail to the cabin, to the confusion of revenues and meddling strangers for ever.

But Adam reckoned without his Eve. These things represented

to him the applied power of wealth, but there slumbered in his dingy cabin an ambition that soared far above his primitive wants. Somewhere in Mrs. Garvey's bosom still survived a spot of femininity unstarved by twenty years of Blackjack. For so long a time the sounds in her ears had been the scaly-barks dropping in the woods at noon, and the wolves singing among the rocks at night, and it was enough to have purged her of vanities. She had grown fat and sad and yellow and dull. But when the means came, she felt a rekindled desire to assume the perquisites of her sex – to sit at tea tables; to buy inutile things; to whitewash the hideous veracity of life with a little form and ceremony. So she coldly vetoed Pike's proposed system of fortifications, and announced that they would descend upon the world, and gyrate socially.

And thus, at length, it was decided, and the thing done. The village of Laurel was their compromise between Mrs. Garvey's preference for one of the large valley towns and Pike's hankering for primeval solitudes. Laurel yielded a halting round of feeble social distractions comportable with Martella's ambitions, and was not entirely without recommendation to Pike, its contiguity to the mountains presenting advantages for sudden retreat in case fashionable society should make it advisable.

Their descent upon Laurel had been coincident with Yancey Goree's feverish desire to convert property into cash, and they bought the old Goree homestead, paying four thousand dollars ready money into the spendthrift's shaking hands.

Thus it happened that while the disreputable last of the Gorees sprawled in his disreputable office, at the end of his row, spurned by the cronies whom he had gorged, strangers dwelt in the halls of his fathers.

A cloud of dust was rolling slowly up the parched street, with something travelling in the midst of it. A little breeze wafted the cloud to one side, and a new, brightly painted carry-all, drawn by a slothful grey horse, became visible. The vehicle deflected from the middle of the street as it neared Goree's office, and stopped in the gutter directly in front of his door.

On the front seat sat a gaunt, tall man, dressed in black broadcloth, his rigid hands incarcerated in yellow kid gloves. On the back seat was a lady who triumphed over the June heat. Her stout form was armoured in a skin-tight silk dress of the description known as 'changeable,' being a gorgeous combination of shifting hues. She sat erect, waving a much-ornamented fan, with her eyes fixed stonily far down the street. However Martella Garvey's heart might be rejoicing at the pleasures of her new life, Black-jack had done his work with her exterior. He had carved her countenance to the image of emptiness and inanity; had imbued her with the stolidity of his crags, and the reserve of his hushed interiors. She always seemed to hear, whatever her surroundings were, the scaly-barks falling and pattering down the mountain-side. She could always hear the awful silence of Blackjack sounding through the stillest of nights.

Goree watched this solemn equipage, as it drove to his door, with only faint interest; but when the lank driver wrapped the reins about his whip, awkwardly descended, and stepped into the office, he rose unsteadily to receive him, recognizing Pike Garvey, the new, the transformed, the recently civilized.

The mountaineer took the chair Goree offered him. They who cast doubts upon Garvey's soundness of mind had a strong witness in the man's countenance. His face was too long, a dull saffron in hue, and immobile as a statue's. Pale-blue, unwinking round eyes without lashes added to the singularity of his gruesome visage. Goree was at a loss to account for the visit.

'Everything all right at Laurel, Mr. Garvey?' he inquired.

'Everything all right, sir, and mighty pleased is Missis Garvey and me with the property. Missis Garvey likes yo' old place, and she likes the neighbourhood. Society is what she 'lows she wants, and she is gettin' of it. The Rogerses, the Hapgoods, the Pratts, and the Troys hev been to see Missis Garvey, and she hev et meals to most of thar houses. The best folks hev axed her to differ'nt kinds of doin's. I cyan't say, Mr. Goree, that sech things suits me – fur me, give me them thar.' Garvey's huge, yellow-gloved hand flourished in the direction of the mountains. 'Thar's whar I b'long, 'mongst the wild honey bees and the b'ars. But that ain't what I come fur to say, Mr. Goree. Thar's somethin' you got what me and Missis Garvey wants to buy.'

'Buy?' echoed Gorce. 'From me?' Then he laughed harshly. 'I reckon you are mistaken about that. I reckon you are mistaken about that. I sold out to you, as you yourself expressed it, "lock, stock and barrel." There isn't even a ramrod left to sell.'

'You've got it; and we 'uns want it. "Take the money," says Missis Garvey, "and buy it fa'r and squar'." '

Goree shook his head. "The cupboard's bare,' he said.

'We've riz,' pursued the mountaineer, undeflected from his object, 'a heap. We was pore as possums, and now we could hev folks to dinner every day. We been reco'nized, Missis Garvey says, by the best society. But there's somethin' we need we ain't got. She says it ought to be put in the "ventory ov the sale, but it tain't thar. "Take the money, then," says she, "and buy it fa'r and squar'." '

'Out with it,' said Goree, his racked nerves growing impatient.

Garvey threw his slouch hat upon the table, and leaned forward, fixing his unblinking eyes upon Goree's.

'There's a old feud,' he said distinctly and slowly, ' 'tween you 'uns and the Coltranes.'

Goree frowned ominously. To speak of his feud to a feudist is a serious breach of the mountain etiquette. The man from 'back yan' knew it as well as the lawyer did.

'Na offence,' he went on, 'but purely in the way of business. Missis Garvey hev studied all about feuds. Most of the quality folks in the mountains hev 'em. The Settles and the Goforths, the Rankins and the Boyds, the Silers and the Galloways, hev all been cyarin' on feuds fom twenty to a hundred year. The last man to drap was when yo' uncle, Jedge Paisley Goree, 'journed co't and shot Len Coltrane f'om the bench. Missis Garvey and me, we come f'om the po' white trash. Nobody wouldn't pick a feud with we 'uns, no mo'n with a fam'ly of tree-toads. Quality people everywhar, says Missis Garvey, has feuds. We 'uns ain't quality, but we're buyin' into it as fur as we can. "Take the money, then," says Missis Garvey, "and buy Mr. Goree's feud, fa'r and squar'." '

The squirrel hunter straightened a leg half across the room, drew a roll of bills from his pocket, and threw them on the table.

'Thar's two hundred dollars, Mr. Goree; what you would call a fa'r price for a feud that's been 'lowed to run down like yourn hev. Thar's only you left to cyar' on yo' side of it, and you'd make mighty po' killin'. I'll take it off yo' hands, and it'll set me and Missis Garvey up among the quality. Thar's the money.'

The little roll of currency on the table slowly untwisted itself, writhing and jumping as its folds relaxed. In the silence that followed Garvey's last speech the rattling of the poker chips in the courthouse could be plainly heard. Goree knew that the sheriff had just won a pot, for the subdued whoop with which he always greeted a victory floated across the square upon the crinkly heat waves. Beads of moisture stood on Goree's brow. Stooping, he drew the wicker-covered demijohn from under the table, and filled a tumbler from it.

'A little corn liquor, Mr. Garvey? Of course you are joking about — what you spoke of? Opens quite a new market, doesn't it?

Feuds, prime, two-fifty to three. Feuds, slightly damaged – two hundred, I believe you said, Mr. Garvey?'

Goree laughed self-consciously.

The mountaineer took the glass Goree handed him, and drank the whisky without a tremor of the lids of his staring eyes. The lawyer applauded the feat by a look of envious admiration. He poured his own drink, and took it like a drunkard, by gulps, and with shudders at the smell and taste.

'Two hundred,' repeated Garvey. 'Thar's the money.'

A sudden passion flared up in Goree's brain. He struck the table with his fist. One of the bills flipped over and touched his hand. He flinched as if something had stung him.

'Do you come to me,' he shouted, 'seriously with such a ridiculous, insulting, darned-fool proposition?'

'It's fa'r and squar',' said the squirrel hunter, but he reached out his hand as if to take back the money; and then Goree knew that his own flurry of rage had not been from pride or resentment, but from anger at himself, knowing that he would set foot in the deeper depths that were being opened to him. He turned in an instant from an outraged gentleman to an anxious chafferer recommending his goods.

'Don't be in a hurry, Garvey,' he said, his face crimson and his speech thick. 'I accept your p-p-proposition, though it's dirt-cheap at two hundred. A t-trade's all right when both p-purchaser and b-buyer are s-satisfied. Shall I w-wrap it up for you, Mr. Garvey?'

Garvey rose, and shook out his broadcloth 'Missis Garvey will be pleased. You air out of it; and it stands Coltrane and Garvey. Just a scrap ov writin', Mr. Goree, you bein' a lawyer, to show we traded.'

Goree seized a sheet of paper and a pen. The money was clutched in his moist hand. Everything else suddenly seemed to grow trivial and light.

'Bill of sale, by all means. "Right, title, and interest in and to" . . . "for ever warrant and –" No, Garvey, we'll have to leave out that "defend," ' said Goree, with a loud laugh. 'You'll have to defend this title yourself.'

The mountaineer received the amazing screed that the lawyer handed him, folded it with immense labour, and placed it carefully in his pocket.

Goree was standing near the window. 'Step here,' he said, raising his finger, 'and I'll show you your recently purchased enemy. There he goes, down the other side of the street –'

The mountaineer crooked his long frame to look through the window in the direction indicated by the other. Colonel Abner Coltrane, an erect, portly gentleman of about fifty, wearing the inevitable long, double-breasted frock-coat of the Southern law-maker, and an old high silk hat, was passing on the opposite side-walk. As Garvey looked, Goree glanced at his face. If there be such a thing as a yellow wolf, here was its counterpart. Garvey snarled as his unhuman eyes followed the moving figure, disclosing long, amber-coloured fangs.

'Is that him? Why, that's the man who sent me to the pen'tentiary once!'

'He used to be district attorney,' said Goree carelessly. 'And, by the way, he's a first-class shot.'

'I kin hit a squirrel's eye at a hundred yard,' said Garvey. 'So that thar's Coltrane! I made a better trade than I was thinkin'. I'll take keer ov this feud, Mr. Goree, better'n you ever did!'

He moved toward the door, but lingered there, betraying a slight perplexity.

'Anything else to-day?' inquired Goree with frothy sarcasm. 'Any family traditions, ancestral ghosts, or skeletons in the closet? Prices as low as the lowest.'

'Thar was another thing,' replied the unmoved squirrel hunter, 'that Missis Garvey was thinkin' of. "Tain't so much in my line as t'other, but she wanted partic'lar that I should inquire, and ef you was willin', "pay fur it," she says, "fa'r and squar'." Thar's a buryin' groun', as you know, Mr. Goree, in the yard of yo' old place, under the cedars. Them that lies thar is yo' folks what was killed by the Coltranes. The monyments has the names on 'em. Missis Garvey says a fam'ly buryin' groun' is a sho' sign of quality. She says ef we git the feud, thar's somethin' else ought to go with it. The names on them monyments is "Goree," but they can be changed to ourn by –'

'Go! Go!' screamed Goree, his face turning purple. He stretched out both hands toward the mountaineer, his fingers hooked and shaking. 'Go, you ghoul! Even a Ch-Chinaman pro-tects the g-graves of his ancestors – go!'

The squirrel hunter slouched out of the door to his carry-all. While he was climbing over the wheel Goree was collecting, with feverish celerity, the money that had fallen from his hand to the floor. As the vehicle slowly turned about, the sheep, with a coat of newly grown wool, was hurrying, in indecent haste, along the path to the court-house.

At three o'clock in the morning they brought him back to his office, shorn and unconscious. The sheriff, the sportive deputy, the county clerk, and the gay attorney carried him, the chalk-faced man 'from the valley' acting as escort.

'On the table,' said one of them, and they deposited him there among the litter of his unprofitable books and papers.

'Yance thinks a lot of a pair of deuces when he's liquored up,' sighed the sheriff reflectively.

'Too much,' said the gay attorney. 'A man has no business to play poker who drinks as much as he does. I wonder how much he dropped to-night.'

'Close to two hundred. What I wonder is whar he got it; Yance ain't had a cent fur over a month, I know.'

'Struck a client, maybe. Well, let's get home before daylight. He'll be all right when he wakes up, except for a sort of beehive about the cranium.'

The gang slipped away through the early morning twilight. The next eye to gaze upon the miserable Goree was the orb of day. He peered through the uncurtained window, first deluging the sleeper in a flood of faint gold, but soon pouring upon the mottled red of his flesh a searching, white, summer heat. Goree stirred, half unconsciously, among the table's debris, and turned his face from the window. His movement dislodged a heavy law book, which crashed upon the floor. Opening his eyes, he saw, bending over him, a man in a black frock-coat. Looking higher, he discovered a well-worn silk hat, and beneath it the kindly, smooth face of Colonel Abner Coltrane.

A little uncertain of the outcome, the colonel waited for the other to make some sign of recognition. Not in twenty years had male members of these two families faced each other in peace. Goree's eyelids puckered as he strained his blurred sight toward this visitor, and then he smiled serenely.

'Have you brought Stella and Lucy over to play?' he said calmly.

'Do you know me, Yancey?' asked Coltrane.

'Of course I do. You brought me a whip with a whistle in the end.'

So he had – twenty-four years ago; when Yancey's father was his best friend.

Goree's eyes wandered about the room. The colonel understood. 'Lie still, and I'll bring you some,' said he. There was a pump in the yard at the rear, and Goree closed his eyes, listening with rapture to the click of its handle, and the bubbling of the falling stream. Coltrane brought a pitcher of the cool water, and held it for him to drink. Presently Goree sat up – a most forlorn object, his summer suit of flax soiled and crumpled, his discreditable head tousled and unsteady. He tried to wave one of his hands toward the colonel.

'Ex-excuse – everything, will you?' he said. 'I must have drunk too much whisky last night, and gone to bed on the table.' His brows knitted into a puzzled frown.

'Out with the boys a while?' asked Coltrane kindly.

'No, I went nowhere. I haven't had a dollar to spend in the last two months. Struck the demijohn too often, I reckon, as usual.'

Colonel Coltrane touched him on the shoulder.

'A little while ago, Yancey,' he began, 'you asked me if I had brought Stella and Lucy over to play. You weren't quite awake then, and must have been dreaming you were a boy again. You are awake now, and I want you to listen to me. I have come from Stella and Lucy to their old playmate, and to my old friend's son. They know that I am going to bring you home with me, and you will find them as ready with a welcome as they were in the old days. I want you to come to my house and stay until you are yourself again, and as much longer as you will. We heard of your being down in the world, and in the midst of temptation, and we agreed that you should come over and play at our house once more. Will you come, my boy? Will you drop our old family trouble and come with me?'

'Trouble!' said Goree, opening his eyes wide.

'There was never any trouble between us that I know of. I m sure we've always been the best friends. But, good Lord, Colonel, how could I go to your home as I am – a drunken wretch, a miserable, degraded spendthrift and gambler –'

He lurched from the table into his arm-chair, and began to weep maudlin tears, mingled with genuine drops of remorse and shame. Coltrane talked to him persistently and reasonably, reminding him of the simple mountain pleasures of which he had once been so fond, and insisting upon the genuineness of the invitation.

Finally he landed Goree by telling him he was counting upon his help in the engineering and transportation of a large amount of felled timber from a high mountain-side to a waterway. He knew that Goree had once invented a device for this purpose – a series of slides and chutes – upon which he had justly prided himself. In an instant the poor fellow, delighted at the idea of his being of use to anyone, had paper spread upon the table, and was drawing rapid but pitifully shaky lines in demonstration of what he could and would do.

The man was sickened of the husks; his prodigal heart was turning again toward the mountains. His mind was yet strangely clogged, and his thoughts and memories were returning to his brain one by one, like carrier pigeons over a stormy sea. But Coltrane was satisfied with the progress he had made.

Bethel received the surprise of its existence that afternoon when a Coltrane and a Goree rode amicably together through the town. Side by side they rode, out from the dusty streets and gaping townspeople, down across the creek bridge, and up toward the mountain. The prodigal had brushed and washed and combed himself to a more decent figure, but he was unsteady in the saddle, and he seemed to be deep in the contemplation of some vexing problem. Coltrane left him in his mood, relying upon the influence of changed surroundings to restore his equilibrium.

Once Goree was seized with a shaking fit, and almost came to a collapse. He had to dismount and rest at the side of the road. The colonel, forseeing such a condition, had provided a small flask of whisky for the journey, but when it was offered to him Goree refused it almost with violence, declaring he would never touch it again. By and by he was recovered, and went quietly enough for a mile or two. Then he pulled up his horse suddenly, and said:

'I lost two hundred dollars last night, playing poker. Now, where did I get that money?'

'Take it easy, Yancey. The mountain air will soon clear it up. We'll go fishing, first thing, at the Pinnacle Falls. The trout are jumping there like bullfrogs. We'll take Stella and Lucy along, and have a picnic on Eagle Rock. Have you forgotten how a hickory-cured-ham sandwich tastes, Yancey, to a hungry fisherman?'

Evidently the colonel did not believe the story of his lost wealth; so Goree retired again into brooding silence.

By late afternoon they had travelled ten of the twelve miles between Bethel and Laurel. Half a mile this side of Laurel lay the old Goree place; a mile or two beyond the village lived the Coltranes. The road was now steep and laborious, but the compensations were many. The tilted aisles of the forest were opulent with leaf and bird and bloom. The tonic air put to shame the pharmacopœia. The glades were dark with mossy shade, and bright with shy rivulets winking from the ferns and laurels. On the lower side they viewed, framed in the near foliage, exquisite sketches of the far valley swooning in its opal haze.

Coltrane was pleased to see that his companion was yielding to the spell of the hills and woods. For now they had but to skirt the base of Painter's Cliff; to cross Elder Branch and mount the hill beyond, and Goree would have to face the squandered home of his fathers. Every rock he passed, every tree, every foot of the road-way, was familiar to him. Though he had forgotten the woods, they thrilled him like the music of 'Home, Sweet Home.'

They rounded the cliff, descended into Elder Branch, and paused there to let the horses drink and splash in the swift water. On the right was a rail fence that cornered there, and followed the road and stream. Enclosed by it was the old apple orchard of the home place; the house was yet concealed by the brow of the steep hill. Inside and along the fence, pokeberries, elders, sassafras, and sumac grew high and dense. At a rustle of their branches, both Goree and Coltrane glanced up, and saw a long, yellow, wolfish face above the fence, staring at them with pale, unwinking eyes. The head quickly disappeared; there was a violent swaying of the bushes, and an ungainly figure ran up through the apple orchard in the direction of the house, zigzagging among the trees.

'That's Garvey,' said Coltrane; 'the man you sold out to. There's no doubt but he's considerably cracked. I had to send him up for moonshining once, several years ago, in spite of the fact that I believed him irresponsible. Why, what's the matter, Yancey?'

Goree was wiping his forehead, and his face had lost its colour. 'Do I look queer, too?' he asked, trying to smile. 'I'm just remem-bering a few more things.' Some of the alcohol had evaporated from his brain. 'I recollect now where I got that two hundred dollars.'

'Don't think of it,' said Coltrane cheerfully. 'Later on we'll figure it all out together.'

They rode out of the branch, and when they reached the foot of the hill Goree stopped again.

'Did you ever suspect I was a very vain kind of fellow, Colonel?' he asked. 'Sort of foolish proud about appearances?'

The colonel's eyes refused to wander to the soiled, sagging suit of flax and the faded slouch hat.

'It seems to me,' he replied, mystified, but humouring him, 'I remember a young buck about twenty, with the tightest coat, the sleekest hair, and the prancingest saddle horse in the Blue Ridge.'

'Right you are,' said Goree eagerly. 'And it's in me yet, though it don't show. Oh, I'm as vain as a turkey gobbler, and as proud as

Lucifer. I'm going to ask you to indulge this weakness of mine in a little matter.'

'Speak out, Yancey. We'll create you Duke of Laurel and Baron of Blue Ridge, if you choose; and you shall have a feather out of Stella's peacock's tail to wear in your hat.'

'I'm in earnest. In a few minutes we'll pass the house up there on the hill where I was born, and where my people have lived for nearly a century. Strangers live there now – and look at me! I am about to show myself to them ragged and poverty-stricken, a wastrel and a beggar. Colonel Coltrane, I'm ashamed to do it. I want you to let me wear your coat and hat until we are out of sight beyond. I know you think it a foolish pride, but I want to make as good a showing as I can when I pass the old place.'

'Now, what does this mean?' said Coltrane to himself, as he compared his companion's sane looks and quiet demeanour with his strange request. But he was already unbuttoning the coat, assenting readily, as if the fancy were in no wise to be considered strange.

The coat and hat fitted Goree well. He buttoned the former about him with a look of satisfaction and dignity. He and Coltrane were nearly the same size – rather tall, portly, and erect. Twenty-five years were between them, but in appearance they might have been brothers. Goree looked older than his age; his face was puffy and lined; the colonel had the smooth, fresh complexion of a temperate liver. He put on Goree's disreputable old flax coat and faded slouch hat.

'Now,' said Goree, taking up the reins, 'I'm all right. I want you to ride about ten feet in the rear as we go by, Colonel, so that they can get a good look at me. They'll see I'm no back number yet, by any means. I guess I'll show up pretty well to them once more, anyhow. Let's ride on.'

He set out up the hill at a smart trot, the colonel following, as he had been requested.

Goree sat straight in the saddle, with head erect, but his eyes were turned to the right, sharply scanning every shrub and fence and hiding-place in the old homestead yard. Once he muttered to himself, 'Will the crazy fool try it, or did I dream half of it?'

It was when he came opposite the little family burying ground that he saw what he had been looking for – a puff of white smoke, coming from the thick cedars in one corner. He toppled so slowly to the left that Coltrane had time to urge his horse to that side, and catch him with one arm.

The squirrel hunter had not overpraised his aim. He had sent the bullet where he intended, and where Goree had expected that it would pass – through the breast of Colonel Abner Coltrane's black frock-coat.

Goree leaned heavily against Coltrane, but he did not fall. The horses kept pace, side by side and the colonel's arm kept him steady. The little white houses of Laurel shone through the trees, half a mile away. Goree reached out one hand and groped until it rested upon Coltrane's fingers, which held his bridle.

'Good friend,' he said, and that was all.

Thus did Yancey Goree, as he rode past his old home, make, considering all things, the best showing that was in his power.

XCVI

Madame Bo-peep, of the Ranches

'AUNT ELLEN,' SAID OCTAVIA cheerfully, as she threw her black kid gloves carefully at the dignified Persian cat on the window-seat, 'I'm a pauper.'

'You are so extreme in your statements, Octavia, dear,' said Aunt Ellen mildly, looking up from her paper. 'If you find yourself temporarily in need of some small change for bonbons, you will find my purse in the drawer of the writing-desk.'

Octavia Beaupree removed her hat and seated herself on a footstool near her aunt's chair, clasping her hands about her knees. Her slim and flexible figure, clad in a modish mourning costume, accommodated itself easily and gracefully to the trying position. Her bright and youthful face, with its pair of sparkling, life-enamoured eyes, tried to compose itself to the seriousness that the occasion seemed to demand.

'You good auntie, it isn't a case of bonbons; it is abject, staring, unpicturesque poverty, with readymade clothes, gasolined gloves, and probably one o'clock dinners all waiting with the traditional wolf at the door. I've just come from my lawyer, auntie, and, "Please, ma'am, I ain't got nothink 't all. Flowers, lady? Button-hole, gentleman? Pencils, sir, three for five, to help a poor widow?" Do I do it nicely, auntie, or, as a bread-winner accomplishment, were my lessons in elocution entirely wasted?'

'Do be serious, my dear,' said Aunt Ellen, letting her paper fall to the floor, 'long enough to tell me what you mean. Colonel Beaupree's estate –'

'Colonel Beaupree's estate,' interrupted Octavia, emphasizing her words with appropriate dramatic gestures, 'is of Spanish castellar architecture. Colonel Beaupree's resources are – wind. Colonel Beaupree's stocks are – water. Colonel Beaupree's income is – all in. The statement lacks the legal technicalities to which I have been listening for an hour, but that is what it means when translated.'

'Octavia!' Aunt Ellen was now visibly possessed by consternation. 'I can hardly believe it. And it was the impression that he was worth a million. And the De Peysters themselves introduced him!'

Octavia rippled out a laugh, and then became properly grave.

'De mortuis nil, auntie – not even the rest of it. The dear old colonel – what a gold brick he was, after all! I paid for my bargain fairly – I'm all here, am I not? – items: eyes, fingers, toes, youth, old family, unquestionable position in society as called for in the contract – no wild-cat stock here.' Octavia picked up the morning paper from the floor. 'But I'm not going to "squeal" – isn't that what they call it when you rail at Fortune because you've lost the game?' She turned the pages of the paper calmly. ' "Stock market" – no use for that. "Society's doings" – that's done. Here is my page – the wish column. A Van Dresser could not be said to "want" for anything, of course. "Chambermaids, cooks, canvassers, stenographers –'

'Dear,' said Aunt Ellen, with a little tremor in her voice, 'please do not talk in that way. Even if your affairs are in so unfortunate a condition, there is my three thousand –'

Octavia sprang up lithely, and deposited a smart kiss on the delicate cheek of the prim little elderly maid.

'Blessed auntie, your three thousand is just sufficient to ensure your Hyson to be free from willow leaves and keep the Persian in sterilized cream. I know I'd be welcome, but I prefer to strike bottom like Beelzebub rather than hang around like the Peri listening to the music from the side entrance. I'm going to earn my own living, There's nothing else to do. I'm a – Oh, oh, oh! – I had forgotten. There's one thing saved from the wreck. It's a corral – no, a ranch in – let me see – Texas; an asset, dear old Mr. Bannister called it. How pleased he was to show me something he could describe as unencumbered! I've a description of it among those stupid papers he made me bring away with me from his office. I'll try to find it.'

Octavia found her shopping-bag, and drew from it a long envelope filled with typewritten documents.

'A ranch in Texas,' sighed Aunt Ellen. 'It sounds to me more like a liability than an asset. Those are the places where the centipedes are found; and cowboys, and fandangos.'

' "The Rancho de las Sombras," ' read Octavia from a sheet of violently purple typewriting, ' "is situated one hundred and ten miles south-east of San Antonio, and thirty-eight miles from its nearest railroad station, Nopal, on the I. and G.N. Ranch consists of 7,680 acres of well-watered land, with title conferred by State patents, and twenty-two sections, or 14,080 acres, partly under yearly running lease and partly bought under State's twenty-year-purchase act. Eight thousand graded merino sheep, with the necessary equipment of horses, vehicles and general ranch paraphernalia. Ranchhouse built of brick, with six rooms comfortably furnished according to the requirements of the climate. All within a strong barbed-wire fence.

' "The present ranch manager seems to be competent and reliable, and is rapidly placing upon a paying basis a business that, in other hands, had been allowed to suffer from neglect and misconduct.

' "This property was secured by Colonel Beaupree in a deal with a Western irrigation syndicate, and the title to it seems to be perfect. With careful management, and the natural increase of land values, it ought to be made the foundation for a comfortable fortune for its owner." '

When Octavia ceased reading, Aunt Ellen uttered something as near a sniff as her breeding permitted.

'The prospectus,' she said, with uncompromising metropolitan suspicion, 'doesn't mention the centipedes, or the Indians. And you never did like mutton, Octavia. I don't see what advantage you can derive from this – desert.'

But Octavia was in a trance. Her eyes were steadily regarding something quite beyond their focus. Her lips were parted, and her face was lighted by the kindling furor of the explorer, the ardent, stirring disquiet of the adventurer. Suddenly she clasped her hands together exultantly.

'The problem solves itself, auntie,' she cried. 'I'm going to that ranch. I'm going to live on it. I'm going to learn to like mutton, and even concede the good qualities of centipedes – at a respectful distance. It's just what I need. It's a new life that comes when my old one is just ending. It's a release, auntie; it isn't a narrowing. Think of the gallops over those leagues of prairies, with the wind tugging at the roots of your hair, the coming close to the earth and learning over again the stories of the growing grass and the little wild flowers without names! Glorious is what it will be. Shall I be a shepherdess with a Watteau hat, and a crook to keep the bad wolves from the lambs, or a typical Western ranch girl, with short hair, like the pictures of her in the Sunday papers? I think the latter. And they'll have my picture, too, with the wild-cats I've slain, single-handed, hanging from my saddle-horn. "From the Four Hundred to the Flocks" is the way they'll head-line it, and they'll print photographs of the old Van Dresser mansion and the church where I was married. They won't have my picture, but they'll get an artist to draw it. It'll be wild and woolly, and I'll grow my own wool.'

'Octavia!' Aunt Ellen condensed into the one word all the protests she was unable to utter.

'Don't say a word, auntie. I'm going. I'll see the sky at night fit down on the world like a big butter-dish cover, and I'll make friends again with the stars that I haven't had a chat with since I was a wee child. I wish to go. I'm tired of all this. I'm glad I haven't any money. I could bless Colonel Beaupree for that ranch, and forgive him for all his bubbles. What if the life will be rough and lonely! I – I deserve it. I shut my heart to everything except that miserable ambition. I – oh, I wish to go away, and forget – forget!'

Octavia swerved suddenly to her knees, laid her flushed face in her aunt's lap, and shook with turbulent sobs.

Aunt Ellen bent over her, and smoothed the coppery-brown hair.

'I didn't know,' she said gently; 'I didn't know – that Who was it. dear?'

When Mrs. Octavia Beaupree, *née* Van Dresser, stepped from the train at Nopal, her manner lost, for the moment, some of that easy certitude which had always marked her movements. The town was of recent establishment, and seemed to have been hastily constructed of undressed lumber and flapping canvas. The element that had congregated about the station, though not offensively demonstrative, was clearly composed of citizens accustomed to and prepared for rude alarms.

Octavia stood on the platform, against the telegraph office, and attempted to choose by intuition, from the swaggering, straggling string of loungers, the manager of the Rancho de las Sombras, who had been instructed by Mr. Bannister to meet her there. That tall, serious-looking, elderly man in the blue flannel shirt and white tie she thought must be he. But no; he passed by, removing his gaze from the lady as hers rested on him, according to the Southern custom. The manager, she thought, with some impatience at being kept waiting, should have no difficulty in selecting her. Young women wearing the most recent thing in ash-coloured travelling suits were not so plentiful in Nopal!

Thus keeping a speculative watch on all persons of possible managerial aspect, Octavia, with a catching breath and a start of surprise, suddenly became aware of Teddy Westlake hurrying along the platform in the direction of the train — of Teddy Westlake or his sun-browned ghost in cheviot, boots and leather-girdled hat — Theodore Westlake, Jr., amateur polo (almost) champion, all-round butterfly and cumberer of the soil; but a broader, surer, more emphasized and determined Teddy than the one she had known a year ago when last she saw him.

He perceived Octavia at almost the same time, deflected his course, and steered for her in his old, straightforward way. Something like awe came upon her as the strangeness of his metamorphosis was brought into closer range; the rich, red-brown of his complexion brought out so vividly his straw-coloured moustache and steel-grey eyes. He seemed more grown-up, and, somehow, farther away. But, when he spoke, the old, boyish Teddy came back again. They had been friends from childhood.

'Why, 'Tave!' he exclaimed, unable to reduce his perplexity to coherence. 'How — what — when — where?'

'Train,' said Octavia; 'necessity; ten minutes ago; home. Your complexion's gone, Teddy. Now, how — what — when — where?'

'I'm working down here,' said Teddy. He cast side glances about the station as one does who tries to combine politeness with duty.

'You didn't notice on the train,' he asked, 'an old lady with grey curls and a poodle, who occupied two seats with her bundles and quarrelled with the conductor, did you?'

'I think not,' answered Octavia, reflecting. 'And you haven't, by any chance, noticed a big, grey-moustached man in a blue shirt and six-shooters, with little flakes of merino wool sticking in his hair, have you?'

'Lots of 'em,' said Teddy, with symptoms of mental delirium under the strain. 'Do you happen to know any such individual?'

'No; the description is imaginary. Is your interest in the old lady whom you describe a personal one?'

'Never saw her in my life. She's painted entirely from fancy. She owns the little piece of property where I earn my bread and butter – the Rancho de las Sombras. I drove up to meet her according to arrangement with her lawyer.'

Octavia leaned against the wall of the telegraph office. Was this possible? And didn't he know?

'Are you the manager of that ranch?' she asked weakly.

'I am,' said Teddy, with pride.

'I am Mrs. Beaupree,' said Octavia faintly; 'but my hair never would curl, and I was polite to the conductor.'

For a moment that strange, grown-up look came back and removed Teddy miles away from her.

'I hope you'll excuse me,' he said, rather awkwardly. 'You see, I've been down here in the chaparral a year. I hadn't heard. Give me your checks, please, and I'll have your traps loaded into the wagon. Jose will follow with them. We travel ahead in the buckboard.'

Seated by Teddy in a feather-weight buckboard, behind a pair of wild, cream-coloured Spanish ponies, Octavia abandoned all thought for the exhilaration of the present. They swept out of the little town and down the level road toward the south. Soon the road dwindled and disappeared, and they struck across a world carpeted with an endless reach of curly mesquite grass. The wheels made no sound. The tireless ponies bounded ahead at an unbroken gallop. The temperate wind, made fragrant by thousands of acres of blue and yellow wild flowers, roared gloriously in their ears. The motion was aerial, ecstatic, with a thrilling sense of perpetuity in its effect. Octavia sat silent, possessed by a feeling of elemental, sensual bliss. Teddy seemed to be wrestling with some internal problem.

'I'm going to call you madama,' he announced as the result of his labours. 'That is what the Mexicans will call you – they're nearly all Mexicans on the ranch, you know. That seems to me about the proper thing.'

'Very well, Mr. Westlake,' said Octavia primly.

'Oh, now,' said Teddy, in some consternation, 'that's carrying the thing too far, isn't it?'

'Don't worry me with your beastly etiquette. I'm just beginning to live. Don't remind me of anything artificial. If only this air could be bottled! This much alone is worth coming for. Oh, look there goes a deer!'

'Jack-rabbit,' said Teddy, without turning his head.

'Could I – might I drive?' suggested Octavia, panting, with rose-tinted cheeks and the eye of an eager child.

'On one condition. Could I – might I smoke?'

'For ever!' cried Octavia, taking the lines with solemn joy. 'How shall I know which way to drive?'

'Keep her sou' by sou'east, and all sail set. You see that black speck on the horizon under that lower-most Gulf cloud? That's a group of live-oaks and a landmark. Steer half-way between that and the little hill to the left. I'll recite you the whole code of driving rules for the Texas prairies: keep the reins from under the horses' feet, and swear at 'em frequent.'

'I'm too happy to swear, Ted. Oh, why do people buy yachts or travel in palace-cars, when a buckboard and a pair of plugs and a spring morning like this can satisfy all desire?'

'Now, I'll ask you,' protested Teddy, who was futilely striking match after match on the dashboard, 'not to call those denizens of the air plugs. They can kick out a hundred miles between daylight and dark.' At last he succeeded in snatching a light for his cigar from the flame held in the hollow of his hands.

'Room!' said Octavia intensely. 'That's what produces the effect. I know now what I've wanted – scope – range – room!'

'Smoking-room,' said Teddy unsentimentally. 'I love to smoke in a buckboard. The wind blows the smoke into you and out again. It saves exertion.'

The two fell so naturally into their old-time good-fellowship that it was only by degrees that a sense of the strangeness of the new relations between them came to be felt.

'Madama,' said Teddy wonderingly, 'however did you get it into your head to cut the crowd and come down here? Is it a fad now among the upper classes to trot off to sheep ranches instead of to Newport?'

'I was broke, Teddy,' said Octavia sweetly, with her interest centred upon steering safely between a Spanish dagger plant and a clump of chaparral; 'I haven't a thing in the world but this ranch – not even any other home to go to.'

'Come, now,' said Teddy, anxiously but incredulously, 'you don't mean it?'

'When my husband,' said Octavia, with a shy slurring of the word, 'died three months ago I thought I had a reasonable amount of the world's goods. His lawyer exploded that theory in a sixty-minute fully illustrated lecture. I took to the sheep as a last resort. Do you happen to know of any fashionable caprice among the gilded youth of Manhattan that induces them to abandon polo and club windows to become managers of sheep ranches?'

'It's easily explained in my case,' responded Teddy promptly. 'I had to go to work. I couldn't have earned my board in New York, so I chummed a while with old Sandford, one of the syndicate that owned the ranch before Colonel Beaupree bought it, and got a place down here. I wasn't manager at first. I jogged around on ponies and studied the business in detail, until I got all the points in my head. I saw where it was losing and what the remedies were, and then Sandford put me in charge. I get a hundred dollars a month, and I earn it.'

'Poor Teddy!' said Octavia, with a smile.

'You needn't. I like it. I save half my wages, and I'm as hard as a water-plug. It beats polo.'

'Will it furnish bread and tea and jam for another outcast from civilization?'

'The spring shearing,' said the manager, 'just cleaned up a deficit in last year's business. Wastefulness and inattention have been the rule heretofore. The autumn clip will leave a small profit over all expenses. Next year there will be jam.'

When, about four o'clock in the afternoon, the ponies rounded a gentle, brush-covered hill, and then swooped, like a double cream coloured cyclone, upon the Rancho de las Sombras, Octavia gave a little cry of delight. A lordly grove of magnificent live-oaks cast an area of grateful, cool shade, whence the ranch had drawn its name, 'de las Sombras' – of the shadows. The house, of red brick, one story, ran low and long beneath the trees. Through its middle, dividing its six rooms in half, extended a broad, arched passage-way, picturesque with flowering cactus and hanging red earthen jars. A 'gallery,' low and broad, encircled the building. Vines climbed about it, and the adjacent ground was, for a space, covered with transplanted grass and shrubs. A little lake, long and narrow, glimmered in the sun at the rear. Farther away stood the shacks of the Mexican workers, the corrals, wool sheds and shearing pens. To the right lay the low hills, splattered with dark patches of chaparral; to the left the unbounded green prairie blending against the blue heavens.

'It's a home, Teddy,' said Octavia, breathlessly; 'that's what it is – it's a home.'

'Not so bad for a sheep ranch,' admitted Teddy, with excusable pride. 'I've been tinkering on it at odd times.'

A Mexican youth sprang from somewhere in the grass, and took charge of the creams. The mistress and the manager entered the house.

'Here's Mrs. MacIntyre,' said Teddy, as a placid, neat, elderly lady came out upon the gallery to meet them. 'Mrs. Mac, here's the boss. Very likely she will be wanting a hunk of bacon and a dish of beans after her drive.'

Mrs. MacIntyre, the housekeeper, as much a fixture on the place as the lake or the live-oaks received the imputation of the ranch's resources of refreshment with mild indignation, and was about to give it utterance when Octavia spoke.

'Oh, Mrs. MacIntyre, don't apologize for Teddy. Yes, I call him Teddy. So does every one whom he hasn't duped into taking him seriously. You see, we used to cut paper dolls and play jackstraws together ages ago. No one minds what he says.'

'No,' said Teddy, 'no one minds what he says, just so he doesn't do it again.'

Octavia cast one of those subtle, sidelong glances toward him from beneath her lowered eyelids – a glance that Teddy used to describe as an uppercut. But there was nothing in his ingenuous, weather tanned face to warrant a suspicion that he was making an allusion – nothing. Beyond a doubt, thought Octavia, he had forgotten.

'Mr. Westlake likes his fun,' said Mrs. MacIntyre, as she conducted Octavia to her rooms. 'But,' she added loyally, 'people around here usually pay attention to what he says when he talks in earnest. I don't know what would have become of this place without him.'

Two rooms at the east end of the house had been arranged for the occupancy of the ranch's mistress. When she entered them a slight dismay seized her at their bare appearance and the scantiness of their furniture; but she quickly reflected that the climate was a semi-tropical one, and was moved to appreciation of the well-conceived efforts to conform to it. The sashes had already been removed from the big windows, and white curtains waved in the Gulf breeze that streamed through the wide jalousies.

The bare floor was amply strewn with cool rugs; the chairs were inviting, deep, dreamy willows; the walls were papered with a light, cheerful olive. One whole side of her sitting-room was covered with books on smooth, unpainted pine shelves. She flew to these at once. Before her was a well-selected library. She caught glimpses of titles of volumes of fiction and travel not yet seasoned from the dampness of the press.

Presently, recollecting that she was now in a wilderness given over to mutton, centipedes and privations, the incongruity of these luxuries struck her, and, with intuitive feminine suspicion, she began turning to the fly-leaves of volume after volume. Upon each one was inscribed in fluent characters the name of Theodore Westlake, Jr.

Octavia, fatigued by her long journey, retired early that night. Lying upon her white, cool bed, she rested deliciously, but sleep coquetted long with her. She listened to faint noises whose strangeness kept her faculties on the alert — the fractious yelping of the coyotes, the ceaseless, low symphony of the wind, the distant booming of the frogs about the lake, the lamentation of a concertina in the Mexicans' quarters. There were many conflicting feelings in her heart — thankfulness and rebellion, peace and disquietude, loneliness and a sense of protecting care, happiness and an old, haunting pain.

She did what any other woman would have done — sought relief in a wholesome tide of unreasonable tears, and her last words, murmured to herself before slumber, capitulating, came softly to woo her, were, 'He has forgotten.'

The manager of the Rancho de las Sombras was no dilettante. He was a 'hustler.' He was generally up, mounted, and away of mornings before the rest of the household were awake, making the rounds of the flocks and camps. This was the duty of the major-domo, a stately old Mexican with a princely air and manner, but Teddy seemed to have a great deal of confidence in his own eyesight. Except in the busy seasons, he nearly always returned to the ranch to breakfast at eight o'clock, with Octavia and Mrs. MacIntyre, at the little table set in the central hallway, bringing with him a tonic and breezy cheerfulness full of the health and flavour of the prairies.

A few days after Octavia's arrival he made her get out one of her riding-skirts, and curtail it to a shortness demanded by the chaparral brakes.

With some misgivings she donned this and the pair of buckskin leggings he prescribed in addition, and, mounted upon a dancing pony, rode with him to view her possessions. He showed her everything — the flocks of ewes, muttons and grazing lambs, the dipping vats, the shearing pens, the uncouth merino rams in their little pasture, the water-tanks prepared against the summer drought — giving account of his stewardship with a boyish enthusiasm that never flagged.

Where was the old Teddy that she knew so well? This side of him was the same, and it was a side that pleased her; but this was all she ever saw of him now. Where was his sentimentality – those old, varying moods of impetuous love-making, of fanciful, quixotic devotion, of heart-breaking gloom, of alternating, absurd tenderness and haughty dignity? His nature had been a sensitive one, his temperament bordering closely on the artistic. She knew that, besides being a follower of fashion and its fads and sports, he had cultivated tastes of a finer nature. He had written things, he had tampered with colours, he was something of a student in certain branches of art, and once she had been admitted to all his aspirations and thoughts. But now – and she could not avoid the conclusion Teddy had barricaded against her every side of himself except one – the side that showed the manager of the Rancho de las Sombras and a jolly chum who had forgiven and forgotten. Queerly enough the words of Mr. Bannister's description of her property came into her mind – 'all enclosed within a strong barbed-wire fence.'

'Teddy's fenced, too,' said Octavia to herself.

It was not difficult for her to reason out the cause of his fortifications. It had originated one night at the Hammersmiths' ball. It occurred at a time soon after she had decided to accept Colonel Beaupree and his million, which was no more than her looks and the entrée she held to the inner circles were worth. Teddy had proposed with all his impetuosity and fire, and she looked him straight in the eyes, and said, coldly and finally: 'Never let me hear any such silly nonsense from you again.' 'You won't,' said Teddy, with a new expression around his mouth, and – now Teddy was enclosed within a strong barbed-wire fence.

It was on this first ride of inspection that Teddy was seized by the inspiration that suggested the name of Mother Goose's heroine, and he at once bestowed it upon Octavia. The idea, supported by both a similarity of names and identity of occupations, seemed to strike him as a peculiarly happy one, and he never tired of using it. The Mexicans on the ranch also took up the name, adding another syllable to accommodate their lingual incapacity for the final 'p,' gravely referring to her as 'La Madama Bo-Peepy.' Eventually it spread, and 'Madame Bo-Peep's ranch' was as often mentioned as the 'Rancho de las Sombras.'

Came the long, hot season from May to September, when work is scarce on the ranches. Octavia passed the days in a kind of lotus-eater's dream. Books, hammocks, correspondence with a few intimate friends, a renewed interest in her old water-colour box and easel – these disposed of the sultry hours of daylight. The evenings were always sure to bring enjoyment. Best of all were the rapturous horseback rides with Teddy, when the moon gave light over the wind-swept leagues, chaperoned by the wheeling night-hawk and the startled owl. Often the Mexicans would come up from their shacks with their guitars and sing the weirdest of heartbreaking songs. There were long, cosy chats on the breezy gallery, and an interminable warfare of wits between Teddy and Mrs. MacIntyre, whose abundant Scotch shrewdness often more than overmatched the lighter humour in which she was lacking.

And the nights came, one after another, and were filed away by weeks and months – nights soft and languorous and fragrant, that should have driven Strephon to Chloe over wires however barbed, that might have drawn Cupid himself to hunt, lasso in hand, among those amorous pastures – but Teddy kept his fences up.

One July night Madame Bo-Peep and her ranch manager were sitting on the east gallery. Teddy had been exhausting the science of prognostication as to the probabilities of a price of twenty-four cents for the autumn clip, and had then subsided into an anæsthetic cloud of Havana smoke. Only as incompetent a judge as a woman would have failed to note long ago that at least a third of his salary must have gone up in the fumes of those imported Regalias.

'Teddy,' said Octavia suddenly, and rather sharply, 'what are you working down here on a ranch for?'

'One hundred per,' said Teddy glibly, 'and found.'

'I've a good mind to discharge you.'

'Can't do it,' said Teddy, with a grin.

'Why not?' demanded Octavia, with argumentative heat.

'Under contract. Terms of sale respect all unexpired contracts. Mine runs until 12 p.m., December thirty-first. You might get up at midnight on that date and fire me. If you try it sooner I'll be in a position to bring legal proceedings.'

Octavia seemed to be considering the prospects of litigation.

'But,' continued Teddy cheerfully, 'I've been thinking of resigning, anyway.'

Octavia's rocking-chair ceased its motion. There were centipedes in this country, she felt sure; and Indians; and vast, lonely, desolate, empty wastes; all within strong barbed-wire fence. There was a Van Dresser pride, but there was also a Van Dresser heart. She must know for certain whether or not he had forgotten.

'Ah, well, Teddy,' she said, with a fine assumption of polite interest, 'it's lonely down here; you're longing to get back to the old life – to polo and lobsters and theatres and balls.'

'Never cared much for balls,' said Teddy virtuously.

'You're getting old, Teddy. Your memory is failing. Nobody ever knew you to miss a dance, unless it occurred on the same night with another one which you attended. And you showed such shocking bad taste, too, in dancing too often with the same partner. Let me see, what was that Forbes girl's name – the one with wall eyes – Mabel, wasn't it?'

'No; Adéle. Mabel was the one with the bony elbows. That wasn't wall in Adéle's eyes. It was soul. We used to talk sonnets together, and Verlaine Just then I was trying to run a pipe from the Pierian spring.'

'You were on the floor with her,' said Octavia, undeflected, 'five times at the Hammersmiths'.'

'Hammersmiths' what?' questioned Teddy vacuously.

'Ball – ball,' said Octavia viciously. 'What were we talking of?'

'Eyes, I thought,' said Teddy, after some reflection; 'and elbows.'

'Those Hammersmiths,' went on Octavia, in her sweetest society prattle, after subduing an intense desire to yank a handful of sunburnt, sandy hair from the head lying back contentedly against the canvas of the steamer chair, 'had too much money. Mines, wasn't it? It was something that paid something to the ton. You couldn't get a glass of plain water in their house. Everything at that ball was dreadfully overdone.'

'It was,' said Teddy.

'Such a crowd there was!' Octavia continued, conscious that she was talking the rapid drivel of a schoolgirl describing her first dance. 'The balconies were as warm as the rooms. I – lost – something at that ball.' The last sentence was uttered in a tone calculated to remove the barbs from miles of wire.

'So did I,' confessed Teddy in a lower voice.

'A glove,' said Octavia, falling back as the enemy approached her ditches.

'Caste,' said Teddy, halting his firing line without loss. 'I hobnobbed half the evening with one of Hammersmiths' miners, a fellow who kept his hands in his pockets, and talked like an archangel about reduction plants and drifts and levels and sluice-boxes.'

'A pearl-grey glove, nearly new,' sighed Octavia mournfully.

'A bang-up chap, that McArdle,' maintained Teddy approvingly. 'A man who hated olives and elevators; a man who handled mountains as croquettes, and built tunnels in the air; a man who never uttered a word of silly nonsense in his life. Did you sign

those lease-renewal applications yet, madama? They've got to be
on file in the land office by the thirty-first.'

Teddy turned his head lazily. Octavia's chair was vacant.

A certain centipede, crawling along the lines marked out by fate,
expounded the situation. It was early one morning while Octavia
and Mrs. MacIntyre were trimming the honeysuckle on the west
gallery. Teddy had risen and departed hastily before daylight in
response to word that a flock of ewes had been scattered from
their bedding ground during the night by a thunderstorm.

The centipede, driven by destiny, showed himself on the floor
of the gallery, and then, the screeches of the two women giving
him his cue, he scuttled with all his yellow legs through the open
door into the furthermost west room, which was Teddy's. Arming
themselves with domestic utensils selected with regard to their
length, Octavia and Mrs. MacIntyre, with much clutching of skirts
and skirmishing for the position of rear guard in the attacking
force, followed.

Once outside, the centipede seemed to have disappeared, and
his prospective murderers began a thorough but cautious search
for their victim.

Even in the midst of such a dangerous and absorbing adventure Octavia was conscious of an awed curiosity on finding her
self in Teddy's sanctum. In that room he sat alone, silently
communing with those secret thoughts that he now shared with
no one, dreamed there whatever dreams he now called on no one
to interpret.

It was the room of a Spartan or a soldier. In one corner stood a
wide, canvas-covered cot; in another a small bookcase; in another,
a grim stand of Winchesters and shot-guns. An immense table,
strewn with letters, papers and documents and surmounted by a
set of pigeon-holes, occupied one side.

The centipede showed genius in concealing himself in such
bare quarters. Mrs. MacIntyre was poking a broom-handle
behind the bookcase. Octavia approached Teddy's cot. The
room was just as the manager had left it in his hurry. The Mexican maid had not yet given it her attention. There was his big
pillow with the imprint of his head still in the centre. She
thought the horrid beast might have climbed the cot and hidden
itself to bite Teddy. Centipedes were thus cruel and vindictive
toward managers.

She cautiously overturned the pillow, and then parted her lips to give the signal for reinforcements at sight of a long, slender, dark object lying there. But, repressing it in time, she caught up a glove, a pearl-grey glove, flattened – it might be conceived – by many, many months of nightly pressure beneath the pillow of the man who had forgotten the Hammersmiths' ball. Teddy must have left so hurriedly that morning that he had, for once, forgotten to transfer it to its resting-place by day. Even managers, who are notoriously wily and cunning, are sometimes caught up with.

Octavia slid the grey glove into the bosom of her summery morning gown. It was hers. Men who put themselves within a strong, barbed-wire fence, and remember Hammersmith balls only by the talk of miners about sluice-boxes, should not be allowed to possess such articles.

After all, what a paradise this prairie country was! How it blossomed like the rose when you found things that were thought to be lost! How delicious was that morning breeze coming in the windows, fresh and sweet with the breath of the yellow ratama blooms! Might one not stand, for a minute, with shining, far-gazing eyes, and dream that mistakes might be corrected?

Why was Mrs. MacIntyre poking about so absurdly with a broom.

'I've found it,' said Mrs. MacIntyre, banging the door. 'Here it is.'

'Did you lose something?' asked Octavia, with sweetly polite non-interest.

'The little devil!' said Mrs. MacIntyre, driven to violence. 'Ye've no forgotten him alretty?'

Between them they slew the centipede. Thus was he rewarded for his agency toward the recovery of things lost at the Hammersmiths' ball.

It seems that Teddy, in due course, remembered the glove, and when he returned to the house at sunset made a secret but exhaustive search for it. Not until evening, upon the moonlit eastern gallery, did he find it. It was upon the hand that he had thought lost to him for ever, and so he was moved to repeat certain nonsense that he had been commanded never, never to utter again. Teddy's fences were down.

This time there was no ambition to stand in the way, and the wooing was as natural and successful as should be between ardent shepherd and gentle shepherdess.

The prairies changed to a garden. The Rancho de las Sombras became the Ranch of Light.

A few days later Octavia received a letter from Mr. Bannister, in reply to one she had written to him asking some questions about her business. A portion of the letter ran as follows:

'I am at a loss to account for your references to the sheep ranch. Two months after your departure to take up your residence upon it, it was discovered that Colonel Beaupree's title was worthless. A deed came to light showing that he disposed of the property before his death. The matter was reported to your manager, Mr. Westlake, who at once repurchased the property. It is entirely beyond my powers of conjecture to imagine how you have remained in ignorance of this fact. I beg that you will at once confer with that gentleman, who will, at least, corroborate my statement.'

Octavia sought Teddy, with battle in her eye.

'What are you working on this ranch for?' she asked once more.

'One hundred –' he began to repeat, but saw in her face that she knew. She held Mr. Bannister's letter in her hand. He knew that the game was up.

'It's my ranch,' said Teddy, like a schoolboy detected in evil. 'It's a mighty poor manager that isn't able to absorb the boss's business if you give him time.'

'Why were you working down here?' pursued Octavia, still struggling after the key to the riddle of Teddy.

'To tell the truth, 'Tave,' said Teddy, with quiet candour, 'it wasn't for the salary. That about kept me in cigars and sunburn lotions. I was sent south by my doctor. 'Twas that right lung that was going to the bad on account of over-exercise and strain at polo and gymnastics. I needed climate and ozone and rest and things of that sort.'

In an instant Octavia was close against the vicinity of the affected organ. Mr. Bannister's letter fluttered to the floor.

'It's – it's well now, isn't it, Teddy?'

'Sound as a mesquite chunk. I deceived you in one thing. I paid fifty thousand for your ranch as soon as I found you had no title. I had just about that much income accumulated at my banker's while I've been herding sheep down here, so it was almost like picking the thing up on a bargain-counter for a penny. There's another little surplus of unearned increment piling up there, 'Tave. I've been thinking of a wedding trip in a yacht with white ribbons tied to the mast, through the Mediterranean, and then up among the Hebrides and down Norway to the Zuyder Zee.'

'And I was thinking,' said Octavia softly, 'of a wedding gallop with my manager among the flocks of sheep and back to a wedding breakfast with Mrs. MacIntyre on the gallery, with, maybe, a sprig of orange blossom fastened to the red jar above the table.'

Teddy laughed, and began to chant:

'Little Bo-Peep has lost her sheep,
And doesn't know where to find 'em.
Let 'em alone, and they'll come home,
And –'

Octavia drew his head down and whispered in his ear.

But that is one of the tales they brought behind them.

XCVII

A Ruler of Men

I WALKED THE STREETS of the City of Insolence, thirsting for the sight of a stranger face. For the City is a desert of familiar types as thick and alike as the grains in a sandstorm; and you grow to hate them as you do a friend who is always by you, or one of your own kin.

And my desire was granted, for I saw, near a corner of Broadway and Twenty-ninth Street, a little flaxen-haired man with a face like a scalybark hickory-nut, selling to a fast-gathering crowd a tool that omnigeneously proclaimed itself a can-opener, a screwdriver, a button-hook, a nail-file, a shoe-horn, a watch-guard, a potato-peeler, and an ornament to any gentleman's key-ring.

And then a stall-fed cop shoved himself through the congregation of customers. The vendor, plainly used to having his seasons of trade thus abruptly curtailed, closed his satchel and slipped like a weasel through the opposite segment of the circle. The crowd scurried aimlessly away like ants from a disturbed crumb. The cop, suddenly becoming oblivious of the earth and its inhabitants, stood still, swelling his bulk and putting his club through an intricate drill of twirls. I hurried after Kansas Bill Bowers, and caught him by an arm.

Without his looking at me or slowing his pace, I found a five-dollar bill crumpled neatly into my hand.

'I wouldn't have thought, Kansas Bill,' I said, 'that you'd hold an old friend that cheap.'

Then he turned his head, and the hickory-nut cracked into a wide smile.

'Give back the money,' said he, 'or I'll have the cop after you for false pretences. I thought you was the cop.'

'I want to talk to you, Bill,' I said. 'When did you leave Oklahoma? Where is Reddy McGill now? Why are you selling those impossible contraptions on the street? How did your Big Horn gold-mine pan out? How did you get so badly sun-burned? What will you drink?'

'A year ago,' answered Kansas Bill systematically. 'Putting up windmills in Arizona. For pin money to buy etceteras with. Salted. Been down in the tropics. Beer.'

We forgathered in a propitious place and became Elijahs, while a waiter of dark plumage played the raven to perfection. Reminiscence needs must be had before I could steer Bill into his epic mood.

'Yes,' said he, 'I mind the time Timoteo's rope broke on that cow's horns while the calf was chasing you. You and that cow! I'd never forget it.'

'The tropics,' said I, 'are a broad territory. What part of Cancer or Capricorn have you been honouring with a visit?'

'Down along China or Peru – or maybe the Argentine Confederacy,' said Kansas Bill. 'Anyway 'twas among a great race of people, off-coloured but progressive. I was there three months.'

'No doubt you are glad to be back among the truly great race,' I surmised. 'Especially among New Yorkers, the most progressive and independent citizens of any country in the world,' I continued, with the fatuity of the provincial who has eaten the Broadway lotus.

'Do you want to start an argument?' asked Bill.

'Can there be one?' I answered.

'Has an Irishman humour, do you think?' asked he.

'I have an hour or two to spare,' said I, looking at the café clock.

'Not that the Americans aren't a great commercial nation,' conceded Bill. 'But the fault lay with the people who wrote lies for fiction.'

'What was this Irishman's name?' I asked.

'Was that last beer cold enough?' said he.

'I see there is talk of further outbreaks among the Russian peasants,' I remarked.

'His name was Barney O'Connor,' said Bill.

Thus, because of our ancient prescience of each other's trail of thought, we travelled ambiguously to the point where Kansas Bill's story began:

'I met O'Connor in a boarding-house on the West Side. He invited me to his hall-room to have a drink, and we became like a dog and a cat that had been raised together. There he sat, a tall, fine, handsome man, with his feet against one wall and his back against the other, looking over a map. On the bed and sticking three feet out of it was a beautiful gold sword with tassels on it and rhinestones in the handle.

' "What's this?" says I (for by that time we were well acquainted). "The annual parade in vilification of the ex-snakes of Ireland? And what's the line of march? Up Broadway to Forty-second; thence east to McCarthy's café; thence –'

' "Sit down on the wash-stand," says O'Connor, "and listen. And cast no perversions on the sword. 'Twas me father's in old Munster. And this map, Bowers, is no diagram of a holiday procession. If ye look again ye'll see that it's the continent known as South America, comprising fourteen green, blue, red, and yellow countries, all crying out from time to time to be liberated from the yoke of the oppressor."

' "I know," says I to O'Connor. "The idea is a literary one. The ten-cent magazine stole it from Ridpath's *History of the World from the Sandstone Period to the Equator*. You'll find it in every one of 'em. It's a continued story of a soldier of fortune, generally named O'Keefe, who gets to be dictator while the Spanish-American populace cries 'Cospetto!' and other Italian maledictions. I misdoubt if it's ever been done. You're not thinking of trying that, are you, Barney?" I asks.

' "Bowers," says he, "you're a man of education and courage."

' "How can I deny it?" says I. "Education runs in my family; and I have acquired courage by a hard struggle with life."

' "The O'Connors," says he, "are a warlike race. There is me father's sword; and here is the map. A life of inaction is not for me. The O'Connors were born to rule. 'Tis a ruler of men I must be."

' "Barney," I says to him, "why don't you get on the force and settle down to a quiet life of carnage and corruption instead of roaming off to foreign parts? In what better way can you indulge your desire to subdue and maltreat the oppressed?"

' "Look again at the map," says he, "at the country I have the point of me knife on. 'Tis that one I have selected to aid and overthrow with me father's sword."

' "I see," says I. "It's the green one, and that does credit to your patriotism; and it's the smallest one, and that does credit to your judgment."

' "Do ye accuse me of cowardice?" says Barney, turning pink.

' "No man," says I, "who attacks and confiscates a country single-handed could be called a coward. The worst you can be charged with is plagiarism or imitation. If Anthony Hope and Roosevelt let you get away with it, nobody else will have any right to kick." '

' "I'm not joking," says O'Connor. "And I've got $1,500 cash to work the scheme with. I've taken a liking to you. Do you want it, or not?"

' "I'm not working," I told him; "but how is it to be? Do I eat during the fomentation of the insurrection, or am I only to be Secretary of War after the country is conquered? Is it to be a pay envelope or only a portfolio?"

' "I'll pay all expenses," says O'Connor. "I want a man I can trust. If we succeed you may pick out any appointment you want in the gift of the government."

' "All right, then," says I. "You can get me a bunch of draying contracts and then a quick-action consignment to a seat on the Supreme Court bench so I won't be in line for the presidency. The kind of cannon they chasten their presidents with in that country hurt too much. You can consider me on the pay-roll."

'Two weeks afterward O'Connor and me took a steamer for the small, green, doomed country. We were three weeks on the trip. O'Connor said he had his plans all figured out in advance; but being the commanding general, it consorted with his dignity to keep the details concealed from his army and cabinet, commonly known as William T. Bowers. Three dollars a day was the price for which I joined the cause of liberating an undiscovered country from the ills that threatened or sustained it. Every Saturday night on the steamer I stood in line at parade rest, and O'Connor handed over the twenty-one dollars.

'The town we landed at was named Guayaquerita, so they told me. "Not for me," says I. "It'll be little old Hilldale or Tompkinsville or Cherry Tree Corners when I speak of it. It's a clear case where spelling reform ought to butt in and disenvowel it."

'But the town looked fine from the bay when we sailed in. It was white, with green ruching and lace ruffles on the skirt when the surf slashed up on the sand. It looked as tropical and *dolce far ultra* as the pictures of Lake Ronkonkoma in the brochure of the passenger department of the Long Island Railroad.

'We went through the quarantine and customhouse indignities; and then O'Connor leads me to a 'dobe house on a street called "The Avenue of the Dolorous Butterflies of the Individual and Collective Saints." Ten feet wide it was, and knee-deep in alfalfa and cigar stumps

' "Hooligan Alley," says I, re-christening it

' " 'Twill be our head-quarters," says O'Connor "My agent here, Don Fernando Pacheco, secured it for us."

'So in that house O'Connor and me established the revolutionary centre. In the front room we had ostensible things such as fruit, a guitar, and a table with a conch shell on it. In the back room O'Connor had his desk and a large looking-glass and his sword hid in a roll of straw matting. We slept on hammocks that we hung to hooks in the wall; and took our meals at the Hotel Ingles, a beanery run on the American plan by a German proprietor with Chinese cooking served à la Kansas City lunch counter.

'It seems that O'Connor really did have some sort of system planned out beforehand. He wrote plenty of letters; and every day or two some native gent would stroll round to head-quarters and be shut up in the back room for half an hour with O'Connor and the interpreter. I noticed that when they went in they were always smoking eight-inch cigars and at peace with the world; but when they came out they would be folding up a ten- or twenty-dollar bill and cursing the government horribly.

'One evening after we had been in Guaya – in this town of Smellville-by-the-Sea – about a month, and me and O'Connor were sitting outside the door helping old *tempus fugit* with rum and ice and limes, I says to him:

' "If you'll excuse a patriot that don't exactly know what he's patronizing, for the question – what is your scheme for subjugating this country? Do you intend to plunge it into bloodshed, or do you mean to buy its votes peacefully and honourably at the polls?"

' "Bowers," says he, "ye're a fine little man and I intend to make great use of ye after the conflict. But ye do not understand statecraft. Already by now we have a network of strategy clutching with invisible fingers at the throat of the tyrant Calderas. We have agents at work in every town in the republic. The Liberal party is bound to win. On our secret lists we have the names of enough sympathizers to crush the administration forces at a single blow."

' "A straw vote," says I, "only shows which way the hot air blows."

' "Who has accomplished this?" goes on O'Connor. "I have. I

have directed everything. The time was ripe when we came, so my agents inform me. The people are groaning under burdens of taxes and levies. Who will be their natural leader when they rise? Could it be anyone but meself? 'twas only yesterday that Zaldas, our representative in the province of Durasnas, tells me that the people, in secret, already call me 'El Library Door,' which is the Spanish manner of saying 'The Liberator.' "

' "Was Zaldas that maroon-coloured old Aztec with a paper collar on and unbleached domestic shoes?" I asked.

' "He was," says O'Connor

' "I saw him tucking a yellow-back into his vest pocket as he came out," says I. "It may be," says I, "that they call you a library door, but they treat you more like the side-door of a bank. But let us hope for the worst."

' "It has cost money, of course," says O'Connor; "but we'll have the country in our hands inside of a month."

'In the evenings we walked about in the plaza and listened to the band playing and mingled with the populace at its distressing and obnoxious pleasures. There were thirteen vehicles belonging to the upper classes, mostly rockaways and oldstyle barouches, such as the mayor rides in at the unveiling of the new poor house at Milledgeville, Alabama. Round and round the desiccated fountain in the middle of the plaza they drove, and lifted their high silk hats to their friends. The common people walked around in barefooted bunches, puffing stogies that a Pittsburg millionaire wouldn't have chewed for a dry smoke on Ladies' Day at his club. And the grandest figure in the whole turnout was Barney O'Connor. Six foot two he stood in his Fifth Avenue clothes, with his eagle eye and his black moustache that tickled his ears. He was a born dictator and tsar and hero and harrier of the human race. It looked to me that all eyes were turned upon O'Connor, and that every woman there loved him, and every man feared him. Once or twice I looked at him and thought of funnier things that had happened than his winning out in his game; and I began to feel like a Hidalgo de Officio de Gratto de South America myself. And then I would come down again to solid bottom and let my imagination gloat, as usual, upon the twenty-one American dollars due me on Saturday night.

' "Take note," says O'Connor to me as thus we walked, "of the mass of the people. Observe their oppressed and melancholy air. Can ye not see that they are ripe for revolt? Do ye not perceive that they are disaffected?"

"I do not," says I. "Nor disinfected either. I'm beginning to understand these people. When they look unhappy they're enjoying themselves. When they feel unhappy they go to sleep. They're not the kind of people to take an interest in revolutions."

' "They'll flock to our standard," says O'Connor. "Three thousand men in this town alone will spring to arms when the signal is given. I am assured of that. But everything is in secret. There is no chance for us to fail."

'On Hooligan Alley, as I prefer to call the street our headquarters was on, there was a row of flat 'dobe houses with red tile roofs, some straw shacks full of Indians and dogs, and one two-story wooden house with balconies a little farther down. That was where General Tumbalo, the commandant and commander of the military forces, lived. Right across the street was a private residence built like a combination bake-oven and folding-bed. One day, O'Connor and me were passing it, single file, on the flange they called a sidewalk, when out of the window flies a big red rose. O'Connor, who is ahead, picks it up, presses it to his fifth rib, and bows to the ground. By Carrambos! that man certainly had the Irish drama chaunceyized. I looked around expecting to see the little boy and girl in white sateen ready to jump on his shoulder while he jolted their spinal columns and ribs together through a breakdown, and sang: "Sleep, Little One, Sleep."

'As I passed the window I glanced inside and caught a glimpse of a white dress and a pair of big flashing black eyes and gleaming teeth under a dark lace mantilla.

'When we got back to our house O'Connor began to walk up and down the floor and twist his moustache.

' "Did ye see her eyes, Bowers?" he asks me.

' "I did," says I, "and I can see more than that. It's all coming out according to the story-books. I knew there was something missing. 'Twas the love interest. What is it that comes in Chapter VII to cheer the gallant Irish adventurer? Why, Love, of course – Love that makes the hat go around. At last we have the eyes of midnight hue and the rose flung from the barred window. Now, what comes next? The underground passage – the intercepted letter – the traitor in camp – the hero thrown into a dungeon – the mysterious message from the señorita – then the outburst – the fighting on the plaza – the –'

'Don't be a fool," says O'Connor, interrupting. "But that's the only woman in the world for me, Bowers. The O'Connors are as quick to love as they are to fight. I shall wear that rose over me heart when I lead me men into action. For a good battle to be fought there must be some woman to give it power.

' "Every time," I agreed, "if you want to have a good lively scrap. There's only one thing bothering me. In the novels the light-haired friend of the hero always gets killed. Think 'em all over that you've read, and you'll see that I'm right. I think I'll step down to the Botica Española and lay in a bottle of walnut stain before war is declared." ·

' "How will I find out her name?" says O'Connor, laying his chin in his hand.

' "Why don't you go across the street and ask her?" says I.

' "Will you never regard anything in life seriously?" says O'Connor, looking down at me like a schoolmaster.

' "Maybe she meant the rose for me," I said, whistling the Spanish fandango.

'For the first time since I'd known O'Connor, he laughed. He got up and roared and clapped his knees, and leaned against the wall till the tiles on the roof clattered to the noise of his lungs. He went into the back room and looked at himself in the glass and began and laughed all over from the beginning again. Then he looked at me and repeated himself. That's why I asked you if you thought an Irishman had any humour. He'd been doing farce comedy from the day I saw him without knowing it; and the first time he had an idea advanced to him with any intelligence he acted in it like two-twelfths of the sextet in a "Floradora' road company.

"The next afternoon he comes in with a triumphant smile and begin to pull something like ticker tape out of his pocket.

' "Great!" says I. "This is something like home. How is Amalgamated Copper to-day?"

' "I've got her name," says O'Connor, and he reads off something like this: "Dona Isabel Antonia Inez Lolita Carreras y Buencaminos y Monteleon. She lives with her mother," explains O'Connor "Her father was killed in the last revolution. She is sure to be in sympathy with our cause."

'And sure enough the next day she flung a little bunch of roses clear across the street into our door. O'Connor dived for it and found a piece of paper curled around a stem with a line in Spanish on it. He dragged the interpreter out of his corner and got him busy. The interpreter scratched his head, and gave us as a translation three best bets: "Fortune had got a face like the man fighting"; "Fortune looks like a brave man"; and "Fortune favours the brave." We put our money on the last one.

' "Do ye see?" says O'Connor. "She intends to encourage me sword to save her country."

' "It looks to me like an invitation to supper," says I.

'So every day this señorita sits behind the barred windows and exhausts a conservatory or two, one posy at a time. And O'Connor walks like a Dominecker rooster and swells his chest and swears to me he will win her by feats of arms and big deeds on the gory field of battle.

'By and by the revolution began to get ripe. One day O'Connor takes me into the back room and tells me all.

' "Bowers," he says, "at twelve o'clock one week from to-day the struggle will take place. It has pleased ye to find amusement and diversion in this project because ye have not sense enough to perceive that it is easily accomplished by a man of courage, intelligence, and historical superiority, such as meself. The whole world over," says he, "the O'Connors have ruled men, women, and nations. To subdue a small and indifferent country like this is a trifle. Ye see what little barefooted manikins the men of it are. I could lick four of 'em single-handed."

' "No doubt," says I. "But could you lick six? And suppose they hurled an army of seventeen against you?"

' "Listen," says O'Connor, "to what will occur. At noon next Tuesday 25,000 patriots will rise up in the towns of the republic. The government will be absolutely unprepared. The public buildings will be taken, the regular army made prisoners, and the new administration set up. In the capital it will not be so easy on account of most of the army being stationed there. They will occupy the president's palace and the strongly fortified government buildings, and stand a siege. But on the very day of the outbreak a body of our troops will begin a march to the capital from every town as soon as the local victory has been won. The thing is so well planned that it is an impossibility for us to fail. I meself will lead the troops from here. The new president will be Señor Espadas, now Minister of Finance in the present cabinet."

' "What do you get?" I asked.

' 'Twill be strange," said O'Connor smiling, "if I don't have all the jobs handed to me on a silver salver to pick what I choose. I've been the brains of the scheme, and when the fighting opens I guess I won't be in the rear rank. Who managed it so our troops could get arms smuggled into this country? Didn't I arrange it with a New York firm before I left there? Our financial agents inform me that 20,000 stands of Winchester rifles have been delivered a month ago at a secret place up coast and distributed among the towns. I tell you, Bowers, the game is already won."

'Well, that kind of talk kind of shook my disbelief in the infallibility of the serious Irish gentleman soldier of fortune. It certainly seemed that the patriotic grafters had gone about the thing in a business way. I looked upon O'Connor with more respect, and began to figure on what kind of uniform I might wear as Secretary of War.

'Tuesday, the day set for the revolution, came around according to schedule. O'Connor said that a signal had been agreed upon for the uprising. There was an old cannon on the beach near the national warehouse. That had been secretly loaded, and promptly at twelve o'clock was to be fired off. Immediately the revolutionists would seize their concealed arms, attack the comandante's troops in the cuartel, and capture the custom-house and all government property and supplies.

'I was nervous all the morning. And about eleven o'clock O'Connor became infused with the excitement and martial spirit of murder. He geared his father's sword around him, and walked up and down in the back room like a lion in the Zoo suffering from corns. I smoked a couple of dozen cigars, and decided on yellow stripes down the trouser legs of my uniform.

'At half-past eleven O'Connor asks me to take a short stroll through the streets to see if I could notice any signs of the uprising. I was back in fifteen minutes.

' "Did you hear anything?" he asks.

' "I did," says I. "At first I thought it was drums. But it wasn't; it was snoring. Everybody in town's asleep."

'O'Connor tears out his watch.

' "Fools?" says he. "They've set the time right at the siesta hour when everybody takes a nap. But the cannon will wake 'em up. Everything will be all right, depend upon it."

'Just at twelve o'clock we heard the sound of a cannon — BOOM! — shaking the whole town.

'O'Connor loosens his sword in its scabbard and jumps for the door. I went as far as the door and stood in it.

'People were sticking their heads out of doors and windows. But there was one grand sight that made the landscape look tame.

'General Tumbalo, the comandante, was rolling down the steps of his residential dug-out, waving a five-foot sabre in his hand. He wore his cocked and plumed hat and his dress-parade coat covered with gold braid and buttons. Sky-blue pyjamas, one rubber boot, and one red-plush slipper completed his make-up.

'The general had heard the cannon, and he puffed down the side-walk towards the soldiers' barracks as fast as his rudely awakened two hundred pounds could travel.

'O'Connor sees him and lets out a battle-cry and draws his father's sword and rushes across the street and tackles the enemy.

'Right there in the street he and the general gave an exhibition of blacksmithing and butchery. Sparks flew from their blades, the general roared, and O'Connor gave the slogan of his race and proclivities.

'Then the general's sabre broke in two; and he took to his ginger-coloured heels crying out, "Policios," at every jump. O'Connor chased him a block, imbued with the sentiment of manslaughter, and slicing buttons off the general's coat-tails with the paternal weapon. At the corner five bare-footed policemen in cotton undershirts and straw hats climbed over O'Connor and subjugated him according to the municipal statutes.

'They brought him past the late revolutionary head-quarters on the way to jail. I stood in the door. A policeman had him by each hand and foot, and they dragged him on his back through the grass like a turtle. Twice they stopped, and the odd policeman took another's place while he rolled a cigarette. The great soldier of fortune turned his head and looked at me as they passed. I blushed, and lit another cigar. The procession passed on, and at ten minutes past twelve everybody had gone back to sleep again.

'In the afternoon the interpreter came around and smiled as he laid his hand on the big red jar we usually kept ice-water in.

' "The ice-man didn't call to-day," says I. "What's the matter with everything, Sancho?"

' "Ah, yes," says the liver-coloured linguist. "They just tell me in the town. Verree bad act that Señor O'Connor make fight with General Tumbalo. Yes. General Tumbalo great soldier and big mans."

' "What'll they do to Mr. O'Connor?" I asks.

' "I talk little while presently with the Juez de la Paz – what you call Justice-with-the-peace," says Sancho. "He tell me it verree bad crime that one Señor Americano try kill General Tumbalo. He says they keep Señor O'Connor in jail six months; then have trial and shoot him with guns. Verree sorree."

' "How about this revolution that was to be pulled off?" I asks.

' "Oh," says this Sancho, "I think too hot weather for revolution. Revolution better in winter-time. Maybe so next winter. Quien sabe?"

' "But the cannon went off," says I. "The signal was given."

' "That big sound?" says Sancho, grinning. "The boiler in ice factory he blow up – BOOM! Wake everybody up from siesta. Verree sorree. No ice. Mucho hot day."

'About sunset I went over to the jail, and they let me talk to O'Connor through the bars.

' "What's the news, Bowers?" says he. "Have we taken the town? I've been expecting a rescue party all the afternoon. I haven't heard any firing Has any word been received from the capital?"

' "Take it easy, Barney," says I. "I think there's been a change of plans. There's something more important to talk about. Have you any money?"

' "I have not," says O'Connor. "The last dollar went to pay our hotel bill yesterday. Did our troops capture the custom-house? There ought to be plenty of government money there."

' "Segregate your mind from battles," says I. "I've been making inquiries. You're to be shot six months from date for assault and battery. I'm expecting to receive fifty years at hard labour for vagrancy. All they furnish you while you're a prisoner is water. You depend on your friends for food. I'll see what I can do."

'I went away and found a silver Chile dollar in an old vest of O'Connor's. I took him some fried fish and rice for his supper. In the morning I went down to a lagoon and had a drink of water, and then went back to the jail. O'Connor had a porterhouse steak look in his eye.

' "Barney," says I. "I've found a pond full of the finest kind of water. It's the grandest, sweetest, purest water in the world. Say the word and I'll go fetch you a bucket of it and you can throw this vile government stuff out of the window. I'll do anything I can for a friend."

' "Has it come to this?" says O'Connor, raging up and down his cell. "Am I to be starved to death and then shot? I'll make those traitors feel the weight of an O'Connor's hand when I get out of this." And then he comes to the bars and speaks softer. "Has nothing been heard from Dona Isabel?" he asks. "Though every one else in the world fail," says he, "I trust those eyes of hers. She will find a way to effect my release. Do ye think ye could communicate with her? One word from her – even a rose would make me sorrow light. But don't let her know except with the utmost delicacy, Bowers. These high-bred Castilians are sensitive and proud."

' "Well said, Barney," says I. "You've given me an idea. I'll report later. Something's got to be pulled off quick, or we'll both starve."

'I walked out and down to Hooligan Alley, and then on the other side of the street. As I went past the window of Dona Isabel Antonia Concha Regalia, out flies the rose as usual and hits me on the ear.

'The door was open, and I took off my hat and walked in. It wasn't very light inside, but there she sat in a rocking-chair by the window smoking a black cheroot. And when I got closer I saw that she was about thirty-nine, and had never seen a straight front in her life. I sat down on the arm of her chair, and took the cheroot out of her mouth and stole a kiss.

' "Hullo, Izzy," I says. "Excuse my unconventionality, but I feel like I have known you for a month. Whose Izzy is oo?"

'The lady ducked her head under her mantilla, and drew in a long breath. I thought she was going to scream, but with all that intake of air she only came out with: "Me likee Americanos."

'As soon as she said that, I knew that O'Connor and me would be doing things with a knife and fork before the day was over. I drew a chair beside her, and inside of half an hour we were engaged. Then I took my hat and said I must go out for a while.

' "You come back?" says Izzy, in alarm.

' "Me go bring preacher," says I. "Come back twenty minutes. We marry now. How you likee?"

' "Marry to-day?" says Izzy. "Good!"

'I went down on the beach to the United States consul's shack. He was a grizzly man, eighty-two pounds, smoked glasses, five foot eleven, pickled. He was playing chess with an india-rubber man in white clothes.

' "Excuse me for interrupting," says I, "but can you tell me how a man could get married quick?"

'The consul gets up and fingers in a pigeonhole.

' "I believe I had a licence to perform the ceremony myself, a year or two go," he said. "I'll look, and –'

'I caught hold of his arm.

' "Don't look it up," says I. "Marriage is a lottery, anyway. I'm willing to take the risk about the licence if you are."

'The Consul went back to Hooligan Alley with me. Izzy called her ma to come in, but the old lady was picking a chicken in the patio and begged to be excused. So we stood up and the consul performed the ceremony.

'That evening Mrs. Bowers cooked a great supper of stewed goat, tamales, baked bananas, fricasseed red peppers and coffee. Afterward I sat in the rocking-chair by the front window, and she sat on the floor plunking at a guitar and happy, as she should be, as Mrs. William T.B.

'All at once I sprang up in a hurry. I'd forgotten all about O'Connor. I asked Izzy to fix up a lot of truck for him to eat.

' "That big, oogly man," said Izzy. "But all right – he your friend."

'I pulled a rose out of a bunch in a jar, and took the grub-basket around to the jail. O'Connor ate like a wolf. Then he wiped his face with a banana peel and said: "Have you heard nothing from Dona Isabel yet?"

' "Hist!" says I, slipping the rose between the bars. "She sends you this. She bids you take courage. At nightfall two masked men brought it to the ruined chateau in the orange grove. How did you like that goat hash, Barney?"

'O'Connor pressed the rose to his lips.

' "This is more to me than all the food in the world," says he. "But the supper was fine. Where did you raise it?"

' "I've negotiated a stand-off at a delicatessen hut down-town," I tells him. "Rest easy. If there's anything to be done I'll do it."

'So things went along that way for some weeks. Izzy was a great cook; and if she had had a little more poise of character and smoked a little better brand of tobacco we might have drifted into some sense of responsibility for the honour I had conferred on her. But as time went on I began to hunger for the sight of a real lady standing before me in a street-car. All I was staying in that land of bilk and money for was because I couldn't get away, and I thought it no more than decent to stay and see O'Connor shot.

'One day our old interpreter drops around and after smoking an hour says that the judge of the peace sent him to request me to call on him. I went to his office in a lemon grove on a hill at the edge of the town; and there I had a surprise. I expected to see one of the usual cinnamon-coloured natives in congress gaiters and one of Pizarro's cast-off hats. What I saw was an elegant gentleman of a slightly claybank complexion sitting in an upholstered leather chair, sipping a high-ball and reading Mrs. Humphry Ward. I had smuggled into my brain a few words of Spanish by the help of Izzy, and I began to remark in a rich Andalusian brogue:

' "Buenas dias, señior. Yo tengo – yo tengo –"

' "Oh, sit down, Mr. Bowers," says he. "I spent eight years in your country in colleges and law schools. Let me mix you a high-ball. Lemon peel, or not?"

'Thus we got along. In about half an hour I was beginning to tell him about the scandal in our family when Aunt Elvira ran away with a Cumberland Presbyterian preacher. Then he says to me:

' "I sent for you, Mr. Bowers, to let you know that you can have your friend Mr. O'Connor now. Of course we had to make a show of punishing him on account of his attack on General Tumbalo. It is arranged that he shall be released to-morrow night. You and he will be conveyed on board the fruit steamer *Voyager*, bound for New York, which lies in the harbour. Your passage will be arranged for."

' "One moment, judge," says I; "that revolution –"

'The judge lays back in his chair and howls.

' "Why," says he presently, "that was all a little joke fixed up by the boys around the court-room, and one or two of our cup-ups, and a few clerks in the stores. The town is bursting its sides with laughing. The boys made themselves up to be conspirators, and they – what you call it? – stick Señor O'Connor for his money. It is very funny."

' "It was," says I. "I saw the joke all along. I'll take another high-ball, if your honour don't mind."

'The next evening just at dark a couple of soldiers brought O'Connor down to the beach, where I was waiting under a coco-nut tree.

' "Hist!" says I in his ear: "Dona Isabel has arranged our escape. Not a word!"

'They rowed us in a boat out to a little steamer that smelled of table d'hôte salad oil and bone phosphate.

'The great, mellow, tropical moon was rising as we steamed away. O'Connor leaned on the taffrail or rear balcony of the ship and gazed silently at Guaya – at Buncoville-on-the-Beach.

'He had the red rose in his hand.

' "She will wait," I heard him say. "Eyes like hers never deceive. But I shall see her again. Traitors cannot keep an O'Connor down for ever."

' "You talk like a sequel," says I. "But in Volume II please omit the light-haired friend who totes the grub to the hero in his dungeon cell."

'And thus reminiscing, we came back to New York.'

•   •   •   •   •

There was a little silence broken only by the familiar roar of the streets after Kansas Bill Bowers ceased talking.

'Did O'Connor ever go back?' I asked.

'He attained his heart's desire,' said Bill. 'Can you walk two blocks? I'll show you.'

He led me eastward and down a flight of stairs that was covered by a curious-shaped, glowing, pagoda-like structure. Signs and figures on the tiled walls and supporting columns attested that we were in the Grand Central station of the subway. Hundreds of people were on the midway platform.

An up-town express dashed up and halted. It was crowded. There was a rush for it by a still larger crowd.

Towering above every one there a magnificent, broad-shouldered, athletic man leaped into the centre of the struggle. Men and women he seized in either hand and hurled them like manikins toward the open gates of the train.

Now and then some passenger with a shred of soul and self-respect left to him turned to offer remonstrances; but the blue uniform on the towering figure, the fierce and conquering glare of his eye and the ready impact of his ham-like hands glued together the lips that would have spoken complaint.

When the train was full, then he exhibited to all who might observe and admire his irresistible genius as a ruler of men. With his knees, with his elbows, with his shoulders, with his resistless feet he shoved, crushed, slammed, heaved, kicked, flung, pounded the overplus of passengers aboard. Then with the sounds of its wheels drowned by the moans, shrieks, prayers, and curses of its unfortunate crew, the express dashed away.

'That's him. Ain't he a wonder?' said Kansas Bill admiringly. 'That tropical country wasn't the place for him. I wish the distinguished traveller, writer, war correspondent, and playwright, Richmond Hobson Davis, could see him now. O'Connor ought to be dramatized.'

XCVIII

The Atavism of John Tom Little Bear

[O. Henry thought this the best of the Jeff Peters stories, all the rest of which are included in *The Gentle Grafter*, except 'Cupid à la Carte' in the *Heart of the West*.]

I SAW A LIGHT in Jeff Peters's room over the Red Front Drug Store. I hastened toward it, for I had not known that Jeff was in town. He is a man of the Hadji breed, of a hundred occupations, with a story to tell (when he will) of each one.

I found Jeff re-packing his grip for a run down to Florida to look at an orange grove for which he had traded, a month before, his mining claim on the Yukon. He kicked me a chair, with the same old humorous, profound smile on his seasoned countenance. It had been eight months since we had met, but his greeting was such as men pass from day to day. Time is Jeff's servant, and the continent is a big lot across which he cuts to his many roads.

For a while we skirmished along the edges of unprofitable talk which culminated in that unquiet problem of the Philippines.

'All them tropical races,' said Jeff, 'could be run out better with their own jockeys up. The tropical man knows what he wants. All he wants is a season ticket to the cock-fights and a pair of Western Union climbers to go up the bread-fruit tree. The Anglo-Saxon man wants him to learn to conjugate and wear suspenders. He'll be happiest in his own way.'

I was shocked.

'Education, man,' I said, 'is the watchword. In time they will rise to our standard of civilization. Look at what education has done for the Indian.'

'O-ho!' sang Jeff, lighting his pipe (which was a good sign). 'Yes, the Indian! I'm looking. I hasten to contemplate the redman as a standardbearer of progress. He's the same as the other brown boys. You can't make an Anglo-Saxon of him. Did I ever tell you about the time my friend John Tom Little Bear bit off the right ear of the arts of culture and education and spun the teetotum back round to where it was when Columbus was a little boy? I did not?

'John Tom Little Bear was an educated Cherokee Indian and an old friend of mine when I was in the Territories. He was a graduate of one of them Eastern football colleges that have been so successful in teaching the Indian to use the gridiron instead of burning his victims at the stake. As an Anglo-Saxon, John Tom was copper-coloured in spots. As an Indian, he was one of the whitest men I ever knew. As a Cherokee, he was a gentleman, on the first ballot. As a ward of the nation he was mighty hard to carry at the primaries.

'John Tom and me got together and began to make medicine – how to get up some lawful, genteel swindle which we might work in a quiet way so as not to excite the stupidity of the police or the cupidity of the larger corporations. We had close upon $500 between us, and we pined to make it grow, as all respectable capitalists do.

'So we figured out a proposition which seems to be as honourable as a gold mine prospectus and as profitable as a church raffle. And inside of thirty days you find us swarming into Kansas with a pair of fluent horses and a red camping-wagon on the European plan. John Tom is Chief Wish-Heap-Dough, the famous Indian medicine man and Samaritan Sachem of the Seven Tribes. Mr. Peters is business manager and half owner. We needed a third man, so we looked around and found J. Conyngham Binkly leaning against the want column of a newspaper. This Binkly has a disease for Shakespearean roles, and an hallucination about a 200 nights' run on the New York stage. But he confesses that he never could earn the butter to spread on his William S. roles, so he is willing to drop to the ordinary baker's kind, and be satisfied with a 200-mile run behind the medicine ponies. Besides Richard III, he could do twenty-seven coon songs and banjo specialties, and was willing to cook, and curry the horses. We carried a fine line of excuses for taking money. One was a magic soap for removing grease spots and quarters from clothes. One was a Sumwah-tah, the great Indian Remedy made from a prairie herb revealed by the Great Spirit in a dream to his favourite medicine men, the great chiefs MacGarrity and Silberstein, bottlers, Chicago. And the other was a frivolous system of pick-pocketing the Kansasters that had the department stores reduced to a decimal fraction. Look ye! A pair of silk garters, a dream book, one dozen clothes-pins, a gold tooth, and "When Knighthood Was in Flower" all wrapped up in a genuine Japanese silkarina handkerchief and handed to the handsome lady by Mr. Peters for the trivial sum of fifty cents, while Professor Binkly entertains us in a three-minute round with the banjo.

' 'Twas an eminent graft we had. We ravaged peacefully through the State, determined to remove all doubt as to why 'twas called bleeding Kansas. John Tom Little Bear, in full Indian chief's costume, drew crowds away from the parchesi sociables and government ownership conversaziones. While at the football college in the East he had acquired quantities of rhetoric and the art of calisthenics and sophistry in his classes, and when he stood up in the red wagon and explained to the farmers, eloquent, about chilblains and hyperæsthesia of the cranium, Jeff couldn't hand out the Indian Remedy fast enough for 'em.

'One night we was camped on the edge of a little town out west of Salina. We always camped near a stream, and put up a little tent. Sometimes we sold out of the Remedy unexpected, and then Chief Wish-Heap-Dough would have a dream in which the Manitou commanded him to fill up a few bottles of Sum-wah-tah at the most convenient place. 'Twas about ten o'clock, and we'd just got in from a street performance. I was in the tent with the lantern, figuring up the day's profits. John Tom hadn't taken of his Indian make-up, and was sitting by the camp-fire minding a fine sirloin steak in the pan for the Professor till he finished his hair-raising scene with the trained horses.

'All at once out of dark bushes comes a pop like a fire-cracker, and John Tom gives a grunt and digs out of his bosom a little bullet that has dented itself against his collar-bone. John Tom makes a dive in the direction of the fireworks, and comes back dragging by the collar a kid about nine or ten years young, in a velveteen suit, with a little nickel-mounted rifle in his hand about as big as a fountain-pen.

' "Here, you pappoose," says John Tom, "what are you gunning for with that howitzer? You might hit somebody in the eye. Come out, Jeff, and mind the steak. Don't let it burn, while I investigate this demon with the pea-shooter."

' "Cowardly redskin," says the kid like he was quoting from a favourite author. "Dare to burn me at the stake and the paleface will sweep you from the prairies like – like everything. Now, you lemme go, or I'll tell mamma."

'John Tom plants the kid on a camp-stool, and sits down by him. "Now, tell the big chief," he says, "why you try to shoot pellets into your Uncle John's system. Didn't you know it was loaded?"

' "Are you a Indian?" asks the kid, looking up, cute as you please, at John Tom's buckskin and eagle feathers. "I am," says John Tom.

' "Well, then, that's why," answers the boy, swinging his feet. I nearly let the steak burn watching the nerve of that youngster.

' "O-ho!" says John Tom, "I see. You're the Boy Avenger. And you've sworn to rid the continent of the savage redman. Is that about the way of it, son?"

'The kid half-way nodded his head. And then he looked glum. 'Twas indecent to wring his secret from his bosom before a single brave had fallen before his parlour-rifle.

' "Now, tell us where your wigwam is, pappoose," says John Tom — "where you live? Your mamma will be worrying about you being out so late. Tell me, and I'll take you home."

'The kid grins. "I guess not," he says. "I live thousands and thousands of miles over there." He gyrated his hand toward the horizon. "I come on the train," he says, "by myself. I got off here because the conductor said my ticket had ex-pirated." He looks at John Tom with sudden suspicion. "I bet you ain't a Indian," he says. "You don't talk like a Indian. You look like one, but all a Indian can say is 'heap good' and 'paleface die.' Say, I bet you are one of them make-believe Indians that sell medicine on the streets. I saw one once in Quincy."

' "You never mind," says John Tom, "whether I'm a cigar-sign or a Tammany cartoon. The question before the council is what's to be done with you. You've run away from home. You've been reading Howells. You've disgraced the profession of boy avengers by trying to shoot a tame Indian, and never saying: 'Die, dog of a redskin! You have crossed the path of the Boy Avenger nineteen times too often.' What do you mean by it?"

'The kid thought for a minute. "I guess I made a mistake," he says. "I ought to have gone farther west. They find 'em wild out there in the cañons." He holds out his hand to John Tom, the little rascal. "Please excuse me, sir," says he, "for shooting at you. I hope it didn't hurt you. But you ought to be more careful. When a scout sees a Indian in his war-dress, his rifle must speak." Little Bear give a big laugh with a whoop at the end of it, and swings the kid ten feet high and sets him on his shoulder, and the runaway fingers the fringe and the eagle feathers and is full of the joy the white man knows when he dangles his heels against an inferior race. It is plain that Little Bear and that kid are chums from that on. The little renegade has already smoked the pipe of peace with the savage; and you can see in his eye that he is figuring on a tomahawk and a pair of moccasins, children s size.

'We have supper in the tent. The youngster looks upon me and the Professor as ordinary braves, only intended as a background to the camp scene. When he is seated on a box of Sum-wah-tah, with the edge of the table sawing his neck, and his mouth full of beef-steak, Little Bear calls for his name. "Roy," says the kid, with a sir-loiny sound to it. But when the rest of it and his post-office address is referred to, he shakes his head. "I guess not," he says. "You'll send me back. I want to stay with you. I like this camping out. At home, we fellows had a camp in our back yard. They called me Roy, the Red Wolf. I guess that'll do for a name. Gimme another piece of beefsteak, please."

'We had to keep that kid. We knew there was a hullabaloo about him somewheres, and that Mamma, and Uncle Harry, and Aunt Jane, and the Chief of Police were hot after finding his trail, but not another word would he tell us. In two days he was the mascot of Big Medicine outfit, and all of us had a sneaking hope that his owners wouldn't turn up. When the red wagon was doing business he was in it, and passed up the bottles to Mr. Peters as proud and satisfied as a prince that s abjured a two-hundred-dollar crown for a million-dollar parvenuess. Once John Tom asked him something about his papa. "I ain't got any papa," he says. "He runned away and left us. He made my mamma cry. Aunt Lucy says he's a shape." "A what?" somebody asks him. "A shape," says the kid: "some kind of a shape – lemme see – oh, yes, a feendenuman shape. I don't know what it means." John Tom was for putting our brand on him, and dressing him up like a little chief, with wampun and beads, but I vetoes it. "Somebody's lost that kid, is my view of it, and they may want him. You let me try him with a few stratagems, and see if I can't get a look at his visiting-card."

'So that night I goes up to Mr. Roy Blank by the camp-fire, and looks at him contemptuous and scornful. "Snickenwitzel!" says I, like the word made me sick; "Snickenwitzel! Bah! Before I'd be named Snickenwitzel!"

' "What's the matter with you, Jeff?" says the kid, opening his eyes wide.

' "Snickenwitzel!" I repeats, and I spat the word out. "I saw a man to-day from your town, and he told me your name. I'm not surprised you was ashamed to tell it. Snickenwitzel! Whew!"

' "Ah, here, now," says the boy, indignant and wriggling all over, "what's the matter with you? That ain't my name. It's Cony-ers. What's the matter with you?"

' "And that's not the worst of it," I went on quick, keeping him hot and not giving him time to think. "We thought you was from

a nice, well-to-do family. Here's Mr. Little Bear, a chief of the
Cherokees, entitled to wear nine otter tails on his Sunday blanket,
and Professor Binkly, who plays Shakespeare and the banjo, and
me, that's got hundreds of dollars in that black tin box in the
wagon, and we've got to be careful about the company we keep.
That man tells me your folks live 'way down in little Hencoop
Alley, where there are no sidewalks, and the goats eat off the table
with you.'

'That kid was almost crying now. " 'Tain't so," he splutters. "He
– he don't know what he's talking about. We live on Poplar
Av'noo. I don't 'sociate with goats. What's the matter with you?"

' "Poplar Avenue," says I, sarcastic. "Poplar Avenue! That's a
street to live on! It only runs two blocks and then falls off a bluff.
You can throw a keg of nails the whole length of it. Don't talk to
me about Poplar Avenue."

' "It's – it's miles long," says the kid. "Our number's 862 and
there's lots of houses after that. What's the matter with – aw, you
make me tired, Jeff."

' "Well, well, now," says I. "I guess that man made a mistake.
Maybe it was some other boy he was talking about. If I catch him
I'll teach him to go around slandering people." And after supper I
goes up town and telegraphs to Mrs. Conyers, 862 Poplar Avenue,
Quincy, Ill., that the kid is safe and sassy with us, and will be held
for further orders. In two hours an answer comes to hold him
tight, and she'll start for him by next train.

'The next train was due at 6 p.m. the next day, and me and John
Tom was at the depot with the kid. You might scour the plains in
vain for the big Chief Wish-Heap-Dough. In his place is Mr.
Little Bear in the human habiliments of the Anglo-Saxon sect; and
the leather of his shoes is patented and the loop of his necktie is
copyrighted. For these things John Tom had grafted on him at
college along with metaphysics and the knock-out guard for the
low tackle. But for his complexion, which is some yellowish, and
the black mop of his straight hair, you might have thought here
was an ordinary man out of the city directory that subscribes for
magazines and pushes the lawn-mower in his shirt-sleeves of
evenings.

'Then the train rolled in, and a little woman in a grey dress,
with a sort of illuminating hair, slides off and looks around quick.
And the Boy Avenger sees her, and yells "Mamma," and she cries
"Oh!" and they meet in a clinch, and now the pesky redskins can
come forth from their caves on the plains without fear any more of

the rifle of Roy, the Red Wolf. Mrs. Conyers comes up and thanks me an' John Tom without the usual extremities you always look for in a woman. She says just enough, in a way to convince, and there is no incidental music by the orchestra. I made a few illiterate requisitions upon the art of conversation, at which the lady smiles friendly, as if she had known me a week. And then Mr. Little Bear adorns the atmosphere with the various idioms into which education can fracture the wind of speech. I could see the kid's mother didn't quite place John Tom; but it seemed she was apprised in his dialects, and she played up to his lead in the science of making three words do the work of one

'That kid introduced us, with some footnotes and explanations that made things plainer than a week of rhetoric. He danced around, and punched us in the back, and tried to climb John Tom's leg. "This is John Tom, mamma," says he. "He's a Indian. He sells medicine in a red wagon. I shot him, but he wasn't wild. The other one's Jeff. He's a fakir, too. Come on and see the camp where we live, won't you, mamma?"

It is plain to see that the life of the woman is in that boy. She has got him again where her arms can gather him, and that's enough. She's ready to do anything to please him. She hesitates the eighth of a second and takes another look at these men. I imagine she says to herself about John Tom, "Seems to be a gentleman, if his hair don't curl." And Mr. Peters she disposes of as follows: "No ladies' man, but a man who knows a lady."

'So we all rambled down to the camp as neighbourly as coming from a wake. And there she inspects the wagon, and pats the place with her hand where the kid used to sleep, and dabs around her eyewinkers with her handkerchief. And Professor Binkly gives us "Trovatore" on one string of the banjo, and is about to slide off into Hamlet's monologue when one of the horses gets tangled in his rope and he must go look after him, and says something about 'foiled again."

'When it got dark me and John Tom walked back up to the Corn Exchange Hotel, and the four of us had supper there. I think the trouble started at that supper, for then was when Mr. Little Bear made an intellectual balloon ascension. I held on to the tablecloth, and listened to him soar. That redman, if I could judge, had the gift of information. He took language, and did with it all a Roman can do with macaroni. His vocal remarks was all embroidered over with the most scholarly verbs and prefixes. And his syllables was smooth, and fitted nicely to the joints of his idea. I thought I'd heard him talk before, but I hadn't. And it wasn't the size of his words, but the way they come; and 'twasn't his subjects, for he spoke of common things like cathedrals and footballs and poems and catarrh and souls and freight rates and sculpture. Mrs. Conyers understood his accents, and the elegant sounds went back and forth between 'em. And now and then Jefferson D. Peters would intervene a few shop-worn, senseless words to have the butter passed or another leg of the chicken.

'Yes, John Tom Little Bear appeared to be inveigled some in his bosom about that Mrs. Conyers. She was of the kind that pleases. She had the good looks and more, I'll tell you. You take one of these cloak models in a big store. They strike you as being on the impersonal system. They are adapted for the eye. What they run to is inches around and complexion, and the art of fanning the delusion that the sealskin would look just as well on the lady with the warts and the pocket-book. Now, if one of them models was off duty, and you took it, and it would say "Charlie" when you pressed it, and sit up at the table, why, then you would have something similar to Mrs. Conyers. I could see how John Tom could resist any inclination to hate that white squaw.

'The lady and the kid stayed at the hotel. In the morning, they say, they will start for home. Me and Little Bear left at eight o'clock, and sold Indian Remedy on the courthouse square till nine. He leaves me and the Professor to drive down to camp, while he stays up town. I am not enamoured with that plan, for it shows John Tom is uneasy in his composures, and that leads to fire-water, and sometimes to the green corn dance and costs. Not often does Chief Wish-Heap-Dough get busy with the fire-water, but whenever he does there is heap much doing in the lodges of the palefaces who wear blue and carry the club.

'At half-past nine Professor Binkly is rolled in his quilt snoring in blank verse, and I am sitting by the fire listening to the frogs. Mr. Little Bear slides into camp, and sits down against a tree There is no symptoms of fire-water.

' "Jeff," says he, after a long time, "a little boy came West to hunt Indians."

' "Well, then?" says I, for I wasn't thinking as he was.

' "And he bagged one," says John Tom, "and 'twas not with a gun, and he never had on a velveteen suit of clothes in his life." And then, I began to catch his smoke.

' "I know it," says I. "And I'll bet you his pictures are on valentines, and fool men are his game, red and white."

' "You win on the red," says John Tom, calm. "Jeff, for how many ponies do you think I could buy Mrs. Conyers?"

' "Scandalous talk!" I replies. " 'Tis not a paleface custom." John Tom laughs loud and bites into a cigar. "No," he answers; " 'tis the savage equivalent for the dollars of the white man's marriage settlement. Oh, I know. There's an eternal wall between the races. If I could do it, Jeff, I'd put a torch to every white college that a redman has ever set foot inside. Why don't you leave us alone," says he, "to our own ghost-dances and dog-feasts, and our dingy squaws to cook our grasshopper soup and darn our moccasins?"

' "Now, you sure don't mean disrespect to the perennial blossom entitled education?" says I, scandalized, "because I wear it in the bosom of my own intellectual shirt-waist. I've had education," says I, "and never took any harm from it."

' "You lasso us," goes on Little Bear, not noticing my prose insertions, "and teach us what is beautiful in literature and in life, and how to appreciate what is fine in men and women. What have you done to me?" says he. "You've made me a Cherokee Moses. You've taught me to hate the wigwams and love the white man's ways. I can look over into the promised land and see Mrs. Conyers, but my place is – on the reservation."

'Little Bear stands up in his chief's dress, and laughs again. "But, white man Jeff," he goes on, "the paleface provides a recourse. 'Tis a temporary one, but it gives a respite and the name of it is whisky."

'And straight off he walks up the path to town again. "Now," says I in my mind, "may the Manitou move him to do only bailable things this night!" For I perceive that John Tom is about to avail himself of the white man's solace.

'Maybe it was 10.30, as I sat smoking, when I hear pit-a-pats on the path, and here comes Mrs. Conyers running, her hair twisted up any way, and a look on her face that says burglars and mice and the flour's all-out rolled in one. "Oh, Mr. Peters," she calls out, as they will, "oh, oh!" I made a quick think, and I spoke the gist of it out loud. "Now," says I, "we've been brothers, me and that Indian, but I'll make a good one of him in two minutes if –"

' "No, no," she says, wild and cracking her knuckles. "I haven't seen Mr. Little Bear. 'Tis my – husband. He's stolen my boy. Oh," she says, "just when I had him back in my arms again! That heartless villain! Every bitterness life knows," she says, "he's made me drink. My poor little lamb, that ought to be warm in his bed, carried off by that fiend!"

' "How did all this happen?" I ask. "Let's have the facts."

' "I was fixing his bed," she explains, "and Roy was playing on the hotel porch and he drives up to the steps. I heard Roy scream and ran out. My husband had him in the buggy then. I begged him for my child. This is what he gave me." She turns her face to the light. There is a crimson streak running across her cheek and mouth. "He did that with his whip," she says.

' "Come back to the hotel," says I, "and we'll see what can be done."

'On the way she tells me some of the wherefores. When he slashed her with the whip he told her he found out she was coming for the kid, and he was on the same train. Mrs. Conyers had been living with her brother, and they'd watched the boy always, as her husband had tried to steal him before. I judge that man was worse than a street railway promoter. It seems he had spent her money and slugged her and killed her canary bird, and told it around that she had cold feet.

'At the hotel we found a mass meeting of five infuriated citizens chewing tobacco and denouncing the outrage. Most of the town was asleep by ten o'clock. I talks the lady some quiet, and tells her I will take the one o'clock train for the next town, forty miles east, for it is likely that the esteemed Mr. Conyers will drive there to take the cars. "I don't know," I tells her, "but what he has legal rights; but if I find him I can give him an illegal left in the eye, and tie him up for a day or two, anyhow, on a disturbal of the peace proposition."

'Mrs. Conyers goes inside and cries with the landlord's wife, who is fixing some catnip tea that will make everything all right for the poor dear. The landlord comes out on the porch, thumbing his one suspender, and says to me:

' "Ain't had so much excitements in town since Bedford Steegall's wife swallered a spring lizard. I seen him through the winder hit her with the buggy whip, and everything. What's that suit of clothes cost you you got on? 'Pears like we'd have some rain, don't it? Say, doc, that Indian of yorn's on a kind of a whizz to-night, ain't he? He comes along just before you did, and I told him about this here occurrence. He gives a cur'us kind of a hoot, and trotted off. I guess our constable 'll have him in the lock-up 'fore morning."

'I thought I'd sit on the porch and wait for the one o'clock train. I wasn't feeling saturated with mirth. Here was John Tom on one of his sprees, and this kidnapping business losing sleep for me. But then, I'm always having trouble with other people's troubles.

Every few minutes Mrs. Conyers would come out on the porch and look down the road the way the buggy went, like she expected to see that kid coming back on a white pony with a red apple in his hand. Now, wasn't that like a woman? And that brings up cats. "I saw a mouse go in this hole," says Mrs. Cat; "you can go prize up a plank over there if you like; I'll watch this hole."

'About a quarter to one o'clock the lady comes out again, restless, crying easy, as females do for their own amusement, and she looks down that road again and listens. "Now, ma'am," says I, "there's no use watching cold wheel-tracks. By this time they're half-way to –" "Hush," she says, holding up her hand. And I do hear something coming "flip-flap" in the dark; and then there is the awfulest war-whoop ever heard outside of Madison Square Garden at a Buffalo Bill matinee. And up the steps and on to the porch jumps the disrespectable Indian. The lamp in the hall shines on him, and I fail to recognize Mr. J. T. Little Bear, alumnus of the class of '91. What I see is a Cherokee brave, and the warpath is what he has been travelling. Fire-water and other things have got him going. His buckskin is hanging in strings, and his feathers are mixed up like a frizzly hen's. The dust of miles is on his moccasins, and the light in his eye is the kind the aborigines wear. But in his arms he brings that kid, his eyes half closed, with his little shoes dangling and one hand fast around the Indian's collar.

' "Pappoose!" says John Tom, and I notice that the flowers of the white man's syntax have left his tongue. He is the original proposition in bear's claws and copper colour. "Me bring," says he, and he lays the kid in his mother's arms. "Run fifteen mile," says John Tom – "Ugh! Catch white man. Bring pappoose."

'The little woman is in extremities of gladness. She must wake up that stir-up trouble youngster and hug him and make proclamation that he is his mamma's own precious treasure. I was about to ask questions, but I looked at Mr. Little Bear, and my eye caught the sight of something in his belt. "Now go to bed, ma'am," says I, "and this gadabout youngster likewise, for there s no more danger, and the kidnapping business is not what it was earlier in the night."

'I inveigled John Tom down to camp quick, and when he tumbled over asleep I got that thing out of his belt and disposed of it where the eye of education can't see it. For even the football colleges disapprove of the art of scalp-taking in their curriculums.

'It is ten o'clock next day when John Tom wakes up and looks around. I am glad to see the nineteenth century in his eye again.

' "What was it, Jeff?" he asks.

' "Heap fire-water," says I.

'John Tom frowns, and thinks a little. "Combined," says he directly, "with the interesting little physiological shake-up known as reversion to type. I remember now. Have they gone yet?"

' "On the 7.30 train," I answers.

' "Ugh!" says John Tom; "better so. Paleface, bring big Chief Wish-Heap-Dough a little bromoseltzer, and then he'll take up the redman's burden again." '

XCIX

The Marionettes

THE POLICEMAN WAS STANDING at the corner of Twenty-fourth Street and a prodigiously dark alley near where the elevated railroad crosses the street. The time was two o'clock in the morning; the outlook a stretch of cold, drizzling, unsociable blackness until the dawn.

A man, wearing a long overcoat, with his hat tilted down in front, and carrying something in one hand, walked softly but rapidly out of the black alley. The policeman accosted him civilly, but with the assured air that is linked with conscious authority. The hour, the alley's musty reputation, the pedestrian's haste, the burden he carried – these easily combined into the 'suspicious circumstances' that required illumination at the officer's hands.

The 'suspect' halted readily and tilted back his hat, exposing, in the flicker of the electric lights an emotionless, smooth countenance with a rather long nose and steady dark eyes. Thrusting his gloved hand into a side-pocket of his overcoat, he drew out a card and handed it to the policeman. Holding it to catch the uncertain light, the officer read the name 'Charles Spencer James, M.D.' The street and number of the address were of a neighbourhood so solid and respectable as to subdue even curiosity. The policeman's downward glance at the article carried in the doctor's hand – a handsome medicine case of black leather, with small silver mountings – further endorsed the guarantee of the card.

'All right, doctor,' said the officer, stepping aside, with an air of bulky affability. 'Orders are to be extra careful. Good many burglars and hold-ups lately. Bad night to be out. Not so cold, but – clammy."

With a formal inclination of his head, and a word or two cor-
roborative of the officer's estimate of the weather, Doctor James
continued his somewhat rapid progress. Three times that night
had a patrolman accepted his professional card and the sight of his
paragon of a medicine case as vouchers for his honesty of person
and purpose. Had any one of those officers seen fit, on the
morrow, to test the evidence of that card he would have found it
borne out by the doctor's name on a handsome door-plate, his
presence, calm and well dressed, in his well-equipped office – provided it were not too early, Doctor James being a late riser – and
the testimony of the neighbourhood to his good citizenship, his
devotion to his family, and his success as a practitioner the two
years he had lived among them.

Therefore, it would have much surprised any one of those zealous guardians of the peace could they have taken a peep into that
immaculate medicine case. Upon opening it, the first article to be
seen would have been an elegant set of the latest conceived tools
used by the 'box man,' as the ingenious safe burglar now denomi-
nates himself. Specially designed and constructed were the implements – the short but powerful 'jemmy,' the collection of
curiously fashioned keys, the blued drills and punches of the finest
temper – capable of eating their way into chilled steel as a mouse
eats into a cheese, and the clamps that fasten like a leech to the
polished door of a safe and pull out the combination knob as a
dentist extracts a tooth. In a little pouch in the inner side of the
'medicine' case was a four-ounce vial of nitro-glycerine, now half
empty. Underneath the tools was a mass of crumpled bank-notes
and a few handfuls of gold coin, the money, altogether, amounting
to eight hundred and thirty dollars.

To a very limited circle of friends Doctor James was known as
'The Swell "Greek." ' Half of the mysterious term was a tribute to
his cool and gentleman-like manners; the other half denoted, in
the argot of the brotherhood, the leader, the planner, the one who
by the power and prestige of his address and position, secured the
information upon which they based their plans and desperate
enterprises.

Of this elect circle the other members were Skitsie Morgan and
Gum Decker, expert 'box men,' and Leopold Pretzfelder, a jew-
eller downtown, who manipulated the 'sparklers' and other ornaments collected by the working trio. All good and loyal men, as
loose-tongued as Memnon and as fickle as the North Star.

That night's work had not been considered by the firm to have yielded more than a moderate repayal for their pains. An old-style, two-story, side-bolt safe in the dingy office of a very wealthy, old-style dry-goods firm on a Saturday night should have excreted more than twenty-five hundred dollars. But that was all they found, and they had divided it, the three of them, into equal shares upon the spot, as was their custom. Ten or twelve thousand was what they expected. But one of the proprietors had proved to be just a trifle too old-style. Just after dark he had carried home in a shirt box most of the funds on hand.

Doctor James proceeded up Twenty-fourth Street, which was, to all appearance, depopulated. Even the theatrical folk – who affect this district as a place of residence, were long since abed. The drizzle had accumulated upon the street; puddles of it among the stones received the fire of the arclights, and returned it, shattered into a myriad liquid spangles. A captious wind, shower-soaked and chilling, coughed from the laryngeal flues between the houses.

As the practitioner's foot struck even with the corner of a tall brick residence of more pretensions than its fellows, the front door popped open, and a bawling negress clattered down the steps to the pavement. Some medley of words came from her mouth, addressed, like as not, to herself – the recourse of her race when alone and beset by evil. She looked to be one of that old vassal class of the South – voluble, familiar, loyal, irrepressible; her person pictured it – fat, neat, aproned, kerchiefed.

This sudden apparition, spewed from the silent house, reached the bottom of the steps as Doctor James came opposite. Her brain transferring its energies from sound to sight, she ceased her clamour and fixed her pop-eyes upon the case the doctor carried.

'Bress de Lawd!' was the benison the sight drew from her. 'Is you a doctor, suh?'

'Yes, I am a physician,' said Doctor James, pausing

'Den fo' God's sake come and see Mister Chandler, suh. He done had a fit or sump'n. He layin' jist like he wuz dead. Miss Amy sont me to git a doctor. Lawd knows whar old Cindy'd a skeared one up from, if you, suh, hadn't come along. Ef old Mars' knowed one ten-hundredth part of dese doin's dey'd be shootin' gwine on, suh – pistol shootin' – leb'm feet marked off on de ground, and ev'ybody a-duellin'. And dat po' lamb, Miss Amy –'

'Lead the way,' said Doctor James, setting his foot upon the step, 'if you want me as a doctor. As an auditor I'm not open to engagements.'

The negress preceded him into the house and up a flight of thickly carpeted stairs. Twice they came to dimly lighted branching hallways. At the second one the now panting conductress turned down a hall, stopping at a door and opening it.

'I done brought de doctor, Miss Amy.'

Doctor James entered the room, and bowed slightly to a young lady standing by the side of a bed. He set his medicine case upon a chair removed his overcoat, throwing it over the case and the back of the chair, and advanced with quiet self-possession to the bedside.

There lay a man, sprawling as he had fallen – a man dressed richly in the prevailing mode, with only his shoes removed; lying relaxed, and as still as the dead.

There emanated from Doctor James an aura of calm force and reserve strength that was as manna in the desert to the weak and desolate among his patrons. Always had women, especially, been attracted by something in his sick-room manner. It was not the indulgent suavity of the fashionable healer but a manner of poise, of sureness, of ability to overcome fate, of deference and protection and devotion. There was an exploring magnetism in his steadfast, luminous brown eyes a latent authority in the impassive, even priestly, tranquillity of his smooth countenance that outwardly fitted him for the part of confidant and consoler. Sometimes, at his first professional visit, women would tell him where they hid their diamonds at night from the burglars.

With the ease of much practice, Doctor James's unroving eyes estimated the order and quality of the room's furnishings. The appointments were rich and costly. The same glance had secured cognizance of the lady's appearance. She was small and scarcely past twenty. Her face possessed the title to a winsome prettiness, now obscured by (you would say) rather a fixed melancholy than the more violent imprint of a sudden sorrow. Upon her forehead, above one eyebrow, was a livid bruise, suffered, the physician's eye told him, within the past six hours.

Doctor James's fingers went to the man's wrist. His almost vocal eyes questioned the lady.

'I am Mrs. Chandler,' she responded, speaking with the plaintive Southern slur and intonation. 'My husband was taken suddenly ill about ten minutes before you came. He has had attacks of heart trouble before – some of them were very bad.' His clothed state and the late hour seemed to prompt her to further explanation. 'He had been out late; to – a supper, I believe.'

Doctor James now turned his attention to his patient. In

whichever of his 'professions' he happened to be engaged, he was wont to honour the 'case' or the 'job' with his whole interest.

The sick man appeared to be about thirty. His countenance bore a look of boldness and dissipation, but was not without a symmetry of feature and the fine lines drawn by a taste and indulgence in humour that gave the redeeming touch. There was an odour of spilled wine about his clothes.

The physician laid back his outer garments, and then, with a penknife, slit the shirt-front from collar to waist. The obstacles cleared, he laid his ear to the heart and listened intently

'Mitral regurgitation?' he said softly, when he rose. The words ended with the rising inflection of uncertainty. Again he listened long; and this time he said, 'Mitral insufficiency,' with the accent of an assured diagnosis.

'Madam,' he began, in the reassuring tones that had so often allayed anxiety, 'there is a probability –' As he slowly turned his head to face the lady, he saw her fall, white and swooning, into the arms of the old negress.

'Po' lamb! po' lamb! Has dey done killed Aunt Cindy's own blessed child? May de Lawd 'stroy wid His wrath dem what stole her away, what break dat angel heart; what left –'

'Lift her feet,' said Doctor James, assisting to support the drooping form. 'Where is her room? She must be put to bed.'

'In here, suh.' The woman nodded her kerchiefed head towards a door. 'Dat's Miss Amy's room.'

They carried her in there, and laid her on the bed. Her pulse was faint, but regular. She passed from the swoon, without recovering consciousness, into a profound slumber.

'She is quite exhausted,' said the physician. 'Sleep is a good remedy. When she wakes, give her a toddy – with an egg in it, if she can take it. How did she get that bruise upon her forehead?'

'She done got a lick there, suh. De po' lamb fell – No, suh' – the old woman's racial mutability swept her into a sudden flare of indignation – 'old Cindy ain't gwineter lie for dat debble. He done it, suh. May de Lawd wither de hand what – dar now! Cindy promise her sweet lamb she ain't gwine tell. Miss Amy got hurt, suh, on de head.'

Doctor James stepped to a stand where a handsome lamp burned, and turned the flame low.

'Stay here with your mistress,' he ordered, 'and keep quiet so she will sleep. If she wakes, give her the toddy. If she grows any weaker, let me know. There is something strange about it.'

'Dar's mo' strange t'ings dan dat' round here,' began the negress, but the physician hushed her in a seldom-employed peremptory concentrated voice with which he had often allayed hysteria itself. He returned to the other room, closing the door softly behind him. The man on the bed had not moved, but his eyes were open. His lips seemed to form words. Doctor James bent his head to listen. 'The money! the money!' was what they were whispering.

'Can you understand what I say?' asked the doctor, speaking low, but distinctly.

The head nodded slightly.

'I am a physician, sent for by your wife. You are Mr. Chandler, I am told. You are quite ill. You must not excite or distress yourself at all.'

The patient's eye seemed to beckon to him. The doctor stooped to catch the same faint words.

'The money – the twenty thousand dollars.'

'Where is this money? – in the bank?'

The eyes expressed a negative. 'Tell her' – the whisper was growing fainter – 'the twenty thousand dollars – her money' – his eyes wandered about the room.

'You have placed this money somewhere?' – Doctor James's voice was toiling like a siren's to conjure the secret from the man's failing intelligence – Is it in this room?'

He thought he saw a fluttering assent in the dimming eyes. The pulse under his fingers was as fine and small as a silk thread.

There arose in Doctor James's brain and heart the instincts of his other profession. Promptly, as he acted in everything, he decided to learn the whereabouts of this money and at the calculated and certain cost of a human life.

Drawing from his pocket a little pad of prescription blanks, he scribbled upon one of them a formula suited, according to the best practice, to the needs of the sufferer. Going to the door of the inner room, he softly called the old woman, gave her the prescription, and bade her take it to some drug store and fetch the medicine.

When she had gone, muttering to herself, the doctor stepped to the bedside of the lady. She still slept soundly; her pulse was a little stronger; her forehead was cool, save where the inflammation of the bruise extended, and a slight moisture covered it. Unless disturbed, she would yet sleep for hours. He found the key in the door, and locked it after him when he returned.

Doctor James looked at his watch. He could call half an hour his own, since before that time the old woman could scarcely return from her mission. Then he sought and found water in a pitcher and a glass tumbler. Opening his medicine case, he took out the vial containing the nitro-glycerine – 'the oil,' as his brethren of the brace-and-bit term it.

One drop of the faint yellow thickish liquid he let fall in the tumbler. He took out his silver hypodermic syringe case, and screwed the needle into its place. Carefully measuring each modicum of water in the graduated glass barrel of the syringe, he diluted the one drop with nearly half a tumbler of water.

Two hours earlier that night Doctor James had, with that syringe, injected the undiluted liquid into a hole drilled in the lock of a safe, and had destroyed, with one dull explosion, the machinery that controlled the movement of the bolts. He now purposed, with the same means, to shiver the prime machinery of a human being – to rend its heart – and each shock was for the sake of the money to follow.

The same means, but in a different guise. Whereas, that was the giant in its rude primary dynamic strength, this was the courtier, whose no less deadly arms were concealed by velvet and lace. For the liquid in the tumbler and in the syringe that the physician carefully filled was now a solution of glonoin, the most powerful heart stimulant known to medical science. Two ounces had riven the solid door of the iron safe; with one-fiftieth part of a minim he was now about to still for ever the intricate mechanism of a human life.

But not immediately. It was not so intended. First there would be a quick increase of vitality; a powerful impetus given to every organ and faculty. The heart would respond bravely to the fatal spur; the blood in the veins return more rapidly to its source.

But, as Doctor James well knew, over-stimulation in this form of heart disease means death, as sure as by a rifle shot. When the clogged arteries should suffer congestion from the increased flow of blood pumped into them by the power of the burglar's 'oil,' they would rapidly become 'No thoroughfare,' and the fountain of life would cease to flow.

The physician bared the chest of the unconscious Chandler. Easily and skilfully he injected, subcutaneously, the contents of the syringe into the muscles of the region over the heart. True to his neat habits in both professions, he next carefully dried his needle and re-inserted the fine wire that threaded it when not in use.

In three minutes Chandler opened his eyes, and spoke, in a voice faint but audible, inquiring who attended upon him. Doctor James again explained his presence there.

'Where is my wife?' asked the patient.

'She is asleep — from exhaustion and worry,' said the doctor. 'I would not awaken her, unless

'It isn't — necessary.' Chandler spoke with spaces between his words caused by his short breath that some demon was driving too fast. 'She wouldn't — thank you to disturb her — on my — account.'

Doctor James drew a chair to the bedside. Conversation must not be squandered.

'A few minutes ago,' he began, in the grave, candid tones of his other profession, 'you were trying to tell me something regarding some money. I do not seek your confidence, but it is my duty to advise you that anxiety and worry will work against your recovery. If you have any communication to make about this — to relieve your mind about this — twenty thousand dollars, I think was the amount you mentioned — you would better do so.'

Chandler could not turn his head, but he rolled his eyes in the direction of the speaker.

'Did I — say where this — money is?'

'No,' answered the physician. 'I only inferred, from your scarcely intelligible words, that you felt a solicitude concerning its safety. If it is in this room —'

Doctor James paused. Did he only seem to perceive a flicker of understanding, a gleam of suspicion upon the ironical features of his patient? Had he seemed too eager? Had he said too much? Chandler's next words restored his confidence.

'Where — should it be,' he gasped, 'but in — the safe — there?'

With his eyes he indicated a corner of the room, where now, for the first time, the doctor perceived a small iron safe, half concealed by the trailing end of a window curtain.

Rising, he took the sick man's wrist. His pulse was beating in great throbs, with ominous intervals between.

'Lift your arm,' said Doctor James.

'You know — I can't move, doctor.'

The physician stepped swiftly to the hall door, opened it, and listened. All was still. Without further circumvention he went to the safe, and examined it. Of a primitive make and simple design, it afforded little more security than protection against light-fingered servants. To his skill it was a mere toy, a thing of straw and pasteboard. The money was as good as in his hands. With his clamps he could draw the knob, punch the tumblers and open the door in two minutes. Perhaps, in another way, he might open it in one.

Kneeling upon the floor, he laid his ear to the combination plate, and slowly turned the knob. As he had surmised, it was locked at only a 'day com.' – upon one number. His keen ear caught the faint warning click as the tumbler was disturbed he; used the clue – the handle turned. He swung the door wide open.

The interior of the safe was bare – not even a scrap of paper rested within the hollow iron cube.

Doctor James rose to his feet and walked back to the bed.

A thick dew had formed upon the dying man's brow, but there was a mocking, grim smile on his lips and in his eyes.

'I never – saw it before,' he said painfully, 'medicine and – burglary wedded! Do you – make the – combination pay – dear doctor?'

Than that situation afforded, there was never a more rigorous test of Doctor James's greatness. Trapped by the diabolic humour of his victim into a position both ridiculous and unsafe, he maintained his dignity as well as his presence of mind. Taking out his watch, he waited for the man to die.

'You were just a shade too – anxious – about that money. But it never was – in any danger – from you, dear doctor. It's safe. Perfectly safe. It's all – in the hands – of the bookmakers. Twenty – thousand – Amy's money. I played it at the races lost every – cent of it. I've been a pretty bad boy, Burglar – excuse me – Doctor, but I've been a square sport. I don't think – I ever met – such an – eighteen-carat rascal as you are, Doctor – excuse me – Burglar, in all my rounds. Is it contrary – to the ethics – of your – gang, Burglar, to give a victim – excuse me – patient, a drink of water?

Doctor James brought him a drink. He could scarcely swallow it. The reaction from the powerful drug was coming in regular, intensifying waves. But his moribund fancy must have one more grating fling.

'Gambler – drunkard – spendthrift – I've been those, but – a doctor-burglar!'

The physician indulged himself to but one reply to the other's caustic taunts. Bending low to catch Chandler's fast crystallizing gaze, he pointed to the sleeping lady's door with a gesture so stern and significant that the prostrate man half-lifted his head, with his remaining strength, to see. He saw nothing; but he caught the cold words of the doctor – the last sounds he was to hear:

'I never yet – struck a woman.'

It were vain to attempt to con such men. There is no curriculum that can reckon with them in its ken. They are offshoots from the types whereof men say, 'He will do this,' or 'He will do that.' We only know that they exist; and that we can observe them, and tell one another of their bare performances, as children watch and speak of the marionettes.

Yet, it were a droll study in egoism to consider these two – one an assassin and a robber, standing above his victim; the other baser in his offences, if a lesser law-breaker, lying, abhorred, in the house of the wife he had persecuted, spoiled, and smitten, one a tiger, the other a dog-wolf – to consider each of them sickening at the foulness of the other; and each flourishing out of the mire of his manifest guilt his own immaculate standard – of conduct, if not of honour.

The one retort of Doctor James must have struck home to the other's remaining shreds of shame and manhood, for it proved the *coup de grâce* A deep blush suffused his face – an ignominious *rosa mortis;* the respiration ceased, and, with scarcely a tremor, Chandler expired.

Close following upon his last breath came the negress, bringing the medicine. With a hand gently pressing upon the closed eye-lids, Doctor James told her of the end. Not grief, but an heredi-tary *rapprochement* with death in the abstract, moved her to a dismal, watery snuffling, accompanied by her jeremiad.

'Dar now! It's in de Lawd's hands. He am de jedge ob de trans-gressor, and de suppo't of dem in distress. He gwine hab suppo't us now. Cindy done paid out de last quarter fer dis bottle of physic and it nebber come to no use.'

'Do I understand,' asked Doctor James, 'that Mrs. Chandler has no money?'

'Money, suh? You know what make Miss Amy fall down, and so weak? Stahvation, suh Nothin' to eat in dis house but some crumbly crackers in three days. Dat angel sell her finger rings and watch mont's ago. Dis fine house, suh, wid de red cyarpets and shiny bureaus, it's all hired; and de man talkin' scan'lous about de rent. Dat debble – 'scuse me, Lawd – he done in Yo' hands fer jedgment, now – he made way wid everything.'

The physician's silence encouraged her to continue. The history that he gleaned from Cindy's disordered monologue was an old one, of illusion, wilfulness, disaster, cruelty and pride. Standing out from the blurred panorama of her gabble were little clear pictures – an ideal home in the far South; a quickly repented marriage; an unhappy season, full of wrongs and abuse, and, of late, an inheritance of money that promised deliverance; its seizure and waste by the dog-wolf during a two months' absence, and his return in the midst of a scandalous carouse. Unobtruded, but visible between every line, ran a pure white thread through the smudged warp of the story – the simple, all-enduring, sublime love of the old negress, following her mistress unswervingly through everything to the end.

When at last she paused, the physician spoke, asking if the house contained whisky or liquor of any sort. There was, the old woman informed him, half a bottle of brandy left in the sideboard by the dog-wolf.

'Prepare a toddy as I told you,' said Doctor James. 'Wake your mistress; have her drink it, and tell her what has happened.'

Some ten minutes afterward, Mrs. Chandler entered, supported by old Cindy's arm. She appeared to be a little stronger since her sleep and the stimulant she had taken. Doctor James had covered with a sheet the form upon the bed.

The lady turned her mournful eyes once, with a half-frightened look, toward it, and pressed closer to her loyal protector. Her eyes were dry and bright. Sorrow seemed to have done its utmost with her. The fount of tears was dried; feeling itself paralysed.

Doctor James was standing near the table, his overcoat donned, his hat and medicine case in his hand. His face was calm and impassive – practice had inured him to the sight of human suffering. His lambent brown eyes alone expressed a discreet professional sympathy.

He spoke kindly and briefly, stating that, as the hour was late, and assistance, no doubt, difficult to procure, he would himself send the proper persons to attend to the necessary finalities.

'One matter, in conclusion,' said the doctor, pointing to the safe with its still wide-open door 'Your husband, Mrs. Chandler, toward the end; felt that he could not live; and directed me to open that safe, giving me the number upon which the combination is set. In case you may need to use it, you will remember that the number is forty-one. Turn several times to the right; then to the left once; stop at forty-one. He would not permit me to waken you, though he knew the end was near.

'In that safe he said he had placed a sum of money – not large – but enough to enable you to carry out his last request. That was that you should return to your old home, and, in after days, when time shall have made it easier, forgive his many sins against you.'

He pointed to the table, where lay an orderly pile of banknotes, surmounted by two stacks of gold coins.

'The money is there – as he described it – eight hundred and thirty dollars. I beg to leave my card with you, in case I can be of any service later you.'

So; he had thought of her – and kindly – at the last! So late! And yet the lie fanned into life one last spark of tenderness where she had thought all was turned to ashes and dust. She cried aloud 'Rob! Rob!' She turned, and, upon the ready bosom of her true servitor, diluted her grief in relieving tears. It is well to think, also, that in the years to follow, the murderer's falsehood shone like a little star above the grave of love, comforting her, and gaining the forgiveness that is good in itself, whether asked for or no.

Hushed and soothed upon the dark bosom, like a child, by crooning, babbling sympathy, at last she raised her head – but the doctor was gone.

C

The Dream

[This was the last work of O Henry. The *Cosmopolitan Magazine* had ordered it from him and, after his death, the unfinished manuscript was found in his room, on his dusty desk.]

MURRAY DREAMED A DREAM.

Both psychology and science grope when they would explain to us the strange adventures of our immaterial selves when wandering in the realm of 'Death's twin brother, Sleep.' This story will not attempt to be illuminative; it is no more than a record of Murray's dream. One of the most puzzling phases of that strange waking sleep is that dreams which seem to cover months or even years may take place within a few seconds or minutes.

Murray was waiting in his cell in the ward of the condemned. An electric arc-light in the ceiling of the corridor shone brightly upon his table. On a sheet of white paper an ant crawled wildly here and there as Murray blocked its way with an envelope. The electrocution was set for eight o'clock in the evening. Murray smiled at the antics of the wisest of insects.

There were seven other condemned men in the chamber. Since he had been there Murray had seen three taken out to their fate;

one gone mad and fighting like a wolf caught in a trap; one, no less mad, offering up a sanctimonious lip-service to Heaven; the third, a weakling, collapsed and strapped to a board. He wondered with what credit to himself his own heart, foot, and face would meet his punishment; for this was his evening. He thought it must be nearly eight o'clock.

Opposite his own in the two rows of cells was the cage of Bonifacio, the Sicilian slayer of his betrothed and of two officers who came to arrest him. With him Murray had played checkers many a long hour, each calling his move to his unseen opponent across the corridor.

Bonifacio's great booming voice with its indestructible singing quality called out:

'Eh, Meestro Murray; how you feel – all-a right – yes?'

'All right, Bonifacio,' said Murray steadily, as he allowed the ant to crawl upon the envelope and then dumped it gently on the stone floor.

'Dat's good-a, Meestro Murray. Men like us, we must-a die like-a men. My time come nex'-a week. All-a right. Remember, Meestro Murray, I beat-a you dat las' game of de check. Maybe we play again some-a time. I don'-a know. Maybe we have to call-a de move damn-a loud to play de check where dey goin' send us.'

Bonifacio's hardened philosophy, followed closely by his deafening, musical peal of laughter, warmed rather than chilled Murray's numbed heart. Yet Bonifacio had until next week to live.

The cell-dwellers heard the familiar, loud click of the steel bolts as the door at the end of the corridor was opened. Three men came to Murray s cell and unlocked it. Two were prison guards; the other was 'Len' – no; that was in the old days; now the Reverend Leonard Winston, a friend and neighbour from their barefoot days.

'I got them to let me take the prison chaplain s place,' he said, as he gave Murray's hand one short, strong grip. In his left hand he held a small Bible, with his forefinger marking a page.

Murray smiled slightly and arranged two or three books and some penholders orderly on his small table. He would have spoken, but no appropriate words seemed to present themselves to his mind.

The prisoners had christened this cellhouse, eighty feet long, twenty-eight feet wide, Limbo Lane. The regular guard of Limbo Lane, an immense, rough, kindly man, drew a pint bottle of whisky from his pocket and offered it to Murray, saying:

'It's the regular thing, you know. All has it who feel like they need a bracer. No danger of it becoming a habit with 'em, you see.'

Murray drank deep into the bottle.

'That's the boy!' said the guard. 'Just a little nerve tonic, and everything goes smooth as silk.'

They stepped into the corridor, and each one of the doomed seven knew. Limbo Lane is a world on the outside of the world; but it had learned, when deprived of one or more of the five senses, to make another sense supply the deficiency. Each one knew that it was nearly eight, and that Murray was to go to the chair at eight. There is also in the many Limbo Lanes an aristocracy of crime. The man who kills in the open, who beats his enemy or pursuer down, flushed by the primitive emotions and the ardour of combat, holds in contempt the human rat, the spider, and the snake.

So, of the seven condemned only three called their farewells to Murray as he marched down the corridor between the two guards – Bonifacio, Marvin, who had killed a guard while trying to escape from the prison, and Bassett, the train-robber, who was driven to it because the express-messenger wouldn't raise his hands when ordered to do so. The remaining four smouldered, silent, in their cells, no doubt feeling their social ostracism in Limbo Lane society more keenly than they did the memory of their less picturesque offences against the law.

Murray wondered at his own calmness and nearly indifference. In the execution room were about twenty men, a congregation made up of prison officers, newspaper reporters, and lookers-on who had succeeded

Here, in the very middle of a sentence, the hand of Death interrupted the telling of O. Henry's last story. He had planned to make this story different from his others, the beginning of a new series in a style he had not previously attempted. 'I want to show the public,' he said, 'that I can write something new – new for me, I mean – a story without slang, a straightforward dramatic plot treated in a way that will come nearer my idea of real story-writing.' Before starting to write the present story he outlined briefly how he intended to develop it: Murray, the criminal accused and convicted of the brutal murder of his sweetheart – a murder prompted by jealous rage – at first faces the death penalty, calm, and, to all outward appearances, indifferent to his fate. As he nears the electric chair he is overcome by a revulsion of feeling. He is left dazed, stupefied, stunned. The entire scene in the death-chamber — the witnesses, the spectators, the preparations for execution — become unreal to him. The thought flashes through his brain that a terrible mistake is being made. Why is he being strapped to the chair? What has he done? What crime has he committed? In the few moments while the straps are being adjusted a vision comes to him. He dreams a dream. He sees a little country cottage, bright, sun-lit, nestling in a bower of flowers. A woman is there, and a little child. He speaks with them and finds that they are his wife, his child — and the cottage their home. So, after all, it is a mistake. Someone has frightfully, irretrievably blundered. The accusation, the trial, the conviction, the sentence to death in the electric chair — all a dream. He takes his wife in his arms and kisses the child. Yes, here is happiness. It was a dream. Then — at a sign from the prison warden the fatal current is turned on.

Murray had dreamed the wrong dream.

WORDSWORTH CLASSICS

General Editors: Marcus Clapham & Clive Reynard

JANE AUSTEN
Emma
Mansfield Park
Northanger Abbey
Persuasion
Pride and Prejudice
Sense and Sensibility

ARNOLD BENNETT
Anna of the Five Towns

R. D. BLACKMORE
Lorna Doone

ANNE BRONTË
Agnes Grey
The Tenant of
Wildfell Hall

CHARLOTTE BRONTË
Jane Eyre
The Professor
Shirley
Villette

EMILY BRONTË
Wuthering Heights

JOHN BUCHAN
Greenmantle
Mr Standfast
The Thirty-Nine Steps

SAMUEL BUTLER
The Way of All Flesh

LEWIS CARROLL
Alice in Wonderland

CERVANTES
Don Quixote

G. K. CHESTERTON
Father Brown:
Selected Stories
The Man who was
Thursday

ERSKINE CHILDERS
The Riddle of the Sands

JOHN CLELAND
Memoirs of a Woman of
Pleasure: Fanny Hill

WILKIE COLLINS
The Moonstone
The Woman in White

JOSEPH CONRAD
Heart of Darkness
Lord Jim
The Secret Agent

J. FENIMORE COOPER
The Last of the
Mohicans

STEPHEN CRANE
The Red Badge of
Courage

THOMAS DE QUINCEY
Confessions of an English
Opium Eater

DANIEL DEFOE
Moll Flanders
Robinson Crusoe

CHARLES DICKENS
Bleak House
David Copperfield
Great Expectations
Hard Times
Little Dorrit
Martin Chuzzlewit
Oliver Twist
Pickwick Papers
A Tale of Two Cities

BENJAMIN DISRAELI
Sybil

THEODOR DOSTOEVSKY
Crime and Punishment

SIR ARTHUR CONAN
DOYLE
The Adventures of
Sherlock Holmes
The Case-Book of
Sherlock Holmes
The Lost World &
Other Stories
The Return of
Sherlock Holmes
Sir Nigel

GEORGE DU MAURIER
Trilby

ALEXANDRE DUMAS
The Three Musketeers

MARIA EDGEWORTH
Castle Rackrent

GEORGE ELIOT
The Mill on the Floss
Middlemarch
Silas Marner

HENRY FIELDING
Tom Jones

F. SCOTT FITZGERALD
A Diamond as Big as the
Ritz & Other Stories
The Great Gatsby
Tender is the Night

GUSTAVE FLAUBERT
Madame Bovary

JOHN GALSWORTHY
In Chancery
The Man of Property
To Let

ELIZABETH GASKELL
Cranford
North and South

KENNETH GRAHAME
The Wind in the
Willows

GEORGE & WEEDON
GROSSMITH
Diary of a Nobody

RIDER HAGGARD
She

THOMAS HARDY
Far from the
Madding Crowd
The Mayor of Casterbridge
The Return of the
Native
Tess of the d'Urbervilles
The Trumpet Major
Under the Greenwood
Tree

NATHANIEL HAWTHORNE
The Scarlet Letter

O. HENRY
Selected Stories

HOMER
The Iliad
The Odyssey

E. W. HORNUNG
Raffles: The Amateur
Cracksman

VICTOR HUGO
The Hunchback of
Notre Dame
Les Misérables: volume 1
Les Misérables: volume 2

HENRY JAMES
The Ambassadors
Daisy Miller & Other
Stories
The Golden Bowl
The Turn of the Screw
& The Aspern Papers

M. R. JAMES
Ghost Stories

JEROME K. JEROME
Three Men in a Boat

JAMES JOYCE
Dubliners
A Portrait of the Artist
as a Young Man

RUDYARD KIPLING
Captains Courageous
Kim
The Man who would be
King & Other Stories
Plain Tales from the
Hills

D. H. LAWRENCE
The Rainbow
Sons and Lovers
Women in Love

SHERIDAN LE FANU
(edited by M. R. James)
Madam Crowl's Ghost
& Other Stories

JACK LONDON
Call of the Wild &
White Fang

HERMAN MELVILLE
Moby Dick
Typee

H. H. MUNRO
The Complete Stories of
Saki

EDGAR ALLAN POE
Tales of Mystery and
Imagination

FREDERICK ROLFE
Hadrian the Seventh

SIR WALTER SCOTT
Ivanhoe

WILLIAM
SHAKESPEARE
All's Well that Ends
Well
Antony and Cleopatra
As You Like It
A Comedy of Errors
Hamlet
Henry IV Part 1
Henry IV part 2
Henry V
Julius Caesar
King Lear
Macbeth
Measure for Measure
The Merchant of Venice
A Midsummer Night's
Dream
Othello
Richard II
Richard III
Romeo and Juliet
The Taming of the
Shrew
The Tempest
Troilus and Cressida
Twelfth Night
A Winter's Tale

MARY SHELLEY
Frankenstein

ROBERT LOUIS
STEVENSON
Dr Jekyll and Mr Hyde

BRAM STOKER
Dracula

JONATHAN SWIFT
Gulliver's Travels

W. M. THACKERAY
Vanity Fair

TOLSTOY
War and Peace

ANTHONY TROLLOPE
Barchester Towers
Dr Thorne
Framley Parsonage
The Last Chronicle of
Barset
The Small House at
Allington
The Warden

MARK TWAIN
Tom Sawyer &
Huckleberry Finn

JULES VERNE
Around the World in 80
Days &
Five Weeks in a Balloon
20,000 Leagues Under
the Sea

VOLTAIRE
Candide

EDITH WHARTON
The Age of Innocence

OSCAR WILDE
Lord Arthur Savile's
Crime & Other Stories
The Picture of Dorian
Gray

VIRGINIA WOOLF
Orlando
To the Lighthouse

P. C. WREN
Beau Geste

DISTRIBUTION

AUSTRALIA, BRUNEI
& MALAYSIA
Reed Editions
22 Salmon Street, Port Melbourne
Vic 3207, Australia
Tel: (03) 245 7111
Fax (03) 245 7333

DENMARK
BOG-FAN
St. Kongensgade 61A
1264 København K

BOGPA SIKA
Industrivej 1, 7120 Vejle Ø

FRANCE
Bookking International
60 Rue Saint-André-des-Arts
75006 Paris

GERMANY, AUSTRIA
& SWITZERLAND
Swan Buch-Marketing GmbH
Goldscheuerstrabe 16
D-7640 Kehl Am Rhein, Germany

GREAT BRITAIN & IRELAND
Wordsworth Editions Ltd
Cumberland House, Crib Street,
Ware, Hertfordshire SG12 9ET

Selecta Books
The Selectabook
Distribution Centre
Folly Road, Roundway, Devizes
Wiltshire SN10 2HR

HOLLAND & BELGIUM
Uitgeverlj en Boekhandel
Van Gennep BV, Spuistraat 283
1012 VR Amsterdam, Holland

INDIA
OM Book Service
1690 First Floor
Nai Sarak, Delhi – 110006
Tel: 3279823-3265303 Fax: 3278091

ITALY
Magis Books
Piazza Della Vittoria l/C
42100 Reggio Emilia
Tel: 0522-452303 Fax: 0522-452845

NEW ZEALAND
Whitcoulls Limited
Private Bag 92098, Auckland

NORWAY
Norsk Bokimport AS
Bertrand Narvesensvei 2
Postboks 6219, Etterstad, 0602 Oslo

PORTUGAL
Isabel Leao **Editorial Noticias**
Rua da Cruz da Carreira, 4B
1100 Lisboa
Tel: 01-570051 Fax: 01-3522066

SINGAPORE
Book Station
18 Leo Drive, Singapore
Tel: 4511998 Fax: 4529188

CYPRUS
Huckleberry Trading
4 Isabella, Anavargos, Pafos, Cyprus
Tel: 06-231313

SOUTH AFRICA
Struik Book Distributors (Pty) Ltd
Graph Avenue, Montague Gardens,
7441 P O Box 193 Maitland 7405
South Africa
Tel: (021) 551-5900 Fax: (021) 551-1124

SPAIN
Ribera Libros, S.L.
Poligono Martiartu, Calle 1 – no 6
48480 Arrigorriaga, Vizcaya
Tel: 34-4-6713607 (Almacen)
     34-4-4418787 (Libreria)
Fax: 34-4-6713608 (Almacen)
     34-4-4418029 (Libreria)

USA, CANADA & MEXICO
Universal Sales & Marketing
230 Fifth Avenue, Suite 1212
New York, N Y 10001 USA
Tel: 212-481-3500 Fax: 212-481-3534

DIRECT MAIL
Redvers
Redvers House, 13 Fairmile,
Henley-on-Thames, Oxfordshire RG9 2JR
Tel: 0491 572656 Fax: 0491 573590